DAZZLE

Judith Gould

AN ONYX BOOK

ONYX
Published by the Penguin Group
Penguin Books USA Inc., 375 Hudson Street,
New York, New York 10014, U.S.A.
Penguin Books Ltd, 27 Wrights Lane,
London W8 5TZ, England
Penguin Books Australia Ltd, Ringwood,
Victoria, Australia
Penguin Books Canada Ltd, 10 Alcorn Avenue,
Toronto, Ontario, Canada M4V 3B2
Penguin Books (N.Z.) Ltd, 182–190 Wairau Road,
Auckland 10, New Zealand

Penguin Books Ltd, Registered Offices:
Harmondsworth, Middlesex, England

Published by Onyx, an imprint of Dutton Signet,
a division of Penguin Books USA Inc.

First Printing, February, 1989
12 11 10 9 8 7

 REGISTERED TRADEMARK—MARCA REGISTRADA

Printed in the United States of America

This book is for
Kathryn Wheeler Gallaher
. . . With Love

All the world's a stage,
And all the men and women merely
   players:
They have their exits and their
   entrances;
And one man in his time plays many
   parts,
His acts being seven ages.
         —William Shakespeare, *As You Like It*

Prologue: Payday

F'lying.
    After all these years, she still couldn't get used to it. She would tense when the plane hurtled down the runway, and only begin to relax once it was airborne and the houses below looked no bigger than those on a Monopoly board. Only on night flights, such as this, El Al's nonstop flight 1002 from JFK to Ben-Gurion Airport, Tel Aviv, could she settle down and sleep. She felt safe in the darkness. Then, once the plane began its descent and her ears started popping, the nervousness would gnaw at her again, and increase its bite until the aircraft touched ground.

    She was a tall, slim woman who held herself with dignity and grace. Her world-famous face blended a disquieting combination of serene aristocrat and jungle amazon. Carelessly combed long straight black hair, so lustrous it shone blue-black, framed her features with a severe Madonna simplicity, but one sensed rather than saw the innate tawny tigress lurking just beneath the veneer of smooth creamy skin. She possessed that alluring quality of devil-may-care beauty that drove men to fantasize about her and women to emulate her. Even casually dressed, there was something disturbingly sensual about her. The cream silk duster from Luciano Soprani lent her the bohemian quality of a serious but highly successful painter, while the wide-sleeved black crepe-de-chine shirt beneath it, open at the throat, hinted at a smoldering sexual perverseness, and the pleated silk pants, the color of dried tobacco, contradicted it all with a kind of inborn Marlene Dietrich élan. Had it not been for the curious looks she'd been getting, those sidelong, knowing flickers of recognition, she would have been able to forget that she was one of the world's three greatest box-office attractions. She, Jane Fonda, and Meryl Streep. And usually in that order.

    Even after nine years, I still don't feel like a movie star. She caught a man across the aisle staring at her, and quickly turned away. *They think they know me. They think I'm some*

11

sort of goddess. They probably wouldn't believe it if I told them I get diarrhea from drinking the water in Mexico.

"Ladies and gentlemen," a disembodied voice announced over the intercom, in English, "the captain has turned on the no-smoking sign. Please extinguish all smoking materials and see that your seats are in the upright position and that all tray tables are stowed. We hope you have had a pleasant flight, and given the opportunity to fly again, you will choose to fly El Al." The message was repeated in Hebrew.

The chief steward appeared from the galley behind her, which separated the first-class section from economy. Solicitously he picked up her empty wineglass and the little square cocktail napkin, then pushed the tiny plastic beverage tray back into the armrest. "We have arranged for you to disembark first, Miss Boralevi." She had been born Daliah ben Yaacov twenty-nine years earlier, but upon embarking on her film career had adopted her mother's maiden name, Boralevi. "One of our representatives will come to the plane to meet you. He'll see to it that you're sped through customs and baggage claim with as little fuss as possible."

Daliah turned her emerald-eyed film-star gaze to meet his. "Thank you," she said throatily, her voice naturally smoky and peculiarly beguiling. "I appreciate it."

He lingered tentatively, hoping to strike up a conversation. "Are you excited about visiting your homeland?"

She nodded, pushing a cascade of glossy hair from her face. She raised her face to his. "Yes," she said softly, "I am a sabra. Born and bred." She smiled.

"I know. Me too." He returned her smile, automatically switching to Hebrew. Then the magic moment was gone: someone was signaling for him. "Excuse me," he told her, and hurried down the aisle.

Daliah smiled slightly. Simply knowing that they were both sabras had given them common ground, something precious to share and cherish. A fierce pride. All native-born Israelis felt it, no matter how many years had passed since they'd been home.

Suddenly a wave of depression and guilt swept through her.

I've been gone eleven years, she admonished herself sternly. *That's how long it's been since I last set foot on my native soil, if I don't count the various embassies and consulates when it came time to renew my passport.*

The jet engines changed pitch, and for a long, drawn-out moment the airliner seemed to stand still in midair. Daliah clutched the armrests with such force that her knuckles stood out whitely on her thin hands. Then the jumbo jet banked and slid forward with another muffled thrust of power.

She let out a deep sigh of relief and, turning back to the window, saw, not the ever-nearing white-capped waves, but images of her family. She wondered if they would meet her at the airport or send a car instead.

They know I love them dearly. They know I haven't deserted them these long, past years. They, better than anyone, understand that I had to go out into the world and make my mark to prove myself. To show them I'm worthy of the Boralevi blood coursing through my veins.

And what blood it was! What a fine, fierce lineage was her heritage!

Her smile returned as she exultantly thought of her distinguished flesh and blood, remembering them in a brilliant flash of absolute clarity the way she had last seen them, in person, not frozen in the photographs they had exchanged regularly by mail over the years: a passionately close, loving family, proudly gathered at the airport to see her off in the silvery World War II-vintage DC-3, its twin propellers already whirling, which was to fly her and twenty other passengers to Athens. From there, connecting flights would take her to London and on to New York.

Daliah could imagine her mother in precise detail on that stark sunny morning, one hand pressing down the crown of her wide-brimmed straw hat against a gust of hot wind. At fifty-four, Tamara had still possessed a startling, eye-catching beauty, with teeth—flawlessly capped back in 1930—as toothpaste-advertisement-perfect as they had been when she was the toast of thirties Hollywood. Tamara's hypnotic emerald eyes, gleaming with jeweled radiance so much like Daliah's own, coupled with the extraordinarily high Slavic cheekbones and plucked, penciled-arch brows, had made her the most fabulous face of them all and had been, on that tearful but exhilarating departure, as theatrically expressive as they were in her old black-and-white films.

During the eleven years of separation, Daliah had religiously watched Tamara's old classics whenever they were played at nostalgia festivals or repeated and re-repeated on the late and late-late shows. She had sat through them enthralled, barely believing that the beguiling film siren on the screen could actually be her mother. By the time THE END flickered on the screen, she always felt a morose, gnawing pang of guilt and homesickness, vowing to fly to Israel as expeditiously as possible for a long visit.

Now Daliah felt a warm pleasure radiate throughout her body, and her eyes sparkled in anticipation of the reunion she had put off so often, and yet waited and longed for with such keen desperation.

Her thoughts and images switched fondly to her father. How incredibly handsome he had looked that morning when he had come to see her off, his starched short-sleeved khaki shirt stained damp under the armpits, his thick, dark chest hair curling out from the V of his open-throated collar. His manner had always been so authoritative, but beneath it lurked a profound strength, an unshakable belief in what he had helped create, and a bottomless depth of love for his family.

General Dani ben Yaacov was more than a family figure-head adored by his worshiping daughter. He had been a fierce Haganah fighter, battling to thrust Palestine into the fledgling state of Israel, and then had hawkishly protected that most precious of almost holy treasures with a mother-like ferocity so that it might remain an oasis of Jewish freedom amid the simmering turmoil of the otherwise Arab Middle East. Since her departure, he had retired from the military, ironically rising in power in the process: a civilian finally, but nevertheless the staunchest of loyal patriots, he had scoffed at the idea of enjoying his golden years in quiet privacy, and had easily been swayed into being a consultant to the Israeli parliament, swiftly emerging as one of the country's most powerful and influential men. National treasure that he was, it was pitiable that the world knew him primarily as the man for whom the legendary movie queen Tamara had given up the dizzying ivory heights of her Holly-wood tower for true love—a love firmly implanted in bed-rock from the beginning, a love which had endured all obstacles and grown in strength with each passing year.

Daliah's thoughts were invaded by the imposing presence of Grandpoppa, Schmarya Boralevi himself. Grandpoppa—the only man alive who could, even now, instill a girlish fear and healthy respect in his sophisticated twenty-nine-year-old movie-star granddaughter. At seventy-two, the one-legged patriarch of the family had already been an unofficially deified living legend, a superhuman monument to the era when Jews still fled the pogroms of the Russian Pale—that area of eastern Poland and the Ukraine which had been a ghetto since the time of Catherine the Great—to the raw, brawny Promised Land. Now Grandpoppa would be . . . eighty-three? Was that possible? Yes, and doubtless he would exude the same robust health he always had.

Ever since Daliah could recall, Grandpoppa had been the easiest member of her illustrious family to conjure up visually, no matter where he might have been at the moment. His gnarled and gaunt body, with its deeply engraved hide toughened and tanned by decades spent in the relentlessly burning sun, and his shock of unruly sun-bleached white hair and long bushy white beard lent Grandpoppa the foreboding portentousness of a biblical prophet. Which, Daliah considered with gentle blasphemy, wasn't that far from the truth. Grandpoppa *had* been a modern prophet of sorts, resolutely envisioning a land for the Children of Israel long before it had ever been concretely fought for. His exploits had assumed almost mythic proportions. "Thundering Schmarya," he'd been reverently and affectionately nicknamed long ago, and the name had stuck. He could rightfully claim his bigger-than-life stance in the annals of Israeli history alongside such fellow luminaries as Chaim Weizmann and David Ben-Gurion, although he incessantly bellowed that he didn't deserve it.

Only Ari ben Yaacov, her tall and handsome older brother, a proud sabra like her, had not yet achieved legendary status.

But he will in time, Daliah assured herself loyally. Ari's made of the same starch and fiber as the rest of us, only he hasn't had the opportunity to prove himself yet. He's a late bloomer, but his time will come. He's liable to outshine us all.

Then the corners of her orange-glossed, sculptured lips puckered into a frown as she was once again confronted with the purpose of her visit. Soon she and Ari would be reunited, but not for long. His wedding loomed two days hence on the horizon, and then he would scoop up his bride and carry her off alone somewhere.

She sighed. Eleven long years had passed; but now Flight 1002 from New York had floated in right on time, and she was home. *Home.*

What a wonderful word that was. Yet . . . A tiny fear nibbled at her. Was this *really* her home? Or had she been gone for so long and had so much changed that she would find as foreign a place as myriads of others she had visited around the globe?

The chief steward's head appeared over the top of Daliah's seat. "Welcome home, Miss Boralevi," he said cheerfully in Hebrew. "I trust you enjoyed your flight?"

She unclasped her belt and turned her face up to his. "Yes, I did, thank you."

He grinned. "If you'll please follow me now, we'll hustle you off first."

She leaned over, yanked her Bottega Veneta shoulder bag from under the seat in front of hers, and got to her feet, cautiously testing her land legs. They could use some stretching and exercise; her calves were in knots.

Swiftly sidling from between the seats, she tossed her hair over her shoulders and followed him to the exit. Her spine was straight, her shoulders squared, and her walk, despite the tingling pinpricks of sleeping feet, was as casually graceful and conquering as the most seasoned model's on a fashion runway. As a stewardess prematurely pulled aside the curtain to economy class, Daliah studiously avoided the sea of upturned prying faces and gaping mouths.

She could imagine what they were thinking. *Look! For Chrissakes! A real-live movie star! Hey, I wonder, could you autograph . . . ? Could I snap a shot of you and the little woman? . . . Did you see her last flick, the one where she did the nude scene with Mel Gibson? Christ, I'd jump in the sack with her anytime.*

The chief steward took his position beside the already open exit to the accordion tunnel connecting the jet to the terminal, a massive square umbilical cord. As promised, an El Al VIP representative was waiting for Daliah.

"Elie's not on duty?" the chief steward asked the VIP rep in surprise. "I thought he was supposed to meet this flight."

"You know Elie," the man said with easy familiarity. "Panics every time his wife or one of the kids as much as sneezes. I'm temporarily assigned to take his place." The VIP man turned to Daliah and favored her with a professional smile. Politely but firmly he touched her elbow and led her toward the terminal.

Frowning, the chief steward watched their receding backs until they turned the corner and were out of sight. Funny, he thought. The VIP man sure was rushing Miss Boralevi.

Hannah, one of the economy stewardesses, rolled her dark eyes at him. "You always get the biggies. Hey! What's the matter? Why the screwed-up face?"

"I . . . don't know." He shrugged. Whatever was nagging at his mind had yet to prod his memory. Meanwhile, he had work to do. Blocking the herd of restless economy passengers, he bid each of the first-class passengers a warm, friendly good-bye. Then he let the economy people out.

Too late, he recalled that Elie lived alone with his mother, who had been left crippled after a PLO raid.

Elie had never married. He records would show that, so he'd never use such an asinine excuse to get a day off.

It was a thought which would scratch at his memory for the rest of the day.

Who, then, was the stranger who had sped Daliah Boralevi so efficiently off the aircraft?

"If you'll give me your passport and baggage claims, Miss Boralevi," the VIP representative was saying to Daliah, "we can skip the usual formalities." He smiled pleasantly, but his eyes were curiously cool as he stuck out one olive-skinned hand, palm up.

Daliah nodded and without breaking her leggy stride dug into her bag, handing him her ticket folder and the Israeli passport, sheathed in thin Mark Cross leather with triangular corners fashioned of smoothly polished twenty-four-karat gold.

Eleven years, but I've still kept my citizenship, she told herself approvingly. *And I'm glad I did. It would have been so easy to become a naturalized American after five years, but I didn't bow to temptation. I might have stayed away forever, but I didn't have the want (or courage?) to cut the umbilical tie to my heritage. That counts for something.*

Doesn't it?

The man marched Daliah swiftly past the backed-up line of passengers from an Athens flight, flashed her open passport to an official behind the counter, who nodded and waved them past. Then the VIP man guided her efficiently through the crowded, noisy terminal, making a beeline for the exits.

"Wait!" Daliah stopped, turning toward him just as he was sliding her passport and the ticket folder with the stapled-on luggage claims inside his jacket pocket. "What about my luggage? And I need my passport!"

His smile was cemented in place. "I'll have the baggage delivered to you by special courier within the hour. The same goes for your passport. Our first consideration is you. We have to be very security-conscious, and you, Miss Boralevi, are an important national treasure. El Al does not like for highly visible celebrities, especially one such as yourself, who hails from a prominent family, to be unnecessarily exposed to possible danger in public areas."

She stood her ground. "Surely there's a VIP lounge," she said with irrefutable logic. "I can wait there while you get the luggage, and save you a lot of trouble. Besides, I can't walk around without my passport. If I remember right, it's against the law here not to carry identification papers at all times."

He smiled at her typical Israeli regard for official law.

"Don't worry," he said airily. "For you, carrying identification has been temporarily waived." Apparently her logic was refutable after all. "I have strict orders, and your safety is our sole concern. The car is already waiting outside."

Her heart surged with eagerness and her eyes glowed with unexpected moisture. *The car—with my family in it, no doubt, waiting to welcome me back within the warmth of their loving fold.*

Without further delay, her Andrea Pfister heels clacked such a rapid staccato on the tile floor that it was the VIP representative's turn to keep pace. She reached the glass doors with such a rush of speed that she had to wait impatiently for them to glide smoothly apart. Then she burst out into a blaze of such stark white-hot sunshine that she was momentarily blinded. Blinking, Daliah groped in her bag for her huge dark sunglasses and slipped them on. Already her body was wilting, recoiling from the heat. After the air-conditioned cavern of the terminal, the dry broiling heat hit her with the hellish intensity of a blast furnace. The heat and sun were much harsher than she'd remembered, unrelenting and undiluted, of an almost surrealistic clarity. How easily one forgot things like that.

The VIP representative was right behind her, guiding her toward a shiny old Chrysler limousine waiting at the curb. Its tinted windows were tightly shut, obviously cocooning the interior's air-conditioned coolness from the ungodly temperature outside. The driver waited behind the wheel, and in the back seat, at the far side, Daliah could make out a shadowy figure.

Only one person's come to greet me, she thought with a pang of misgiving. Who would it be? Dani? Or Ari? Perhaps Tamara?

The El Al representative gripped the rust-speckled chrome handle and yanked open the rear door. Daliah ducked inside the big car. Then she clutched the doorframe, her stomach heaving in fear.

It wasn't any of her family come to greet her, but a hawk-nosed, dark-skinned stranger, who was not offering her a welcoming bouquet but a victim's-eye view of the round, malevolent barrel of a revolver. It was lined up point-blank with her suddenly wary green eyes.

Time came to a standstill.

"Welcome to Israel, Miss Boralevi," the stranger said with a ghastly smile, his Hebrew heavily accented with an Arab dialect.

She blinked and turned slowly as another pistol prodded

her spine. The man posing as a VIP representative pressed close behind her, shielding his pistol from any curious onlookers with his body. On the sidewalk behind him, she caught sight of two wiry policemen in short-sleeved uniforms. Her heart gave a hopeful surge.

"I would get in very quietly if I were you," the voice behind her whispered threateningly. "If you try anything, you'll get shot, and innocent bystanders will get killed too. We have people staked out all over the airport."

She didn't doubt him one bit. Wordlessly she climbed into the car. The bogus VIP man got in beside her. The door slammed shut against reality. Two pistols, one to either side of her, pressed through her expensive clothes, into her flesh.

"What's going on?" she demanded as the big car surged off smoothly. Her face was bleak, drained of its naturally creamy color.

The men remained silent.

"Tell me. What do you want with me? I've done nothing."

"Ah. So you too are one of the holy innocents." The man who had been waiting in the back seat barked a short laugh. "You have more than your share of skeletons rattling in your family's closet, *film star*," he spat out harshly. "It is time someone paid for them."

"Paid?" She nearly laughed hysterically, choked it down with an immense effort. "Whatever for?"

"Let us say . . . for the sins of the fathers and the mothers." His smile was fixed.

"You won't get money from them. They refuse to buckle in to kidnappers' demands. You should know that."

"It's not money we want."

Her face burned feverishly. "What, then?"

"To pay them back . . . in kind. Call it payday, if you wish."

"You know what you are," she said with a blunt, cool vehemence, somehow managing to keep her voice subdued and steady. "You're nothing but common criminals. *Criminals*," she pronounced a second time, as though needing to make her point twice.

But her mind was racing. What did he mean by "the sins of the fathers and the mothers?" Was he being metaphorical? Or was she meant to take it literally?

I
Senda
1911–1922

Composers, playwrights, choreographers, and dancers found favor, fame, and fortune in prerevolutionary Russia, but because of the fleeting popularity of its stage stars and the lack of records on film, only a solitary name has survived from the stars of the theater of that pre-motion-picture era—the legendary Senda Bora.

—Rhea Gallaher, Jr.,
Stage and Screen: A History of World Entertainment

The pale afternoon sun cast weak, shifting shadows on the soft mossy ground in the birch forest. The canopy of tender green leaves overhead diffused the light even further, softly dappling Senda's purposeful features with a luminous glow. She was humming softly to herself, the tune one of the lighthearted lullabies Grandmother Goldie used to sing to her at bedtime as a child. Now the tune was especially appropriate, she considered. It was soft and lulling, light and innocent, and she appreciated the innocence it conveyed because she knew that the tryst toward which she was hurrying was anything but.

She lifted her heavy quilted skirt and with a swiftly bouncing step darted through the trees, ducking here and there to avoid the low-hanging branches. She breathed the brisk chill air and laughed to herself. Spring had definitely dawned, last night's frost had disappeared. She took it as a good omen and hurried even faster. Soon she left the village far behind, and only once she crested the hill and reached the familiar clearing did she stop to catch her breath.

This was her favorite spot. To her right was the wellspring of the stream which flowed past the village, the water in the small pool clean and crystal clear. She treasured the solitude this spot afforded, and proprietarily thought of it as her own—and *his*. Here they could make love together, far from prying eyes. Here, too, she could be at peace with only the sounds of the babbling water, the rustling of the leaves, and the chirping of the birds. Surveying the countryside from the clearing, she felt that the world was at her feet, the tiny rustic cottages built of mud, wattle, and wood appearing tinier yet, but the distance made the mean poverty of the village fetching, with the most important building, the synagogue, standing apart, larger and therefore more imposing.

Her breathing returned to normal, and she spun around, her skirt swirling about her legs. Her eyes searched the trees. She was alone.

The anticipation of seeing Schmarya again brought a glowing flush to her cheeks, intensifying her already natural startling beauty. Her face was a blend of her father's finely chiseled features, far too beautiful and delicate in a man but striking in a woman, and her mother's more harsh and determinedly disciplined, though no less eye-catching, strength. In Senda, the distillation was arresting, lending her a peculiar, other-worldly beauty all her own. Her face was a perfect oval, with striking Slavic cheekbones, exquisite Botticelli hair, and dazzling emerald eyes. Seen close, they were not perfectly emerald, but touched with glints of hazel and slivers of aqua, each a perfect jewel set within a star of copper lashes which matched her thick, gleaming hair. Her eyebrows were bewitching and decidedly witchlike, slanting upward at the ends at an elfin angle, and her skin had the luster of pearl touched ever so slightly with a faint healthy pink glow. There was a naturally poetic lilt to her carriage, and she was by far the most beguiling young woman in the village, far more lovely, it was said, than even Grandmother Goldie had been, and Goldie Koppel was still as famous for her long-lost beauty as for her razor-sharp tongue. At the tender age of sixteen, Senda's beauty was in its flowering prime. Seated against the thin, supple trunk of the birch under its vast umbrella of green, with her knees drawn up close to her chin, Senda looked remarkably like one of the wood nymphs which populated the fairy tales she'd been told as a child. Not even the voluminous, shapeless quilt of a skirt in its drab shade of mud brown, and the modest off-white peasant blouse, unadorned with any finery, not even an inch of lace, could detract from her magical appearance. Her sole feminine adornment was her precious bright scarlet scarf, tied like a sash around her waist. As soon as she'd left the village behind, she'd snatched it off her head and wrapped it around her. It was a desperate attempt at beautification, at the finery she hankered for but knew would forever elude her in this poor, puritanical village. But no matter what she wore, her nineteen-inch waist and well-matured breasts could not be disguised, to the chagrin of her shrewish, domineering mother, her sedate, archconservative husband, Solomon, and her disapproving in-laws. "She's far too beautiful for her own good," her mother-in-law, Rachel Boralevi, was all too fond of suspiciously uttering to any sympathetic ear she could find.

Not that Rachel Boralevi didn't have a point. But for all her suspicions, even she had begun to admit that maybe Senda wasn't all that bad, and that she had, thank God, settled down since she'd married the apple of Rachel's eye—her dear brilliant and sensitive Solomon. But Rachel Boralevi saw what she wanted to see. She had even begun to take Senda's afternoon walks at face value, and Senda, knowing there was little love lost between them, tried her best to conceal her true self. At home she was demure, almost decorously prim and silent, not so much because she wanted to give a false impression of herself as because she was trapped in a loveless marriage—a marriage which was slowly killing her spirit. And it was this sullen spiritlessness that let Rachel Boralevi breathe a little easier. She was blind to the fire which burned within Senda's emerald eyes. It glowed constantly and turbulently, pleading for the three things she treasured most: freedom, adventure, and true love.

Senda's breasts now heaved with a painful sigh. She knew she was lucky to have managed to leave the house and come here. Only here in the forest clearing could she really be herself. Only here could she breathe freely, without being stifled, without being physically and emotionally fettered in a match not made in heaven. The forest gave her respite from the arranged marriage she so despised. And most important, it gave her the opportunity to steal the few precious hours of love which made life worth living and kept the fire from dying within her eyes.

Her extraordinary features sagged into a most unattractive frown. "Only me, Grandmother Goldie, and Schmarya," she said aloud, voicing her misery to a pair of sparrows darting through the trees. "Why are we the only ones who know how much I despise this marriage? Why?"

Neither the trees nor the birds could answer her question. She fell silent, her frown deepening, remembering that day last year when the *shadchen* and her family had arranged her loveless union.

"She's not built for childbearing," pronounced a woman's shrill voice. "You have only to look at her hips. Did any of you notice how narrow they are?" There was a prolonged silence. "You see!" the woman cried dramatically, smacking her hand resoundingly on her knee with the force of a gunshot. "What did I tell you? One look at her, and you can see that she'll never give birth! And tell me, what good is a woman who can't have children, eh? You tell me!" Her prognostication was punctuated by the sudden creak of her chair as she sat back in triumph.

Senda felt Grandmother Goldie's gentle hand on her arm and resisted the impulse to stick her head through the open window to give Eva Boralevi a piece of her mind. Instead, she peered cautiously around the edge of the window frame, her face hidden from sight by the dark night and the curtain shifting in the breeze. Through the lace patterns she could see the kitchen of the Boralevi cottage. It was the main room, and it was warmly lit by flickering oil lamps. The faces of all those in the room were aglow with the yellow light. The Boralevi family counselors, six of them; the *shadchen*, the official matchmaker who arranged marriages between families; the Valvrojenskis, her own parents, who had been relatively silent; and Uncle Chaim, her father's brother, and, his wife, Aunt Sophie, who had debated vehemently, pointing out her outstanding qualities, one by one, as the Boralevis had seized upon every potential defect. In all, there were eleven people crowded in a semicircle on three-legged stools; only Rachel and Eva Boralevi occupied chairs with backs.

The meeting had already lasted for over two hours, and the debate had just begun to heat up. Now, with Eva Boralevi's grim verdict on childbearing, the debate came to a temporary standstill. Eva Boralevi was the local midwife, and no one dared argue with her when it came to matters of giving birth. Nor did any family want to be saddled with a barren woman.

"I think," the *shadchen* said hastily, sensing that the debate had gotten totally out of hand, "that it's time to take a break and have a nice cup of hot tea."

"So now we should stay to have tea?" Uncle Chaim growled. "It's obvious that our Senda isn't good enough for the high-and-mighty Boralevis."

"Ssssh, ssssh!" Aunt Sophie hushed her husband quickly. Then she smiled around the kitchen. "Some tea would be very nice."

Senda felt Grandmother Goldie pulling her aside, away from the window. She let herself be led around the corner, out of earshot. "I have to go back inside now," Grandmother Goldie told her. "I left because I said I had to use the outhouse. I can't stay out here with you forever."

Senda nodded in the dark. "But . . . but I don't *want* to marry Solomon!" she cried in a low voice. "You know that, Grandmother Goldie. Meanwhile, they're tearing me to shreds in there—dissecting me like a piece of meat! If they don't want me, why don't they just come out and say it and leave me in peace?" The pale moonlight shone weakly on her miserable features.

"It's not that, Sendale, and you know it. They do want you—"

"But I don't want *them*!" Senda interrupted vehemently. "Not Solomon or any of his family!" She sniffed noisily. "I want nothing to do with any of them!"

"Not *any* of them?" Grandmother Goldie asked shrewdly.

"Well, Schmarya, yes," Senda admitted in a voice filled with longing. "But he's not like the rest of the Boralevis." Suddenly her emotional dam broke and the words tumbled out of her mouth. "I love him, Grandmother Goldie! Oh, how I love Schmarya. And he loves me too!"

"I know. I know," the old woman whispered gently, "but Schmarya is out of the question. Your parents would never allow you to marry him."

Senda hung her head. "I know," she said miserably.

"And if you know what's good for you, you'll stay far away from him." Grandmother Goldie's voice grew harsher. "Schmarya everyone tries to avoid like the plague, and with good reason. Even his parents have washed their hands of him. He has dangerous ideas. You mark my words, one of these days he will come to no good."

Senda remained silent.

"Now, cheer up." Grandmother Goldie smiled and took Senda's chin in her hand, raising her granddaughter's head. "And be very quiet so nobody hears you eavesdrop. When the negotiations are winding up, hurry home. It's not seemly for a young woman to be found eavesdropping. You know how upset finding that out would make your mother."

"Why should I care about her?" Senda asked, her low voice none the less savage for its softness. "Mama doesn't want what's best for me."

"Senda!" Grandmother Goldie hissed sharply. "Your mother loves you. That you know. She only wants what's best for you *and* the family. And it's up to you to do what's best for the family too." She paused, her voice growing gentler. "Now, pull the shawl tighter around you so you don't catch your death." She patted Senda's arm and almost reluctantly left her outside while she went back into the cottage.

Senda retraced her steps to the kitchen window.

"You were certainly gone a long time," Senda's mother complained to Grandmother Goldie when she returned to the Boralevis' kitchen. "For a moment I thought we should have to check on you. We were afraid the wolves had gotten to you."

"I should make excuses for my health?" the old woman

27

snapped. "If you should be so unfortunate to live as long as I have, Esther, it's trouble you'll have with your bowels too."

Esther Valvrojenski's jaw snapped audibly shut. Outside the window, Senda couldn't help but grin. Grandmother Goldie was the only person who wouldn't let her daughter get the better of her.

"Here, I kept your tea warm for you." Aunt Sophie handed Grandmother Goldie a steaming glass filled with amber liquid. The old woman took it, popped a lump of sugar into her mouth, and took a sip of tea.

"It's good tea, no?" Senda's mother said gushingly. "Mrs. Boralevi knows just how to brew it perfectly."

"So now it takes special talent to brew tea?" Grandmother Goldie sniffed. The way the marriage negotiations were proceeding, she couldn't see any reason to suck up to the Boralevis. She chewed quickly on the sugar with the good teeth on the right side of her mouth, swallowed the lumpy granules, and put her cup down after the one sip and pushed it away. Now that she'd tasted the tea and the others had had the chance to simmer down, it was time to get the negotiations back on track. *"Nu,"* she said coolly, fixing the *shadchen* with a hard gaze. "Are we going to socialize all night or finish what's begun? We've plenty of work awaiting us, and there are plenty of families who'd give their eyeteeth for our Senda's dowry."

The *shadchen* flashed Eva a stern warning look. It was clear that the Boralevis had gone just a little too far; the *shadchen* could sense that Senda was slowly slipping out of the Boralevis' grasp. Mention of the dowry did it: the Boralevis might be more prominent socially, but the Valvrojenskis were far better off financially. If things didn't proceed with more caution, then Senda, and therefore the dowry, would be forever lost to them.

"Dowry aside," Aunt Sophie put in, smacking her lips, "it's like an angel our Senda cooks. Of course, she learned from her mother and me. There's no better homemaker in all the village than our Senda."

Grandmother Goldie leapt into the melee. "And wasn't *I* skinny? And didn't *I* have a fine daughter?" She thrust her jutting chin at Esther. "And didn't Esther have the fine daughter we're now discussing? Who's to say that Senda cannot have children?" She glared at Eva Boralevi. "You yourself delivered Senda from hips as narrow as those you hint are barren, or did you forget that?"

Eva suddenly looked nonplused, and Rachel, Solomon's

mother, took over for the Boralevis. "But can Senda manage household accounts?" she asked smoothly. "A Talmudic scholar is learned beyond belief, but a way to live in riches it's not."

"Senda knows how to manage things," Esther Valvrojenski put in quickly. "Didn't I myself teach her?"

"But can Senda live on the good graces of many?" Rachel insisted. "Or is she too proud? Like I said earlier, Solomon, being a brilliant scholar, depends upon the entire village for his livelihood."

Adroitly Grandmother Goldie picked up the thread of conversation. "Solomon we bless for all the hours he spends at the *shul*. But being a scholar isn't exactly the way a fine young man can take care of his family, is it?"

Rachel and Eva looked scandalized. It was blasphemous that anyone should dare question a Talmudic scholar's calling.

Grandmother Goldie seized upon their silence. "Perhaps our Senda should marry someone more . . . more comfortably well-off?" she suggested, tapping her folded arms with her fingers.

"But why?" Eva asked, her feathers more than ruffled. Her voice grew shrill. "All of us contribute to the care of Talmudic scholars, no one more than us Boralevis. So tell me, you think once our Solomon is married we'll withdraw our support?"

Grandmother Goldie let her silence speak for itself.

"You forget," Rachel Boralevi said importantly, "a Talmudic scholar makes an enviable addition to any family," stressing the word "any."

Grandmother Goldie looked at Rachel shrewdly. "The way I see it," she said with her usual practicality, "Solomon needs our Senda and her dowry much more than our Senda needs your brilliant scholar. And of course," she goaded, laying her trump card out on the table, "we don't even know if Senda wants to marry him, do we?" She turned her back on them, a sly, gloating smile lighting up her ancient face.

The Boralevis were shocked into silence. No self-respecting family let the feelings of a mere child enter into such important decisions. It was unheard-of. What did a girl of fifteen know, anyway? When the negotiations had begun, the Boralevis had been certain it was they who held all the cards. They hadn't expected such a fierce onslaught from Senda's family. What Grandmother Goldie had voiced was true, but it wasn't the kind of thing decent people said—not with a Talmudic scholar at the center of the argument.

"My mother is right," Esther Valvrojenski boasted proudly.

"My daughter's dowry is one this village hasn't seen the like of for years. No girl will bring more to a marriage." She sniffed and wiped her nose. "Senda is all we have. Even our cottage someday will be hers."

"And ours will be Solomon's," Rachel retorted, not to be outdone. Her voice and attitude expressed miffed indignation.

"Mrs. Boralevi!" Aunt Sophie exclaimed. "How can you say such a thing? It's two sons you have. And Solomon is the younger. Traditionally the older son inherits. Surely they both can't?"

Rachel suddenly looked flustered. She had walked into a trap of her own making. She cursed herself for her stupidity. All evening long, she had adroitly avoided any mention of Schmarya. She did not like the twist these negotiations were taking, not at all. Somehow the tables had turned on her, and the strong position she and her family had started out with had suddenly been undermined. "Schmarya is not one for the life in a small village," she murmured weakly, her gaze suddenly occupied by studying her folded hands in her lap.

"Then you're disinheriting him?" Grandmother Goldie asked slyly.

Outside the window, Senda had been listening to the negotiations with a mixture of quickening interest and revulsion. She despised Solomon and couldn't for the life of her conceive of sharing his life and bed; nor could she help her morbid fascination with the drama unfolding before her eyes. She prayed fervently that Solomon would never be hers. At the same time, she couldn't help but feel delight at the beating the Boralevis now took. But the moment Schmarya was brought up, the most intense hatred she had ever felt prickled hotly behind her ears. How dare they? she felt like screaming. What right did they have to discuss him? she asked herself savagely. What did they know about Schmarya? Only *she* knew him . . . knew how he spoke out against injustice . . . knew how he tried to fight their serflike servitude and the anti-Semitic life they were all locked into. He was the solitary outspoken critic of Wolzak, the landowner who bled them all dry, and Czar Nicholas II, whose unfair laws allowed him to do so. Solomon hid behind his books, the entire village buried their heads in their work, and only Schmarya had the courage to speak out.

Inside the kitchen, the mention of Schmarya quickly brought preliminary negotiations to a close, and the bargaining began in earnest. Schmarya was the black sheep of the Boralevi family—indisputably, the black sheep of the entire village.

Everyone in the room knew that although they had never been proven, the rumors that Schmarya was involved with a band of anarchists were undeniably true. Which was why Solomon was having such a difficult time of it finding an appropriate wife. Even the rabbi would not permit his homely daughter, Jael, to marry into a family tainted by such a volatile son, although no one would dare speak of it. It was surely only a matter of time before tragedy struck Schmarya. And when it did, then perhaps the entire Boralevi family would suffer the consequences along with him.

"Forty silver coins more," Eva was saying firmly. Gone suddenly was the careful, crafty game-playing, the verbal shifting of musical chairs. She was seriously bargaining for Senda's dowry now, greed glinting in her sharp dark eyes. "Plus the hope chest, and the original twenty silver coins you have offered already."

"Four more silver coins and nothing more," Senda's father said gruffly.

"Fifteen silver coins more." Rachel Boralevi eyed the Valvrojenskis shrewdly. "You should want your only daughter to starve?"

"So maybe if she stays at home and doesn't marry Solomon, she'll eat, *nu*?" Uncle Chaim interjected heatedly.

"Ten silver coins more," the *shadchen* put in quickly, trying to get back into the act of bargaining. So far, the matchmaker had let the negotiations be taken out of her hands, and if she let the others seal the bargain without her, then she was in danger of losing her commission.

"Five coins more," Senda's father said adamantly, "as well as the original dowry."

Rachel Boralevi glanced at her husband. A silent signal seemed to pass between them. Her husband sighed heavily and shook his head sadly. He sat hunched over, as though in great pain. Finally he shrugged. "Seven more silver coins and we'll call it quits," he said, "but as God is my witness, my family for this will suffer."

"It's settled then," Senda's mother said quickly.

"We'll drink a toast!" Rachel Boralevi sat up straighter, her eyes shining eagerly. "Not the *chazerei* we drink every day. The good wine we've been saving for the holidays."

Then everyone began talking excitedly all at once. Forgotten now were the tough, cruel accusations of only moments ago.

Suddenly they were all the best of friends.

Outside, Senda clutched the windowsill unsteadily and

shut her eyes. She let out a silent moan of intense pain. She felt drained, numb. Her entire world had suddenly collapsed about her. She wished she were dead.

Clapping a hand over her mouth, she stumbled home, tears flooding from her eyes. When she reached her family's cottage on the far side of the village, she fairly flew through the front gate, rushed at the front door, and the moment she burst into the tiny bedroom she shared with Grandmother Goldie, slammed the door shut with such fierce force that the entire cottage shook under the impact.

She flung herself on her narrow bed and sat huddled there, her arms wrapped protectively around her as if she suffered from a mortal wound. Her head lolled forward against her chest, and her face was streaked with tears. She didn't move from her pathetically childlike and vulnerable position. She didn't even lift her head when she heard her parents, Aunt Sophie, Uncle Chaim, and Grandmother Goldie finally return from the Boralevis'. Normally she would have jumped up and run to embrace them, but tonight she didn't care if she never saw them again, with the exception of Grandmother Goldie. Not for as long as she lived. Not after they had so cold-bloodedly bargained for a marriage she found loathsome in her heart and soul.

She heard chairs scrape and creak. In the kitchen, everyone talked at once, and she could hear snatches of the conversation, then the clinking of a bottle as tiny glass cups of precious celebratory wine were half-filled to toast the completion of the marriage negotiations.

"I'm so *relieved*!" Senda's mother was exclaiming. "For a moment there, I thought I should suffer a heart attack!" She allowed herself a low laugh, now that the ordeal was over.

"You deported yourself very well, as usual," her father said loyally.

"Yes, I rather did, didn't I?" Her mother sounded pleased. "Imagine *us*, the Valvrojenskis, related to the Boralevis! And Solomon a Talmudic scholar, yet! Such an honor!"

"Yes, a fine young man he is," Aunt Sophie agreed heartily. "A good catch. Nothing like that no-good brother of his."

"For a moment," Uncle Chaim interjected, "I was afraid it was all off."

"And it would have been, too, " Aunt Sophie retorted angrily, "had I let you walk out like you threatened! Fine things you get us into, Chaim! It's God I thank that I had the finesse and the fortitude to gloss over your outburst. If I hadn't, poor Senda would still be husbandless!"

I don't count, Senda thought angrily as the voices rose and fell, carrying clearly into her room. There they sit, congratulating themselves on what a fine match they've found for me. Well, the hell with *shadchens* and tradition, that's all I've got to say! I won't stand for being haggled over like a piece of meat! I will not be a sacrificial lamb for my mother's social climbing!

Once again her eyes overflowed with tears. She threw herself facedown on the bed, sobbing soundlessly into the pillow as she railed against the injustice of it all. She clapped her hands over her ears to try to drown out the voices from the kitchen, but she only succeeded in muting them somewhat.

"L'Chaim!" her father's voice rang out all too clearly.

"L'Chaim!" came the answering chorus. Glasses were clinked, and the toast drunk.

"Ah. Good wine," Uncle Chaim said with a deep sigh of contentment. "Better than the Boralevis'."

In the kitchen, Grandmother Goldie had watched the others throw back their heads and swallow the wine, their faces flushing slightly under the glow of the rich ruby-red liquid. She looked down at her untouched glass. Now the others stared at her.

"You should think Senda would be invited to join in the toast," Grandmother Goldie said quietly.

Senda's mother, who was seated beside her husband, smiled vaguely. Now that the negotiations were over, she was breathing easily, and the wine was making her feel heady and expansive. "Oh, I don't think Senda would be interested," she said. "What's she to do with it?"

"It's her life," Grandmother Goldie reminded her daughter. "It's she who has to live with Solomon Boralevi."

Senda's mother caught the unmistakably brittle tone in Grandmother Goldie's voice. "And it's a fine young man he is," she responded without hesitation. "Senda's a very lucky girl."

"Certainly she is," Aunt Sophie echoed. "She should count her blessings. It's not every girl who catches a Talmudic scholar. Such prestige."

Grandmother Goldie stared first at her daughter-in-law, Sophie, then at Esther, her daughter. This was unbelievable. A marriage should be built on a firm foundation. And should not love be a part of it? Had they all forgotten that? And hadn't Senda made her feelings about Solomon clear, time and again? Yes, but nobody had chosen to listen. "Senda doesn't love Solomon," she stated quietly as she set her

33

untouched wine on the kitchen table. "Has that not occurred to any of you?"

Senda's mother waved her hand in irritation. "Then she will come to love him in time," she said quickly. "Love has to grow. In the beginning, it's like it was with us . . . all of us." She nodded at her husband. "From duty springs love."

"That's all you have to say about it, then?"

Senda's mother nodded emphatically with self-righteousness. "That's our final decision. The marriage ceremony will take place as planned next month."

Later, when the cottage was quiet, Grandmother Goldie tiptoed softly into the little bedroom she shared with Senda. The window was open, and the curtains fluttered with the chill night air. She looked down at her grandchild. Senda was lying under the covers, her face turned toward the wall. Her breathing was coming regularly, as though she were asleep, but Grandmother Goldie knew she was pretending.

"Sendale, child, I know you're awake."

Senda let out a stifled sob.

Grandmother Goldie took a seat on the edge of Senda's narrow bed. "It's not the end of the world, child," she tried to reassure her softly.

Senda didn't turn around. When she spoke, it was in a thick, muffled mumble. "Yes. It is."

Grandmother Goldie sighed heavily. "Please, Sendale, listen to what I have to say to you."

Obediently Senda sat up and faced her grandmother in the dark.

"That's better." Grandmother Goldie spoke haltingly, choosing her words with care. "Like it or not, a few things in life you must understand and accept. Now you are fifteen, almost sixteen, not a child anymore. You are a woman, and it is our lot to be hardworking and obedient."

"And suffer through marriage to someone revolting?"

"Don't be so stubborn!" Grandmother Goldie whispered. She shook her head. "You may be a woman now, but you are still a child in many ways."

"Am I?" Even in the dark, Grandmother Goldie could feel her granddaughter's challenging gaze burning into her.

"No, you're not," the old woman admitted at long last. "But you must go through with this marriage nevertheless, no matter how distasteful it may seem to you. It would break your poor parents' hearts if you didn't. The shame of it! They'd never be able to live it down."

"But I can?" Senda countered in a low voice. "*I'm* the

one who has to live with him. *I'm* the one who's expected to give birth to Solomon's children." She paused. "Grandmother Goldie . . ." she began haltingly.

Goldie reached out and embraced her granddaughter. "Yes, child?"

It was then that the torrent of misery broke and the words burst forth from Senda's lips. Quietly keening, she cried into her grandmother's warm, gaunt bosom. "Oh, it's not Solomon I love," she moaned over and over. "It's his brother, Schmarya. What will I do? I can't live without Schmarya!"

"You mustn't speak such things! You must get Schmarya completely out of your mind. Do you understand?"

"How can I?" Senda cried. "It's him I love. And he loves me."

"You must!" Grandmother Goldie insisted sharply. "This is evil! To think of your betrothed's brother in such a way!"

Senda was silent.

"Promise me!" Grandmother Goldie's voice was sharper than Senda had ever heard it. "You must never speak of this again! You must banish it from your mind forever!"

Senda's eyes were as lackluster as the dark.

Grandmother Goldie shook her. "Promise me!" she hissed, her fingers digging into Senda's arms.

Senda shrugged. "If you insist," she mumbled without conviction.

"*Promise me!*"

"I promise."

Goldie let out a deep breath of relief. Then she held her only grandchild in her arms, rocking her back and forth as though she were a baby. She too was crying, not for lost loves, but because she knew that by insisting Senda marry Solomon, she had betrayed her grandchild, the person on earth she loved above all others. "You'll see," she murmured soothingly, "everything will be for the best."

Gently Senda pulled herself out of her grandmother's arms. "Marriage entails . . . so many things."

"It is only your duty you have to do."

"But I'll have to . . . you know, nights . . ."

"That will come naturally," Grandmother Goldie told her sternly. "You should think of your physical duties now? In time, you'll get used to it."

But Senda never did.

The night of her marriage, when Solomon stiffly stepped out of his best clothes, folding each piece neatly on the chair before taking off the next, a nauseating revulsion held Senda in its grip. She turned away from him, able to bear him in his nakedness even less than she could when he was clothed. She was sickened by his thick facial beard and even thicker pelt of dark body hair. His pale scrawny body and thin, erect penis disgusted her even more. When he slid naked under the covers beside her, she lay there unmoving, unyielding as a rock. "Good night, Solomon," she said with abrupt finality, pulling the quilt higher around her neck.

His hands moved under the covers. "I love you, Senda," he said softly.

"I'm tired," came her reply. She wanted to jump out of bed, run outside in her flannel nightgown, and dash home to her own comforting little bed in the room she had shared with Grandmother Goldie. Yet she knew she didn't dare. She was honor- and duty-bound to share Solomon's life and bed. Anything else was unthinkable.

She cringed as she felt him plant a clumsy wet kiss on the nape of her neck. "I . . . I don't feel well," she pleaded, fighting down the nausea rising in her throat. "Maybe it was all the wine, or the dancing . . ."

"Don't you love me?" Solomon sounded hurt. He nudged closer to her, and Senda could feel his moist penis rigid against her buttocks.

"Of course I love you, Solomon," she said with resignation. She could feel his piercing gaze, and was grateful that she had turned away from him, her rich, gleaming copper hair covering her face like a veil. It made her feel safer, more withdrawn, and he couldn't see the look of revulsion on her face.

"Is something wrong?" he insisted.

"Nothing's wrong that a little sleep won't cure," she lied. "Now, please," she begged, "turn out the lamp and let me go to sleep. Maybe tomorrow . . ."

But when tomorrow came, she found another excuse, and the following night, yet another. Tomorrows without love-making blended into tomorrows, until Solomon gave up completely. Senda was his wife in every way but one.

"Many women don't like it," his father told him. "In time, they come around."

But Senda never fulfilled Solomon's physical passion. She satisfied her own in the forest clearing with Schmarya, exposing for him what she could never allow herself to expose to his brother, her husband.

To Schmarya she offered the jutting, proud strawberry nipples of her well-formed breasts and her softly muscled belly.

36

To Schmarya she offered up her lean hips and the curly copper pubis arrowhead which nestled softly and secretively at that part of her which was all woman.

It was Schmarya's, not Solomon's, engorged phallus that entered her, bringing her to bursting climax again and again, making her feel loved and complete.

Which was why now, once again, she waited with bated breath and surging blood for him to come to their secret clearing in the birch forest. She could imagine his strong body on top of hers, his mouth devouring hers, his tongue running over her breasts, down between her legs, until finally she begged him to enter her. Oh, God, how she loved it with him, could never get enough as they untiringly coupled again and again in their stolen hours spent together.

The snap of a breaking twig brought her out of her reverie. She sat bolt upright, her sparkling emerald eyes searching the trees to catch sight of him. "Schmarya," she called out softly, her heart hammering with anticipation. "Schmarya, I'm over here. *Schmarya*! In the name of God, Schmarya! What happened to you?"

Her hand flew to her breast, her fine thin nostrils flared, and her eyes grew large as saucers. For one long, terrifying instant, her heart stopped dead. After a moment, her heart began pounding.

Schmarya did not speak. Arms outstretched, he weakly wove his way toward her, as though drunk, but she knew, knew for certain deep within her heart, that it was not drink which made him stagger. Whatever he had been up to, he had gotten hurt. Oh, dear God! His forehead was cut open and was bleeding.

Uttering a cry, she summoned her legs to move and darted swiftly through the trees toward him. When she reached him, she clasped him under the armpits, and he let himself be helped down into a sitting position, his head leaning back against the peeling bark of a birch. "Don't worry," he panted. "Got thrown. Off a horse. Am all right."

"Don't talk now, just rest," she ordered briefly, hurrying back to the spring. When she reached it, she whipped her precious scarlet scarf from around her waist, knelt at the edge of the tiny pool, and plunged the scarf into the icy water, making certain the wool absorbed as much water as it could. Then loosely rolling the soaked scarf into a ball, she hurried back to him, the wet bundle dripping water all over the front of her voluminous skirt.

She dropped to a squatting position beside him, gently

cleaning his head wound. Water trickled down his face, dripped into his collar.

He sat expressionless, his eyes closed as she dabbed at the blood, his long booted legs, thick with powerful thigh muscles, stretched out straight in front of him. Sixteen years old, like her, over six feet tall without his boots, and she couldn't help admiring his manliness even now that he was her patient, his face with its proud bone structure caked with blood and his golden hair disheveled. He was large-boned and hard of muscle, but didn't carry a spare ounce of fat on his body. He had the healthy complexion of one who spent life out-of-doors. And handsome . . . so incredibly handsome he made her heart ache, with his lusty, naturally red lips, bold blue-sapphire eyes always glinting with amused contempt, and his clean-shaven face with its strong cleft chin jutting almost insolently out at the world.

After a few minutes his face was clean. She sat back on her heels. "There." She was relieved, but her face was set in anger, as if she wanted to attack him for causing her such fright. Instead, her voice was soft and soothing. "It's only a surface wound, thank God." She paused briefly, furrowing her slanting brows. "Schmarya, what in God's name have you been up to?"

He tilted his head forward and bridged her sharp gaze, his face filled with unspeakable anguish. Then he heaved a massive sigh, as if the weight of the world was upon him alone, let his head fall back upon the yielding trunk of the young birch, and shut his eyes and began to weep. Soundlessly, without even heaving his chest. But the tears rolled steadily down his cheeks.

"Schmarya!" she whispered. She was more frightened by his tears than she had been when she'd first glimpsed his wound. Schmarya wasn't one to cry. She had seen him clamp his teeth together and scoff at the pain when he'd once gotten badly hurt while chopping firewood.

"*Schmarya.*"

He did not speak, and in the heavy silence which hung over them, the sound of far-distant hoofbeats came whispering on the wind. Soft and muted, far away, but quickly growing louder, as if many horses were galloping furiously toward them.

Schmarya tensed and his eyes flew open with a start. He wiped away his tears with the back of a hand, stumbled unsteadily to his feet, and swiftly lurched toward the far end of the clearing, with its fine vista of the village below. He kept staring down. Then suddenly he turned to her. "We've got to warn them," he said grimly.

"Warn whom? About what?" She stared at him, her eyes wide and scared.

"There's no time to explain. Quickly! We've got to get to the village!" Without another word, he ran off through the trees, stumbling and sliding downhill.

For a moment she stared after him, hands on her hips in perplexed indecision. What could there possibly be to fear? What danger had he sensed? Her eyes darted about, searching the forest. Overhead, the birch branches shivered and rustled softly in the cool breeze. Birds swooped and sang in the sky. She could smell the fresh earthiness of spring all around her, could feel the comforting moistness of the cushiony moss beneath her feet. Everything seemed crystal clear somehow, as though all five of her senses were heightened. Something, she knew—*something*, whatever nameless, faceless danger it was—threatened from nearby.

Finally she caught up with Schmarya, but there was no sweet victory in winning this footrace. When they'd begun running, she had been well-rested, while he had already been half-dead on his feet. And although he'd started running with a burst of speed, she could feel his pace was already flagging. It was obvious that he had summoned his last reserves of strength for this run.

She raced beside him now, bosom heaving, heart hammering. Her lungs felt as though they were on fire from the exertion. She was so winded she could barely breathe, and her legs felt heavier and heavier, as if weighed down with lead. Still, she forced herself to keep pace with him.

If he can run in his condition, then I can keep up, she told herself resolutely.

She stole a sideways glance at him. Schmarya's face was set in fierce lines of determination.

"Schmarya," she finally gasped, "I can't. Can't run anymore. Got to rest. You too."

"No." He was short of breath, but breathing evenly, steadily, conserving what little strength he had left. "Got to make it." His words were clipped, disjointed, in rhythm with his breathing.

"But why? Tell me! Why?"

"Horses."

"So? Not the first time. Horses here. Horses ride past. All the time."

"Not like that. Not so many." He clenched his fists as he

spurred himself on faster, head tilted skyward, eyes half-shut. "Pogrom."

"What!"

Despite the sweat which bathed her, her blood suddenly ran cold at this dreaded word. What Jewish child in Russia didn't know the meaning of "pogrom"? *Sanctioned death. Slaughter of the innocent. All because of a circumstance of birth over which they had no control.*

"No. Can't be." Tears pushed out of the corners of her eyes. She didn't want to believe this. Couldn't begin to believe it. Pogroms were a thing of the past. "Hasn't been one." She panted for breath. "For years. Why now?"

"Pogrom," Schmarya repeated doggedly.

"But why? What reason—" She clamped her lips shut. How stupid of her! From the stories she'd heard, there didn't have to be a reason for a pogrom. Being Jewish was excuse enough.

"Wolzak's house. Someone burned it. I tried to stop them, but I was too late."

So there *was* a reason. She stared sideways at him, her attention on him instead of the ground up ahead. Suddenly she let out a scream as she tripped on a fallen log. She somersaulted forward headfirst, her skirt and petticoat flying. She landed facedown and felt the air being knocked out of her lungs.

Dazed, she raised her head. Then she shook it angrily, as though to clear it. She scowled. Schmarya hadn't stopped to help her. He hadn't so much as shot a backward glance at her. He kept on running.

Because of the pogrom.

Oh, God. She stifled a sob, pushed herself to her feet, and took a few careful, tentative steps. Tears seeped from her eyes. She'd twisted her ankle when she fell, and the pain shot upward, halfway to her knee.

With a grimace she fought to keep from crying out, and forced herself to limp after him. Her lips tightened in self-loathing. Schmarya would soon approach the edge of the forest. She was so far behind now. All because of a stupid sprained ankle. If she didn't hurry, she would be too late.

She took a deep breath. Well, she wouldn't let it slow her down. Not if what Schmarya feared was true. What was her pain compared with the lives of so many?

She forced herself to race ahead, closing her mind to the splinters of fire shooting through her leg. Mustn't think of the pain, she told herself over and over. It's nothing compared with—

—the pogrom.

She picked up speed now, her hair flying in the wind. She was just about to catch up with Schmarya, and could see that he had nearly reached the edge of the forest. The hoofbeats rang out much louder now, a steady, resounding bass pounding off the earth. She forced herself to speed up, as Schmarya was doing, for the final homestretch, and just as she reached the extreme edge of the forest, Schmarya instinctively stopped in his tracks. Senda was about to shoot past him, but his right arm shot out, slammed into her breasts, and sent her flying backward through the air. She let out a cry, half in anger, half in pain, as she landed heavily on the ground. "What the—"

But Schmarya dived to the ground and clapped a hand over her mouth.

The Cossacks burst past, sabers and rifles glinting evilly, their sweating steeds throwing off glistening drops of hot sweat, their powerful hooves tossing up clumps of dirt. They were very near, but the heavy forest underbrush completely concealed Senda and Schmarya from the Cossacks while offering them a bird's-eye view of the village.

The life seemed to drain out of Schmarya. His face was contorted in agony. "We're too late," he wept softly, covering his face with his hands.

As they watched in horror, wholesale slaughter began; it was as if the gates of hell had suddenly flung open, and bizarre demons and devils were unleashed upon the earth.

The Cossacks wielded whips, guns, and sabers in their black-leather-gloved hands, their huge fur hats pressing down over their brows. They split into two groups, taking opposite ends of the village and working bloody paths toward the center.

What came was no battle. It was a massacre, pure and simple—the systematic butchering of peaceful, unarmed villagers by a horde of ruthless, bloodthirsty savages.

The first victims were Gilda Meyerov and her children. With the Cossacks' arrival, Senda had seen Gilda rush out of the nearest cottage, protectively gather up her three children who had been playing outside, and herd them into the deceptive safety of the cottage, slamming and bolting the door behind them. When the cottage was set on fire, it was a matter of minutes before Gilda and the children stumbled back out, gasping and coughing. The children were shot, and Gilda Meyerov, frozen in horror, never saw the powerful arc of the saber that decapitated her. Her severed head flew through the air and landed on the ground, bouncing twice before rolling away like an obscene ball.

The tranquil village became a sea of blood. No one and nothing was spared, whether human or otherwise. Senda had heard accounts of pogroms in the past, but they had always seemed distant, only stories—something that happened to other people. Nothing had prepared her for the horrors of the reality. She witnessed her father being shot in the chest and crumpling to the ground, then saw her screaming mother throw herself atop his lifeless body, wailing and sobbing as she held his head in her hands, only to have her back hacked open lengthwise by a Cossack leaning over his mount.

The slaughter took only a few minutes, but to Senda the massacre seemed to last a lifetime. No matter in which direction she looked, horror after unspeakable horror piled up before her eyes.

She saw a gangly woman take flight from one of the burning cottages, fleeing toward a shed which stood halfway between her cottage and the forest. Her escape was cut off by two Cossacks who galloped around her in ever-narrowing concentric circles until she fell and was trampled to death under the iron-shod hooves of their horses. Senda shut her eyes. She had recognized Hannah Jaffe, who lived in the cottage next door and was so proud of her cooking. She always brought her neighbors a piece of cake when she baked one, or brought over steaming pots of chicken soup if someone was ill. She would never cook and bake again. The Cossacks had seen to that.

Senda watched, heartbroken, as Solomon, the husband she did not love, made a valiant attempt to rescue the sacred Torah from the synagogue. When he ran out of the temple with the scrolls tucked under his arm, a Cossack's whip expertly lashed out, coiling itself around him and the scrolls. Totally immobilized, Solomon stood stock-still, eyes lifted skyward, as a band of Cossacks hacked his body and the scrolls into bloody bits. Senda grieved terribly for that one instant. So he had not been a coward. He had died bravely, and she now felt shame for the way she had treated him.

But soon that fragmented emotion was replaced by another, for the most terrible sight of all now greeted her eyes. Her beloved Grandmother Goldie, white-blond hair tied back, feet still shod in the mules she wore indoors, socks too big for her sagging around her ankles, came marching through ragged clouds of smoke down the one road which bisected the village, her eyes narrowed in grim determination. All around Goldie, the slaughter took place with furious speed and brutal efficiency, but her pace never flagged. She was not one to suffer death without a fight. Twice, once with her heart, and another time with her liver, she had cheated the grim reaper, and she wasn't about to stand still and wait for the Cossacks to finish the job. Not if she could help it. She held her boning knife poised high in the air and headed straight for the nearest mounted Cossack, her stride never breaking. Before she could reach him, he threw back his head and laughed, then reined in his horse, forcing its front legs high, and when they swiftly descended, the hooves crushed Grandmother Goldie to the ground as easily as other horses had crushed Hannah Jaffe.

Senda could bear no more. She was sickened by the violence, the needless slaughter; repulsed by the devilish joy the Cossacks seemed to derive from it. And then, miraculously, she saw an opportunity to try to help one person.

Despite her size, Aunt Sophie had avoided the slashing sabers on three occasions in as many minutes, and she was racing as fast as her plump legs could carry her toward the very bushes behind which Senda and Schmarya were hidden. She was running breathlessly, her thick arms stretched out in front of her, as though waiting for invisible hands to pull her. When she caught sight of Senda parting the bushes and reaching out to her, hope gleamed in Sophie's eyes.

"Hurry!" Senda called encouragingly, her heart hammering wildly. "Hurry, Aunt Sophie!" And she prayed as the gap between the two of them narrowed. *"Hurry!"*

At that moment, a Cossack cut Aunt Sophie off and aimed his rifle. Senda screamed as she heard the report. Aunt Sophie's body seemed to jump into the air; her head snapped backward. Her face was shattered, spraying everything around her with fragments of tissue, bone, and blood. Senda could feel warm drops of it raining down on her face and arms.

She squeezed her eyes shut, too shocked to scream any longer. Numbly she allowed Schmarya to pull her back into the shielding safety of the bushes. For several minutes she lay there in white-faced shock. Then she heard Schmarya curse.

She turned to him and opened her eyes. "What is it?" she asked tremulously, afraid of the reply. She was afraid of so many things suddenly.

Schmarya's face seemed to have undergone a metamorphosis. Whereas anguish had contorted it earlier, a silent, seething rage was now burning.

"Schmarya . . ."

"They're not all Cossacks," he muttered grimly. "At least one of them isn't."

"What!"

"Look for yourself," Schmarya whispered. "It's the collector. See? Over there, on the horse."

Senda carefully parted the bushes and peered out. Until Schmarya had pointed him out, she hadn't noticed Wolzak's tax collector. Her attention had been focused on the massacre, and the collector had been waiting quite some distance away on a horse far inferior to those of the Cossacks. His back was turned from the slaughter, as though by not watching it he would be absolved of any moral responsibility. Only when the massacre was over and every building was burning furiously did the leader of the Cossacks bellow for the collector. The collector wasted no time; the huge burly bear of a Cossack inspired fear even in him. With his perpetually scowling expression, fierce mustache, bushy black beard, and fiery eyes, the Cossack leader was enough to make anyone turn tail and run. During the massacre, his black lamb hat had gotten lost, and his glistening, frightfully smooth hairless skull threatened all who looked upon him, as did the massive raised white welt of a scar which coursed down the left side of his face from his brow to the corner of his mouth.

Senda turned to Schmarya. "But what's the collector doing here? There's nothing to collect." Her voice was choked.

"Not anymore, there isn't."

"Yes, but he knows everyone in the village."

Senda watched the collector. His conversation with the leader of the Cossacks over, he swung down off his horse and started walking among the corpses.

Senda frowned as she saw him consult a black ledger and make a note of each of the victims. "He's checking the dead against some sort of list!"

"Don't you see?" Schmarya hissed. "The collector knows every man, woman, and child—even newborn babies—in this village. His ledger lists everyone. Now he's taking inventory of the dead."

Senda shook her head. "But . . . why? I don't understand. If everyone has been butchered—"

"To make certain everyone's accounted for," Schmarya said grimly. "Don't you see? *Everyone* is to have been killed. Every man, woman, and child in this village." He shook his head in disbelief. "*Everyone*! It was cold-bloodedly planned that way!"

"Which means . . ." Senda gasped and her throat worked slackly. ". . . that when they find out we're missing . . ."

"I'll kill that bastard first!" Schmarya growled. He jumped to his feet and clenched his fists at his sides.

Senda clung to his legs and pulled him back down, out of sight. "No, Schmarya," she said softly. "You won't. You'll only get yourself killed."

"So what?" he retorted bitterly. "Everyone else is dead. Why shouldn't I die too?"

"*Why?*" she whispered vehemently, shaking him with quiet fury. "I'll tell you why. If we die too, then nobody will ever know what happened here. We have to live to keep the story alive. Besides, if we die too, then who's to mourn the dead?"

His shoulders sagged. "I suppose you're right," he murmured. Then he reached out and embraced her. They clung to each other for meager comfort. Once again Senda felt as if each of her senses was heightened, only this time she did not smell the moist freshness of the earth or hear the singing of the birds. The birds and the whirring insects were still. The foul stench of blood and excrement assaulted her senses. She could almost taste the coppery, metallic aftertaste of blood in her mouth. Death hung in the air.

Oily black plumes of smoke billowed skyward. Soon there would be nothing left of the village, only piles of ashes and scorch-scarred earth.

The Cossack leader burst through a wall of smoke on his horse and looked about with grim satisfaction. "Well?" he bellowed to the collector, who had finished his inventory. "Did all the Jews get what they deserved? Are they all accounted for?"

Senda held her breath, waiting to hear Schmarya's death notice—and her own—pronounced. This was the moment of reckoning, she knew. For she understood that if the Cossack learned that they'd escaped, the countryside would be searched until they were found and killed.

The collector consulted his ledger and then looked stonily around him. He was dumbstruck by the holocaust. His throat throbbed, and his face was ashen. Suddenly he bent over and retched noisily. When he finally finished, he wiped his mouth with the back of his hand and looked up at the Cossack. He nodded weakly. "They're all accounted for."

Only after the Cossack turned his back did the collector

quickly mark off the names of the two villagers unaccounted for on the list.

So there had been enough death. Even for him.

Senda let out a sigh of relief.

The Cossacks regrouped, the collector swung himself up on his horse, and the leader raised his saber high. Then he brought it down, signaling their departure.

The saber no longer gleamed. It was mat brown with dried blood.

The scourge rode off as noisily and swiftly as it had come.

As the pounding hoofbeats receded, Senda felt Schmarya gripping her arm. "All right," he said wearily. "Let's go."

"Where?"

"Anywhere, as long as it's far away from here."

She shook her head. "We can't," she said. "We have to bury and mourn the dead."

"No." He shook his head. "We must leave everything as it is. If they return and see that somebody . . ." His voice trailed off, leaving the unfinished threat hanging heavily over them both.

Senda pursed her lips. Finally she nodded. He was right. If they stayed to bury or burn the dead, then Wolzak and his Cossacks would know some villagers were left alive. Horrible though it was to leave the victims lying scattered, it was their only hope to escape alive. Overhead, a shadow had crossed the darkening sky. Senda glanced up and shuddered: a flock of black carrion birds wheeled around, already attracted by the prospect of a feast.

She nodded at Schmarya. Her eyes were awash with tears, but a peculiar hardness had come into her face, a strength which had never before been there. "Let's go," she said quietly.

And she never looked back.

Prince Vaslav Danilov relaxed comfortably on the forward-facing velvet seat of his barouche. It was one of forty carriages he owned in St. Petersburg alone, but one of only seven he had ordered converted into a sleigh so that the coach slid easily over the hard-packed snow and ice on smoothly polished gold-plated runners and swayed ever so gently on its well-mounted, shock-absorbing springs. This particular barouche, its sides emblazoned with the gilded coat of arms of the Danilovs, as were the thirty-nine other carriages, was pulled by his six finest matched black horses, and His Highness's privacy from the prying eyes of curious commoners was assured by brocade curtains drawn tightly across rolled-up windows. Outside, the early afternoon had already become nighttime, and an icy Baltic wind whipped through the city, lashing at anyone unfortunate enough to be caught out-of-doors. But Prince Vaslav, unlike his driver and footmen, who were exposed to the bitter elements, was well-protected from the Russian winter. He was warmly dressed and draped with a thick bearskin rug, and the little coal braziers built into the sides of the barouche glowed with heat. A compact custom-made silver samovar, filled with hot tea, was strapped to the narrow burl-wood shelf behind the facing seat, as were crystal decanters of vodka and kvass and crystal glasses and cups engraved with the Danilov coat of arms.

Prince Vaslav was happiest when he rode in any of his multitude of sleighs or carriages, or when on horseback. For him, half the pleasure of going somewhere lay in the method of transportation, and he believed that there was nothing as elegant, enchanting, or indubitably Russian as horses and horse-drawn vehicles. Never mind that one wing of the great Danilov Palace on the Neva had recently undergone conversion to accommodate his fleet of motorcars. It had been his wife's idea, and he had bowed to her wishes. The Princess Irina was not one to let any of her social competitors—each of whom owned garages full of cars—outdo her. Were it up to him, he would banish the imported Mercedeses, Rolls-Royces, Citroëns, Bentleys, and Hispano-Suizas from the streets and stately boulevards of St. Petersburg forever, and the sooner accomplished, the better. But he was realist enough to know that motorcars were here to stay, whether he personally liked them or not. There were some things even a prince was powerless to change.

With his forefinger he moved the curtain aside a crack and glanced idly out of the coach as it made a sweeping turn and sped across the Neva on the lamplit Nicholas Bridge. A confectioner's delight, the bridge never failed to remind him of Paris. Ah, Paris . . . Like the *bon ton* of the City of Light, the aristocrats of the Prince's Paris of the North walzed through endless months of operas, ballets, concerts, banquets, official receptions, private parties, and extravagant midnight suppers. Even cultured Paris, resplendent though it was, lacked the magic that was St. Petersburg, the staggering elegance and riches which he had so enjoyed since the moment of his high-placed birth. True, the palaces here were more reminiscent of those in Venice than Paris—many of them Mediterranean in style, thanks to the Italian influence from the armies of architects and artisans imported over the centuries—but even this Italianate dominance had its decidedly Russian twists.

He smiled. In no building was this more true than in his own daunting palace, which he had just left. The Danilov Palace itself sprawled over four square blocks and was decidedly baroque in style, beautifully designed like a colossal capital C, with the open end becoming a massive circular courtyard and the closed side looking down upon the stately Neva, frozen hard as steel during this and every winter. Its five stories were painted, plastered, and ornamented in yellow and orange, and it boasted three massive square towers, two at each end of the C and a third at the colonnaded curve facing the Neva. Each tower culminated in a splendid cluster of five gilded, spired onion domes. What magnificent buildings did Paris have to compare with this, especially when viewed, alternatingly, in the sun- and water-dappled summers, the swirling snowstorms of winter, or on those particularly prized, though rare, winter days when the oppressive, monotonous gloom was broken and the sky became silvery blue, causing the snow-shrouded palace to glare so brightly in the sun that one had to shield one's eyes? Or, as now, with the incredibly iridescent vertical fires of the aurora borealis hanging like a coral-and-amythyst necklace suspended above it in the premature darkness of the Arctic sky?

Nothing. Nothing on earth could compare with St. Petersburg, especially not now, in January, when the 1914 "season" promised to be a glittering one. The season had begun a week earlier, on New Year's Day, and would continue until Lent.

He was about to withdraw his finger and let the curtain fall back into place when the coach suddenly slid to an abrupt halt, jolting him.

He sat bolt upright and made a mental note to admonish his driver once they arrived at their destination, which would be the jewelry emporium of Carl Fabergé. With its solid soaring granite pillars and rich atmosphere of Byzantine opulence, it was a thief's paradise of glittering gold, sparkling gems, dazzling silver, and gleaming enamel. The Prince had decided to pick up his wife's birthday present in person. Her birthday was in two days' time, on the ninth, and now that she had daringly taken up smoking long, thin black Turkish cigars, he had ordered her an exquisite customdesigned cigarette box of translucent dusty-rose enamel, its edges on both sides lined with rows of fiery pink diamonds. But her gift was not the only reason he had decided to take the opportunity to honor the shop with his presence: he had decided to buy a little ready-made something—a diamond bauble, perhaps, or an emerald or ruby bracelet—for his mistress, Tatiana Ivanova.

Tatiana Ivanova was the reigning star of the St. Petersburg theater, and what she lacked in dramatic talent she more than made up for in beauty and a fiery temperament, both enhanced by her extravagant costumes. The last night he had seen her, he had been a little forceful in their game-playing, and had injured one of her nipples. Not that he'd meant to actually hurt her. It had been an accident. But she had screamed bloody murder and thrown him out, threatening to tell everyone what a sadistic bastard he was.

Well, the tart would be appeased and her silence bought with a bauble. Still, he had decided it would be prudent to find himself a new mistress. Sooner or later, Tatiana was going to be trouble. He was tired of her threats and tired of her.

The barouche-sleigh had not yet begun to move. Irritated, first by the abrupt stop and now by the delay, the Prince reached up to yank the tasseled bell-pull connected to the bell behind the driver's seat. It was not necessary: a knock came on the door.

He parted the curtain and peered out. It was one of his well-bundled footmen, his nose exhaling a plume of white vapor, the gold buttons of his massive blue greatcoat raised in relief with the Danilov coat of arms.

Prince Vaslav cursed under his breath and rolled the window down a crack. "Now what is it?" he demanded angrily, at once sorry he'd assumed that tone. It wasn't like him; he'd been taught from an early age to treat servants, if not with a modicum of respect, then at least with politeness. He realized that his irritableness was a reflection of his own growing annoyance with Tatiana.

"I'm sorry, your Highness. A wagon was overturned up ahead and is blocking the street. Would you like for us to turn around and try another route?"

"See how long the delay will be. And find out who they are and if anyone has been injured."

"Yes, your Highness." The footman bowed low. Etiquette required that he face his employer as he withdrew, so he took a few steps backward, turning only when his polished boot heels hit a high, frozen snowbank. Then he hurried forward to the scene of the accident.

The Prince rolled his window all the way down and stuck his head out into the icy dark. Looking beyond the impatient horses of his own coach, he could see a small crowd gathered in the illumination of a streetlamp. He could also see a portion of the overturned wagon, its wheels still spinning in the air. Two horses had gone down along with it. One was getting unsteadily to its feet, but the other, although someone had already unhitched it, kept falling back down.

The footman hurried back. "Well?" the Prince demanded, turning his cold blue eyes on his servant.

"It will take a quarter of an hour, your Highness. Perhaps longer."

"Is anyone injured?"

"No, your Highness. There were no passengers. The people were in the two forward wagons. The driver jumped off in time. Apparently he was trying to avoid a motorcar which was skidding."

"I'm not surprised." The Prince nodded gravely. "And the horses?"

"One seems to have no injuries, your Highness."

"And the other?"

"Someone has gone off to fetch a gun."

The Prince pursed his lips. He could not bear to think of a horse in agony. He knew that pain frightened horses, and finding someone with a gun to put it out of its misery might take time. Meanwhile, the horse was suffering.

He reached under his seat for the Karelian birch gun case in which he kept two loaded pistols. He always had them there in case of trouble: these were troubled times, with marchers and strikers taking to the streets in droves. Too, there were altogether too many reports of anarchists roving the shadows of the city.

He checked a pistol, waited for a footman to open the door of the barouche, then passed him his heavy sable-lined coat. The footman took it, unfolded the step, and helped him down. Since the Prince did not hold out his arms, the footman took it as a sign to merely drape the coat capelike over His Highness's broad shoulders.

"Follow me," the Prince ordered without looking at his servant, making it plain that it was he who would lead the way. He strode forward like a general, the pistol at his side, and his servant hurried after him.

The small crowd gathered around the scene of the accident took one look at Vaslav Danilov and fell silent. Here was a personage of the uppermost crust, they could tell. Here was a man who took command of a situation at once. He was striding purposefully toward them, as though daring the treacherous ice to cause him to slip and fall. Despite the seeming recklessness of his pace, his movements were calculated and precise.

The crowd drew back as one, respectfully putting more distance between the Prince and themselves. He was a man who commanded such respect, a man born to the power he exuded, and a presence to be reckoned with. He was a big man, and his towering height and wide shoulders gave an imposing impression. His bare head was dark with medium-length thick black hair combed backward and cut close above the ears. His beard was carefully trimmed, and his magnificent moustache made two sweeping handlebar curves. His eyes and noble brows were those of a grandee.

These autocratic hooded blue eyes now came to rest on the unfortunate horse, and without a word he held out the revolver, aimed it downward at the animal's head, and fired.

The horse immediately sagged and was then still.

Many people watching had shut their eyes at the gunshot, but Prince Vaslav never flinched. Nor, he noticed, had one young woman. Her ratty fur hat was pulled far down over her forehead, and the lower half of her face was hidden behind a thick woolen scarf so that she exuded an aura of challenge and mystery much like a Muslim woman hiding her face behind a veil. He knew the scarf was to shield her from the bitter cold: she and the others had obviously been riding on one of the two open lead wagons, exposed to the cruelty of the bitter elements. Her coat, despite its size, was too threadbare to offer any real warmth, and she shivered continuously. Yet her dancing green eyes were uncomplaining. Something about them was frank and startling, as though they were sizing him up; the pink flush on the narrow exposed portion of her face, he thought, was not a result of the cold. She held a well-bundled child of two or three years in her arms.

He lowered the pistol and walked around the overturned wagon, inspecting it closely. He noticed that neither axle had been broken and that the tarpaulin which had been tied down over the cargo, and on which the wagon and its contents now rested, was strong and had not come undone. He turned to the quiet crowd and gestured at the wagon. "Whose wagon is this?"

There were some murmurs, which he gathered meant it belonged not to an individual but to the small crowd.

"What is in it? Any breakables? One of you can explain for the group." His eyes swept the crowd. "Which of you is your spokesman?"

The Prince was astonished when a tall golden-haired young

man, sapphire-blue eyes gleaming with amused contempt, stepped quickly forward. He held himself boldly erect, as though he considered himself the Prince's equal.

The Prince sized him up in surprise. Despite the ragged appearance of his dirty clothes, he was quite the most extraordinarily handsome and self-assured young man he had ever seen.

"I am the spokesman, your Highness," the young man said quietly.

The Prince nodded, choosing to ignore the mocking look in the young man's eyes and the somehow disrespectful emphasis on the words "your Highness." There was an indefinable air about the young man—he could not put his finger on it yet—but he instinctively recognized him as arrogant and dangerous. "What is in the wagon?"

The young man replied, "Theatrical props and costumes, your Highness. We have just arrived here this afternoon after a tour of the provinces."

"You are a theater troupe, then?"

"Yes, Highness, and I am the business manager."

"And you'll be performing here in St. Petersburg?"

The young man shrugged. "If we can find a theater to perform in."

The Prince looked thoughtful. Despite himself, he was intrigued. "What sort of plays do you perform?"

"Drawing-room comedies, satires, the usual repertoire."

"Where did you last perform?"

"In the town of Sestrovetsk. We came directly from there. The Princess Sviatopolk-Korsokoff herself came to see us and congratulated us on the performance."

The Prince did not register his surprise, but disgested this information in silence. Anastasia Beletnova Sviatopolk-Korsokoff moved in his circle. She had just come to St. Petersburg from her country palace outside Sestrovetsk, and now that he came to think of it, only two days ago when he and Irina had spoken to her during intermission at the ballet, she had mentioned something about a marvelous theater troupe she had recently seen.

"Chekhov. Do you perform him?"

"We have, your Highness, but . . ." The young man shrugged. "Chekhov is a master, and we . . . we are not that experienced."

"And for the Princess . . . what did you stage when she came?"

"La Dame aux Camellias."

The Prince looked surprised, then nodded approvingly. "An amusing piece, and quite popular." And harmless froth, he thought. "I have seen it twice myself, and it is among my wife's favorites. Who among you plays the ill-fated Marguerite?"

They looked at each other in silence, and the young man stared at the ground. "Her name was Olga, but she caught pleurisy and died."

Like most members of the Russian nobility, the Prince did not concern himself with the misfortunes life doled out to strangers—certainly not itinerant entertainers—only by how they affected him. "Then you cannot now perform it, I assume."

Suddenly the green-eyed woman holding the child stepped eagerly forward. "I can perform the part. I have watched Olga countless times, and have memorized the lines."

The young man turned to her. "Senda, you've never played that part. You've had only minor roles—"

"Please, Schmarya," she pleaded. "I am ready for it. I know it."

The Prince caught sight of the most expressive, mesmerizing pair of emerald eyes he had ever encountered. "She is your wife?" he inquired politely.

"No, your Highness. She is the widow . . ." He paused. ". . . of my brother."

"She is a very young widow."

"Sometimes," the young man said bitterly, "it is the lot of the young to suffer misfortune or death."

"Yes, yes." The Prince made a gesture of irritation. He did not like to involve himself with the problems of the lower classes. Still, something about the woman wove a spell. He was silent a moment longer and then made up his mind. "Come to my palace. We have a private theater. Two days from today is my wife's birthday, and I shall expect you to perform *The Lady of the Camellias* then. My majordomo will find you accommodations in the palace. You will be well-paid."

The young man nodded toward the dead horse. "It will be our honor to perform it without pay. Lodging and board for two nights are enough. We are grateful that you put our horse out of its misery." His voice was proud.

"It is settled then. The Danilov Palace on the Neva. If you have difficulty finding it, ask anyone for directions." The Prince turned to leave and then caught a movement out of the corner of his eye which caused him to turn back around. The woman named Senda had reached up and lowered the scarf from around her face and pushed the fur hat back on her head, a seductive gesture even in this cold and public place.

Prince Vaslav's breath caught in his throat. She was extraordinarily beautiful. She met his gaze unblinkingly, and he nodded abruptly, then tore his eyes from her and strode quickly back to his barouche.

All in all, he felt extremely pleased with himself. And as he heard the snapping of the whip carrying backward in the wind, another, even more pleasant sensation swept over him.

He closed his eyes, conjuring up those two huge emerald eyes, impossibly green and striated, so full of life.

He had found himself another actress. So . . . Tatiana would not get her bauble after all. He relished that.

Placing one elegantly manicured finger on his lips, he made a mental notation.

Emeralds.

Fabergé was certain to have just the thing.

Senda had watched as the driver of the magnificent barouche walked the six beautifully matched black horses around in a tight circle, climbed back up on his high seat, and cracked his whip. She stared after the receding coach-sleigh in amazement. "I've never before seen a sleigh quite like that one," she marveled, shaking her head. She glanced at Schmarya. "Do you suppose that yellow metal was real gold?"

"I wouldn't doubt it," Schmarya said bitterly. "The rich only get richer by walking all over the likes of us. Then they turn around and rub it in our faces."

"But he seemed nice."

Schmarya's eyes flashed. "Nice. Sure." He compressed his lips into a grim smile. "I'm certain even Wolzak was nice to people if he chose to be. It didn't stop him from slaughtering everybody in our village, though, did it?"

She turned away at the memory. After all this time, her eyes still filled with tears.

Schmarya didn't seem to notice. He turned around and raised his arm. "All right!" he yelled out. "All of you! Let's get this wagon back up on its wheels!" The wheels of the wagon clattered on the ice as they uprighted it. Senda, standing off to one side, held the child in one arm and the reins of the surviving horse in her free hand. For a moment she looked longingly down the street to catch one last glimpse of the departing fairy-tale barouche, but it had turned a corner and was already out of sight.

"It's time we got this show on the road!" Schmarya yelled. "Everybody back up in the wagons! Alex, hitch the horse back up."

The man named Alex frowned and slowly scratched the back of his neck. "It's an awful heavy load for just one horse."

"In that case, we have no choice but to substitute a horse from one of the front wagons for the one that's dead. Which means all of us had better walk except the drivers."

There was a chorus of groans, but no one voiced outright refusal. They'd had enough trials and tribulations on the road to view this as no more than a slight discomfort.

Senda fell into step beside Schmarya as they slowly made their way on foot alongside the creaking wagons. She was bone weary, cold, and hungry. The icy wind which had battered her relentlessly since early morning had taken its toll. All she wanted now was to eat, have something hot to drink, and then crawl into bed under mountains of warm covers.

"Want me to hold her for a while?" Schmarya asked, reaching for the child.

She shook her head and smiled. "No, I'm fine. Tamara's really not very heavy. And we'll be warm soon. It's fate, don't you think? We had no place to go, and because the wagon flipped and that coach stopped, now we do."

"It's only for two nights," he growled.

Her gaze was level. "Two nights in a palace is better than sleeping in a barn in the freezing cold." She paused and tightened her lips. "Schmarya, why did you insist we perform for free?"

He did not reply.

"You know how desperately we need the money! We can't afford not to get paid. We can hardly eat as it is, and now with a horse dead . . . how can we afford to buy another?"

He hunched forward against the wind, hands in his pockets, eyes focused on the ground. "He did us a favor by shooting the horse, and we're returning the favor. I don't want to owe anybody anything. Especially not the enemy."

"The enemy!" she scoffed. "Hearing you talk, one would think everybody's the enemy."

"Have you forgotten what happened three years ago?" he asked her softly. "Has it been so long that you don't remember!"

"No, I haven't forgotten."

He lowered his voice. "Then have you forgotten why we joined up with this troupe of no-talent has-beens?"

She shook her head, thinking back to that night soon after the pogrom when they had stumbled upon the gypsylike theater troupe, which was playing the villages in and around the Pale. They had unquestioningly, even eagerly, welcomed Senda and Schmarya into their little band since a young couple had recently eloped and left them short of help.

Schmarya answered himself: "So we could work our way to St. Petersburg or Moscow. So we could get out of the Pale once and for all and live decent lives."

She shook her head. "That wasn't it and you know it. You only wanted to come so you could join up with the revolutionaries in the cities." It was her turn to sound bitter. "That's why you really wanted to join the troupe and come here, isn't it?"

When he looked at her, his eyes were shining. "Yes, it was. And it still is. The wealthy oppressors must be fought and defeated. There'll be no freedom in Russia until the blood of the rich stains the soil. Senda, you just don't understand. I know you want what's best for Tamara, but you're unable to look past the hearth. Don't you see? All things in society have to change for the better if our daughter's to be assured a peaceful future. You, better than anyone, should have learned that by now. It doesn't matter if you refuse to have anything to do with it—others will change this world as we know it. And I will help. It's only a matter of time."

She shivered suddenly, and knew it was not from the cold.

Now that she'd allowed fear to creep into her consciousness, two other thoughts crept into her mind. Schmarya always carried a loaded pistol. He hadn't used it to put the horse out of its misery because he didn't want anyone to know he had it. People weren't supposed to be armed. If the police caught him with the weapon, he'd immediately be suspected of anarchy, clapped behind bars, and shipped off to Siberia. And hidden in one of the barrels stuffed with costumes were the ten sticks of dynamite he'd picked up in Riga.

She was afraid to venture a guess as to what he might have in mind once they arrived at the Danilov Palace.

"Itinerants though you may be, you are considered neither guests nor servants in this palace. You are subject to the same stringent rules and regulations governing any unknown transients passing through this household. Unless you are specifically given permission otherwise, you are to remain here in the servants' wing. On the grounds you are not to wander any further than the servants' garden. The public rooms, private apartments, and remainder of the grounds are strictly off limits. There will be no exploring the premises. On those occasions when one or more of you need to leave this wing and gain access to the theater, which is located among the public rooms, you will do so escorted by one of the footmen. Never, for any reason, will any of you venture about this palace unescorted. This rule shall be strictly obeyed. If even one of you fails to follow it, you shall all find yourselves unwelcome here."

The theater troupe was in the servants' wing, located above the stables and garages. They were facing Count Kokovtsov, the Prince's second cousin, chief adviser, and right-hand man. The Count was everything the Prince was not. Overbearingly imperious, sallow, and effetely elegant, he was a tall, crisply unemotional machine of efficiency and no-nonsense who looked more like a spidery-fingered undertaker than a member of the aristocracy. Beside him stood a plump, rubicund woman in her fifties wearing the uniform of chief housekeeper. Her cream-puff hands were laced in front of her, and her usually merry features were dour and compressed. Minutes earlier, Mrs. Kashkin had welcomed them warmly in the sparsely furnished but pleasant servants' parlor. Upon seeing the obviously hungry and frostbitten condition of the actors, she had sent a girl scurrying for a samovar and sweet cakes, and another to run hot baths. Then Count Kokovtsov had arrived, and a pall had descended upon them all. Since traveling with the troupe, Senda had met her share of unpleasant characters, and something inside told her that Kokovtsov was not a man one crossed lightly, if one dared cross him at all.

"Despite its size and splendor, this palace is a private home and is to be regarded as such. It is filled with treasures from around the world, and because of that, the rules I have outlined must be followed to the letter, as much for your protection as for that of Their Highnesses. This way, should anything be damaged or missing, none of you will be held accountable. I assume I am making myself perfectly clear?"

All too clear, Senda thought bitterly as she levelly returned the Count's pompous gaze. Obviously he was trying to instill fear in all of them, thereby causing each of them to spy upon the other. Well, she could voice her opinion about *that*.

Clearing her throat, she stepped forward and conveyed her opinion that so many strictures might stifle the creative impulses so important to acting.

The Count cocked an eyebrow and regarded her coldly. "Be that as it may, I assume that you are seasoned professionals? As such, you have surely played a variety of places, each of which has had certain rules of etiquette. So it is here. Obeying our household rules should be second nature. As long as you do not abuse the privileges provided you here, there is nothing to worry about. You need only concern yourselves with giving a good performance."

Later that evening, after eating, bathing, and putting her tiny daughter to bed, Senda considered the restraints the Count had put upon the troupe. Much as she despised any rules, whose bases were deeply rooted distrust, she felt curiously relieved. Surely under such stringent observation Schmarya would find himself unable to do anything which might further his vengeful goals, thereby sabotaging the troupe's chances for success. He was occupied now with several other men of the troupe, examining the theater.

Breathing a sigh of relief, she concentrated on familiarizing herself with the script of *The Lady of the Camellias*. She gave silent thanks that, during their countless afternoon trysts in the forest, Schmarya had taught her to read—and that she'd continued learning on her own over the past three years. But she didn't study long. Soon she turned off the solitary lamp in the room she shared with Schmarya and Tamara and fell into the most sound and peaceful sleep she had enjoyed in weeks.

Four o'clock in the afternoon the next day, Senda was alone, pacing the stage of the private theater in the Danilov Palace. The servant whose duty it was to keep an eye on her had left her in peace and was waiting outside in the hallway. Senda's face was screwed up in concentration, deepening her dimple as she recited her lines, summoning them from memory. Her voice rose and fell with thick emotion. " '. . . and my impulses unquestioningly. I had found such a man in the Duke, but old age neither protects nor consoles, and one has other needs. Then I met you. Young! Ardent! Happy! The tears I saw you shed for me, your anxiety over my health, your mysterious visits during my illness . . . your honesty. Your enthusiasm . . . your enthusiasm . . . your enthusiasm . . .' " She had to consult the script again. "Oh, damn!" she blurted out, then bit down on her pink underlip and scowled. Tears of frustration welled up in her eyes. Hers was the central character, and as such, she had the most lines. Many, many more than she had anticipated. She realized now her unmitigated gall. Acting the part of Marguerite Gautier was not the simple matter she had convinced herself it would be. And to think she had believed that she knew the entire play by heart! By *rote!*

She sighed heavily, her bosom rising slowly, then falling. It was a fine time to discover that she had deluded herself. Not that the lines weren't on the tip of her tongue at all times. But getting them out at will, adding the necessary emotions, and following the stage directions—well, it was simply too much to have to concentrate on all at the same time.

Frowning, she tapped the open script against her right thigh. Her heart-shaped face was creased with anger and disillusionment. Could it be that she was trying to force things too much? After all, the rehearsal earlier that afternoon hadn't gone so badly. She'd only needed to be prompted . .

. . . only about two dozen times or so. *Only!*

Far too often.

But still . . .

Wearily she tossed down the script and sank onto a silken red Empire settee which was to be used as a prop. She silently gazed out at the empty theater. She nodded to herself, already feeling herself untense a bit. Now she could at last take the time to study the little theater. And what a jewel box it was!

She marveled at the unabashed luxury surrounding her. Never in her wildest dreams had she imagined such fairy-tale trappings to exist in real life. It was a feast for the eyes. Each seat was Louis XVI in style, handsomely hand-carved and heavily gilded, with plush powder-blue velvet upholstery —a hundred and sixty seats altogether. Added to that was the balustraded, magnificently curved little balcony at the back, a rococo symphony of design which could seat another thirty spectators, as well as the two individual wedding-cake boxes, swagged with rich draperies, which overlooked each side of the stage. Those seated six apiece.

She shook her head incredulously as the numbers sank in. It seemed unbelievable that this theater—a private theater in a private home—could have a capacity for an audience of two hundred and two. Most theaters in the provincial towns they had played were much smaller than this. And nowhere near as lovely.

Her visual inspection over, she tightened her lips determinedly and pushed herself to her feet. Enough lounging. It was time to get back to work.

She scooped up the script and once again took her position at center stage. She stood there for a long moment in the silence, then drew a deep breath.

" ' . . . The tears I saw you shed for me, your anxiety over my health, your mysterious visits during my illness . . . your honesty. Your enthusiasm. Everything about you led me to see in you the one I had been calling to from the depths of my loud solitude—' "

From the box above her right came the abrupt claps of lone applause. Startled, she stopped in mid-sentence, took a few steps backward, and looked up. The Prince, dressed in a beautifully tailored charcoal Edwardian suit, was stepping from behind one of the swag curtains. The top half of him seemed suspended in midair; his face was in deep shadow. But his eyes, brilliant and concentrated, conveyed his emotional keenness. Otherwise, his face was carefully composed in an unemotional mask.

"That was quite an extraordinary soliloquy," he said softly in the well-modulated speech of the upper class. "As a rule, I am not taken with theatrical performances. Most of them bore me, put me to sleep, and if they don't, I nevertheless find it difficult to suspend my sense of reality sufficiently to be transported into a world of make-believe. However, you have entranced me. You are quite the consummate actress."

Senda bowed her head slightly. "Your Highness is too kind. It is not I who should take credit for having entranced you, but Monsieur Dumas. Surely it was his writing which appealed to you, not I."

"On the contrary, madam. You do yourself a great injustice. You are a very gifted young actress." The Prince paused, poising his fingertips on the gilded railing of the box. "For a moment you actually made me believe that you were the ill-fated Marguerite Gautier. My heart went out to you." He stared at her steadily. "And if you will forgive me for speaking the truth, you are extraordinarily beautiful as well."

She locked eyes with him. Despite the shadows, his luminous gaze was so powerful, so penetrating, that she found herself blushing. "That is the magic of theater, your Highness. It is all an illusion. Greasepaint. Costumes. Sets." She gestured elegantly around the stage.

"Ah, but my eyes do not deceive me." He smiled and wagged an admonishing finger at her. "Your beauty is no illusion."

She was silent. His intense gaze seemed peculiarly hypnotic, and burned with a fierce fire. She forced herself to focus slightly to his left to avoid the focus of those unsettling, glittering eyes.

"Beauty," she murmured, "is only in the eyes of the beholder."

He half-smiled. "If you say so, so be it." For a long, uncomfortable moment he was silent, staring down at her so intently that she could feel the heat of his gaze. For some reason, she felt the beginnings of a deeply rooted fear knotting her insides.

Finally he broke the lengthy silence. "In any case, you *are* the lady of the camellias. I can feel it in my heart. That was not playacting I was watching." He shook his head. "The emotions were very real. Far too real to have merely been an illusion."

She turned away and nervously paced the stage as he drew back into the shadows. She could hear his footsteps echoing on the marble steps as he left the box. Somehow she knew he had not finished saying what he had started. Nor was he leaving; he was on his way to the stage. To her.

She tightened her lips across her teeth, wishing he would go away. Compliments usually filled her with glowing warmth, but the Prince's words of praise had had the opposite effect. Surely he had ulterior motives, was leading up to something. But what? And why did he make her feel awkward, like a blushing schoolgirl?

She took a series of deep breaths to steady her nerves and waited until he leapt onstage and towered prepossessingly over her. She flinched as he reached out without warning, held her chin in his hand, and raised her face to his. Her eyes shone richly in the spotlights. "You have the most incredible emerald eyes," he murmured slowly. "It is my sincerest wish that you remain in St. Petersburg for the entire season."

Flustered, she stepped back and looked down at the script in her hands. She was gripping it so tightly that her knuckles were white. "Your Highness." Her voice was so thick she had to clear her throat before continuing. "Your Highness, we are but a humble theater troupe touring the provinces and cities. We go wherever there is an opportunity to perform. The morning after the Princess's party, we will have to depart."

"For where?" His look was keen with real interest, but his smile mocked. "Parts known? Or unknown?"

She dimpled at the effort of summoning a suitable reply. "Wherever work beckons."

"It beckons here," said the Prince. "You see, you really have no choice. I demand that you remain here."

A sudden chill, caused in part by his temerity, in part by his self-assurance, rippled up and down her spine like fingers strumming the width of a harp. Much as she tried to convey force, her voice trembled as she spoke. "Your Highness, I'm afraid I must continue rehearsing to be prepared for tomorrow's performance. Otherwise—"

"I will leave momentarily," he said softly. "In the meantime, I beg you to hear me out. I do not wish to boast, but the Princess and I wield considerable influence in this city. I am certain we can arrange for your troupe to perform here for the entire season. There are many private theaters in the various palaces, quite a few public theaters begging for use, and a shortage of entertainers. Such an opportunity should be a godsend for what you call a humble troupe searching for work. Especially since I personally guarantee to pay for every empty seat." He paused. "For the entire season, I might add."

She raised her head and met his gaze. "With all due respect, your Highness wouldn't, by any chance, be making advances to me? For if you are, I'm afraid I must warn you ahead of time. It is a waste of your time as well as mine."

A fire flared within his eyes, then died as quickly as it had appeared. "You are an actress."

"And the mother of the child you saw me carrying."

"And a widow."

"Widows," she said firmly, "are not necessarily loose women."

"Perhaps not." He was smiling directly at her. "But a star?" he asked, his voice a whisper. "I have it within my power to make you the toast of St. Petersburg. You can have all Russian society worshiping at your feet."

She stared at him, her heart beating wildly. There was something predatory, almost satanic, about the hypnotic glint of his eyes and the amused self-assurance of his manner. How tempting it was to listen to his soft-spoken promises. Yet how angry they made her also. How dared he think she could be so easily swayed!

Now her eyes flashed. "Your Highness," she said unsteadily, "I think enough has been said. I don't think I would care for the way"—she swallowed the lump blocking her throat—"the way I would have to repay you for the favors of which you speak." She lowered her lashes and sucked on her lower lip. "Now I think I had best continue to rehearse."

"Ah, but I do admire spirit. So, you are under the impression that I am trying to buy you." His face was so close to hers that she could feel the warmth of his breath.

"Are you?" Despite her defiant voice, she rather enjoyed this badinage.

"What do you think?"

She looked shaken. "I think," she murmured, "that this conversation has gone far enough."

He smiled. Not unpleasantly. "But you have no idea what I was about to propose."

"I think that is obvious," she countered crisply, her face suddenly flaming red.

He was silent for a moment. "So you cannot be bought for the sake of your troupe. Very well. However, long experience tells me that everyone has a price. Only the currency changes from one person to the next." He shook his head again. "Those eyes . . . so expressive . . . so haunting . . . as though they have seen much suffering. You attract me, that is no secret." He paused. "And I intend to have you."

Her voice was hushed. "I'm sorry, your Highness, but I'm not on the auction block."

"Not for your troupe perhaps. But these?" He reached into his jacket and took out a long, slim velvet case. He held it out to her.

She shook her head and instinctively drew back, as from a snake.

"You have not looked inside," he said. "Perhaps the contents will change your mind. There is much more from where these"—he held up the case—"came."

"No," she said quickly, adding quietly but firmly, "no, thank you."

"You owe it to yourself, and to me, to look at least."

Sighing, she took the case and opened it slowly. Then she let out a gasp. The necklace was a length of huge square-cut stones the color of her eyes surrounded by icelike baguettes. Shakily she snapped the case shut and thrust it at him. "I don't want it!" she hissed, turning away.

Shrugging, he slipped the case back into his pocket. "That is today," he said equably. "Perhaps in time you will change your mind." He smiled tightly.

"I . . . I'm afraid I won't. Change my mind."

He nodded. "I see that neither jewels nor a season of bookings can sway you," he said. "I was mistaken. You must forgive me. You are far too beautiful and talented—and independent—to be bought so easily. You are not interested in materialistic gain."

She turned to him, her eyes unwavering. "Your Highness, only two things matter to me," she said with soft frankness. "My career, at which I must work and achieve with my own God-given talent, and my daughter, whom I want to make proud of me. Since my husband's death three years ago, I have had no other ambitions."

He was staring raptly at her.

She turned away and took a few steps across the stage.

His voice was the merest whisper, but it carried the force of a physical blow. "Then the child is not your husband's," he said matter-of-factly.

She whirled on him, her face suddenly ashen.

"The child is too young." His deceptively lazy lapis-lazuli eyes deepened to twin pools of dark indigo. "I should have known. There is someone else."

A stab of fear clutched her insides, twisting her stomach into a tight knot.

"Indeed, it seems you were right." His voice was cool and dignified. "It *is* time you continued rehearsing your lines." He smiled. "You are an actress, and a fine one at that. I expect a remarkable performance tomorrow."

"Yes, your Highness." She curtsied formally, careful to avoid his gaze. "I trust I will not disappoint you."

"You have already disappointed me," he said softly. "But I am the Prince Vaslav Danilov. A very rich, very powerful, and very determined man. You will find I do not generally take no for an answer."

Her cheeks stung hotly, as though she had been slapped.

He stood poised at the edge of the stage for a moment, as if pausing between lines to gauge his invisible audience. "And in the end, no matter what it takes, I always get what I want."

She looked up sharply then, but he was a mere fleeting shadow. Then she heard footsteps echoing, the sound of a door closing, and, finally, silence. She knew she was alone in the theater.

She shuddered and took a deep breath. She could not remember ever having felt quite so frightened of anyone in her entire life.

Outside in the hallway, Count Kokovtsov slipped silently out of a doorway and caught up with the Prince. The dour Count had to hurry to keep pace with his cousin. Overhead, the cold glitter of chandeliers of fruit-shaped rock crystal flashed and seemed to fly past with the speed of storm clouds; underfoot, the richly inlaid marqueterie seemed to rush toward them, gleaming mirrorlike and crackling with every step. The Prince did not look at his cousin. "So you heard it all?" he asked grimly, his eyes focused straight ahead.

The Count's face assumed a hurt expression. "You know me better than to accuse me of eavesdropping, Vaslav," he said innocently. "What need have I to do that?"

"Sometimes I wonder. And the answers I come up with, cousin dear, are not very pleasant."

A vein in Count Kokovtsov's tall, domed forehead twitched with anger. "I had just arrived when you came rushing out," he said. "Even had I wanted to, which I certainly did not, there would hardly have been the time to overhear anything." He sniffed disdainfully. "Besides, you yourself instructed me to thoroughly search the theater troupe's belongings. It was my understanding that you wished to be informed immediately if I found anything unusual."

The Prince stopped walking. "And did you?"

The Count's thin lips curled into a smile of satisfaction. "I have discovered two things that are decidedly of interest. First, a loaded pistol. An unimportant-enough item, considering the actors are itinerants constantly on the road. But I asked myself: Why a pistol? Why not a rifle? That in itself strikes me as rather suspicious. The answer, of course, is that a pistol is far more easily concealed than a rifle. But the second item—or items, I should say—it is they which truly worry me." Count Kokovtsov paused dramatically for effect.

"Well, out with it, man!"

Count Kokovtsov's twisted lips widened into a compressed smile. "What do you say to ten sticks of dynamite?"

"What!" Prince Vaslav took a deep breath.

"You heard correctly. Ten sticks of dynamite." Count Kokovtsov shook his head lugubriously and rubbed his elongated hands together. "I am afraid my worst fears have been borne out. This acting troupe, which you so generously—and unsuspectingly—invited into your home, seems to be a cover for other, far more sinister activities."

"Mordka Vyauheslavich, sometimes even you manage to surprise me," the Prince said calmly. "You constantly see anarchists and assassins lurking behind every bush."

"Perhaps," Mordka Vyauheslavich Kokovtsov conceded acidly, "but if you kept more in touch with what is going on around you, maybe you would do likewise. You would find it wise to do so, instead of chasing after every actress you see."

"That is enough!" the Prince snapped. His eyes blazed

menacingly. "I have turned a blind eye on you and your stableboys and footmen long enough!"

"Touché." The Count sighed and made a fluttery gesture with his hands. "Far be it from me to cast stones in that department. However, I strongly suggest that you toss this particular troupe out of the house. Immediately."

The Prince considered this in silence. Neither a fool nor an alarmist, he had to concede that his cousin was for once right on all counts. Obviously there was at least one terrorist among the theater troupe. This could only cause him terrible trouble—at the very least, a sense of agitation and foreboding—until the troupe was gone. But then his mind's eye conjured up those magical, glittering emerald eyes of the lady of the camellias. She was a young goddess if there ever was one, and surely with enough surveillance and caution. . .

His mind made up, a tight smile crossed his lips. "Noooo . . ." he said slowly, "the entire troupe will stay."

"And the dynamite?" Count Kokovtsov hissed. "Surely we're not to condone—"

"Do as I say, Mordka," the Prince cut in wearily. "I know what I am doing."

"I certainly hope so, because whatever misfortune descends on us as a result of this is upon your head alone," his cousin replied grimly. "I am washing my hands of this entire affair."

"No, you are not. In fact, your stealth will come in very handy. I want every member of the troupe kept under constant surveillance and the pistol and dynamite watched around the clock. It is up to you to make certain they are not touched. Have whoever tries to get to them arrested. If you must, requisition extra policemen and guards. Meanwhile, we will let the troupe perform at the soiree tomorrow as if nothing is out of the ordinary. The day after, they will be gone anyway."

"But . . . but half of St. Petersburg society will be here tomorrow!" the Count sputtered. "Perhaps even the Czar and Czarina!"

"Then it is your responsibility to see that nothing tragic happens. You are capable of doing that, I presume?"

The Count's eyes flashed fire, then died to dull embers. He nodded unhappily.

"Good. It is settled then. Now, do as you've been told. Meanwhile, I have other things to occupy myself with. Oh . . ." The Prince reached into his pocket and handed the jewelry case to the Count. "Return this to Fabergé."

Then he walked off.

Behind him, Mordka Kokovtsov threw up his hands in a gesture of defeat. He could only wonder what his cousin was up to now. Little did he know what a wild idea had blossomed in the Prince's mind.

How simple it would be! Vaslav Danilov thought as a footman threw open a pair of gilded double doors which led into yet another massive hallway. He would get his emerald-eyed goddess even sooner than he had expected.

As that dark, icy winter afternoon melded into an even icier evening, and finally into a brittle arctic night, a light snow began to fall, powdering St. Petersburg and muffling its city sounds. The crystalline snowflakes sparkled in the avenues and streets, on the thousands of windowsills and mullioned panes, and in the lamplit parks as though an especially munificent god had sprinkled giant handfuls of diamonds over the earth. The baroque and Renaissance-style palaces skirting the ice-sheathed Neva were a vision out of a Pushkin fairy tale, with both electric and candle lights glittering through the haze of flakes.

The entire three blocks of the Winter Palace was floodlit from without and glowed richly from within. The Czar and Czarina were staying in, retiring after their evening prayers, a late dinner, and an hour at which the Czarina worked on needlepoint with her daughters in their private apartment and the Czar helped his young hemophiliac son, Alexis, complete a picture puzzle that had been purchased at the English Shop on Nevski Avenue.

In the Danilov Palace, which was second in size and splendor only to the Winter Palace, the lights glowed brightly. Three hundred retainers worked furiously but silently around the clock to prepare for Princess Irina's fiftieth birthday celebration the following day. The lights glowed in all windows of the palace save those of two private apartments and rooms in the servants' quarters above the garages and stables.

"Thank you." Senda smiled at the young footman who had escorted her from the private theater past squads of servants dusting, polishing, and arranging massive bouquets of hothouse flowers in giant vases and urns. She closed the door softly behind her. After the endless trek through gargantuan, glittering hallways and towering reception rooms, the small room under the eaves, which connected with Schmarya's, seemed especially tiny and utilitarian. The thick plaster walls were cracked and the plain furnishings looked scarred and uncomfortable. She couldn't help but feel a twinge of regret and resentment. She had hoped for lodgings far more luxurious, for the palace was grand beyond her wildest imaginings. Except for the servants' quarters.

She tightened her lips and suppressed her pique. She knew her resentment was without foundation. She should count her blessings. After all, they had a roof over their heads, food was bountiful, if plain, and there was an abundance of firewood.

Briskly she rubbed her arms with her hands. She glanced about the room. Only a solitary lamp was burning, throwing dark shadows up the gray walls. The fire in the grate had almost burned itself out. The room was chill. At first she thought Schmarya was asleep, but now she saw that the bed was still made, the covers drawn so tautly across the thin mattress that a kopeck tossed onto it would have bounced off.

Then she noticed him at the narrow window, half-hidden behind the thick double draperies which served to cut down on the insidious, stealthy drafts which wormed their way through every crack and crevice. He was standing motionless, gazing out into the night. He didn't turn to greet her. Perhaps he had not heard her come in.

She moved to the right, paused, and peered down into the crib the housekeeper had arranged to move in from the nursery. The ornate gilded carving and satin coverlets seemed incongruous in the room, but Senda smiled placidly as she pulled the blanket closer around the angelic little face. Tamara was sound asleep, one tiny thumb stuck in her mouth. Senda, remembering Grandmother Goldie's admonition that thumb-sucking made a child's teeth grow in crooked, bent over and disengaged the thumb from the child's lips, but gently, so she wouldn't awaken her. Tamara needed a good night's sleep. At least until the day after tomorrow she would be warm and cozy. Senda was grateful for that. Tamara had had to suffer more than her share of discomfort and cold since birth.

Convinced that her daughter was comfortable, Senda picked up a poker, jabbed at the dying embers in the grate, and added another birch log to the fire. The dry wood crackled and quickly caught fire. Satisfied by the amount of heat radiating forth, she moved toward the window and stood behind Schmarya. He had still not turned around. He had surely heard her by now.

Tenderly she encircled his powerful chest with her arms and placed the side of her head against the warmth of his back. He stood there tense and unmoving.

She frowned, but forced a lightness to her voice. "I think I've got all the lines memorized," she said.

Still he did not respond.

After a moment she stepped back and began to knead the knots out of his shoulders. "You're very tense."

"What else would you expect?" he asked, his voice filled with a quiet bitterness.

She drew away in surprise. "What's wrong, Schmarya?" she asked in a low voice so as not to awaken the child. "Aren't you glad I'm finished for the day? Now we have the rest of the night to ourselves."

"I've barely seen you all day."

"I had to go over the lines until I memorized them all. You knew that."

He whipped around to face her. In the dim light, despite the guardedness of his pale face, the savageness gleaming through his narrowed eyes shocked her. They stared at each other for an interminably drawn-out moment. Then he turned back around to face the window. "This acting bug is going to your head," he said gruffly. "So is the blatant luxury here. The servants' quarters aren't good enough for you, I suppose? That's why you've been down in that theater all day and half the night."

She stared at his back in surprise. "But . . . you yourself agreed that we were to perform here tomorrow. And we need the work." She moved closer again and reached for him, but anticipating it, he stepped adroitly out of her grasp. He moved across the room, away from her.

Her eyes were huge and hurt. "Schmarya." Tears blurred her vision. "What's wrong? What's suddenly come between us?"

"Nothing." He dug his hands into his trouser pockets and stared down at the floor. "It's just that I feel caged up here, I suppose. There's always somebody spying on us. Following us around as if we were common thieves. Maybe I just need some fresh air."

She stared at him, then let out a soft sigh. "You're sure that's all it is?" she asked doubtfully. "Just a feeling of being locked up?"

"What else could there be?"

In puzzlement she stared at the scowl of hatred twisting his face into an ugly mask. She was at once astonished and devastated by his vehement reaction. Until recently, unless she brought up his political activities, he had generally been warm and loving.

"If it's that important to you, we can leave here right

now," she decided quietly. "No performance is worth seeing you so unhappy. We have too much love to share."

"You just do what you have to," he said coldly, "and I'll do what I must."

"Let's not fight, Schmarya," she pleaded softly, plucking desperately at his sleeve. Somewhere deep inside, a smoldering fire, half-hope, half-desperation, rose and burned intensely. "Let's make *love*! Let's forget this squabbling and . . . and recapture what we used to share." She paused and lowered her voice huskily. "If not for our sakes, then for Tamara's?"

He stared expressionlessly at her, and on an impulse she reached up, wrapping her arms around his neck. She stepped up on tiptoe and kissed him, closing her eyes as her tongue sought his, but her lips brushed a mouth carved of stone, as cold and lifeless as one of the multitude of statues which lined the endless corridors of the palace.

Sighing, she let her arms drop heavily to her sides. In a daze, she moved over to the window on leaden feet and parted the curtains with a forefinger. The snow fell heavier now, but she didn't notice. A solitary tear slid a rivulet of moisture down one cheek; then it was followed by another, and another. How many months had it been now since she and Schmarya had made love? Since Schmarya had held her in his passionate embrace and kissed her, seeking the intimacy of her body, urgently needing the fulfillment that only the bottomless well of their mutual desires could provide? The well, she was beginning to realize with a sinking heart, had dried up, at least as far as he was concerned.

And all because of a misunderstanding. Because he believed she had turned her back on their heritage, and thus him.

She sobbed soundlessly. How much things had changed! How little Schmarya really understood her. What she had done had not been to hurt him, but to make things easier for all of them. In Russia, Jews were outcasts only because of religion. Conversion to Russian Orthodoxy provided acceptance for any Jew, even in the highest circles of society, and many Jews had thus obtained enviable positions in the loftiest ranks of czarist Russia. And four months earlier, in order to spare herself, and especially Tamara, any more anguish and heartache resulting from future persecution, Senda had converted to Russian Orthodoxy. In their travels she had met other ambitious actresses who had done the same thing and told her about it.

It was, to her, a simple matter of ensuring their safety.

Social acceptance had never entered her mind. The memories of the pogrom were still all too real. How often the nightmares about it still caused her to awaken in a cold sweat. Schmarya might have understood that, had she not, despite his violent opposition, had Tamara baptized in the Russian Orthodox Church at the same time. He had taken it as a personal insult, an insult against all he held dear. Senda simply viewed her actions as practical necessity, insurance against the future for both herself and her daughter.

The question haunting her now was: Would Schmarya *ever* find it in his heart to forgive her? Would he ever get over what he considered her treachery against their faith, their heritage, and love her again the way he once had? The way she still loved him in so many, many ways.

These terrible thoughts swirled in her mind as thickly as the snowflakes outside.

The tears blurred her vision, but it was not her own crying which finally brought her out of her reverie. She swiftly crossed over to the crib. The little room was chilly again. The fire had burned itself out. The cries were coming from Tamara. She had awakened, and was hungry and cold. Or, Senda wondered, could she somehow sense that something was wrong, even in the depths of her sleep, and need comfort as badly as she herself?

It was then that Senda realized Schmarya was no longer in the room. She hadn't heard him leave during her miserable soul-searching. She shivered, but it was not from the cold. Icy fingers of dread rippled through her, bringing new fears along. Where was Schmarya? Where had he gone? And what in heaven's name was he up to now?

Oh, God, she prayed silently, let him do anything he feels he must as long as it will not ultimately bring harm to Tamara.

It was an interminable wait before the guard ambled along to the far end of the narrow hallway, turned his back, and lit a cigarette. Then Schmarya saw his opportunity. He shut the door soundlessly, and furtively dashed down the narrow staircase to the ground floor. Avoiding servants was no easy matter. While the Danilovs slept, a small army worked in a quiet frenzy to prepare for the next day's celebration. Once he reached the grand public rooms on the ground floor, he thought he had a chance to escape undetected.

The floors of the hushed corridors and reception rooms were masterpieces of their makers' craft: finely inlaid marquetry swirls and checkerboards with a polished, honey-rich

71

glow. Despite the heat radiating from the porcelain ovens and steam radiators, Schmarya could feel the relentless damp chill soaking through the arabesques of wood, numbing his stockinged feet. No amount of heat could completely dispel the damp arctic chill as he tiptoed soundlessly, boots in hand, and flitted in and out of the shadowed niches, pressing himself against the icy statues at any distant sound. Finally slithering behind two sets of heavy curtains, he unlatched a tall beveled-glass French door in one of the splendid reception rooms and slipped outside, wedging the door shut again with a large splinter of wood so that he could open it from the outside once he returned. He pulled on his boots in the dim yellow glow of light which spilled out from a window on the floor above. He was on the balustraded terrace overlooking the park which sloped down to the frozen river.

It was deathly cold out. Although well-bundled, he instantly felt the raw wind turning his blood to ice. The moisture in his nostrils crystallized, and he wound his scarf around his nose and mouth. He was both terrified and exhilarated by the sudden overwhelming sense of freedom.

For long silent minutes he stayed concealed in the shadows, wary of being seen or stopped or, worst of all, tracked to his ultimate destination. When he was fairly certain no one had spied him leaving, he crept along the palace, keeping as close to the wall as possible. Drawn near the servants' entrance by a cacophony of clanging and banging, he noticed a solitary sleigh drawn by two impatiently waiting dray horses.

Creeping closer, Schmarya wrinkled his nose in disgust. This was no luxurious passenger sleigh, he realized. This was winter's version of a garbage truck being piled high with the day's refuse. The kitchen and house servants were dark shadows scurrying in and out to dump the contents of boxes and barrels into the back.

As the garbage was being loaded, Schmarya crept nearer. Soon he was but a few feet from the sleigh. He could see that it was roughly built, the boxlike utilitarian body formed by uneven slats of weathered, splintery wood atop a pair of thick, solid metal runners. He let out a breath of satisfaction. Since the boxlike construction towered above the drivers' seat, it would be child's play to climb up the back without being noticed.

He wrinkled his nose in disgust and pulled his shabby scarf higher above his nostrils. He couldn't believe that the smell was so powerful in weather this cold. Because of it, however, he didn't think he would have to worry about the guards at the gate poking in the garbage.

When the trash was finally loaded, he watched the two burly drivers climb heavily up onto their seats. One took a swig from a flask and passed it to his partner; afterward only their eyes showed from under their low-pulled caps and above their upturned collars and tightly wound scarves. The servants' door banged shut. He could hear a bolt being thrown across it. It was much darker now.

The snow suddenly turned to fast-falling sleet. Schmarya cursed under his breath. As if the cold were not enough. But he had little time to consider this change in the weather. He tensed as a whip cracked mightily in the night. The horses whinnied their protests, and the sleigh immediately began to hiss swiftly away, its jingling bells warning anyone in its path of its hurried approach.

Now was the moment, Schmarya knew.

Crouching low, he ran after the receding sleigh and flung himself facedown as he made a grab for one of the runners. He allowed his prone body to be dragged through the snow for several yards. Then swiftly he pulled himself closer, clutching first one and then the other of the upright struts which rose from the runners to the sleigh bed, until his feet found purchase atop the runners. He glanced down. The white ground seemed to fly past in an ever-quickening blur. Without further ado he climbed up the towering body of the sleigh, using the wide cracks between the slats like the rungs of a ladder. At the top, he nimbly vaulted over into a heap of trash.

The hellish stench was worse than he had anticipated. He had to breathe through his mouth, but even so he nearly gagged and had to fight the impulse to retch. Silence was imperative. Even dry heaves might attract the drivers' attention.

Moments later, the garbage sleigh slid to a halt at the gates. Schmarya peeked out from between two slats. The guards, obviously well aware of the stench, kept their distance. They unlocked the double gates and quickly waved the sleigh through. It crossed the Neva on the bridge beside the Petropavlovsky Island Fortress, and then raced down a straight stretch to the Little Nevka before crossing yet another bridge to Kamenny Ostrov. Unfamiliar though he was with the city, Schmarya sensed it was time he got off this infernal conveyance.

He climbed to the top slat and braced himself for the leap. For long seconds he crouched there. Then he jumped. He seemed suspended in midair before he tumbled painfully onto a snowbank.

Testing his limbs, he rose slowly to his feet. No broken bones or sprains, thank God; the most he likely suffered from the leap was a few bruises.

He whistled to himself. At least he had found a way to escape the Danilov Palace. Why anyone chose to live there, he could not for the life of him imagine. However gilded it might be, it was a prison, a self-imposed prison for the rich. It not only locked undesirables out, it locked the Danilovs in. He wondered if they ever gave that any thought.

He glanced up and down the street, his eyes wary. Few pedestrians were about, as it was not a night for idle strollers. The weather was working in his favor.

Satisfied that he hadn't been followed, he started walking, remembering what his revolutionary "brother" in Kiev had shared with him: the secret St. Petersburg address was engraved in his memory forever.

"They're our kind of people, Schmarya," Sasha Sergeyevich Kraminsky had whispered to him. "Working with them, we can achieve wonders. Give them this dynamite . . ."

Well, he hadn't brought it with him. It was still hidden safely among the props and costumes. Before he handed it over, he had to see if Sasha's friends were as motivated as he. If they deserved the explosives, or if they would waste them. Soon he would find out. But first, he had to find his way to their house. Find out if they were still together as a group. Find out . . . Butterflies stirred in his stomach. He would have to be careful. They might have been discovered and arrested already. The house could be under surveillance.

At last he came to a streetcar stop. He waited for nearly half an hour for the electric trolley, but it never came. An old woman, head hunched down against the relentless blasts of stinging sleet, finally passed, mumbling about it snowing too hard for the trolleys to run.

He asked her for directions, and she pulled back away from the smells emanating from his filthy clothes. She pointed in the opposite direction and shuffled off.

Thanking her, Schmarya made his way on foot. It was when he had nearly reached the street he was looking for that he felt the hairs at the nape of his neck stirring. For an instant he froze. This instinctive reaction had served him well in the past, and he had learned to rely on it.

So he was being shadowed after all.

Or . . . was he simply imagining it?

Sneaking a glance over his shoulder, he saw that he was not alone on the sidewalk. Half a block behind, two men, one burly and one slightly built, were pale shadows in the sleet coming toward him. As he turned, they seemed to . . . slow down? Engage in conversation? Or was he imagining that too? They did seem to be hurrying in his footsteps. But their strides . . .

Although they seemed to be walking casually, their strides were long. Very long. If he didn't hurry, they would gain on him.

He walked on, his footsteps faster, and turned left suddenly at an intersection. He found himself on a smaller, more deserted street. He chanced a backward glance again and saw that the two men had turned at the same intersection and were gaining on him.

His immediate reaction was to run, but he knew he must conserve his energies for later. Besides, he didn't want them to know he was onto them. His heart racing, he broke into a graceful ballet of a speedwalk. Behind him, he could hear the staccato echo of footsteps speeding up. So they *were* pursuing him, and no longer disguised the fact. He smiled grimly, his lips twisting savagely under his scarf. All pretense was abandoned. They were the wolves and he their quarry.

Fear and instinct were a potent mixture: fists clenched, he began racing as fast as he could now, his eyes glued straight ahead on a well-lit intersection which seemed dismayingly distant. Still the footsteps sounded ever closer behind him. Gaining rapidly on him. Panic-stricken, he wondered if he could take both men on should the need arise. He heard a sudden yelp of surprise followed by a dull thud and a bellowed curse. Obviously one of the men had slipped and fallen on the ice. Schmarya's heart leapt and he felt a new surge of determination.

The well-lit street grew in size as he summoned up all his reserves and hurtled forward with a final burst of speed. Another twenty meters, he estimated . . . just fifteen more . . . ten . . . nine . . .

The distance melted to two meters, then one, and suddenly he burst out of the shadowy street and was caught in a throng milling about on the sidewalk. There was more of a crowd then he had dared hope. He guessed that a theater must have just let out or a restaurant had closed for the night.

Ruthlessly he shoved his way through couples and groups of well-bundled, happily chattering friends, elbowing them aside as he stumbled on. A man grabbed at his arm, but he shook him off. A woman screeched after him, "Watch it, you idiot!"

Finally Schmarya stopped, slipped into a dark entryway,

and flattened himself against a door. Swiftly he faced left and craned his neck.

His hopes sagged. Whichever man had fallen had not suffered a broken bone. Both emerged from the smaller street and glanced up and down the congested sidewalk, their eyes searching for him. The burly one spotted him, pointed, and they started after him again. Schmarya observed, with more than a hint of grim satisfaction, that the slight one had developed a pronounced limp, which slowed both of them down.

Then a miracle happened. The crowd through which he had savagely elbowed his way had no intention of being shoved again. Tempers intensified, and as he watched, the men's path was blocked. People began to yell, and the shouting match swiftly turned into a fight. Arms flailed and fists flew. More and more people pressed around in a circle, attracted by the spectacle.

Schmarya slipped unnoticed from the doorway and disappeared. Now his pursuers were stranded in the center of the melee. No matter how hard they tried, they would be unable to catch up with him. He could hear the spectators excitedly egging the fighters on, and he grinned to himself. There was nothing like a fight to bring out the worst in people.

Schmarya reached his destination half an hour later, cautiously backtracking along a different route. It was a small, bleak old house squeezed between a block of others identical to it. Only the peeling numbers on the doors differed.

He cautiously slipped inside and shut the door softly behind him. The hall was narrow and cold, with weak bare bulbs spilling sickly pools of light down the rickety, narrow wooden stairs. As he climbed up toward the top floor, the steps sagged and creaked under his weight. Warning anyone of his approach, he thought dismally, at the same time feeling a respectful gratitude for someone's extreme caution in having chosen this place. God forbid, he did not want to deal with fools. He had a feeling he wasn't, but he had to be sure.

On the second-floor landing the lightbulb was burned out. No light shone down from the third floor either. He had to let his vision adjust in order to see where he was going. Dark shadows merged into Stygian darkness, and he cursed the dangerous steps.

When he took his first step up to the third floor, a shadow detached itself from the wall behind him, and he felt the cold muzzle of a pistol against the back of his head at the same instant that he heard an unmistakably loud click.

"Take one more step," a whispery voice warned, "and I'll blow your head off."

Mordka Kokovtsov lay awake in the well-heated second-floor bedroom of his lavish apartment in the easternmost end of the Danilov Palace. Mordka had been staring up from his down-filled pillows with closed eyes for so long that he could imagine ghostly shapes and ephemeral apparitions hovering in front of his shut eyelids. The dreamy, shadowy boy-angels fluttered tantalizingly toward him, nimbus bodies with giant erect penises. Not like that damned Mikhail.

Mikhail!

With that thought, Mordka quit stroking his penis, and his eyes snapped open in anger as he shot up to a sitting position.

Where the hell was that boy? He'd kept him waiting for . . . how long?

Mordka furiously snapped on the black-shaded bedside lamp. He squinted at the tiny ormolu clock. It was nearly midnight.

Midnight! Why, he'd been waiting for *hours*! Was that possible? he asked himself, his eyes glaring as his lips curled downward in fury. Had the hashish he'd smoked earlier so dulled his perception of time?

He flung aside the down filled comforter and lunged out of bed. He prowled the room with naked restlessness. His penis shriveled, and he breathed deeply and evenly to try to control his burning fury. He uncorked a crystal decanter, poured himself a brandy with shaking hands, and threw back his head as he quaffed the liquid in one gulp. He banged his glass down on a marble topped bureau, threw himself onto a tufted green velvet armchair, and waited for Mikhail, all the while his long fingers drumming impatiently on the arms of the chair.

"Where the hell is that infernal Mikhail?" he thundered.

As if on cue, he heard the parlor door opening and shutting softly, then the muffled sibilance of harsh whispers, interspersed with moans. As soon as the sounds reached his ears, he knew that something had gone wrong.

Damn. He jumped up from his chair and hurried naked into the parlor to investigate. He drew in a sharp breath and froze in the doorway. His jaw hung open.

The sight which greeted him was not a pretty one. Ivan was carrying Mikhail, as if he weighed nothing, to the sofa, where he deposited him lengthwise. Mikhail let out a sharp yelp as he was put down. His head lolled on a cushion. His clothes were torn and filthy, there was a deep gash on his forehead, and the left side of his face was brownish-red and puffy, caked thickly with drying blood. His eyes were closed, whether from shock or fear, Mordka had no way of telling. But in one sweep of his hooded eyes he could see that Ivan's wounds were far less drastic. Ivan, Mordka's faithful retainer, was a Cossack, burly and tough, unlike the frail blond fourteen-year-old.

Mordka swallowed his irritation and approached Ivan. "Well?" he snapped. "Are you going to stand there like the village idiot all night? Get some hot water, towels, and bandages! And whatever you do, don't let anyone in!"

Ivan felt the sweat break out on his forehead and almost ran from the room. His head hung low after Mordka's verbal onslaught.

Tightening his lips in annoyance, Mordka drew closer to the sofa.

Sensing his presence, Mikhail tried to raise his head. Slowly he opened his eyes. His gaze was glazed and distant, somehow otherworldly. He tried to smile. "I'm sorry," he whispered, his voice a thick mumble as the words squeezed past his cut, swollen lips. "I . . . failed you." Then his eyes drooped shut, whether from fatigue or shame, it was difficult to tell.

Mordka's love had turned to stone the moment he had set eyes on his damaged lover, but he felt compelled to comfort him. "There, there," he said softly, although his eyes glittered with a peculiar icy hardness. "All is well now. You're safe." Mordka dropped to his knees beside the sofa, stroking the boy absently with his cool hand before undressing him. He flinched when he caught sight of the ugly amoeba-shaped bruises already welling up on the otherwise flawless young skin.

A draft breathed into the room as Ivan returned carrying a pitcher of steaming hot water in an enamel bowl, clothes, and bandages. Mordka gestured for him to set them down on the floor beside him. Carefully he dabbed the boy clean with a wet cloth and dressed his wounds. The child flinched constantly and sucked in his breath in pain. The hissing sounds gave Mordka a modicum of satisfaction. Finally finished, he rinsed his hands. Heaving a sigh, he rose to his feet and stared expressionlessly at Mikhail. The boy deserved no sympathy. He had failed. At long last Mordka motioned for Ivan to follow him into the bedroom.

Mordka closed the door quietly behind them and faced his servant. "Who did this?" Mordka demanded quietly. "Was it someone from the theater troupe?" He was still quietly composed, and only the nervous tic at his right temple warned Ivan of his master's scarcely contained fury.

Ivan averted his gaze and hung his head, studiously concentrating on the swirling patterns of the green carpet. He was not about to meet his master's penetrating gaze. Slowly he shook his head. "We followed one of them," he said sulkily, "but he gave us the slip. We were trying to get to him when this angry crowd—"

Mordka lifted a hand, palm facing outward. "Spare me excuses," he snapped wearily. He turned his back on Ivan, tucked one hand in the small of his spine, and paced the room with elegant, measured steps, unconcerned with the fact that he cut a ridiculous figure wearing nothing but a giant ruby ring on one finger. "You had but two tasks to perform," he said grimly. *"Two!"* He paused dramatically. "The first, an act of simple surveillance with Mikhail to help you if need be. The second, to see that no harm befell Mikhail. You have failed magnificently at both." Mordka whirled about with the speed of a striking cobra and froze just as suddenly in the pose, still as a statue as he regarded the Cossack through narrowed eyes.

Ivan lifted his immobile bronze face and looked at his master with direct dignity. Enough was enough. In his veins flowed the proud, fearless blood of his warring ancestors. Cossacks were not ones to plead for mercy.

Mordka locked eyes with him and smiled coldly. His high forehead flushed with excitement, and his prominent cheekbones quivered. "Sometimes I wonder why I keep you on, Ivan," he said chidingly, as if lecturing a disobedient child. "It has occurred to me that lately you've become more of a disappointing liability than I would like to admit."

Mordka's words were simple, but all the more lethal because of the quiet conviction of their delivery. Ivan was familiar with the workings of Mordka's mind; therefore he knew the voice with which his master rebuked him was the very same usually reserved for ordering someone's death. Too, his demeanor bespoke the same frigid detachment with which he confronted his hapless victims.

There was unspoken death in the air.

Ivan's mind was a flurry of conflicting hopes and fears. He wondered: Which am I to be today? The executioner? Or the victim? There was no doubt in his mind but that Mordka could easily get rid of him, his trusted killing machine. Ivan took a deep breath. He had to divert his master's raging anger to other channels. "I swear that what happened tonight will not happen again," he said shakily. "I underesti-

mated the man we were following. He was no fool." Ivan
paused momentarily. "But all is not necessarily lost," he
said softly, tempting Mordka's curiosity.

Mordka's lizard eyes blinked, and he looked at Ivan sharply,
with renewed interest. "Then you know where the man
went?" he asked.

Ivan hesitated, buying time to think.

"Yes? Yes?" Mordka could barely contain his impatience.

"A house on Potyomkin Street," Ivan said slowly. "I
know the block, but I'm not quite certain which house.
After he gave us the slip once, I thought it best not to follow
too closely when I caught up with him again."

"When *you* caught up with him again? In other words,
you were alone. You left Mikhail to fend for himself. Which
doubtless accounts for the fact that he is seriously wounded."

Ivan bit down on his lip. What he was about to say now
would either vindicate him or seal his doom. He took a deep
breath and nodded. "Yes." He waited, his heart pounding,
then continued. "Then, once satisfied of the general location
of our quarry's destination, I backtracked to aid the boy,
then brought him here. I figured I could narrow down the
house another time."

Mordka considered this in silence. From his expression,
Ivan was unable to guess his thoughts. "So you admit that
you deserted Mikhail."

Ivan bowed. "I hope that does not disgrace me in your
eyes," he murmured obsequiously.

Mordka appeared not to have heard. He stepped up to the
mantel, one arm draped across it, and stood staring unseeingly
at his reflection in the gilded mirror above it. He had to
come to a quick decision. He had never caught Ivan in a lie.
On the other hand, the Cossack was clever enough to know
that a boy—even one he could trust to sleuth for him as he
had Mikhail—was easily replaced. Far easier than finding
another devoted Cossack who followed any and all orders
with no questions asked. Was he telling the truth?

Mordka drew himself up, turned from the mantel, and
again paced the room in silence. His eyes seemed to have
changed color. They were bleak, and the skin was stretched
tautly across his protruding cheekbones.

Seeing his expression, Ivan was barely able to keep the
terror from showing on his face. "The boy will heal quickly," he
said hastily in a quivering voice. "In no time at all he will be
as good as new. I shall take him to the Georgian masseur on
Orlov Street. They say he has the power to heal in his
hands."

Mordka shook his head. His voice was calm. "No, no, no. Mikhail is inept and stupid, but that is beside the point. I will not tolerate damaged goods." He poised his pinkie on his lips, the ruby a giant drop of blood on the bony finger.

Mordka nodded to himself. Like it or not, it was time to get rid of the boy. While washing him, he had noticed with horror that the peachlike fuzz on the boy's face was developing into a beard. It was not very obvious yet; indeed, he'd never noticed it before. But close up . . .

Yes, it was high time for a transfusion of youth and new adventure. The boy *had* begun to bore him. New, young blood was in order. As if to acknowledge that fact, the vision of a new child brought a stirring to his loins. "Do not bother with the masseur," he said offhandedly. "That boy is a disgrace. I want no part of him."

Ivan felt the tight knot in his gut slowly unravel. So the ax would not descend upon him, but upon the boy. Quickly he looked away so that Mordka could not see the relief in his face. He had bought enough time, he was certain, to discover where the man had disappeared. With a lot of footwork and a little luck, he would surely find out soon. Mordka would be pleased with the results. Perhaps even reward him.

Mordka's thin voice cut into Ivan's reverie like a knife slicing through butter. "You may go now. And take the boy with you."

"Yes." Ivan hurried toward the door and opened it.

"And, Ivan?"

His hand on the door handle, Ivan turned to face his master. "Yes?"

"See that he doesn't suffer too much pain, will you?"

"As you wish."

Mordka sighed deeply. "On the other hand, he should suffer somewhat. After all . . ." He allowed himself a tight, humorless smile. "He was really a rather dreary disappointment."

Princess Irina's birthday did not start auspiciously, at least not for Senda.

At seven-thirty in the morning she was awakened by a series of sharp, businesslike raps on the door. The knocks continued, sharper, louder, more insistent. Then they awakened Tamara, who began wailing angrily.

Damn.

Senda flung the covers aside, jumped out of bed, and grabbed a flannel robe, quickly slipping it on. She rubbed her arms briskly with her hands. The room was icy cold; the floorboards felt like frozen wood beneath her bare feet. The fire in the grate had long since burned out. As she breathed, wisps of vapor trailed from her nose and mouth. She caught sight of herself in the mottled mirror on the wall. She stopped, peered into it, and gasped. She was startled by the ravaged visage staring back at her. Her eyes were puffy and red-rimmed. She did not look at all well-rested.

The knocks on the door continued without letting up. Angrily she turned from the mirror, stalked to the door, and flung it open. A woman in a gray uniform and starched white apron quickly jumped back, one hand poised over her heart. Obviously the suddenness with which the door had burst open, coupled with Senda's fierce scowl, gave the woman quite a scare. Senda blinked and gazed at her blearily.

Frizzy flaxen hair fought the confines of the braids coiled on top of her head in the Germanic fashion and was winning the battle, but the face was far from unkempt, young and glowing with health as it was. She had a button of a nose, apple-red cheeks, and naturally pink lips, all highlighted and brought to sparkling life by a pair of lively inquisitive cornflower-blue eyes. Senda guessed her age to be twenty, twenty-one at most. Only a year or two older than she herself, she mused.

The woman smiled tremulously and let her hand drop from her breast as she stepped forward.

"Yes?" Senda inquired politely, pasting on a smile to compensate for her abruptness.

The young woman bobbed a quick curtsy. "I'm Inge Meier, my lady. I've come to fetch the baby," she said in halting, heavily accented Russian. "His Highness suggested I take the child to the nursery in the family wing of the palace and care for it there." She hesitated, quickly looked away, and added softly: "He said to tell you it was probably best you concentrate on other things, seeing as how you have to perform tonight."

"*He* told you to tell me that?" she asked incredulously.

"Yes, my lady."

"I see." Senda tightened her lips and her smile froze in a bleak, humorless line. Annoyed, she raked her fingers through her hair. How dare he interfere with her family, she thought rebelliously. She wasn't about to let Tamara out of her sight, let alone hand her over to a total stranger. Yet what choice did she really have? She guessed that a "suggestion" from Prince Vaslav Danilov was actually a polite euphemism for an order.

Slowly the irritation seeped out of her. She couldn't really hold him at fault. Lord knows, she owed him the best performance she could give. That would take all the concentration she could muster. Today was one day it wouldn't hurt not having to care for Tamara on top of everything else.

"Very well," she said at last. "Wait here, please."

"Yes, my lady."

Senda went back inside, half-closing the door to shield Schmarya's sleeping form from the nurse, and approached the crib. Tamara stared up at her and reached out with tiny, pudgy fingers. Senda lifted her out and kissed her, hugging her tightly, then nuzzled her face. Instantly the wails with which the child had awakened turned to happy laughter.

"You be a good girl," Senda whispered to her daughter. "You hear? Don't do anything to shame me. I'll try to drop by to visit if I can." Then she went to the door, forced a smile, and met the other woman's cornflower gaze. "You'll take good care of her?" she said anxiously, handing Tamara over to her.

"Oh, I will, my lady! As if she were my own!" The nurse leaned low over the bundle in her arms and cooed softly. Tamara laughed happily in return.

Senda smiled, liking the young woman's honest eyes and self-confidence. "I don't think I caught your name."

"Inge, my lady," the young woman said, an answering liking shining in her eyes.

"And I'm Senda Bora. You may call me by my first name. Please."

Inge looked surprised that anyone she worked for would be so casual. "Yes, my lady," she said formally, rocking Tamara in her arms.

Senda smiled her thanks, shut the door, and stumbled wearily back to the bed. She wanted to go back to sleep. She let herself fall into bed without taking off her robe. Shivering from the cold, she buried herself under the covers. Suddenly she had to stifle a paroxysm of laughter.

" 'My lady'!" The nurse had actually called her "my lady"! Now, that was a first, Senda thought.

Minutes later she had shut her eyes and drifted back to sleep, when another series of knocks interrupted a dream.

"Oh, my God!" she cried, sitting bolt upright, her heart skipping a beat. Her nerves unraveled and fear shot through her like a bolt of lightning. A thousand potential disasters short-circuited her usual composure and practicality. Tamara! The nurse had dropped her! There'd been an accident. There—

She flew from the bed to the door and threw it wide, but

83

her panic was immediately replaced by relief as she squinted down at another stranger, a short barrel of a woman who gazed unblinkingly up at her through thick metal-rimmed glasses. Senda leaned against the doorframe, shut her eyes, and murmured a quiet prayer of thanks.

"Are you quite all right, my dear?" the woman asked anxiously.

Senda nodded, waiting for the rush of adrenaline to dissipate. "Yes. I'm fine." She opened her eyes and saw the woman's genuine concern. "Really I am. For a moment . . ."

"For a moment you looked quite as though you were ready to faint. You gave me quite a fright, actually." The woman laughed weakly. "Calm, you know," she said, wagging a finger at Senda. "Inner calm and optimism. They change your entire perspective on life, you know. Of course, they are rather a difficult state of mind to achieve. Higher planes always are, don't you agree?"

Senda couldn't help but smile. She had no idea what the woman was babbling about, but something about her cheerful spirits and energy boosted her own flagging morale. So did her bizarre figure and costume. She'd never seen anyone quite like her. She was short and plump, with a massive, thrusting bosom and gentle turquoise eyes hugely magnified behind the bottle-thick spectacles. Her uniqueness was further accentuated by the gloriously plumed, top-heavy hat swaying precariously atop her head. Beneath it, the shiny scrubbed face peering up at Senda was round and lady pink, with a succession of chins which wobbled as she spoke. She had that flawless complexion so often seen in overweight women. She smelled of Pears soap and lilac.

"So you are the actress," she said, studying Senda with as much fascination as Senda studied her. "Vaslav told me you were beautiful, but he didn't begin to describe how enchanting . . ." She waved her wrist limply. "Never mind, there's so much to do and so little time. We'll show them we can move mountains, shan't we!" And then, out of the blue: "How soon can you be ready, my dear?"

Senda stared at her, trying to follow the incessant chatter and abrupt changes of subject without success. "Ready? For what?" She was confused. "I don't have the least idea what you're talking about," she protested.

"Of course you don't. He wanted to keep it a surprise!"

"But what, may I ask, is the surprise?" Senda pressed her thumb and index finger against her forehead, as if she had a massive headache.

"Why, the fitting, of course! How stupid of me. I keep

forgetting that it's a surprise. He hasn't told you." The woman laughed, and the running litany came to an abrupt end as she placed her hands on her hips and her giant eyes swept Senda's figure up and down. "Now, let me think . . . the pink or the dove gray? Noooo . . . the white! It will look so inspiring on you. So virginal. It will suit you to a . . ." The giant eyes sparkled happily. "Come, come. We've wasted enough time chattering. In we go. There's so much more I've still . . ." She dashed past Senda into the room and skidded to an abrupt halt. "Oh . . . oh, dear!" The woman suddenly looked flustered. "Oh. Ohhh! How thoughtless of me." She turned to Senda, balled up a hand, and brought it to her lips. "I didn't realize—"

"—that there's a man sleeping in the bed?" Senda completed the sentence for her, smiling slightly.

The woman nodded unhappily. "You must excuse me, my dear. I didn't mean to pry. I mean, whatever anyone . . . Well, just put something on, my dear. It doesn't matter what. And don't worry about bathing or doing your hair. There's plenty of time for that later. Princess Irina has the most divine hairdresser. I know for a fact that at least one princess and two duchesses tried to get her to defect to their households. But that's another story entirely." Then she whispered conspiratorially, "I know this palace backward and forward, you know. There is no end of staircases and halls, some which everyone's forgotten about. We'll smuggle you to the fitting room so quickly that no one will see you."

"The fitting room? What's the fitting room?"

"Why, precisely what its name implies. The room where magic is made, what else?"

"Magic?"

"Sewing, my dear."

"But . . . what for?" Senda asked, flabbergasted.

"What for?" The woman looked shocked. "My dear . . ." Shaking her head, she took Senda by the elbow and guided her to the far side of the outside hall. "You are performing tonight, aren't you?" She looked up at Senda questioningly.

"Yes."

"And afterward you are attending the ball? I mean, no one in his right mind would dare turn Vaslav down. He does have such a temper . . ." She saw that Senda was staring at her blankly. "Now, my dear, whatever is the matter?"

"The ball?" Senda's heart skipped a beat. "I'm supposed to go to the ball?"

"After the performance." The giant hat nodded briskly. "Yes. Didn't Vaslav invite you?"

"No one invited me."

"Oh, dear. It's slipped his mind. He is like that, you know. So much to do. He told me . . . yesterday, I think it was. Yes, yesterday! When I asked him if there was anyone he had neglected to invite, he named several people. You among them. Then he told me you probably wouldn't have anything to wear, so I assured him Madame Lamothe—she's the seamstress—would be able to cook up a little something. Of course, when I talked to her she complained endlessly, claiming she was overbooked and overworked. She's such a dragon that sometimes I wonder why we put up with her, though I know. She sews like an angel. Well, I soon got her to see things my way, as usual. Beside, she wouldn't dare do anything to upset me, and especially Vaslav. We send too much business her way. If we stopped going to her, then everyone in St. Petersburg would avoid her like the plague, you see. A little blackmail never hurts. And now that she's here . . . you see, my dear, we can't keep her waiting, as she's got less than twelve hours to complete your gown— now, can we?" The woman smiled brilliantly, as if what she'd said made perfect sense.

"But . . . but this is so sudden!" Senda argued weakly. "I didn't expect—"

"Good. Expectations are for children." The woman clapped her little pink hands together. "Now, in you go, and put on a dress and some shoes at least. I know you won't keep me waiting long." Gently but firmly she placed her hands in the small of Senda's back and propelled her forward.

In the doorway, Senda paused and turned around. "I know it sounds ridiculous, but we haven't been introduced. I don't even know your name!"

"Oh, dear. And I've completely forgotten yours!"

"Senda Bora—" Senda caught herself just in time. When she'd converted to Russian Orthodoxy, she'd discarded the "levi" at the end of her name. She was simply Senda Bora now. Schmarya had refused to follow suit, but his name never appeared on playbills or posters, an absence which pleased them both.

"And I am Countess Flora Florinsky, but you must call me Flora, my dear." The Countess's sentence was punctuated by laughter. "Flora Florinsky does sound rather redundant, don't you agree? Anyway, I'm a very minor relative, and an even more minor countess . . ." And before she completed the sentence, she made little shooing gestures with both limp hands, and Senda was left with no choice but to shut the door and hurriedly dress.

*   *   *

In the fitting room, Madame Lamothe impatiently awaited them, tapping her folded arms with slender manicured fingers. Behind her stood her two young apprentices.

Senda's heart fell, and she stole a sideways glance at Countess Florinsky for moral support. Madame Lamothe, she thought, was not a mere dragon, as the Countess had warned; she was surely an arrogant fire-breathing dragon, as haughtily impressive as even the most titled of St. Petersburg nobility.

Senda caught Madame Lamothe's eyes settling on Countess Florinsky's concoction of a hat, and saw her thin humorless lips turn slightly downward in disapproval. Then her gaze rested on Senda, and the frown deepened even further.

Senda flushed and glanced away. She felt shabby in her scratchy underclothes, worn boots, and faded green wool dress which was all the worse for wear because its white jabot had turned a ghastly shade of bilious gray-green through repeated washings. Worse, it smelled musty and desperately needed ironing: it was wrinkled from being packed for so long. Yet it was the best dress she owned, and she had made an effort to look presentable. Despite Countess Florinsky's suggestion to the contrary, she had even taken the time to run a comb through her hair, and had hastily pinned it up, but it was already coming loose and hanging in tendrils all around.

Senda glanced studiously about the high-ceilinged room in order to avoid Madame Lamothe's sharp gaze. She could not remember when she had ever felt so intimidated by someone as she was by the dressmaker, a tall, spare, imposing woman, even taller than Senda herself. Her jet-black hair, artfully streaked with stripes of gray, was pulled back into a perfect chignon, and her eyes were a clear, glacier blue. The simple dove-gray dress she wore was of silk, and its cut was superb. Her sole adornment was a pair of heavy gold-rimmed spectacles hanging from around her neck on a heavier gold chain. Her scent was expensive, and her face was pale and classic, like the finest, most flawless white marble; indeed, her perpetually dour expression seemed to be chiseled and carved. She was not a woman in whom one could inspire fear, that much was plain.

Her two young apprentices, Senda sensed, were in complete awe of their mistress. Both girls were quite pretty, plainly dressed in black wool, and their only adornment was yellow cloth measuring tapes draped decorously about their necks.

As though sensing her discomfiture, Countess Florinsky slid an arm through Senda's and steered her forward. The Countess was filled with cheerful chatter and that particular *joie de vivre* which was hers alone. "Here she is in the flesh, Madame! St. Petersburg's newest and finest actress."

Senda cast the Countess a sidelong glance, but the Countess didn't seem to notice.

"And this, Senda, my dear," Countess Florinsky prattled on, "is Madame Lamothe. Madame Lamothe has the distinction of being the city's finest couturière. She once had a salon in Paris. I'm certain she'll take the very best care of you."

Awkwardly Senda held out her hand in greeting. For a moment Madame Lamothe cast a long cold glance at the proffered hand before deeming it necessary to smile fixedly and shake the offending thing. Her grip was loose and dry, Senda noticed, and the fingers felt cold as stone. The last thing on earth Senda wanted was to be left alone with this indomitable creature.

Senda didn't realize how unfounded her fears were.

For her part, Vera Bogdanova Lamothe was, for once, totally nonplussed. She was at a loss for words when confronted with Senda's guileless greeting, and she viewed it, not with the contempt and disgust with which it was interpreted, but with fascinated astonishment. This simple gesture went against everything she had been taught and learned in St. Petersburg court life.

Vera's youth had been ruined, as she saw it, by a courtly Frenchman, one Gerald Lamothe, who had wed her and left her, and she had come to her middle years hating life in general and men in particular. If she remained aloof and withdrawn, shrouded, as it were, in a far-off world of her own creation, it was simply because it was the sole armor she could don to protect herself from the unforgiving lack of fairness which was life. Her aloofness had served her well. Dowagers and debutantes alike felt comfortable in her imperious silence, mistaking it for respect and veneration. The nobility looked upon their couturières as they did their maids, shopkeepers, jewelers, and butlers—necessary conveniences who were there to cater to every whim with quiet respect, dignity, and sealed lips.

As a result, not once in the thirty-five years of her professional career had Vera Bogdanova Lamothe encountered a client who actually proffered her hand to shake. It was simply not done. With no choice but to shake Senda's hand, she tried to comprehend this most-unheard-of breach of etiquette. Only as she swiftly withdrew her hand did it dawn on her that the young woman—a mere child, really—had not meant to commit such a *faux pas*. A total innocent, she simply didn't know how to deport herself.

As the initial horror of the familiarity seeped out of Vera Lamothe, she tried to put herself into the young woman's shoes. If she herself hadn't been raised from birth to her station as dressmaker to the nobility, would she have behaved any differently? Probably not. Certainly not if she had suddenly been thrust from modest obscurity—perhaps even poverty, from the looks of Senda—into the inner folds of the most ostentatiously grand court on earth.

And that was something Vera found immensely refreshing.

Well, she would have to put the child—woman—at ease, Vera decided then and there. Obviously Senda was clinging to the Countess out of pure terror. But the girl wouldn't be uncomfortable for long, not if she, Vera Bogdanova Lamothe, had anything to say in the matter. And say it she would, with needle, fabric, and thread. She knew that she didn't sew gowns so much as she sold dreams, and therefore self-confidence and self-worth. Didn't everyone on whom she draped a magnificent gown not only assume a sense of marvelous style but also absorb it as part of her natural inner character as well?

Vera's professionally calculating gaze swept Senda from head to toe and back up. She nodded to herself with satisfaction, though her face revealed nothing. Her heart began to beat just a little quicker. Transforming the shy, unassuming woman into a fairy-tale princess, at least for tonight's performance and the ball, would not be a difficult task at all. Behind eyes still filled with sleep and beneath obvious insecurities and the loathsome clothes, lurked a fine figure for clothes. A noble figure, rare and remarkable. Long waisted torso, long legs, all crowned with that head of spectacularly abundant, if unruly, wild red hair. Indeed, the more closely she inspected her, the more inspired Vera became. The girl really did possess a devilishly rarefied and radiant beauty which could easily be accentuated and brought to full bloom. Like a tightly clenched rosebud brought into the warmth to open.

Yes!

She studied Senda closely, prowled slow, measured circles around her, feeling at once exhilarated and defeated. *How?* How was she to conjure up a dream of striking ethereal beauty, one which would bewitch and tantalize, waltz and polonaise through the night, and put all those filthy-rich, multititled society dowagers to shame? Then the lightning bolt of inspiration flashed, crackled, and caused her to freeze in mid-step. She caught her breath, dared hardly breathe.

Youth.

Innocence.

Simplicity.

Dusty rose.

Suddenly she was swept away, her mind reeling. She could already see it: a vision in taffeta the color of fading roses.

Vera Lamothe lived for those moments when she could revel in the potency of her creative talent and power. But she kept her face carefully composed, entirely neutral. She motioned for Senda to turn around slowly, and she spoke calmly, almost wistfully. "Very well," she said shortly, glancing at Countess Florinsky. "I shall see what I can do. But I'm making no promises." Vera held herself regally erect, smug with the satisfaction of what she was about to achieve.

"Oh, thank goodness!" Countess Florinsky trilled happily, flinging her arms across her massive turquoise bosom in a gesture of pleasure. "I knew I could count on you, Madame! How delighted you've made me! Such a weight you've taken off my shoulders." The Countess turned to Senda, held both her hands, and squeezed them affectionately. "Well, my dear, I do wish I could stay and keep you company, but alas, duty calls." Unexpectedly the Countess hopped on tiptoe and deposited a quick kiss on Senda's cheek.

Senda was touched by the gesture, but appalled that she would have to suffer through her first fitting alone. "You must leave?" She sounded stricken. "Just when my fairy godmother appears out of nowhere, she disappears again." She bit down on her lip nervously.

"No, no, no, my dear." The Countess flapped a hand in Vera's direction. "I'm not your fairy godmother. She is."

"You are far too kind, Countess," the seamstress murmured, working to hide her pleasure behind the mask of inscrutability she had perfected over the decades.

"Well, I must be off!" the Countess sang. "I've dallied far too long. There is so much . . . Heavens! The flowers!" She slapped herself gently on the cheek. "Goodness, I'd forgotten them." She smiled at Senda. "You see, it isn't easy to arrange a fete like the Princess's birthday celebration. There are so many responsibilities, you've no idea. The food . . . the music . . . the floral arrangements. Oh, dear, my head is spinning. I'm afraid I might faint!" She hesitated, glanced about frantically, and spied a square of cardboard on a worktable. She seized upon it and began fanning herself furiously with it. "Maybe . . ." she said haltingly, "maybe

I'll sit for a moment . . ." Her words trailed off as she seemed to slowly wilt and sag.

Alarmed, Senda reached out to catch her, but with a single nod from Madame Lamothe her two assistants sprang forward. They helped lower the Countess's considerable bulk into a mahogany armchair.

"Ah, yes, yes. That is so much better. What got into me? It's so unlike me . . ." Her makeshift fan a blur, the Countess closed her eyes. Senda was saying something, and she hadn't been paying attention. Abruptly she ceased fanning. "I'm sorry, my dear. I think my mind is filled with cobwebs. You must forgive me."

"You said that you're in charge of the fete?" Senda asked. "I didn't know that."

"Of course!" the Countess said negligibly. "Everybody knows that. Helping give parties is how I earn my living." The Countess felt compelled to explain, seeing Senda's puzzled expression, and her giant, distorted eyes took on a faraway look. "You see, when my Boris died, God rest his soul—he was a Hussar officer, so tall and handsome . . . so dashing and slim. Imagine, his elkskin breeches fit so tightly that it took two servants to pull them on! His shoulders were so wide, and with those epaulets . . . I'll never for the life of me know what he saw in me." She paused, and when she continued, her voice took on a feeble tone. "Of course I know. Everyone knows. Boris' commission took nearly every ruble his parents had left, and he was under the impression that I was wealthy."

"Oh." Senda's heart went out to her newfound friend. "How awful it must have been for you to discover that."

"No, you mustn't think badly of him. It's a very long story, my dear, but suffice it to say that my dear Boris gambled away every ruble, and then . . . oh, my dear . . . committed suicide and left me alone with enormous debts. So I took the bull by the horns, as they say, and went to work to pay them off and make a life for myself." She fanned furiously for a moment and then continued. "I refused to live off the kindness of family and friends, like someone's dreary maiden aunt. So for years I've arranged fetes and so on for a fee. I began working for Vaslav's father and have managed to keep going. Thank God for dear Vaslav and his friends." She laughed affectionately. "So you see, Senda, my dear, although I am titled, I'm really a simple workingwoman." She caught Madame Lamothe's stern, disapproving gaze and ignored it, fingering the gold locket which hung from her neck. She snapped it open to reveal a watch.

The Countess regarded the time in wide-eyed shock, and then snapped the locket decisively shut and dropped her makeshift fan to the floor. She recovered her equilibrium remarkably well, leaping up from the chair in such an energetic bound that it put a lie to her dizzy spell. "I mustn't dally another minute!" she cried. "The flowers should have arrived from the Crimea, and I must see to the decorations. Oh, and I'm certain camellias are among them. I will see to it that a bouquet is delivered to the theater." She embraced Senda swiftly, enfolding her in her lilac-scented breast, waddled hurriedly to the door, and then turned her head. "Toodles!" she sang, wagging her fingertips and blowing a kiss as she shut the door behind her.

Madame Lamothe sighed with relief, but Senda couldn't help smiling. The Countess needn't have shared her circumstances with her; she had done that to make her feel at ease. Silently Senda blessed her. She was such a guileless, charming, and honest woman that she'd won Senda over completely.

Madame Lamothe apparently wasn't happy with the interruption at all. As soon as the door closed, she turned to Senda and clapped her hands sharply. "Come. We have wasted enough precious time. Now we must measure you . . . madame . . . mademoiselle?"

"I am a widow."

"Madame, then. Undress completely." Madame Lamothe's patrician eyebrows arched imperiously, suggesting that Senda had best hurry.

Nine hours later, Senda stared critically at herself in the cunningly angled reflections of four tall, floridly carved cheval mirrors. Madame Lamothe stood off to one side, hands clasped primly in front of her, an almost pleased expression softening her usually stolid features. She was flanked by the two assistants, each of whom gaped at Senda openmouthed.

"That's . . . me?" Senda gasped incredulously, taking her eyes off her reflection for a few seconds and staring sideways at Madame Lamothe.

The dressmaker nodded. "Yes. Indeed it is."

"My God. I'm . . . I don't know what to say." Senda turned back to the mirror facing her and shook her head. "I look . . ."

"Breathtaking?" Madame Lamothe ventured softly.

Senda nodded wordlessly, as if speaking would break the spell. She was uncomfortable with preening and primping, especially with three sets of appraising eyes watching, but she was unable to keep her eyes off her reflection. She

92

turned hesitantly and studied herself from the back. The skirt of the gown rustled and moved with her every motion, as if it had a fluid life of its own. She could scarcely believe the vision of loveliness which mimed her every move. She was . . .

Was it possible? Was that extraordinarily exquisite creature really she?

Swallowing her embarrassment at such self-centered fascination, she realized that the young woman in the mirrors—perhaps they were magic mirrors?—was sophisticated, aristocratically regal, and yet somehow touched with an elusive, innocent vulnerability. The pale ashes-of-roses taffeta highlighted her naturally rosy complexion, shining even pinker under the scrutiny of the prying eyes. The elegant low-cut bodice fit snugly and her shoulders were left bare. Her breasts were pushed upward, making them appear to be two perfect creamy orbs, larger and more sublime than she knew them to be in reality. The puffy short sleeves were like delicate taffeta epaulets, cloudy afterthoughts perched ever so lightly just off her shoulders. Senda marveled at her almost nonexistent waist. Pinned just above her left hip was a single silk camellia, identical to the one attached to her right shoulder. The effect was superbly balanced. On the flaring skirt Madame Lamothe had applied pale silk camellias near the hem, each blossom holding up resplendent curving swags of taffeta which barely swept the parquet. The matching velvet gloves reached to mid-bicep, complimenting her perfectly.

More than ever now, she was firmly convinced that Madame Lamothe did indeed possess a league of diabolical, otherworldly powers.

Senda daringly moved her hips from side to side, feeling not only the luxuriant sensuality of the gown as it swayed smoothly with each rhythmic motion, but a thrill of exhilaration. Then, on a sudden impulse, she pirouetted on the toes of the slippers Madame Lamothe had magically conjured up, and the taffeta shimmered and billowed about her legs.

Her eyes sparkled, radiating pleasure she had never known existed. She looked spectacular indeed, and she *felt* beautiful. From within.

Earlier, while needles were positively flying, Senda had bathed, and then the Princess's English hairdresser, Alice, had done her hair, pulling it tightly back from her face and pinning it up with barrettes. A last silk camellia crowned her forehead like a tiara.

Spellbound with herself, Senda saw Madame Lamothe

93

and her assistants recede into the background as if they were ghosts in a dim dream. Forgotten were the observant, critical eyes. Senda discarded the last vestiges of her inhibitions, daintily pinched the skirt between thumb and forefinger, and began waltzing around the room, humming softly to herself.

Just as she danced past the fitting-room door, it burst open without warning. Startled, Senda froze in mid-step and stared wide-eyed at the intruder.

A breathless Countess Florinsky, gowned in age-yellowed brocade encrusted with seed pearls on the bodice, froze, as had Senda, the closed silver fan she carried in one hand poised in midair. Two golden medallions, like gleaming earmuffs, covered the Countess's ears, and these were attached to each other by a wide gold band sprouting a gloriously excessive concoction of fluffy white egret feathers atop her head.

Time came to a standstill. Nothing breathed. Nothing moved—nothing except the egret feathers, which swayed and quivered on the Countess's startled head. Silence reigned, save for the gilded clock on the mantel, which ticked away unperturbed, each tick seeming to grow louder and louder, building up to a climax. Unexpectedly, the clock chimed the hour. Everyone jumped, and reality once again descended upon the room.

"What's wrong?" Senda cried, staring at the Countess's stunned expression in dismay.

"What's *wrong*?" The Countess found her feet, flung open her arms, and rushed forward, embracing Senda with her pump arms. She cocked her head sideways and smiled happily at Madame Lamothe. " 'What's wrong?' she asked. Imagine!" The Countess's face glowed, and she permitted herself a spurt of laughter. "*You,*" she emphasized, pressing Senda even closer, "you're so lovely that I think I shall *cry* at any moment. Normally I save my tears for weddings and funerals. Oh, my dear, you are glorious! You will indubitably be the belle of the ball!"

And with that, the Countess lifted her chin, resolutely took Senda's arm, and led her out, wondering how on earth it was possible that this humbly born and innocently bred girl could possess that bewitching, captivating charm and glamour everyone high-bred and highborn worked so hard to achieve—and most of them with scant success.

Already the muted sounds of partying emanated from a distant wing of the palace.

The sounds brought Senda a new attack of gnawing misgivings. Only minutes before, in the excitement of those magical reflections miming her every move in the mirrors, it had seemed that the Cinderella gown and her newly pinned-up hair were weapons enough to vanquish any and all terrors she might have to face. But now she was incapable of enjoying the dreamy metamorphosis wrought by Madame Lamothe's extravagantly fertile imagination and fanciful, nimble fingers. Each sober step she took was an effort, bringing her closer and closer to the ordeal she began dreading with a rising passion: facing her audience and carrying an entire play.

Resolutely she raised her chin, but a sickening, sour feeling coiled itself venomously in the pit of her stomach.

No matter how hard she willed herself to ease the tension, her nerves were still stretched as taut—and were as fragile—as a crystal violin's blown-glass bow.

Senda made her request of Countess Florinsky on the way to the theater. "Could you show me to the nursery?" she asked. "I must stop by there," she told her firmly. "I haven't seen my daughter since the nurse, Inge, fetched her early this morning."

Countess Florinsky hesitated in mid-waddle for a moment, and then her wobbling plumes nodded their acquiescence. It was a small-enough request, and there was just enough time. The Princess's birthday celebration had been carefully orchestrated, but despite the minute-by-minute planning—cleverly juxtaposing the performance of *The Lady of the Camellias* between the caviar-and-champagne reception and the midnight dinner-ball—the festivities were getting off to a late start. As they neared the nursery, they heard a strange whirring noise, punctuated by a child's shriek of delight. Senda exchanged startled glances with the Countess and then, since the nursery was not guarded by doormen, slowly turned the handle and opened the door. She could only gasp and stare in amazement into the room.

This was no ordinary nursery, she realized in one glance. This was a huge zoo of silent stuffed animals, turreted castlelike playhouses, and literally hundreds, if not thousands, of toys. And Tamara, her beloved daughter, whom she had been so certain was screaming grievously for her, was having the time of her life. The little girl was happily seated astride a large, authentically detailed electric-powered locomotive which ran on narrow-gauge foot-wide tracks around the room, pulling three empty wagons, each of which was large enough to seat another child in slat-railed safety and tufted, cushioned splendor. In the center of the room stood a doll's house carved of malachite, trimmed with fili-greed gold; the rails passed through its tunnellike entrance at the front, emerged out the back, then ran in a figure eight between the widespread stance of a giraffe that towered to the sixteen-foot ceiling. All around the room, the tracks were lined by handsome carved wood rocking horses, mam-moth furry elephants, period dolls of all sizes in assorted finery, uniformed toy soldiers with cannon and wooden swords, and faithfully reproduced dollhouses with miniature rooms that boasted minuscule tassels on curtains and tiny electric crystal chandeliers. In that first breathtaking glance at this magical miniature kingdom, Senda noticed small chil-dren's chairs set around a perfectly laid-out tea table, with child-size dishes, silverware, and a distressingly real assort-ment of cookies, cakes, tortes, tarts, candies, and whipped cream. Cookies *and* cakes? Candies *and* whipped cream? She had never heard of all of them served at one sitting.

Senda felt a surge of anger toward Inge, the nurse, but then realized she was reacting to the display of wealth and luxury which she could not provide Tamara. It intensified the hunger they had so often felt and the battle they waged with the bitter elements just to stay alive.

"You see?" said the Countess, "there's nothing to worry about. She's enjoying herself immensely."

Senda could only nod. What child wouldn't enjoy this world of sugarplum dreams? Inge, the beaming nurse, stood up, bobbed a curtsy, and reached for a switch high on the wall—so high that no child could reach it, Senda was grati-fied to notice. The whirring died away and the train slid to a halt. Tamara instantly began sobbing and throwing her tiny fists about in a tantrum.

Senda was shocked. Her Tamara never threw tantrums. Never! Nor did the angry wailing let up even as Inge picked up Tamara and deposited her ever so gently in her mother's arms. Senda tried to comfort her child, but for once the little girl would not be pacified. Her own daughter did not seem to recognize her! And why should she? Senda wondered. I must look a stranger to her. I've never been dressed in such finery before, or had my hair done in this particular fashion. And then she realized that this was not what lay at the root of the problem. For the moment, at least, Tamara did not want to be in her mother's arms. She had been seduced by the train, and wanted to be back on it.

Yes, Schmarya had been right. It had been a terrible mistake to come here. Before having been exposed to this blatant luxury, they had all been so satisfied, never noticing

what they had missed, and they had been so grateful for so
many little things. *Any* little things. Even Tamara, in her
young life, had never acted as spoiled as she had on this one
single day. On the road with the theater troupe, eking out
the most meager of existences, they had somehow been
happier. Closer. Used to poverty, they were now glimpsing
the other side of the coin—everything that money could buy,
things which they could never dream to enjoy again. And
Senda sensed that somehow their lives had been altered,
that none of them would ever be the same again.

She glanced down at the squirming bundle in her arms,
and for the first time noticed Tamara's clothes. Her little girl
had been bathed and newly clothed in a tiny outfit suited for
a princess.

Angered, Senda shut her eyes for a moment. "These
clothes . . ." she murmured. "They're not hers."

Inge shook her head. "No, my lady," she said apologetically. "I was told to choose something appropriate from the
children's wardrobe next door. It seems there haven't been
children here in decades, so perhaps they're a little out-of-
date . . ." Flustered, Inge fidgeted with her hands.

Senda laughed quietly, without humor. She wasn't surprised to find that she was shaking. "It's not that," she
assured Inge quietly.

*It's that the best I could ever do for my own daughter was
scrounge up some rags to dress her in and pray that they
would keep her warm enough.*

Again she found herself wishing they had never come
here. She wished she didn't have to face this little princess
who was her daughter. It shamed her to have to face yet
another reminder of how she'd failed to provide as a mother.
She was also certain that Schmarya and the rest of the
troupe had not been showered with fancy clothes like she
and Tamara had. They would be envious.

She shivered, trying to remember the Prince's exact words
in the theater. What had he said? Something about always
getting what he wanted.

*He wants me. He thinks a new gown and entertaining my
daughter will buy me, just as he tried to buy me with that
necklace.*

She could see it so clearly. The sardonic Prince who always got what he set his sights on; herself, young and seemingly available. Actresses were always thought to be easily
available. And widows.

She ground her teeth stubbornly.

Well, this time he's made a mistake. I won't be bought. Not for money, jewels, or anything else he might try to tempt me with. Or my daughter.

She and Tamara had been satisfied with their bleak existence, because they had known no other way to live.

But now we know what is hidden on the other side of that damned coin.

Tamara squirmed like a wet eel in her arms, piteously howling to get back to the magical locomotive. Gently Senda planted a somber kiss on her daughter's forehead before handing her to Inge, who set the child back in the seat of the locomotive.

Tamara's howls turned into squeals of delight and she clapped her hands in anticipation. "Momma!" she screamed happily. "Looky, Momma!"

Inge flipped the switch and Tamara whirred past on the locomotive, headed straight for Mad Ludwig's miniature castle. Senda watched the tunnel entrance swallow up the train and joined the Countess at the door.

"Let's go to the theater," she told Countess Florinsky in a strained, world-weary voice. "Let's get the show over with."

Senda parted company with Countess Florinsky outside the stage door. "My dear, you are a vision!" The Countess was positively glowing with unrestrained excitement, and held both of Senda's hands in hers, squeezing them affectionately. "You are indisputably going to radiate on that stage!"

Senda tightened her lips apprehensively. "I hope I'll be adequate," she murmured.

"Nonsense! You'll be heavenly!" Another warm squeeze of the Countess's hands punctuated her faith in Senda. "I have every confidence in you, and so should you." The countess embraced her warmly, and Senda wished she could return her embraces as easily, but other than Grandmother Goldie, her family had never shown much affection, seldom ever touched, so she felt that her returned embraces were rather limp.

Countess Florinsky had a few last well-meaning words of advice. "Now, remember, my dear," she bubbled, "if you want your lips to look redder and fuller, just bite them gently. But whatever you do, don't draw blood! If you wish for slightly pinker cheeks, pinch them slightly, but not in public, I daresay. Oh! And one more thing!" The Countess dug around in her bosom and fished out a tiny glass vial filled with amber liquid. She placed it in one of Senda's hands and made sure Senda's fingers closed around it.

Senda brought her hand closer to her face and slowly unclenched it. "What is it," she asked jokingly, "hemlock? In case I should fall flat on my face?"

Countess Florinsky fluttered. "Oh, my dear! You daren't speak that way! It makes me feel quite faint, you know. You'll be a great success, I know it. That vial contains a bit of rosewater. The Grand Duchess Xenia herself has it imported from Floris of London. It's divine! Dab a drop behind your ears, and another in your bosom, and it will drive men literally to distraction. But just a dab, mind you. It's quite concentrated, and you don't want to smell like one of the women on . . . Anyway, I must fly. See you soon. And the best of luck!" The Countess held up her crossed fingers, then uncrossed them and waggled the fingertips of one hand in that peculiar way of hers before waddling away with startling speed for someone so short.

Alone now, Senda turned to the stage door with trepidation. A flurry of muffled, shouted orders, scraping furniture, and excited, high-pitched chatter reached her ears. Her knees were wobbly, and she felt as if her feet had been permanently glued to the spot, making it impossible for her to take that single step required to reach the door. Sickly fears and anguished emotions raged in her bosom.

She was terrified to go backstage. The upcoming performance was strain enough on her fragile nerves, but having to face Schmarya in her new splendor was an even more frightening thought. She wanted desperately to share things with him, not create an unbridgeable chasm, God knows, she thought, enough of a gulf had separated them lately. How was he going to react to her metamorphosis? To her having been invited to the ball, and his having been left out? How was she going to explain? She visualized his accusing eyes, his quivering clenched knuckles—the anger which he used to mask his hurt.

Sighing painfully, she finally composed herself, forcing her slumping shoulders square and raising her drooping chin in an effort to arm herself with the only weapons she knew to do battle with. Hastily she tugged the bodice of her gown higher, steeled herself, and yanked the door open before she could change her mind. She let out a gasp.

Schmarya stood on the other side of the door. He was obviously as surprised to see her as she was to see him.

She almost laughed aloud with hysterical relief. He was dressed as she had never before seen him, in sartorial splendor: an exquisitely tailored formal black suit with a detachable wing collar, tails, and white tie.

99

For a long moment they ogled each other's new finery with critical eyes. Then simultaneously they burst out laughing, and any hard feelings either of them might have been harboring vanished miraculously into thin air.

"I feel like a penguin," he growled in mock anger, showing her his tails.

"But you don't look like one," she said soothingly. She swept closer to him, her gown rustling richly, and she instinctively straightened his tie. Then she took a step backward and looked down at herself. "Don't feel so bad. I feel like an expensive doll."

"And you look it. My compliments, madam."

They laughed and held each other close, something they hadn't done in so long that even now her heart ached for having missed his wondrous, loving embrace for so long. She marveled with pride at how truly handsome, how virile he looked. His hair had been trimmed, his fingernails manicured, and his teeth flashed whitely against his naturally healthy complexion.

"Black suit and golden hair," she murmured softly. "Mmmmm, a rather disquieting combination."

"Well, it looks like we've both been invited to the ball," he said casually.

She smiled and touched his cheek with her hand. "And to think that I was beginning to feel quite guilty that you'd been left out."

"It sure surprised me," he said. "There I was, sound asleep, when I was rousted out of bed and rushed to a fitting room, where an English tailor from Nevsky Avenue was waiting."

She smiled at him. "With assistants," she said slyly.

He laughed. "With assistants."

She shook her head wonderingly. "How many fitting rooms do you think there are in this palace?"

He shrugged. "Beats me. One for men, I suppose, and one for women."

"Probably even one for children."

They laughed again. It was good, so good, she thought, to share something again.

Unexpectedly, she caught her breath as he drew her into a shadowy corner, away from prying eyes. Gently he nuzzled her neck. "Promise me the first dance?" His lips were warm and moist against her cool, fragrant skin. His breath was fresh, scented with cedar.

She gazed at him and prayed: Oh, God! Please let it be like this from now on. Let us share our laughter and our love, our very souls. . . .

But this litany was soundless, and what Schmarya saw were mischievously fluttering vixen eyes. She tossed her head capriciously. "Maybe I'll be so popular you'll have to stand in line and wait your turn."

"Bitch," he said good-humoredly.

Suddenly she clutched his arms in such a tight grip that she left wrinkles on his sleeves. "Oh, Schmarya, I'm so scared," she whispered. "All those people I'm going to have to face. What . . . what if I make an ass out of myself?"

"You?" He threw back his head and laughed, deep, rich, reverberating peals of laughter like in old times, and suddenly it *was* like old times. "If I know you, and I think I do, you'll have the audience wrapped around your little finger."

Slowly she extricated herself from his embrace. "I'd better go hone up my lines. And I've got all that greasepaint to smear on . . . Schmarya! Let me go!" She giggled with delight, captured in his steely arms.

"On one condition."

She raised her brow questioningly.

"That you kiss me first."

"I love you, Schmarya," she whispered.

He kissed her lightly on the forehead, nose, ears, and lips. Then he kissed her deeply, long and fierce, his strong hands pulling her so tightly against him that even through all the layers of fabric, she could feel the bulge of his erection.

"I love you so much," she gasped, her heart pounding, tears of joy in her eyes. "I'll love you forever. For eternity." Then she whispered intensely: "You're getting me excited! Now, stop it! My legs are already wet. What if it seeps through the gown?"

Suddenly he released her and grinned devilishly. "Let it."

"Schmarya!" She feigned shock.

"There's a little storeroom in the back . . ." His voice, a soft, appealing challenge, drifted languidly into the unspoken world of promises. "It's empty. And the door locks."

"Someone will notice." But she didn't glance about.

"Let them."

She met his challenging gaze and held it. "Then by all means," she concurred, before practically yanking his arm out of its socket. "What are you waiting for?"

"This." Effortlessly he swept her off her feet and carried her to the little storeroom. It was dark and cold and smelled musty, but she didn't care. When he set her down and slid the lock in place, she could only stand there rooted to the floor, her heart surging. She felt like a giggling young lover sneaking away to a tryst. As she used to do in the Pale.

"I want you to touch me," she said softly, reaching behind her and undoing the top of her gown by feel. Then she could feel his hands.

She sucked in her breath, visualizing him in this dark cocoon, his fingers brushing her breasts, his lips rolling her nipples between his teeth. Then she felt him lifting up the full heavy skirt of her gown. "Hold it up," he said, "while I undo your underwear."

"Just make sure I don't get this gown dirty."

"Women." He laughed. "Here we are, about to make love, and you only care about your dress."

"That's not true,"she said soberly. "I care for you."

"I know that." He kissed her deeply, and then he felt beneath her gown, pawing his way past layers of petticoats and finally unfastening the silk panties with their single fragile button.

Something tinkled to the floor.

"Damn!" he swore.

"What is it?" she asked.

"The button popped off your panties."

"I told you to be careful!" she hissed. "Now what will I do?"

"Nobody'll notice if you don't wear them."

And then he felt her curly pubis. She let out a moan and heard him fumble with his trousers. Then suddenly she could feel his swelling hardness growing even bigger and harder against the juncture of her legs. She reached down to touch it, her hand gripping the familiar firm, warm thickness. She thought she could hear his breath quickening.

She held the gown up higher. "Put it in," she said. Then, as she felt him sliding himself inside her, she gasped. "Oh, God," she moaned. "That's so good."

Eagerly she thrust her hips, letting him stand still as she slid herself along the engorged shaft, jamming him inside her, sliding herself off, jamming him back inside.

Finally he could stand it no longer. He let out a gurgling moan and breathed hoarsely, clinging to her now, as if for dear life, his own in-and-out thrusts turning pitiless and savage as he threw all his weight against her vagina.

In and out he slammed, and her mouth gasped in delirious pleasure as she felt wave after crashing wave of orgasm roll through her. "Oh, yes!" she whispered. "Oh, yes, yes, yes!"

And she could feel him climbing closer, ever closer to his own orgasm. Overwhelmed by his onslaught, she picked up his rhythm and desperately began hammering herself against him. Faster, faster they thrust, his great engorged being swelling up even larger as he rode her furiously. And then he bellowed as if he'd been wounded, reared back, and hurled himself into her for one last time, letting his excruciating warm stream of liquid mingle with hers.

He still clung to her, groaning at the afterjolts of pleasure, the spasms racking his body, and then caught his breath. She could feel him growing smaller inside her, and she let out a little gasp of disappointment as his penis slid from within her.

"That was too fast," she panted.

"We still have time," he whispered between gulps of air. "I haven't used my tongue yet."

She smiled to herself. She couldn't remember when she had last been filled with such indescribable joy.

It was indeed a night of wizards and fairy godmothers and magic.

The performance of *The Lady of the Camellias* was scheduled for eight o'clock.

Since six o'clock, guests had begun drifting to the palace, as eight o'clock approached, they were arriving in droves. Countess Florinsky dispatched a messenger backstage to announce that the start of the play had been postponed an hour. This news was greeted by a chorus of groans from a jittery cast, but the message, shouted to Schmarya and Senda through the storeroom door, was greeted with delight, at least by Schmarya.

Outside the Danilov Palace, the coral strands of the aurora borealis hung like a succession of muted, shimmering silk veils in the crystalline black night above the onion-domed spires. The weather had cleared completely, as though a royal edict had specified a glorious night for the Princess's birthday celebration. The ice-sheathed circular drive was lined on both sides with thousands of festive electric bulbs glowing with the Princess's favorite color, sapphire blue, and was jammed with a steady procession of stately cars and horse-drawn coaches bearing the guests come to help celebrate. Other, more enterprising guests took an alternate route in small red horse-drawn sleighs, skimming the frozen Neva on hissing runners and gliding into the parkland through the giant palace gates. But no matter from which direction they came, they were treated to a most breathtaking spectacle. Both the front and rear facades of the palace were strung with sapphire-blue electric bulbs in the shape of the Princess's monogram; the huge stylized IND's—Irina Nicolaevna Danilova—seemed suspended in midair, each letter three stories tall.

If enough electricity to light a small town glittered outside the palace, candlelight reigned supreme inside; the crystal-and-gold chandeliers and candelabra flickered their rich golden glow on the corridors, staircases, and grandiose public rooms, which echoed resoundingly with excited conversation, gracious music, and an abundance of good cheer. Many a kingdom's worth of diamonds, emeralds, sapphires, and rubies outglittered each other as the guests, many of the ladies in white satin, swept into the great Colonnade Hall, where they were met by an army of servants who took their ermine, sealskin, lynx, sable, and fox coats. From the second-floor gallery set between the jasper columns which gave the hall its name drifted the gentle strains of baroque chamber music. No one carried gifts; for the past week, a steady procession of deliveries from St. Petersburg's finest shops had filled an anteroom to overflowing.

Leaving their wraps behind, the guests ascended the neo-baroque grand staircase, its marble steps red-carpeted for this special occasion, at the top landing of which they were required to queue up until the majordomo announced their entrance into the Malachite Room.

After paying their respects to the regal Princess, who was flanked by the Prince, Count Kokovtsov, and the Princess's baptizer, the ancient and resplendently bearded archbishop, the guests mingled in animated groups, spilling into the adjoining Agate Vestibule, where a black jazz quartet from New York played the latest rage in American music. In the Blue Salon an orchestra of stirring balalaikas animated spirits with rousing, traditional Russian folk melodies, and in the Cabinet Doré, a jewel box named after its profusion of ormolu moldings and furnishings, a string quartet played sedately elegant music in keeping with its severely classical decor. Liveried servants circulated with gold and sterling trays bristling with cut-crystal champagne glasses filled to overflowing with bubbling Louis Roederer Cristal, the same imported French champagne delivered to the Czar; on tables, enormous silver bowls set in huge tubs of ice held forty kilos of grosgrain beluga caviar.

After the reception, the guests were gently herded to the private theater, where the chamber orchestra from the Colonnade Hall now appropriately played the overture to *La Traviata*, Verdi's opera based on *The Lady of the Camellias*.

Behind the thick, muffling red velvet puff curtain which had yet to rise, the audience's excited anticipation could be both heard and felt.

Electricity crackled in the air.

Unnoticed by the audience, Senda carefully pushed the edge of the puff curtain aside a crack. She peered out at the theater through one roving eye. The rows of gilded Louis XVI seats had already filled up. It took her by surprise that there were more people than seats: the back of both the orchestra section and the balcony were crowded with standees. Still, the two drapery-swagged boxes, swelling from the walls on either side of the proscenium like immensely ornate bombé chests, were empty.

A murmur swept the theater, and all eyes focused on the left box, just above her, from which the Prince had applauded and addressed her during rehearsals only yesterday. The Danilovs and a party of four, who Senda was certain constituted the most important guests, were making a late but grand entrance.

Intrigued, Senda studied the woman who must be Princess Irina, for she led the way into the box with exquisite natural grace. She was slightly older than the Prince, pale-skinned and fragile, and there was something watery and translucent about her. She wore a pearl-beaded gown of silver and pale blue brocade, and the faded yellow hair piled atop her head was completely encircled by what appeared to be a tiara—if tiaras could be made of polished ice. Around her thin, patrician throat she wore a lacelike choker of more ice; a larger baroque pearl necklace hung down into her décolletage, as did an even longer simple string of enormous pearls. Most other women among the audience were similarly bejeweled, though these particular chunks of glittering ice were by far the largest, and thereby probably the most valuable. At first Senda didn't know what to make of the jewels—she had never seen any like them. But she knew instinctively what they had to be, although she had only heard tell of them. diamonds.

My God, I've never seen so many jewels, she marveled silently to herself, her free hand self-consciously touching her bare throat. The fact was, she had hardly ever seen *any* jewels, except in the towns and cities where they had played, and then they had been mostly modest and inexpensive—a thin band of gold on a finger or, more likely, gold on silver, and no stones more valuable than amethyst or topaz. She felt positively naked now, and how would she feel at the ball? She could only hope the silk camellias Madame Lamothe had sewn so strategically to her gown were adornment enough, though everyone, it seemed, wore masses of cut gems with total abandon. Why, the Princess actually wore *three* necklaces.

Despite the size of the Princess's stones, there was something else about her which set her apart from the other women. Perhaps it was her poise, or her fragile beauty, or the way the audience, which was already seated, eyed her covetously.

Then, with a mixture of bewilderment and shock, Senda realized that all the money in Russia could not cure Irina Danilov's hands. It was these which set her apart. They were hideously crippled claws, demonically obscene, although she didn't look old enough to suffer arthritis.

Only after the Princess was seated between the archbishop and the Prince did the other people in their party take their seats behind them.

Senda could hear the overture reaching its end. In fifteen or twenty seconds the curtain would rise, and she was about to let it fall back into place and hurry into the wings when, instead of completing the overture, the orchestra prolonged it. There was a ripple of whispers and a rustling of clothing as the entire audience faced the still-empty box to the right, opposite that of the Danilovs. Senda eyed it curiously, wondering what was happening, but all she could see were four splendidly uniformed officers entering to inspect it, as though they were searching for something. Obviously satisfied, they stepped out again. Ever so smoothly, the orchestra switched from the overture of *La Traviata* to a regal anthem of pomp and grandeur.

The entire audience rose as one and faced the box.

Senda's mouth opened in astonishment.

Chin held high, diamonds ablaze, a regal woman swept into the box. She was dressed in white, and her creamy shoulders were bare. A magnificent jewel-encrusted tiara rose from her curls and a cascade of fine lace draped from it flowed down her back. She had about her an air of indefinable breeding and assurance, of a woman born to power.

Her escort followed behind. He stood five-feet-seven and was slim, with a handlebar mustache and clipped brown beard. His beautifully tailored dark blue uniform glittered with ribbons, medals, and gold: gold braid, gold epaulets, gold belt, and gold collar. A red satin sash slashed importantly across his chest, but his expression was rather gentle and shy. As his gaze swept the curtained stage, Senda almost felt as if he had found the chink in the curtain and was looking straight at her.

In the recesses of her mind a flash of blinding intuition flared brilliantly, leaving her weak and reeling. She swiftly let the curtain fall back in place. In that one paralyzing moment her heart had stopped beating, and she took a giant breath of air. She turned and beckoned to Schmarya. Quickly he drew up behind her, and she could feel his warm, comforting body pressing against hers. He peered out from behind the curtain.

Her hand poised on her fluttering breast, Senda looked questioningly at him. "It isn't . . ." She didn't dare complete the sentence.

Schmarya's bright blue eyes were dancing with a wild, dangerous fire. "You will give the performance of your life tonight, Sendale," he said dryly. "It seems you are not only going to entertain the cream of Russian society, but our revered Czar and Czarina as well."

If she noticed the sarcasm in his tone, she gave no indication. "Oh, God," she moaned, feeling herself shrinking inside her gown as she stared at him in dumbfounded bewilderment, the greasepaint making her stricken expression all the more grotesque. She was drenched in a sudden ice-cold sweat. Her legs felt as though they would buckle under her. She wanted to die on the spot.

The orchestra switched back to the last few notes of the overture. With a swift movement, Schmarya pulled her into the wings. The actors playing the Baron de Varville and Nanine hurried silently past them to their places onstage. Senda watched with growing dread as Nanine slipped into a chair, quickly placed some sewing in her lap, and busied herself. The baron took a seat in a bergère by the fireplace. The curtain rose slowly to expose the Paris boudoir of Marguerite Gautier. It was a set which looked very much like a real boudoir, even close up from the wings. The very real, very fine furnishings and carpets had come from rooms within the palace, and even the marble fireplace mantel was genuine. It had come from one of the storage rooms.

The play began with the ringing of a doorbell.

"I'm scared!" Senda whispered, turning to Schmarya. She clenched her teeth to keep them from chattering. "Schmarya, I can't go on. I *can't*."

His voice was soft and sure, but the lines coursing from his nose to the sides of his mouth were tense. "Of course you can. You know your lines backward and forward. You'll sail through them."

" 'Someone is ringing,' " the actor playing the Baron said loudly in his rich stage voice.

"I'm going to make an ass out of all of us." Senda gave Schmarya a searching look and clung to him as if for dear life.

His face nuzzled into her hair. "You'll be magnificent," he assured her.

"No, I won't." Her whisper was a squeak. "Oh, God, why did I have to get myself into this mess?"

"So you have a little stage fright. Hey. What are you worried about? You'll knock 'em dead." His strong fingers sought to soothe her.

"Schmarya . . ." Her fingers dug into his arms.

Onstage, de Varville was saying, " 'God forbid.' "

She grasped his arms even more fiercely, her body trembling.

"That's your cue!"

"I forgot my lines!" she hissed in a panic.

" 'Nanine, Nanine,' " he said.

She gulped, nodded, and took a series of deep breaths. Her heart felt as though it would burst. " 'Nanine! Nanine!' " she called out from offstage, her voice sounding surprisingly strong even to her ears. In amazement, she looked at Schmarya.

He blew her a kiss. Then she felt him turning her around. His fingertips applied pressure to the small of her spine.

"Off you go, Marguerite," he whispered softly.

She found herself propelled gracefully forward by his little push, for a moment blinded by the white glare of the footlights.

Off you go, Marguerite!

Schmarya had called her Marguerite!

I *am* Marguerite, she thought, and the stage floor suddenly seemed to tilt at a slight angle. The footlights receded into a blur, and the audience was forgotten. Almost without her knowing it, she wafted toward Nanine. " 'Go, order supper, Nanine,' " she sang out clearly. " 'Olympe and Saint-Gaudens are coming! I met them at the opera!' "

From the wings, Schmarya watched the beautiful, coquettish young woman. He stared entranced, then came to with a start. He swore to himself in disbelief. "Well, I'll be damned!" he whispered aloud to himself. "That isn't Senda. Hell, that's Marguerite Gautier!"

Reality became illusion.

And illusion reality.

The audience in the small baroque theater sat shrouded in dark, spellbound silence, not daring to move and break the magical spell. From the moment Senda walked onstage, everyone from the Czar and Czarina down to the other players awaiting their cues could feel the electricity like invisible currents in the air. As the heart-wrenching story of Marguerite Gautier unfolded, each one of them felt transported from the theater to a picture-window view of someone else's life, an eavesdropper privy to the most private moments of the tragic heroine.

Before the intermission the unanimous response was simply: a performance nothing short of miraculous.

Except for Senda, the other actors were seasoned troupers all—some had toured the provinces for more than a decade—but it was her bravura performance in the lead role which caused the sensation. She shed her own skin and enveloped herself in the persona of the consumptive heroine, eliciting the finest performances ever from her usually jaded fellow players at the same time. She was titillating. Teasing. Fresh. Young. Doomed. She had the audience wrapped around her little finger, playing on their deepest, innermost, heartfelt emotions.

They cared for her.

They loved her.

There was an appealing vitality to her character which the audience only now realized they had missed during other performances of the play.

The curtain dropped. It was intermission.

"But she is fantastic!" the Princess whispered to her husband. "Vaslav, wherever on earth did you find her?"

The tearjerking performance caused Countess Florinsky's eyes to water incessantly, and she was forever poking a handkerchief behind her new gold-rimmed glasses to dab at her eyes.

During the short intermission, the curtain draping the Czar's box was drawn shut so that the royal couple might be afforded total privacy from prying eyes. Servants circulated with massive trays of champagne. The only talk among the glittering audience was of the performance.

"It is magic," Princess Olga Alexandrovna was heard to declare.

"She should be at the Théâtre Français," said Princess Marie Pavlovna.

"And to think it's in Russian," Prince Golitsyn told Admiral Makarov. "Quite novel, that, don't you think? I've only seen it in French before."

Raves, raves.

Backstage in the wings, Senda dropped wearily into a chair between hulking props and painted backdrops. Some-

one pushed a glass of water at her and she sipped it gratefully. Schmarya solicitously sponged her sweating brow. "I
was right!" he crowed. "You're knocking them dead!"

"I'm knocking *myself* dead," she gasped, her breasts heaving. "My throat's sore from all that coughing, and I'm emotionally exhausted." She shut her eyes and let her head loll
back. "I hope I can continue like I've been doing."

"Of course you can. You've gone through two acts. There
are only two more, and they're a lot shorter."

"And a lot tougher," she reminded him, letting out a
long, resonant sigh. She opened her eyes and stared up at
the ceiling. "You think I'm all right?"

"All right?" He grinned. "You're a damned marvel!"

She rolled her head sideways to face him and smiled her
thanks.

"Mind you, I'm not sure whom I prefer, though," he said
pensively.

"What do you mean?"

"You, or Marguerite."

"Bastard." Restrainedly amused, she punched him playfully. Then she frowned and touched her throat in concern.
"My voice is starting to go. It's all the coughing I've had to
do. Maybe I should ease up a little."

They watched in silence as the set was rearranged for the
third act. Then from the other side of the red puff curtain,
the orchestra started up again. She tensed, her hands tightening on the arms of the chair.

"Sit tight. You still have a few minutes. Rest."

"I can't." She got up and began pacing nervously, fidgeting with her hands. Her face was screwed up in concentration. Schmarya stood silently back, letting her metamorphose
into Marguerite.

Marguerite's prolonged death from consumption caused
velvet-sheathed fingers to dab lace handkerchiefs at moist
eyes. An occasional sniffle could be heard.

Senda, caught in the beam of the spotlight, stood with her
arms at her sides. Slowly she lifted them and stared at her
hands. Her eyes gleamed with an almost beatific light, and
her voice held the hushed tones of a revelation. " 'I'm not
suffering anymore. It seems as though life were pouring into
me.' " She floated, wraithlike, across the stage. " 'I am
going to live! Ohhhhh, how well I feel!' " She swayed,
tottered unsteadily, and crumpled so suddenly that the audience let out a communal gasp.

The actor on a chaise sprang up and ran to her, collapsing

atop her. " 'Marguerite!' " he cried with rising terror. " 'Marguerite! Marguerite!' " Then he let out a scream, and with an immense effort tore his hands from her. He drew back, wild terror blazing in his eyes. " 'She's dead!' " he sobbed. He jumped up and ran over to the man and woman standing quietly off to the side. He sank down to his knees in front of them. " 'My God, what's to become of me?' " he cried.

The couple looked stoically down upon him. " 'How she loved you, Armand,' " the man who was standing said softly, shaking his head. " 'Poor Marguerite.' "

The tableau was frozen. Then the red puff curtain rippled swiftly down over the stage.

For a long moment the audience sat in stunned silence.

The applause, when it finally came, was spontaneous and deafening. It shook the small theater, reverberating from the rococo walls. Slowly Senda lifted her garishly made-up face off the floor and looked up in wonderment as the first shout of "Bravo!", muffled by the thick curtain, stirred something deep within her drained emotions.

Dazed, she could only watch as the rest of the cast swiftly assembled in a row, hooking their arms together.

"Quick!" Schmarya hissed at her. He pulled her unceremoniously to her feet and shoved her into the center of the row of performers. Arms to her left and right linked through hers.

She twisted her head around. "What did you think?" she asked Schmarya.

He grinned. "Just listen to them!"

"I can hear what *they* think," she said a little breathlessly, her eyes bright with excitement. "I asked for your—"

Swiftly Schmarya jumped back out of sight as the curtain rose again. The row of performers faced the audience and bowed together. The curtain began to descend again. Swiftly lifting her eyes, Senda stole a brief upward glance at the box the Czar and Czarina had been occupying. She could see nothing. The curtain was already tightly drawn across it. An odd disappointment came over her and she tightened the corners of her mouth. She hadn't been watching the box, so she had no idea if they'd even stayed to the end. That realization sobered her, tainted the triumph somewhat.

The applause remained steady.

In the wings, Schmarya quickly paired off the individual performers in couples, starting with the least important ones. Holding hands, they hurried onstage for their curtain calls, their order of appearance determined by the importance of the parts they had played. Senda and the actor playing Armand were last, and received the heaviest applause.

Then, turning on her prettiest smile from a repertory of dozens, Senda went out to take her solo curtain call. The mighty and the powerful, the titled aristocrats of Russia, not only applauded in a frenzy, but for once they dropped their stiff-upper-lip veneers and went wild. Shouts of "Brava! Brava!" echoed from all corners. Finally the men in formal dress or dress uniforms and the ladies in gowns and jewels rose to their feet in unison to give her a standing ovation.

Standing there alone, bowing again and again, Senda felt the waves of their adulation rushing over her. When she finally danced back offstage and the curtain descended, the applause was no quieter. She had to come out again and again.

Her nerves quivered like fine-tuned antennas, and she felt more alive than she had ever felt. Her heart throbbed wildly, as though it would burst out of her body. Exultation surged through her, more potent than any drug.

It was unbelievable. She had conquered them all. They were no longer just her audience. One and all, they had become her admirers. They adored her; they worshiped her; in a period of two hours, she had totally seduced them and had become the toast of the town.

Finally the curtain rippled downward for the last time. Dazed, she waltzed dizzily toward a chair, her arms extended, and when she dropped into it she found little peace. The rest of the cast rushed toward her, mobbing around in a tight circle. Each of them heaped kudos upon her.

"You were marvelous!"

"If we'd only known you were so talented, we'd have given you starring roles long ago!"

"We'll probably be able to stay in this city for the rest of the season!"

Accolades and kisses, merriment and compliments abounded.

"Hey," Schmarya finally said good-naturedly, "I hate to have to break this up, but give the star some breathing space so she can unwind. She's got a ball to attend."

Reluctantly the other cast members began to drift away.

Senda was in euphoria. She felt invincible, capable of doing everything she had never done before. Although the reception she'd received from the audience had been electrifying, the warm praise from her fellow actors meant even more. Much more.

But the most important thing now was going to the ball—with Schmarya. That, she knew in her heart, topped it all. Made everything worthwhile.

"Well?" Schmarya asked her after she'd washed off the

greasepaint and rested awhile. "What are you waiting for? Don't you want to go?"

They were alone in the dressing room. The others had long since gone. The little theater was like a tomb. "Go?" she asked. "Where?"

"Where do you think?"

"Say it," Senda said gently.

"Why?"

She smiled tolerantly. "So I'll always remember that you asked me to the ball."

The gracious one-two-three, one-two-three strains of a waltz grew progressively louder the nearer they got to the ballroom. Despite the labythrine succession of rooms and halls branching off in all directions, Senda was certain she could have found the ballroom without the liveried footman leading them, by simply following her ears and nose, heading in the direction of the music and the fragrant, flowery scents that drifted like incense in the air. The strains of the waltz drew her like a magnet.

Halls merged into progressive halls, salons opened into larger salons. Then, suddenly, all the massive rooms seemed inconsequential as the last door opened up to the second-floor gallery of the cathedral-size ballroom. Senda drew to a halt to take it all in. She was bedazzled.

Dozens of guests milled about in the wide gallery which completely encircled the second floor of the ballroom like a wraparound balcony, the balustrade punctuated every four meters by Ionic columns soaring majestically from the dance floor to the inverted-coffin ceiling.

Finding her feet, Senda forgot the footman and anxiously tugged Schmarya toward the balustrade. She leaned over excitedly. Below, the dancers were Lilliputian in proportion to the room itself. She caught her breath as she hungrily took it all in. Oh, the sight which fed her eyes! The ballroom floor was a sea of elegant couples, the women in rustling, billowing gowns floating in the arms of their partners, their lace petticoats frothing like whipped cream under flowing hems, their delicate ivory shoulders bare, their patrician throats, heads, and arms encrusted with a staggering collection of precious jewels. And the men! They were the handsomest, most elegantly turned-out men she had ever had the pleasure of laying eyes on—tall and graceful for the most part, clean-shaven and neatly bearded, in formal attire or resplendent gold-braided dress uniforms with mirrorlike boots, they rivaled the exquisitely gowned ladies for attention. The oval dance floor was thronged with guests spilling into the adjoining chambers under the palm-lined colonnades. They talked, laughed, exchanged delicious tidbits of gossip, or eyed the graceful couples swirling on the glassy floor under the twin rows of massive crystal chandeliers, twelve in all, each one sparkling as brightly as diamonds. Four tiers of creamy, flickering beeswax candles bristled from each one. In a cul-de-sac of hothouse palms at the far end was the orchestra.

Oh, the sweet sounds! The splendid sights.

"There you are!" Countess Florinsky chirped breathlessly as she hurried toward Senda and Schmarya as fast as her short legs would carry her. With flutters of her open fan she waved the waiting footman away. "My dear, your performance was positively magnificent!" she crooned, blowing three noisy kisses past each of Senda's cheeks. Then she stepped back and regarded Schmarya closely. "Handsome," she said, nodding. "Yes, quite, *quite* handsome indeed." She narrowed her eyes at Senda. "If you're not careful I shall steal him for myself!" After introductions, she happily slipped her arms through theirs, a bubbly, effervescent plump child-woman. "Now, come, darlings, and do hurry, please," she tittered. "The Princess is simply dying to meet Camille! I was to bring you to her the moment you arrived!"

Countess Florinsky guided them around to the nearest of the two balustraded marble staircases which swept down, facing each other, to a common landing where the two staircases converged into one.

"This used to be called the Ambassador's Staircase, though heaven only knows why," the Countess chattered excitedly. "I think everyone's forgotten the reason!" When they reached the landing, she squeezed their arms with hers and let them go. The Prince and Princess stood side by side greeting guests who had not been invited to the performance.

The Princess smiled at a buxom woman in an off-white lace gown and turned. "Ahhh!" she intoned in the lilting, well-modulated French of the upper classes. *"Voilà notre Mademoiselle Marguerite!"*

Since Senda did not speak a word of French, all she could catch was the name Marguerite, but she guessed at what the Princess had said. The Countess made introductions. "Your Highness," Senda murmured in Russian. "Happy Birthday." As protocol demanded, she dropped a graceful curtsy, conscious of Schmarya grudgingly bowing beside her. Senda willed him to be on his best behavior. No one knew better than she what he thought of the ruling class.

"Thank you, my dear. And do rise," the Princess told Senda in a kind voice, switching easily from fluent French to native Russian. "I wanted you to know that your performance was quite stunning. We enjoyed it ever so much. It was my favorite birthday present. I must thank you."

"Your Highness is too kind."

"I think not. Even Their Imperial Majesties asked me to convey their congratulations on a dazzling performance."

Senda's eyes widened in surprise, and at that moment she looked exceedingly girlish.

"But you are so young!" The Princess studied Senda closely, then looked at her husband. "Why, she must be barely twenty, Vaslav!"

"But quite talented," the Prince said mildly, as though he had little interest in Senda. But his intense, unwavering blue eyes belied his words as he looked at her strangely.

The Princess, apparently unaware of her husband's keen interest in Senda, patted his hand affectionately. "My husband is right, as always. You are very talented. And now, I'm sure that you are anxious to have some refreshments and perhaps dance."

A gentle but obvious dismissal. "Thank you, your Highness," Senda said.

"It is my pleasure. Do circulate."

Curtsying again, Senda could still feel the Prince's steady gaze. A flush heightened her features with glowing pink. She quickly took Schmarya's arm and led him over to where Countess Florinsky was waiting.

Together, the three of them descended the seven steps to the dance floor.

"I don't know what Vaslav would have done for entertainment had he not run across you," the Countess was telling them. "Irina loves the theater so. Sometimes I get the feeling she would rather be onstage than playing the role of princess." Countess Florinsky gave a little shrug. "At any rate, what's important is that everyone agrees you were simply divine. Divine . . . hmmmm, yes. *La Divina.* That is what I shall call you. The divine one."

Senda laughed. "That's carrying it a bit far, I think."

At that moment, two dowagers passed by, flicking surreptitious glances in Senda's direction.

"De près elle est encore plus belle." Senda could hear one dowager whispering behind her fan. *"Et elle est si fraîche."*

"Si j'étais homme, je pourrais facilement m'enamourer d'elle," the other dowager whispered back, nodding. *"Je crois qu'Irina devrait prendre garde . . ."*

115

"You see?" Countess Florinsky said triumphantly, her magnified eyes twinkling. "You are already the talk of the town!"

Senda flushed again, but she recognized the compliment and was secretly pleased. "But what did they say? I couldn't understand a word."

"Never mind *what* they say, as long as they keep talking. Anyway. I must be getting back to work and leave you two to enjoy yourselves." The Countess pulled the décolletage of her gown higher. Then she tilted her head, looked around, and breathed deeply with satisfaction. "It does look rather romantic, even if I do say so myself," she said a little wistfully.

"I still can't believe you arranged all this," Senda told her.

"It's easy," the Countess said with a negligible wave of her hand. "All a good party requires is money. *Lots* of money." She giggled and fluttered her fan. "Other people's money is so easy to spend! Well, off I go. And do enjoy yourselves, my dears!" She blew three parting kisses past each of Senda's cheeks and pressed Schmarya's hand warmly. Then she was gone.

Senda and Schmarya exchanged smiles and watched as the short plump woman waddled along the edge of the dance floor with that inimitable breathless bounce. When she was out of sight, Schmarya turned to Senda and took her hand formally. His touch was warm and gentle and mocking, but underlying it was an unmistakable possessiveness. "A dance, my lady?" he asked teasingly as the orchestra switched to a lively mazurka.

Senda's smile dazzled. "I would be honored, kind sir."

They swiftly danced into an opening on the dance floor, where they were swallowed up amid the rustle of swishing silks and the heavenly fragrances of perfumes. The huge room rose and dipped and whirled around her. Though the theater troupe knew nearly every conceivable dance step, and often entertained itself by dancing, none of their dances, on or offstage, had ever been like this, Senda thought.

The mazurka flowed into a quadrille, the quadrille into a chaconne, and the chaconne into a polonaise.

"Schmarya, I'm exhausted!" Senda had to gasp finally.

He grinned. "And I'm hungry. Let's take a break." Taking her hand, he led her off the dance floor. "Now that we know how the other half lives, let's go see how they eat."

Extraordinarily well, it turned out. The lace-and-damask-draped buffet tables behind the colonnades groaned under the weight of overladen gold and sterling platters. It was difficult to choose among the delicacies—roast duck with raspberry sauce, cold sturgeon, pheasant, salmon mousse with crayfish sauce, whole squab, rack of lamb, shashlik, blinis, white marzipan flowers, petits fours, and cakes of all kinds. All this, plus four enormous gold bowls containing four kinds of caviar—large-grained grayish beluga, small-grained black sevruga, and golden nutty-flavored osietra, as well as red-salmon keta. And there were no fewer than ten varieties of fresh-baked bread, their thin slices artfully stacked to create the base of an enormous butter sculpture of the Princess.

"Can you believe it?" Senda breathed, ogling the lifelike meter-high likeness of Irina Danilova with wide eyes. "It's actually made of *butter*." She had come to a stop with her plate extended, and thinking she wanted squab, a waiter with sterling tongs fished a whole tiny bird from a flock of crisply burnished squab and placed it on her plate with a flourish.

She eyed the bird suspiciously and moved on to the next tables.

Luxury was heaped upon luxury. For the sweet-toothed, one table was devoted exclusively to crystal bowls of out-of-season fruit brought in from the Crimea. Another held more cakes—fruitcakes, pale almond cakes, and deep, dusky chocolate tortes. A third table of pastries held only white-frosted cakes, sugar-iced cookies, and white candies, all arranged among a sumptuous tableau of gilded nuts and masses of lustrous strung pearls.

Their plates filled, they carried them into one of four chambers adjoining the ballroom being used as dining rooms. From the other diners there was an almost simultaneous *Nasdrovya* as they raised their glasses to toast Senda. Blushing, she returned the cheer and proceeded to a table. Each of the small tables had been set with an exquisite centerpiece: silver candelabra were hung with heavy garlands made of pink roses. Senda and Schmarya saw lavishly wrapped boxes at each place and, following the lead given by other guests, opened theirs. They were stunned beyond words. For the men, Schmarya included, there were solid gold lighters, and for the women solid gold compacts. All were engraved with the date and the Princess's monogram. When they were finally recovered enough to eat, Senda picked up a heavy knife and fork and cut a crunchy piece of squab. She bit hungrily into it. "I'm starved," she said, beginning to chew. "I haven't had anything to eat all day." Suddenly she stopped chewing and looked stricken, her eyes bulging.

"What's the matter?" Schmarya asked.

With her tongue she shoved her food into the pocket of one cheek. "This bird is all bones."

He looked at her with amusement. "Well, chuck it, then."

She reached under the tablecloth and pinched his thigh. He jerked his leg, banging his knee on the table.

Countess Florinsky, her egret-feathered headpiece bouncing, swooped down upon their table. "Enjoying yourselves, my dears?" she sang.

Senda nodded. "Except for this bird, whatever it is." She scowled at her plate.

"It's squab, I believe."

Senda jabbed it with her fork. "I thought it was a particularly starved pigeon."

The Countess trilled with laughter. "You do say the most amusing things."

"What do I do with the bones? I have a whole mouthful of them."

"I think you're supposed to chew and swallow them." The Countess frowned. "Or is that with partridge? Dear me, I keep forgetting. I can't see my way to eating fowl. They're really a delight to watch or wear"—she patted her headpiece affectionately—"but I simply can't eat the little creatures."

"Oh," Senda said, "well, I'm having trouble eating this one myself. I'm afraid to swallow the bones. I'll choke to death."

"Then spit the bones out into a napkin. If you're discreet, no one should be the wiser. By the way," she said casually, looking around, "you didn't happen to run into Vaslav?"

"Earlier, with you. When we came in."

"No, no. Since then." The Countess's eyes roved the tables. "I ran into him. He told me he was looking for you."

"For me?" Senda stared at her. "I wonder what he wants."

"To dance, probably. Oh! There he is. Vaslav!" The Countess got on tiptoe and raised her fan, waving it briskly to catch his attention. "He's coming, and off I go, my dears!"

Vaslav Danilov approached their table. "I hope you are enjoying your repast, Madame Bora?"

"Thoroughly, your Highness," Senda assured him, though she wished she had something to eat other than the brittle, bony squab.

"Good."

"Countess Florinsky said you wished to see me?"

He smiled. "Later, after you have eaten. I was going to ask you for a dance." He paused and looked at Schmarya. "With your permission, of course, monsieur?"

"By all means," Schmarya said, gesturing magnanimously.

"Then why not right now?" Senda asked. She swallowed, dabbed her lips with a heavy linen napkin, and pushed back her chair.

"But your food," the Prince pointed out. "You haven't finished."

"I'm really not at all hungry," Senda said. Especially not for squab, she thought, rising and proffering her crooked arm. "Your Highness?"

"With pleasure." Taking her arm in his, the Prince led her back to the ballroom, where an elegant Viennese waltz was playing. "Johann Strauss," he said, his eyes sweeping the dance floor. "A very sweet melody, though I am not at all certain that sweetness becomes you. A steamy Argentine tango, perhaps, or the wild new American jazz I have had the pleasure to hear on occasion."

"Oh?" She lifted a studied eyebrow. "And why should that be?"

"Because"—he smiled—"I sense passions smoldering within you."

"Then perhaps you have overestimated the power of your senses, your Highness. Perhaps they have misread me?"

"They never misread anything," he said quietly.

She turned away quickly, a flush intensifying the red of her hair, the slivers of aqua in her emerald eyes dimming as though a veil had descended over them. "I think we had better dance," she said soberly, casting furtive glances around her. "Everyone's looking at us."

"And why shouldn't they? I am, after all, Vaslav Danilov, and you are the evening's star attraction. And a beautiful woman by anyone's standards."

"You are making me feel conspicuous and uncomfortable."

"You will soon be over that."

"Shouldn't you be dancing with the Princess? It *is* her birthday."

"I led her in the first dance of the evening. Besides, Irina would rather not dance."

"Oh?"

"She dislikes showing her hands to disadvantage."

Out of the corner of her eye Senda could see Countess Florinsky and the Princess staring in their direction. She caught the speculative glances of other guests, the openly appreciative looks of the Hussars in their elkskin breeches, and she could hear whispers carrying gossip on sibilant lips. "I think," she said rather unsteadily, "that if we do not begin to dance soon, this waltz will be over before we start."

"This waltz is unimportant." He looked down at her keenly, a film glistening over his eyes. "It is the next dance which interests me. I asked for it myself."

"And what would that be?"

"Something infinitely more Russian. Livelier and, I daresay, closer to your heart."

Even as he spoke, the waltz reached its last honeyed strains, and then, without warning, furious balalaikas broke through the last note, thundering into that most Russian and soul-rousing of music, an authentic Gypsy dance. The couples on the dance floor were momentarily at a loss. They looked about in astonishment.

"So wild music is closer to my heart, is it?" Senda asked, raising her chin challengingly. Her eyes sparkled. "Then so be it!"

She did not wait for him to lead, but tossed her hair and clicked her heels as if a fine madness had swept over her. To her surprise, the Prince did not hesitate. He dropped his stiff aristocratic veneer. The other couples on the dance floor parted as swiftly as if Moses himself had ordered the Red Sea to recede. The floor was theirs, and theirs alone. Except for the balalaikas, silence descended. The two of them, she in Madame Lamothe's exquisite gown, and he in his black, gold-laced formal uniform, swirled and stomped and kicked with their hands on their hips.

As the ballroom bounced and jumped and spun madly around her, Senda caught a fleeting glance of open mouths, of guests jockeying for a view from the packed balustrades above, of Countess Florinsky's fan stopping mid-flutter, of the Princess's inscrutably veiled eyes, and then Schmarya's amused grin from the perimeter of the dance floor. So he had been drawn by the music too.

Knowing he was watching, she let herself go, flinging aside any inhibitions which remained, and assumed the dervish moves of a devilish Gypsy gone berserk on the steppes. When the racing instruments finally reached their crescendo and stopped, spontaneous applause thundered in the ballroom.

Senda reeled dizzily. She was panting.

"And now," the Prince whispered between gulping lungfuls of air, "we can catch our breaths during a waltz."

She felt his hands gripping her as he led her to "The Blue Danube." One by one, other couples began to whirl around them, and soon the ballroom was as before, elegant with the sweetness of civilized music and the expensive rustling of billowing gowns. Senda couldn't help thinking that she had preferred the Gypsy music. It had had torment and ecstasy and soul.

The Prince was in his element. He grinned at her and danced faultlessly. "I was right, you know," he said softly.

"Right?" Senda frowned. "About what, your Highness?"

She could feel the breath of his words on her bare shoulder. "The smoldering passions I was so sure you possessed."

Her eyes narrowed. "And if they smolder, your Highness," she countered tartly, "I think it best you take care before you're burned."

"For them, I daresay I would gladly burn anywhere, hell included." Despite the soft timbre of his voice, he seemed to loom over her. There was an animal surety glowing in the depths of his eyes.

She couldn't help laughing. "I don't know whether you are incorrigible, or merely persistent."

And then the perfect ball was marred.

"Vaslav Danilov!" a loud, sharp voice cracked whiplike from behind them above the strains of Johann Strauss. "Your . . . Highness!"

Still waltzing, the Prince turned his head in the direction of the voice, his face puzzled at the menacing tone. Senda turned also. They waltzed in place.

The man in evening dress was short and pudgy, and his corpulent face was red and quivered with rage.

The Prince's eyebrows lifted. "Do I know you, monsieur?"

"You damn well know my wife!" the man yelled in so loud a rage that the dancers around them stopped in midstep and the orchestra's music slowly faded. A hushed and pregnant silence suddenly hung over the ballroom.

"I am afraid this charming lady is not your wife," Vaslav Danilov said with amused restraint, but his features had hardened. "Now, if you will be so good as to— "

"Don't humor me!" the man screamed, his dark eyes flashing fire. "Of course *that's* not my wife. *My* wife's at home! Pregnant with *your* child!"

The Prince was silent while he collected his thoughts. "Monsieur, *if* your wife is indeed pregnant, and you decide to lay the blame at my doorstep, this is neither the time nor the place to discuss it. Now, if you will excuse me—"

"Bastard!"

"Begging your pardon, monsieur . . ." the Prince said quietly through clenched teeth, his temper simmering.

"Don't pretend innocence, you sanctimonious bastard!"

"I think you had best leave at once," the Prince suggested coldly, fighting to keep control of himself. He signaled to his private guards, but they froze the instant the man reached for a revolver and held it outstretched in both hands, the barrel pointed at the Prince.

Simultaneously, a gasp rippled through the guests surrounding them.

Senda gripped Vaslav's arm, but he slowly pushed her aside, out of harm's way. "I suggest you put that thing down before something happens which you might regret," he told the man with steely calm.

"Regret!" the allegedly cuckolded husband screeched in a blind rage. "*You're* the one who should regret what he's done!" The revolver clicked malevolently as he cocked it.

Shivers of terror ran up and down Senda's spine. She uttered a silent prayer, knowing a miracle was called for.

Apparently undaunted by the danger, Vaslav took a step forward, his hand outstretched, palm up. "Give it to me," he said softly.

"No!" the pudgy man's eyes ran rivulets of tears. "Don't come any closer!"

"Give it here." The Prince took another step forward. "Nothing will happen to you."

"Get back!" the gunman wept. The gun wavered, and just as the man pulled the trigger, a Hussar standing near Senda lunged for the gunman, deflecting his aim as he wrestled him to the floor. The shot rang out like a clap of thunder. A woman screamed, and overhead, a chandelier shook and tinkled; then several crystals, brittle wax stalactites, and pink roses rained down around them with a clatter. A bright bubble of ruby blood welled up on the Prince's forehead and trickled down his cheek. It was a moment before Senda realized the scream had come from her.

"It is nothing. I have only been grazed," the Prince said mildly, reaching for a handkerchief and dabbing his wound. Senda watched, still paralyzed, as the gunman was dragged off, weeping noisily.

No one dared move. In the silence, one could have heard a pin drop. Perhaps it was her imagination, but it seemed to Senda that the moment the gun had gone off, the candles in the chandeliers had flickered and dimmed, the cut pink roses had drooped and rotted, and the fairy-tale world had been fouled by the stench of jealousy and violence.

Wordlessly she ran toward Schmarya, while the Princess raced to her husband's side. Schmarya enfolded Senda in his warm, comforting arms. Her eyes filled with tears. "I want to go back upstairs," she whispered bleakly.

He nodded, leading her by the arm toward the Ambassador's Staircase. She climbed the steps blankly, as though hypnotized. Below, the interrupted waltzing began again.

"It's funny, isn't it?" Schmarya said softly as he led her back through the succession of enormous rooms. "I can think of a dozen revolutionaries who would have given their eyeteeth to have a crack at the Prince. And with every good reason under the sun. Now, someone tries to kill the son of a bitch, but for the wrong reason. A woman." He shook his head in disbelief and laughed mournfully. "It seems our Prince has made one too many beds for him to safely lie in."

Senda spent most of the following two days in the Leather Room of the Danilov Palace, where she was comfortably curled up in a leather armchair. The name of the room derived from the burnished brown and gold tooled French leather covering the walls, as well as the similarly clad bindings of the volumes lined neatly in the shelves and stacked with military preciseness on the gleaming tables all around. A tole lamp cast a warm circular glow of light from the table next to her. Its gleaming surface was cluttered with the piles of hardbound plays she had selected to read, the ubiquitous steaming silver samovar, a plate of petits fours, and glass cups set in sterling holders with sterling handles. There were used cups left over from her last visitor.

Eight times that day, she had had surprise visitors dropping by for tea.

She forced herself to concentrate on the open book in her lap. It seemed unbelievable that after having to share a single precious, tattered copy of a play with the entire cast, here she was, ensconced like a queen, lap robe and cakes on hand, with every available published play bound in tooled leather and printed on the thickest, most expensive rag paper.

Would the luxuries never end? she wondered from time to time. She was so grateful that they had been invited to remain at the palace. They had been informed by Count Kokovtsov that the ever-generous Danilovs were certain the troupe would be receiving invitations for work elsewhere in St. Petersburg and were welcome here until plans were worked out.

Thoughtfully she flipped a page, forcing herself to forget her visitors for a moment and focus all her attention on the lines. Silently she mouthed a few to herself and nodded. Of all the plays she had been thumbing through, Chekhov's *The Cherry Orchard* impressed her the most. It was definitely the best bet by far. She was glad her first visitor had specifically asked for *The Cherry Orchard* to be performed at the party soon to be given at the Yussoupov Palace. Princess Yussoupov was the niece of the Czar, young, but not to be taken lightly. And she had dropped in unannounced, as casually as she would have gone shopping, to ask Senda if she would agree to perform it.

Senda had never felt so dizzy from excitement in all her life. Princess Yussoupov! A real-life princess had come to *her*, hoping to hire the troupe for a performance at her palace.

She was euphoric with joy.

But even more surprising was what followed: a steady succession of visits from the Shuvalov, Sheremetev, and Stroganov palaces had kept her busy all morning and half the afternoon over tea in the Leather Room while discussing the possibilities of performances in their various palaces during the following weeks. Incredibly, during that one afternoon it would have been possible to actually do the impossible—book the entire season.

With every new offer, her eyes had glowed as she tried to conceal the triumphant excitement building within her. They had done it. *She* had done it. They were the rage. This unknown theater troupe which had trudged hungrily from province to province was suddenly the talk of the capital of all the Russias. She couldn't wait to tell Schmarya and the others, but for the moment she kept the secret to herself, cherishing it until she could spring it on them.

Distracted by a mysterious thumping, she glanced down at her feet. Tamara had been playing quietly since Inge, the nurse, had brought her in, but now she was disgustedly shaking the stuffed pink bear she'd dragged in with her.

Smiling, Senda placed the open book flat on her lap and regarded her daughter with fond pride. She shook her head in disbelief. It was hard to imagine Tamara was over two years old.

She was delicate but large, with white-gold hair and inquisitive solemn eyes. Her features and character were developing at an amazing rate. The lovable if somewhat irascible child had inherited Senda's beauty and Schmarya's temperament. Those pale, green eyes, almost almond-shaped, were like her own, but she had definitely inherited Schmarya's boundless energy, curiosity, and cunning. She fought constantly to gain everyone's attention, lurching with determination after any adults within her sharp eyesight, tugging at their legs for the attention she so desperately sought, and assuming a heartbreaking expression if it was not instantly forthcoming. Attention had always been showered upon her, if not by Senda or Schmarya, then by the doting members of the troupe. Tamara had been unofficially adopted by them all.

She's really become quite spoiled, Senda realized. Why haven't I noticed before?

"Surprise!"

Startled, Senda jerked as Schmarya burst into the library with sudden fanfare.

"My God, you gave me a scare!" she reproved him gently as he picked his way around the tables and bent down to kiss her cheek.

Tamara tottered swiftly toward him, whooping: "U'cle Schmarya! U'cle Schmarya!"

"How's my favorite princess?" He scooped Tamara high in the air and twirled her around like a madly flying bird, his lips making the buzzing noises she adored so much. She flushed with pleasure, squealed with delight.

Senda's eyes filled with tears. They usually did when she heard their child calling him "uncle" instead of "poppa." For the thousandth time she cursed their decision of two years before. It had been a mistake, she often thought. After fleeing the pogrom, they should have pretended to be husband and wife, but when they had first joined the troupe of players it had been easier on both their consciences not to have to lie too boldly. Of course, there had been no end of questions. Even actors were not without curiosity. Why did they not get married? Especially since she was with child?

How could they have begun to explain?

It would have been easy enough to marry. Solomon was dead, and marrying his brother would have brought no shame upon any of them. Indeed, under Jewish law Schmarya would have been expected to marry her. But curiously enough, both she and Schmarya shared the belief that it would somehow be morally wrong to legalize and sanctify a union which had begun as the most dreadful of all sins. It was yet another problem which on occasion had threatened to tear them apart, and at the root of it all lay guilt: her guilt for disgracing her husband, his guilt for stealing his brother's wife, their combined guilt for having survived the pogrom.

Schmarya was saying, "Hey! Senda! Why the morose face?" He swept Tamara through the air, her arms spread like wings, steered her toward a chair, and plopped her down in a smooth, sweeping landing. Then he grinned, flashing Senda a triumphant sparkly smile. "I've got wonderful news! Guess what?"

She reached for his hand. "What?" She smiled.

"I've found us a theater!" Excitedly he crouched beside her chair, his eyes glowing. "Put on your best dress, lover, we're going out on the town. We're all going to celebrate. But not too formal, eh? No gowns tonight." He laughed, obviously pleased with himself.

Senda was too stunned to speak.

He'd found them a theater?

Senda felt a thin cold knife slicing into her belly, and she had to avert her gaze, staring down at *The Cherry Orchard* on her lap so that he would not see her dismay.

"Where is . . . this theater?" she finally managed to croak.

"Well, not in the best section of town, naturally. I mean, we can't expect that. We just came here. It's across the river in the Vyborg section; it's poor and industrial. We're certainly not going to become rich, but we'll have everything we need. It's a *theater*, Senda! I couldn't believe my luck. Some acquaintances of mine knew about it and steered me there. We can rent it for a song. The last troupe which played there put on socially significant plays. So will we. What do you think?"

"And how did the last troupe fare?" she asked pointedly.

He ignored her. "It seats two hundred and has an adequate stage. Nothing fancy, and not much in the way of wings, though . . ."

Suddenly she felt fearful. There were so many questions she'd avoided lately. Questions she'd adroitly sidestepped or silenced before they reached her tongue. Questions such as: Where were you last night? Questions whose answers she was afraid to hear.

She sighed deeply. She had always tried to avoid making so-called wifely noises, knowing how he hated them. But now she felt compelled to ask one of those questions, fear of the answer aside.

"Just who are these acquaintances of yours? And where did you meet them?"

"Can't tell you that, my love," he said lightly. He jumped to his feet, tugged off his jacket, and flung it over his shoulder. He stooped to plant another kiss on her unyielding cheek. "I've got to go change. I can tell by your expression that you're surprised. I would be too, in your shoes. Who can believe such luck?" He laughed again.

She had to clear her throat in order to speak. "Schmarya," she said shakily, no longer sure of herself, "I have something to tell you too."

"Later," he said breezily. "Over dinner tonight."

"No! It's important."

"Can't be as important as the theater, can it?" His eyes twinkled as he swaggered past the tables piled high with books. "Especially not with your stage blood. No, I didn't think so." He was already at the door. She had watched his progress as though in a dream. "Now, run along and get changed. We'll break the news to the others over the wine."

She nodded numbly. "All right," she whispered tightly as the door shut. She sighed deeply and pressed her forehead with her fingers. She'd been too startled, too shaken, to interrupt and tell him about Princess Yussoupov and the others.

The afternoon seemed suddenly to have darkened, as if an evil cloud obscured the sunshine. Which was ridiculous, of course. There was no sun. Darkness had already fallen.

She slid out of the chair and went stiffly over to the window. She wrung her tapered fingers nervously. The night shone with moonlit clarity, throwing ghostly shadows of the palace's onion domes and spires across the snow-sheathed park.

She shut her eyes in a mournful pain. Like it or not, she had no choice but to upstage Schmarya's find. Steal his thunder. Hers was the golden opportunity of a lifetime. If they didn't seize upon it immediately, it was unlikely to come within reach again.

And yet she couldn't shake the terrible feeling that just as things between the two of them seemed to be on the mend, her news would drive yet another stake, perhaps a fatal one, into the heart of their already strained relationship.

Aloud she prayed, "Not an ultimatum. Please, Schmarya, don't make it an ultimatum."

He exploded.

"Damn you!" Schmarya yelled, bringing his fist crashing down on the plank table with such force that the crockery danced and glasses fell on their sides. One of them rolled off the table in the ensuing silence and crashed to the floor, shattering upon impact. Everyone seated at the long rectangular table jumped. "Damn all of you!"

Senda's face flushed as she felt the eyes of the other diners in the restaurant riveted on their table. In the shocked silence she could have heard a pin drop.

"Please Schmarya," she begged softly. "Everyone's watching. Can't we discuss this quietly, like adults?"

"You bitch!" he stormed, his face a bright crimson as his fury built and brewed like a madly roiling cloud. His body trembled with rage. "You goddamn bitch! You couldn't tell me about all this this afternoon?"

Her embarrassed gaze held his flashing, accusing eyes. "I wanted to . . . I *tried* to, but you were so geared up about the theater that you never gave me a chance!"

He laughed insanely, and she cringed. She had never seen him like this. "*You* never got the chance?" he bellowed. "What about me?" He planted his splayed hands on the rough table and leaned over it, toward her. "How could you let me make an ass of myself jabbering on and on in front of everybody about the theater I found and then break in, oh so *innocently*"—he proceeded to toss his head and mimic her sarcastically in a high-pitched feminine voice—" 'Schmarya, I didn't have a chance to tell you this before, but we've had some offers . . .' "

She shut her eyes against the hateful spray of his spittle.

"And *you*. And *you*. And *you*!" He focused his madly burning eyes on each of the other members of the troupe in turn. They sat there stiffly, wide-eyed with shock. "When we joined up with you, what were you doing? Playing *villages*! Who brought you to the towns and cities? Who brought you *here*? Who always scouted ahead for theaters?"

There was silence.

"I'll tell you who brought you here! *Me*! I've had the vision and courage to look ahead for you . . . you *spineless* second-rate idiots! And what do I get for thanks?"

No one dared breathe.

"I'll tell you how you've thanked me! By deciding against me. All for this"—he pushed himself away from the table, straightened, and primped with grotesque feminine gestures— "this Princess Yussoupov!"

"Schmarya, this is nothing personal against you," Alex, the old troupe member, murmured, his gaze concentrated on the pine table. "It's just that the Princess and all the other private performances guarantee us the best chance."

"Chance? For what?" Schmarya sneered. "Fame? Fortune? Is that what you want?"

Alex compressed his lips tightly, his cheekbones flexing. He would say no more. It was as impossible to break through Schmarya's ramparts of rage as it would have been to knock through the stone battlements of the Petropavlovsky Fortress barehanded.

"Well, I'm through with all of you, you hear? I'm packing my bags and leaving!"

Senda reached out to touch his arm, but he recoiled as though from a serpent. "Bitch!" he whispered.

Her eyes were shining. "Please, Schmarya, don't be so angry. It's the opportunity of a lifetime. Can't you see that?"

"Listen to yourself. You're stage-struck." He eyed her mockingly. "The big actress. The leading lady." He gave a hollow laugh. "Well, so be it. I wash my hands of you. All of you! See how far your kowtowing and ass-kissing get you with these princesses and countesses, but don't come running back to me." He snatched a bottle of vodka off the table and, although he was not drunk, lurched heavily to the door.

Only Senda was aware of how truly hurt he was. Otherwise he would never have lashed out like that. "Schmarya . . ." she pleaded one last time.

He whirled around and flashed one last withering glance back at her.

Senda jumped up and ran to the door. She grabbed his arm frantically, somehow feeling that if she couldn't sway him now he would be lost to her forever. "Schmarya, *please*," she begged. "Don't walk out on me and Tamara. We love you. Nothing is worth losing you."

He stared at her grimly. "Does that mean you'll turn Princess What's-her-name down?"

Senda hesitated. "We have to consider her offer. All of us," she said carefully. "Don't you see? It's just that . . . well, hers is better than yours."

"Better, eh?"

She tightened her lips and nodded miserably. "Come back to the table and talk it out."

"Bitch." She barely saw the blur of his hand coming, and even after the slap knocked her backward against the wall, she still couldn't believe it had happened. She looked at him in surprise, her hand flying up to her cheek, where his handprint stood out whitely. Schmarya had never hit her. Never. No matter how angry he might have been.

"Bitch!" he hissed again under his breath. Then a gust of arctic wind blasted into the warmth of the little dining room, causing the candles to sputter and die. Only the dim glow of the electric lights coming from the open kitchen doorway illuminated the restaurant.

When the door slammed, the walls shook.

He was gone. She had lost him. *Lost* him. And through the flood of tears, she couldn't help blaming herself.

It was the day her career as Russia's biggest star began.

And the day when Schmarya's love for her completely died.

* * *

That night Vaslav Danilov summoned Mordka Kokovtsov to the Chinese Room of the palace. "Well?" he asked his cousin. "Did all our friends respond to my suggestion?"

"Wholeheartedly, I would say," the Count replied dryly. "Of course, I wouldn't have expected otherwise. Especially in light of the fact that you'll be footing the entertainment bill for half the city for the entire season."

The Prince ignored the pointed gibe. "Arrange to have the director of the Théâtre Français invited to every palace where she'll perform."

"Really, Vaslav!" Count Kokovtsov raised his brows. "She doesn't even speak French. She can only perform in Russian. It's unheard-of!"

"She can learn French quickly enough. I would say she is one person who can learn almost anything quickly. You would do well not to underestimate her. Arrange for the director to find her a tutor. And be discreet."

"Very well. No one will be the wiser that you have contrived it. But you don't really think her acting is good enough for the Français, do you?"

"I do." The Prince steepled his hands and sat back thoughtfully. "She's very, very good. A little unpolished, perhaps, but her performance was spellbinding nonetheless." He paused. "She has it within her to become Russia's greatest living actress. Why not speed her on her course? The Français's director can see to it that she is schooled in acting, also."

"You must want her very badly, my cousin."

"That I do," the Prince said mildly. His eyes looked bland. "And she will be mine."

"Very well." The Count rose and walked to the door.

"Oh, and one more thing, Cousin Mordka. Tatiana Ivanova."

"What about her?"

"She has become rather . . . tiresome." The Prince gestured wearily. "She is no longer in favor."

Which means, the Count mused as he walked the extravagantly inlaid parquet halls on his way back to his apartment, that that slut Tatiana is finished.

Mordka was not surprised. He had aided his cousin through countless affairs.

Aloud he found himself murmuring, "The Prince giveth, and the Prince taketh away."

Senda withdrew from the world and took to her bed, resolved it would be her coffin. Shut out behind the thick, perpetually drawn draperies, the days and nights blended into one single interminably bleak stretch of timeless agony. She was blinded by tears until there were no more to shed, and for many days thereafter her eyes felt swollen and scratchy from dehydration. She had vague recollections of Countess Florinsky bustling cheerfully in and out of the dark chamber, Inge bringing Tamara on short visits, and listlessly sitting forward to accept spoonfuls of thick, fatty chicken broth fed to her by alternating members of her increasingly alarmed troupe. She waited in vain for Schmarya to come rescue her from her despondency, but she saw nothing of him. When she asked Inge whether he had tried to see Tamara, the young woman averted her gaze.

Senda's heart echoed listlessly: his capacity for cruelty was not such that he would desert his daughter. Was it?

No, he loved Tamara. He *had* to return soon.

But he didn't. It was as though he had died, and something inside her whispered that he had left her forever. She could only hope she was wrong. She loved him so deeply, profoundly, and needed him desperately. She could not come to terms with the fact that he could turn his back on that love.

Living without him was not even an existence. She felt empty. Desolate. Lifeless. It was as if when he had stalked out of the restaurant, he had stolen her soul, taken it with him. Which in a way was what he had done.

Over and over she found herself cursing her decision to put Princess Yussoupov's offer above him. She should never have hesitated at the door of the restaurant. She should have told him his decision had been the right one. If only she had.

But she hadn't. And now the joy of living had gone out of her.

It was on the afternoon of Senda's sixth day of self-imposed mourning that Countess Florinsky panted into the Prince's drawing room. Her face was unnaturally white and drawn, and for once her gushing, inherently ebullient nature was subdued. As though to emphasize this fact, she was dressed in black bombazine, her huge black hat, as wide as her own generous girth, loaded down with an impossibly abundant bush of shiny black satin roses.

She found Vaslav Danilov seated behind the desk centered squarely in the midst of a palace-size Aubusson carpet. She did not like this room. In fact, it chilled her spirits even further. The polished furniture was classically austere, not at all to her liking, and even the parquet floor lacked the arabesque splendor of the rest of the palace. But the oval room itself, with its succession of three domed ceilings supported by columns at each end and two sets of caryatids facing each other mid-room, was an architectural tour de force. Nothing was allowed to detract from this monumental magnificence.

"Have a seat," the Prince offered, pushing aside a thick sheaf of documents. He looked mildly surprised. "If I didn't know better, I would say you look slightly . . . agitated." He frowned.

Sniffing, she glanced around for the chair offering the most upholstery, found one to her liking, and plopped into it. She produced a handkerchief and dabbed ineffectually at her eyes.

She sniffed. "I won't beat around the bush, Vaslav," she declared stiffly. "Frankly. I'm *quite* worried." She nodded tremulously, as though to herself. "She still hasn't begun to snap out of that horrible depression. When I speak to her she turns away. I was told she even has to be hand-fed."

"She will snap out of it soon enough," he said casually, pushing his chair back. "She is a woman of reason."

"Well, I hope to *God* you are right. She is heartbroken, the poor dear."

He rang for a servant, and after the Countess was ceremoniously poured tea, she blew on the steam and took a sip. She sighed appreciatively and set her cup and saucer on the desk. "Nothing like hot tea to take away the winter chill. Now. I take it there is something you would like me to do, eh?"

"There is. First, here is the balance of what you're due for the ball." He slid an envelope, weighed down by a narrow velvet box, across the desk toward her.

For a moment her tears were forgotten. She seized upon the box with pudgy fingers and pried it open. "Oh, Vaslav!" she breathed. Her giant, magnified eyes shone mistily.

"Well, put them on. Let us see what they look like."

Countess Florinsky made a production of slipping off her old metal-rimmed spectacles and looping the new gold-framed ones carefully over her ears.

"Even the prescription is correct!" She appeared deeply moved.

He waved his hand negligibly. "A token of my gratitude for a delightful fete." As he spoke, she placed her old spectacles in their case and slid it and the envelope of money into her black satin bag. When she yanked the tasseled string shut, the gaping mouth of the bag closed hungrily over its treasures with the speed of a gulping fish. She let the bag drop to the floor beside her and settled back, suddenly brusque and businesslike. "Now, my dear. You didn't ask me here to give me the glasses, I take it?"

He stared at her "My dear Flora! You wound me," he said, as if offended. "You can't believe that I don't find the pleasure of your company reason enough?"

"I'm afraid I find that *very* difficult to believe," she sighed. "I do know you, Vaslav."

His face was a mask, but his voice bore grudging respect. "You're a shrewd woman, Flora."

She waited, sipping her tea.

"As I said before, Madame Bora is strong, but severely depressed. Which is why I am counting on you."

"Indeed."

"Yes. You, if anyone, can help speed her recovery."

"Ah, but it isn't her health that concerns you."

He shrugged eloquently. "Her health concerns me, of course. As does anyone's under my roof."

The Countess wasn't fooled. "I see," she said, folding her plump pink hands in her lap.

"You are her only friend, I think?"

It was the Countess's turn to shrug.

"And as such, her speedy recovery is of interest to you as well."

"She is going through a great personal crisis, and crises are hardly the stuff of which good health is made. She is dying inside. A man has deserted her, Vaslav. A tragedy . . . if ever there was one. I'm afraid we shall find it rather difficult to give her life new meaning."

He nodded. "Difficult, perhaps. But impossible, no. I think I have come up with the antidote she requires."

"Which is?"

"We will arrange for her to do that which she loves best: acting. She will be doing something constructive which will take her mind off her present situation. She will have no time to languish in her depression."

Countess Florinsky thought it over before nodding approvingly. She permitted a slight smile to appear on her lips. "I think you are right."

"Good. You will help with it then, Flora. Give her moral support. Urge her to get to work, to forget that man, and so on. I think you understand?"

She nodded.

He smiled. "Then it is settled. Come to think of it, I am

133

rather pleased. Not only will Madame Bora benefit enormously, but you also."

"How?"

"There will be many fetes and performances for which you will receive considerable commissions."

"I am her friend, Vaslav," she said gravely. "As such, it is my duty to protect her."

"From what?"

"You."

"Me!" He laughed, but his voice bore a trace of amused respect. "Even if it is not in your own best interests?"

"That depends. She is lovely, marvelously naive, and dangerously impressionable. And despite your noble veneer, Vaslav, you are a shark."

He regarded her thoughtfully. "I have been called many things," he mused, rubbing his chin, "but never a shark."

"A shark who needs constant feeding. I don't need to mention that Tatiana Ivanova has left the Théâtre Français?"

"Oh, has she now?"

"She has indeed," the Countess sniffed, "as if you didn't know."

He nodded and rose to his feet, towering above her. "Then I can count on enlisting your help?"

She sighed deeply. For once her hugely magnified eyes were sad and lackluster. "What choice do I have?" She looked up at him.

He smiled tightly. "You are always free to do as you choose."

"Am I, now . . ." she murmured. "I wonder, sometimes."

"I think you know what is best for you both." He paused. "You have always trod the line between duty to others and duty to yourself with remarkable agility. I do not think that that particular talent will desert you now. of all times."

"This is different . . . I have to think it over. She could get hurt in the process. I prize her friendship, and I have no desire to jeopardize it."

"Of course not." He stared blandly at her. "There is no need to."

She returned his gaze.

"I am convinced that within the week you will have her up and about. She will be grateful to you for having helped her."

The Countess tightened her lips. "Well, I do hope you know what you're doing," she said agitatedly.

"Flora, as long as things work out as planned, she will get what she wants, namely a career onstage, you will get what you want, a deepening friendship . . . and a little money. And I . . ." His voice trailed off.

"You will get *her*," she finished pointedly.

He smiled easily and showed her to the door. "I am counting on you, Flora. You know that."

She nodded and stepped out into the cool hall. Before he closed the door she turned to face him. "What I'm going to do," she said softly, "is not for you or the money, but for her. Because it is as you said. She needs something to occupy her mind."

"Does that mean you don't want money?"

"Thirty pieces of silver for delivering her to you?" Her giant hat wobbled precariously as she shook her head. "No, I don't want any money for this."

"You are a strange woman, Flora," he said.

"And perhaps a foolish one. Time will tell."

"Time always tells."

"Just don't hurt her, Vaslav. That's all I ask. She's special. She's not another Tatiana Ivanova."

He stared at her and closed the door softly. Slowly she made her way along the giant hall. For once she was vaguely frightened. The Danilovs wielded too much power.

Too much, it occurred to her now, for their own good.

And far too much for the good of many others.

A week later, Vaslav Danilov summoned Count Kokovtsov to the Chinese Room. He was leafing through a sheaf of documents, occasionally making notes in the margins. "What have you to report?" the Prince inquired mildly, seated behind his big tulipwood *bureau plat*.

"Madame Bora's friend has moved into an apartment above a bookstore on Zaytsev Street," the Count intoned in his usual lugubrious manner. He crossed to a cabinet, poured himself a generous glass of vodka, and downed it in one swallow.

The Prince did not look up from his pages. "And?"

"We have stumbled upon a hornet's nest. The apartment is leased to a student. A radical student, I am told," the Count added distastefully. "It is suspected that as many as ten or twelve students, all involved in varying degrees of anti-Czarist politics, may be sharing the same premises." He visibly shuddered at the thought.

"Men?" Vaslav asked. "Women? Or both?"

"Both."

"I see." The Prince pushed the papers aside thoughtfully. "That many people will make surveillance difficult."

"On the contrary." The Count took a seat, the huge shiny surface of the desk between them a visible barrier between their separate stations. "As you ordered, Captain Dimitrov of the Okhrana has taken over surveillance duties. He now has his men stationed in an apartment they have temporarily . . . ah, appropriated . . ." —the Count coughed discreetly into his cupped hand—". . . directly across the street from the bookstore. I am but the liaison, as planned."

"Good," the Prince said with a nod. "And our star-to-be? Has she been placed yet?"

Count Kokovtsov nodded, his normally pained expression unchanged. "She has," he answered, "although she does not know it yet. I might add that Monsieur Guerlain was quite unhappy about the arrangement. I received a rather pompous dissertation on artistic integrity and other such nonsense. Of course, it all boiled down to the fact that"—the Count paused and then mimicked Monsieur Guerlain's patrician French vowels, his own voice taking on a high-pitched, effetely fluent tone—" 'The Théâtre Français can never, never allow its standards to be lowered, or its integrity to be compromised. Never, Monsieur le Comte, under any circumstances or for all the money in the world!' "

"One never says 'never,' " the Prince murmured pontifically with an idle wave of his hand. "I take it that what we wanted is precisely what was agreed upon, in the end?"

"It was."

"It is amazing, is it not, Cousin Mordka, what a difference a little money can sometimes make in a person's outlook? How it can tempt the most conscionable of men?"

The Count nodded again. "Money and death, the great equalizers. At any rate, Madame Bora will become the understudy for Olga Botkina within a month's time. That does not give *us* much time, considering that she does not speak so much as a word of French."

The Prince was not bothered by simple logistics. With enough money to smooth the way, such things could be seen to easily enough. "Acting is but the memorization of words and emotions," he said. "She will learn fast."

"I hope so," the Count said unhappily. "If not, we will become the laughingstock of St. Petersburg."

"Indeed not!" the Prince said haughtily. "Secrecy is of paramount importance. You have stressed that, I take it!"

"I have."

"And you have also seen to it that the arrangements cannot be traced back to me?"

"I have done that too. However . . ."

"However, what?" The Prince sat forward and stared at his cousin keenly.

"Countess Florinsky." The Count's lips curled in distaste.

"Your having involved that woman in the project makes secrecy . . . well, less than . . ."

"Are you trying to tell me that she has trouble holding her tongue?"

"Precisely."

"You needn't worry about Flora. Since her utmost concern is not for any commissions she might earn, but for Madame Bora's welfare, her silence is assured."

"If you say so, cousin," Count Kokovtsov said dubiously.

"I do." The Prince stared down at his desk. "Now, the least I expect, aside from the private performances in Russian which Flora is scheduling at the various palaces, is for Madame Bora to star in the last five performances at the Théâtre Français this season."

The Count looked shocked. "Surely you are jesting!"

The Prince shook his head. "I assure you I am not. In due time Olga Botkina is to become ill and Madame Bora will replace her."

"I am afraid that illness cannot be contrived as conveniently as you like to think," the Count said dryly.

"But a short tour of . . . perhaps, Paris?"

"If you insist upon squandering the family fortune, yes." Count Kokovtsov sighed heavily and made as though to rise from his chair.

"One moment. There is another subject I wish to discuss with you." The Prince consulted the papers on his desk. "The day after tomorrow, you will leave for Moscow. I want the sale of our Ural estates to be concluded as hastily as humanly possible."

"The Ural estates!" The Count sucked in his breath. This was the first he had heard of this new development. "But . . . we are hardly what you would call financially strapped! If anything, we have an overabundance of cash."

"Be that as it may, there are other reasons for disposing of the property."

"But that could take months to do. Years, even. Vaslav, do you have any idea of how difficult it is to sell twenty-nine million acres?"

The Prince forced a smile. "I do. Finding a buyer for that massive tract would not be easy, although there are several families who might be interested. But I suggest you subdivide it into smaller parcels, say, of one million acres apiece. That way, I think we will not only be rid of it quite readily, but make a substantial profit besides."

For a moment they sat in silence.

"Vaslav, as your financial adviser," the Count said at last, "I can only urge you to reconsider this."

The Prince held his cousin's gaze unblinkingly. "And hold on to all our real-estate holdings?"

"As your father, and his forefathers before him," the Count said silkily, relieved to be back on familiar turf instead of the murky world of footlights and stage props. "Need I remind you that a large part of the Danilov fortune is based on land acquisition and ownership? Do you have any idea how much money flows in from the timber, the mines, and the rents?"

"I have all your figures right here at my fingertips," the Prince replied gravely, fanning the papers out on the desktop. "Now, as my financial adviser, may I ask you a few questions?"

"Ask what you will."

"Then I shall speak candidly, and expect you to answer likewise. Mordka, do you have any idea of what is happening to this country?"

"You mean . . . politically?"

The Prince nodded.

"Well, there is quite a bit of unrest, of course. But what country doesn't experience those difficulties at times?"

"Mordka. Mordka. Put aside, for once, your rationalizations and blind faith in the Motherland. Look beyond our palace grounds and the vaults of our banking institutions."

"So?"

The Prince sat forward. "So what do you see?"

"Well . . ." Mordka's mind was suddenly a maelstrom of thoughts. "To tell you the truth," he said uncomfortably, "I haven't given it much thought."

"As I was afraid. But *I* have, Mordka." Frowning, the Prince got to his feet and slowly paced the Chinese Room, his hands clasped in the small of his spine. "I am concerned, Mordka, far more than most, about the current political unrest, and its repercussions down the road. I'm afraid I have trouble playing the ostrich, hiding my head beneath the sands of reality like so many of our fellow nobles." He paused and sighed deeply. "Have you listened carefully to what is going on all over Russia? I don't mean among our peers, but among the majority. The peasants. The students. Their teachers."

"Of course I've gotten wind of silly notions such as revolution." Count Kokovtsov waved his hand irritably. "Who hasn't? But you can't really believe—"

"I do, Mordka." The Prince laughed bitterly. "It must not go beyond these four walls, but I've kept my ear to the ground. For quite some years now, I have been paying a network of . . . informants, and handsomely. Their prognosis, I hate to say, is not good."

"Prognosis! You make it sound like . . . like some disease!"

"Mordka, Russia *is* suffering from a disease. A terminal social disease. But then, why should you be aware of it? You are insulated from day-to-day life and its tragedies. Everyone else within our circle is. I would be too, were it not for my informants. I realize, naturally, that when the time comes, they too shall turn against me. Even now, only the gold I distribute so lavishly among them assures their loyalty. That too will soon change."

"And this . . . disease you fear so greatly, cousin. What is it, exactly?"

"Poverty, Mordka," Vaslav Danilov said gravely. "For centuries now, we have lived on the sweat and toil of millions—millions of slaves—and it is catching up with us. I fear we are hopelessly outnumbered. Perhaps we will even become extinct."

"Extinct!"

"In the future, the same fate shall befall us as befell the slave owners in America and the aristocracy in France."

Vaslav continued, "I also want you to start cataloging and shipping our finest art treasures and antiques to the estate in Geneva. I feel they will be safer there."

Dumbfounded, Mordka could only nod again, and wonder for how long Vaslav had been planning this. He seemed to have thought of everything.

Vaslav consulted another paper and pushed it aside. He sighed heavily again. "As soon as you've parceled the property in the Urals," he continued, "I want the proceeds of each sale to be deposited immediately in the Banque Danilov in Geneva. I do not want to wait for it all to accumulate before being sent. By then it might be too late, and the losses would be astronomical. Also, convert most of our cash assets into Swiss francs and have them sent out of the country."

"As you wish." Mordka's mind was swirling with such a blizzard of thoughts that it was impossible for him to sort them all out. For the time being, he found it simplest to agree to anything his cousin ordered.

"And one last thing, Mordka."

"Yes?" What else could there possibly be?

"Our train."

"What about it?"

"It is ready for immediate departure?"

"At our usual railroad siding, yes."

The Prince's lips tightened. "From now on, it will be

waiting in readiness wherever we happen to be, whether in the Crimea, Moscow, or here. I want it fully fueled and crewed at all times. That does not mean a skeleton crew, either. Oh, and have two extra wagons of coal added to the front."

"Really, Vaslav—"

The Prince gestured to the Count. "I have not finished. I also want six empty boxcars and two passenger cars added to the existing train, ready to be loaded within a few hours' notice."

The Count stared, tongue-tied, transfixed.

Vaslav Danilov remained silent.

When he recovered enough to find his tongue, Count Kokovtsov's voice was shaky. "Vaslav!" he whispered in strangely pitched words. "You're giving me quite a fright!"

Vaslav still did not speak.

The Count shuddered. "I mean, a contingency plan is fine and well, but something on such a massive scale as what you're suggesting . . . well, don't you think you're carrying this a bit *too* far?"

"I am not carrying it far enough, I fear. Now, it is important that the train look ordinary and unostentatious in case we are forced to make a rather hasty . . . ah, departure. Our coats of arms are to be sanded off the engine and the coaches, and painted over to look like any normal train."

The fear which already choked Mordka coursed ever more coldly through his veins. "Vaslav, I hope for all our sakes that you are not clairvoyant."

"So do I, believe me, so do I. Meanwhile, follow my instructions to the letter. And do not fail me." The Prince gestured with authority. "Now, go. You have plenty to occupy yourself with."

Count Kokovtsov rose and beat a hasty retreat, his mind spinning out of control. He was glad to leave so he could sit down to sort things out in his muddled mind.

Once alone in his parlor, Mordka rang for iced vodka and drank straight from the bottle while he brooded, his eyes fixed on the dancing fire. After a while the icy heat of the vodka and the warmth emanating from the redolent spruce logs began thawing his ice-cold fears.

Vaslav obviously had matters well under control, so why worry himself unnecessarily about the fickle future? he asked himself. Besides, there was a sterling-silver lining to the particular storm clouds Vaslav was predicting. If anything . . .

Mordka's heart skipped a beat and he suddenly sat bolt upright.

If anything, the winds of political change only played into his hands. He usually received a five-percent commission on all purchases and sales conducted for the Danilovs, and would earn likewise on the sale of the Ural estate. Five percent of twenty-nine million acres would amount to a tidy sum. Plus this was the ideal opportunity to skim a little off the top. After all, with twenty-nine million acres, one or two million wouldn't be missed.

Hell, he thought, taking another swig from the bottle, he stood to make a bloody fortune.

In the meantime, more and more of the Danilov fortune would seep quietly into Switzerland.

Senda's energy and resolve began to return in mid-January.

Finally forced to accept the fact that Schmarya had deserted her and that languishing in the palace might be the stuff of romantic heroines but highly inconvenient in real life, she drew on all her reserves of strength and came back to life with a new surge of direction. Although she had missed performing *The Cherry Orchard* at the Yussoupov Palace, Countess Florinsky had arranged for two other shows to be performed soon, one at the Yelagin Palace and the other at the Stroganovs'.

"It's too soon, Flora!" Senda had tried to beg off numbly when Countess Florinsky informed her of the impending productions. "I just can't! Not yet!"

"Oh, but you simply must!" the Countess had cried. "Not for yourself, of course. We can always take care of you and the little one. But what about the rest of the troupe? My dear, I do believe they're counting on you. If you don't accept these offers, what is to happen to them?"

What indeed? Senda asked herself morosely, seeing no way out of her predicament.

The next weeks were crammed with all the exhausting exigenies necessary for Senda's resurrection. It was a tiring but welcoming period of transition, and she had little time to mourn for Schmarya, a fact for which she was extremely grateful. And Countess Florinsky had magically produced what seemed to Senda an astronomical sum of money.

"It's just an advance installment, my dear. The second half is coming," the Countess told her, folding Senda's hesitant fingers around the crisp new bills. And she added, lying glibly: "Of course, I've already taken out my commission, so you needn't worry about that."

By the beginning of February, Senda was almost completely back on her feet. On the morning of Friday, the sixth of that month, Countess Florinsky steered her to what she called "a modest but respectable" high-ceilinged apartment near the Academy of Arts, with tall rectangular windows overlooking the Neva.

"I know it's on the *wrong* side of the river," Countess Florinsky apologized, "but it *is* furnished, and rather nicely, and it does have three bedrooms, along with this nice parlor. It's just what you need for holding your salon."

"My . . . *what?*" Senda peered at her friend closely.

"Your *salon,* of course! It goes without saying, my dear, that you'll have to do a bit of entertaining. It's the thing to do, you know."

Slowly Senda explored the apartment, peering into closets, roaming from one room to the next. Even in the bitter, windswept freeze of deep winter there was a decidedly warm and elegant air about the apartment. The salon was simply furnished and spacious, with heavy wooden furniture, a ceramic fireplace, and a black grand piano. There were classical chiaroscuro prints on the walls, a brass and glass-globed chandelier, and bentwood chairs. Heavy opaque puff draperies and gossamer white sheers hung over the windows, and the sofa was covered in tapestry. The glossy wooden floor was warmed by several geometric-patterned Oriental rugs, and occasional tables were draped with thick embroidered cloths. The small dining room off the salon was austere, with lilac-colored walls, a heavily carved armoire, and four chairs around a plain white-draped square table over which hung another brass chandelier. Senda was delighted with the smallest of the three bedrooms, for which the Countess had shamelessly looted some of the treasures from the Danilov nursery: a crib, playpen, pint-sized chairs, and a profusion of toys. Tamara would be in heaven, Senda knew, and thanked Countess Florinsky profusely for having thought of it. "Eh? But it is nothing," the Countess assured her with an idle wave of her hand, looking rather pleased with herself despite her modesty. The largest of the bedrooms was any lady's dream, Senda thought. The walls were covered with pale blue watered silk, and the brass-framed botanical prints and flowered glazed-chintz curtains gave it a gardenlike cheer. But it was the kidney-shaped dressing table, which flaunted three layers of ivory lace flounces, that made it so decidedly feminine. On its glass-topped surface were laid out all the implements necessary for feminine grooming—two silk-shaded lamps flanked a round silver-framed mirror, and around it were arranged silver combs and brushes, bottles of lotions, perfumes, and eau de cologne, and a delicate crystal vase of pink tea roses. And the Spartan, utilitarian third bedroom, Flora informed her, was for a live-in servant.

"But I've never had a servant!" Senda moaned with dismay. "I wouldn't know what to do with one!"

"You don't have to do anything, which is the point of having a servant. I think a general housekeeper with nurse's training is best. You don't really need more than one servant for the time being, but you do need a housekeeper and a nurse for Tamara. After all, you can't drag her to the theaters for rehearsals every day, and then to performances every night, can you? She would become an exhausted wreck, the poor thing. Besides which, all respectable families have at least one live-in."

"When do you think we can move in, then?" Senda asked softly. She barely trusted herself to speak, so afraid was she that vocalizing anything to do with her good fortune would somehow cause her to awaken from this cornucopia-filled dream.

"Anytime, I suppose," Flora said with surprise. "After all, it's yours. The pantry is stocked and there are linens on the beds. The kitchen has all the pots and pans and dishes you are likely to need."

Senda took a deep breath and barely hesitated. "This afternoon, then," she said firmly.

Countess Florinsky smiled. "As long as it makes you happy," she said warmly, hugging Senda tightly.

The palace slid out of sight as the sleigh carrying Senda and Tamara turned down an *allée* of ice-frozen trees, their skeletal branches glassy with the veneer of crystalline ice. Nightmare trees, she thought, each one a solitary sentinel well-spaced from the next. A sob caught in her throat. Damn. Those wintry trees were but a reflection of her own life.

The sleigh picked up speed, the bells on the horses jingling with false merriment. She blinked her eyes and sniffled. A lump blocked her throat and the mist in her eyes welled up into a blur of full-fledged moisture. Lost forever, she feared, was the warm, welcoming touch of Schmarya's body. The safe haven she had sought in his arms. His loins. His heart. His soul. She drew a quivering breath and dabbed ineffectually at her eyes with a gloved knuckle. Her stomach was squirming and the length of her intestines gnarled into a tight, spastic cord.

You're alone, alone, alone! a voice within her chanted its singsong message. *You're now father and mother both. You're the breadwinner of the household and solely responsible for your daughter. Nothing you want counts for anything anymore! You've made your choice and you won a career. But you're alone, alone, alone!*

Alone!

Impulsively, as though to draw strength from her daughter, she leaned forward and pressed a trembling kiss against the back of Tamara's bright red knit cap, resting her lips on the scratchy wool in a long, drawn-out kiss of anguish.

She could feel Tamara's strong arms and feisty legs as she squirmed impatiently on her lap. For a moment longer she held her child close, then let her go. Even before she loosened her grip, the little girl was clambering about the seat.

She closed her eyes, making the rest of the short journey in self-imposed darkness. She dreaded facing each long, empty minute remaining of that year. That month. That week.

Especially the rest of that day.

To her surprise, however, there was no time to spend considering the bleakness of her situation. Tamara explored every nook and cranny of the new apartment, mesmerized with the roomful of toys and insisting that Senda play with her. Then she was hungry, and Senda made them both something to eat. To her astonishment, she herself had a ravenous appetite

The afternoon was gone.

That night, when shadowy self-recriminations over losing Schmarya were sure to engulf her, promising to keep her awake, it was other doubts which preyed on her mind. Turning down her new bed, she let out a cry of dismay, dropping the sheet as she recoiled. She stared at the white linen as if she'd found a snake lurking under the covers

In a way, she had.

Elegantly but discreetly embroidered in white silk thread, the comforter, sheets, and pillowcases all displayed the small but unmistakable twin-headed eagle crest of the Danilovs.

She sat heavily on the slipper chair, wearily covering her face with her hands.

So the bedding was the Prince's.

Her mind began to reflect unhappily on the probable course of events.

If the bed linens were the Prince's, didn't it only make sense that the pots and pans in the kitchen belonged to him also?

And if they did, wouldn't the furniture? And perhaps even the apartment itself?

What, then, about the stage roles which she was scheduled to play at the various palaces? Had they, too, been arranged through the Machiavellian machinations of Vaslav Danilov?

Could he want her *that* badly?

She gazed at the incriminating bed. Had he provided her with these ornate bed linens because he expected to share them with her eventually?

With an immense effort of will she pushed the thoughts out of her mind, but not before glimpsing the ugly truth that perhaps, just perhaps, she had been cleverly manipulated all along. And was still being manipulated.

It was something she did not relish. She decided she would confront Countess Florinsky in the morning.

But when morning came, she never got around to asking any questions. Countess Florinsky, all splendid wobbly hat, sweet flowery toilet water, and bubbling *joie de vivre*, burst in clapping her hands and crying, "Hurry, my dear! We're already late!"

Senda eyed her curiously, wondering at her friend's state of excitement. "We've got to go somewhere?" she asked. She looked down at herself. It was the first she had heard of it, and she still wore her flannel nightgown.

"Of course. You do need clothes, my dear, if I say so myself, and I'm afraid this time you'll have to help choose the fabrics. We're expected at Madame Lamothe's within the hour."

Senda stared at Countess Florinsky with the same bewilderment one might expect on the face of a fairy-tale heroine when confronted with the tangible assets bestowed upon her by a benevolent fairy godmother: surprise, awe, wonder, but above all, fear and confusion. She had the unsettling feeling that velvet gloves had somehow pried her destiny from her own hands and put it in the hands of others, that things might never again be as they once had been.

"Really, Flora," she said hesitantly, "it's all good and well, but . . . do I really *need* new clothes?"

Countess Florinsky was taken aback. "Do you *need* new clothes? My dear, you not only need new clothes, but a new wardrobe, as anyone in society can tell you. From this moment on you are a star, and as such, you must begin to think like one. In case you didn't know it, theatrical stars are the fashion plates of our society. What you are seen wearing, both onstage and off, will set new styles and be copied by others. In fact, you will *owe* it to your adoring public to be a constant fashion sensation. In time, people will expect you to wear a different dress every day. Tatiana Ivanova never wore the same one twice. Of course, an entire wardrobe can't be put together overnight," Countess Florinsky continued, hooking an arm through Senda's and adroitly steering her toward the bedroom. "That takes time, but a few things are absolutely necessary to start. I would say that several dresses for day and evening wear, a few really good gowns—you never know when you might need them in this town—and of course, a riding habit—"

"Riding habit!" Senda looked horrified. What more could possibly be expected of her? Evidently there was more to being an actress than simply performing onstage.

Countess Florinsky did not break her confident stride. "Don't look so shocked, my dear, and for heaven's sake, *do* get ready. We're running quite late as it is." And with that, she gave Senda a firm prod in the small of her back, propelling her into the bedroom.

Senda turned. "But, Flora. What about Tamara? I can't leave her here alone."

"I've already seen to her, my dear. A temporary servant is on her way. Now, on *your* way!"

So the whirlwind which was sweeping Senda up into its vortex continued. Perhaps it was a well-meaning conspiracy; perhaps not. But there never seemed time to sit down and ask the brutal questions she needed answered so desperately.

"But . . . can I really afford this?" Senda whispered to Countess Florinsky. It was an hour later, and they sat on gilt ballroom chairs in Madame Lamothe's plush atelier on Nevsky Avenue, fingering a rich emerald bolt of extravagantly priced silk beneath a shimmering rock-crystal chandelier.

"Ssssh!" the Countess looked scandalized at the mention of cost. *"Au contraire,* my dear," she trilled softly, frantically fanning her bosom with a pink peacock plume. "Of course you can afford it, and quite easily at that. Besides, I simply cannot stress enough how imperative it is that you keep up certain standards. If what I anticipate will happen does occur, you will find that you are living . . . well, if not quite frugally, then far below your means."

And of course the Countess was proven right. Monsieur Guerlain, the director of the Théâtre Français, sought her out and insisted she accompany him and a small group of his friends for an impromptu midnight supper. Before she could decline, off she was whisked in a whirlwind of furs in one of a flotilla of small red sleigh taxis, racing to the fashionable Restaurant Cuba, where, over a late dinner of sturgeon, shashlik, caviar, and champagne, Monsieur Guerlain endlessly—and to his own surprise, genuinely—praised her talents to the skies. Senda listened quietly, a part of her detached, as if he were discussing someone else and not her. But of course they *were* discussing her, and the undetached part of her mind knew this. Everyone at the huge round table listened raptly to each and every word of Jean-Pierre Guerlain's dissertation while she listened politely, first with slight amusement and then with a growing horror, all the while a gracious smile she did not feel pasted on her lips as she studied her new mentor's physical attributes. Whereas Madame Lamothe was a witch of sorts, surely Monsieur Guerlain was a warlock of equal, if not even more prodigious, powers. One look at him and you knew for certain that he was larger than life. Marvelously animated, splendidly special. A sorcerer.

That he was. Jean-Pierre Guerlain had reigned supreme among the elite of the St. Petersburg theater for the past twenty-five years; he was to acting what Serge Diaghilev was to dancing and Rimsky-Korsakov was to music. In Senda, he realized, he had come across that rarest and most beguiling of pure illusionists, a natural, authoritative stage presence, as yet untrained. Which only meant that no well-meaning director had as yet had the opportunity to ruin her spontaneity, meddle with her God-given natural talents, or, heaven forbid, teach her that most disastrous of all catastrophes— bad acting habits which he would first have to exorcise before turning her into a true star. Now, she threw herself wholeheartedly into the role she played with refreshing, if somewhat amateurish fervor, baring her innermost soul for all to see. What she lacked in training, she more than made up for in raw, unadulterated talent.

Her flawless physical beauty, while only secondary to her other attributes, was by no means a hindrance. The marriage of talent and beauty he saw in her . . . well, Senda Bora was precisely what Jean-Pierre Guerlain was constantly on the lookout for, and had found only once before.

The excitement he felt was nearly uncontainable.

She was the Kohinoor diamond in the rough. Indeed, with her natural resources and his vast expertise and unrivaled power, he would single-handedly create Russia's greatest living theatrical treasure: a living legend. Senda Bora would not reflect badly upon the Théâtre Français, he decided. Nor would the healthy sum of money which that fool Count Kokovtsov had dangled in front of him reflect adversely upon his bank account.

Within the first few minutes of their meeting, Monsieur Guerlain offered a startled Senda a position near the head of his elite company's roster of impressive stars, French-language tutors, and daily acting lessons.

"A grueling regimen, if ever there was one," he warned her.

Nearly speechless, and ever practical, Senda could only wonder aloud: "Yes, but . . . but how will I be able to pay for all this?"

"I will provide everything," he said, gesturing expansively. "As long as you fulfill your end of the bargain, consider everything paid for."

Senda was too awestruck to take it all in.

"Let us not fool ourselves. You are a very beautiful woman, Madame Bora. Not only that, but a major talent as well." He leaned across the white-draped table, obsidian eyes gleaming predatorially.

She looked demurely at her untouched dessert, pastry cream and apricots in an airy, flaky walnut crust. The last thing on her mind at this moment was food, however beautifully served. She was certain that he was not telling her the entire truth, that he had ulterior motives. She slowly sipped at her champagne, afraid to drink it too quickly. This was no time to get light-headed and giddy.

"You are not listening," he chided softly.

"I am," she said, turning to him. "It's just . . . well, I'm not used to things like this happening." She shrugged her silk-puffed shoulders eloquently, all the more beautiful for her lack of jewels. "Ever since I came to St. Petersburg," she murmured, "life has been a fairy tale. I wonder when it will all end."

"Why should it? In any case, fairy tales have happy endings."

She shook her head. "Even they are not as perfect as this."

He laughed. "Ah, I suspect you are not a romantic, but a realist, after all. So much the better. But consider this. You are no stranger to compliments, I take it." It was a statement, not a question which needed a reply.

She felt his fingers discreetly grazing the inside of one thigh. Ripples of longing, mixed with revulsion, crawled up and down her leg.

"You are going to be our greatest star, Senda," he whispered, using her first name for the first time.

Despite the overheated room, she found herself shivering. She sidled away from him, clearing her throat. "Monsieur Guerlain," she said shakily, "my grandmother used to have a saying. 'If you don't want to get eaten by the bear, then stay out of the forest.' "

"I am the bear in question?"

"All I'm trying to say . . ." She faltered, blushed suddenly, and lowered her lashes. Her voice was cold, but so whispery that he had to lean close to hear her words. "My body is not part of the bargain."

He threw back his dark head then, and burst out laughing, as though at something exceedingly funny. Finally he had to dab his eyes dry with a corner of his napkin. "My dear, I am not a dirty old man, despite what you may fear. You must excuse an old man's familiarity. We are that way in the theater, I'm afraid—quite fraternal, you know. Believe me, I have no ulterior motives as far as your virtue is concerned." He swallowed champagne, still sputtering on laughter. "How could I?" he finally asked her solemnly.

"I . . . I don't think I understand."

His obsidian eyes searched hers gravely. "You really don't, do you?" he asked softly.

She shook her head.

"Then you are indeed someone out of a fairy tale. A princess lost deep in the forest." He smiled warmly and patted her hand, this time in an obviously paternal gesture. "Whatever you do, keep your virtue as intact as your innocence. It is quite refreshing, believe me. Especially in this cultured jungle they call St. Petersburg. And even more so in the cutthroat jungle of the theater."

"And your touching my leg?" Her voice was trembling.

He looked at her steadily. "That was a test, Madame Bora. Something for me to go on. You are quite the mystery to me, you know."

She sat silently for a moment. "And why did you have to test me?"

His expression did not change. "To understand where I stood with you." He paused. "Or perhaps, where you stand with someone else."

She shook her head in disbelief. "Then . . . it is true that you really do not desire me. You're not doing all this . . ." Her voice was crackly, and she swallowed a gulp of champagne to soothe her parched throat. The chilled sparkly wine was so refreshing she drained the glass. Somehow it helped loosen her tongue as well. ". . . for my body?" She smiled shyly.

"Good heavens, no!" He made as though to shiver. "Do you have any idea as to the legions of young women who try to throw themselves at me each week in order to get a role? *Any* role! Of course I want your body. In my own way. Up onstage, in whichever role you are to lose yourself in. But if I were after you physically . . ." His eyes took on a faraway look. "Well, then, I expect even I would be finished in this town."

She looked shocked. "Finished? *You?*" Her voice quivered. "But . . . why?"

But he never got to reply, for the tall blond baroness on his left said something clever, everyone was obliged to laugh, and the conversation lightened and swept off in another direction. The moment of his sharing any chilling, secretive knowledge was past, her opportunity to learn it robbed by a clever comment.

There would be no more chances to get champagne-loosened answers, times to share dinners or private chats together. For the very next morning, they got seriously down to work.

Senda was a natural student who could soak up a plethora of subjects all at once and, most remarkably, seemingly at will. She surprised even herself, although at first being a student was a real struggle. In the Pale, little had been expected of her, so she had never had the opportunity to prove herself in the classroom; no woman had. She had been born and bred for housework and raising children, and the learning had been left to those rare male scholars such as her husband, Solomon. Had it not been for Schmarya's teaching her and her own studying, learning would not have come as easily.

Her parlor had become the scene of an accelerated-course university, with so many teachers and tutors coming and going that one would inevitably be arriving just as another would yet be preparing to leave. Within a week, there were so many demands made upon her, and so much traffic through her new home, that she often came to wish she had never been "discovered" and would just be left alone in peace and quiet and privacy.

Countess Florinsky had been right, Senda came to realize after the first few days of living in the apartment without help. She couldn't clean, cook, take care of Tamara, *and* study, all at the same time. There simply was no time to juggle. But she couldn't hand over her daughter to just any nanny or nurse, either. She had to find someone who loved children, who was eminently capable and, most important, someone whom Tamara liked. After interviewing six women, none of whom suited both Senda and Tamara, it was Countess Florinsky who came up with a solution.

"What about the nurse at the Danilov palace?" she asked. "The one who took care of Tamara during your fitting."

Senda looked pensive. Of course, she thought. The young nurse with the German accent and cornflower-blue eyes.

What was her name? Ingrid? No, Inge. *Inge*. She was a possibility she hadn't thought of, although she was rather young.

Sensing Senda's hesitancy, the Countess suggested, "Why don't you hire her for a trial period, my dear? If she works out, fine. If not, you can always look for another nurse."

Senda had to hand it to her friend. The suggestion made sense. "But can we lure her from the palace?" Senda wondered.

"Of course we can, my dear," the Countess told her definitely. "I will see to it immediately."

It was arranged and Inge Meier with her crown of flaxen braids and cornflower-blue eyes, moved into the small spare bedroom next to the nursery.

To Senda's surprise, she felt herself relaxing immediately. From the start, Inge was a jewel who made her life easier. And best of all, Inge adored Tamara, and Tamara adored her in return. It was a mutual admiration such as Senda had never hoped for. There was nothing Inge wouldn't do, and she wore many hats around the house: she was nanny, cook, and lady's maid all rolled into one. She never needed to be told what to do, and always took the initiative without asking questions. Mornings, she would get up before anyone else was awake and make breakfast; when Senda's tutors began arriving, Inge and Tamara would disappear, shopping or laundering. While Senda was at the theater, the house was cleaned as though by magical elves. Senda couldn't believe her luck in having obtained Inge's services, and thus began a friendship that would never disappoint, never fail.

All in all, Senda often considered, with the exception of Schmarya's ever-lengthening absence, St. Petersburg had been wonderful to her. She was beginning a career, she lived in a lovely apartment, she had a countess for her best friend, and a nurse for Tamara who was becoming less a servant and more and more a devoted member of the family.

Except for Schmarya, what else could she possibly ask for?

But there was no time to think about him now, for the lessons to groom her for stardom continued in earnest.

Each day turned into a grueling blur of lessons, a contest of wills between Senda and her tutors. Mademoiselle Clayette for French, Madame Rubenova for elocution, Monsieur Vesier for singing, and from six until nine o'clock at night, another French tutor, Mademoiselle de Rémy-Marceau, took over combined duties as cook, maid, and language instructor.

There's so much to learn, Senda realized soberly. I'll never get it all right.

Even over dinner with Mademoiselle Rémy-Marceau, Senda was obliged to speak French. At times, never being allowed to speak Russian in her own house was infuriating.

With frustration, she wondered how it could be that Tamara, whom Inge was amusing in the nursery during the highly vocal language lessons, was learning French through the walls faster than she was next to her instructors.

"What color upstages all other costumes onstage?"

"White."

"Where is stage right as I am sitting now?"

Pointing: *"There."*

"Which note is this?"

"C flat."

"Qu'est-ce que c'est?"

"Une fourchette."

The little free time she had, she spent with Tamara, stealing a half-hour here, getting up an hour earlier there, so they could share some part of the day.

But harried though those weeks were, it was at night, lying on her pillow in a state of absolute exhaustion, with only the throbbing of her heartbeat to keep her company, that she realized how truly lonely she was.

Schmarya had still not contacted her by March.

It would soon be nearly two months since she had seen him last. But her days were too grueling, and sleep so precious, she spent little time lying awake.

Then on the night of the nineteenth of March, Olga Botkina became ill, and Senda, as her understudy, took over her role at the Théâtre Français for the remainder of the St. Petersburg season.

Overnight, she was adulated by critics and audiences alike. It was the greatest event of her life.

And the most memorable, it would turn out, for on the night of her greatest triumph onstage, she had to share the headlines with Schmarya.

At precisely the same moment that Senda took her last curtain call, ten sticks of dynamite exploded across the Neva at the base of the Troitekoi Bridge.

The resulting explosion killed no one and the bridge survived the blast, but Count Kokovtsov's spies had seen to it that the secret police waited in ambush. They killed every anarchist but Schmarya, and as it turned out, his dead friends had been lucky.

*   *   *

The Prince was impatient. It was not patently obvious, but Count Kokovtsov had learned to recognize the symptoms: the irregular tic in his cheekbones, the shortened attention span, the set frown on his face. Finally, the intensity of the impatience took a blatant, uncharacteristic turn: Vaslav Danilov moved to the windows overlooking the drive and parted the curtains. A reedy sigh escaped his lips.

"She will soon be here," the Count assured his cousin confidently. He was sitting comfortably in an armchair sipping his tea from a delicate Sèvres cup.

"I am beginning to wonder," the Prince said slowly. He turned away from the window and took a seat. "She is not like the others."

"Unpredictable though she may be, you should bear in mind that she is nevertheless a woman. And women tend to follow their hearts. Their emotions."

"Perhaps she did not see the newspapers?"

"That is highly unlikely. After all, yesterday was her debut performance at the Théâtre Français. Since she is an actress, and actresses seize upon the critics' every word, she is sure to have scoured the reviews. Actresses are like moths drawn to the flame of publicity."

"Perhaps she cares more for her craft than what is written about her."

"Nevertheless, there is no way she can miss the headlines. They scream at you from every kiosk and shop. Under ordinary circumstances, the item might have been buried. Unrest, bombings, and assassination attempts have become so commonplace that it is beneficial for us to bury such items to keep the general public from getting ideas. Luckily, we can influence the major newspapers in this town, so it was easy to splash her brother-in-law's name across the headlines."

"Still, why should she come to me?"

"Really, Vaslav." Count Kokovtsov laughed softly. "Since I have seen to it that she will get no answers at the prison, she has no choice. You are the only person in a position to help her. She will turn to you."

At that moment there was a soft knock at the door. Both men turned to face the majordomo. "Excuse me, your Highness, but something . . . well, highly irregular has occurred. A young woman has come to call, without an appointment or even a calling card. She said you would see her."

"Indeed. It would not be Madame Bora, by any chance?" The majordomo looked surprised. "Yes, your Highness."

"In that case, send her up," the Prince said. He turned to

his cousin, who could barely mask his triumph. "I will see you later, Mordka. I want to be alone with her."

The count nodded lugubriously. "Of course." He put down his cup and saucer, rose to his feet, and left the room.

Several minutes later, Senda was shown into the study by the majordomo. Hearing her arrive, the Prince rose and advanced toward her. "Madame Bora," he said, feigning surprise. "What a pleasure that you should visit!"

"Your Highness," Senda murmured in a lackluster voice, her fingers twisting the thin silver ring on one hand in agitation.

"Please, have a seat." He waved toward the armchair Count Kokovtsov had vacated only minutes before and waited until she was seated before he sat in the facing chair. "May I offer you something? Tea, perhaps?"

She shook her head. "No," she said hoarsely, "thank you."

He studied her dull, downcast eyes and pale, pinched features. It was unusual of her to look anything less than radiant, and the compassion he felt for her was genuine. Such a pity, he thought, that this luminous creature should look so miserable. And misery it was. The serene spirit and vivacity natural to her were subdued, so that there was a quiet resignation in her eyes, red-rimmed and hollow now, and a slack droopiness to her usually defined, firm full lips. Creases which had never lined her flawless face lined it now, more than hinting at a tragic futility and inner turmoil, and the refractions of light in her jewellike eyes had bleared, causing the emeralds to become dull pinpoints of opaque glass. She looked vulnerable as only the most defeated can look vulnerable, and there was a kind of wild desperation and pent-up helplessness underlying it all. She had the look of a woman at the end of her rope.

He moved his chair closer. "You do not look well," he said gravely.

She turned to him sharply, her body tensed, as if preparing for a high-pitched battle, but she sighed and seemed to crumple within herself. "No, I suppose I don't." She met his gaze directly. "Something . . . terrible has happened."

"But I heard you had a great success last night. All St. Petersburg is talking."

"Are they?" She sighed again, twisting the ring some more. She had all but forgotten her triumph the previous night.

"Would you like to tell me what is wrong?"

She nodded, tucking her chin into her chest. "I know it is forward of me to have come."

"Ah, but you are always welcome here. I thought I made that quite plain."

"But I have no right to come and beg favors of you."

"On the contrary," he said expansively, lighting a cigarette and exhaling a plume of smoke. "You don't strike me as the type of woman who begs. You ask, perhaps, but beg? No, I don't believe so. You have much too much pride for that." He paused and added cunningly, "Nor do I believe you would ask for a favor without returning it in kind. You are the type of person who always pays her debts."

She smiled bleakly and turned her face up to his. "If I had elsewhere to go, your Highness—"

He shook his head. "Vaslav," he interrupted softly. "In private you need not address me formally. You must call me Vaslav."

She inclined her head, frightened by his easy familiarity, but not showing it. Far more frightening things preyed on her mind.

"Now, what is it that I can do for you, Senda?" he asked softly.

"Your power and influence . . ." she began in a labored voice, then stopped. "I'm afraid not even they can help me."

"That remains to be seen." He smiled encouragingly. "It may sound egotistical of me, but I like to think that I wield quite a lot of both."

She cleared her throat and swallowed. "It concerns my brother-in-law, Schmarya. Perhaps you have seen today's newspapers?"

He shook his head. "Not yet," he said. Which, he reflected, was the truth.

"Then you cannot know that he has been imprisoned."

He stared at her. "I see," he said at last, sitting back and looking thoughtful. He rubbed his chin with his thumb and forefinger. "And the charges?"

Her voice was a stiff, hollow whisper. "Treason."

"What!" He cringed. "Good Lord. Tell me what happened."

Senda quickly related what she knew.

"I will see what I can do," he said slowly. "But it will be very difficult, even for me. Larceny . . . rape, if a member of the nobility was not the victim . . . murder, even, are one thing. But treason! Surely you must know that the automatic penalty for treason is death?"

Senda moaned, her face going from pale to chalky white. "Please!" She reached for his sleeve and dug her fingers into his arm. "Help him, I beg of you!" She shook his arm desperately.

He continued to stare at her silently.

"You have to understand," she babbled quickly. "Schmarya is misguided. There were others. He wasn't alone. And he never, *never* meant to hurt anyone!"

"Did he?"

She stared. "I really don't know." She shut her eyes against the ugly thought, sighed hopelessly again, and slumped, once more collapsing within herself. "Then you think it is hopeless," she murmured in a monotone.

"I don't want to get your hopes up, but nothing is ever entirely hopeless. I have arranged for pardons before."

"Then you *will* help!" she said eagerly.

He raised a hand to silence her. "Please hear me out. As a rule, pardons are expensive, but not impossible."

"I will repay you," she blurted. "I don't care what it costs, or if it takes the rest of my life!"

"Yes, yes," he said gently. "But we are talking about *treason*. You must remember, the political situation being what it is today . . . well, needless to say, it's an uncomfortable situation under even the best of circumstances. And the last few months . . . well, the powers that be are going to scream for his blood."

"But . . . but you are one of those powers, a-aren't you?" she stuttered.

"An astute observation." He allowed himself the slightest smile. "But I am merely *one* of them. One of *many*. Others are involved in this. They will try to make an example of him. They have to, you understand, because otherwise they are condoning an act of subversion. If he is let go, then the enemies of the Czar will think they, too, can get off. The result would be . . . chaos."

She buried her face in her hands. "If I could only see him, speak to him!" she moaned. "I've visited the prison, but they won't let me in."

He nodded slowly. "Arranging a visit should be a rather simple thing. But a pardon?"

"Then you can arrange a visit?" Her voice was tiny.

"I will see what I can do."

She let out a long, deep breath, her eyes holding his gaze. "You won't regret it," she promised huskily. Then she swiftly lowered her eyes. "And I will show my gratitude," she whispered. "As you said before, I pay my debts."

He hid the smile of triumph. "We shall discuss that later. Now let me see what I can arrange. If I am successful, I will send an envoy and a carriage to pick you up at your house and take you to the prison."

She nodded and rose to her feet, her eyes glistening moistly. For a moment she hesitated, then bent down over him and brushed his cheek with her tragic lips. Her warm, sweet breath lingered on his face, so delicious and overpowering he thought he would moan aloud.

But he received the kiss impassively, hiding his emotions behind his usual stoic mask. The kiss was an unspoken pact, a handshake, a contract. She would honor it. Therefore she would be his . . . she *was* his now. She had come to him for help, understanding that it would not be freely given. That she would have to give something in return. And if one could not call it love, freely and willingly offered, then it was a reasonable facsimile, at least, and that would be enough.

Then, stifling a convulsive cry, she was gone, her swift, receding footsteps echoing her haste.

For a long time he sat there, sweetly drowsy. The room seemed chillier now that she was gone. He couldn't entirely fathom her effect on him. None of his other mistresses had affected him quite like her. It was as if she warmed the very air around her with her presence.

And now she was his.

His.

Unconsciously he lifted his hand and touched the spot where she had kissed his cheek.

The dreaded Okhrana, the Russian secret police, like its predecessors before it—and its descendants to come—thrived on its infamous reputation of omnipotence and horror. Okhrana three short whispered syllables long on effect, enough to strike terror in the hearts of all who heard them. For it was the Okhrana which came stealthily in the night and snatched suspected enemies of the state from their beds, never to be heard from again. It was the Okhrana which had on all too many occasions arrested the wrong man, dumping him back on his doorstep so beaten that he had lost his reason. Specific evidence of crimes was unnecessary: suspicion, surveillance, even mere unfounded gossip was all that was needed to have the merchants of death materialize. And the very word "Okhrana" had become yet another synonym for "oppression," for the sins and crimes of the Czarist regime. Always the word was whispered, and only after people looked suspiciously over their shoulders to make certain no one was eavesdropping. It was as if mentioning it too loud would somehow give it more credence, could possibly even summon the dreaded secret police by mere association with its spoken name.

It was to one of the bleak Okhrana prisons that the Prince's envoy took Senda to visit Schmarya.

Outside the fortress, the muffled sounds of traffic and occasional furtive voices passed quickly by, as though everyone knew of the dark doings inside the dank stone walls and wanted to put as much distance between the fortress and himself as swiftly as humanly possible. There were rumors that even birds were afraid to roost on its roofs and crenellated battlements.

Inside the fortress, it was even darker, damper, and chillier than the outside walls promised. Metal-caged bare bulbs cast grotesque shadows on moist, sweating walls of cells, halls, and torture chambers. The place was evil incarnate, as though it was a living, breathing monster, and the misery of its short-lived, transient population was scarred everywhere—dried rust splashed on floors and walls from shed blood, agonizingly deep scratches on stone from fingernails gone mad. Constant sounds of terror hung in the air. Ghosts of whispers and sighs. Shrill soprano screams. Hollow clanging ringing out and reverberating from around corners. All pierced by the bloodcurdling shrieks of agony, the cracks of whips and bludgeons, the reports of guns.

Senda was certain that if she had to stay here for more than a few minutes she would surely go mad. It was impossible to think of Schmarya being held captive here. The image of him running free kept springing into her mind. He had always loved the outdoors, the fresh air, the great vast bowl of the skies. He would not take easily to confinement. Nor to keeping his tongue. There was too much of the freedom-loving rebel in him. Surely he had already antagonized his captors. Possibly had even taunted them. *Dared* them.

The guard who led her to Schmarya's cell had "Okhrana" written all over him, as had the hard-eyed administrator, the other guards, the doctors. No telltale uniforms for them, though the expressions etched into their faces—blank faces set with the terribly cold, unfocused eyes of automatons—were a uniform of sorts, and their quietly ruthless authority their chevrons and ribbons.

Down, down he led her on rough-cut, winding stone stairs into the bowels of the fortress. She had to walk with extreme caution. The steps were slippery and had been worn concave over the centuries. Claustrophobia moved in on her, squeezing her, trapping her, making it difficult to breathe. Somewhere further below, water dripped steadily on stone, ringing out with bell-like clarity. Rats screeched and shot past her feet, and the further the stairs coiled underground, the lower the temperature dropped. The intermingling stenches of feces, urine, and vomit were sickening, and she wondered why the guards didn't bother to wash down the cells. Perhaps it didn't bother them anymore; possibly they had grown immune to it. Or was it just an added torture for the prisoners?

The stairs, green and slimy above, had turned to slick, smelly sheets of brown ice. Something wet dripped down on her forehead. She glanced up and shuddered. The vaulted stone ceiling above was covered with stalactites of fecal ice. She wiped her forehead furiously with her sleeve.

Finally she and the guard reached the end of the labyrinth of vaulted mazes. The guard stopped at the last thick iron door. Heavy sliding bolts were riveted into the iron. Senda noticed that this particular cell did not have a pass-through window.

"This is it," the guard said, speaking for the first time.

She watched wordlessly as he selected a large key from a ring and unlocked the door, then slid the bolts out of the wall. Slowly he pushed the door inward. The creak from unoiled hinges and the scraping of metal on stone shrieked with unearthly eeriness, the sounds of ghosts and things ghastly.

"I have to lock you in," the guard said. "I'll be back to get you in ten minutes."

Her jaw tightened. "That's all the time I'm allowed?"

"I think you'll find even ten minutes is too long in there." He grinned, showing long, clavier-key teeth yellowed from tobacco. "We call this cell 'Paradise,' on account of it's the worst of 'em all. Nobody's ever been locked in there and come out alive."

She spun her face toward him, her eyes blazing cold hatred. "Well, *I* know two people who will!" Refusing to show her fear, she pushed past him into the small unlit stone-lined chamber. Like a narrow chimney it soared ten meters up to the ceiling. She didn't think she had ever seen anything so oppressive as this cell. She would never have considered putting a rabid animal in here, let alone a human being.

And the stench! It caused the bile to rise in her throat. Then her heels slipped in something mushy, and she fought to retain her balance. Feces. Were there no sanitary facilities in any of the cells?

Behind her, the iron door screeched shut, and the bolt was slammed back in place. She was locked in. The cell was dark, with only the shaft of thin light slashing down from the single bulb high above. "S-Schmarya?" she whispered tentatively, her eyes slowly adjusting to the darkness. "Schmarya?"

There was a sound at her feet and she looked down. The rat was the size of a huge cat. She let out a piercing scream and pressed herself flat against the cell door. The iron felt cold as ice.

Then she heard the moan. It came from her left. Slowly she turned toward it and sucked in her breath.

There had to be some mistake! she told herself. The man curled in a fetal position in the corner was not Schmarya. He could not be. Schmarya was tall and blond and stalwart. Not at all like this filthy, broken, disheveled shell of a man cowering in the corner.

Trembling, she stepped closer and stared down at the blanket-draped man with an expression of growing horror. Then she blinked and gulped. Blood rushed to her temples. The room reeled and she had to clutch the wall to steady herself.

It *was* Schmarya.

Disregarding the filthy frozen floor, she dropped to her knees beside him and, cupping his face in her hands, gently turned him to face her. His eyes looked faraway, withdrawn, and glazed over in unseeing pain. "N-no more h-hurt," he mumbled thickly through swollen lips.

Somewhere deep inside her, a fire kindled and began to roar. He didn't recognize her! What had they done to cause this! What kind of monsters were in charge of this place?

She tried to smooth back his filthy, blood-matted hair with reassuring fingers, and leaned closer to his face. This was not the Schmarya she knew and loved. Instead of the familiar, youthfully healthy face of the man she had loved, the face which stared uncomprehendingly back at her was that of an aged man, lifeless and swollen and beaten. His usually clean-shaven cheeks bristled with the stubble of a beard, and his jutting, proud cleft chin had somehow receded in pain and misery.

She squeezed her eyes shut against the horror. "Schmarya, Schmarya," she whispered as she wept, "what have they done to you?"

But he only continued to stare at her blankly.

Recovering herself, she dried her eyes. Bending low over him, she embraced him ever so lightly, just enough to comfort him, let him know she cared, but not enough to cause him pain. She wrinkled her nose at the sickening, offensively putrid odor emanating from his body.

"I'll get you cleaned up as best I can," she began chattering in a low voice, as much to keep her own tortured mind occupied as to soothe him if he could hear. She swiftly lifted her skirt, and without hesitating, tore at her petticoat, shredding off a large piece of it, and deftly began dabbing at his face with it. She tried to smile bravely. "And I've started working on your release. I'll see if I can bring some food and blankets in the meantime, maybe even get you transferred to . . ."

She lifted the thin, moth-eaten tatters serving as his blanket to fold it double, and then she let it slip suddenly through her fingers. "God!" she screamed, squeezing her eyes shut against what she thought she had just glimpsed. "God, don't let it be true!" And then she took a deep, foul breath of air and began gabbling to herself in a frenzy. "No, no, it isn't possible. It's a trick of the lighting. Yes, that's all it is. It's so dark in here, it's no wonder I didn't see right."

Shaking, she knelt by his side, unable to look again and double-check to see if her eyes had somehow tricked her Then, after a long moment, she gathered up her courage, forcing herself to lift the blanket with infinite care from his leg again to investigate the wound more closely. But even as she sat back on her legs and forced herself to shoot a swift anguished look at his left leg, she wanted to scream, and scream, and never stop screaming. She knew then that what she was seeing was no trick, no hallucination. It was a very real nightmare come to haunt the waking hours.

Her mind screamed in protest. His foot! His left foot was gone!

For all that remained of Schmarya's left leg was his thigh, knee, and a small portion of his calf that ended in a stump wrapped in dreadfully filthy rags. From there emanated the festering sweet smell of decay.

She thought of how he had always walked, so proudly, so swiftly, each footstep a stride. She recalled that terrible afternoon of the pogrom, when he had raced to the village, trying to warn everyone of the impending slaughter. He had always treasured his freedom and his health so, and now fate had conspired to deprive him of both. If he did not die, he was surely badly crippled for life.

I have to help him, she thought slowly, regaining her wits. It's up to me to see that he doesn't die.

Carefully she began unwrapping the wounded leg, holding her breath as she released a horrible miasma of decay. She quickly turned her head away and vomited. Maggots crawled in the wound. The flesh and bone were not neatly severed and cauterized. The wound was green and black, and even to her untrained eye, definitely gangrenous. Whoever had wrapped the tourniquet around his leg would have done him a greater favor by letting him bleed to death.

Tears flowed silently from her eyes. Schmarya was barely conscious, barely alive. With trembling fingers she lovingly smoothed his head and murmured soft words of comfort. Sweat stood out on his forehead in bold relief, his temperature raging from the infection, although he could surely freeze to death in this cell. As it was, he wouldn't have long to live. Suddenly she caught her breath. He was no longer deliriously moaning, but completely silent.

Then with immense relief she heard his wheezing breath and saw the faint rise and fall of his chest. He hadn't died yet, at least. He had gone back into shock.

Her eyes now totally accustomed to the darkness, she glanced around in desperate search of anything with which to make him more comfortable, but the cell was barren. There wasn't a stick of wood, an extra rag, a lumpy pallet. The food bowl on the floor had been overturned, its contents in all likelihood devoured by the rats. The water in the tin pitcher had long since frozen into a block of unyielding ice.

Nothing, she thought in disgusted despair. There was nothing with which to even cover him other than that thin rag of a blanket. On impulse, she slipped out of her coat and spread it over him. The smelly, icy air instantly hit her full force, chilling her to the bone, but he needed the warmth it provided far more than she.

What he must have, she knew, was immediate medical attention. And that was something she was helpless to provide.

She felt frustrated, useless.

It was then that she heard the soft skittering sound beside her. Without moving her body, she ever so slightly turned her head. The audacious rat which had confronted her upon entering had crept up beside her. With horror, she saw that it had begun gnawing through the tourniquet of Schmarya's ruined leg.

It was eating him!

A shiver ran through her and for a moment she froze. Then she screamed as she threw herself at the rat. The rodent eluded her and snapped its jaw at her, backing up a few steps, watching intently, its eyes glittering.

Senda drew a deep, shuddering breath. Where was that damned guard? How long had she been in this godforsaken freezing and festering hellhole anyway? She had to leave this instant, and get Vaslav Danilov to arrange for having

162

Schmarya immediately moved to a hospital. Rage and worry alchemized into action. She flung herself up and on flying feet attacked the iron door, beating on it until her clenched fists ran bloody.

Where was that guard?

Why wasn't he waiting outside for her signal?

Then she remembered. I specifically told him that I wanted more than ten minutes with Schmarya, she thought miserably. Now each extra minute he's giving me has become Schmarya's enemy, precious wasted minutes during which his life is running out.

At last she heard distant footsteps. She pounded on the door with renewed fury. When the guard finally got the door open, she pushed past him and raced up the stairs, oblivious of the precarious ice and the cold assaulting her now that she no longer had her warm coat. Schmarya's impending death gave her impetus, terror somehow gave her strength.

The following days were sheer torture. Even after the Prince miraculously arranged for Schmarya's transfer to a hospital, it was only the beginning of Senda's sleepless, nerve-racking vigil. Only by spending every waking hour near Schmarya could she keep her sanity intact and self-recriminations at bay.

She realized that she was laying the blame for what had happened to him at her own doorstep, but she felt she deserved to blame herself. If I had done as he wanted, she rationalized, and joined him in producing socially significant plays, then I could have watched over him more closely. Seen to it that he didn't get involved with the wrong people and come to any harm. He would have his leg. Tamara would have a father.

Here she was now, a physical and emotional wreck, camping out in the hospital's chilly waiting room. Schmarya's leg had been amputated far above the gangrene, halfway up his thigh. She was missing her lessons, her rehearsals and performances. But of what consequence were those?

Schmarya would never walk like a man again.

Senda jumped up from the waiting-room bench as the nurse approached. "How is he?" she asked anxiously.

"Why don't you go see for yourself? You may visit him now." The nurse's voice was cold and professional, but her gray eyes crinkled warmly. "Five minutes, not a second more."

Senda was unable to contain the flood of excitement.

"Thank you!" she blurted so fervently that the nurse scowled, said "*Ssssh!*" sharply, and placed a warning finger on her lips.

But nothing could dampen Senda's rising spirits. She had the sudden devilish urge to laugh and sing. As she rushed to the ward, it seemed her feet never touched the floor.

Schmarya was out of danger! He would make it!

Miracles did indeed happen.

When she got to the ward, she suppressed her excitement, opened the door slowly, and peered inside. Her heart sank when she didn't see him immediately. A sea of enameled iron beds, each squeezed as close to the nightstand of the next one as possible, fifty along each wall, one hundred in all, with an icon above each headboard, met her confused gaze. Her eyes scanned the many faces from afar, her ears assaulted by moans, whimpers, and occasional cries. All the beds were filled, and she could almost feel the roiling, invisible cloud of pain which hung over the ward. The patients looked so pathetic, she thought, so helplessly vulnerable, not so much like grown men as like . . . like frightened children.

She shut the door softly behind her, and frowning studiously, moved slowly along the rows of beds, shifting her gaze from left to right, left to right, as she searched for Schmarya's familiar face. She had to step right up to some of the beds in order to make out the features of the men who seemingly lay asleep. Many were awake and greeted her arrival hopefully; then, realizing she had not come to visit them, they would lie back resignedly once again. She would favor them with a smile, a kind word or two, and move quickly on.

And then her heart gave a symphonic surge.

There he was, his head turned sideways on the crisp white pillow, his eyes closed, his mouth slightly open. Sleeping peacefully.

For what seemed like countless minutes she just stood there silently, staring down at him. She felt a warm glow radiating inside her. His skin was sallow from loss of blood, and his face was gaunt and haggard, but she could see he'd been scrubbed antiseptically clean, and his hair shone golden. Someone had even gone to the trouble of combing it.

This was more like it, she thought; this was the Schmarya she loved. Not that broken, filthy, frightened shell of a man she had found at the prison fortress. She quickly dismissed that terrible scene as a nightmare from which they'd both awakened happy, so jubilantly happy that he had rejoined the ranks of the living that she wanted to yell it to the world. He'd lost one leg, she thought. Well, thousands of other men had lost theirs and functioned quite well with wooden prostheses. It was remarkable, the inventions the doctors and engineers had come up with nowadays. All that mattered was that he was *alive*, that the gangrenous rot had been severed from his otherwise healthy body, and that he was recovering from the ordeal of the operation quite nicely. One leg or two, she loved him the same.

Senda was so relieved at seeing him that tears shone in her eyes. Close up, he still looked shockingly bloodless, but she was thrilled beyond belief that he had recovered this much in three days' time. If she knew Schmarya, he'd be up and about as soon as he was fitted with an artificial limb.

She looked around for a chair, spied one on the other side of the room, and tiptoed to get it. When she returned, she stared down at him again. His eyes were still closed and his breathing, quiet but regular, indicated a relaxing, convalescing slumber.

Slowly, without taking her eyes off him, she felt for the chair and lowered herself into it.

Her expression was rapt with tenderness as she watched him sleep. For the time being, he was going nowhere. He belonged to her. And she had never felt happier, more relieved, or fulfilled. She could feel the radiant glow of her love for him strengthening and burning with a pure white intensity, and after what she knew he'd been through, she felt a fierce maternal protectiveness toward him which she had never before known. She saw him in a different light now, as more vulnerable and infinitely more human. As precious as life itself. Now that he was stripped of his forbidding strength and independence, she felt herself more a part of him than ever before.

Her love for him was nearly unbearable.

With a jolt she realized that he had opened his eyes and was staring warily at her.

"Schmarya," she breathed softly, bending forward and kissing him. She moved her hand to take his, but he moved it away, slid it under the sheet. Perplexed at this bizarre behavior, she nevertheless continued smiling and moved the chair closer to the bed. "You look so *much* better," she said warmly, trying to make her voice cheerful.

He grunted something unintelligible.

Undaunted, she quickly continued, "When I found you, you were half-dead. It's a miracle that you're recovering so fast."

He gave an ugly, savage bark of a laugh. "You want to talk about miracles?" he snarled, his voice weak but intense. "Let me tell you about a miracle, something the Okhrana does to Jews."

"Please, Schmarya," she begged, fighting back the tears but feeling them sliding down her face nonetheless. From the beds all around came the rustling of linen, the eavesdropping stares and quick turning of heads. She could feel the piercing scrutiny surrounding her, and she wished Schmarya would lower his voice. "Say what you want," she said in a low voice, "but for heaven's sake, does everyone here have to be party to it?"

"Well, dammit . . . I'll show you! Then *you* tell *me* whether I should keep quiet or not!"

Stinging under the rebuke, she bit down on her trembling lip, fighting to hide her private agony from the prying eyes around her.

"Look . . . closely, if you like . . ." His voice rose shrilly in the stillness of the ward.

Flustered, she looked away as he grabbed the corner of the sheet.

"Look, Dammit!"

She turned slowly as he flipped the sheet in the air. It billowed like a soft cloud before settling slowly at his solitary foot. She could see that he wore only a long striped nightshirt. He couldn't wear pajama bottoms because of the thickly bandaged stump. *The thickly bandaged, even shortened stump.* "Oh, God," she moaned silently, "did they really have to cut off so much?"

He watched her closely as he lifted the tail of his nightshirt. "Look!" he hissed.

She looked. And the world exploded in a million fragments. She clapped a hand over her gaping mouth.

His crotch was as heavily bandaged as the stump of his leg, with only his shriveled penis exposed for the necessary ablutions. And as Schmarya and the bed reeled in her vision, a whirling dervish out of control, the rush of his words slammed into her: "They castrated me, the bastards!" he sobbed, tears flowing unchecked down his face. "They cut off my goddamn balls so that I'll never be a man again!"

She held her hands pressed against her mouth, her face white.

He stared at her, his sobs increasing. "Why didn't you leave me there to die?"

She crumpled to her knees, one hand still clamped over her mouth, the other desperately searching under the bed for the chamber pot. Then she closed her eyes and retched. Between the rushes of lumpy bile she heard the nurse come running, comforting her, wiping her mouth, pulling her to her feet.

"Please, Madame Bora," the nurse urged in a whisper. "You'll only upset everybody . . ."

Senda stared back at Schmarya even as she was gently pulled out of the room. A hundred faces were turned toward her, two hundred prying eyes witness to her anguish. Her tears seemed to boil, searing her eyes.

She wanted to burrow away somewhere, into a dark, warm void, a womb where she would be sheltered and untroubled and safe.

But there would be no time for mourning Schmarya's terrible loss. Not tonight, at least.

Whether Schmarya liked it or not, the Prince had saved his life.

And tonight she had to pay the piper.

Like a hidden jewel, the mansion was tucked away behind high stone walls that hid it from prying eyes.

Senda stood at a window, her warm breath making a halo of fog, burning a perfect circle through the thin frost sheathing the windowpane. The night was dark, but she could see a rim of light from the window of the octagonal garden pavilion below, its sloping roof and steeple mounted with smooth drifts of new snow, its fretted white gingerbread eaves hanging like perforated icicles. Suspended incongruously inside the bare, unheated, glassed-in interior were the crystal swags of an elegant chandelier.

"When I was a child, I would have loved that little folly," she murmured wistfully. "All those glass panes, the chandelier, the steeple   like a tiny play castle of one's own."

The Prince stood behind her, so close she could feel his every breath rippling on her bare shoulders. "You like it still," he said softly, "and so do I. Exquisite, isn't it? It brings out the child in us all."

She turned slowly. "I cannot believe there is a child inside you still."

"There is one in us all. Only the games we play are different when we grow up. That, or we forget how to play at all." He paused. "So you like this house?"

She inclined her head. "Very much."

"Good." He smiled. "Then you must move in here, and we will use your apartment for a meeting place. It is a pity to maintain this large house for only occasional lovemaking."

She did not reply and he traced a finger lightly along her profile.

"A beautiful woman," he said, "is like a masterpiece in a museum. She deserves beautiful surroundings to show her off."

Senda did not reply, but walked past him to the *lit bateau*, the enormous mahogany-and-ormolu boat bed draped with heavy blue-and-gold silk hangings. She scooped her champagne glass from the nightstand and sipped.

She knew that it was time. To do what she had come to do. There was no use delaying it further. The sooner it was over with, the better.

"Your daughter," he was saying. "Perhaps the garden folly will please her also?"

She would not allow him to use Tamara as a pawn in this game. It was simply another way to get her to owe him even more. She looked at him over the rim of her glass. "She would, but we like where we live now. Besides, you have done more than enough for us already, Vaslav." She paused. "I cannot repay you for all your kindnesses as it is."

He came to her, stroked her creamy shoulders, then held her at arm's length. "Being with you is repayment enough," he said softly.

She did not reply, and he reached into his jacket pocket.

"I want you to wear this while I make love to you," he said softly.

She looked down at his hand and gasped. He was holding a necklace of tiny bronze freshwater pearls with a huge chalcedony clasp. She moved her surprised gaze up to his eyes.

"Wear them while we make love at least," he urged softly. "It would please me."

For a moment she just stood there; then she turned around and held her head high, exposing her neck. She could feel him draping the pearls around her throat, then clasping them shut.

"Ouch!" she exclaimed. "They're so tight I can scarcely breathe!"

His breath was a whisper against her ear. "Just the way I like it," he said, giving the clasp a slight tug.

The pearls dug into her throat and her hand flew up to tug the necklace forward. She gasped for breath.

"You are very beautiful," he said. "Pearls suit you." Then she felt his hand under her chin, gently turning her around and lifting her face to his. She stared deep into his eyes as his lips descended to hers.

She felt rooted to the carpet, afraid to encourage him, afraid to flee. Her heart was pounding. She had never gone to bed with a man behind Schmarya's back, had never been to bed with any other man. Not even with her lawful husband, his brother. But now I must, she thought. I must please Vaslav. He's used his power for Schmarya to escape the clutches of the Okhrana.

She forced her lips to part, forced her mouth to his, accepting his long soft kiss.

"Senda, how I want you," he breathed softly, his words muffled by her lips.

She closed her eyes against the lull of his voice, letting it lap at the edges of her consciousness.

"I have waited so long for this moment. At last you are mine." He kissed her deeper, more urgently, his mouth clamping down on hers in a fury of possessive passion, his tongue probing hers, tasting her mouth, her smooth pearly teeth.

For a moment she let herself succumb. Then her eyes flew open.

No! something inside her screamed suddenly as he pressed his hips against hers. Even through the restricting fabric of his trousers and multitudinous folds of her silk gown she could feel his swelling hardness pressing against her. The hardness which for Schmarya would be forever futile . . . at least for its biological purpose, she couldn't help thinking.

"I need you so much," he murmured, "so very much . . ."

I don't want to be needed! she wanted to shout. I need to be loved!

His hips continued to grind against hers, and suddenly her heart slowed. A wave of stifling nausea surged through her. It was as if her blood was fired with bile. Her head swirled with a peculiar lightness, much like it had at the hospital after Schmarya had exposed his wounds to her.

I mustn't get sick now, she pleaded with herself, clutching Vaslav's arms for support. Oh, God, if I do that . . .

But he misinterpreted her desperately clawing grasp as a sign of her passion, and he kissed her with renewed fury.

Her ears pounded while her blood surged madly. This is wrong! she wanted to cry out. I can't go through with it! Not after what they've done to Schmarya! I can't go to bed with a man, feel him in me . . . not after Schmarya's suffering. Not after they've made him a eunuch.

She tensed, feeling his hands tugging savagely at the bodice of her gown. Every muscle of her body drew taut, the marrow in her bones chilling. A sudden flash of heat boiled in her stomach, caused beads of sweat to stand out on her forehead. Then she heard the fabric tearing. Her breasts leapt free, the strawberry nipples erect and surrounded by gooseflesh. The night air rippled cool against her bare back.

A terrible voice inside her kept raging: *You whore! Making love to this man after your lover's been castrated! Whore!*

She struggled to twist out of his grasp, but his hands dug deeper into her flesh, made red depressions in her arms that hurt to her very bones. He jerked her closer to him, crushing her to his chest as he buried his tongue deep in her throat.

She made little whining noises, trying to pull away. "Please," she cried, trying to wrench herself out of his grasp, but the word was garbled, smothered by his intense lips. And all the while his fingers roamed, clutching her even more fiercely against the unyielding muscular flesh of his chest.

She could feel her body going faint.

Her lips were free at last, and they felt swollen and puckered. He bowed his head into her elongated neck now, his lips making little sucking noises. Her back arched and a million minuscule tremors crawled up and down her spine, tingled along her arms, danced ghostlike along her legs. Both his hands cupped her breasts, massaging them in circles, and then he massaged downward, rolling the gown to her hips.

It occurred to her that this was her last opportunity to draw back, to call an end to this travesty of lovemaking.

But I need him. Schmarya needs him desperately. When Schmarya is well enough to stand trial . . . Well, it mustn't happen. That's why I'm doing this, Schmarya. For you.

And then, curiously, the nausea she had felt was replaced by a surge of lusty warmth. But she stood there resolutely, trembling, afraid to give in to it. It had been so long since she had slept with a man. She had almost forgotten what it was like to be held. The last time had been with Schmarya, just before he had left.

Vaslav slid a hand down to her groin. She could feel his smooth fingers gliding over her mound, seeking her womanhood.

She sucked in her breath and shivered in sweet agony, powerless to stifle the need rising within her. She could already feel the long-forgotten moistness welling up between her thighs.

Her hands moved, as though of their own volition, slipping inside Vaslav's open shirt, her fingertips crawling on the crisp, curly hairs of his chest, kneading his nipples.

Suddenly his arms blurred, and he tore the gown completely from her body. She let out a sharp cry as the fabric bit into her flesh before sliding to a useless heap at her feet. Effortlessly he ripped at her underwear, shredding it with a few concise tugs. She felt herself beginning to tremble all over, her mouth dry, the moistness between her legs increasing, running blatantly down her thighs. She felt naked, vulnerable, yet strangely excited in a way she could never remember ever having been before.

Without warning, he bent over, scooped her off the floor, and carried her to the bed like some sort of medieval conqueror bringing her to his altar. She felt herself bounce lightly on the mattress as he put her down, and she quickly slid around on the quilted blue-and-gold silk to face him, her breasts brushing against the sleek rich covers, her round, contoured buttocks feeling the slight chill in the air.

She felt herself go weak as he stripped himself to the waist in front of her, staring at her all the while, moistening his lips with the tip of his tongue. She was unable to tear her eyes off his body. His chest was tantalizingly wide and taut, swathed with curly hair, and the muscles, burnished bronze from the dim bedside lamp, seemed molded to his very bones. For so large and strong a man he was surprisingly lithe and slender and agile.

Her heartbeat was now an endless, quickening triphammer. Schmarya had always radiated a strong sexuality, an animal attraction, but suddenly Vaslav Danilov was the most irresistible man she could imagine. It was not only his body, but the power he wielded in everyday life, his self-confidence, his aloofness, his riches, his title.

He stepped casually out of his trousers, the sculptured planes of his face gleaming like bronze, his phallus huge and red and angry. She could only stare openmouthed at it. The size of his organ was fascinatingly shocking, all the more so because of the way he seemed to display it with such indifference, as though it were a casual threat. She could imagine it deep inside her, disappearing into the bush of her coppery hair, causing her insides to bubble and burst with shards of pleasure. Gone now was all memory of her earlier revulsion. Her face glowed lustily.

Totally naked now, he straightened his back and stared at her, and she felt herself drawn into his hypnotic, glittering gaze. She caught her breath. Promises of a thousand pleasures glowed back at her.

Greedily her eyes swept him from head to toe. He was hairy. Besides his mustache and trimmed beard, short black hair swirled dark vortices on his chest and started again below his navel, spreading into a thick hairy scrotum. Shorter, curly hairs traced the curving furrow of his buttocks. He was like Schmarya in that way, although Schmarya was blond and his phallus was very curved. The Prince's, she could see, was ruler-straight, thicker, and came to a blunt end. When he entered her, it would be head-on and deep.

Tentatively she reached out to touch his phallus, but he slapped her hand away. She drew back, looking up at him with an expression of hurt, her eyes wide and frightened.

Without taking his eyes off her, he reached into the nightstand drawer and produced two long white silk scarves.

Her breathing grew quick and shallow as she wondered what they were for.

Wordlessly he took her hands, and before she knew what he was doing, he pressed her wrists together and wound one of the scarves swiftly around them several times in a tight figure eight. His fingers nimbly knotted the ends.

She could only stare at her tied hands in frozen shock. Then she flicked a swift upward glance of apprehension at his face, but what she saw was not comforting. His eyes flashed with a bewilderingly sinister, merciless glint. With another swift motion he looped the second scarf around her bound wrists and jerked her arms back as he secured them to the bedrail. She shook in horror. Now she was completely helpless.

The entire procedure had taken him mere seconds.

The necklace around her throat made breathing difficult. She began struggling furiously to twist her wrists free, but the silk held. It was far too strong to tear.

A thousand fears flashed unbidden through her mind.

What was going on, she wondered, and why had he tied her hands like a captive? What did he have in mind? Maybe he liked to play these sorts of games, but she didn't. And . . . and what if . . . what if this *wasn't* a game? What if he intended to really hurt her?

Well, if he did, it was too late for her to struggle against it.

"Please," she whimpered. "D-don't do this to me. D-don't hurt me."

Her pleading received no reaction from him, which only made everything seem all the more ominous.

"Oh, God." The tears welled up in her eyes. What on earth had she gotten herself into?

Before she could come to grips with the situation, he swung himself up on the bed. She tensed and held her breath.

What was he going to do?

She felt herself growing red with anger, and she waited with bated breath. Waited for an opportunity to somehow wrench herself loose and escape. He squatted over her, straddling her belly with his legs. Her eyes followed his fingers as they slowly reached for her nipples. Then he squeezed the roseate nodules between his fingernails.

She let out a shriek. The pain was razor sharp, agonizing as fire. "You bastard!" she screamed, writhing helplessly. Every nerve in her body screeched with hatred. "You fucking bastard, I'm going to kill you!"

His fingernails pinched again in reply, cutting off her tirade with another wave of red-hot, excruciating pain.

"So I am a bastard, am I?" He grinned down at her.

She was flushed, breathing hard, and confused. "Yes! I mean *no!*" She seemed to slump as the fight went out of her. "Let me go," she whispered wearily. "I'm not enjoying this."

"Ah, but we have just begun."

She shut her eyes and sighed.

"There. That is much better." He nodded, slid further toward her feet, and fingered her groin.

Despite herself, she shivered and moaned as he massaged her vulva with his hands. Then he spread her vagina with the tips of two fingers, closely studying the exposed moist purple clitoris. She moaned again as he suddenly stuck a finger up her anus while simultaneously stroking her moist labia.

"You are getting even wetter," he marveled softly. "That is not so bad, is it?"

She shook her head, her eyes glazed over with an odd look. "Be gentle?" she pleaded in a tiny voice.

He slid himself higher toward her face, straddling her chest with his knees. His huge phallus poked her nose and mouth. She found herself grimacing. Then, with one hand, he grasped her behind the back of the head and savagely thrust his penis toward her mouth.

Involuntarily she clamped her lips shut against it before he could slide it into her mouth.

"Open up," he commanded softly. "I want you to eat me."

She stared up at him, once again shaking her head.

He shifted slightly, making room to reach her nipples. Even as she felt his fingers tightening on them, she realized she must do as she was told. Swiftly she opened her mouth wide. For an instant her fear overwhelmed her; then he shoved himself deep inside her. For one long, terrible moment she felt her throat muscles quivering, and she thought she would choke. Her teeth tightened instinctively against the intrusion, and she heard his sharp yell.

"Bitch!" he hissed. "Don't use your teeth!"

She immediately opened her jaw wider, and he slid partially out again, then thrust back inside, and his penis seemed to come alive within her.

He thrust his hips rhythmically against her face, using her throat mercilessly. She shuddered, half from fear and half from indulging in this forbidden pleasure. Schmarya had buried his face in her mound, licking her, but she had never taken a man in her mouth before.

It seemed to last forever. She lost all sense of where she was, what part of her body he was using. She became a forest of tingling nerves, and everywhere he touched her, she shivered and trembled.

Her initial anger fading, she submitted to him, sucking eagerly, her mouth making soft gurgling noises. As his thrusts quickened, she wondered if she felt violated . . . or ecstatic? Could it be both?

And his penis was doing the impossible, growing thicker, harder, longer, pressing savagely into her mouth and out again.

Finally she could sense the shudders preceding his orgasm. She sucked even harder, but then, at the last moment, just before letting go, he withdrew from her mouth.

She lay there gasping, madly gulping for air. Her lips seemed swollen, her throat raw, her arms tingling sleepily from the constant strain of the silk bonds.

He poised himself, lifting her hips with his hands, and then he started to slide into her. She let out a yelp of surprise. For a moment she could scarcely breathe. He was so huge, so impossibly swollen that she was afraid she could not take him.

But then he was suddenly inside her as far as he could go. The sharp, piercing pain radiated inside her, stabbing throughout her belly.

He pulled back slowly, and the constricted feeling in her groin ebbed away with his movement, like a receding surf. Afraid that he would pull out completely, she clamped her wet insides against him, trying to trap him there through the sheer force of her vaginal muscles.

Slowly, deliberately, he began to thrust half in, and then out again. She shuddered and stared at his purposeful expression. His mouth was open, his face agonized, as though hurting from concentration, and a silvery thread of saliva formed on his lips and dripped down to her breasts.

She scissored her legs tightly around his buttocks, forcing him to enter her more deeply.

In response, he began to pump away at her in earnest.

It was nothing like anything she had ever experienced before. She knew that this mating ritual had nothing to do with love, but it was as intense a lust as lust could get. He was like a man possessed. With his every thrust, she could feel his scrotum bouncing against the cleft of her splayed thighs.

And he seemed indomitable, pumping on forever, relentlessly pounding himself into her, stopping if his passion threatened to burst forth, and then continuing on as it subsided. His skin was sheathed with a veneer of glistening sweat.

She had never known anything like it.

She closed her eyes, giving herself over completely to the warm friction of his manhood, to this pleasure which seemed to have no beginning, no end. She felt like she could go on like this forever. Her entire body was filled with it, and she forgot the cramps in her bound arms, the constriction of the tight necklace. In fact, she began to enjoy her helplessness.

On and on he savagely assaulted her open thighs, jolting her with each inward thrust.

Then suddenly she let out a cry. Stars seemed to burst behind her closed eyelids, pinwheels spun wildly, the sweat dripping down off him seemed to hiss and sizzle and spark on her skin like drops of water falling into hot oil. Wave after wave of numbing, crashing orgasm rolled through her, repeating like a mad symphonic crescendo with no end.

And still he continued.

"Please!" she whimpered. "Please, please, give it to me! Hurt me! Vaslav, *hurt me!*"

Her voice took on the hellish chant of obscenity, each word punctuated by a thrust of his pummeling hips.

"More . . . oh, yes, more, *more*, harder, *harder!*"

And then he let out a savage howl. She opened her eyes and squeezed him tighter into her scissoring legs. His body bucked, jerked, and he thrust so deep into her that she cried out in pain, and then he clung to her as if for dear life and she could feel him spouting inside her.

It was as if a dam had burst, and her own last shuddering orgasm sent her wetness to mingle with his.

This time, she did not refuse his gift. When she left the

house in the early hours of the morning, she wore the pearl necklace home.

And every time she saw him in the weeks that followed, he presented her with another jewel, each more priceless than the last. But they all had one thing in common: they were tightly constricting necklaces or bracelets. Never rings or brooches. Never earrings. Whether diamonds, sapphires, emeralds, or rubies, gold or platinum, they were all, in one way or another, symbols of his power over her. Slave collars and slave bracelets.

And she found herself hungering for even more of his twisted passion.

"And if I don't want to leave?" Schmarya's voice was low. "What happens if I decide I like Russia?"

They were alone in the empty examining room. The doctor who had adjusted Schmarya's new wooden leg had left several minutes earlier.

Senda took a deep breath and forced the words out of her lungs. "In that case, he says he won't be able to help you."

He turned his back on the hospital window. "The Prince this," he grunted irritably, "the Prince that. Suddenly the two of you are as thick as thieves."

She blushed and bit down on her lip. "I'm only trying to help you," she said. "Is there something wrong with that?"

"And him? I suppose *His Highness*," Schmarya said sarcastically, "wants what's best for me too?" He leered at her.

"Why shouldn't he?"

"I'd like to know what he's getting out of being so damned helpful! Doesn't it strike you as suspicious?"

"Suspicious?" she repeated softly, gazing down into her lap. "Why would it?"

He stalked the length of the room, the wooden leg thumping stiffly on the floor. The left leg of his hospital pajamas had been cut off several inches below the crotch in order to facilitate the bulky leather straps and buckles of the prosthesis. The ugly contraption was bare, and Senda winced as she looked at it. Somehow the leather boot which encased the bottom part of the artificial leg made it even worse, somehow obscene. As if it were a travesty of a real leg.

"Stop playing games with me!" Angrily Schmarya kicked out at a chair with his prosthesis and sent it toppling on its back. "You think I've lost my brains along with my leg?"

Senda cringed. It occurred to her that this was no longer the Schmarya she had known and loved. The Schmarya she had given her heart so selflessly to had died three days after the ball, and it seemed as if an even angrier—and more pitiful—man had taken his place.

She wriggled forward on her chair and clasped and unclasped her hands in agitation. "Schmarya, can't you be reasonable?" she urged. "Must you always be so pigheaded? Why . . . *why* are you unwilling to see that this is for the best? All you'll have to do is travel to Finland and wait for me there. It's just a hundred and thirty kilometers across the gulf. I'll follow with Tamara in a few days' time and join you. From there we can go anywhere we want—Europe, England, America, even Palestine! What's so difficult about that?"

He scowled. "All I want to know is, why can't we leave together?"

She shut her eyes and sighed. "Because . . . because it's . . . well, it's *easier* this way."

He gave a bark of a laugh. "In other words, we've got to sneak out of the country separately because His High and Mighty doesn't want us to be together, is that it? Because he wants to come between us. He's hoping to keep you here. That's what you're really trying to tell me, isn't it?"

She bit her lip and hesitated. Vaslav had never put it that way, but she had to admit that it *was* an unspoken tactic on Vaslav's part. What other reason would there be for the gown, the ball invitation, the apartment, and now the house? Why would he have pulled so many strings to get Schmarya transferred from the jail to the hospital? She was realist enough to know that he hadn't done any of these things to satisfy any altruistic urge. He wanted her. It was as simple as that. And he'd had her—several times now. She had two necklaces and a diamond-and-aquamarine bracelet to show for it. Yes, he wanted her. Wanted her all to himself. Yet, when Vaslav had told her that Schmarya must not remain in Russia much longer, his argument had made perfect sense. Altogether too many legal papers had been filed against him. Too many newspaper articles had involved him, had virtually passed sentence on him. If it had merely been an arrest report, that could easily have been mislaid and destroyed. So, too, if it had been the police who had caught him. But the Ohkrana? The secret police? They were virtually a law unto themselves. She knew it had been no easy matter for Vaslav to have Schmarya transferred to the hospital, stolen, as it were, right out from under their fingers. Even here, in the hospital, the Okhrana regularly came to check to make certain he had not escaped.

But *if* Schmarya managed to get to Finland—with Vaslav's

help, of course, since the necessary travel papers had to be in order—then he could travel on from there.

And if he was stubborn enough to stay in Russia? Then he would have to face the music, and it promised to be a far-from-pretty tune: in all likelihood, the melody was certain to be a death song.

She sighed deeply to herself. The ice she was treading was treacherously thin, and if she made one wrong move it would be Schmarya, not her, who would inevitably face disaster. His blood would be on her hands as surely as if she'd killed him herself.

She had to make him see the light. Somehow, she had to cut through his deliberately nasty baiting. There was no time to waste on that.

But his accusation had hit all too close to home. Although she railed against his suspicions—he was totally wrong in assuming she wanted him out of her way—she had to admit he had been right on one count.

She did not dare jeopardize his chances for escape by letting Vaslav know she was planning to flee as well. Under no circumstances must Vaslav suspect that. For if he did, she was certain that he would not be willing to help Schmarya.

"Well!" Schmarya had been watching her silently, and now he stomped toward her with his ungainly gait, his weight on his good leg. He looked down at her. "Is that question so difficult that you've got to *search* for an answer? I would think a simple yes or no would suffice."

She lifted her head to meet his eyes. "It . . . it was never discussed," she said stiffly.

"You make me sick!" he said contemptuously.

She flushed and pressed her lips tightly together.

He began to stomp madly around the room, his wooden leg thumping. "I must admit, it's a fine little plot the two of you have hatched. I'm damned if I stay, and I'm damned if I leave."

"Why is that? I think it's all rather simple."

"Why?" He stopped pacing and stared at her. "Because if I leave first, then you won't have to follow me, will you? You can always stay behind, be detained for any number of convenient excuses."

"That's not true!" she cried heatedly, jumping to her feet. "I *will* follow you." She shook her head in disbelief. "Schmarya, what's happened between us that makes you not want to believe me? I'd go to the ends of the earth with you!"

His lips curled into a grim smile. "Why would you want to do that?"

She held his gaze, her eyes growing moist. "Because I love you," she whispered simply.

He threw back his head and roared with laughter. "That's rich!" he sputtered. "By God, that's really rich!"

She stared at him. "I don't understand what's so funny," she said quietly. "Would you care to share the joke?"

The hysterical laughter died in his throat. "You want to hear a joke, I'll tell you one!" His eyes became narrowed slits and he fumbled with the drawstring of his pajama bottoms, yanking them down. There was only a small bandage taped to his groin now, since his wound was healing, but it emphasized the terrible loss he had sustained. "There," he said hoarsely. "There's your joke."

She laid a hand on his arm. "That's not everything, Schmarya, and you know it," she said softly. "So we can't have another child. We don't *need* another child. Tamara is all we need. She gives enough love to last us several lifetimes. And she needs and loves you. You don't know how terribly she misses you. She asks about you all the time. I wish you'd at least see her. Why make her suffer for something she's far too young and innocent to understand?"

He turned away from her and pulled the trousers back up. "And you?" His voice sounded strangled. "What does this do to *your* needs?"

She shrugged. "What about them?"

He whirled on her. "Tell me that this doesn't make a difference," he said bitterly, gesturing at his groin.

She shook her head. "You know it doesn't," she said quietly. "I love *you*, Schmarya . . . not just a piece of your anatomy. I love everything about you." Her voice broke.

She thought: I must be patient with him. I must show only my love for him, never pity. Then perhaps in time the anguish which racks him so relentlessly will lessen, and the healing process can finally begin.

She knew she was making excuses for him, but didn't he deserve them?

"Schmarya, listen," she said urgently. "What's happened has happened. I know it's unpleasant—"

"*Unpleasant*! That's a slight understatement."

She sighed again and started over, her voice a little stronger. "I know it's dreadful, but much as we'd like to, we can't change what has happened. What we need to do now is to deal with it, to cope with it and try to rebuild our lives and prove we can go on despite everything. Can't you see we have to? For both our sakes, and Tamara's. Schmarya, *please*." The words came out in a rush. "We have to go on living! You must believe me when I say what they did to you hurts more than anything that has ever happened to us." Her vision blurred with tears. "But the way I feel about you?" She shook her head. "It doesn't make a bit of difference. If anything, I love you all the more."

"You pity me," he snapped, turning away. "That's not love. You're feeling sorry for me. You're only humoring me. Patronizing me. You don't really want me. Not anymore."

"But I *do*."

"Then prove it."

"P-prove it?" she stammered.

That crazy light was dancing in his eyes again. "Make love to me." He waggled a finger for her to come closer. "*Now*."

"Schmarya," she begged, beginning to cry, "don't do this to us. I know you've gone through a lot—"

"You were the one who said it doesn't make any difference," he reminded her in a chilly tone. "Now I want you to prove it. You can start by getting undressed."

A sudden cold fright chilled her to her very bones. "You're crazy!" she hissed. Her eyes holding his gaze, she started to back away from him, edging carefully toward the door.

"So you don't really want to do it, do you?" He began to take a step toward her for each of her steps backward. He leaned his head toward her. "This has all just been a lot of talk, hasn't it?"

This can't be happening! she told herself. What's gotten into him?

"Schmarya . . ." Her voice had taken on a warning tone.

Without warning, his hand flashed out and he grabbed a fistful of her hair, jerking her head up and pulling her closer. Her scalp felt as if it were on fire, and she stifled a cry of pain.

He glared at her, his own face inches from hers. "Now let's see how much you love me," he whispered, every word punctuated by a spray of spittle.

Her face suddenly drained of color, and her unblinking eyes were wide with fright. Her heart thundered so loud it was impossible for her to think. Then her trembling fear gave way to icy anger. "Let me go," she demanded.

He burst into high-pitched, maddened laughter and tugged harder on her hair.

She winced, but fought the impulse to flay at his arm. "Schmarya, not like this," she said quietly, gritting her teeth. "It will only destroy what little we have left."

"What's wrong? Do you want to get out of it already?"

She struggled to pull away from him, but he held tight.

Then, still clutching her clump of hair with one hand, he whirled her around, slashed his hand across her back, and tore wildly at the pearl buttons of her dress. They popped from the fabric, raining iridescently down at her feet and scattering over the floor. Then he tugged her dress down to her knees and attacked her petticoat with the same savage fury. When she stood naked, her clothes gathered about her legs, he twisted her around to face him. He fumbled with his drawstring.

Hatred blazed in her narrowed eyes. "Are you through behaving like an animal?" she asked coldly. "I think it's time that I left."

The fight had suddenly gone out of him, his demeanor now that of a pathetic, broken man. She wondered whether he would ever heal from this. He was silent while she slipped into her clothes and put on her coat. When she reached the door, his strangled voice stopped her. "How long will it take to get my papers in order?"

"A few days," she answered stiffly. "Perhaps a week."

He seemed to consider that. "All right," he said finally, nodding.

"Schmarya . . ."

"I think you were right," he said softly, tears streaming down his face. "I should leave as soon as possible."

She stood there, her feet rooted to the spot, her hand frozen on the cold door handle. "Where will you go?"

He shrugged. "Who knows? Palestine, probably."

She nodded, her eyes immeasurably sorrowful, her soul implacably sad. Only after she shut the door of the room behind her did she crumble. Forcing herself to move down the hall, she cried for the loss of her first and only love.

Five days later Senda walked slowly toward the glass-windowed front door of the hospital and looked out. Schmarya was outside, gripping the iron railing as he awkwardly negotiated the front steps, his wooden leg swinging stiffly in an arc with every step he took.

She didn't move. She could only stand motionless, her heart pierced by a stiletto stab of pain as she watched his distorted image through the wavy glass, watched yet another part of her life draw to a close.

At least he'd agreed to flee Russia. At least his life would be spared.

But at what a cost.

She sighed painfully to herself as he was helped into the sleigh that would whisk him to the harbor and the ferry bound for Helsinki, from which he would go on to . . . where? Then the sleigh driver climbed up onto his seat, snapped the reins, and the sleigh jingled off into the steel-gray morning.

Senda glanced down at the envelope in her hand. Schmarya had refused the money she tried to give him to get beyond Helsinki. He had stonily accepted the travel papers, the one-way ticket across the gulf, and the sleigh ride. He wouldn't take anything else.

For nearly an hour after he left, she stood there, unable to move, and then she sank down onto a hard waiting-room bench. She had always believed that their love could survive anything, that they would weave their lives together to infinity and beyond. But this was where their love had finally gone.

Their parting had been like that of total strangers.

The hot Crimean sun shone brilliantly, dappling the emerald waters of the Black Sea below with millions of silver knife points. Senda sat on the breezy terrace wearing a wide-brimmed ivory silk hat which matched the loose-fitting brocaded tunic she wore over a long skirt of chestnut silk. She watched Inge leading Tamara toward the steep steps cut into the rock leading to the tiny private beach below. "Be careful!" Senda called out.

Inge waved, acknowledging the warning. "Are you sure you don't want to come?" she called back.

"No, I have to stay close by." Senda sat back, crossed her arms behind her head, and gazed contentedly out over the balustrade.

The breeze quickened, lifting the soft ends of her hair, curling the hem of her skirt and tunic, raising the brim of her hat.

Paradise, she thought.

Oh, what a perfectly dreamy summer it was turning out to be. She had loved Livadia from the instant she had arrived seven days earlier. Inge had come on ahead two weeks before that with Tamara, and she had looked forward to being reunited with them. Naturally, their being together made the vacation all the sweeter, but even had she been alone, Livadia would have enchanted her. It was a stupendous natural setting, with spectacular craggy cliffs plunging into the warm sea, lavish palaces tucked away among the flower-fragrant hills, and strawberry-sheathed slopes where even a blind man had to do little more than reach down to pluck a handful of the luscious fresh fruit at random.

Now, relaxing in the sun, she knew it had been a good idea to come. The past six months had been torturous, with hardly a moment to herself, and now that she could relax, she realized how much she had needed the break. Too, her ten performances on the way from Moscow—five at Kiev, and then five at Odessa—had been total triumphs. The two theaters had pulled out all the stops for their august guest star, and it warmed her to know that her reputation had preceded her.

She was abruptly brought out of her dreamy recollections by the shrill ringing of the telephone inside the villa. For a moment she turned around and stared at the house, unsure whether to go in and answer it. At any moment, she was expecting Vaslav's swift motor launch to round the little promontory from the Danilov Palace, and then, while it docked at the stone jetty of the neighboring villa, she would have to hurry along the footpath to meet him halfway.

She stood up and glanced down at the sea. The launch was not yet in sight.

The telephone continued its insistent jangling.

She rushed inside to answer the shrill rings. "Hello?"

It was Vaslav. "I've been detained," he said without preamble. "Something has come up. I had better stay here and keep trying to get in touch with the Czar. I've been trying to reach him for some time, but he is on the *Standart*. The Imperial family is taking their annual two-week cruise along the Finnish coast, so it might be hours before I finally get him. Don't wait for me; do whatever you want."

So she would not see him today. Just as well, she thought. She would spend the rest of the day with Tamara. But her curiosity had been aroused. She wondered what had happened. It had to be important for Vaslav to interrupt His Imperial Majesty's vacation.

"It's something serious, isn't it?" she asked, a note of worry creeping into her voice.

"It could very well be," the Prince said cautiously. "The people I have spoken to are shrugging it off, but I am not so sure that's wise. Which is why I have to get in touch with the Czar. Someone has to apprise him of the serious repercussions the incident might have."

"Vaslav, what has happened?" she asked.

He paused, then said quietly, "Archduke Ferdinand."

"The Hapsburg prince?"

"Yes. The heir to the throne . . . or he was."

"What do you mean?"

"He and his wife were assassinated in Sarajevo."

"Oh, no." Senda was startled. The news, despite his calm delivery, caused a chill of dread to ripple along her spine. She had a sudden premonition of chaos and death.

"What . . . what does this mean?" she whispered.

"That is what I have to talk with the Czar about. War is my guess. Everyone else thinks not, and I'm afraid that is the opinion his advisers will try to push on the Czar."

"But you're not so certain."

"No, I'm not."

"I hope to God you're wrong, Vaslav."

"Believe me, so do I. Meanwhile, don't wait for me. I'll call you back in a few hours. But it is safe to say we probably will not meet today."

She slowly replaced the earphone. For a moment she just stood there gazing through the French doors at the sparkling, deceptively peaceful sea. It was June 28, a calm, sunny day all over Europe, but beyond the blue horizon, invisible storm clouds were gathering.

The long summer of 1914 had begun.

Few people in Europe and Russia believed the Archduke's assassination could trigger war.

In Paris, the respected newspaper *Figaro* confidently declared: "Nothing to cause anxiety."

The German Kaiser, Wilhelm II, was shocked by the news and thundered against what he thought was the most heinous of all crimes—regicide. He did not, however, believe it to be a preamble to war.

Neither did King George V of England. With the typical British penchant for understatement, he confided in his diary: "Terrible shock for the dear old Emperor."

Aboard the Russian Imperial yacht *Standart*, another tragedy hit far closer to home, taking precedence over the events in Europe. The day before, news had reached the Empress that Rasputin, the monk, had been stabbed in the stomach, and the doctors' contention was that he could not possibly survive: the slash had exposed his entrails. Empress Alexandra, who had long believed that Rasputin was the sole hope for her hemophiliac son, was frantic with worry. While almost everyone on board the yacht secretly prayed that the mad monk would indeed die, the Empress prayed constantly for his life and received daily cables informing her of Rasputin's condition.

In Livadia on the afternoon of June 30, after Senda and Vaslav both came to orgasm, they lay quietly in bed, catching their breaths. It was two days after the Archduke's assassination. The shutters were closed against the bright afternoon sun, and the bulky furniture lurked like murky purple shadows in the corners of the room. A hornet, trapped behind the open window, buzzed angrily, trying to escape its prison of glass.

Vaslav lit a cigarette and smoked silently beside her, his eyes thoughtful, as though studying the ceiling. Senda reached for her champagne glass on the nightstand and took a sip. She grimaced. It had stood there untouched for the last hour or so, and the fine smooth taste had gone flat. She was just pushing the glass away when Vaslav casually announced, "I will be leaving for St. Petersburg in the morning."

"What!" Senda sat up straight and stared at him, the sheet falling away from her breasts. "Vaslav, we've hardly more than gotten here!"

He looked at her strangely. "Summer holidays are all very well," he said, his voice assuming a brisk, businesslike tone, "but my interests, and especially Russia's welfare, must take priority."

"Of course." She looked at him steadily, not certain what else she should say.

"There is little choice. The way I see it, if the Czar is as blind as those useless ministers of his, then I'll be forced to take it upon myself to try to convince him otherwise."

"Then he's returned to St. Petersburg?" she asked.

He barked a low laugh, a plume of blue smoke escaping his nostrils. "No, our revered 'Father of all the Russias' and his family are still enjoying their cruise." His voice was tinged with an acidity she had never heard him use before. "Apparently the events in Europe aren't of consequence enough to justify his cutting their vacation short."

She was shocked. "But he's the Czar! Surely, as our leader, if it's as serious as you fear—"

"The Czar is weak, obstinate, incompetent, and misinformed," Vaslav interrupted derisively. "And his ministers are useless, puffed-up ostriches."

She stared at him. This was all startling news to her. She was not usually privy to this kind of information, and it was the first time she had ever heard a member of the nobility speaking less than favorably about the ruler. It did little to inspire confidence, and she was becoming quite alarmed.

"So you understand," he said, stubbing out his cigarette in a crystal ashtray, "why we really have no choice but to return to St. Petersburg."

And Senda thought: We. Why do *we* have to return? Why

not just you? What's this got to do with me? If war came, surely it wouldn't touch Livadia.

But deep down inside, she knew that it had everything to do with her. She should have guessed his intentions the moment he had decided to cut the summer short and return to St. Petersburg. Wherever Vaslav went, she was to follow. It had never been put into words, but that was what he expected her to do.

She, Tamara, and Inge were supposed to drop everything and pack.

She had easily adapted to life in the sun-drenched villa by the sea, just as she had quickly grown accustomed to the adoring crowds, the abundance of luxuries, and a way of life few people in the world could sustain. Now the perfect summer was shattered.

She thought savagely: I'm not his toy. I'm not his plaything. He can't order me around like one of his servants.

But she knew he could, and that was what filled her with a sudden burst of anger and self-disgust. In many ways, she had less freedom than his servants.

They returned to St. Petersburg within a day of each other, Vaslav and the Princess on the Danilovs' private train, and Senda, Inge, and Tamara in a first-class compartment on the regular express train.

For the first time since their affair had begun, Senda was truly miserable. She knew she was being selfish, but she couldn't help herself. Didn't he realize that her first responsibility had to be to Tamara? That she had promised her daughter a vacation, sent her to Livadia, and that, because of him, something she could not possibly explain to the young girl, they had been forced to cut the summer short? He was too self-important, altogether too autocratic to think of anyone's needs but his own. He was the same way in bed.

The world revolved around Vaslav Danilov.

It was the nineteenth of July before the Imperial yacht steamed into its home port. Even then, the Czar refused to heed the Prince's warnings. However, the Imperial household had calmed down: the Empress's prayers had been answered, for Rasputin, who she believed was blessed with miraculous healing powers, proved to his countless enemies that this was indeed so. Despite his massive injuries, he rallied and pulled through, and the Empress was convinced he was more sainted than ever.

Ten days later, the Austro-Hungarian artillery sent the

first salvos of shells across the Danube, disregarding the white flags of truce fluttering from the rooftops of Serbia's capital.

The shelling had begun.

And with it, war.

The instant Senda stepped out onto the balcony to join Inge and Tamara, the sweltering heat hit her with the intensity of a blast furnace. Inside, the heavy drawn curtains and the lofty ceilings kept the rooms cool, but outside, the summer sun broiled the city and baked its buildings. It was the afternoon of August 2, and below, the quay along the Neva was wall-to-wall people; she could see that the crowd of tens of thousands was packed even more densely around the Palace Bridge. Everyone waved banners and shouted and cheered. Strangers kissed strangers. People danced little jigs with partners they had never seen before. Vendors, attracted by the crowds, sold iced lemonade and fruit drinks. Excitement was at its most feverish pitch.

Horns blasted and tooted on the Neva. The river swarmed with a flotilla of steamers, yachts, sailboats, rowboats. Anything, it seemed, that could possibly float had been launched, and each craft was dangerously overloaded with spectators and flew at least one Russian Imperial banner.

It was as if there were an impromptu festival and all of St. Petersburg had joined in the celebration.

Suddenly a ripple of excitement swept the crowd; the banners waved and dipped with renewed vigor. Unbidden, a massive tidal wave of cheers rolled through the spectators and echoed up to the hot midsummer sky.

Inge reached down and lifted Tamara high so that she could get an unobstructed view above the balustrade. Senda drew up beside them. "It's the Czar and the Czarina, I think," she said, squinting into the distance.

"See, child?" Inge told Tamara. "There is the father of your country. See how people love him?"

Tamara wiggled in Inge's arms until she faced her mother. "It's exciting, Mama! Is it Easter again? Does it mean we're going to color eggs?"

Senda couldn't help laughing. "No, angel cake, it's not Easter." She tousled the youngster's hair and then her eyes and voice took on an implacable sadness. "It means war, I think."

"It looks a lot more exciting than Easter!" Tamara breathed, bobbing her head. Her eyes were shining.

Now the crowd began to chant as one: "Father! Father! Lead us to victory, Father!"

"I wish we were closer," Tamara said with a frown. "I can't see much. They're so far away."

"If you look closely at the bridge, angel cake," Senda said, pointing, "the woman in white with the big picture hat is the Czarina, and the man in uniform beside her is the Czar. I think those are the four young Grand Duchesses behind them."

In unison, as though commanded by an unseen conductor, the crowd of thousands upon thousands suddenly began to sing the Imperial anthem, its lyrics set to the final rousing crescendo of the *1812 Overture* by Tchaikovsky: *"God save the Czar, Mighty and Powerful, Let him reign for our glory . . ."*

"Ooooh, Mama! It's so pretty! Do you know the words? Can you sing it too?"

As the emotional crowd sang on and wept during the last three stanzas, Senda could only shake her head in disbelief. Her lips were tight and white, and her body was tensed, as though she was confronting some hidden horror.

". . . For the confusion of our enemies," the crowd sang, *"The Orthodox Czar, God save the Czar . . ."*

"God save their souls," Senda murmured, and Inge glanced at her sharply but said nothing.

Senda glanced out over the swelling crowds one last time. It was too much. Praying for death and destruction, calling upon God to help achieve it. It was ridiculous and disheartening. If they wanted to pray for peace, that was one thing. But war? There was no point in watching these fools beg for their own destruction.

She went back inside, but the voices followed her. There was no escaping their thunderous praise for the Czar, and God, and Holy Russia.

Suddenly she began weeping, but not out of any surge of patriotism. She wept for the foolish foibles of silly men.

That night, as the Russian Imperial banner flew alongside the French tricolor and the Union Jack, a violent mob attacked the German embassy in St. Petersburg. Suddenly anything German in Russia was suspect and hated. When she heard the news, Senda sat down with Inge and said quietly, "You're German, Inge. How do you feel about all this?"

Her cornflower-blue eyes lit up. "They are behaving like foolish children!"

Senda nodded. "I quite agree. But . . . if you feel you have to leave and go back to Germany . . ." She left the sentence unfinished.

"Why should I want to do that?" Inge asked in surprise.

Senda shrugged. "You were born in Germany. The Russians are suddenly so rabidly anti-Teutonic. Perhaps you have family or friends . . . I just thought . . ."

"I have no other family and my place is here with you," Inge declared loyally. "I don't care if you're Russian or Swedish or Japanese. Unless, of course . . ." She hesitated and studied her hands. "Unless you mind that I am German."

Senda clasped Inge's hands warmly. "*Me* mind? Goodness no! Inge, why should I? You're . . . well, you're Inge!"

And from that moment on, they were friends for life.

On the thirty-first of August, another tangible sign of Russian loathing for all things German was proven when the capital's name was officially changed from the German, St. Petersburg, to the Slav, Petrograd.

For the next few days Inge was quiet, tight-lipped. When she took Tamara to the park or along the quay, she avoided speaking to anyone, other nannies included, lest someone catch her German accent.

Always keenly aware of other people's sensitivity, Senda shrewdly spoke for Inge when she was with her. And since Inge was suddenly afraid to even go out to do grocery shopping, Senda hired a day maid named Polenka to do such chores; Polenka's husband, Dmitri, became Senda's chauffeur. Vaslav had bought her a new car, but she soon retired it. Gasoline had to be conserved, and although it was easy enough for high-placed people to obtain it, and through Vaslav her supply could have been endless, Senda preferred to travel by horse-drawn coach. She also knew that flaunting such luxuries might be asking for trouble in the long run.

At first, most Russians were convinced the war would have a swift outcome in their favor. How could it be otherwise? they rationalized. Victory shimmered so tantalizingly near that they felt they had but to reach out and pluck it. The Russian Army was, after all, a colossus the likes of which the world had never before seen—the British press went so far as to call it "the Russian steamroller."

And a steamroller it was, albeit an ineffectual, outdated one. During the war, fifteen and a half million men marched on behalf of Holy Russia to fight her enemies. However, the predicted swift victory proved elusive. Except for her sheer numbers of seemingly limitless troops, Russia was not prepared for war.

For every Russian mile of railroad tracks, Germany had ten.

Russian troops had to travel an average of eight hundred miles to the front; German troops traveled no more than two hundred miles. The Russian railroad system was in such shambles that on one occasion a troop train from Russia to the front took twenty-three days to get there.

German factories spewed out weapons and ammunition around the clock. Russia was so short of ammunition that her artillerymen were threatened with courts-martial if they fired more than three rounds per day.

Last but not least, Russia was a behemoth which sprawled across two continents, reaching from the Baltic Sea in the east to the Pacific Ocean at its westernmost border. Its very size and geography made it impossible for the Allies to help. A German blockade of Russian seaports proved swift, effective, and strangling: during the war, Russian imports dropped ninety-five percent, and exports ninety-eight percent. In Great Britain, ports docked 2,200 ships a week, but due to the blockade, Russian ports docked a mere 1,250 ships annually.

To make matters worse, Russian military commanders hated and distrusted one another, and rations were scarce, sometimes nonexistent.

Meanwhile, in Petrograd the rounds of sumptuous balls, glittering nights at the opera, ballet, and theater, and midnight champagne suppers continued as they had while the city had been called St. Petersburg. And Senda Bora danced and dined with the most noble of Petrograd's elite, while conquering role after role on the stage of the hallowed Théâtre Français. Her admirers were legion, and her life of astounding luxury had become taken for granted. She was now in Society with a capital S. And to paraphrase the trite old phrase: Society danced while Russia bled.

But Russia seemed to have an endless supply of fresh blood.

The battles and bloodshed dragged one.

Despite the war, perhaps because of it, Senda's career skyrocketed. Entertainment took people's minds off the seriousness of countless battles won and lost and the terrible loss of human life. For the next three years she basked in the adoring public limelight; virtually overnight, she enjoyed that fickle and most elusive of celebrity status—being thrust to the uppermost of ivory towers and becoming a living, breathing legend.

With her beauty and talent she seduced audiences and critics alike. Each of her performances received more lavish praise than the last, and every time the curtain descended on the final act of one of her plays, a contest between herself and her fans ensued: they were determined she break all records for the number of curtain calls.

During a matinee performance, when her hairdresser had come down ill and stayed home, a long wave of her red hair escaped her hat, and it was deemed a new style and suddenly became all the rage.

When it was learned she had a daughter named Tamara, the newspapers reported that six of every seven newborn girls christened in one week in Petrograd were named Tamara.

Everything Senda said or did was seized upon, dissected, imitated. Madame Lamothe's cash register sang the happiest tune it ever had because Senda's clothes were scrupulously copied. So was her manner of walk and the way she held her head. She even made a short silent film—*Romeo and Juliet*—and thousands flocked to the cinema week after week to see her flickering image captured on the silver screen. Because the sole achievement of a stage actress could be measured only by the duration of a live performance, it was the one accomplishment Senda felt would outlive her; indeed, at the time it was considered a cinematic milestone, since most stage actresses snubbed the screen. Seventy years later, it was still a cult classic.

To her adoring public who flocked to her plays, she was to Russia what Sarah Bernhardt had been to Europe and America—the nation's foremost theatrical star and beauty, a national treasure, the brightest jewel in the glittering Czarist crown.

But her life was too full for public appearances to play more than a minor role. Inge was marvelous with Tamara, but the child needed a mother, and Senda lavished time and love on her daughter—time which was in shorter and shorter supply. For every hour she spent onstage, a hundred hours were spent in rehearsal. When she was not rehearsing or acting or spending evenings with Tamara and Inge or Vaslav, she was studying. The few hours she had left to herself were likely to be Sunday afternoons, and these, as it turned out, became legend.

Countess Florinsky had been right: it was inevitable that Senda should hold a salon. She had never given it a thought or deemed it important, and it started simply, accidentally really, with a few theater friends dropping by; soon, to drop by Madame Senda Bora's was *the* fashionable way to spend Sunday afternoons. Her salon was reputed to be the finest and most interesting not only because her friends were accomplished celebrities but also because she had an unerringly keen instinct for sniffing out newcomers with as-yet-unproven talent. It was circulated that her salon was all the rage due to sheer snob appeal, a rumor invariably heard from those not invited. If Senda's salon was elitist, it was only because she gravitated toward scintillating, brilliant conversationalists, people she could learn from. And her friends were among Russia's most interesting and accomplished artists, composers, musicians, dancers, and writers. Among her circle of friends, most of whom were fated to become famous the world over, she listened and learned, fussed over them and entertained them, and it was said that every man who met her was to fall under her spell.

Senda treasured these Sunday afternoons. Her friends stimulated her mind, forced her to grow creatively, to live and *think* creatively, and they nurtured each other. They were demanding and gifted, accomplished and ambitious, and they were each other's worst, and therefore best, critics. Merely having money, no matter in what staggering amounts, or a title, even on the highest rungs of the Imperial social ladder, was not enough to gain one's entry into the exclusive domain of this artistic circle. What made one welcome was brilliant talent, or at least creative accomplishment and passion about one's work.

But what Senda loved best of all about her salon was that Tamara was never far away. Tamara usually stayed in the nursery while Senda entertained. The child swiftly became an accomplished eavesdropper and mimic, and the people she overheard were the best possible teachers on earth. Senda was gratified that Tamara was picking up an education and hearing debates from masters in their fields—an experience which would have been unlikely for even the wealthiest child to dream about.

One evening at bedtime, when Senda kissed her daughter good night, Tamara had declared staunchly, "Mama, I want to become an actress."

Senda laughed lightly as she tucked the blanket around her daughter. "And if I remember right, angel cake, last week you wanted to be a pianist, and the week before that, a dancer."

"Oh, but actresses have more fun! And they have many

more boyfriends, don't they? You have more boyfriends than anybody, Mama."

Senda looked startled; she'd never categorized her friends in terms of male or female, but it was true, most of her salon *did* comprise men.

"And besides, you're the only actress. And a lot prettier than anybody else."

Senda smiled and kissed Tamara's forehead. "And now you'd better get your beauty sleep, young lady," she advised with mock gruffness, turning off the bedside lamp. "Otherwise you'll never grow up to be a beautiful actress."

As Senda shut the door, she heard Tamara sigh happily and murmur, "I want to be just like you, Mama."

Senda felt a slight shudder quivering through her, the thin strands of hairs at the nape of her neck prickling.

Don't be too much like me, she prayed silently. I've had more than my share of misery. I wouldn't want you to suffer that. I want only what's best for you, a life of peace and happiness.

She felt a sudden rush of guilt. She was trying her best to raise Tamara well, but she was never able to convince herself that she could be a decent model for an impressionable child. Trying to juggle the responsibilities of mother *and* father, she felt she failed at both. She wished she could provide a real family for her daughter, even a surrogate father.

Nearly two years had passed since Schmarya had walked down the hospital steps and out of their lives forever. Not a card or letter had come, not even for Tamara, and Senda didn't know whether he was in Europe or had made it to Palestine. He had left a void in her life, a blankness which nothing could fill. Senda continually felt loneliness gnawing at her, the company that only a man she loved could have relieved. It seemed overwhelmingly ironic at times that among her friends and fans, thousands of men would have been ecstatic at the opportunity of sharing her life.

But the only man she could love had deserted her, never to return.

Not that she was celibate. Far from it. She had Vaslav, and it was true that they harbored a certain fondness for each other, but it was a fondness of the flesh. It was Schmarya she hungered for, and she would have gladly traded every last gem and coin of her newfound wealth and fame to follow him back to poverty if the chance had come.

"Sometimes I have the impression that you are really not here with me," Vaslav once complained.

What made the Sunday afternoons at Senda's so continuously prized was that her salon was founded upon two principles of enormous integrity—honesty and freedom of speech. Everyone was encouraged to speak on any subject close to his or her heart, without fear of the opinions being ridiculed or violated; above all, without fear of outside retribution. By common agreement, no matter how radical or unpopular, no discussion ever went beyond the four walls of Senda's salon.

Thus, it was only natural that as 1916 sped to a close, and the war had been dragging on for nearly two and a half years, it was politics instead of art that was the major subject of conversation among the peace-loving intellectuals that gathered each Sunday.

This was becoming the norm all over Russia.

Again, frightening talk of revolution began creeping back into everyday conversation. Again, violence was becoming widespread. The outbreak of the war had initially united all Russians, regardless of political or social leanings. But the festive days of soldiers marching proudly off to finish the Germans was a dream of the long-gone past. Victory had been an elusive rainbow; harsh reality had set in. Among all strata of society, the war was now being seen as a useless, ceaseless drain on Russia, and in one way or another it had touched upon everyone's life. Its continuance was threatening to tear the nation asunder: the ravenous war machine was devouring lives, food, and the economy. Hunger, which had always been widespread, was now rampant. Starvation had become commonplace. People were freezing to death in their homes and on the streets.

Anger, frustration, and hatred were piling up in dangerous quantities, and the objects of these lethal emotions were invariably the Czar and his Czarina.

The heartfelt cries of *"Batiushka! Batiushka!"*—Father! Father!—had weakened in strength, and were no longer heard by the Czar.

To further complicate matters, there was endless talk of the Czarina and her relationship with the monk Rasputin and her possible pro-German treachery. Even at the highest rungs of the nobility, people assumed the Czarina and the monk were having an affair. It was widely believed that Rasputin, a known drunk and womanizer, was consorting with German spies, and he was murdered in 1916. Others were convinced the Czarina still harbored fierce German loyalties and sentiments, and went so far as to suggest she be tried for treason. Even the simplest acts of kindness on her part, as innocent and humane as sending prayer books to wounded German officers in Russian hospitals, did not escape the ire of her growing ranks of enemies.

It was becoming the national consensus that the Czar was weak and incapable and had to be removed from power. And his Czarina, the lovely German-born Alexandra, called "*Nemska*," the German Woman, was fast becoming the most hated monarch's wife since Marie Antoinette.

Russia was ripe for revolution and Lenin.

It was the beginning of the end.

On Thursday, March 8, the silent, endless breadlines in Petrograd erupted into chaos. All over the city, the hungry and the starving, no longer willing to wait for their pitiful starvation-level rations, violently stormed the bakeries and grabbed whatever goods were in sight. Simultaneously, protesting workers marched from the industrial Vyborg section across the Neva bridges to converge in the center of Petrograd. Another demonstration, nearly all women, marched up and down the Nevsky Prospekt chanting: "Give us our bread! Give us bread!" Peaceful though the march was, mounted Cossacks patrolled the Prospekt through the night in anticipation of violence.

Over a simple dinner of potato pancakes that night, Senda was filled with a growing sense of anxiety, Inge uncharacteristically picked wordlessly at her food, and Tamara, always a sensitive barometer of the moods around her, was curiously subdued and quiet. Matters had gotten to a very bad state indeed, Senda considered, when even her privileged household was feeling the punishing strain of food shortages so severely.

Since the arrival of Polenka and Dmitri, Polenka's duties had been to cook, clean, do laundry, and shop. Except for certain long-lasting staples, Polenka shopped every morning for whatever the day's menus would require, carrying the purchases home in two net shopping bags. Since Senda was a stickler for fresh, nutritious food, and because the pantry was too warm in the winter, perishables were bought on an as-needed basis. These arrangements had worked out perfectly—that is, until this very morning, when Polenka had gone shopping with a clutch purse full of money and had not returned. Finally, when it had been safe to assume that something had happened which made it impossible for her to return with the groceries, Senda and Inge, rummaging through the distressingly bare pantry, found a few staples and little else. There was no meat, fowl, eggs, or fresh vegetables. The potatoes and oil had been transformed into the pitiful pancakes, but there was no applesauce, no sour cream—nothing moist and tasty to perk up the pancakes' greasy tastelessness.

Inge pushed her plate away, saying, "I'm not hungry."

"Me either," Tamara grumbled, letting the heavy sterling fork drop on her plate with a resounding clatter. "Yech! I *hate* potato pancakes! They taste like newspaper."

Senda, equally depressed and uninterested in the rubbery, unappetizing rounds of shredded potatoes, drew on her apparently limitless wellspring of indomitability and good cheer. "I know they're terrible, angel, but they're all we've got today. Tomorrow we'll feast extravagantly and make up for it."

Inge raised her eyebrows and tartly said, "Tomorrow is going to be as bad or worse, mark my words. If you ask me, it's all that Polenka's fault. She probably took the shopping money and ran off with it. I hope at least she and Dmitri are eating well!"

"Inge! We can't make such assumptions," Senda cried sharply. "You know there were riots and demonstrations all day. In all probability, Polenka couldn't get back here."

"Oh no? And what about Dmitri? He's got your horse and carriage, hasn't he? I've checked downstairs in the stable and they're not there. He could have driven her here."

"Maybe they've been injured."

"Maybe they're plain thieves."

"Tomorrow," Senda said wearily, "will be a lot better."

"Tomorrow, I'm afraid," Inge mumbled pessimistically, "is going to be a lot worse."

Unfortunately, Inge was proven right.

The next morning, crowds of even greater magnitude filled the streets. More bakeries and food shops were looted, and the ubiquitous Cossacks, who appeared anywhere at the first sign of trouble, patrolled the streets once again, although this time without their whips. The significance of whipless Cossacks was not lost on the demonstrators—whips were the traditional method of crowd control. The whipless Cossacks, greeted cheerfully by the mobs, also assured them they wouldn't use their guns.

But even the lack of whips and bullets could do little to assuage hunger.

"So now what?" Inge growled unnecessarily. "It's past noon and neither Polenka nor Dmitri has shown up. Not that I miss them, especially that shifty-eyed Dmitri, but we can't wait much longer for them. If we do, we'll starve."

She and Senda were in the kitchen going through the bare pantry shelves and cupboards. "Meissen porcelain and sterling silver are very nice, but we can't eat them. We've got to get hold of some food. The two of us can get along on a lot less, but it's Tamara I'm worried about. She's a growing girl and needs all the nourishment she can get."

"I know, I *know!*" Senda snapped, reaching the end of her strength and patience and finding herself in a morass of irritability, frustration, and growing anger. She turned on her heel, marched briskly out to the foyer, and began pulling on her thick, warm sable coat and matching hat.

"And where do you think *you're* going, all dolled up like the Queen of Sheba?" Inge demanded, arms akimbo.

Senda turned to blink rapidly at Inge from within the starburst of sable framing her oval face. "You know it's cold out. Besides, I always dress like this," she said in surprise. "I'm going out to try to buy some food."

"Not in that outfit, you won't," Inge said grimly. "The way tempers are flaring on the streets, it's best to melt into the crowd. I should think it would be a lot safer for you to wear something old and suitably ratty. Right now, those people out there aren't going to be impressed by displays of wealth. They're liable to rip that coat right off your back."

Senda stared at her, then nodded. Inge was right. In fact, she should have thought of it herself. Silently she slipped off her coat and hat and rummaged through her closets trying to find something plain and inconspicuous. She sighed as she slid aside padded hanger after padded hanger. She'd had no idea that her wardrobe was filled with so many extravagant clothes. Only now, searching for something that would not draw attention from the starving multitudes, did she realize the extent of her beautiful wardrobe. In the end, she settled for her oldest astrakhan cape and one of Inge's plain black woolen scarves. She scowled at herself in the mirror. "I look like an old *babushka*," she said with a tight grimace.

"Better a live old *babushka* than a dead princess," Inge retorted gently.

Senda left, and when she finally returned from shopping, it was three hours later. She was exhausted and her feet ached, but considering the circumstances, she'd scored a triumphant coup. It didn't matter, she told herself, that she'd had to pay ten times what the groceries would normally have cost; at least she'd managed to buy some wilting turnips, limp string beans, a scrawny chicken, six brown eggs carefully wrapped in newspaper, a brittle wedge of moldy cheese, and a box of rice. Still, in light of the fact that most of the food stores had been shut, it was going to be a glorious feast.

"If this is any indication of what's to come," Inge told her grimly through clenched teeth as they put the precious groceries away, "then God help us all."

They would need God's help. The following day, Friday, March 9, the wheels of Petrograd ground to a complete standstill. Almost to the last man and woman, the workers staged a citywide strike. The trains stopped running. The trolleys never left their terminals. There wasn't a single cab in sight. Not one newspaper was printed. Massive crowds, this time carrying the enormous red banners which were to become a familiar sight, marched through the streets chanting, "Down with the *Nemska*! Down with the war!" The two cries echoed from the crowded streets throughout the day.

At last the seriousness of the situation was making itself felt. Even those privileged people at the highest levels of society could no longer ignore the impending doom. Hardly anyone went out that night; at the Maryinsky Theater, Georges Enesco gave a violin recital to an audience of less than fifty. The restaurants were empty.

Senda, due to open in a revival of the ever-popular *La Dame aux Camélias* at the Théâtre Français, prudently decided to stay home behind locked doors. As it turned out, so did the rest of the cast, and the audience.

Throughout Petrograd, the food situation became even more critical. Without transportation, the little there was could not be distributed. If it was, the stores were ransacked before the first customer could purchase anything. The Czar, five hundred miles away and unaware of the extent of the problems plaguing his capital, naively telegraphed his orders— carefully veiled instructions clearly meaning that military troops were to shoot to clear the streets.

As luck would have it, bloodshed was kept to a minimum, thanks to the lack of disciplined troops. The well-trained veterans had long since perished fighting the Germans, and what remained of the better fighters were entrenched on the faraway front. The garrison at Petrograd was filled with raw, inexperienced recruits, many hailing from the working-class suburbs of the city itself. Due to a severe shortage of officers and arms, many had not been trained at all.

Still, on Saturday, March 10, fifty people were killed or wounded on the Nevsky Prospekt after soldiers fired into the crowds. Altogether that day, the death toll rose to two hundred dead civilians throughout Petrograd.

Scores more would have been killed had the soldiers obeyed

orders. One company, urged by its screaming officer to shoot into a crowd, turned on the officer and shot him instead. Another regiment emptied their rifles into the air rather than shoot into a mob.

That night, a telegram was sent to the Czar. THERE IS ANARCHY IN THE CAPITAL, it read.

The Czar promptly responded by sending reinforcements, but by Sunday afternoon, scores of soldiers were starting to mutiny and join the rebels.

By Tuesday, one solitary outpost of czarism remained in the city: fifteen hundred troops loyal to the Czar were holding the Winter Palace. The rebels gave the troops twenty minutes to evacuate or else face bombardment.

The troops fled.

It was a scene out of Dante's *Inferno*.

The majestic, once-well-ordered city was in the midst of a revolutionary hurricane. Mobs rampaged, looted, and pillaged. The rattle of gunfire was heard day and night. Screams rent the air. At the naval base outside Petrograd, sailors slaughtered one officer and buried a second alive beside the corpse of the first. Nothing was sacred, life least of all. Centuries of hunger and oppression were vented in one ghastly spree. Armored cars rumbled through the streets, their tops and sides packed with cheering rebels flying huge red banners. Arson was in many a heart: flaring red sheens lit the night sky as buildings were put to the torch. When the fire department arrived, the firemen were invariably chased away. Killing and burning were a catharsis of sorts. Mobs danced like driven devils around the massive pyres which had once been government buildings and stately homes.

Hearing a volley of nearby shots followed by a cheering roar, Senda stepped to the French window, parted the curtains a hairline crack, and ventured to peer out. She drew in her breath sharply and stood very still. Through the icy glass she could see yet another of the uncountable manifestations of violence. Directly across the frozen river another building was going up in flames. Sparks exploded through billowing smoke, their fiery spores racing skyward in the wind. The dancing orange glow was mirrored on the ice-sheathed river, doubling the terrible sight.

The thunderous cheers that accompanied the burning sounded like the crowd in a sports stadium. It was a long moment before she realized whose home it was.

Why, it's Mathilde Kschessinska's mansion! Senda thought

with growing horror. What could they possibly have against a ballerina? Aren't even artists safe from this madness?

Fleetingly she thought of how often the .prima ballerina had been part of her Sunday salons; how Tamara had idolized her. Indeed, one of Tamara's prize possessions was the paste crown Mathilde had worn in a performance of *Sleeping Beauty*, and it occupied the place of honor among the treasures in Tamara's bookshelves.

And now Mathilde's mansion had been put to the torch.

Senda could only hold her breath and pray that her friend had somehow escaped the mob and found safety.

"Mama? What's going on?" a tiny voice asked from behind her.

Senda let the curtain fall back in place and turned slowly to face her daughter. The sight of the girl tore at her heart. Tamara's eyes were wide with fear, and her cheeks were wet with tear tracks. She was dragging her favorite teddy bear by the arm.

"It's nothing, angel," Senda lied softly, reaching for her daughter's quivering hand. She tried to compose her own tautly frightened features. "Everything is fine."

"But when I looked out my window—"

"I thought I told you to stay away from the windows!" Senda hissed, her voice suddenly as sharp as a newly honed knife. "How often must I tell you! Someone could have seen you and . . . and . . ."

"But I'm frightened, Mama . . . all the noise and the fires . . . I could see the orange light through my curtains." Tamara's voice rose to a terrified squeak.

The initial burst of anger, fueled by worry, seeped out of Senda. "I'm sorry, angel," she whispered. "I didn't mean to take it out on you. Of course you're frightened. We all are."

"You're frightened too?" Tamara looked up at her mother in awe.

Senda forced a smile and pulled her close. "Even mamas get a little frightened every now and then. Of course, it doesn't last very long." She knelt down and pressed Tamara tighter to her breast. "What you have to remember is that everything looks worse than it is. We're safe and we're together. That's all that's important. Together, we are strong, invincible. I want you always to remember that." She pulled away from Tamara and dabbed a large tear from her daughter's soft cheek. "You won't forget that? Ever?"

Tamara shook her head solemnly.

The sudden pounding on the front door froze them and Senda's face went ashen. It sounded like a battering ram.

Her every instinct screamed that they must flee. But there was only that one door.

"Gott im Himmel!" In the kitchen, Inge forgot herself and let out a sudden stream of German.

"I'd better go see who it is," Senda muttered.

"Mama, it's *them!*" Tamara cried shakily. "They've come to burn us!"

"Ssssh!" Senda said more forcefully than she felt. She placed a quieting finger on Tamara's lips. "'Everything is all right, angel, you go to your room and stay there."

"Open up! We know you're in there!" a rough voice called from out in the stairwell.

Senda rose to her feet, pushed Tamara toward her room, and clutching the front of her robe together with one hand, started for the foyer. "I'll get the door!" she called to Inge. Her voice, despite her worst fears, was miraculously untouched by panic. It was as though something deep within her character gave her strength and a shrewd insight. Whatever happened, it was imperative that she remain calm and collected. Under no circumstances must she panic. All three of their lives could be at stake.

When she reached the foyer, she stared dumbly at the door; it was shaking under the repeated impacts of knocks and kicks. She could hear the wooden panels splintering. Another minute and they would have it broken through.

Automatically, as though receiving guests, she turned to the pier glass and ran a hand through her hair, aware of the ludicrousness of the gesture, but unable to stop herself. It was as if any last vestige of normalcy, however ill-timed it might be, was suddenly of paramount importance. If she simply gave in and met them looking haggard, then she would be conceding defeat before the battle even began.

She took a deep breath, squared her shoulders, and opened the door.

It burst inward with a crash, sending her staggering backward. Five heavily armed, unshaven men, led by Dmitri and Polenka, pushed past her into the apartment, four of them leveling their rifles at her. The last man pulled a long red banner behind him. From the mudstains on it, it appeared to have been trampled on repeatedly. Somehow, that revelation gave the scene the air of a farcical comic opera. For a moment Senda thought she would burst out laughing, but the laughter died in her throat before it could emerge.

"How many of you are here?" the leader of the men demanded. For some strange reason, Senda was mesmerized by his round wire-rimmed glasses and the thick, ugly purple scar tissue coursing down his left cheek, from the corner of his eye to the corner of his mouth. Never afterward would she be able to reconstruct his face, but those glasses and that scar would be engraved in her mind forever.

"*How many?*" he barked, his face so near to hers that their noses almost touched.

Senda recoiled, shrinking back against the wall as she stared at him, her eyes blinking against the wave of spittle and alcohol.

Her face was drawn and thin, but her mind was racing. Oddly, she thought she had never been able to think quite so clearly as now. It was as if the simmering violence and the very real danger obliterated everything but the most necessary thoughts and actions.

If he had been drinking, she thought, then the others might very well have been too. And if they were drunk, as well as armed, that made them doubly dangerous. They could all too easily be trigger-happy. She would have to humor them, do as they wanted, but she mustn't jump as soon as they told her to, either. That would only prove her terror. She had to show her strength, however feeble it might be in reality.

She raised her head challengingly, her eyes flashing with an all-consuming anger. "What right do you have to come barging into my home?" she demanded icily, her hands clenched stiffly at her sides.

"What *right*? *You* dare ask me what right *I* have?" The leering man grinned horribly, raised his hand, and it flashed suddenly through the air. She tensed, bracing herself for the impact, but when it came she wasn't ready for it. She spun away from him, crashing into the opposite wall, her skull banging on the doorframe. Her cheek burned, and his handprint stood out whitely.

"I have *every* right! Do you understand?" His face was next to hers again. "Get things straight, *elegant* lady, I have the *people's* right!"

Polenka tugged at his sleeve for attention. "I keep telling you, there's only the three of 'em. This whore, the German woman, and the kid. All women." She spat derisively.

"Mama!" Tamara's plaintive cry pushed through Senda's fog, and she shook her head to clear it. Her ears were ringing, but she had heard enough to know her daughter was close by . . . too close to these animals. Turning to her left, she spied Tamara peering around the corner from the salon, only one huge expressive eye and one small white hand visible. "Did they hurt you, Mama?"

Senda could feel her underlip swelling, and she tasted the coppery blood. She shook her head. "No, angel, Mama isn't hurt. Go to your room and wait." Despite her efforts to stay calm, she could hear her voice rising to a shrill yell: *"And stay there till I fetch you!"*

Out of the corner of her eye she caught sight of Inge, like a protective mother hen, scurrying from the kitchen, sweeping Tamara off her feet, and scooping her off into the nursery. The door slammed shut and a key turned noisily in the lock.

The man laughed. "So *that's* your very own *Nemska*, is it? A skinny bitch."

Senda raised her pale face, her eyes calm. There was a burning protectiveness in her that she had never known existed. "That *Nemska*, as you call her, has more decency in one little finger than all of you so-called men put together. At least she doesn't terrorize women and children!" She tensed, waiting for another slap, but it didn't come. "So now that you're here," she added coldly, "what is it you want?"

"We came to try you and find you guilty on five counts," the man said wearily, as if by rote.

"Indeed. So you're a *judge?*" Senda asked incredulously, laughing almost inaudibly. "You could have fooled me."

"On the first count," he intoned in a judicial monotone, his glasses catching a reflection of light, rendering his expression strangely blank, "harboring a *Nemska*, an enemy of the state and a suspected spy, you are hereby fined ten thousand rubles."

"What!" Senda's mouth popped open.

He ignored her. "On the second count, buying foodstuffs from known racketeers and supporting the black market, you hereby are fined twenty thousand rubles."

Senda turned to stare at Polenka; her former servant's eyes gleamed triumphantly.

"It was *she* who did the shopping," Senda said tightly. "Why don't you ask around, and you will discover that these trumped-up charges should be leveled against her. Not me."

"And on whose orders did I shop, Madame High-and-Mighty?" Polenka sniffed virtuously.

"Did I tell you where to shop?"

"With all the luxuries you needed, where did you think I would come up with them? The greengrocer with bare shelves? The flour mill which hadn't seen a dusting of grain for the last six months?" Polenka's dark eyes flashed passionately. "You should have seen the sugar they consumed here! Like it was going out of style! The cakes! The pastries! The delicacies! Caviar from "

Senda turned to the leader of the group. "You're all mad!" She gave a hollow bark of a laugh. "Who in *hell* do you think you are, marching in here and holding some sort of kangaroo court?"

He drew himself up with self-importance. "I am Comrade Padorin, the elected leader of the neighborhood coalition for the revolutionary committee," he said gravely. "Now, if you will remain silent for a moment, we will get this over with and go about our business."

"By all means," Senda said, feeling suddenly weary. "You are so right. The sooner we get this travesty of justice over with, the better. I, for one, have better things to do with my time."

"I advise the accused to hold her tongue, unless she chooses to be charged with contempt," Comrade Padorin said coldly. "On the third count, promoting decadence in public theaters and thereby propagating foreign imperialist propaganda, you hereby are fined twenty thousand rubles." He peered at Senda over his shiny round glasses to see if she had anything to say in her behalf.

But she stared at him silently, and she could swear a look of disappointment crossed his face.

"On the fourth count, profiting from the misery and oppression of the people, you hereby are—"

"Oh, for God's sake, spare me the rest of this silly gibberish," Senda moaned, throwing her hands into the air in frustration. "If it's money and valuables you've come to steal, then take them and get out."

"As I was saying before you so rudely interrupted me, on the fourth count, profiting from the misery and oppression of the people, you hereby are fined twenty-five thousand rubles."

Senda rolled her eyes.

"On the fifth count, consorting with the criminals who until now have composed the so-called upper classes, you hereby are fined forty thousand rubles."

"I suppose," Senda said dryly, "that you really believe you are carrying out justice?"

"By the power invested in me by our local council, yes."

She took a deep breath. "What are you," she asked, a challenging smile flaring in her eyes, "a law student who failed to pass his bar examination?"

His face went purple with fury. "You *cunt!*" he screamed. His hand flashed as he slapped her again, but this time she stood her ground; only her head whipped sideways. Even while her ears were ringing, she turned slowly and smiled tauntingly at him, holding his gaze as she touched her face gingerly, her fingertips coming away sticky with blood. She had scored a triumph, meager though it was. Despite the pain, she felt better. Perhaps she had been right about him. She had certainly hit a raw nerve.

"I do not take my position lightly," he warned her icily, trembling to contain his anger. "I warn you, Comrade Bora, you had best keep your tongue in check."

"I am not *Comrade* Bora," she said coldly. "I am *Madame* Bora."

"In Russia, all are now equal. There are no longer any class distinctions."

"Oh, really? Then what is your purpose here—simply to terrorize me?"

He struggled to retain the composure which had deserted him. "Are you, Comrade Bora, willing to pay the total fine of one hundred and five thousand rubles as levied against you by the revolutionary committee?"

Senda had to laugh. "As anyone can tell you who has five rifles pointed at him, I'm really in no position to argue."

"A wise decision, I am sure."

"However, I don't keep a fraction of that amount here. And, as you very well know, the banks seem to have declared a holiday."

"She has jewels!" Polenka piped up craftily, her eyes glinting with greed. "Such gorgeous jewels they make your heart ache! You should see them!" She closed her eyes to envision them, her thick peasant fingers involuntarily creeping to her throat. "They rival even the *Nemska*'s. Rubies the size of pigeon eggs. Emeralds set in filigreed—"

"That is quite enough, Comrade Petrova," Padorin admonished Polenka sternly. "There is no need to get carried away."

Polenka's hand dropped and she smiled ingratiatingly. "I wasn't extolling their virtues, Comrade Padorin. On the contrary, I was merely doing my duty by informing you—"

"You low-down, thieving, conniving, snooping, trashy little sneak!" Senda hissed at Polenka. "So *that's* why you were so anxious to work for me. Just to sniff out what valuables I might have."

"I'm not a thief."

"Oh? Then where is the grocery money you absconded with?"

"It has been put to good use," Polenka said quickly, her face reddening. "It has fed hungry stomachs."

"Yours, no doubt, while my daughter's was empty."

Polenka glared at Senda. "What does that spoiled child know about hunger? She's had more than her share of the good life."

Senda turned to Dmitri. "And my horse and carriage? I haven't seen them for quite some days now. You wouldn't happen to know where they've disappeared to, would you?"

Dmitri looked away, but Polenka exclaimed triumphantly: "They have been requisitioned by the revolutionary committee! Everything is now the property of the people!"

"You being the 'people,' I gather?"

"You bitch," Polenka spat.

"Enough!" Padorin bellowed, silencing the argument. He looked at Senda and lowered his voice. "We will accept the jewels in lieu of the levied fines. Where are they?"

"If you want to steal them so badly, why don't you search for them? Maybe you'll discover they're in a bank vault."

"They are not!" Polenka shouted. "She keeps them hidden in the secret bottom drawer of her dresser. I'll get them." She started for Senda's bedroom, but Padorin caught her by the arm.

"Not so fast," Padorin told her, nodding at one of his cronies. "Yevgeni, check out the dresser."

Polenka glowered as Yevgeni went to see about the jewels.

"What's the matter, Polenka?" Senda asked saccharinely. "Don't they trust you? Perhaps they know you'd try to pocket most of them?"

"Shut up!" Polenka snapped. She raised her hand to slap Senda.

Senda, seeing what was coming, had no desire to suffer yet another slap. She ducked, adroitly avoiding the blow, and caught Polenka by the wrist. "My, my, how brave we are," she murmured.

"I told you to shut your fucking mouth!" Polenka screamed, struggling to writhe out of Senda's grasp.

Senda dug her fingers even more firmly into Polenka's wrist. "Your language leaves as much to be desired as your honesty."

"Bitch!" Polenka spat into Senda's face. Senda, momentarily nonplussed, loosened her grip, and Polenka took advantage of it, squirming out of her grasp. She thrashed out at Senda with flailing arms.

Senda stepped backward to avoid the wildly swinging arms, but Polenka, her dark eyes burning, followed her step by stalking step. On impulse, Senda feinted to the right, caught Polenka unawares, and grasped her by the left arm. She twisted it around the woman's back and yanked it upward.

Polenka howled with pain, arched her spine, and reached backward with her right hand, grabbing a fistful of Senda's hair.

Tears suddenly sprang up in Senda's vision. Her scalp burned as if on fire. Gasping from the pain, she let Polenka's arm drop and groped blindly for Polenka's hair, but the serving girl wouldn't let her get close enough. Arm extended, Polenka had her like a puppet by the hair, forcing her to move in whatever direction she jerked.

"Look at Madame High-and-Mighty now!" Polenka crowed smugly, tugging ever harder at the fistful of copper curls. "Look at the rich bitch dance!" Suddenly she let out a scream as Senda grabbed a fistful of her dark hair. "Let me . . . go!" Polenka screamed.

"Now who's the bitch?" Senda asked grimly, tightening her lips.

Polenka stared with wild eyes. "You are! I mean, I . . . I mean . . ." Polenka suddenly went limp as Senda let her slip to the floor. Then Polenka suddenly jumped back to her feet. One foot flashed out and the heavy boot tip caught Senda in the shin.

Senda moaned and stumbled. Lightning bolts of pain shot through her leg and starlike patterns danced kaleidoscopically before her eyes. She shook her head to clear it. The pain was severe, but the adrenaline pumping mightily through her seemed to obliterate all else. A surge of power filled her, blossomed, mushroomed. Without warning, she lunged, tackling Polenka around the waist, and the two madly scrabbling women crashed to the carpet, knocking over a table and a lamp as they rolled over and over. For half a minute, neither of them had the upper hand. Then Polenka suddenly rolled atop Senda, caught her around the throat with her clawlike hands, and began to choke her.

Gasping for air, Senda felt her face glowing with a red-hot heat. She wheezed heavily, but no oxygen could pass her strangled windpipe.

"Should we stop 'em?" she heard one of the men asking another.

"Hell no," replied a second voice, laughing. "Too good a show. Haven't seen anything like it for a long time. Let 'em have a go at it."

A strange light-headedness came over Senda. The voices receded into the distance, sounding ever further away. Her blood seemed to rush noisily through veins and arteries. In a moment, she knew, she would surely pass out for lack of oxygen. If she allowed that, the crazed woman might kill her.

With a massive effort Senda clapped a splayed hand up into Polenka's face and dug her nails deep into the flesh. Grunting, Polenka screwed her face into a grimace, but her clasp of steel held on to the delicate throat. Desperate, Senda lowered her crab grip on Polenka's face. Making a fist, and putting all the force she could muster behind it, she smashed her knuckles up into Polenka's face. There was the unmistakable crunching of bone and cartilage. Polenka's screams rent the air. Her fingers instantly loosened from round Senda's throat. While Senda lay gasping for air, Polenka crawled hysterically on hands and knees, a shrieking, wounded animal heading for the protective lair offered under the belly of the grand piano. She crouched there, her eyes looking in cross-eyed fascination down at her nose. With her fingers, she gingerly moved it back and forth, from one cheek to the other. Her eyes blazed with horror as she screamed: "My nose! You broke my nose, you bitch! You b-broke it!" Suddenly she broke down and began to weep.

A heavy silence hung in the room, punctuated only by Senda's heavy panting and Polenka's quiet weeping. Gaining her strength, Senda grasped a chair, pulled herself unsteadily to her feet, and staggered to the piano. Leaning down, she grabbed Polenka by her collar and slid her roughly around to face the foyer. "Get out of my house before I kick you down the stairs," she muttered thickly, her voice weak and scratchy from the choking.

Polenka stared daggers at her through the wildly swaying curtain of madly disheveled hair. "I'll kill you if it's the last thing I do!" she swore. Her eyes darted wildly about like a madwoman's, and as she pulled herself to her feet she spied the blue-and-white Oriental vase on the piano. Her eyes glittered in frustrated agony. Then she made a swift lunge for it, but before her fingers could encircle the weapon, the porcelain exploded in a roar.

Senda jerked around, staring at Padorin in surprise. Smoke drifted out of his rifle barrel as he lowered the weapon. He was looking at her peculiarly. "You must excuse Comrade Petrova," he apologized stiffly. "She is quite passionate about the cause, and sometimes allows herself to get carried away in her enthusiasm."

"I think somebody had best take her out of my sight before her precious *cause* sees an end to her," Senda advised him grimly. "She is mad."

Dmitri rushed to his wife's side and fell to his knees beside her, tentatively examining her face. He glanced quickly at Senda, who glared back at him without pity. Then, turning his full attention upon Polenka, he pulled her solicitously toward the foyer, consoling her softly.

At that moment Yevgeni came out of the bedroom. His eyes were wide. "Holy Mother of God, look at all this stuff!" He held out a cylindrical tan leather hat box, its round lid yawning wide. Into it he had stuffed all of Senda's jewels. The jumble of rare gems, semiprecious stones, gold, and silver sparkled and gleamed richly.

Padorin let out a low, impressed whistle. Senda's hand instinctively touched her bare throat, and Polenka drew closer to the box, reaching out to touch the jewels with a shaky hand.

Senda slammed the lid shut on her fingers. "It's bad enough that they're being stolen, but I'll be *damned* if I'll let you touch them while they're still under my roof."

Polenka glared venomously at her.

Senda turned to Padorin. "In case you haven't noticed, their value comes to a lot more than a hundred and five thousand rubles," she said. "Each piece alone is worth at least that."

"The Soviet can put it to good use," he said.

Senda took a deep breath and drew her head up. "You have what you came to *steal*. What are you waiting for? If it's my blessing, don't waste your time."

Padorin frowned sternly at her. "We are not stealing, Comrade Bora," he corrected her in a slightly miffed tone. "We are requisitioning your property for the good of the people. I hope you will come to understand that."

"I understand nothing of the sort," she said. Then she pushed past him and went to stand at the open stairwell door, one hand poised on the handle. She still breathed heavily from the exertion of the fight, and her voice was shaky. "Now, would you leave?" she said with quiet dignity.

The men exchanged glances and began to file out, Dmitri protectively hugging Polenka against him, but Padorin stopped and looked levelly at Senda. "Are you so insensitive to the suffering of this country's people that money and jewels mean more to you than food for their stomachs?"

She raised her chin stubbornly. "No, *Comrade* Padorin, I am not. For your information, for the first nineteen years of my life there was not a night that I didn't go to bed hungry. As did the rest of my village."

"Then you, better than most, should understand what a great time this is for Russia."

"I understand what I was taught when we were poor."

"And what is that?"

"That there is no excuse—none whatsoever—that gives us the right to steal, to plunder," she said softly, closing the door on him.

Emotionally and physically depleted, she slumped against the door. Once again her fingers felt her bare throat. It felt naked, as if something were missing. And of course there was. She had no more jewels.

It was not the loss of the jewels she mourned, but what they represented. Her nest egg. Her means of converting easily transportable valuables into immediate cash should she, Inge, and Tamara need to flee.

"Bastards!" Senda screamed suddenly, clenching her fists in futility. "Thieves!" Then she slumped once more and covered her face with her trembling hands. "Now what do we do?" she whispered to herself. "They took everything of value. *Everything.*"

"No, not everything." Inge had come to her quietly.

Slowly Senda lowered her hands. She looked at Inge with a puzzled expression. "What . . . do you mean?"

"I'll show you." Inge gestured for her to wait, marched to her own room at the other end of the apartment, and was gone half a minute. "Remember the yellow diamonds you wanted to have reset?" she asked softly when she returned.

Senda drew a short breath. "The ones you were going to drop off at the jeweler's—" Her voice trailed off and she stared at Inge.

"And the jewelry shop was closed because of the troubles. *Ja.*" Inge nodded and then smiled. Raising her clenched hands, she held them out. Slowly she let her fingers uncurl. Nestled in the palm of each hand was a scintillating jewel—a brooch with a garnet center and yellow diamond petals in the shape of a sunflower, and a matching ring.

Taking a deep breath, Senda reached out shakily to touch them, to reassure herself that they were no mirage, no mere hallucination.

The diamonds felt cold . . . and very real.

"Inge . . . how did you . . ."

"They were in my good purse, and with all that has happened, it slipped my mind to return them to your jewelry box. Until now, I'd forgotten all about them."

Senda closed her eyes and said a silent prayer of thanks. The brooch and the ring weren't much—especially not compared to the jewels she'd had. But they *were* more than nothing. Enough to tide them through an emergency.

"Inge," she said softly with admiration, "you just might well have saved our lives."

The situation in Petrograd kept deteriorating. The crowds taking to the streets became ever larger and more violent. Bloodshed increased. Soon, Senda realized that unless she, Inge, and Tamara fled the city—and left the country—they might never live to see things return to normal.

"If we stay and something happens to Tamara, I'll never forgive myself," she told Inge.

"Nor will I forgive myself," Inge replied.

They exchanged long looks. No words were necessary.

They both knew they needed Vaslav Danilov's help—if he had any influence left.

"Oh, what's the use!" Senda asked herself with weary frustration. She stared accusingly at the earphone in her hand. Despite her disgust, she carefully replaced the earphone on its hook. She had been tempted to drop the useless instrument and kick it across the room, enjoying a perverse pleasure in seeing it shatter, just as she had been tempted to leave the porcelain shards of the Oriental vase scattered about the salon. While sweeping them up, she had wondered why she was doing it, but now she understood the reasoning behind her curious actions. Habit and order. Even if it was not safe to stay here any longer, by leaving the mess behind she would be as bad as the animals who had caused it. Now, more than ever, she felt it was important to go through the ordinary, civilized motions of everyday life. To keep her sanity in a world gone insane.

Behind her she heard Inge and Tamara coming out of the nursery. She turned around. Inge carried a small brown valise in each hand, and she and Tamara were already bundled up; their shawls hung loosely from around their necks, waiting to be tied once they got downstairs.

"Did you get through?" Inge asked anxiously.

"No," Senda replied tightly with a shake of her head. "There's still no telephone service."

"I shouldn't wonder, the state things are in. The world's falling apart around us." Inge paused, adding wistfully: "It makes you appreciate the way things were, doesn't it? I wonder if they'll ever be the same again."

"I wouldn't count on it," Senda said regretfully.

Inge set the two valises on the floor. "I only packed the minimum of necessary clothes, like you said."

Senda looked at the valises. "Good. But . . . the luggage

looks a little too new, don't you think?" She glanced at Inge.

"That's because I take care of my things," Inge said.

"I know, but the idea of leaving the Vuitton behind and using your luggage is so we won't draw unnecessary attention to ourselves. I think it would help if it looked . . . well, a bit scruffier."

Inge looked to see if Senda was joking. She made a painful face. "Once we're outside, I'll drag it along the pavement to scuff it up and dirty it a bit."

Senda nodded. "That should do it, I would think."

"Mind you, it goes against my grain."

Senda smiled. "Mine too, Inge, but sometimes we've got to adapt to the changes around us in order to blend in and survive."

"It hurts, though," Inge said, "having to ruin the little we'll have left. I can't imagine leaving all that expensive luggage of yours behind. And the good clothes. But most of all . . . mostly, I get sick thinking of the valuables in here . . ." Her voice trailed off thickly as her gaze swept the salon fondly. "You worked so hard for all this!" Inge blurted suddenly, the tears misting her eyes. "And for what, I ask you?"

"I know, and so do you," Senda murmured, though she was beginning to wonder herself. "The last few years have been good ones."

"Yes."

"Even now, it's not as bad as you think. It won't be the first time I've had to start from scratch." Senda gave a low, mirthless laugh. "Wherever we end up, I guarantee you we'll be resettled in no time. I'm becoming quite the professional at it. I'd better get my coat," Senda said. "And then we'd best leave right away. We've dallied long enough. The sooner we get to the Danilov Palace, the better."

Inge followed her out into the foyer. "And what if the Danilovs have already left?" she asked tremulously as she lifted Senda's coat from the polished brass coat tree. "Or what if they can't help us?"

Senda's cheeks twitched involuntarily. "We'll worry about those bridges only if we absolutely have to cross them," she said resolutely, but despite the false note of optimism in her voice, Inge had brought up her one real worry—the most difficult obstacle they might have to face. The Danilovs could very well have already left for parts unknown. And if they had, how could she begin to guess where? Their estates sprawled over every conceivable part of Russia, and they had houses in countless European countries as well. If Vaslav were gone, who would help her then? Where would she get the money they needed for traveling? Who else could possibly help ease their way across the war-torn borders?

She sighed and slipped into the coat Inge held. It wasn't one of the six priceless furs she had become so accustomed to; it was a thick charcoal-gray woolen coat, but she consoled herself that at least the fleece lining would keep her warm. Still, she couldn't help the bitter thought that wormed unbidden into her mind: who would get her hard-earned furs now? Who would swathe themselves in their soft, profligate lushness? Someone who would never appreciate them, no doubt; someone who would let the moths feast on the hand-stitched lining, who would drag the perfectly matched pelts in the dirt, perhaps heedlessly spill things on them.

She turned to the pier glass to inspect her reflection—another vain, everyday action born of habit. Even in the wool coat she looked eminently respectable and elegant—too much so for comfort in these inflammatory times. Tossing her well-styled copper hair with her fingertips so that it appeared an unstyled jumble, she made a mental note that, like the two valises, the coat too could use a little dirtying. It didn't look nearly shabby enough. Simply cut though it was, it was too beautifully tailored.

"Get a pair of scissors," she told Inge.

Inge hurried to get them from the sewing table, and when she returned, Senda turned her back on Inge.

"Quickly undo the seams on the sides and at the back of the waist too," she instructed, stooping over to lift the hem, which reached her finely boned ankles. She hit at the seam threads and tugged with her fingers, ripping a portion ragged while Inge slid the edge of one blade through the carefully hand-stitched seams around the waist. Senda turned to the mirror again. She nodded with satisfaction. The coat looked much less tailored now. At least she wouldn't be presenting a refined, elegant figure to the angry crowds on the prowl.

Her glance lingered, and she shook her head mournfully. It seemed impossible that the last few years could be summed up by the unobtrusive clothes on their backs and the meager contents of Inge's two inexpensive valises. They had no cash save for the household money Inge had kept tucked away even from Polenka's prying eyes.

Wordlessly Inge reached down and picked up her valise. "I wonder what will happen to Russia now." She shook her head. "I can't believe the Czar has abdicated!"

"I suppose he had no choice." Senda shrugged. "I don't

think it matters much anymore. The only thing that can be counted upon is human nature, and humans are greedy on all levels. Polenka proved that. If the 'people,' as they call themselves, take everything away from the aristocracy, then money, valuables, and privileges will still be here." She smiled tightly. "Only shifted from one pocket to another."

"I suppose you're right," Inge said.

On their way out, Senda took a last deep, fond breath of the familiar, lingering scents of furniture polish and baked apples, a last glimpse of the consoling comforts of home. Then she switched off the lights. It was yet another mundane action born of habit. Not, she thought with wry humor as she snapped the door shut, that she'd have to worry about the electric bill. Now that she thought of it, it was amazing that the electricity was still on. Everything else seemed to have ground to a halt.

When they reached the street door, Senda turned to Inge. "This is your last chance," she said tremulously. "If you want to stay, or go somewhere on your own and not be saddled with Tamara and me . . . well, we'll understand." She smiled bravely through a sudden blur of tears. Over the past few years Inge had become such an integral part of their lives that it seemed impossible to live without her. She had become a second mother to Tamara, a sister to Senda.

"I've made my decision," Inge said bluntly. "I thought we'd agreed that wherever you decide to go, I will go too."

"We might have difficult times ahead of us," Senda warned.

"So? You and Tamara are the only family I've got," Inge said simply. "Despite everything, I can't see deserting those I love. We swim together or we sink together. It's as simple as that."

"Thank you, Inge," Senda said huskily. She put her valise down and embraced Inge. For a long moment, neither woman spoke. Finally Senda extricated herself from their embrace. "Now, remember, if we run into any mobs we can't avoid, we'll try to hold hands. It doesn't matter if it means we have to get rid of one of the valises. It's more important that we don't get separated."

Inge looked at her. "We've been over all that already," she said gently with a sad smile. "Now it sounds as if you're the one who's stalling."

Senda smiled bleakly. "If we get separated, we'll meet at the Danilov Palace." She looked down at Tamara. "Are you ready, angel?"

Tamara looked up, her emerald eyes wide, her face particularly vulnerable, peculiarly fragile. She nodded bravely.

Senda set her chin firmly. "Inge?"

Inge fussed with Tamara's collar and scarf, then flipped her own russet shawl around her throat. She took a deep breath. "I'm as ready as I'll ever be."

"Well, here's to luck," Senda murmured, opening the massive, heavy carved door to the sharp blast of the mid-March night.

"Amen," Inge said quietly, and then, instinctively leaning forward against the prevailing wind, they headed along the lamplit quay on foot.

"Quick! Into the bushes!" Senda hissed as they approached the gatehouse of the Danilov Palace. Without a word, Inge drew Tamara into a cluster of scratchy leafless winter shrubbery. Even on foot, their progress had been surprisingly swift and, until now, blessedly uneventful. By taking turns carrying Tamara rather than matching her slower pace, they had crossed the Neva bridge and reached the forbidding palace walls in no time at all.

"What is it?" Inge asked with alarm. "What do you see?"

"Sssh!" Senda hissed, squeezing Inge's wrist to silence her. She pushed a branch aside and peered ahead into the darkness. Two men had come out of the gatehouse. One of them carried a ladder and the other peered cautiously through the filigreed wrought-iron bars before unlocking the gate. Their furtive apprehension nagged at her, and she watched quietly as in the white glow of the ironwork lanterns mounted on the stone piers at either side of the gate, they began to work quickly. First they unfurled long red banners.

A roiling sickness clutched her belly. Red, she thought with an involuntary shudder. Why does that bright, crimson red strike such terror in me? Despite the cold, a faint mist of perspiration sleeked her features.

Finished hanging the banners, the two men began to affix a wooden sign on the gate bars. Close enough to see what they were doing, Senda was too far away to make out the words. But she could see that they, too, were painted in red.

Inge tugged at her sleeve. "Shouldn't we leave?" she whispered sibilantly. "What if they find us here?"

Senda didn't reply. Her squinted gaze was fixed on the men. Suddenly she understood their furtiveness and laughed softly to herself. Her tensed muscles relaxed and the warm rush of relief she felt as she recognized one of the men was good. The tall, thin, praying mantis of a figure was unmistakably Count Kokovtsov.

"Well, I'll be," she marveled, shaking her head in wonder. "Clever. Very clever."

"Ssssh!" Now Inge silenced her.

"We don't have to whisper anymore," Senda said, raising her voice above a whisper but still speaking softly. "I think it's safe to approach now. But stay back with Tamara a little, while I do the talking."

"You're sure?" Inge asked hesitantly.

Senda nodded definitely and branches rustled as she emerged from the bushes. Brushing her woolen coat with her hands, she hurried toward the gate.

Hearing the briskly approaching footsteps, Count Kokovtsov turned slowly to face her. She heard his sharp intake of breath, and in the wash of the lamplight she could see a single eyebrow arch into a poised question mark on his high, domed forehead.

"Count Kokovtsov," she said pleasantly.

"Madame Bora," he said tightly. He was momentarily at a loss; she was the last person he had expected to see. "What . . . what a . . . pleasant surprise."

Senda forced a smile. "The pleasure is mine, Count," she answered in a civil tone, the irony of her own words not lost on her. She looked questioningly at the burly, short-haired man beside him.

"Ivan, my manservant," the Count replied to her questioning look.

She nodded and turned to the sign they had affixed to the gate, reading the crudely painted red letters as she slid her hands into her coat pockets:

NO TRESPASSING!
THIS HOUSE IS THE PROPERTY OF THE
PETROGRAD SOVIET!
PRINCE VASLAV DANILOV AND
PRINCESS IRINA HAVE BEEN REMOVED
TO THE FORTRESS OF ST. PETER
AND ST. PAUL!

The Count watched her with an inscrutable expression, one hand tucked in the small of his back. To either side of them, the long red cotton banners flapped and sighed like sails in the wind. The Count turned to his servant. "That will do, Ivan," he said.

Bowing, his servant picked up the ladder and carried it through the open gate.

The Count turned his full attention to Senda, fixing her with an imperious gaze.

"Monsieur le Comte," she said softly, "I have come to see the Prince."

His eyes were hooded. "Madame Bora," he intoned patiently, "you can undoubtedly read; therefore, the sign should be self-explanatory."

Senda squared her shoulders. She was determined not to let his haughty superiority intimidate her. She gripped his arm. "I must see him!" she whispered urgently.

"As you can see for yourself, madame," he said obliquely, freeing himself from her grasp, "it is impossible for me to assist you. I am truly sorry." He gestured elegantly at the sign. "I suggest you rely on your own, shall we say, somewhat formidable resources. Perhaps you would like to pay him a visit in the fortress?"

"Count Kokovtsov." She smiled chidingly. "What do you take me for? I know it's merely a ruse. The sign, the red banners, the shuttered windows. It's a ploy to divert the revolutionaries who would otherwise ransack the palace and surely imprison you."

He looked surprised. "Why should we want to do such a thing?"

"To buy time in order to escape." She nodded. "Shrewd. Very clever."

"Believe what you will." He turned away in irritation and began to head through the gate.

"I watched while you and Ivan hung the banners and the sign."

He began to shut the gate on her.

Her voice rose. "Don't you dare lock me out! I demand to speak to Vaslav."

"Vaslav, is it now?" He smirked. "My, my, but we *are* familiar."

"I'm going to see him." Her voice took on a knife edge of warning.

"And if you can't?" Kokovtsov's smile was wide but humorless. A death's-head grin, she thought.

She smiled grimly. "In that case, Count Kokovtsov, I shall be forced to camp out here . . . *and* tear down your precious sign and banners."

"You are bluffing."

She raised her chin stubbornly. "Try me." Her eyes flashed challenging fire.

His eyes blazed hatred, his cheeks ticked, but she had to say one thing for him. Somehow he managed to salvage his cold pride and keep his voice under control.

"Very well, Madame Bora." His voice lowered. "You

give me no choice. However, I shall not take the responsibility for having let you in."

"I am willing to take responsibility for my actions."

He swung the gate open. "I see you have brought your daughter and a servant. The three of you will have to wait in the Jasper Vestibule while I inform the Prince that you are here. He is with the Princess. I should think you would not wish to barge in on them."

"Thank you, Count Kokovtsov." She was pleased to see that despite the breakdown of society, etiquette and discretion were practiced here. She turned, motioning for Inge and Tamara to follow, and slipped through the gate. Count Kokovtsov locked the gates behind them. Then they hurried along the curving drive to keep up with his swift stride.

As she walked, Senda glanced around. Nothing seemed to have changed in the three years since she had first set foot here. Except for the shuttered windows, everything looked the same. To either side of her, the specimen trees were bare, skeletal, and in front loomed the massive palace, its signature cluster of five onion domes poised pitch black against the deep purple velvet of the night sky. The palace grounds seemed deceptively peaceful, giving her the feeling that the walls could forever keep the world at bay. Overhead, amid the canopy of winking, incandescent stars, the coral strands of the aurora borealis hovered like brilliant necklaces in midair. For the first time since the start of the revolution, she began to feel a measure of peace and tranquility. The heavy burdens which had weighed her down lifted from her shoulders.

Vaslav will help us, she thought.

Count Kokovtsov closed the door on the Jasper Vestibule and smiled at Ivan, but his lips were humorless. "There. That should keep them out of our hair for a while."

"You are certain they will wait, master?"

"For a half-hour or more, yes." The Count's voice was cold. "The woman is a fool. She believes whatever she is told. Is the car in readiness?"

Ivan bowed his head. "I have filled it with petrol and warmed up the engine, as you instructed."

"Good. We will be leaving at once. Wait for us in the garages . . . *No!*" He poised a finger lightly on his lips, his ruby ring glinting crimson. "On second thought," he said slowly, "hitch up a carriage."

"A carriage!" The burly Cossack looked at him in surprise. "But the car will get us to the train so much faster!"

"It will also draw undue attention to us. Haven't you noticed, Ivan? There *are* no cars on the streets."

Ivan looked at the Count with glowing respect. "I hadn't thought of that, master."

The Count smiled benignly. "That is why I am your master, and you are my servant. In the meantime, I shall go see the Prince and the Princess. Have the carriage waiting. Five minutes." The Count held up a hand, splaying his five fingers. Then he strode off. After a few steps he halted and turned around. "And, Ivan?" he called out.

"Yes, master?"

"Affix one of those infernal red banners to the carriage."

"Yes, master. It is as good as done."

The Count hurried to the Danilovs' suite of apartments in the far wing of the palace. He smiled to himself with satisfaction, congratulating himself on his quick thinking. Despite the initial shock he had felt when that actress had arrived, he had kept his wits about him and gained the upper hand. He hadn't planned to have to deal with her, but matters were under control. He had chosen to have her wait in the Jasper Vestibule for the very reason that it was the public room furthest from the Danilovs' apartments. There would be no danger of her running into Vaslav.

His lips tightened across his teeth. Infernal woman! Who did she think she was? Damned if he was going to help her and that miserable child of hers escape the country. Not if he could help it. And help it he could. So far, everything was going altogether too smoothly to let her put a crimp in his well-laid plans. Even the revolution was playing right into his hands. Once he and the Danilovs reached Geneva . . .

He found the Prince where he had guessed he would be—in the Chinese Room. His cousin was still feeding sheafs of documents into the roaring flames of the fireplace. The Prince looked up. "What is it?"

"Are you soon finished?" Mordka asked silkily. "I thought all the necessary papers had already been transferred to the train."

The Prince fed another batch of documents into the fire, his face flickering in the light of the dancing flames. "They have, but I see no reason why these should be left lying about to make things easier for those criminals."

"I do," Mordka lied smoothly. "We had best get to the train immediately. Is the Princess ready?"

The Prince nodded. "She is in the next room." He studied the folder in his hand.

"Good. We will leave at once." The Count took the

folder out of his cousin's hand and dropped it to the carpet. "You must forget about burning the rest of the papers. They will be burned more efficiently by others."

"What do you mean?" Vaslav stared at his cousin.

"I have just received word that a mob is headed this way. With the intention of burning the palace."

The Prince's face paled, and for a moment he could not speak.

"The train!" the Count urged, grabbing Vaslav's arms and shaking him. "The train is waiting, cousin! Don't you understand? We can't procrastinate any longer! Do you want us to die at the hands of a mob?"

"Of course not. Have you received word from the messenger I had you send to Madame Bora?"

The Count nodded. "She has already left her apartment and is headed for the train," he lied glibly. "She will meet us there. I have arranged that she and the child travel with our personal servants. The Princess need not be compromised in any way."

Satisfied, the Prince drew himself up with dignity. "Then we can go," he said.

"But quietly." The Count held up a cautioning finger. "There is no need to advertise our departure."

Five minutes later, the Count, Ivan, and the Danilovs drove swiftly off into the night, leaving the palace gates yawning open behind them.

As the minutes torturously dragged by, Senda's impatience increased to the verge of panic. Where was Vaslav? Why was he keeping her waiting so long? Couldn't he get away from the Princess for even a few minutes? He'd always found time for her before. Didn't he *want* to see her? Had she overstepped the boundaries of propriety by coming? But these tumultuous times certainly required initiative, didn't they? Dread and irritation rose like bitter bile within her, twisting her stomach, stabbing her heart. He owed it to her to help, dammit. She'd shared her bed with him. He'd kept her.

Damn him to hell!

She glared at the steadily ticking lyre clock on the jasper-sheathed console and froze. Thirty-two minutes had passed since they had been ushered into this room! "Something's wrong," she muttered tightly, tucking her chin into her chest and heading for the door.

"Where are you going?" Inge called out.

"Stay here," Senda said grimly. "I'll be back."

She marched purposefully through the corridors, not beginning to know where to look. She knew only too well how enormous the palace was, how easy it was to get lost in it. Without help, it could take hours to find Vaslav, searching from room to room, wing to wing, top to bottom. There were hundreds of rooms. Counting vestibules, anterooms, stairwells, hallways, and bathrooms, the number could easily swell to the thousands.

It was too daunting a search.

Suddenly she stopped, cocking her head to listen. Then she swiftly continued down the endless corridor. She scowled. How many doors were there in this palace? She'd never had to open so many. And where had the footmen gone? She thought she heard something again, and now, as she was inexorably drawn to the source of the sound, it increased in volume. She tightened her lips in annoyance. Music? she thought in disgust. So many, *many* voices? Singing? It sounded like a party! And in the midst of all the violence and turmoil! It was unthinkable! Unbelievable!

But the fiendish sight which greeted her when she flung open the doors of the Music Chamber was even more incredible. She could only gasp and take a staggering backward step.

A party *was* in progress. A drunken, celebratory bacchanalia of servants who at long last could savor for themselves, however fleetingly, the good life they had spent their lifetimes helping provide their masters. Champagne corks popped and flew across the room; Cristal and Dom Perignon gushed lavishly out of foil-wrapped bottlenecks and spewed, unheeded, onto the priceless parquet floors and Savonnerie rug. In front of a mirror, a cluster of maids preened in finery that obviously belonged to the Princess. In a corner, a footman sang mournfully, strumming the large gilt harp between glassfuls of champagne. Dirty boots and shoes rested on marquetry tables, oblivious of the treasures they marred; behind a sofa a gardener and a maid necked, and a lively parlor maid was stretched out atop the Bösendorfer grand piano on her belly, kicking downward with the tips of her bare toes to produce teeth-gnashing chords. A fat female cook, still in her grease-splattered kitchen whites, was wrapped in a lynx stole, and puffed teary-eyed on a cigar, laughing and coughing intermittently. All the while, the gramophone blared raucous American jazz from its speaker horn.

One of the footmen spied Senda. "Wellllcome!" He laughed drunkenly, throwing her a noisy wet kiss. He swigged from a bottle of Cristal and spat it out, weaving happily around the room. "Join the parrrrty! Pa-arrrty, everybodddddy!"

Senda stared, her face putty-colored, and then she hurried after him. "Wh-where is the Prince?" she managed to stutter.

"Parrrrty! It's a parrrrty!"

Senda clenched her fists and shook them in frustration. With everyone drunk, who was able to tell her where Vaslav was? She gazed around in desperation, her eyes searching for help. Then the maid slid off the piano, nearly fell, and somehow managed to regain her equilibrium. Scooping up two champagne classes, she traipsed carefully toward Senda, walking with that concentrated, overly cautious poise of the inebriated. "Have champagne," she slurred, thrusting a glass at Senda and burping noisily.

"No, thank you," Senda declined politely. "But I'd appreciate it if you could tell me where I might find the Prince."

"Who cares?" The maid's tawny eyes gleamed drunkenly. "There's food, cham . . ." She paused to burp again. ". . . pagne, clothes, and cigars for the taking!" She tossed her head back, drained one glass in a single draft, and tossed it against the wall, where it shattered, showering the floor with crystal shards. "No money, though," she said with a pout. "They took all that. But you can't 'spect everything. Can you?" She leered and giggled.

Drawing the maid aside, Senda lowered her voice confidentially. "You see, I'm supposed to bring the Prince something. I have to get it to him." A lie, but what did lies matter, now?

The maid's face wiggled toward her, the tawny eyes open in perfect twin O's. "In Shwisherland?"

"Switzerland!" The very word made Senda's knees go weak. "But I was told he is *here!*"

"*Was* here. Left. Over half an hour ago. To Ge-ne-*va!* Been drinking ever since!"

"Left? For Geneva?" Shivers of cold dread passed through Senda, chilling her to the very marrow of her bones.

"Left." The maid was nodding emphatically again. "To their train. Overheard 'em. It's been waitin' for 'em."

Senda clutched the maid's arm and shook it. "Do you know *where* the train is?"

The maid shook her head.

"If you know, you must tell me!"

"Ouch! You're hurtin' me!" The maid pouted and stared down at the deep red impressions Senda's fingers were gouging in her forearm.

"I'm sorry," Senda apologized quickly. She withdrew her

hand. "But you see, it's urgent. If I reach the Prince in time . . ." Lies born of desperation were beginning to coast glibly off her tongue, coating the untruths with promises. "He'll give whoever brings it to him five . . . thousand . . . rubles."

Tawny eyes blinked, bulged. "F-five th-thousand?"

Senda heard the sharp intake of breath and nodded. "Five thousand," she repeated shamelessly.

"Vladimir! Vladimir knows!" the maid cried triumphantly. "He took some stuff to the t-train."

"Which one's Vladimir? You must tell me!"

Now it was the maid who clutched Senda's arm. "I gets half!" she slurred, greed glittering like diamonds in her eyes. "Two thousand, five hundred rubles."

"Yes!" Senda promised. "Yes! You get half! And Vladimir gets a thousand!"

Lies, lies, but what did they matter?

"Half!" the maid cried. "Half!"

It was like riding with the devil.

Miraculously, less than six minutes had passed since the maid had last shouted "Half!" Vladimir, drunk but spurred on by the prospect of a thousand rubles, unerringly led them to the very car Ivan had warmed up, pulled on the driving goggles, and let out the clutch of the open-topped Hispano-Suiza touring car. With a roar, the car shot out of the garages, its left fender crashing into the partially open door, tearing it off its hinges. The car swerved as Vladimir steered drunkenly toward the open gates. Then the wheels screeched in protest as he slammed on the brakes to take the turn, skidding brilliantly, as if he had chosen to do exactly that. After one and a half revolutions, the hood nosed in the right direction, and with a screech of tires they were off.

"Careful!" Senda cried from the back seat, pressing Tamara's terrified face into her bosom, while beside her Inge, forgetting herself, let out an indecipherable stream of thick German which closely resembled the Lord's Prayer.

Petrograd flew past in a blur. One second, they were on the near side of the Neva; the next, the car shot over the far side of the bridge.

"This car and no traffic?" Vladimir turned around and grinned at Senda. "We might get to the train yet!"

"Just watch where you're driving!" she shouted back above the roar of the wind. "Don't look at me! Look at the street!"

Laughing wildly, Vladimir floored the gas pedal. Senda let

out a cry. Ahead of them, an angry crowd of protesters blocked an intersection.

"Vlaaaadiiimiiiiir," she yelled, shutting her eyes.

He headed straight for the center of the crowd and leaned on the air horn. The crowd flew apart.

"We'll get there!" he shouted again, swigging from an open bottle of champagne.

Oh, God, let us hope so! Senda prayed, adding an amendment: In one piece, dear Lord. In one piece.

On its shunting, beyond the farthest reaches of the remote Vyborg quarter, the Danilovs' train stood in readiness, enormous white clouds of steam billowing up from the undercarriages of the locomotive, coaches, and boxcars before being shredded to pieces and torn away by the wind. Inside the richly appointed main carriage with its opulent paneling, shaded ormolu wall sconces, and rich jewel-box furnishings, Vaslav Danilov stirred restlessly in an armchair upholstered in crimson brocade. The lace-draped table beside him held a silver samovar, books, bibelots, a cigar humidor, and a large crystal bowl filled with sevruga caviar set in a larger bowl of shaved ice.

The Prince looked at the caviar, then the humidor. He had little appetite for either food or tobacco. Suddenly he got to his feet and crossed to the far window, cupping his hand against the glass to shadow his own mirrored reflection. The night was as dark and still and empty on this side of the train as it was on the other.

He tightened his lips and cracked his knuckles. He was as tense as a wound-up cat.

Princess Irina studiously kept her eyes on the open book in her lap. "Sit down, Vaslav," she said gently, turning a page. "Nervousness on your part will not help her get here any sooner."

He turned to her in surprise. "You knew?" he asked hoarsely. "All along?"

"Whom we've been waiting for? And why?" She marked her place carefully with the thin velvet ribbon she used as a bookmark and looked up at him. "About her, yes. And the others. Everyone knew. Why shouldn't I?"

"But . . . but you never *said* anything."

"I could not blame you," she said calmly, "so why should I have said anything? After all, I am not an especially attractive woman." She glanced down at her arthritically clawed hands and sighed. "These are not the hands of a model lover."

He took the chair opposite hers, lifting his trousers with a pinch of their knifelike creases, and sat forward with his hands dangling between his splayed legs. "I haven't been a model husband to you, have I?"

She looked at him gently, reached out, and touched his arm. "You have given me everything you were able to give," she said softly. "You shared your life with me in every way but one. Is that so bad?"

He grimaced painfully.

"I am not complaining, Vaslav. I only want you to know that I have understood. Just as I understand now why you are nervous that she is not here."

"And you are not jealous?"

She permitted herself a tinkling little laugh. "I am, I must admit. Especially of her. The others . . . well, they did not count much. But she must be very special. She was the first woman you saw monogamously for a period of more than three years." She slipped across to his chair and sat on the brocade arm, stroking his head with her deformed fingers.

"I have let you down," he said stonily. "I thought I was discreet—" His voice broke suddenly.

"And you have been. I have no complaints."

The tears welled in her eyes as she regarded him with a fondly tilted head. She loved him so much, had given herself to him in every way that she could. What fault was it of his that so soon after their marriage the arthritis had set in and systematically destroyed her beauty? True, she still ached to feel his body beside hers, inside her, but how much more could she have asked of him than a steady if passionless love? She herself was disgusted by her hands. How could she expect him to want her to touch him?

"We'll wait for her as long as we can," Irina said unexpectedly. "I wish her no harm. You must believe that."

He took one of her hands and pressed it against his cheek. "I will not see her again," he promised, "but I must help her. I owe her that much."

The Princess nodded. "Yes, you do."

They both looked up as they heard the door at the end of the carriage sliding open and shut. Count Kokovtsov approached them stiffly, his hands at his sides. "We cannot wait much longer," he intoned lugubriously. "The danger increases with every additional minute of delay. This train has been ready to depart for half an hour."

"We will wait twenty minutes longer," the Princess said firmly, cutting off any further argument.

She felt Vaslav's meaningful response in the way he pressed her hand. It was his silent way of thanking her.

She turned to him and smiled at the way he was looking at her so wonderingly, and she waited until the Count was back in the forward carriage before she kissed her husband quickly on the lips.

"Sometimes I wonder why I deserve you," he said softly.

"Because I love you," she replied. "That we cannot share everything does not make my love for you any the less." She gazed into his eyes. "Do you know how often I reminisce about when we first met?"

"It was at the Bal Blanc, and I had a hell of a time getting a dance with you between all those handsome officers in their tight uniforms and that chaperoning sphinx."

"Aunt Xenia!" she whispered, delighted that he remembered.

"Yes, Aunt Xenia. A regular dragon. She never did approve of me."

"Hush. She liked you very much. She just never showed her emotions."

They both smiled, the memory as alive as though it had all happened only yesterday.

Count Kokovtsov's face was devoid of emotion. "Twenty minutes have passed," he murmured.

The Prince nodded calmly. "Tell the engineer to pull out."

Irina reached for her husband's hand and held it. She knew he was feeling as if a part of him was being wrenched loose from his body.

Now there is only me for him to love, she thought. I don't have to share his affections with anyone else. The one mistress he has truly loved is out of his life. I should feel elated.

Why don't I?

The Hispano-Suiza shot past the derelict warehouses and rattled over the expanse of deserted, horizontally laid rails. Each time the tires hit the raised ties or rails, the car jumped and Senda could feel her teeth jarring under the impact. Her face was streaked with tears from the force of the wind. She kept wiping her eyes and craning her neck. Where was that train?

Suddenly she saw it. "There!" she cried. "To the right! It's the train!" She pointed and stood up, clutching the leather-upholstered back of the driver's seat with one hand for support.

Vladimir wrenched the steering wheel and they rode parallel to the rails now, the ties thumping beneath the tires.

"It's starting to move!" Senda screamed as the locomotive's smokestack spewed a shower of sparks skyward. "Drive faster, dammit! Get closer!"

Vladimir took another swig of champagne, wiped his sleeve across his mouth, and drew his lips back across his teeth in a grin. He floored the gas pedal, steering directly toward the train so that the car jumped from one track to the adjacent one, then steering forward again on a parallel course before jumping to the next set of tracks. Still on her feet, Senda clung to the driver's seat for dear life.

"Hurry!" she urged Vladimir. "Hur-*rrrry*!"

The brightly lit windows of the three passenger coaches glowed yellow in the night. The fierce pounding of her heart and the rushing of her blood roared in her ears.

They were racing alongside the train now. The air smelled heavily of smoke, and Inge pressed Tamara's face into her bosom so that the child might be spared the stinging orange showers of sparks. She kept slapping her own face each time she felt the piercing barbs and screamed in German. Beside the car, the slowly moving boxcars which comprised the rear of the train flew past in a blur as the car started overtaking the train. The last of the three passenger coaches behind the coal tender was coming up, the big square windows radiant with light.

Splaying her legs in a precarious stance for balance, Senda began screaming and waving her arms frantically as she saw the back of the Princess's neatly coiffed head sliding into view. Then her heart surged as she caught sight of Vaslav's familiar, unmistakable profile.

"Vaslav!" she yelled. "Stop the train! Vaslav!"

Inge joined in the screaming. Vladimir leaned relentlessly on the air horn, filling the night with its raucous blare. Metal train wheels clicked and roared.

Then a face filled the window, and Count Kokovtsov smiled chillingly down at her, the fingers of one hand curling slowly up and down in a wave.

"What on earth is that infernal racket?" the Princess asked fearfully. She glanced at Mordka, her eyes lined with worry. "Is there trouble?"

"Nothing we need worry about." The Count's lips tightened and he swiftly loosened the tie-back curtains, drawing the velvet draperies across the window. "But I suggest you do not show yourselves. I believe it is a band of revolutionaries."

"Then all is lost!" the Princess exclaimed in horror.

"No," the Count said, shaking his head and talking loudly

in order to drown out the shouts and honks coming from outside. If only the car horn continued to blare, he hoped; it drowned out the voices.

"But if it is the revolutionaries—" the Prince began.

"We are just meters from the canal bridge," Count Kokovtsov explained. "Once we cross it, they will not be able to follow. We will be safe."

The Prince started toward the next window to look out. Mordka swiftly stepped in front of him to bar his path. "It is too dangerous, cousin," he said solicitously. "You have too many responsibilities. We cannot afford for you to come to harm. They might shoot, you know."

"Vaslav, please do sit," the Princess begged. "I do not want you to get hurt!"

The Prince hesitated, and Mordka held his breath.

Reluctantly Vaslav took a seat.

"You *can't* slow down!" Senda screamed. Disregarding any thought of safety, she began pummeling Vladimir's head and shoulders with clenched fists. "Speed up, I tell you! We've got to catch *up*!"

Vladimir grimaced under her glancing blows, unable to shield himself. Without warning, he hit the brakes so hard that they locked. The car swerved, lurched, and finally skidded to a halt so suddenly that Senda nearly toppled over the windshield. She managed to grab it just in time. For a moment no one moved. Then slowly each of them let out a deep breath and began to test their joints.

"Whew! That was close." Vladimir upended the champagne bottle but it was empty. He scowled.

"Why did you stop?" Senda cried, tears of frustration streaming from her eyes. "We were so close, dammit. So close."

"See for yourself," Vladimir said grimly.

She sniffled and looked to her right. The train was picking up speed, steadily click-clacking across an iron-girdered bridge. Then she threw a glance forward and sucked in her breath. There were no more tracks at this end of the railroad yard except for the solitary set of rails crossing the bridge. And small wonder. The car's headlights shone out across black, brackish water. For a moment she could only stare.

They had come to a halt on a jutting embankment, and the hood of the car hovered in midair. Four meters below was water. Another half-meter and they would have plunged into the icy waters of the canal.

It had been a close call.

She gazed after the departing train. Her throat clogged as

she watched the last boxcar disappear across the bridge in a shower of sparks. Then the huffing locomotive sounded fainter, was receding into the stillness of the night.

Slowly Senda sank down into the seat. Her face was ashen. Suddenly she felt the cold, empty numbness of defeat. "What do we do now?" she asked in a strained whisper. "What do we do now?"

She felt Inge reach across and envelop her in her arms. "Now," Inge said simply, "we will just have to get to Geneva on our own somehow. If you taught me one thing," she said, her blue eyes sparkling, "it is never to give up."

Senda looked at her in surprise. "I did?"

"You did." Inge leaned back in her seat, folded her hands in her lap, and burst out laughing as Vladimir put the Hispano-Suiza in reverse. "I wouldn't like to do this again, but I must say, I've never experienced anything quite as exciting as this ride."

Suddenly Senda joined in the laughter. Perhaps it was relief after the close brush with death; whatever it was, it felt good to be alive. Maybe things weren't so bad after all.

"Back across the Neva?" Vladimir called over his shoulder.

"No, to the ferry station," Senda said.

"You're going to Finland? Well, I hope you have papers. The Finns are sticklers for such things."

"Papers?" Senda repeated dully.

"You know, documents. Passports. Things like that."

Senda shook her head. "No, we don't."

"Then you'll find it easier getting papers in Poland. I heard the Polish border is much more relaxed. I'd better take you to the train station."

"But slowly," Senda begged as he shifted gears. "Please drive slowly."

They arrived in Warsaw a little more than two months later. The stop-and-go journey had taken its toll.

Senda took ill. At first she dismissed her coughs and bouts of fever as nothing more than a cold she couldn't throw off. She had always enjoyed the best of health and wasn't too worried. But when the coughs erupted from deep within her lungs, and the fevers persisted, and her thick phlegm was tainted with blood, Inge became alarmed. She insisted that Senda see a doctor.

"No. No doctor," Senda insisted weakly with as much emphasis as she could muster. "We can't afford one." Sick as she was, the incessant worries about money took precedence.

Inge did not argue. If this wasn't an emergency, she didn't

know what was. She put Senda to bed and waited until she was asleep. Then she cut open the lining of Senda's coat, where the yellow diamond sunflowers had been sewn, and went out seeking the best jeweler in town.

So what if she only got a fifth of what the brooch was worth? Now there was enough money to get them through another few months—and to summon a doctor.

Inge knew her priorities, and Senda's health came first.

Dr. Buchsbaum was a short, gnomish man who despite his kindness was one to never mince words. "I'm afraid the prognosis is not very good," he told Senda with a frown. "I'm not quite certain yet, but I think it's safe to assume that you suffer from pulmonary consumption."

"Consumption!" Senda looked at him incredulously.

He nodded gravely and reached out a quieting hand. "I'm afraid so. But given rest, care, and fresh air, it needn't be the end of the world."

Senda shut her eyes, allowing the dread to wash over her. She hadn't been expecting good news, but *this*? For a moment she wanted to laugh hysterically. What irony! Just when they had escaped the revolution unscathed, her health had to deteriorate! More ironically yet, was she doomed to become a real-life *Lady of the Camellias*? And how was she going to care for her daughter . . . and for Inge . . . if she had consumption? What was she going to do for money? For Tamara's future? A few months more, and the ring would have to be sold too.

Long hours after the doctor left, Senda lay in her bed, coughing up blood.

Tamara tugged at her arm and sniffled. "Mama! Are you going to be all right?"

"Of course I am, angel. I'm just a little tired." Senda smiled briefly. "All I need is some rest. Even mamas need their rest sometimes, you know."

After Inge gently shooed Tamara out, Senda lay there, weak and worried.

She needed help, and she knew of only one person who could give it.

Suddenly, it was more important than ever that they reach Geneva . . . and Vaslav. With her own declining health, Tamara's future loomed large and uncertain.

The Danilov estate outside Geneva was rivaled only by the gargantuan palaces they had roamed about in Russia. More moderate in scale and grandeur than their magnificent

Russian homes, Château Gemini was nevertheless the most splendid residence along Lac Léman. Set in a magnificent park of venerable trees and manicured statuary-decorated lawns which sloped gently down to the edge of the lake, it afforded an unrivaled vista of sailboat-studded blue water and spectacular mountain ranges—the silver-peaked Alps capped with dazzling dentures of blinding white snow. From the lake one could catch a glimpse of the massive, nineteenth-century mansion rising like a stone island from behind the thickly leafed oaks and ancient conifers, but from land the view was severely restricted because a cornice-crowned sixteen-foot-high stone wall completely encircled the forty-six-acre park.

During the past five weeks, Senda had become increasingly and frustratingly familiar with the château. Now, once again facing the imposing ornate gates topped with the gilded crest of the Danilovs, she was reminded of that first time she had stood here and rung the buzzer.

It had taken her two full weeks to track the Danilovs down after she had arrived. The Prince and his entourage kept an extremely low profile, and had she not had a sudden burst of inspiration, it might have taken much longer. Only when she spied the golden domes of the Russian Orthodox Church gleaming above the rooftops near the Musée d'Art et d'Histoire, did she know her search was over. Expatriate Russians flocked together like lost pigeons, and no matter how high or low their social station, their lives invariably revolved around the church.

Who knew his flock better than the local priest?

The unsteady pounding of her heart throbbed loudly in her ears as she pulled wide the heavy door and stepped into the church. Outside was Geneva, sunlight sprinkling silver dapples on windswept Lac Léman, but inside the church, it was as if a giant, invisible hand had somehow transported her back in time, into the past, to Russia.

Tears welled in her eyes. This church looked like the churches in Russia and even smelled the same—heavy and oppressive, thickly fragrant with incense and the hot wax emanating from the banks of flickering candles. Multitudes of dark unmoving eyes stared down at her from icon-hung walls, as though watching her every move and penetrating her very being. There was a hauntingly beautiful quality about it, but the overwhelming, even threatening, sense of déjà vu compelled her to forget her reason for coming, compelled her to back out into the world of sunshine. For it was in a church much like this that she had renounced her

Judaism, had turned her back on all she had ever been and known, had vowed to embrace and uphold the tenets of Russian Orthodoxy.

Painful memories swept over her, all the more painful because her conversion had been the catalyst that had pried apart the first menacing crack in what she had once been so certain was the stubborn, organic bedrock of the relationship she and Schmarya had shared.

She wanted to flee in desperation.

"Can I help you?" a voice asked softly out of the gloom in heavily accented French.

Startled, she whirled about and was confronted with an old white-bearded priest who had stepped from behind a marble column. His slippers whispered on the stone floor and his heavy dark vestments rustled mysteriously about him. There was a gentleness in the sound of his baritone, and somehow his voice soothed her.

"You are crying, my child."

Abruptly she made to leave. "Perhaps I should not have come here," she replied in Russian. She turned to go.

"Nonsense." He caught her arm, and led her to a pew. He sat beside her, folding his hands in his lap. He tilted his head and regarded her curiously. "I have not introduced myself. I am Father Peter Moskvin."

"Senda Bora."

"A refugee." It was a statement, not a question.

She nodded in silence.

"Can I be of assistance to you, Senda Bora?"

"Do you know my friends, Father?" Senda asked eagerly, her pulse quickening. One part of her was desperate for the reply; the other was afraid of what she might hear. "The Danilovs? Prince Vaslav and Princess Irina?"

The old man's eyes lit up. "Yes, I do, and they are here," he said, smiling. "But they never come into town to worship. They have a private chapel on their estate, which I myself blessed at their request."

She looked at him directly. "I must try and reach them. Could you tell me where they live?"

He smiled. "Of course," he said, patting her hand reassuringly. "It is the Château Gemini, on the far side of the lake. Anyone can give you directions."

Armed with the address of the Danilovs' lakefront estate, she hurried back to the boarding house where she, Inge, and Tamara rented rooms, stopping at a stationery shop along the way. She splurged on a creamy vellum envelope and several sheets of thick rag paper.

As soon as she reached the boarding house, she hurried from the foyer up the steep stairs, pausing at both landings to catch her breath. Coughs racked her, and she hacked into her handkerchief before balling it up and continuing her climb to the three tiny rooms they shared under the sloping eaves.

Inge, apparently alerted by the coughing seizures, was holding the door open. Breathlessly waving away her greetings, Senda headed for the little desk pushed against the dormer window. She sat down and with trembling hands took pen, inkwell, and blotting paper out of a drawer. She slipped the precious sheets of vellum from the plain brown wrapper and then stared, deep in thought, out past the lace curtains at the thin slice of lake visible between two buildings. After several moments of deliberation, she dipped the pen into the jar of ink, and then the nib swooped unhesitatingly down on the paper, scratching its confident message in graceful letters.

Your Highness

Brows furrowing, she frowned at the salutation. How she despised this form of address when she wanted so badly to scrawl "Dear Vaslav" instead. After sharing his bed and affections for so long, it seemed ludicrous to have to be so stiffly formal, yet propriety required she keep the message distant and polite. There was always the possibility, however remote, that her message could be intercepted by carefully drilled servants, misconstrued, and subsequently tossed out with the day's garbage, thereby never reaching Vaslav's hands. Best it be veiled and courteous, and that he receive it.

It has been a long time since we last saw each other, but I have finally reached Geneva. It would be marvelous— and to our mutual advantage—if we could meet and renew our past acquaintance. I can be reached at 21 rue de Moillebeau, number 6, and am waiting to hear from you.

Senda paused, as if too weary to compose the required closing. The pen moved slowly now, each letter of each word harder to form. Strange, now that the message was written she should feel so empty, so depleted, the pen so heavy, as if it had been fashioned of gunmetal.

I am, of course, available at your convenience. Mean- while, I remain, respectfully,

Your humble servant,
Senda Bora

She sealed the envelope, and for a long moment held it in front of her, staring at the name and address. It was done. The rest was up to him.

Then a sudden thought occurred to her. No, it was not quite done.

She picked up the pen again and scrawled the word "Personal" in both Russian and French on the front of the envelope and underlined them with a single fluid slash.

Now it was done.

Inge didn't need to be told what was up. Wordlessly she took the envelope, glanced expressionlessly at it, and pulled on her loden coat, trotting out to hand-deliver it to the Château Gemini immediately.

Like a caged tiger, Senda prowled the rooms, anxiously awaiting Inge's return. Her eyes flitted constantly to the clock. The minute hand moved so slowly that at first she was certain the clock had stopped. But it ticked on noisily, proof of her own fraught nerves.

Darkness had fallen by the time Inge returned. Senda rushed to her eagerly, eyes questioning, but Inge only shrugged and sighed and went to hang up her coat. Senda followed at her heels. "Well?" she prompted, her eyes gleaming with a mixture of fear and anticipation. "What happened?"

"At the Château I knocked, and when he answered the door, I handed the envelope to the majordomo. He took it."

"And?" she demanded passionately.

"I was told not to wait for a reply." Inge shrugged negligibly. "If there will be one—"

"There will!" Senda interrupted with an indignant hiss. *"There has* to be!"

But no message arrived from Vaslav that day, or the next. As day after day crept by and there was still no word from him, Senda became increasingly moody and cantankerous. She was irritable toward Tamara and Inge, and actually had to restrain herself from lashing out at them.

It was like living in a pressure cooker.

By the eighth day, Senda knew there was only one avenue left open to her. She would have to go see Vaslav unannounced. She had followed the rules of etiquette to the letter by sending the note first. Since that had failed, she now had no other choice.

Baroque in design, the gates were so intimidatingly lavish that they were a startling reminder of the mean circumstances she, Inge, and Tamara had been reduced to. But how well she knew that proud polished brass crest embellishing them! It seemed a lifetime had passed since she had last seen it.

By reflex, she patted her hair, adjusted her felt hat, and smoothed her plain, forest-green cloth coat. Two years earlier, she would have been dressed in sumptuous furs and beautifully tailored dresses, and would have arrived by car, or a carriage with both a driver and a footman in attendance instead of having to take public transportation and endure a long, seemingly endless walk. But times had changed, and she'd had to change along with them, a rudimentary rule of survival. Were it not for her adaptability, would she have survived this long or gotten here at all? Wouldn't she have succumbed to her disease instead of fighting for life? Still, the plain, ankle-length dove gray dress was a painful reminder of how her fortunes had changed.

But some things never changed. One look at the Château Gemini and it was obvious that the Danilovs still had a great deal of their massive fortune intact—reason enough for her to thank her lucky stars.

As she pressed the buzzer set into the nearest of the two massive stone piers surmounted with carved pineapples, Senda could hear a bell jangling somewhere behind the wall. An elderly green-uniformed gatekeeper immediately shuffled out to answer the summons.

He eyed her dubiously from behind the thick curlicued iron bars and made no move to unlock the gates. "Yes, madame?" he asked, eyeing her with dry disapproval.

So her apparel, which had seen far better days, was not lost on his wily old eyes.

"I have come to see his Highness," she stated succinctly.

"Is his Highness expecting you?"

Senda hesitated for only the briefest fraction of a second. "My good man, would I have wasted my time and come had I *not* been expected?"

He put his face close to the gate and peered out sideways in both directions. "Madame does not have a vehicle?" he asked in surprise.

"It is a glorious day and I chose to walk. I had the car sent back to town." She raised her chin, knowing that affecting airs was necessary. "I shall be picked up later. If a car arrives for Madame Bora, please allow my driver admittance."

He hesitated, then unlocked a pedestrian gate so ingeniously crafted that it was impossible to tell it was set into one of the two larger ones.

She smiled her thanks and slipped inside before he could question her further. She could hear him locking the gate behind her. "The château is at the end of the drive," he called after her, pointing. "Just keep on the drive and eventually you'll reach it."

She turned and waved. "Thank you," she called back over her shoulder.

The sweeping drive was longer than she had anticipated. On either side of it, the parkland was beautifully maintained, studded with enormous old trees, artfully pruned shrubs that gave the impression of having been not so much clipped as *shaved,* and marble copies of Greek and Roman statuary. She heard loud shrieks and turned her head, gasping at their source: An army of snow-white peacocks, pulling their heavy tails behind them like proud brides, strutted, impossibly beautiful, between the trees.

Even as she neared the château, she could see little of it. As though they wanted to hug it protectively within their leafy bosom, the trees suddenly thickened, and she could only glimpse a sea of verdigris-aged copper rooftops rising above them. Then the trees abruptly cleared and the château reared its magnificent symmetry before her.

Squaring her shoulders as if preparing to go into battle, she climbed the low stone steps to the intimidatingly scaled double doors, tossed back her head, and reached forward to lift the enormous brass knocker. Almost magically, the door opened from within before she could touch it. Startled, she withdrew her hand and instinctively moved a step backward.

"Can I help Madame?" a man croaked disapprovingly.

Senda stared. Standing before her, his bald head glossy from polish or wax, was a thin ugly man in the formal attire of the majordomo. The black tailcoat and detachable wing collar of his shirt did little to soften his angular features. In the shadows behind him stood two immobile men with inconceivably wide shoulders. Guards of some sort, she surmised.

Senda said softly, "I have come in the hope of speaking with Prince Vaslav."

"Madame does not have an appointment." The majordomo's voice was a froglike croak.

Senda shook her head ruefully. "No," she admitted, "but he . . . and the Princess . . . and I were close friends in Russia. Tell his Highness Madame Bora requests to see him."

Did the name spark a flicker of recognition within those bulbous eyes? Or had she imagined it?

"Perhaps an appointment would be possible," he said smoothly. "Could you leave your calling card, please?"

She glanced closely at his face, but an inscrutable veil seemed to have slithered down over his eyes. If he had shown any recognition at her name, it was impossible to tell now.

"Then they are not in?" she asked.

He shook his head regretfully. "I am sorry, but they have left for several days."

She tightened her lips, and cleared her throat, struggling valiantly to retain her poise. "In that case, I see that I will have to leave my card." She could feel him waiting stoically as she opened her purse and reached inside. Her fingers groped among its meager contents, keeping up the charade. She would never admit that she had no calling cards. Finally she sighed and smiled disarmingly, a wry expression in her eyes as she snapped the purse shut. "I seem to have left them at home," she said. "How silly of me."

He appeared unperturbed. "If Madame will be so good as to wait a moment, I shall get something to write with." He left the door open, with her standing on the other side of the threshold. A mere doorway, she thought, has become a visible line of demarcation I dare not cross uninvited. Then she looked up. He was back with a polished sterling silver salver on which lay a tiny gold pencil and miniscule pad. She wrote her name and address, smiled her thanks, and turned, leaving with as dignified a carriage as she could muster. Tears of frustration stung in her eyes.

Suddenly she stopped dead in her tracks. Ice, not blood, coursed through her veins as realization dawned.

The gates.

The gatekeeper had let her in. *After* she had told him that she wanted to see the Prince. The gatekeeper, better than anyone, would know his employer's comings and goings. He would have told her Vaslav was gone. Wouldn't he?

Her face felt as if it were on fire, an unbearable coughing fit racked her chest, burned her lungs. So Vaslav *was* in. Only she couldn't get to him.

Why. *Why?*

In his second floor study in the Château Gemini, Count Kokovtsov stared at the tiny slip of paper in his hand. The veins and arteries stood out on his high domed forehead as his glassy, lacquered fingernails drummed a steady tattoo on the finely inlaid Louis XV desk. His brow was furrowed, his teeth clenched.

Common sense told him that he should not feel consternation or surprise at the woman's unannounced visit. He knew better than to believe she could be as easily evaded as the intercepted letter to Vaslav could be burned. Senda Bora was, after all, a determined, resourceful bitch. Hadn't he anticipated her coming in person after receiving no reply to her letter? And wouldn't the bitch return time and again? Yes, and he was certain that eventually, despite any obstacles he might erect in her path, she would connive some devious way to contact Vaslav.

Which was precisely the one thing he could not afford to let happen.

Thoughtfully, he pushed back his chair and moved over to the tall French doors overlooking Lac Léman. He parted the heavy curtains swagged over the windows. Through the glass, he could make out two small figures down by the lakeside. Then he saw a third figure climbing the steps of the stone jetty to join the other two waiting on top.

Mordka scowled contemptuously before letting the curtain sway back into place. So Vaslav had just finished his daily swim in the chilly waters of the lake, the usual two attendants waiting subserviently to drape his shivering body in heavy, heated robes. Despite his state of mental and physical depletion, Vaslav Danilov still insisted on taking his daily dip, just as he had in Russia, no matter how frigid the weather, or how freezing the water.

Mordka's lips curled into an ugly smile as he turned away from the window and paced the study. Unconsciously, he crumpled the slip of paper into a tiny wad.

Well, his cousin wouldn't be taking these refreshing little dips much longer, he thought with satisfaction. Soon now, Vaslav would be out of the picture, and the mighty Danilov fortune would be his, and his alone. From the desk he took a sheaf of documents, representing another parcel of the Danilov fortune which would be his, then pausing to stare at the tiny ball of paper still in his hand, he strode swiftly toward the fireplace and tossed it in. The flames licked greedily at it, turning the paper black before consuming it altogether. With the physical evidence of her visit destroyed, he already felt much better. Then he went downstairs to take tea in the salon overlooking the lake. The papers were tucked under his arm and he hummed softly to himself, his mood buoyant and self-congratulatory. He felt utterly confident.

After all, weren't the Danilovs always so bovinely content, so idiotically manageable and agreeable at tea?

Come to think of it, they were becoming more and more agreeable all the time!

Her second visit.
This time she was received quite differently at the château.

The same majordomo opened the door, but his manner was decidedly less superior. "If Madame will be so good as to follow me?" An unctuous, sweeping hand invited her to enter.

Startled by the change in his demeanor, Senda allowed herself to be ushered wordlessly through a series of silent halls to a small salon. She was oblivious to the priceless masterpieces glowing on the walls, the giant Sèvres vases and urns on marble-topped consoles. Her heart throbbed and sang, and she could barely contain her excitement. So Vaslav *had* gotten her message! So he did wish to see her! Thank God she had had the notion to come today, rather than wait another day or two. Something had told her to come. Five days had already passed since she had been here last.

"If Madame will please wait here?"

Senda nodded. Too nervous to sit, she paced the huge wine-colored Oriental carpet. The wait was interminable.

Finally, her ears caught the distant but unmistakable sound of approaching footsteps. Her skin prickled hotly, and she forced herself to stand still, taking a series of rapid breaths to ease her fluttering nerves. To stifle the painful cough, which always threatened.

The door opened and she turned slowly toward it, forcing the same expressionless facade on her face she had used in Russia when her path happened to cross Vaslav's in public. Her "public face," she had called it.

Count Kokovtsov entered the room.

The moment she saw him, her face drained completely of color. *What on earth!* she thought. *Where was Vaslav?* She stifled the cry of disappointment before it left her lips.

Slowly he drew shut the door and turned to face her, his expression reserved and aloof. "Madame Bora," he murmured. He came closer, reached for her hand, and suavely raised it to his lips. The pigeon-blood ruby adorning his long thin finger glowed obscenely. His dark eyes glittered, and she suppressed a shudder. "It is a pleasure to see you again." He regarded her inquisitively. "We . . . were afraid some tragedy might have befallen you. It pleases me to see that it has not."

She forced a smile she did not feel. All too fresh in her mind was that terrible scene at the railroad yard when the Danilovs' train had pulled out. The Count had deliberately turned the Princess's attention away from the window so that she could not see Senda, and then he had stared back at her, his smile triumphant and mocking. She reminded herself not to be taken in by any display of sincerity on his part. He was a dangerous man, not to be underestimated.

"And it is a pleasure to see you also, Count Kokovtsov. It has been a long time."

He nodded gravely. "Nearly two years. That is indeed a long time." He motioned to a chair. "Won't you have a seat?"

Senda tucked her long skirt beneath her before sitting down.

He lowered himself soundlessly into a chair facing hers, his every motion somehow insectile, as if he were a giant, poisonous spider. "You are looking well, as always," he said mildly. "You were always beautiful."

"On the stage, it was a marketable commodity," she said modestly, lowering her eyes. "Here . . ." Her voice trailed off and she shrugged. Then she raised her head. "And the Prince?" She was succinct. "How are he and the Princess taking their exile?"

He was silent for a moment. "Not well, I fear," he said slowly. "It has made for some drastic changes. There is a significant difference between visiting a place by choice and being forced to live there in exile."

She smiled bleakly.

He looked thoughtful for a moment, and then heaved a painful sigh. "About the Prince . . ."

"Yes?" she asked sharply, sitting up straighter.

"He told me about your letter and your previous visit."

She drew a deep breath and waited, her heart hammering, her pulse speeding.

"I have tried to tell him repeatedly that exile does not necessarily mean one has to lock oneself away. However—" He sighed again and shook his head mournfully. A tight sad smile hovered on his thin lips. "I had hoped that you could be of assistance."

"Me?" Puzzled, Senda tilted her head to one side. "How?"

"He is no longer the Prince you . . ." Mordka paused and coughed delicately into a fist. ". . . you once knew."

"Why?" she asked, suddenly alarmed. "Is he ill?"

"His illness is not of the body, I fear. We have had a parade of the finest doctors and specialists in all of Europe through here. Their consensus is unanimous. The Prince suffers from a malaise of the spirit." Count Kokovtsov looked at her. "He will see no one. *No one.* I am truly sorry. This comes as a severe shock to you, I can see. But believe me, Madame Bora, it is what *he* wants. What *he* has ordered."

Is it? she couldn't help thinking. She bit down on her lip. He was describing a different man altogether, not the Vaslav she knew. Could the Prince have changed so much? Or was it a clever fabrication, another Machiavellian ploy by this arthropod of a man?

"These are trying times for everyone," Kokovtsov said with finality. "The Prince and the Princess . . . myself . . . surely for you. You must understand, he will not see you."

"I don't believe that. I cannot!"

"I have my orders. He will see no one." Hardly aware of his doing it, Kokovtsov led her out through the halls, back to the soaring foyer, past the curving marble staircase to the front door. "I will arrange for a car to take you back."

A million thoughts assailed her mind with hailstorm intensity. Had Count Kokovtsov spoken the truth? Or had she been tricked? And now she was being pushed aside, hustled out—and quickly. *Something was wrong at the château. Terribly wrong.*

Somehow, she just knew it.

Well, she would have to find a way to get back in there, to confront Vaslav face to face and see for herself. She could not, *would not*, take the Count's words at face value. He had tricked Vaslav into leaving her behind in Russia. She certainly could not trust him now.

Count Kokovtsov watched her departure from a second floor window. "The bitch will be back," he told himself in a low, sure voice. His fingers ticked against the sides of his trousers. "I only wonder what her next move will be."

Unknown to him, so did Senda.

Less than two weeks after Senda's second futile visit to the château, the plan she had wracked her brains to create was unexpectedly dropped in her lap.

It was Saturday, and Inge had spent the morning shopping. When she came back from bargaining at the open-air market, her breathing was labored and her face was flushed beet red and glistened with a fine sheen of perspiration from hurrying. "Hello! Hello!" she called, heading straight for the kitchen. "I've picked up a very intriguing piece of news."

"Well?" Senda demanded.

"One of the finest homes in the area is looking for part-time help."

Senda jerked. She turned around slowly to stare open-mouthed at Inge, who was coming out of the pantry. "You don't mean—"

"You get three guesses," Inge cut in, her cornflower-blue eyes sparkling brightly.

"It couldn't be . . ." Senda could not bring herself to pronounce the name aloud.

"Now it's down to two guesses." Inge smiled.

241

"It . . . it *can't* be . . ."

"It *is*," Inge crowed triumphantly. "The Château Gemini!"

The following Monday, Senda was back at the château, this time as a part-time maid. Nobody had stopped her because no one had recognized her—not the gatekeeper or the majordomo, not even Count Kokovtsov, who she passed twice in the halls, her eyes and face demurely lowered. She had put all her theatrical make-up tricks to good use. She looked dourly plain, an effect increasingly simple to achieve: her features had become austere and bony from the steady weight loss she had suffered since the onset of her illness. She had powdered her tell-tale hair nearly snow white, wore it pulled severely back, and had added shading to her already too-hollow cheeks. She looked like a gaunt, old woman twice her age. She was virtually unrecognizable.

The following afternoon, she spent lunchtime walking in the parkland in front of the château. Just as she came out of the cluster of trees that hid the château, she was forced to stop and wait. Her path was blocked by an army of strutting, snowy white peacocks crossing the drive, dragging their magnificent plumes behind them. Between their persistent, ear-splitting cries of *"Pf-ow! Pf-ow!,"* she could hear an engine up ahead, coming from the direction of the gate. The noise grew louder as it approached. Turning her head, she saw its source. A huge open white touring car was rounding the curve, bearing down on the peacocks. Not twenty-five feet away, the car coasted to a halt to let the unperturbed birds by when—was it possible?—or was she hallucinating?

Seated in the front of the phaeton was a tan-uniformed chauffeur, his head crowned by a peaked cloth cap. And sitting in the rear, flanked by Count Kokovtsov on his left and the Princess on his right, was her former lover and protector!

She couldn't believe her eyes. "Vaslav!" she screamed suddenly, her voice reverberating with new-found strength. Her hands clapped a rhythmic tattoo on her lips as she jumped up and down. *"Vaslav!"*

Hearing his name, he turned his head slowly.

She bore down on the car, racing toward it.

Count Kokovtsov leaned forward, rapping the raised glass divider with his knuckles. *"Drive, you idiot!"* he shrieked at the chauffeur. *"Drive!"*

The chauffeur twisted around to face him. Even above the idling engine, Senda could hear his every word with crystal-like clarity. "But the peacocks—"

"Never mind the goddamned birds!" Kokovtsov screamed. *"Run the hell over them!"*

The chauffeur hesitated, and Vaslav stared at Senda stupidly all the while, as though through an invisible haze. His lips were turned down in a frown as if he should know her, but couldn't remember her name. The Princess appeared to stare at the floor, never raising her head or moving her eyes.

"Vaslav, it's me! Senda!"

She had reached the car. Her hands clutched the glossy door and she leaned across it, ignoring the Count's baleful face as she searched Vaslav's eyes. They were curiously shiny and unfocused. Her face whitened, and she felt she was going to be sick. Vaslav continued to stare at her . . . *through* her really . . . as if he were catatonic.

What was wrong with him?

Of course. Her scarf! Her white hair! How *could* she expect him to recognize her in this disguise?

With a swift tug of her hand she tore the scarf off her head and in a desperate frenzy began slapping the white powder from her hair.

Still Vaslav Danilov regarded her with that curious faraway look, and the Princess continued to stare at the floor as if in a trance.

"Vaslav!" Senda sobbed. "For God's sake, *why* don't you recognize me? It's *me!* Senda!"

"Drive!" Count Kokovtsov screeched at the driver again. *"Drive, I tell you!"*

This time the chauffeur jumped into action. The rear tires dug tenaciously into the drive, kicking up gravel and spraying it backward. The car surged forward with a sudden burst of speed. Unprepared for its abrupt departure, Senda was still clinging to the door, her feet dragging a deep furrow through the gravel. Then she uttered a cry of dismay as her grip loosened. The breath was knocked out of her as she hit the ground and rolled over twice.

Thump-thump-thump.

She drew in her breath sharply and shut her eyes at the terrible sounds: the car had plowed through the peacocks. When she opened her eyes again, a cloud of white feathers billowed up into the blast of exhaust before snowing slowly groundward. Out of the corner of her eye she saw the car careening around the wide curve, toward the house. The chauffeur had taken the corner so fast that for a moment it appeared as if the phaeton was balanced on its left tires alone. Then the car was out of sight, screened by the thick foliage of the trees.

Vaslav! Her heart was a triphammer, her blood surging. This was her one opportunity to speak with him—perhaps the only one she might ever have! She had to take advantage of it, to find out what was wrong with him.

Why didn't he recognize her? Or did he?

She struggled to her feet and raced toward the château, cutting across the lawn. She glanced at the blood-splattered carcasses of three prize peacocks, and quickly averted her gaze. It had been a mistake to look, and she had to fight to keep from retching. Nothing could drown out the agony of one mortally wounded fowl's ear-piercing death shrieks.

"Butcher!" she hissed aloud, angrily cursing Count Kokovtsov. Then she ducked through the trees and ran straight into the waiting arms of two guards.

She fought them like a captured banshee, her arms flailing. "Let me . . . GO!" she screamed. *"Vaslav! Vaslav!"* Then she shouted at the guards: "You don't understand! Something's *wrong!*" Squirming like an eel, she nearly eluded her captors, but then they pinioned her arms behind her back and dragged her forcibly to the gates, her heels furrowing the gravel.

"If you value your job, you'll see that this one never gets in again!" one of the guards snapped to the wide-eyed gatekeeper. Then they flung Senda out with such force that she all but flew through the air. She landed painfully on the pavement but, curiously, hardly felt the impact. She only knew that she had to get back into the estate, and that the gate was already swinging shut.

She stumbled dazedly to her feet and rushed the closing gate, but it clanged shut in front of her, locking her out forever with the same loud foreboding clang of finality as a jail door.

Her eyes streaming tears, she grasped hold of the curlicued bars of the gates, clutching them in desperation as she sank to her knees under the iron and gilt coat of arms of the Danilovs.

"Vaslaaavvv," she howled in the keening, unearthly wail of a wounded animal. *"VAAASSSLLLAAAVVVvvv . . ."*

Two days after Senda's ignoble eviction from the château, Inge returned from the market with a newspaper folded under her arm. She slapped it down on the kitchen table. "There, it's all in black and white. No wonder you could never get to the Prince," she announced.

Senda raised her eyebrows in puzzlement. She had no idea what Inge was talking about.

"It's all there!" Inge pointed a wavering index finger at the newspaper. "You thought something was wrong. Well, your intuition was right!"

Slowly Senda approached the table and looked down. She sucked in her breath. She could never forget that elegantly evil face, not for as long as she lived.

Count Kokovtsov.

Her blood ran cold as she stared at the bold, page-wide headline: COUNT INDICTED IN MURDER PLOT

Her lips trembled and her hands shook as she read the second bank of smaller headlines: RUSSIAN EXILE CHARGED WITH CONSPIRACY, ATTEMPTED MURDER

Shaken, she snatched up the page and began to read.

Count Mordka Kokovtsov, the Russian nobleman, was arrested last night on charges of grand larceny, conspiracy, and attempted murder. His intended victims were Prince Vaslav Danilov and his wife, Princess Irina Danilov, Russian expatriates who fled the Bolshevik revolution and live on the outskirts of Geneva. On his attorney's advice, Count Kokovtsov remained silent and refused to respond to police questioning.

Police sources say Kokovtsov, 53, a cousin of the Prince and the Danilovs' chief financial advisor, had been slowly poisoning the Danilovs over an extended period of time. During afternoon tea, a household tradition, Kokovtsov laced the Danilovs' tea with scopolomine.

Police were alerted by Daniel Delauney, president of the Banque Danilov. The bank, headquartered here in Geneva, is privately owned by the Danilovs. Apparently Delauney had become increasingly alarmed as the effects of the scopolomine became more and more evident in the victims.

Scopolomine, a sedative hypnotic which depresses the central nervous system, can kill in large quantities. In small, regularly ingested doses, it causes a weakening of mental faculties and subsequently leads to a slow, often undiagnosed or misdiagnosed, death.

According to Delauney, the Danilovs were becoming increasingly "idiotic," with a near-total loss of memory. "It was as if they moved slowly in a dream world," he told reporters.

Delauney says he first became suspicious of Kokovtsov when the Danilovs signed over or sold to him a number of multi-million-franc businesses, including a munitions factory in France and many thousands of acres of timberland, at a fraction of their worth.

Doctors told this reporter that the Danilovs should slowly regain their health and memory as the scopolomine works out of their systems . . .

The newspaper slid through Senda's fingers and fell to the table. "So I was *right*!" she whispered. "I *knew* that something was wrong, only I had no idea what! When I saw Vaslav he . . . he seemed to stare straight through me, as if I wasn't there. At least now I know why."

Dazed, she sank slowly onto one of the kitchen chairs, her face drained of color. Her temples pounded mightily, and the ever-present coppery taste of blood in her throat, now further tainted by the rancid acidity of bile, turned her stomach. For a long time she stared into space.

Inge stooped down and put an arm around Senda's shoulders. "Are you all right?" she asked in concern. "Can I get you something? You look like you're going to be sick."

Slowly Senda shook her head back and forth. "I . . . I'm all right. Really, I am." Then she sat quietly. Almost a full minute passed before she realized she was staring at the newspaper. Savagely, she grabbed it and flipped it upside down. She had had her fill of Count Kokovtsov. Seeing his photograph staring up at her was more than she could bear.

"Well, it's time that evil man was put away!" Inge said grimly, gesturing at the newspaper. "The few times I saw him, he gave me the willies. Just seeing his picture makes me feel like our home's been invaded."

Senda nodded. "At least we know one thing now. When Vaslav's well again, I won't have any trouble seeing him, but it might take some time if these doctors are right."

"We've waited this long." Inge shrugged. "What's a few days or a few weeks more at this point? As long as he'll be healthy again, that's all that matters."

Eight days later, Senda's renewed surge of hope was dashed once and for all. The Danilovs' names were once again splashed across the headlines: both the Prince and Princess had been murdered.

"An execution, the newspaper says it was," Inge whispered hoarsely as she read the article which Senda could not bring herself to read.

"Executed!" Senda cried. "You mean murdered in cold blood, don't you?"

"I'm just telling you what it says here," Inge said. "And it says that a gun was held against the tops of their spines. All it took was a single shot each. Death was apparently instantaneous."

"Oh, God," Senda said softly, shuddering as if something cold and wet had rubbed against her.

A single shot each. That was all it had taken . . .

"It's supposed to have been the way the Okhrana executed Bolsheviks during the reign of the Czar. But now . . ." Inge's whisper dropped even lower as her eyes scanned ahead to the next paragraph. "Now the Bolsheviks' Cheka is hunting down White Russian émigrés abroad, killing them in the same fashion! Good Lord, it says it's happened in Berlin and Paris, too!"

"And now here." Another icy chill slithered through Senda. She covered her face with her hands. No matter which way she turned, it seemed defeat was all there was to greet her.

Inge shook her head and pushed the newspaper aside. "Ironic, isn't it?" she said softly. "A crook like Kokovtsov is safe and lives in jail while his intended victims are dead. Murdered by someone else."

Senda felt suddenly too weak to move.

Death. Death and violence. For too long, they had been part and parcel of her life. Was there no escape?

Senda's health took a sudden swing for the worse. She had put so much stock in Vaslav's helping her secure a future for Tamara that the news of his murder was the final nail in her coffin. Her racking coughs increased. Her lungs burned with an even fiercer, more unbearable fire than before. Each day her handkerchiefs became soiled with larger amounts of blood.

Inge cared for her as best she could, summoning expensive doctors who could do little but prescribe cures at expensive spas. Senda refused to go. The money from the sale of the brooch was all gone, and Inge had already had to sell the ring as well.

She wasn't about to let any more of the precious, dwindling money be spent on her deteriorating health.

Only one last dream kept Senda going. For too long, she, Inge, and Tamara had been roaming without a country, citizens of nowhere. Even if she herself would not live long enough to enjoy a secure future, Tamara could—with Inge's help.

"We're leaving, Inge," Senda said one evening. "We're going to Hamburg. With luck, there'll be just enough money to get us to America."

Inge stared at her, wondering if Senda was lucid. "America!" she exclaimed. "This is out of the blue! You're not in any condition to tra—"

"America." Senda's voice, weak and wheezing though it was, left no room for argument. Then she doubled over suddenly. She wrapped her arms around her belly as she coughed. She spat into the handkerchief and quickly balled it up. She was afraid to look at it. "America," she said again between rasping gasps.

Inge shook her head. "We don't even know any English! We might not even have enough money! How do we know things in Russia won't improve soon? We might be able to return to St. Petersburg . . ."

Senda said, "We're leaving for Hamburg tomorrow. My mind is made up. Once there, we'll see about steamship tickets."

Senda refused to listen to Inge's arguments to the contrary. If it was the last thing she would live to do, she would see to it that the three of them—and if that wasn't possible, then at least Inge and Tamara—would sail to New York.

For wasn't it in America, she'd heard, that golden opportunities awaited everyone?

Well, Tamara would have them.

Senda slept quietly throughout most of the exhausting train journey from Geneva to Hamburg, and Inge let her. She knew that Senda needed her rest. She didn't try to wake her until they pulled into the railroad station at the end of the line.

"Senda, we're here," Inge said softly, giving Senda a shake. And then she froze.

Senda was dead. She had died enroute.

Fate had reserved its cruelest trick for last.

The liner *Lübeck* shuddered and creaked as it plunged through the dark troughs of the North Atlantic. In the cramped confines of the windowless inside cabin, Tamara sat wordlessly on the lower bunk, her lips tightly compressed. She looked down at her hands, in which she clutched a picture of her mother. "I loved Mama," she whispered, the tears sliding down her cheeks. "I still love her. I want her to be proud of me."

"And she will be, child," Inge assured her. "So she will."

"She loved acting." Tamara licked the salt tears off her lips. "She loved it so." Tamara nodded emphatically. "And so will I." She turned to Inge. "I want to become an actress too."

"We will see, dear." Inge smiled gently. "You've plenty of time to make up your mind."

"My mind *is* made up." Tamara furrowed her brows and studied the picture in her lap. "I'm serious, Aunt Inge. I want to become the greatest actress in the world. And I *will*!" Her little voice faltered, and she clenched her small hands and shuddered. Then she raised her tear-streaked face to Inge's, and at that moment the Boralevi strength shone in her eyes, brilliant, faceted emeralds catching the light. "I'll do it for Mama," Tamara said resolutely, her face hardening with an adult determination. "And myself."

It was at that moment that Inge first became truly aware of how much her mother's daughter Tamara truly was. She could not stifle the uncanny sense of déjà vu coursing through her. Tamara's force and determination reminded her so much of Senda that a stab of pain sliced through her. Now that she thought about it, Tamara reminded her of Senda in many ways. She had the same translucent, pearly skin, identical luminous eyes, and precisely the same thin-boned elegance. Only her hair was different, not coppery, but a lustrous, corn-silk gold.

"I *will* make her proud of me!" Tamara said forcefully. "I *will*." Then together, she and Inge wept throughout the night.

Interlude: 1926

The stage for modern Mideast crises was set long before the British control of Palestine. To truly understand the powderkeg that characterizes today's Arab-Israeli conflict, one must study the very first actors in this ongoing drama, the Biblical Israelites of Moses. In the centuries since, the play itself has remained much the same; only the actors have changed.

—Contrucci and Sullins,
The Mideast Today: Strategies to Cope with the Seeds of Yesteryear

"Eieeee, but this is some climb," Schmarya growled breathlessly to himself. Grunting as he summoned up a last great effort of will, he pulled himself up the one remaining outcrop of rock at the flat crest of the sun-scorched cliff. He cursed his useless wooden leg; as usual, the leg which was no longer part of him ached and throbbed fiercely.

Digging his elbows into the sandy limestone, he crawled forward for a few yards, thankful that he hadn't let his artificial leg hamper his getting around. His body had in some ways compensated for his deficiency, and for that he was extremely grateful. His arms, upon which he had to rely to offset his one useless leg, had become extremely powerful and packed with hard muscle. And his good leg had become much stronger than it had been initially.

Using his arms and his good leg, he stiffly scrabbled up into a semi-kneeling position, and then pushed himself up. Spread out gloriously below him, as far as the eye could see, was the magnificently arid Negev, its apocalyptical, naked brown hills interspersed with haphazard jumbles of red and purple cleft rock. Overhead, the cloudless sky was blue, the brightest, most uniform shade of incandescent blue imaginable. Far up in that ultramarine a solitary bird circled slowly, a falcon or a hawk cruising for prey. He could only shake his head at the beauty of it all and wonder, not for the first time, if the desert's spectacular ruggedness would ever become monotonous. He didn't think it would. He considered it home.

To its few hardy, scattered inhabitants, the word "Negev" was synonymous with "desert," and when Schmarya had first arrived, he'd been under the mistaken impression that the two words were interchangeable. He soon discovered the Hebrew word meant "south," and as such, there was no real geographical boundary to it.

Schmarya had become a "southerner" by chance and by choice, and in many ways he epitomized the hardy pioneering spirit of those who had settled this ancient, unforgiving

253

land. At thirty-one, he was no longer the handsome, dashing youth filled with vague dreams. Over the years his blue eyes had taken on maturity, and the slight, parched creases in his sun-darkened skin bespoke both purpose and determination, of dreams becoming concrete reality. The fiery-eyed youth of the Ukraine who'd fought against oppression and left Russia ten years ago had, if anything, become an even more determined, though still fearless, man out to change the world. But now he was armed with a mental blueprint of what he wanted to achieve.

The journey from Petrograd to Palestine was one he would never forget. It had been long, arduous, and roundabout, some six thousand miles traveled on trains, ships, wagons, and foot. He'd left Russia with nothing other than the thin, torn prison garb he'd been wearing when he was released; the ticket the Prince had arranged for had taken him only across the gulf to Finland, and from there he had been on his own, with no money, no home, no friend or acquaintance, and not even clothes enough to keep him warm. Only his heritage and his determination to help create a Jewish homeland in Palestine had kept him going against all odds. Somehow he'd persevered; it had taken him three long, torturous years to work his way to Palestine and begin to fulfill the dream of all ardent Zionists. The most exciting moment of his life was when he'd gotten off the steamer at Haifa. Overcome by emotion, he had clumsily dropped down on his good knee and bent his head forward to kiss the soil of this land so rich in Biblical history and promise for all Jewish people.

It had taken many months, working at any menial job he could find, to make his way to Jerusalem, where he found work and a home with a family of Arab street merchants. During this time he learned both Hebrew and Arabic and honed his ambition to join the kibbutz movement. In the holy city, he met up with a small group of Jews heading south to a dot in the Negev where once there was an ancient well. Schmarya joined them, and now, many weeks later, stood atop the wind-whipped cliff surveying the majestic silent terrain. Only the roar of the sandy wind and the flapping of his clothes disturbed what down below would be an awesome, unearthly silence broken only in places where the hot wind managed to penetrate gaps in the canyons so that they moaned and whistled eerily. Overhead, the solitary bird still wheeled lazily, high in the dazzling blue sky.

He turned slowly, his body buffeted by the wind, but with his back turned to it, the sand no longer blew into his eyes.

The force of the wind against his back made walking easier, as though invisible hands propelled him forward with every gust.

He whistled softly to himself. His fellow inhabitants of Ein Shmona would kick up a fuss when he got back, because for three days he'd been off exploring on his own. He himself had laid down the inflexible ground rule that no one was ever to wander out of sight alone.

He grinned to himself. What was good for the goose was not always good for the gander. He who made the rules could break them. Besides, they ought to be grateful that he had done so. When he shared his discovery with them, they would have to muzzle their complaints and be thankful to him. Just at the fledgling kibbutz's darkest hour, his sleuthing had provided the salvation for their most pressing problem.

The well which had initially drawn them into the desert had been slowly drying up, creating a panic. Now, with a little inqenuity and a lot of hard work, the panic could be staved off forever. Halfway up the north face of this cliff, deep in a narrow cleft, he had discovered an abundant source of water—clear, cool, sparkling water which gushed from a hidden place in the rocks and then plunged into a narrow crevasse, where it roared down into a deep green pool before joining an underground stream. He'd discovered it not so much by looking for it as by listening for it, which was the very reason he hadn't wanted anyone to accompany him. He'd needed to concentrate. The faint splashing of water could easily have been muffled by conversation, footsteps, or even breathing. Alone, the silence had guided him to it. The only thing which subdued his discovery's excitement somewhat was that with his artificial leg he hadn't been able to shimmy down into the narrow crevasse and investigate further. One of the athletic young men on the kibbutz would be only too happy to do it. With help, he would get down there somehow, plant some explosives, and blow clear part of the forbidding wall of rock. Then a few miles of pipe could reroute the flow and bring the precious water across five miles of desert to Ein Shmona. The new source of water would more than make up for the stingy well: it would make it obsolete. The source he'd found was pure and apparently infinite. It would bless Ein Shmona with its life force and bring the cracked desert fields surrounding it bursting to glorious life for a hundred years to come. He felt very pleased with himself.

He limped forward, dragging his wooden leg. He was nearly at the edge of the cliff, at the spot where he'd climbed up. He planted his legs in a wide stance, leaned his torso forward, and looked down. He bared his teeth and cringed. It would be much more difficult getting back down than it had been climbing up.

He dropped to a prone position and crawled to the edge of the cliff. He stuck his head over the ledge and studied the drop with its outcroppings of rock. Below were gigantic rocks, some the size of houses, jagged and menacing, like pagan altars awaiting their sacrifices.

Carefully, with infinite slowness, he began his creep downward.

Veins and bubbles of sweat stood out on his forehead in bold relief, more from fear than from the exertion. One wrong foothold, one loose rock . . . He mustn't think of that. He had to keep his mind clear and concentrate on one thing, and one thing only: getting safely to the base of this cliff. Nothing else mattered.

Ever so slowly, he continued to descend, his feet slipping from the skimpy foothold, his hands raw from grasping the outcroppings. But steadily, inch by precarious inch, then foot by foot, the ground was coming closer.

Now his blood surged and boiled from the effort and the excitement. This was danger. This was life. This was laughing squarely in the face of death.

Forgotten suddenly was his useless leg. Clinging to the rock face began to make him feel omnipotent. He had set out to conquer, and conquer he would. It was Schmarya Boralevi alone against the forces of nature, and it didn't matter that he was handicapped. He was in command of his body, and his adrenalin pumped mightily. He could almost hear its powerful rushing roar.

Pebbles sang and laughed as they slid and bounced. And then the outcropping he grasped in his right hand suddenly cracked loose from the cliff. He cried out silently in surprise, and hung there, one-handed, for a single long, drawn-out moment before his left handhold too snapped clean from the cliff. For an instant he felt suspended in midair, and then the tunnel of wind rushed upward to meet him as he dived down, down, down through nothingness.

"Allahu akbar . . ."
God is Great . . .
The muezzin's chanting prayer rang out clearly in the small Arab oasis village of al-Najaf. The villagers caught out-of-doors dropped to their knees and faced the huge red setting sun and Mecca far beyond. Indoors, the faithful had

already unfurled their precious prayer rugs and bowed low, their voices echoing the prayer.

"*. . . A shhadu allaa ilaha illa llah . . .*"

I bear witness that there is no God but God . . .

The prayer rose in a powerful chant from within the tiny stone houses, from the men still out in the fields, from the camel tenders of the bedouins who had pitched their goat-hair tents outside the oasis, and from the man tending the noria, the huge, antiquated water wheel which scooped up precious dippers of water from the oasis pond and deposited them into the irrigation channels from which the surrounding fields were watered. Only the creaking of the wooden wheel and the restless movements of the animals disturbed the ethereal, cathedrallike aura suffusing the oasis during the evening prayer.

After the last melodic note of the prayer died into the dusk, Naemuddin al-Ameer got to his feet, brushed sand off the knees of his robe, and hurried home.

At forty-three, he was a tall, imposing man with a craggy presence, a full black beard and flowing mustache, a magnificent hawk's beak of a nose. He surveyed the oasis and the surrounding fields with a countenance which belonged to the prophets of the Old Testament. His eyes were sharp and canny, his black, flowing *bisht* the same as that of his people, but what distinguished his position was his cleanliness, the maroon-and-black patterned head dress wound around his head, and the gray-and-black fringed shawl beneath it. Only the most important man in the little settlement could afford to wear cloth of such fine quality.

As the leader of the village, it had been up to him to visit the bedouins camped nearby, who would depart long before daylight, and he had just left their huge black tents when the call to evening prayers had caught him out-of-doors.

He left behind the miraculously lush and fertile furrowed fields as he made his way toward the date palms which marked the perimeter of the oasis itself. Here a sandy path led past the mean tents and rickety lean-tos of the poorer inhabitants, and then he reached the inky pool of water with its magical water wheel splashing gently, the miniature waterfalls it created flowing from its dippers like liquid crystal. He stood still for several moments, marveling at its wonderful power as he did each time he passed it, ever since he had been a child. Without it, the village would cease to function and its inhabitants starve. It was a miraculous invention indeed, as were the large, delicately carved Archimedes' screws which, when the farmers rotated them by hand, raised water from the lower level of the six main irrigation channels into the higher ones which crisscrossed their own small, individually owned fields. Al-Najaf was an agricultural community, and except for its meager trade with passing bedouins, relied solely on its few goats, sheep, and crops for survival.

He continued his evening walk, exchanging greetings with neighbors and waving when he caught sight of his eight-year-old half-brother, Abdullah, who was leading the family's three cherished goats homeward. And then, when he caught sight of his own home, a small but sturdy square of rough-hewn rock, he paused as always to admire its clean lines in the setting sun, each stone glowing radiantly as though from within.

His evening inspection over, he opened the small door to his house and ducked his head as he entered. His wife, Jehan, wearing her black headcloth and *abbeya,* was squatted on the floor, grinding *kibbe,* a lamb-and-cracked-wheat dish, with a wooden pestle in a large hollowed square of rock. She smiled up at him with her heavy-lashed eyes. Despite the harsh desert climate and years of toil which had creased and cracked her once-soft skin to a tough leathery hide, she was, at forty, still a handsome woman of angular planes and profound strength.

"How is our guest, my wife?" he asked softly.

"He has awakened twice and eaten," she whispered, smiling. "A few more days and he will be up and about." She quietly continued to grind the *kibbe.*

Naemuddin pushed aside the curtain which sectioned off the single large room. Quietly he approached the pallet in the dark far corner and looked down. The man was asleep.

Naemuddin nodded to himself. Rest was what the patient needed now, and food and water, but only in small amounts. Feeding him too much too quickly after his near-starvation and exposure to the elements would only make him sicker. It was nothing short of miraculous that the nomadic bedouins who had brought him here had found him, an even greater miracle that he had not died.

"Life or death," Naemuddin murmured gravely. "Which ever destiny had been chosen for him is the will of Allah."

Allah's will, too, Naemuddin thought, had brought him here, into his house. Yet the stranger was an enigma he could not fathom: hair the color of the desert sand, one leg, and feverish jabber in many tongues, including fluent Arabic. Yet Naemuddin was certain that Allah, in his good time, would unravel that mystery when ready to do so.

Naemuddin started to turn and leave, when the man suddenly moaned in his sleep. He recognized at once that the sound was one not of pain, but of terror.

Schmarya emitted another strangled sob. In his sleep, he was once again falling through that horrible tunnel of empty air, the wind whistling and shrieking, the jagged fingers of rock coming closer, closer, ever closer . . .

With a scream he awakened and tried to sit up, but the effort proved too costly. His head slumped wearily back down upon the pillow. It was a moment before he became aware of Naemuddin. He stared at him as though seeing an apparition.

"Who are you? Where am I?" Schmarya was certain he shouted the questions in Russian; in actuality, his voice was weak, barely a raspy croak.

Naemuddin did not reply. He squatted down and hunkered there, smiling gently.

Schmarya repeated his question, in Hebrew this time.

Naemuddin shrugged and held out his hands helplessly.

Schmarya tried one last time, in Arabic.

Naemuddin's eyes lit up. "I am Naemuddin al-Ameer, and you are in my house," he replied in Arabic.

"Your house?"

"The house of my father, and his father before him. You are at the oasis of al-Najaf."

Schmarya let out a deep sigh. "Then I am not dead."

Naemuddin chuckled. "No, you are not. Indeed, you are very much alive." For a moment he felt compelled to ask Schmarya many things. Who he was. Where he was from. How he had learned such surprisingly fluent Arabic for one with the fair skin of the British. But he stifled his curiosity. Questions and answers would only tire the man. There would be time enough to ask them tomorrow, or the day after.

Weakly Schmarya tested his limbs. He grimaced at the pain which shot through him, but he felt relieved. It didn't feel as if any bones had been broken. Then he suddenly realized he was not wearing his wooden leg. His eyes danced with terror. Without that most precious possession he would not be able to walk. Would not even be able to stand.

"My leg!" he whispered hoarsely. "My *leg!*"

"That?" Naemuddin gestured toward the corner, where the prosthesis was propped against the wall.

Schmarya nodded and sighed a breath of relief.

"The bedouins were puzzled by it. They found it lying beside you."

"It must have come loose when I fell. Thank God they didn't leave it behind." Schmarya shuddered at the possibility.

"The bedouins who brought you here said you had suffered a severe fall," Naemuddin told him. "It was a miracle, they said. You landed in a pocket of sand which cushioned your fall. Otherwise . . ." Naemuddin cursed himself silently. What a stupid, callous thing to have let slip. "You will be fine," he reassured Schmarya. "We have no doctor here, but several of us are wise in the ways of accidents and their remedies. A few more days of rest and then—"

"A few *more* days!" Schmarya looked horror-stricken. "How . . . how long have I been here?"

"Five nights."

"Five nights! And . . ." His throat was suddenly dry. "And how long was I out there before I was found?" he asked in a whisper.

"That I do not know precisely. Three days. Four." Naemuddin frowned. "The bedouins could only guess from your condition."

Five nights and . . . three or four days! Could that be possible? It would mean that he'd dropped off the face of the earth, so to speak, for eight or nine days altogether, and adding the three days he had already been gone from the kibbutz before the accident had occurred . . .

Schmarya could well imagine the consternation he had provoked at Ein Shmona. He must send a message . . .

"Perhaps tomorrow," Naemuddin told him. "For now, I think you should get more sleep."

Schmarya gazed into the gentle liquid eyes of this man who had taken him into his house and was selflessly nursing him. He was beholden to him for his life. And to the bedouins who had found him. He owed them the greatest debt a man could incur.

"I owe you so much," he said heavily. "How will I ever repay you?"

"If a man finds another in the desert, he does not rescue him in order to be repaid," Naemuddin said quietly. "We are all travelers on the same sandy sea. In other circumstances, you would have done the same for one of us. Now, sleep."

Schmarya shut his eyes. Sleep. He could already feel it drifting over him in a dark, peaceful mantle. "Yes, you are right," he murmured thickly. "A little sleep . . . And then tomorrow . . ."

"Yes, tomorrow."

But Schmarya was already snoring steadily.

Under Naemuddin and Jehan's care, Schmarya's strength increased with remarkable alacrity. The next morning, he stepped outside the house for the first time and took a short walk in the sun. The day after that, he explored the entire oasis. Everyone stared at him with curiosity, but he paid no heed to the attention he received. He was too busy comparing al-Najaf with Ein Shmona.

The two settlements, he learned, were a mere twelve miles apart, which made them neighboring villages, but other than himself, the inhabitants of neither village had ever met those of the other.

The settlements shared much in common, but al-Najaf, with its ready supply of oasis water and several hundred years of inhabitation and cultivation, enjoyed a more comfortable and placid existence. At Ein Shmona, all that had awaited the settlers was the stingy well and a nearby cliff face where rock could be quarried and hewn. Ein Shmona did not boast the fields which had been laid out and irrigated for several hundred years. But there was a pioneering spirit at Ein Shmona which al-Najaf perhaps once had had and no longer needed. Yet the industriousness of the inhabitants of both settlements was equal. The major difference Schmarya noticed was that while everything at Ein Shmona had to be done by trial and error, the people of al-Najaf had accumulated a wealth of knowledge passed down through the centuries. Coaxing an existence from the desert was second nature to them. The difficulties between man and desert had long since been resolved. This not being the case with Ein Shmona, Schmarya was especially excited by the two priceless discoveries he made—the water wheel and Archimedes' screws.

With those, the final pieces of Ein Shmona's water problem fell into place. He realized now that rerouting the water from the spring he had found, and piping it to Ein Shmona, was but the first step toward irrigating the kibbutz. These two ancient, time-honored tools—this simple wheel and the giant, delicately carved wooden screw—were the final necessary implements. With improved variations on these ingenious instruments, far more desert fields could be watered and brought to fruition than he had ever dared dream possible.

The Negev could indeed flower.

Now he could hardly wait to get back to Ein Shmona, bringing with him not only the gift of water but also a solution for distributing it to the surrounding desert.

Suddenly the Promised Land held more promise than ever.

*　　*　　*

Fourteen months later, when the five miles of six-inch water pipe carried a ceaseless flow of fresh cool spring water to the kibbutz, everyone cheered and celebrated. Schmarya was toasted repeatedly, and spoken of in awe. He had become the hero of the settlement.

The combination of radiant sun and abundant water soon blanketed the surrounding irrigated fields with fertile vegetation and a bumper crop so fruitful that truckloads of produce were shipped to Jerusalem and Tel Aviv, where they brought a tidy profit. More desert was converted to fields as quickly as humanly possible; more crops were planted. It seemed to Schmarya and the inhabitants of Ein Shmona that they had only to expand further and further out into the desert, and the crops would multiply.

The possibilities were endless, and the newfound wealth attracted more and more families to Ein Shmona. The original twenty-three settlers quickly burgeoned into a village of one hundred and twenty. A second pipeline was installed two years later; then a third. The fields thirsted for the water and gave ever-more-bountiful crops in return. Water, which would otherwise have joined an underground desert river going nowhere, had been tapped and put to mankind's most noble use.

No one, least of all Schmarya, realized that with each additional pipeline, the water level at the oasis of al-Najaf, twelve miles distant, was dropping steadily.

With the completion of the third pipeline, so much water was being diverted from the source that the pool at al-Najaf was fast drying up and came to resemble a mere puddle.

The rumblings from al-Najaf were too distant to be heard. And anyway, the settlers at Ein Shmona were too busy to stop and listen.

II
Tamara
1930–1947

To this day, moviegoers are still divided on whether or not Tamara's beauty was natural or whether, as with Garbo, Hollywood moguls decided to improve on nature's gifts. If they did, it remains one of filmdom's few secrets.

—Nick Bienes,
Those Fabulous Thirties

It was still dark in Los Angeles when Tamara was dressed and ready to leave. Not that she could part the curtains and look out the window—the large airless room was dark and windowless, its walls hung with heavy maroon velvet draperies. The stifling smells of tallow and flowers hung cloyingly sweet and heavy in the air, barely masking the stronger, all-pervading odor of death.

She glanced at her watch. It was nearly six o'clock.

She snatched her coat, umbrella, and script off the Murphy bed and laid them on the nearest of the forty metal folding chairs lined up in rows of five, twenty on either side of the center aisle, like silent soldiers facing forward in a stiff military formation.

She shoved the Murphy bed up into the wall and closed the doors over it. Now that it was hidden, the room regained its chapel aura. Any indication of the living was obliterated from this grim place in which she slept alongside death.

She avoided looking around as she picked up her coat, umbrella, and script. She had been living here over ten months, and the Mourning Room of Paterson's Mortuary was engraved on her consciousness. It was a room designed for peaceful contemplation, a place where mourners came to say their tearful farewells to loved ones. Sometimes, when the Murphy bed was folded down and she tried to sleep, she imagined she could hear their sobs long after they'd gone.

And small wonder, for centered precisely at the front of the room, like an altar on a raised dais, there was always a casket, its style dictated by the pocketbook and taste of the loved ones. It was invariably surrounded by reeking giant wreaths and massive floral arrangements, usually dominated by cheap chrysanthemums. Hanging against the velvet folds of the maroon curtains above the casket was a cross, a crucifix, a Star of David, or nothing at all, depending upon the faith—or lack of faith—of the deceased currently in residence. At the moment, the gruesome crucifix was suspended, its emaciated thorn-crowned plaster Jesus slumping in agony, eyes rolled heavenward.

She couldn't wait to move out of this place.

I'm impatient because so much is at stake today, she thought. Today will either mark the day I begin to work toward getting out of here, or it will mean I'm trapped here for months, perhaps even years.

This morning was the screen test she had waited so long for, the potential film role which could open the door to a new life. Everything hinged upon her performance. Either her life would change because of it, or . . . Well, she would try not to think of the alternative.

Still, she knew she should consider herself fortunate. When they'd first moved here, Inge had volunteered to sleep in this room, but Tamara had vetoed that suggestion. So Inge slept in a far less depressing room upstairs, with a stove, a cot, and a window overlooking the garbage-strewn backyard. Inge had taken a job as a part-time receptionist at Paterson's, which came with boarding privileges, and these benefits were combined with Tamara's job as a part-time waitress at the Sunset Restaurant, which also had its advantages, meager though they might be. She was usually free to go to auditions when they came up because somebody could fill in for her, and what other job would have allowed her that? Her income at the restaurant, augmented by the few days a month she worked as an extra on the movie lots, let them squeak by.

Mouthing a silent prayer for the screen test to which she was headed, Tamara shrugged into her coat and grabbed her purse, script, and umbrella. Then she sailed into the adjoining room, Paterson's lurid showroom. Casket lids yawned half-open to display their plush, guilted linings.

Tamara groaned. In the glow from the streetlights, the big plate-glass window facing the boulevard was streaked with rain. It was still pouring cats and dogs; it hadn't let up for days now. The Southern California rainy season had begun with a bang.

Halfway across the showroom she heard muffled footsteps and turned to see Inge rushing down the carpeted stairs to intercept her, her normally braided crown of flaxen hair hanging to her waist. Still clad in her nightgown, she held a steaming mug of coffee.

"You don't have to see me off," Tamara said. "Go back to sleep."

"Sleep!" Inge's features creased into a mock scowl. "How you expect I sleep this day?" she asked in her broken, thickly accented English. "I have to wish you luck." She skirted the coffins and embraced Tamara, careful not to spill the coffee. Then she handed her the mug.

Tamara took a long, grateful swallow and handed the mug back to her. Her hands were shaking, and she took a few deep breaths, repeating to herself silently, I'll do it. I've *got* to do it! For Inge. For the memory of my mother. For *me*!

"Don't you be nervous," Inge said. "You get good part, mark my word. You be big star. You have Senda's talent. Soon we buy castle in hills and ride with a chauffeur, *ja*?" She tilted her head to one side and smiled hugely, her cornflower-blue eyes regarding Tamara with affection.

Tamara squeezed her eyes shut. "I hope to God you're right, Inge," she said fervently.

"Always I'm right." Inge's smile never faltered; but then, neither had her belief in Tamara. Ever. "Of course you get role, *Liebling*. Now you go and it's dead you knock them!"

Tamara laughed. "You mean 'knock 'em dead,'" she corrected.

Inge shrugged and waved her free hand through the air. "Whatever," she said expansively. "Just you do it."

Tamara pecked Inge's soft cheek. "I promise I will. Now I'd better get going or I'll miss the bus."

"No bus."

"Huh?"

"You take no bus. Not today."

"Not Mr. Paterson's hearse," Tamara begged. "It's bad enough sleeping next to the embalming room without having to ride around in a hearse as well." She shivered. "I'd as soon wait for the bus."

"No, no hearse," Inge answered her. "Not for this. See? I arrange car." Proudly Inge pointed out the window as a car horn blasted twice. Tamara recognized the 1928 four-cylinder Plymouth which sailed to a halt at the curb, its front wheels parting massive sheets of water as if it were a speedboat flinging aside a giant bow wave. The car belonged to Inge's closest friend, Pearl Dern, a makeup artist at International Artists. Pearl had used her considerable contacts at IA to arrange for Tamara's screen test.

Tamara gave Inge one last swift hug. "You're a dear," she told her warmly. She hesitated, looking at Inge's expression, and saw that that kindest of faces reflected a stony certainty combined with a touch of rapture. She knew then that Inge was convinced she had what it took. Dear Inge, she thought, she believes in me as much as I believe in myself. Thus reassured, she turned without another word, unlocked the door, and ducked out into the lashing rain.

Pearl pushed the passenger door of the Plymouth open and Tamara jumped in. " 'Morning, Mrs. Dern," she said breathlessly, slamming the door shut. "Ugly day, isn't it?"

"Tell me about it," Pearl said grumpily. Her voice was deep, raspy, and resonant, a voice tempered by decades of chain-smoking unfiltered Lucky Strikes. "It's rained steady all week. I heard on the radio that those fancy houses on the hillsides are sliding down like skiers in Sun Valley. Thank God I can't afford to live up in the hills." She shook her head. "In summer you got to worry about the damn fires. In winter you got to put up with the rain." She put the car in gear and moved slowly out into the nearly deserted street.

"I really appreciate the ride, Mrs. Dern," Tamara said gratefully.

"Don't mention it." Pearl Dern flicked a sideways glance and flashed a little smile. "And what's all this 'Mrs. Dern' shit anyway? You're eighteen and not a kid. You're a woman. If we're going to be friends I think it's high time you called me Pearl, don't you?"

"Pearl, then," Tamara said.

"That's better. Now, about your screen test." Pearl leaned forward over the wheel, driving with care. She was a tall, farmerish-looking woman. Her features were sharp, her complexion tanned, and her short-cropped hair was bleached light brown. Her eyes were the color of faded denim, with crow's feet at the corners, and her body was severely mannish, all jutting angles and gangly hard edges which she made no effort to soften and feminize. Her chest was flat as a man's, and her man-tailored jacket and long skirt were of heavy Scotch tweed. "I'm going to do your makeup, like we planned. Wouldn't trust anybody else to do it, not in this case." She smiled conspiratorially. "Especially seeing as how we have to please the high-and-mighty Louis Ziolko. Have you ever worked with the prick before?"

"I've never set foot inside IA. I've only played extra at MGM, Paramount, and Warner's."

"So much the better," Pearl said. "That bastard likes to discover his own stars. He doesn't like to think he's overlooked anybody, especially if the person in question was right under his nose. He prides himself on sniffing out new talent without anybody else's help. Know what I mean?" She paused. "You memorized the lines?" Her searching glance lingered on Tamara's perfect profile.

Tamara nodded. "Inge went over them with me all week long. I've got them down pat."

Pearl nodded. "I read the script. It's good. Very good. There isn't an actress in this town who wouldn't give her eyeteeth—and a lot more—for that role. Rumor has it that Constance Bennett and even Garbo are begging to be loaned out to IA for it. Not a one of them gives a damn that *The Flappers* is the most glamorous film to come along in ages. It's the *part* they're after. They say there hasn't been a role with that much juice in it for years."

Tamara looked at her challengingly. "Then what do you think my chances are?" she asked. "With stars like Bennett and Garbo after the part."

Pearl laughed her throaty laugh and patted Tamara on the knee. "Don't worry. You'll be *the* flapper. By the time I get done with you, hell, even Inge wouldn't be able to recognize you. Besides, they say that Oscar Skolnik—the shit owns the studio—wants to cast an unknown, so that's a point in your favor. *I* think Ziolko will insist on casting you—*if* you come across on the screen like you did the other night when you read the part for me." She paused. "This is your big chance, kid, so give it all you've got, and then some."

"I won't disappoint you," Tamara said confidently. "I know you've gone out on a limb for me on this. I mean, I wouldn't want you to get into any trouble—"

"Trouble? Horseshit!" Pearl rested a hand on Tamara's thigh. "Listen, kid, somebody owed me a favor," she said, patting the young woman's leg, "and I called it in. That's the way this business works. You scratch my back, I scratch yours."

Tamara flushed and then put on her best smile. "But . . . how can I ever return the favor? I mean, what could I possibly do for you?"

Almost reluctantly Pearl removed her lingering hand. "Don't worry that beautiful head about it now, kid," she said cryptically, meeting Tamara's eyes. "We'll think of something when the time comes. Okay?"

Tamara nodded slowly. Then Pearl was facing forward again, her denim eyes on the road. For some peculiar reason, Pearl reminded her of a shark circling its prey.

But she was too excited to give Pearl much thought. Her mind was filled with one thing, and one thing only—*The Flappers*.

Everybody in the business knew about *The Flappers*. It was a lively story about three fun-loving chorus girls who work in a Chicago dance hall. Leila, the main character, is wooed by a tough Irish cop but falls in love with his nemesis, a notorious gangster, and soon becomes his moll. The light-hearted partying turns to deadly seriousness when Leila witnesses her gangster lover and his cronies committing murder. The policeman, who still loves her, finds it his duty to turn her into an informer. In the final shoot-out between the gangsters and the police, Leila must choose which of the two men should live. Snatching a revolver, she shoots the gangster, only to be shot by one of the policemen. She dies in her policeman-lover's arms.

It had all the ingredients of a mediocre action picture and could easily have become a run-of-the-mill, good-guys/bad-guys, woman-caught-in-the-middle kind of picture, except for one thing. Its intelligent script had been authored by a first-rate novelist. It featured crackling dialogue, deft characterization, marvelous dance sequences, and moments of hilarity which offset the heavy plot. The role of Leila, a character who metamorphoses from good girl to bad and back to good, called for a beautiful, spirited young woman who could give a virtuoso performance.

Now Tamara had her chance to be Leila.

As she and Pearl drove along, they passed the dream factories of Paramount, MGM, and Universal, sprawling on the gigantic lots, masses of huge industrial-looking complexes which did not at all resemble the sort of places in which most people imagined the movie wizards conjured up their magic. Behind their walls lay acres of mundane factory buildings and immense soundstages, but their glamourless appearance did nothing to subdue their attraction.

Tamara pulled back her sleeve and glanced at her watch. In the sparse early-morning traffic they were making good time. It seemed no time at all before they reached the famous IA lot. Pearl turned right and coasted to a halt at the security booth centered on its little island of concrete.

Tamara leaned down and glanced up at the rainbow arch curving from one massive pillar to the other, forty feet above her. Even in the rain, the rainbow-colored legend was dazzling. Full of promise. While Pearl rolled down her window, Tamara read and reread the mesmerizing sign.

INTERNATIONAL ARTISTS
Home of the Stars

And just to the right was a huge billboard. Slowly she mouthed the five-foot-high rain-swept letters:

Her heart began to hammer fiercely. This was the dream factory. Here visions became reality, printed on celluloid for posterity. With luck, here her own dreams could be nurtured, could come to life.

" 'Morning, Sam," Pearl called out.

" 'Mornin', Mrs. Dern," the old green-uniformed security guard replied in greeting. "It's supposed to rain for two more days."

Pearl growled in exasperation. "How about sharing some good news for a change, Sam?"

"Nothin' I can do about the weather." Sam leaned into the open window and looked questioningly at Tamara.

"This is Tamara Boralevi," Pearl explained. "She's got a test scheduled on Stage Six."

Sam consulted his plastic-sheathed clipboard. "She's as good as marked off, Mrs. Dern. And good luck, Miss Boralevi." Sam smiled and saluted; Pearl stepped on the gas and the Plymouth surged forward under the imposing rainbow.

"Oh, my God!" Tamara's voice was a strangled gasp as she turned to face her visage in the lightbulb-lined mirror. She drew back in disbelief, her eyes echoing shock, finding it difficult to believe that the face which stared back at her could be her own.

Slowly, under Pearl's inscrutably hooded, ever-watchful eyes, Tamara leaned closer into the reflection. Then, ever so gently, she lightly touched her face with her fingertips.

"Careful," Pearl warned.

Tamara nodded, careful not to mar the expert job Pearl had done, but she *had* to touch herself to prove it was she. The skin felt strange and mud-caked to her elegantly tapered fingers, but yes, her very own flesh did indeed meet her very own flesh. Was such diabolical alchemy possible?

"What do you think?" Pearl, standing off to the side, arms folded across her flat breasts, asked in a matter-of-fact voice.

Tamara shook her head in continuing disbelief. She knew now why Pearl was said to be the most respected makeup artist in the business. Slowly she turned from the mirror and faced Pearl. "It's . . . it's truly *me!*" she whispered, gesturing dramatically with her beautifully manicured hands.

Pearl looked at her steadily. "It is," she said, shrugging her shoulders with that mannish manner of hers.

"You've . . . you've worked magic!"

"It's what I do, part and parcel of the job," Pearl grunted simply. "Besides, kid, you're easy. And lucky. You've got the bone structure and everything that goes with it. All I've done is play with it."

"But it's more than that!" Tamara insisted softly. "It has to be!"

Pearl was silent for a moment. Then she shook a cautionary finger and lowered her voice confidentially. "Just take one piece of advice. If you forget everything else I've told you, fine, but always keep this one thing in mind."

"What's that?" Tamara questioned.

Pearl stuck a Lucky Strike in her mouth and lit it with a match. She inhaled deeply. "The most basic rule in this business, kid," she replied through the blue smoke curling up around her, "is one too many little starlets tend to forget once they've made it big." She paused dramatically. "Whoever you battle with . . . or make friends with . . . never, *ever*, under any circumstances, make enemies with the cameraman. He can either be your best friend or your worst enemy. He captures what you do on film, and he can make you look very, very good . . . or very, very bad. Learn whatever you can from him—all the rules and tricks of the trade. Especially your best and worst angles. Work *with* him as if he were part of you. Learn everything he knows, ask questions, study the view through lenses if he lets you so you can see what the camera sees. Then, if you do make it in this cutthroat business, believe you me that will do you more good than anything else you can imagine."

Tamara nodded soberly. "I was always under the impression that it was the director who was most important."

"He is," Pearl replied shortly. She inhaled deeply and blew out a column of smoke. "He usually gets what he wants, even if it means thirty different takes of one scene." Pearl smiled faintly. "Of course, that's *if* the rest of the crew obliges and gives it to him. Often, it's up to them—not him—how many takes a scene requires until he gets the precise effect he wants."

"In other words, the lighting director can sabotage the lights, the cameraman can make a star look bad, the makeup artist—"

"You're learning fast, kid," Pearl said with a note of respect in her raspy voice. "Now, turn around and let me get this thing off you." Deftly Pearl untied the smudged protective white robe Tamara had worn while being made up, and whipped it off her with an expert flick of her wrist. Then Pearl stood back, frowning thoughtfully through a veil of cigarette smoke as she studied Tamara critically one last time. Quickly she stabbed her cigarette out and stepped closer. With an extremely steady hand she penciled in the slightest adjustment to the liner around Tamara's eyes. She held the young woman's gaze steadily. "Well, kid, now you're out of my hands and into theirs."

Even as she spoke, the waiting wardrobe mistress and the dresser descended upon Tamara with the lightning speed of hungry wolves.

The wardrobe mistress was clearly in charge. She was tall and skinny, with hyperthyroid eyes which studied Tamara with cold, capable judiciousness for some time. The dresser, on the other hand, was the antithesis of her superior: tiny, plump, and snappish, she fussed with her hands constantly, never quite able to stand still. Despite their opposing looks and personalities, the two women worked together with unusual, almost telepathic efficiency, and were mysteriously capable of communicating without speaking more than one or two key words. Tamara did not enjoy enduring the exhausting process of their choosing a costume for her, but she suffered through it with a quiet docility unlike her, not uttering a word of complaint. She only wished the two women, each of whom referred to the other by surname— the dresser, she soon discovered was "McBain," while the wardrobe mistress was "Sanders"—would make up their minds about her costume once and for all and be done with the tedious process.

McBain and Sanders were seasoned, uncompromising professionals, not about to be rushed, and the staggering choice of outfits available made speedy selection an impossibility. So Tamara gritted her teeth, knowing that what they were doing was not only their job but also a favor to her. There was nothing short of life itself which was as important as sailing through the screen test with absolute perfection. She wanted this role so badly, needed it so tremendously, that it was an almost palpable hunger.

Besides, their costume selections so far had inspired her confidence. They were the attire which made up the wardrobe of a dazzling film idol, clothes that suited her newly created face and the happy-go-lucky sophistication of the flapper's life of unabashed luxury. There were exciting beaded bodices, beautifully scalloped necklines, rustling silks, shiny satins, smooth velvets; every manner of sparkle, glitter, and glamour to further enhance her exquisite visage. Her jewelry was to be selected from boxloads of dazzling paste earrings and pins, necklaces and bracelets, rings and brooches—all flawless re-creations of the best money could possibly buy. And the headbands and boas! Ostrich and peacock, egret and marabou . . .

Oh, the staggering beauty of it all!

Tamara's ambition to become an actress had been fueled, in the beginning, by the sharply focused, unwavering memories of her mother, by Senda's unrivaled talent for storytelling and acting out various roles in different voices as she did so, effortlessly altering her features as if they were a mask that could be instantly adapted to any part without the aid of makeup or costumes. After Tamara and Inge had arrived in New York, the older woman had tried her utmost to steer Tamara away from such a feckless career as acting. To no avail, of course. Tamara soon discovered that the ambition to act burned deep within her. It flared within the very marrow of her bones. She was not about to be prodded in a different direction, and disregarded Inge's gentle persuasions and concerned admonitions to the contrary. It was the only thing in which she had ever opposed Inge, and with staunch, stolid belief and a mysterious, almost psychic surety, at that. In all other things she obeyed Inge to the letter. Well, almost. Inge had, after all, become a surrogate mother to her, but without having tried to sweep Senda aside and step into her footsteps. On the contrary, Inge wisely and frequently regaled Tamara with memories and anecdotes, embellishing them with each retelling, of course. Senda had conquered the Russian stage, and Tamara was more determined than ever to do the same in New York.

Yet the theater in New York, on which she had pinned so much fervent young hope, had proved a fickle and pointless exercise in futility. The stage blood within her, however, was not subdued by constant rejection. It only continued to boil with more effervescence than before. After a while, even Inge began to prod Tamara in that direction, doing everything within her power to help make the fantasy a reality. In fact, Inge had happily agreed with Tamara's decision that they leave New York for the greener, and hopefully more fruitful, pastures of Hollywood.

Tamara was so deeply engrossed in her thoughts that she became accustomed to the hands of the wardrobe mistress and the dresser touching her body. Only now, after a few minutes of no more fingers groping or tugging at her, did she snap out of her reverie and realize the women must have finished.

The wardrobe mistress stepped back and rubbed her chin thoughtfully. "That's it," she said with finality. "Just the right effect. McBain?"

The plump dresser's head bobbed up and down. "That's it, Sanders," she agreed.

Tamara slid her eyes sideways to catch a glimpse of herself in the mirror. She drew in her breath sharply.

"Well?" the wardrobe mistress asked. "What do *you* think?"

"Now that you ask, I . . . I look positively fabulous, don't I?" Tamara boldly ventured.

"Precisely." The wardrobe mistress regarded her with satisfaction. A feisty little number, she thought. Then she grinned for the first time and gave a thumbs-up signal. "Good luck," she said sincerely.

"Break a leg," the dresser added.

Before Tamara could thank them, the two women departed, leaving her alone with Pearl. As soon as the door shut, Tamara slumped in all her sequined and bejeweled glory, her shoulders drooping heavily as the reality of it all suddenly sank in. She staggered toward a chair, squeezed her green eyes shut, and gripped its back until her knuckles shone white.

"What is it, kid?" Pearl asked anxiously as she stepped quickly forward.

"It's just that . . . I mean . . . I'm really *ready*!" Tamara's eyes flew open as she stared at the stranger in the mirror. "But now that I've waited for this moment so long, and studied so hard, I . . . I can't remember one line." She bit down on her lip and turned slowly to stare at Pearl in horror. "Not a *single* line!" Her voice took on the sibilance of a terrified whisper.

"You'll remember every word once we hustle you over to the soundstage." Pearl laughed her throaty rasp.

"Could this be stage fright?"

"Now, now." Pearl pulled Tamara close, making her lose her grip on the chair back. Tamara looked into the older woman's face.

Pearl smiled and gripped Tamara's hands. "You'll do fine," she said in a soothing voice.

"Yes! I've got to be!"

"Have a seat and give yourself a minute to calm down." Pearl guided Tamara to the sofa. It felt unyielding, not at all comfortable. "Now, breathe deeply."

Tamara took a series of deep, steadying breaths.

"Just relax, kiddo. Pearl will take care of you," she said in a peculiarly soft voice. She stood behind the sofa, hesitated, and then her fingers massaged Tamara's shoulders through the exquisitely beaded gleam of silver and white silk and chiffon. "Just close your eyes and clear your head. Everything else will come to you."

Tamara nodded obeisantly, and Pearl continued kneading her tensed muscles, her hands creeping lower and lower, until they were near the young woman's nubile breasts. Tamara, though she was not totally innocent and guileless, if inexperienced in some matters, let the touch of the other woman soothe her. Pearl was proving useful, after all. The fingers felt so gentle, so light, so . . . caressing.

There was a sudden knock on the door, and both women jumped. Pearl jerked her hands away.

"It's time, Miss Boralevi," a stagehand called out. "Mr. Ziolko should be on the set at any moment!"

Naked or dressed, Louis Frederic Ziolko was too impressive a man to easily melt into a crowd. For one thing, there was his great height, his naturally wavy black hair, his princely Renaissance nose, his sensual, arrogant lips, and his penetrating obsidian eyes. For another, he had the toned, well-developed body of the natural athlete. He looked a casting agent's dream for that ultimate Hollywood prop, the quintessential playboy. And playboy he was, when the opportunity presented itself.

To outsiders who didn't know any better, making movies seemed the ultimate casual life, consisting of forty-five percent glamour and forty-five percent parties, with an occasional ten percent of lackadaisical work thrown in, when in reality the exalted citizens of this celluloid fiefdom thrived on the greatest work to lowest relaxation ratio known since slavery. Filmmaking being a grueling six-day-a-week business with inhuman hours that stretched from sunup well past sundown, these relentlessly driven workaholics naturally took spirited advantage of their one well-earned day of rest—Sunday. Sunday afternoons consisted of endless rounds of swimming parties, tennis matches, and social get-togethers. These legendary events in the Hollywood Hills—most notably Lookout Mountain—actually began on Saturday nights, with stars roaming from house to house, carrying their cocktails with them. Appian Way on Lookout Mountain became known as the Gold Coast, and if it didn't provide enough action, the stars would descend from their roosts, dressed to the nines, and head for Ciro's and the Trocadero to dine and dance. In many ways, these much-celebrated parties were just an extension of work. No one dared turn down the imperial summons of a studio chief's invitation, even if it was well known that he wanted his lawns sprinkled with stars, starlets, directors, and writers to be photographed for the ravenous newspapers and magazines or for the studio's very own newsreels, thereby creating news out of play and exploiting it as a great public-relations event. Not surprisingly, then, Hollywood parties turned into the stuff of legends.

For his part, Louis Ziolko was a regular feature at all these Sunday gatherings, seemingly none the worse for wear after dancing the night away with a beauty on the Sunset Strip. He was a demon on the tennis courts and a fish in the pools, which kept him in superb physical condition. He appeared more mature than his thirty years, and since he was an extraordinarily handsome, cultured, well-mannered bachelor, and women in Hollywood are no different from women the world over, he had more than his fair share of beauties breathing down his neck for friendship, marriage, or a casual tumble in bed in exchange for helping further their careers, or sometimes simply for the pure pleasure of it.

He reveled in this female attention. These Saturday nights and Sunday afternoons helped create Louis Ziolko the legend: the successful, debonair, rich, and sexually heroic young director-about-town. More than one woman had let herself be seduced by him in the mistaken hope of obtaining a ring for her finger; but only one woman ever had, and like most ex-wives, she was but a fading memory to Louis, except when alimony time rolled around.

Despite the torrid affairs and scandals which brewed with the regularity of clockwork, especially in the Hollywood Hills, the film community was a close-knit one, and most studio bosses were downright prudish when it came to matters of sex. Consequently Louis was discreet regarding his more notorious sexual affairs. Otherwise, he was dauntless in his actions and beliefs and cared not an iota for the opinions of others. While he sometimes bedded women who spread the word of his prowess, it was also to his advantage to pay for the gratification of the female company he craved—a thirst he slaked by picking up various prostitutes whose daily paths he would not be in danger of crosssing. Paying for sexual favors was not abhorrent to him, it was practical. He welcomed paying for services rendered, followed by a swift good-bye, with no questions asked, nothing known about him to his partner and vice versa, and above all, no lingering relationships. This was preferable to involved, potentially dangerous affairs that might eventually explode out of proportion and become more complicated than he wanted them to be.

If anything made his life less than perfect, it was the fact that he was unmarried. The trouble was, he had yet to meet a woman he thought he could stand to live with.

While Tamara waited with bated breath for Louis Ziolko's imminent arrival, she had no idea that he was not then on the set, that he had no intention of going there, and that he was certainly not in a good mood. Last night he had spent drinking and screwing vigorously; this morning he had awakened to the worst headache in memory, and worse, he could see everything he'd ever worked for slipping away. Literally. Right in front of his eyes.

Yesterday his troubles had begun when his burgundy-and-black model J Duesenberg had given up the ghost in the middle of Wilshire Boulevard and had had to be towed to a garage, where, he'd been informed, it would have to "set for a week or two till them parts come from Dee-troit." He'd have to use his dark blue Chrysler. Later that night, he'd had to thumb through nearly every page in his "little black book" before he'd finally struck paydirt and found a girl who was available for the night. He'd never used her before but had heard she gave good service.

This morning, he'd awakened to an ominous rumble. His first thought was: My house!

Even in his sleep, he'd heard the ear-splitting groan, and he could have sworn that the house had actually bucked like a goddamn bronco in a rodeo. The terrible thought which haunts all Californians had flashed instantaneously into his mind: Quake! *The* quake! The *killer* quake!

His heart had leapt to his throat as he'd jerked bolt upright from the midst of his peaceful, dreamy sleep, only to catch the call girl rifling his baubles, making a neat pile of his gold-and-diamond cufflinks, diamond evening studs, gold lighter, Cartier cigarette case, and gold Rolex watch.

Then, just as he'd leapt from the bed to throttle the two-bit whore, a horrible cracking sound rent the air. A deep, shuddering rumble had followed, and they'd both been thrown to the deep-pile carpet.

Unlike Louis Ziolko, who was Brooklyn-born and -bred, the girl was a seasoned Californian and found her feet first. Forgetting the expensive baubles on the bureau, she bawled: "Quake!" and made a naked beeline for the nearest doorway.

Yanking that particular door open proved to be a dreadful

mistake. It opened onto the narrow walk-around deck facing the rising vertical hillside of the canyon behind the house. Ziolko was suddenly wide-awake, horrified by the wall of glutinous mud flowing ceaselessly through the door like brown vomit spewing from a monstrous mouth. He knew in a flash that unless he acted fast, both of them would be smothered within seconds.

He yanked the terrified girl by the arm and they both escaped by making a dash for the balcony door on the other side of the room. Even as they ran across the balcony toward the driveway, Ziolko couldn't help wishing that he'd let the thief drown in the morass of mud, but this belated thought instantly fled from his mind as another, more treacherous one took sudden precedence: the balcony underfoot, which hung three hundred feet above Los Angeles, was actually groaning and heaving, its huge concrete slabs buckling one after the other.

Earthquake! Ziolko's mind still screamed in silent terror. *The killer quake's here*!

Only once they stood on the still-unmoving driveway did it occur to Ziolko that the ground all around was steady. Only the hillside on which the house was perched was sliding down the canyon in a sheet of liquid mud.

Now, standing naked in the torrential icy blast of rain, Ziolko screeched, "It's a mud slide! A goddamn mud slide!" Shivering with cold as they stood on the relative safety of the driveway, both he and the girl riveted their eyes on Ziolko's pride and joy—his house. The cantilevered Art Deco structure, all concrete beams, sturdy pilings driven deep into the hillside, and streamlined balconies that jutted proudly out over Los Angeles, had never been intended for this nearly vertical site, a fact which the previous owners, an asbestos tycoon and his young starlet wife, had taken no heed of whatsoever. They instructed the worried contractor to sink pilings into the soft hillside so that the ocean-liner superstructure of the house looked as if a massive tidal wave had detached it in toto from a seagoing hull out in the Pacific and washed it up against the hillside.

A year later, the wife of the tycoon had developed a passion for all things Latin and moved into a Spanish stucco "hacienda" in Bel Air complete with a new Cuban playboy husband whose sexual endowment and endurance were legendary.

When Ziolko learned that the house was for sale he'd promptly purchased it, had a huge swimming pool blasted into the hillside at the far end of the house, dotted the rooms sparsely with sleek-veneered Art Deco furnishings, and settled in contentedly, laughing at the spoilsports who in turn laughed and condemned the canyon-hugging folly.

But now it was he who was damning the house, all five vertical acres of sparsely vegetated grounds, the sixteen huge rooms and four-car garage, the granite-tiled patio surrounding the heated swimming pool—he was cursing, in fact, everything and everyone. Angrily he watched his beautiful house crack neatly in half, one part sliding piecemeal down the steep hillside, the other still perched precariously to the hill. For a long, intensely sad moment he had a child's-eye view of the rear of a dollhouse—three stories of exposed, cut-away rooms: the sweeping, monumental staircase, the dining room, and the bedroom where the mud was still gushing through to fall in a perfect brown waterfall down into the canyon bed three hundred feet below.

"Goddamn sons of bitches who sold me this fucking place!" he thundered. "I'll sue their goddamn asses off!"

"My watch!" the girl sobbed quietly. "My clothes." She stood there pathetically trying to cover her exposed breasts and the blond patch of hair between her thighs. "All of my best things were in that bedroom!" she wailed, her teeth chattering and her body racked by shivers from the cold.

"Fuck *you*, you two-bit whoring thief!" Ziolko bellowed. "It's my goddamn house I'm worried about!"

Ziolko and the girl, staring from their ringside spot beside the Chrysler, watched awestruck as, with a doomsday rumble and a decidedly Cecil B. De Mille effect, the remainder of the house cracked into four giant pieces, alternately sliding and somersaulting down the rain-drenched hillside. Tons of molten mud slid down after it, a slow-moving river to bury it forever.

Slowly Louis Ziolko lifted his rain-and-tear-streaked face. Abruptly he threw back his head and began to laugh uproariously, the rain pouring down his face, not caring that the girl thought he was a psycho bound for the loony bin.

What a farce!

Hell, now that he'd had a minute to think things out, they weren't all *that* bad after all! At least he'd managed to obtain this grand house in the first place, he still had his enviable position as the number-one director in a town full of directors, and as such, wielded immense influence and power—no easy feat for anyone to obtain, let alone Louis Ziolko from Williamsburg, Brooklyn. Thank God he'd managed to escape *that*. It hadn't been easy, but he'd always had sense: street sense, business sense, art sense, motion-picture sense. The senses he hadn't been born with, he'd simply cultivated.

"My son, the *macher*," his mother, Zelda, used to complain disparagingly to anyone who would listen. "Too smart for his own good, he is. He'll come to no good. I know it. A nogoodnik he is."

But these very qualities had served him well in the past and were serving him well now. Otherwise, he'd never have had the foresight to sign an enormously expensive insurance policy to go along with the deed to the house. The place was tremendously overinsured.

Hell, he'd end up *making* money!

Things were looking better and better. Who would have believed it? If he'd needed the money, which he didn't, and if he'd tried to sell that goddamned white elephant of a house, he would have had to wait for years to find a sucker. So right there, he was coming out ahead. The insurance company might scream and tear out its hair, but it had no choice but to pay up.

And as far as the film business went, his position had never been better. The Depression was bringing out moviegoers by the droves, perhaps because it got people's minds off their problems. His studio boss, Oscar Skolnik, O.T. as he was known, the legendary wunderkind of International Artists—what Irving Thalberg was to MGM—had already slated him to direct three new pictures for IA over the next eighteen months. Another ninety thousand dollars there.

Indeed, California wasn't called the Golden State for nothing!

"Now what do we do?" the girl wailed plaintively, yanking Louis Ziolko back to harsh reality, to the rain-drenched, menacing present of the chill Los Angeles hillside.

Ziolko didn't waste time or words. "We drive out of this hellhole before the rest of the goddamn hillside ends up down there and buries us along with it," he said grimly. "That's what we do." He yanked the driver's side of the midnight-blue Chrysler's door open and climbed inside, gratified to see the key. The leather upholstery felt like sticky ice against his bare wet buttocks, but he scarcely noticed the discomfort. He reached across the seat and flung open the passenger door for the girl. She stood there stupidly, not knowing quite what to do.

"Well, get in!" Ziolko ordered tersely.

The girl glanced around uncertainly, as if she had any other option, then slid in awkwardly beside him. "I haven't got any clothes," she complained morosely, staring out the rain-streaked windshield.

"You'll get some." Ziolko turned the key and stepped on the starter. The engine hesitated, sputtered, and abruptly died. Ziolko cursed and pressed on the starter again, careful not to wear out the battery. After a few more coughs and stops, the engine finally turned over steadily. He let out a sigh of relief. "Goddamn rain," he muttered. "How come it never rained like this in New York?" he growled.

"Because it snows in New York," the girl muttered sullenly.

Ziolko ignored her and switched on the windshield wipers. They began squeaking slowly to and fro, barely able to keep up with the blinding buckets of rain the sky seemed to fling against the glass. Finally a vague, blurry arc of vision appeared. He jerked at the stickshift, threw the car into reverse, and looked over his shoulder in vain to make out the end of the drive through the rain-streaked rear window. The rear bumper made unceremonious contact with the hillside behind them, and both he and the girl were flung forward in their seats.

"Jesus!" the girl breathed, gingerly touching her forehead. "I hit my head on the windshield. I could have been killed, you bastard!"

"Not soon enough," Ziolko grunted under his breath. All he knew was that the further he got away from this goddamn sliding hillside, and the sooner he dumped the girl, the better. After that he'd have a chance to get resettled, to think. The last thing he needed now was a shrew.

But he consoled himself with the fact that the engine throbbed steadily in anticipation, and he swerved the car in a half-circle and nosed the hood straight up the steep drive, more by memory than vision. He didn't bother to come to a stop at the intersection, and swung right onto the canyon road. He figured that chances of a collision were rare; the road was hardly ever used, especially not in miserable weather like this.

Ziolko sneaked a glance sideways. The girl sat hunched over, shivering convulsively, her teeth chattering and her flawless, sculptured skin textured with gooseflesh. At least she was keeping quiet about his lethal driving on the hairpin curves.

After a long silence, the girl slid a sideways glance over at Ziolko. "Got any cash to tide me over?" she asked in a small voice. "I need to buy some clothes to replace those. Besides, you didn't pay me yet."

Ziolko burst out laughing, a laugh from the depths of his

guts. It was the first good laugh he'd had all morning, and it did him a world of good.

"What's so funny?" the girl demanded belligerently, furtively sliding further down in her seat.

Ziolko slammed his fists on the horn for emphasis. "I'll tell you what's so funny. Money! You want money, I'll back up the way we came and you can go scavenging around down where the house is. That's where my fucking money is!"

The girl muttered a curse under her breath.

"Reach in back. There're some lap blankets on the seat. Give me one of them, you take the other. Least we won't be naked as jaybirds. That's all we need now, being thrown in the clink." Ziolko pulled over to the shoulder of the road, screeched to a halt, and they wrapped themselves into the scratchy plaid shetland wool. "Where should I drop you?"

"I told you. My apartment's down near the Strip."

Ziolko reached past her, punched the walnut glove compartment open with a stab of his finger, and fished out a five-dollar bill he kept handy for gassing up in emergencies. "Here's a fin. Take it. I'll drop you off and send the rest to you later today."

The girl palmed the money eagerly, and sat in a less sullen silence. Ziolko tried to guess her age. She claimed to be twenty-one and looked it, but close up, seventeen was probably more like it. Well, the younger the better.

The girl looked surprised when Ziolko made a sudden left turn into a deserted side road, the branches of wet trees brushing and whipping the car. Then he slammed the brakes so hard they were both thrown forward once again.

"Where are we?" the girl demanded. "You crazy or something? We aren't even in town yet."

"You got your fin, didn't you? So we aren't quite finished with our business deal yet." He grinned lasciviously, flipped open the lap blanket at his groin, and grabbing the girl by the neck, pulled her down into his crotch. "Just because I lost my house doesn't mean we've finished."

The girl glared up at him with murderous eyes. Then the fight seemed to go out of her and she slumped, bending forward. Her lips found Ziolko's penis and she began licking and sucking halfheartedly.

"You can put a little more effort into it than that." Ziolko grabbed her hair and yanked it. Then he leaned back on the headrest, shut his eyes, and moaned as her moist mouth slid up and down his tumescent shaft.

"You see?" Ziolko asked himself. Everything isn't so bad after all. It's all what you make of a situation.

A half-hour later, Louis Ziolko, with characteristic dauntlessness and a blasé disregard for what anyone might think, screeched to a stop in front of the Beverly Hills Hotel. Then, tossing the Shetland blanket around him like a matador's cape, he emerged from the car, ignoring the gaping parking attendant's openmouthed expression. The doorman, who thought he had seen everything in his thirty-year career guarding the gates of America's premier hotels, would have snapped into action under normal circumstances, hurrying forward holding his huge protective umbrella aloft. However, he seemed as incapable of moving as the tubbed topiary bushes atop the steps, and stared at Ziolko with a mixture of incredulity and shock.

Ignoring their expressions, Ziolko held his head high as he strode confidently up the steps and pushed his way past the ogling doorman. It was only then that the doorman recognized this drenched, nomadic-looking apparition. Realization dawning, he snapped suddenly to, clicked his heels together respectfully, and held the door wide.

"I'm sorry, Mr. Ziolko," the doorman called out sincerely to Ziolko's back. "I didn't recognize you—"

Ziolko waved away his apologies without turning around and hurried barefoot into the lobby, seemingly impervious to the incredulous stares he received as he marched up to the concierge's desk. Unfortunately it was not manned by any familiar face, but a man who could only stare at him in shock. Ziolko glared right back at him. Then the concierge cleared his throat in one cupped hand and discreetly signaled for the security guard with the other.

"I want a bungalow—number one if it's available," Ziolko demanded of the nonplussed clerk, who looked positively apoplectic. "And a double cabana by the pool."

The concierge's shock was immediately replaced by an obvious smirk. "I'm sorry, sir," he said smoothly, recovering his composure, "but we're booked up." He busied himself with some letters he was sorting and turned his back.

"What do you mean, you're booked up? There's *always* a bungalow available for me. If not bungalow one, then another." Ziolko clicked his fingers. "Snap to it!"

The concierge turned around and sighed with exasperation. He leaned over the desk, wiggled a forefinger for Ziolko to draw nearer, and lowered his voice. "Look, mister," he said harshly, "we don't want any trouble here. Understand?"

Ziolko fixed the concierge with his most intimidating glare. "Straighten your tie, it's crooked!"

Seeing the concierge's hand instinctively fly to his collar made him feel slightly better. But not for long. He felt a firm pressure on his bare right arm.

Twisting around, Ziolko came face-to-face with the house detective. He, too, apparently was new and didn't recognize him.

Where *was* everybody when you needed someone?

"If you'll leave quietly, we won't be forced to call the police," the detective said in a firm but soft voice. He spoke out of the corner of his mouth.

Ziolko shrugged the detective's hand off and brushed the spot where he had been touched. From his expression, it was clear that the staff had gone too far. "Call the police, if you like, but time is money and you're wasting mine. I demand to speak to the proprietor this very instant. That is, if you value your jobs." He raised his eyebrows questioningly and stared from one man to the other.

And then, before either employee could come to a decision, he heard a familiar friendly voice. "Louis?" a man called out with a good-humored laugh. "Is that *you* under that abominable blanket?"

Ziolko turned, relieved to see that the proprietor himself, possibly sensing a potential problem through the power of some secret antennae known only to hoteliers, was bearing down on him in the flesh.

As he approached, the hotelier snapped his fingers, and the detective slid silently away and the concierge hurriedly busied himself sorting the mail in order to hide his embarrassment.

"Yes, it's me under this blanket," Ziolko said testily. He shivered, for the first time really feeling cold and wet. "And for your information, it's Shetland wool, which can hardly be called abominable."

"Indeed. So it is."

Quickly Ziolko explained his situation.

"The key to bungalow one." The proprietor held his hand out to the concierge for the key. "And have a hospitality basket delivered to Mr. Ziolko with our compliments. Got that?"

The concierge apparently did. He reddened, gulped, and sprang into action. He didn't need to be told more.

Two hours later Louis Ziolko, wearing a thick terry-cloth robe supplied by the hotel, felt completely rejuvenated.

Warmed by a steaming hot bath and a full bottle of vintage French champagne, which had been furtively delivered by a room-service waiter—and smuggled into the country by rum-runners from Mexico—he was comfortably ensconced on a velvet sofa, his lifeline to the outside world, a black telephone, at his side. He was feeling better with each passing minute. His insides were positively beginning to glow, the bungalow was dry and heated and safe, the rain was kept at bay, and except for the fact that the pool and its famous deal-making environs were closed due to the weather, he couldn't have asked for anything more. Even the critical essentials necessary to a gentleman were on their way. He had telephoned the proprietor of his favorite haberdashery, which had his sizes on file, and he would soon have enough clothes to tide him over while new custom-made ones were being fitted and sewn. On the coffee table next to him, the enormous hospitality basket overflowed with polished fruit and fresh cheeses; if it was less than perfect it was only because it did not contain a single ounce of liquor. But he couldn't fault the hotel for that: it was Prohibition, and the champagne was more than adequate, a pleasant surprise, in fact.

His stomach began growling, informing him that it was past his usual breakfast time. Never one to deny himself anything, he picked up the phone and ordered a hearty breakfast from room service. Next, he called Zelda, his mother, who lived in a house he'd bought her in Pasadena—near enough so she couldn't complain that he was too far away, and far enough away that she couldn't simply drop by whenever the whim seized her. Last, but not least, he called the studio and cancelled all his appointments.

"But you've got three screen tests for *The Flappers* lined up!" Janice Frauenfelder, his secretary, protested.

"Make them tomorrow. No, tell you what, beautiful. Better yet, reschedule them for the day after."

He hung up on her protests.

When room service wheeled in his breakfast, he lifted the silver domes covering the eggs Benedict, fruit platter, and bagels liberally swathed with cream cheese and thinly sliced smoked salmon. Just as he was about to attack the eggs, he was interrupted by the messengers delivering his clothes and jewelry. He let his fork clatter back down on the plate and, once the messengers were well-tipped and gone, poured himself a cup of steaming black coffee and let the food grow cold.

Now that he had clothes to wear and, thanks to the

proprietor who, without having to be asked, had loaned him $200 out of his own pocket for "walking around" money, Ziolko no longer felt hungry. Indeed, what he was most in need of was a prowl, not food. The girl last night hadn't fulfilled him in the least, especially after the mud slide.

As if to punctuate that fact, his penis grew tumescent under the robe.

Whistling softly to himself, he quickly pulled on a sweater, trousers, shoes, and raincoat. Already he could feel himself rising to the challenge of the hunt. He'd cruise the streets, he decided, searching the protective doorways for a pickup, and if he struck out doing that, he'd drop by a few drugstores for coffee. There were always hungry girls to be found nursing a cup of coffee or a glass of soda on rainy days. Maybe he'd strike it lucky and pick up a dreamboat.

"Ah just wish you'd make up yer mind once and fer all," Jewel said testily in her Southern accent. "We all have to make plans, ya know."

Juliet "just-call-me-Jewel" Haynie was forty-nine years old, a seasoned waitress fighting the losing battle against time by dying her hair a garish flame orange and concealing her ruddy complexion under a ton of makeup; she was also one of a handful of women in Los Angeles who considered her waitress job her real calling, and had never had the slightest ambition to break into show business in any way, shape, or form.

"I know, Jewel, I'm sorry," Tamara said contritely. "Really I am. It's just that today's test was called off. It wasn't my fault."

"It ain't never nobody's fault," Jewel sniffed snappishly. "Sometimes Ah wonder why Ah'm so good to you kids. It's always 'Jewel this, Jewel that!' " She squinted her fluttery, heavily made-up violet eyes.

"Is it all right if I work today and you take over my shift the day after tomorrow instead?" Tamara held her breath.

Jewel placed a hand on her hip, sighed deeply, and rolled her eyes in exasperation while nonchalantly popping an enormous bubble of gum. "Oh, all *right*. Just this once, y'heah?" She waggled a chipped, brightly lacquered fingernail at Tamara.

"I hear." On impulse Tamara embraced Jewel and beamed for the first time since she'd been told the screen test had been cancelled.

Jewel made a production of scowling and pushed her away. "You'll wrinkle mah uniform if you don't watch it."

287

They were in the sweltering kitchen of the Sunset Restaurant, a glorified coffee shop which stayed open from six in the morning till ten at night. The place was narrow and deep; up front, a big plate-glass window looked out from the dining room at the traffic swishing silently along the rain-swept boulevard. Maroon-upholstered booths for four lined the window as well as the two side walls; smaller tables made up little islands in the center of the room. The ubiquitous counter with its maroon swivel stools separated the aisle behind the soda fountain from the kitchen, and the pass-through window to the kitchen was already stacked with heavy plates in anticipation for the noon rush. If, that was, there would be a noon rush in this weather. Even shoppers from Woolworth's next door weren't drifting over like they usually did on sunny days.

More through a remarkably well-honed sixth sense than by ordinary sight or sound, Jewel sensed that the front door of the coffee shop had opened and shut. Signaling for Tamara to stay put, she squeezed past José, the Mexican cook, and got up on tiptoe and leaned forward, peering out the pass-through window to check on who had arrived or departed. She saw beads of rainwater glistening silvery as a new arrival eased out of his creamy coat and shook the rain off it before hanging it up on one of the hooks by the door. From the look of it, it was an expensive coat, and Jewel's calculating mind instantly translated it into potential tips. She was an expert at guessing generosity and miserliness just from the looks of customers, and she was seldom wrong.

This one would tip well. Thank God.

The rest of the patrons looked far less well-off; they were obvious refugees from the streets, driven indoors by the rain. At the counter, a scrawny, toothless old lady in a dirty turban slowly gummed a sugar doughnut, rinsing tiny bitefuls down with a glass of water, trying to make it last. A quiet, reserved young man occupied a booth by the far wall, taking nervous little sips from his coffee cup, which he held wrapped in his hands as if trying to absorb the warmth through his fingers. He had been coming in for a week now, and from flirting with him, Jewel had learned that he was an unemployed actor trying to break into the movies. She'd had her eyes on him ever since he'd first walked in. He was just her type, even if she was old enough to be his mother. Grandmother, even, but she didn't want to think about that, and pushed it out of her mind.

"Ah'll be right out," she called to no one in particular, then rocked back on her heels and turned her attention to

Tamara again. "By the way, Janet called up earlier. She won't be in, so we're the only two workin' today. 'Fraid we'll both have to stay till ten. Shouldn't be too bad, though, what with the rain an' all. Just hope the tips won't be too bad. Got me a nice dress on layaway an' Ah wanna wear it 'fore it goes outta style. Still, Ah cain't blame nobody fer stayin' away in this godawful weather. Ain't no time to be out 'lessen you have to."

"I'll say."

"Damn right it ain't." Jewel cocked her head and frowned, then tapped Tamara on the arm. "Lissen, somebody else just come in. Ah gotta run, honey. If Ah don't, the customers'll be screamin' bloody murder. You can take the counter soon as yer changed. Ah'll chat with you later." She paused. "Plus there's that cute young actor Ah tol' you 'bout. He's waitin' on his burger." Jewel gave two well-timed snorts, wiggled her shoulders in a sexy shudder, and added, "Wish he'd sink his teeth into me 'stead o' that old meat."

Tamara had to laugh. "You're incorrigible, Jewel."

Jewel flapped her hand limply. "Ah ain't incorrigible, honey. Ah'm horny!" And with that, Jewel tucked her chin into her chest, leaned forward as if into a wind, extended an arm straight out to push on the swinging door with her flat palm, and marched purposefully out into the dining room. The door flapped shut behind her.

"Don' know 'bout that Jool," José muttered, shaking his head as he flipped a sizzling burger over on the grill. The grease splattered him as he pressed it flat with a spatula, but he had long since become inured to it. Then, turning his back to the grill, he moved over to the big chopping block and began slicing a huge onion with a big, sharply honed knife. "Sometime, she get into big trouble. You wait an' see."

"Oh, I wouldn't worry about Jewel so much, José," Tamara told him. "Bet she knows how to take care of herself better than you or me."

"Yeah, bot how 'bout the poor *hombres*, huh? She take a big bite out of this one and dat one an' then spit them out again. I seen her do it again an' again." He shook his head morosely. "For two years already I tole her I love her, an' she always reject me. How you like that?"

Tamara looked surprised. This was news to her. "You?" she asked incredulously. "*You've* been after her, José? Seriously?"

The cook nodded unhappily, his drooping Zapata mustache making him look all the sadder. "Only she wan' all the others, but she don' wan' me."

"She's a heartbreaker, Jewel is," Tamara consoled soberly. Then she patted him on the back. "Maybe she'll wake up and come to her senses one of these days." She smiled reassuringly.

"You really tink so?" José asked, his hopes rising.

"Maybe. You can never tell. Just don't be too depressed, and don't get your hopes up too high either."

"You a nice girl, Señorita Tamara. Now, why Jool not be nice like you?"

"She *is* nice, under all her hardness and flirting." It was high time she got moving. "Well, I better hurry up and change. See you later, José." Tamara gave a wave and hurried toward the storeroom in back, which doubled as a changing room, while José continued slicing onions.

At that moment Jewel's face appeared at the pass-through window. "Where's that well-done burger fer my cutie pie?" she hissed darkly at José. "An' stop gossipin' 'bout me, 'fore Ah take that knife away from you an' leave you singin' soprano!"

José looked up at her and continued slicing the onion, not paying attention to what he was doing. His soulful, hurt dark eyes were filled with tears from the onions.

"Well?" Jewel snapped, slapping the window's counter sharply with the flat of a hand. "What're you waitin' fer?"

José jumped at the report, and the onion slipped from his grasp and went flying. It was then that the accident happened. The razor-sharp knife descended, chopping his thumb with a sickening crunch.

"Aieee!" José let out a sudden shriek, stared at his hand with bulging carp's eyes, and dropped the knife on the floor with a clatter. He staggered backward. "Now look wha' you make me do!" he screamed.

"*Laws!*" Jewel gasped, her face turning putty through the thick pink powder. She gulped noisily. Then she found her feet and disappeared from the window. "Ah'll be right in, José!" she called urgently. "*T'mara!*"

Hearing her name screamed out, Tamara quickly backtracked to the grill. She saw why she had been summoned so urgently, and she clapped a hand over her mouth. Her stomach lurched and roiled, and for a long, terrible moment she was certain she was going to be sick.

José's hand poured an enormous, steady stream of blood, and his thumb seemed to hang away from the other fingers at an absurdly crooked angle. The sharply honed knife had obviously sliced it neatly, even severing the bone at the first joint. The spray of blood was crimson, a bright, wet red against his neat, starched cook's whites.

She gripped the edge of the worktable to steady herself.

"My feenger!" José was screaming, dancing around in horror. "My feenger! I gonna die!"

Jewel burst through the swinging door like an angel to the rescue. "Ah'll take care of this," she called out as she rushed past Tamara and took over. Not for nothing was she in charge of the restaurant. She had been working around kitchens most of her life, and had seen plenty of accidents. First aid came naturally to her. The first thing she did was sit José down, grab a handful of ice shavings, wrap them in a towel, and press it tightly around the severed thumb. Then she turned to Tamara. "He'll have to be driven to the hospital immediately," she told Tamara. "This here thumb needs stitchin' and settin' bad. Here, hold this tight while Ah go see 'bout somebody drivin' José to the emergency room."

"Is he going to be all right?" Tamara asked tremulously, pressing down around the thumb.

" 'Course he's gonna be all right!" Jewel snapped fiercely. "Just make sure you keep pressin' it tight to stanch the blood." Jewel disappeared, and returned in a flash with a clerk from Woolworth's next door. Just jumping out and back in had gotten her soaked, but she didn't seem to care. "Hank here's got a car," she announced crisply. "José, you take over holdin' that thumb and go with him. Us girls'll hold down the fort. Keep holdin' it tight!"

Before Hank and José were out the door, Jewel was already busy washing blood from the worktable and counters. "It's all my fault. Ah shouldn'ta been at him, the po' thang."

"It wasn't your fault," Tamara said. "It was an accident."

"Never mind what it was. There ain't no time fer us to chat. We're shorthanded now. Lucky fer us that your test's been postponed and you come in today."

Yes, and unlucky for me, Tamara thought. And for Inge too. She started back to the storeroom to change into her uniform.

"Fergit 'bout changin'," Jewel said. "There ain't no time." Jewel reached for an apron and looped it over her head. "T'mara, git on out in the dinin' room. You do all the waitin' an Ah'll do the cookin, God help 'em all!"

Tamara hurried out the swinging door.

Without Jewel's competence, the dining room had quickly turned into bedlam.

Despite the rain, a sudden crowd had descended upon the restaurant. Unfortunately, everyone was in a hurry to eat, and the weather brought out the worst in tempers. They were the most demanding customers Tamara had had to serve to date. She dashed nervously from one table to the next, taking orders and rushing back again with filled plates and pots of steaming coffee. In her nervousness she dropped one plate of food, mixed up three orders, and tripped and spilled coffee all over the guest whose trench coat was hanging by the door. Tamara stared at him in horror, wishing the floor would open up and swallow her whole.

"Ooooh . . . I'm *sor*-ry!" she blabbered in horror. "I've ruined your beautiful sweater!" Her face burning scarlet, she rushed back to the counter, grabbed a stack of paper napkins, and began dabbing ineffectually at the spreading brown stain on the man's sweater. Clearly it was ruined. She wanted to die.

But the man didn't seem to mind. He was staring mesmerized at her, as if he'd found a particularly priceless gem.

She stopped dabbing at his sweater and took a step backward. She was fast becoming disconcerted by the way he kept staring up at her. "Is something the matter?" she asked shakily. "I mean . . . other than the coffee I spilled on you?"

Louis Ziolko grinned and grabbed her arm as she was about to scurry away. "Hey, beautiful. How'd you like to be in pictures?"

International Artists, Inc., had been started eight years earlier by a husband-wife couple, two disgruntled motion-picture stars, Laura Banker and Clyfford Shannon. For ten years they had reigned as *the* show-business couple, the brightest stars in a dazzling firmament, but even so, they were disgusted with the roles forced upon them, the hold their previous studio had on them contractually, and their inability to express themselves creatively. Luckily they had amassed a considerable fortune. Even more luckily, their names were money in the bank. When it came time to renew their contracts, they figured that they were far better off starting their own studio than they were indenturing themselves for another period of five years.

So International Artists, popularly known as IA, was born. The company, relying on the box-office power of its star owners, became a major success virtually overnight. Then, three years, seven Banker-Shannon films, and twenty-nine other pictures later, the world's most celebrated screen couple died in a fiery automobile crash.

International Artists was left adrift, without a captain at its helm and minus its two most bankable stars. For a year the company floundered. The banks threatened to call in their loans. Bankruptcy was visible on the horizon.

The heirs of Banker and Shannon decided to sell.

Enter Oscar Tenney Skolnik.

At age thirty-four, Skolnik was already well on his way to becoming a full-fledged American legend. It seemed there was nothing he couldn't do if he set his mind to it. His exploits were legion. He was the first of the big-time corporate raiders, and so proud of that fact that he wanted everyone to know it, unwittingly creating a moneymaking public-relations firm in the process. He relished giving birth to corporations, pirating companies, building a nationwide conglomerate, gaining ever more power, and basking in celebrity. He couldn't get enough publicity. Naturally, there were men richer than he who enjoyed their wealth quietly, but during those bleak, dark years of the Depression, the multimillions he flaunted fired the imagination of a depressed, starving public. It pleased him to no end when he read in the New York *Times* that the new equation for wealth was "Skolnik = $."

Of course, what he didn't advertise was the fact that he hadn't been born into poverty. Far from it. He'd had a nice head start in becoming wealthy. In 1915, an inheritance of a quarter of a million dollars was a healthy-enough jumping-off point—more than enough seed money to sow a sprawling empire. Still, his achievement was astonishing. He had a truly magic flair for making money multiply. In the fifteen years following his father's untimely death aboard the torpedoed liner *Lusitania,* the nineteen-year-old Skolnik parlayed his inheritance into a seventeen-million-dollar fortune, an almost-unheard-of sum. By then, his companies and investments were such that they would from that point on continue multiplying astronomically, ad infinitum.

Later, critics and armchair economists would deride his spectacular successes, pointing out that the achievements were minimal: the time had simply been ripe for picking up invaluable companies, and investments and financial wizardry had had little, if anything, to do with it. After all, thanks to the Depression and the misery of millions, companies were going begging for ridiculously cheap prices to anyone who had any money. Too, the period following World War I was a technological wonderland, more dazzling than the previous ten centuries combined. The world had taken quantum leaps forward, bursting into a future few people could predict.

But Oscar Skolnik could and did. He was among the first visionaries to predict the eventual decline of the railroads and the advent of air travel. Thus he began his own fledgling airline—Trans U.S. Airways, more commonly known as TUSA—which began with government-contract mail routes, and in later decades revolutionized travel and became a mammoth multibillion-dollar carrier, with its distinctive blue-and-white planes logging millions of miles each year.

He borrowed liberally from Henry Ford's pioneering genius, applying the method of assembly lines to building aircraft—Skolnik Aviation.

In 1920 Skolnik had been one of the first men in the United States to foresee the popularity of radio not as a novelty but as a major business with limitless opportunities. He subsequently purchased the third license to broadcast in the United States, thus creating WSBN—Skolnik Broadcasting Network. In later years he was to apply his radio know-how to television, with even greater success.

But above all, Oscar Skolnik was a dedicated womanizer. None of his myriad business interests or daredevil exploits could compare with his passion for women. The truth of the matter was, he loved women, all women, but the more beautiful and celebrated they were, the better. Indeed, it was this passion for the female of his species which first attracted him to motion pictures. Figuring that the film industry was filled with the most glamorous, sought-after women in the country, he decided that he should have a film studio of his own.

As it had in all his other ventures, luck smiled on him in this one. He didn't even have to go through the trouble and expense of setting up a studio. International Artists happened to be going begging at just the right time.

Under him, IA was not only saved. With his famous Midas touch it quickly flourished and became a power to be reckoned with. Soon he moved his entire business headquarters to Los Angeles in order to keep his eagle eye on his favorite business and be close to his beloved women.

It became immediately apparent to him that IA suffered from one crucial problem. It was missing the most fundamentally necessary asset of any film kingdom: a major, full-fledged female star of its own, one with enormous, sure-fire box-office appeal. At first he had managed to get around the problem by relying upon loan-outs from other major studios but he knew that was no solution. To secure IA's future, he needed his own Gloria Swanson, his own Greta Garbo, his own Constance Bennett—or better yet, all three.

In the past, IA had depended too heavily upon its deceased actress and actor owners. Insecure as only creative people can be, no matter how successful, they had loathed competition, and had been adamant about being their company's only major, bankable stars. They hadn't been about to share the limelight with anyone else.

Now, without any major stars, IA was in peril.

Skolnik had instinctively recognized this problem. However, he hadn't anticipated the sheer difficulty in finding, or creating, a bankable star. Though he had systematically raided talent from other studios with promises of huge salaries when their current contracts expired—Louis Ziolko, the celebrated director from MGM, and Miles Gabriel, the debonair leading man from Paramount, had been among those, as well as a host of solid supporting players—IA continuously suffered from the lack of a leading screen siren to pair with Miles. Not that Skolnik's talent scouts hadn't tried. He'd been kept well-informed, and knew that his scouts had been everywhere, turning over any rock where the elusive star he was looking for might be hiding. Nationwide, they had scoured local theaters, attended talent contests, beauty contests, and county fairs. Either something was lacking in the possible candidates, or another studio had gotten there first. He had gone so far as to negotiate for untried but promising new talent from other studios, prepared to buy out their contracts for far more than they were worth, but thus far the six starlets he had depended on had fizzled like defective firecrackers, despite IA's mighty publicity machine.

The public simply hadn't warmed up to them, and Oscar Skolnik, unaccustomed to failure, didn't like it one bit. He was outwardly calm and emotionless, but the very idea of Hollywood getting the better of him rankled deeply, burned in a silent rage within him.

"Goddamm it!" he fumed over and over. "There's got to be a bewitching woman out there somewhere!"

Among the first things Oscar Skolnik had done upon acquiring IA was to set up weekly Monday-morning meetings —nuts-and-bolts meetings which focused mainly on the behind-the-scenes workings of the studio. Regulars at the Monday meetings generally included Milton Ivey, head of the legal department; Marty Scher, head of accounting; Edward Brain, who handled distribution and was in charge of IA's chain of three hundred outrightly owned nationwide cinemas; Skolnik's severe but efficient secretary, Miss Schultz, who took copious notes and kept her first name a jealously guarded secret;

Rhoda Dorsey, who headed the reading department, where fifteen full-time readers pored over books and plays and wrote reports on their viability as possible film properties; Bruce Slesin, vice-president in charge of publicity; Roger Callas, the general manager of IA and Skolnik's right-hand man, whose duty it was to keep the cogs of the studio's business machinery humming; Carol Anderegg, whose scouts were always out sniffing for new talent; and, unless he was involved in shooting, testing, or in production, Louis Ziolko. Other studio executives and managers were summoned on an "as-needed" basis, depending on the subjects under discussion.

The Monday meetings focused upon finances, distribution, production schedules, projects under consideration, projects in the works, who was available for loan from other studios, how many inches of film had been shot per dollar, whom they should or shouldn't cast and in what, safety procedures and legal liability for stunt crews, and, invariably, the subject would somehow always roll around to Skolnik's pet peeve: finding and developing a beautiful, talented major new star.

On this particularly dreary, rain-lashed Monday morning in January, Skolnik looked around his conference table with the deceptive lack of emotion typical of him and asked, "Where's Ziolko?"

The others glanced at Louis Ziolko's empty leather chair and shrugged, but then Miss Schultz, seated off in one corner, spiral-bound shorthand pad poised on her crossed legs, spoke up and said, "Mr. Ziolko was *supposed* to be testing."

"*Supposed* to be?" Skolnik asked without turning around to look at her.

"Yes, sir," Miss Schultz sniffed. "But according to his secretary, he won't be in today. It seems his house slid down the canyon."

"Beats hell out of me why anyone'd want to live on a mountainside," Skolnik grumbled, eliciting some chuckles. "But he's all right?"

"I believe so, O.T."

"Then why the hell didn't he come in to work? Doesn't he realize that a screen test costs an average of four thousand dollars whether it's made or not?"

Louis Ziolko could scarcely contain his excitement. His body temperature rose feverishly, and his heart thumped at twice its normal rate. He was dizzy with delirium and felt like dancing and shouting for joy.

He had *found* her! *Her*! That ephemeral presence, that new face for which everyone at IA had been fruitlessly scouring every nook and cranny of the country, that face which, like Helen of Troy's, would be capable of launching a thousand ships, inspire a million dreams, drive men insane with lust, and miracle of miracles, had been right here all along, practically under all their very noses!

The very notion that she'd been the proverbial hop, skip, and jump from the studio struck him as being too, *too* delicious. It was, he considered, not at all unlike finding a wish-wielding genie inside a Coca-Cola bottle.

Would he ever knock Oscar Skolnik's black silk socks off when he brought *her* in! He couldn't wait to see Skolnik's face. He had made the once-in-a-lifetime discovery, and it was his, and his alone. Posterity would see to it that he would receive the credit for having discovered her. Whether or not she could act was a bridge he would cross when he came to it. At any rate, it wasn't a worry which would eat at him days and keep him awake nights. Somehow he would cajole her, prompt her, teach her, and patiently direct her, drawing a performance out of her by using his own genius and conducting her as carefully as any nimble conductor led his orchestra. After all, films weren't like the stage, where acting ability counted for everything. In films, too much talent and overacting could kill a scene more swiftly than an untalented youngster who could be herself and follow direction. He much preferred to direct a fresh newcomer he could mold into *his* vision of a star than deal with a talented name saturated with other directors' mistakes. It was far easier to create than to destroy and re-create, do than undo.

"*Mister!*" Tamara's sharp hiss intruded into his spiraling, convoluted thoughts. "You're keeping me from my work!"

He stared into the limpid pools of her uncanny, glossy emerald eyes, and it was as if he were being inexorably swept into the hypnotic, spiraling depths of a slowly moving maelstrom. "Huh?" he said dreamily.

"I said, I've got to *work*."

He said nothing in reply, dismissing her with good-natured impatience, his eyes agleam.

She looked down at her arm, which he was still clutching tightly, and tried to shake him off. "Please! Let go of me!"

He narrowed his eyes to squints and, without asking her permission to touch her, raised a trembling hand to her chin and moved her face this way and that, studying her profile, calculating her superb, startling facial angles with keen professional interest.

Abruptly she jerked her head back angrily. "What's the matter with you? Are you crazy or something?"

"Sssssh! Keep still."

"What the—" For the third time Tamara tried to shrug his hand off. This time she succeeded.

He was in euphoria. No, he was definitely not dreaming! he thought exultantly. She was very, very real indeed.

"Sit down, please listen to me," he urged quickly, starting to pull her down into the booth. "Just give me a minute to explain."

"It's against the rules, I'm afraid." She laughed good-naturedly, but stood her ground and refused to budge.

"Rules are made to be broken," he said solemnly.

"Unh-unh." She tossed her head. "Not here they aren't. Not if I want to keep my job."

"What you want to do that for? You're beautiful. Why would you want to work in a place like this?"

"If you haven't figured it out already, I'll spell it out for you. I've got to eat."

"Don't you want to be in movies?" he asked curiously. "You can sign a contract today."

She blushed and then laughed. "Mister, that's got to be the oldest line in this city. Now, excuse me, but I have better things to do."

He looked genuinely hurt. "Listen, you want to check up on me? See if I'm kosher? There's a pay phone over there." He nodded toward the entrance.

"I work here," she reminded him stiffly. "I know very well where the phone is."

"Good. Here, I'll even give you change." He dug deep into his pocket, and she took the opportunity to make her escape.

"Hey!" He jumped back to his feet. "Where're you going?" he called out in surprise. "Don't you want to call the studio and check up on me?"

"I've got tables to wait." She strode swiftly toward the counter, trying to ignore the other patrons, who were now staring at her with new interest.

He was at her heels. "I don't even know your name!" he said loudly.

"And I don't know yours either, do I?" she said casually, trying to keep her voice low so the entire restaurant wouldn't be privy. She grabbed two plates from the pass-through window, pirouetted, and smiled sarcastically at him. "That makes us even, don't you think?"

"Mine's Louis Ziolko," he said quietly. "What's yours?"

She was so startled that she dropped the plates. They fell to the tiles with a clatter, and he had to jump back to avoid being splattered by eggs and pork links.

"What's the matter with you?" he asked. "You look like you've seen a ghost or something."

She grabbed his sweater precisely where lapels would have been had he been wearing a suit, and shook him. "What did you say?" she whispered incredulously. Her face had suddenly gone ashen.

"I said, my name's Louis Ziolko. Now, would you be kind enough to tell me yours?"

She released his sweater and took a stagger backward. Hands on her hips, she sighed hopelessly, rolled her green eyes, and shook her head. "Tamara, my dear," she said aloud, "sometimes you can be a first-class bimbo."

"Cut!" Louis Ziolko roared malevolently into his megaphone as he shot up from his director's chair. "Cut-cut-*cut*!" He stamped around noisily, muttering curses under his breath. He interrupted his pacing just long enough to throw a withering glance in Tamara's direction.

What have I done wrong *now*? Tamara wondered in dismay. She stared at Ziolko. This was the twenty-eighth time he had had her repeat this simple scene, and once again he had brought filming to an abrupt halt. She could sense that his perfectionist's patience was beginning to wear dangerously thin.

He lifted the megaphone to his lips. "Kill the lights!"

Instantly the blazing hot klieg and spotlights high in the catwalks faded into crackling darkness, and Pearl Dern and the skeleton crew of fourteen seasoned technicians who were casually dressed and wore their boredom with the same casual ease with which they performed their various duties turned away and took the opportunity to light cigarettes.

Tamara instantly felt the humid, biting chill of the unheated sound stage raising gooseflesh along her arms. Shivering, she rubbed them briskly with her hands. A girl from wardrobe hurried over to carefully drape a blanket around her shoulders, and Tamara managed a grateful smile as she exchanged the white feather boa for the blanket, clutching it tightly around her. Involuntarily her teeth began chattering, which was not in the least bit surprising. The moment the blinding lights were switched to maximum wattage on her, she would break out into a sweat so that her face and shoulders had to be dusted with an absorbent powder; invariably, as soon as the lights dimmed, the chill would take hold of her again. Hot, cold. Hot, cold. She had seldom had to endure such temperature extremes, and she feared that if she wasn't careful, she would come down with pneumonia, or pleurisy at least. Her otherwise splendid costume, a short, skimpy white silk bodice dress, heavily sequined, with two rhinestone-studded spaghetti straps looped over her shoulders, ostrich-plume fan attached to her waist, and feathered headband, did as little to keep her warm as the two long strands of pearls hanging low from her neck and the paste diamonds around her wrists and on her fingers.

Tamara turned away as Ziolko bore down on her, so that he wouldn't see her blinking back tears. "What did I do now?" she asked in a timid voice, as though addressing the wall in front of her. For obviously she must have done *something* wrong again; why else would he have stopped the cameras from rolling? Still, she was almost certain she had been playing the scene perfectly.

"This time it isn't anything you've done wrong," he said in a voice of weary resignation. "It's those damn spots."

"Spots?" She turned to face him. "What spots?"

He slid the blanket off her shoulders. "Those."

She looked down and inspected her shoulders. A little whimper of surprise escaped her lips. Everywhere the feathers of the boa had touched her skin, red splotches rose up into ugly raised welts.

She was allergic to feathers.

Damn. This was a fine time to discover that.

He leaned close into her face. "What I want to know is, why didn't you say something about having allergies?" he demanded, his voice none the less threatening for its low tone.

"How was I supposed to know?" she shot back angrily. A rivulet of tears slid out of one superbly made-up eye, damaging the exacting makeup with a streak of black mascara. "It's not as if I dress up in chicken feathers all the time!"

His expression softened as he sighed. "Okay, okay. Just don't cry, huh? It's ruining your makeup." He motioned Pearl over to repair the damage. "Put enough makeup over her back and shoulders to hide the welts," he said irritably. "That'll do it, don't you think?"

Pearl nodded and looked at Tamara sympathetically.

Ziolko clicked his fingers at the wardrobe mistress. "Exchange the boa for a white fur wrap."

The wardrobe mistress hurried off.

Tamara looked at Ziolko in surprise. "But won't the makeup ruin the fur?"

He shrugged and looked at her steadily. "Maybe, but what's the alternative? Who cares about a piece of fur as long as the scene works out?"

Fifteen minutes later they shot the scene again. "Take twenty-nine," Ziolko boomed through his megaphone. "Silence on the set!"

The assistant cameraman leaned in front of Tamara. His wooden clapper snapped together like two noisy jaws, and the camera began to roll yet again.

"Action!"

Tamara clutched the fur stole casually around her and ignored the sudden blazing heat of the lights. For all of thirty seconds she walked slowly toward the camera, her face registering the haunted, faraway look of a person whose life was over. Then her footsteps slowed, she paused, and caught her breath. Though she did not know it, the lights shimmered on her sequined dress like molten silver. Her breasts rose and fell.

Her breathing quickened. Her eyes gleamed and held a look of disbelief, and her lips parted in a hint of a smile. And then her ever-quickening footsteps brought her rushing toward the camera, a look of hope imprinted on her exquisite features. The assistant cameraman caught her just before she could collide with the camera.

"Cut!" Ziolko's reverberating voice yelled through the megaphone. "And *print!*"

He grinned at her. The twenty-ninth take was a charm.

Still, in the end the entire five-minute screen test was to take two-and a half days of shooting, and this was only to prepare her for the final test, a scene with dialogue and dancing with none other than Miles Gabriel, IA's leading man. The green-eyed young hopeful was more terrified than ever.

"T'mara! It's fer you!" Jewel shrilled excitedly. She held out the telephone receiver and did a series of feverish hops. "It's that Silko guy you been waitin' to hear from!"

"Ziolko?" Tamara said blankly. She finished refilling the big chrome coffee urn and plonked the lid down on it. She wiped up the spills. She glanced at the pass-through window and then checked the customers hunched over the counter. The two orders she'd given José weren't ready, and the customers were either busy sipping their coffees or eating. Only then did she slowly approach the phone.

"Sweetie!" Jewel hissed. "What the *hell's* the matter with

you? The suspense is killin' me!" She thrust the receiver at Tamara and did another impatient little dance, her fists clenched.

Tamara lifted the receiver to her ear. "Mr. Ziolko?" she said tremulously.

For a moment she could only hear the static and rushing sounds on the line. "Louie," he finally said. "I thought we agreed you'd call me Louie."

"Louie." Her voice sounded as weak, indistinct, and far-away as his.

Jewel was gesturing frantically. "What's he say?" she mouthed silently.

Tamara turned her back on Jewel and tightened her grip on the receiver. "It's bad news, isn't it?" she said into the shiny black instrument.

There. The dreaded fear had been spoken aloud. It hung like a poisonous snake in the air.

"Bad news?" Ziolko's voice came back. "What's bad news?"

She could have strangled him. Why was he toying with her like this?

"The screen test," she found herself saying. "What else?"

He sounded surprised. "What makes you think it turned out badly?"

Her heart was going *bam . . . bam . . . BAM*, like a sledgehammer steadily pounding away at an anvil. She could almost see the sparks fly. "Then . . . how *did* it turn out?"

"I'll let you see for yourself. What are you doing day after tomorrow, at seven?"

"In the morning?"

"Evening. Seven P.M. We're invited to O.T.'s for dinner."

"O.T.'s? You mean Oscar . . . Skolnik's?" She couldn't trust her ears. "The head of IA?"

"Don't know of any other." He laughed easily. "It's a date, then, I take it."

"But what about the screen test?" she cried in anguish.

"O.T.'s house has a screening room. You'll see it then. Afterward we'll talk about it."

"But we're talking now!"

"Listen, there's no point in discussing it over the phone." He paused. "It's a little complicated."

Complicated! Oh, God, she could see her world crumbling already.

"Where do I pick you up?"

Her voice was subdued. "Paterson's Mortuary."

He laughed. "Paterson's Mortuary?"

"That what I said."

"Well, just don't go killing yourself in the meantime. We want you alive, not dead."

Her heart gave a hopeful surge. Was that to be construed as a positive sign, that they wanted her after all? She was dying to ask, but she said instead, "I live there."

"Okay." He didn't sound surprised. "I'll pick you up at six-thirty."

And with that he clicked off.

"A new dress?" Inge asked at dinner that night. "Well, *ja*, I suppose we can afford it. I manage to put aside a little money. Why not? Is not every day my actress is invited to studio Mongol's home."

"Mogul," Tamara corrected without malice. Inge herself had demanded that she be corrected each time she misused English. "A Mongol's from Mongolia."

Inge waved her soup spoon airily. "Mogul, Mongol, is all the same to me. We go tomorrow to Goodwill."

Tamara's face fell. Somehow she managed to get the ungrateful-sounding words out before they strangled her. "I'm not trying to be an ingrate, Inge," she pleaded, "but can't we get something new? Just this once?"

Inge fell silent and looked thoughtfully down at her soup bowl, where a large white dumpling floated in fatty yellow chicken broth. Then she managed a smile. "Why not? We find you something nice to wear to your Mongol's."

Tamara's eyes lit up. "It's got to be something smart, though," she said slowly.

"Smart?" Inge asked. Her eyes flicked suspiciously sideways. "How a dress can be smart? It thinks, huh?"

"It's an expression. You know, like chic. Elegant. Classy."

Inge shook her head. "Glassy clothes. Smart clothes. What will they think of next?"

Tamara let the "glassy" slide. All she had thought for was her new dress with the strand of pearls shimmering around her throat. She loved those pearls, and took every opportunity to wear them. That they were inexpensive fakes from Woolworth's didn't matter one iota. What did matter was that she'd had her eyes on them ever since she'd seen a photograph of Constance Bennett wearing pearls. That had done it. And the Woolworth pearls made her feel right up there along with Constance Bennett.

At two-thirty the next afternoon they entered Dorothy's Dress Shoppe, Inge looking out of place and older than her thirty-seven years in her dowdy, shapeless gray coat, heavy, sensible brown shoes, large frayed handbag, and the shapeless little black hat she wore whenever she stepped out-of-doors. Tamara set her magnificent chin firmly and refused to be intimidated by the elegant surroundings of the emporium she had, until now, only been able to gaze longingly at from outside. Dorothy's! she thought ecstatically, taking in its hushed, almost ecclesiastic silence. What incredible luxury! She looked around the shop in wonder. Why, there was even plush carpeting on the floor!

"Oh, Inge! Isn't everything too divine?" she breathed, dancing along an aisle, her fingertips rippling the glorious dresses hanging from racks on either side. She paused, breathless, and danced back toward Inge, rippling the dresses again. "Isn't it all to *die* for?"

Even Inge had to admit that while the clothes at Dorothy's were certainly not worth the price of death, they were very fine indeed.

A patrician saleslady in a well-tailored dove-gray dress and immaculately coiffed silver hair approached them, revealing only for a fraction of an instant her unqualified disapproval of Inge's hopelessly frayed outfit before a mask of inscrutable professionalism slid smoothly over her features. "Madame is looking for something?" she inquired with only a modicum of disdain.

Inge shook her head and lowered her eyes shyly. "Not for me, sank you." She touched Tamara's shoulders and pushed her gently forward. "Is for her," she said proudly, lifting her shiny eyes. "She needs a glassy dress."

The saleslady raised her eyebrows. "A *glassy* dress?"

"She means elegant," Tamara explained.

Inge nodded and lowered her voice confidentially. "She is invited to dinner at film Mongol's house in the Beverly Hills! I want her to look nice, like she belong."

"Here at Dorothy's we pride ourselves on helping our customers look their best," the saleslady sniffed. "The finest people in the city patronize us. What did you have in mind?"

Inge gave an expressive, helpless shrug. "Tamara, she know. She read all the magazines."

The saleslady looked Tamara over to gauge her size. "Is it to be formal?"

"I . . . I don't know, ma'am."

"I see." The saleslady pursed her lips thoughtfully. "I suggest a dress, then, not a gown. You have a good figure and very nice legs. There's no need to hide them. You'll also be able to wear it days and evenings both."

"That sounds good," Inge declared, nodding.

"And the, er, price range you have in mind?" The sales-lady looked at Inge.

Inge steeled herself. "Ten dollar?" she ventured, naming what was to her an astronomical sum.

"I see." The saleslady sighed. "That limits our selection, I'm afraid. However, we do have a few rather nice sale items left over from last year. One in particular should suit the young lady quite nicely. I'll go get it and she can try it on."

"It must be decent," Inge warned. "I want her to look a lady."

"Of course," the woman said, "and she shall." She strode off to find the dress, and when she returned, Tamara took one look at it and uttered a swift, fervent prayer that it would fit her. And it did. Standing in front of the three-way mirror, turning this way and that to catch her reflections, she could scarcely believe her eyes. It was a body-hugging sheath that came up to the armpits and reached to mid-calf, was made of lightly gathered satin the color of perfectly ripe raspberries, and had thick black velvet straps which looped over her shoulders. It could be worn with the extravagantly gargantuan matching satin bow pinned near the hem on one side for formal wear or without it for a more casual look. Her face was flushed with pink excitement at the anticipation of acquisition. She looked, she knew, in a word, sensational.

She was enchanted, bewitched, in love with the dress.

Even Inge knew a sight for sore eyes when she saw it. She nodded her approval. "*Ja,* that looks goot. How much it will cost?"

"It's a beautiful dress," the saleslady praised lavishly. "Handmade, not mass-produced. Originally it was priced at twenty-four dollars."

"So much!" Inge looked horrified.

"It has been reduced to twelve."

"Twelve dollar," Inge muttered, the corners of her lips twitching.

Tamara was crestfallen. She knew that look of Inge's only too well; equally well, she knew how far Inge could stretch those twelve precious dollars.

After a thoughtful silence Inge asked, "Do you have something else nice for less money?"

Tamara silently offered up another, even more fervent prayer. She had to have this dress, this extravagant fantasy which made her look and feel beautiful. She couldn't bear the thought of having to part with it.

The saleslady shook her head. "I'm sorry, this is the least expensive, I assure you."

Tamara held her breath, staring at Inge's reflection in the mirror. This was the moment of reckoning. She could see Inge's fingers tightening on the handbag. Another bad sign.

"You like it, Tamara?" Inge softly asked at long last.

Tamara nodded swiftly, too shaky to speak.

"Then you shall have your glassy dress," Inge announced under a sudden fusillade of happy hugs and noisy kisses.

"Damn!" Tamara wailed as the unmanageable stray curl escaped her newly coiffed hair and spiraled down the middle of her forehead. Disgusted, she tugged it back up with the Bakelite tortoiseshell comb. "Why does it have to come undone now, of all times?"

It was nearly six-thirty and she was still planted in front of the bathroom mirror, comb in one hand, bobby pins sticking out from between her lips like a mouthful of spiky porcupine quills. She had draped herself with a bedsheet to protect her precious new dress from water spots or stray hair, and longed, not for the first time, that instead of this mottled, distorting, cracked mirror she had an honest-to-goodness sit-down vanity with a large, well-lit mirror. She would give her eyeteeth for one.

She raked the comb through her hair again and then shook her head. The shoulder-length waves bounced as easily and naturally as springs. Aha! Triumph at last! The recalcitrant curl had finally been tamed.

She put down the comb, spat out the bobby pins, and let the bedsheet slide off her shoulders. She rumpled it into a ball and shoved it under the sink. Then she rubbed her bare arms briskly while experimenting with various seductive poses in the mirror. Damn, it was chilly. No matter how cold it got, Roland J. Paterson's bathroom in this apartment was never heated; still, she was grateful to have it.

"He is here!" Inge burst excitedly into the bathroom. "I never seen such a giant car!" Then she gasped, stepped back, clasped her hands in front of her, and shook her head. "*Du bist so schön!*" she marveled admiringly in disbelief, reverting to her native German as she always did when something frightened, shocked, or impressed her unduly. "*So schön.*"

"You're sure I'm all right?" Tamara asked worriedly. "You're not just saying that to please me?"

Inge smiled and tilted her head. "*Ja.* I'm sure," she said gently, her eyes glowing warmly with love. She placed the palm of her hand on Tamara's cheek and held it there. She shook her head sadly. "*Mein Liebchen.* Already you go out into the world. Soon you have use no more for your Inge."

"Of course I will!"

Before her emotions could overcome her, Inge drew back and said gruffly, "Leave everything be. Later I clean up here." She thrust a crocheted black stole into Tamara's hands. "It is cold out. Put around you." She paused. "Now, go. Go."

Tamara turned to the mirror one last time, attacking her cheeks with inspired pinches to bring out a healthy, rosy glow."

"Stop that." Inge gently slapped her hands away. "You want red marks on your face? Enough is enough."

Tamara hurried lightly down the steep stairs, one hand on the banister, the other dragging the crocheted stole behind her.

Louis Ziolko was waiting just inside the front door, holding a match to a thick Belinda cigar. The match flared and his cheeks inflated and deflated like a bellows as he sucked on the flame. Hearing her footsteps, he glanced up through the blue cloud of smoke. God Almighty! The match slipped from his fingers. He could feel the muscles contracting painfully in his gut, as if he'd been punched. What was wrong with her? Didn't she know better than to leave herself wide open for sexual assault? Hadn't she given *any* thought to the way that horizontally gathered satin clung to her hips so . . . so *obscenely,* that giant bow off to the side only inviting lecherous leers to follow the shapely perfection of her magnificent legs? Didn't she realize that the very act of totally concealing her bosom just begged one to rip it free? And those sedate pearls—a masterfully ladylike, demure touch if there ever was one, but one which played havoc with her ribald sensuousness.

And clear out of the blue it hit him, as incisive a bolt of knowledge as if lightning had struck. At the coffee shop, and then again during the screen test, he had encountered a glorious girl, but this was no girl who was coming down those stairs now. Far from it. This was a woman, a sleek, poised, shapely siren, a natural star if ever there was one. What an entrance! "Well, I'll be goddamned," he muttered under his breath.

Seeing him, Tamara slowed to a dignified walk the rest of the way down. She smiled. "Am I late?" she asked in that throaty, haunting voice which caused cool ripples to course across his flesh.

"N-no, you aren't late . . . ." He took two steps toward her, seized her hand, raised it awkwardly to his lips. ". . . you're beautiful, princess."

She flushed with pleasure and he took the stole from her and draped it solicitously around her shoulders. He frowned inwardly. He had never felt like this before . . . why was he feeling this way now?

The chauffeur snapped the rear door gently shut after Ziolko climbed in alongside her, and walked around to the front, to the separate driver's compartment. Then she heard the engine purr, and the big car surged majestically forward, swinging out into the lane as if on a cloud. Beside her, Ziolko unfolded a leopard lap robe and spread it over her. "Hmmm," was all she said. She smiled at him gratefully and snuggled into the far corner, unaware that he was staring at her with the same kind of keen, mesmerized wonder with which she stared down at the rare fur. She stroked its sleek, spotted softness with her newly varnished, elongated fingers. How warm and potently satisfied she felt.

Ah, to have such resources at her beck and call, she thought dreamily. This was the life. How invincibly superior and flush it made her feel! She sighed luxuriantly. How easily a girl could get used to this.

The Duesenberg climbed up the curved, tree-lined roads into Beverly Hills. Through the rain-streaked windows Tamara caught occasional glimpses of lights glowing in the windows of the immense secluded mansions which had been built by the film-colony elite. This was her first time here, and she was thrilled to the bone. She had always wanted to see Beverly Hills for herself, but until now it had been part of that elusive, unattainable world she had only read about in the movie magazines. Even though she'd never seen it before, she knew all about Beverly Hills. Who didn't? For the most part, it was still a separate entity from Los Angeles, a sparsely settled wilderness where privacy could be treasured without being jealously guarded, and where an occasional deer or wolf could be glimpsed roaming about. She knew it was a community which, sadly but ironically, had been born of necessity with the influx of the ever-growing ranks of the motion-picture people. Movie stars and industry honchos were frowned upon by the Los Angeles old guard, who viewed them as nouveau-riche upstarts and parvenus at best, and perverted hell-raisers at worst, so they had been driven up here, far from the fine old addresses and into the hills where no one in his right mind had wanted to live until now. These newcomers went about systematically creating an exclusive gilded ghetto all their own.

"It must be beautiful up here during the day!" Tamara marveled with suppressed excitement as acres of dark, untouched land slipped by in the empty tracts between the far-flung houses. "It feels like we've left the city behind and gone to the country."

Ziolko nodded. "For now it's still like that, but just wait a few years. Every year more and more houses are going up. Soon, I'm afraid there won't be any privacy left. Land prices have gone through the roof. What used to be tracts of land are now little parcels being zoned smaller and smaller. Soon there'll be giant houses, swimming pools, and tennis courts on postage-stamp lots. Mark my words."

"Do you live up here?" She turned to him curiously.

He shook his head. "Not yet." He was watching her eyes carefully in the dim glow of the coach light. "Why? You like it?"

She nodded and breathed deeply. "I smell eucalyptus." She smiled at him.

"Wait'll the flowers come out. Then it smells like a god-damn florist's. Flowers grow here like weeds. Well, here we are."

She sat up straighter and stared out her side window as the chauffeur steered the car into a narrow white gravel drive which crunched and popped beneath the pneumatic tires. The drive was bordered on both sides by a wild, overgrown jungle of shrubbery. Occasionally a thorny branch would scratch against the polished sides of the car, causing Ziolko to grimace in anguish. Except for the pristine drive, it looked for all the world like a forest road leading nowhere. Then suddenly the shrubs cleared to reveal a massive floodlit mansion sprawling amidst a floodlit, formally landscaped garden. So this was where Oscar Skolnik lived, Tamara thought. She was impressed. Somehow the estate was exactly as she had imagined, and it certainly befitted a multimillionare tycoon turned movie mogul.

Slowly the car crept to a halt, the chauffeur got out, swiftly unfurled an umbrella, and held the rear door. The giant carved house door swung open and a butler stood stiffly erect in the bright rectangle of light.

"Good evening, Frédérique," Ziolko greeted. "How you doing?"

"Fine, thank you, sir. Miss." The butler inclined his head a second time. "Mr. Skolnik and the other guests are waiting in the sitting room," Frédérique murmured. "If you will be so kind as to follow me, please."

Ziolko nodded and took Tamara by the elbow. She was grateful for his touch, for otherwise she would have stood there rooted to the spot, wide-eyed in wonder at the luxurious house.

They followed Frédérique through an atrium, past slender, shallow green Alhambra fountains, whose plashing drowned out the persistent drumbeat of rain on the glass roof overhead. Looking up, she couldn't believe her eyes. An arched gallery completely encircled the atrium, and everywhere, pots of exotic hothouse orchids bloomed in riotous splendor. She drew in her breath and shook her head. Her eyes had already become so numbed by the grand displays of splendor that she felt as if she were drifting through a dream. This was more, far, far more than she had ever dared anticipate.

Frédérique led them under another set of arches and then swung open another heroically scaled carved door.

Tamara was bedazzled. This was an enchanted world; these were the cultivated furnishings of a hedonistic sultan. A fire leapt and crackled in each of the large Adam fireplaces which faced one another across the expanse, scenting the air with eucalyptus and fruitwood while chasing away the damp chill. Despite the staggering thirty-six-foot-high ceiling and the room's auditorium scale, it nevertheless gave the impression of being a cozy, welcoming, and much-used and much-loved room.

If a person's home was an indication of his personality, then Tamara was completely bedeviled by Oscar Skolnik. Everything pointed to his being a very complex and not easily understood man.

She noticed him the moment she entered the room. She had never seen him, but even from a distance of seventy feet it was impossible to overlook him. He was seated in a wing chair in the semicircular end of the room, apparently holding court. The other men present were all standing. A large painting on an easel was propped up to face him, and four men in evening attire stood to the left and right of his chair, their expressions dubious and thoughtful. Their attention was focused on a brittle praying mantis of a man with a lugubrious expression and a pointed Vandyke beard who stood beside the easel. Two women in pale floor-length sheaths sat off to the side, each holding a flute of champagne. It was an exceedingly elegant tableau, so perfectly composed and lighted that it seemed to have been contrived for effect.

At first, no one took notice of the new arrivals, and Tamara was grateful. For a moment she hesitated and glanced pleadingly at Ziolko, but he smiled reassuringly, placed a hand in the small of her spine, and propelled her forward.

"What we have to do is acknowledge the symbolism," the man with the Vandyke was saying with low-keyed but intense passion. "In other words, we must scratch below the surface, dig deeply beyond the obvious representation, as it were, in order to find the Place of Truth—" He broke off suddenly when he realized no one was paying attention any longer: all eyes were on the newcomers.

The silence grew prolonged. No one spoke. No one blinked. One of the women rose soundless as a ghost in order to have a better view of Tamara.

One could have heard a pin drop on those priceless Bessarabian carpets.

Tamara's initial rapturous delight at the house was immediately replaced by a severe attack of the jitters. Her entire body trembled as she moved forward, her earlier assurance deserting her as her sweeping gaze focused upon the unmoving figures bathed in soft lighting, a lamp catching the intensity of their stares and causing their eyes to glitter glassily; the lovely room which at first glance had dazzled now shifted slightly to take on a leering, intimidating quality, and the elegant tableau of men and women did a transmutation, taking on the severe, menacing presence of a panel of presiding judges. Tamara's impulse was to flee this minatory scene, these awe-inspiring surroundings. She was all too acutely conscious of the seven sets of hard, appraising eyes that were not so much looking at her as picking her over.

A stab of resentment caused her cheeks to prickle and flash becomingly. She couldn't help but think that she was not a woman—not anymore—but a slab of meat at the butcher's, waiting to be grabbed, poked, prodded, and sniffed at by finicky customers, as prone to rejection as acceptance. It was a humiliating, inhuman, and unjust position to be in.

Yet somehow, despite it all, her heart pounding in her ears, she kept on moving with a queenly stride, her chin raised, her head held at a regal angle. All outward indications said she was the self-assured, quintessential beauty, a siren, a heartbreaker.

Miraculously, she made it across the room without stumbling. As she approached Oscar Skolnik he noticeably sat up straighter, raising his crystal blue eyes to meet her gaze. In response, she readjusted her line of vision accordingly by raising her own gaze further, somehow managing, at the same time, to paint what she hoped was a cool confident smile on her face. But the smile was not real. It was a Bakelite smile, as plastic as the shell of the radio in Inge's room.

"Ah, just what we need!" Skolnik said when she halted beside the easel, facing her panel of judges from a distance of five feet. He sat back in a deceptively casual pose, crossing one leg over the other, but his sharp eyes never left her for an instant. "What do *you* think of it?"

His voice made her start, its sudden sonorous baritone breaking the acute silence as a gunshot might a hushed tomb's.

"Wh-what?" Her vision lowered, meeting his eyes for the first time, and she stared at him blankly.

"I asked what you thought of it." His crystalline eyes bore into hers. "Sometimes a fresh, impartial opinion sheds a good deal more light on such matters."

Opinion? She felt her heart stop for an agonizing moment. *An opinion of what?*

She flitted a sideways glance at Louis Ziolko, but he was no help. He gave her a lopsided little grin. She turned her head and looked now directly into Skolnik's face.

Everything about the man seemed bigger than life. He was too rugged to be called distinguished; he was a man thoroughly capable of the exploits that were part and parcel of his growing legend. Just as other men could instantly give off the impression of being oily or unctuous or fastidious, he exuded raw, potent, unadulterated power. He was clearly a man to be reckoned with. He smoked a pipe, drank champagne, and never gambled—other than on big business deals, which were gamble enough—and was a man who appeared, remarkably, to have only one vice, an exorbitantly expensive one: women, women, and more women. Rumor had it that he had bedded all the single women worth having in Hollywood, and had then gone on to raid Los Angeles' marital bedrooms, gossip Tamara wouldn't have doubted the truth of for an instant. There was a way he had of undressing a woman with his eyes, something of which she was uncomfortably aware at the moment. His eyes were the pale blue of arctic ice and conveyed the deceptive laziness of a riverboat gambler.

He wore a paisley silk dressing gown with turkish slippers, and was puffing on a clay pipe. His hair was prematurely gray.

His voice was cultured, a melodious, rich baritone. He was saved from the fate of being merely handsome by the network of telltale facial scars, evidence of the dangers of aviation: he had crashed three times in prototype aircraft of his own design, and had lived to tell the tales. Yet for all the scars, possibly because of them, there was something brutally attractive about him, a blatant quality of bursting sexual vitality. Every crease and scar told of a man who had already crammed a lifetime of living into a few short years.

She forced herself to pull back from Skolnik's smoldering magnetism. He was certainly no man to treat casually; she had the distinct feeling that a woman could easily get hurt around him. But still, she couldn't help conjuring up an unbidden picture of him naked. It seemed to jump up before her eyes. A lion! That was what he was. A jungle creature. A hungry, predatory beast forever on the prowl.

She realized with a sudden start that he had been studying her with the same frankness with which she was studying him, almost as if he had been able to seize on her inner life force and pull it out of her. Frightening.

Then, with an easy grin that disarmed, that redeemed his improbably stony features and his deeply rooted lusts, he said, "You must excuse me. Of course you can't know what we've been discussing." He thumbed a gesture toward the canvas beside her. "Well? What's your opinion? Should I buy it or not?"

Tamara peered cautiously around the easel, then took two steps forward and turned her back on the group. She stared at the painting. It was a large rectangle, painted off-white. Off-center near the top was a perfect black square, its angles lining up with the edges of the canvas. Another, smaller perfect red square under it was painted slightly on the diagonal. She furrowed her brow, trying to make sense of it. *What could she say?*

"I really know nothing about art," she said slowly, furrowing her brow. "I *do* find it . . . interesting, though."

She could hear Skolnik chuckling.

Bernard Katzenbach, the man with the Vandyke beard, was, above all, a salesman. He raised his beard-pointed chin defiantly. "It is *more* than interesting," he intoned indignantly, displaying glossy rabbitlike teeth. "All art is interesting, of course," he went on in sepulchral tones, "since even the worst creative efforts have the redeeming quality of giving us a glimpse of the artist's soul. But this . . . this is an interesting, a heroic, a *majestic* vista of a tormented soul which has ultimately reduced life's myriad complexities to their simplest, most manageable and profound forms."

Two squares *profound*? Tamara couldn't believe her ears.

"Tell me," Skolnik interjected laconically with a lazy twirl of his index finger, "is it worth two thousand dollars?"

"Is it . . ." Kazenbach sputtered. "Is it worth . . . can a monetary price *ever* be put on such genius? Why, it's a Malevich—"

"I asked the lady," Skolnik said easily.

Oh-oh, Tamara thought, and said nothing.

"Well, Miss Boralevi?" Skolnik prodded gently. "Would you spend two thousand dollars on this painting?"

She turned to face him and was silent for a moment. "Two thousand dollars?" She managed to laugh lightly. "I don't *have* two thousand dollars, never have had, so there is absolutely no way I can begin to imagine spending it. I'm afraid you've asked the wrong person."

Did she hear a palpable sigh of relief emanating from the stick figure that was the art dealer? Or was it her imagination?

"Well-said," Skolnik said approvingly. "You must have been bred for sociability. An important asset in a star when it comes to dealing with the press and the public."

Did this mean she had passed his test, whatever it was? And he'd mentioned the word "star." Did this mean he really intended to make her one?

"Louie," Skolnik said without rising, "I think you should introduce us to the beautiful lady."

Louis Ziolko nodded. "As you all know, this is Tamara Boralevi, whose screen test you have all seen." He turned to Tamara. "Tamara, I'd like you to meet the powers that be at IA. To start with, seated in the chair, Oscar Skolnik, president of IA."

Tamara nodded. "Mr. Skolnik."

"Standing directly to his left, Roger Callas, our general manager. Next to him is Bruce Slesin, vice-president, publicity. And on the right, the gentleman nearest O.T. is Milton Ivey, our general counsel."

"Gentlemen," Tamara said.

Except for Oscar Skolnik, who remained seated, each man stepped forward and shook her hand in turn, each of them murmuring that he was pleased to meet her.

"And the gentleman on the right?" she asked.

"Claude de Chantilly-Siciles," Ziolko said, "our art director. Claude gives our pictures their unique look."

The short, dapper Frenchman bowed low over Tamara's hand. "Enchanté, Mademoiselle Boralevi," he said gallantly, his breath prickling the back of her hand.

"Don't let his continental manners and phony accent fool you," Ziolko added with a chuckle. "Claude's as American as apple pie, and a slick old lecher to boot. So don't say you weren't forewarned."

Claude de Chantilly-Siciles put on a pained expression. "They are jealous!" he said fervently with a mock scowl. "Can I help it if the ladies find me attractive?"

Tamara laughed along with the rest of them.

"And then, of course, representing the talent divisions are the ladies," Ziolko continued. "Seated beside Mr. Skolnik is Miss Rhoda Dorsey, who heads the reading department. It is she who provides us with the various properties we might wish to consider buying and making into films."

"Miss Dorsey," Tamara inclined her head. "I hope I have the chance to overtax your department's workload."

The woman wearing heavy horn-rims, her hair pulled back into a no-nonsense bun, laughed. "I only wish you would. Sometimes I think my readers are nothing more than lazy bookworms enjoying themselves."

"And the lady who is standing is Mrs. Carol Anderegg, vice-president, talent. It is her department which combs the country for suitable talent."

Mrs. Anderegg's eyes were glassy hard and appraising, and her voice was clipped. "Miss Boralevi." She inclined her silver-haired head ever so lightly.

"I'm pleased to make your acquaintance," Tamara said.

"Ah, and we mustn't overlook Mr. Katzenbach," Skolnik said from his chair, his lips smiling thinly. "Art historian, adviser, purveyor of beauty, and salesman nonpareil. Many are the times I wish he'd work for me, selling motion pictures to the public instead of talking me into buying expensive painted pictures for myself."

"But this time you have no intention of buying," the art dealer countered shrewdly. "You lured me here for the sole purpose of judging Miss Boralevi's beauty, I take it?"

"Guilty." Skolnik partially raised both hands in surrender but looked at Katzenbach with newfound respect. Then he gestured for a chair to be pulled up and smiled at Tamara. "Have a seat, my dear. We are having champagne. Of course, if you'd prefer something else, I'm known to have the best-stocked bar in this city. Not moonshine, either, mind you. French champagne and the best liquor money can buy. Nowadays I find a good rumrunner to be as important as a good marketing analyst, and nearly as hard to find as a treasured butler."

"Well-said!" Milton Ivey, the attorney, interjected warmly. Ivey's cheeks, a network of florid burst blood vessels, shone redly. Clearly, despite Prohibition, liquor was not all that difficult to come by.

"A little champagne, please," Tamara said softly, "though this is a first for me." She smiled artlessly. "I've never drunk anything alcoholic before."

Skolnik nodded approvingly. "And well that you should be cautious about drinking." He glanced momentarily up at Milton Ivey, who quickly looked away. "But I think you'll like the champagne. It's Dom Perignon, the very best. And with dinner, I propose a bottle of 1898 Château Latour. I've been saving it for a special occasion."

"Is this a special occasion, then?" Tamara asked boldly, unable to keep silent any longer about her chances of a stab at stardom.

Skolnik laughed. "Every day is special, especially one graced with the presence of such a beautiful, talented young woman."

The words were sweet music, and she reveled in them.

"I must have seen your screen test thirty times," he continued, "so this occasion certainly warrants celebration. I must tell you, though, that your photographed image does not do you justice—you are even more beautiful in person than on the screen. You see, Miss Boralevi . . . may I call you Tamara?"

She smiled brightly, glad to be rid of the awkward surname. "I'd be delighted."

"Good." He looked pleased. "And you must call me O.T., as everybody does. As I was about to say, it is not every day that a potential star joins the IA stable."

"Then . . . then you're really hiring me?" she asked huskily, barely daring to speak.

"That depends," he replied vaguely. "Not to crush your expectations, but I'd like you to see your screen test first; then you'll hear our proposal and decide."

Tamara's stomach lurched and all glimmers of hope dulled. "Oh. Then there are . . . problems?"

"Not problems, just a few . . . minor details, none of which are insurmountable, I assure you." He spied his ever-present butler approaching soundlessly. "Ah, here comes your champagne. Enjoy it and try to relax. I have a rule of never discussing business on an empty stomach; too many good meals have been ruined that way. After dinner we will get down to it."

She wished they could have done away with dinner altogether; as it turned out, despite her nervousness, she found herself enjoying it immensely. It was an entirely new experience: a meal to remember, a fugue for the senses. Every detail was perfectly orchestrated by the small army of soundless servants, so soundless that she was almost certain they were required to wear rubber-soled slippers. She would never have believed that such intoxicatingly aristocratic cooking could exist. For an appetizer, the Filipino busboys trouped in and placed two small plates and a bowl in front of each guest—quail served three different ways: paper-thin sliced breast of quail with sautéed shallots, a satiny quail consommé, and a perfect tiny leg of quail in a round pool of rich red wine sauce. Over the main course of three different freshwater fish served in a duck-liver sauce and accompanied by the palest, youngest green asparagus tips she had ever seen, Skolnik and the others regaled her with anecdotes of stars she'd seen on the screen or read about; at regular intervals everyone at the table casually threw questions at her, shrewdly prying from her everything they might need to know about her background, a subtle but clever tactic. The smooth champagne and impressive, velvety dinner wine made it seem less an interrogation than a social event. By the time dessert arrived—a trio, of course, raspberries, blueberries, and strawberries served with crème fraiche—Skolnik and his handpicked top rank knew enough about her to have something to go on. The fact that her mother had been a great Russian stage actress and the favorite of a prince excited them; thanks to the wine loosening her tongue, she had even let it slip out that she and her guardian needed money rather badly.

"Bruce," Skolnik asked as the butler came around with a humidor of Cuban cigars, "do you have enough for your publicity department to start work on?" He lit his pipe, forgoing a cigar.

Tamara's scalp prickled. So they *were* serious!

Bruce Slesen grinned, selected two cigars, and pocketed them. "More than enough!" he crowed. "This little lady's background is dynamite. A little embellishment here and there, and we have a history like you wouldn't believe. For instance, we'll simply say her mother was a great Russian actress and her father was a bona fide prince. No one will come forward and contest that, believe me. In my experience, people believe what they want to believe, and they'll want to believe this for sure. Anyway, as far as I know, most of the White Russians who escaped the revolution are either too busy trying to plot their return to take time out to tattle on her, or else they're scared stiff the Bolshies will find them, so they're staying hidden. What we'll do with Tamara, here, is give her the royal treatment. Don't forget, having a prince for a father makes her a princess."

"A princess, eh?" Skolnik mulled that over and smiled. "I like it."

"I don't." Tamara leaned across the table, her perfect arched brows drawing sharply together. "It's . . . it's simply not *true*!" she insisted in a vehement whisper. "I'm *not* a princess! I never was! And my father wasn't a prince!"

Slesin grinned easily at her. "Sure he was. And sure you are."

She stared first at him, then at Skolnik, shocked at how easily they could spin a web of half-truths. Was everything she had ever read about the stars of Hollywood only partially true . . . perhaps even total fiction?

Skolnik turned to the head of his talent division. "Carol? Any comments?"

"Except for the details we discussed yesterday, I believe she seems to fit most of the requirements we've been looking for," Carol Anderegg said carefully without committing herself.

There it was again, Tamara thought with a sinking feeling, another mention of those damn "details," whatever they might be.

Skolnik's piercing eyes bore in the direction of the art director. "Claude?"

Claude de Chantilly-Siciles nodded slowly. Gone now was the flippancy, the continental demeanor he liked to affect; things had obviously gotten down to brass tacks. "I think we could structure a whole new look, a total *style* around her," he said thoughtfully, toying with his rococo teaspoon. "From what I have seen of the screen test, her acting could use some sprucing up, but that's the director's problem, not mine." He glanced at Ziolko, who sat there impassively. "On the whole, I'd say she has that elusive star quality that instantly makes you sit up and take notice." His eyes flicked around to the others, who nodded silently. "And I like that princess angle," he continued. "It gives us something definite to shoot for. She's regal, but not overly so. She's charming and fresh—sexy, even—but she doesn't mock these attributes; indeed, there's nothing blatant about her, just enough of a hint, which is far, far more effective than any blatancy. I think our watchword with her should be 'class,' because she's definitely got it, but we must be careful to exploit it without *over*exploiting it. What it boils down to is this: I think she has all the makings of a glamour queen. I see her all white—almost white-blond hair, white wardrobe, white furnishings, white sets, sparkling jewels, white furs . . . white borzois on a leash—that kind of thing. I think we can

318

create the film sensation of the thirties if, and I repeat *if,* she decides to play along with us and agrees to our suggestions."

Skolnik sat back and puffed leisurely on his pipe for a few moments. For her part, Tamara managed to sit through the discussion with quiet poise and dignity. Tight-lipped, she looked around the table. She was at once fascinated by the workings of these creative minds, able to witness firsthand the gears of the industry brains swiftly clicking and turning, and at the same time she seethed with monstrous anger. Her hands were clenched in her lap in two red balls, a hidden barometer of her emotions, which rose and plunged alternately with euphoria, anger, humiliation, and fervent hope. She struggled to keep her face carefully composed, but the corners of her lips were pinched, beginning to show her growing anger and annoyance. On the one hand, she basked in all this attention, but on the other, they were discussing her as dispassionately as a convention of butchers talking about a skinned steer, and that caused her blood to boil. Who did they think they were, jabbering on and on without even once stopping to consult her! And there hadn't even been a whisper of a contract yet. She was ready to burst into tears of frustration.

Skolnik turned now to the art dealer. "Bernie, like you said earlier, I had an ulterior motive when I invited you. Well, here it is. I've trusted your judgment enough so far to have bought . . . what, twenty paintings off you?"

The art dealer waited.

"Now I want your professional opinion of Tamara. Not your *personal* opinion, mind you, but the art critic's. Don't be afraid to be harsh. I want you to be truthful. What does your expert, appraising eye tell you when you look at her? Be as objective as if she were a painting you'd consider buying and selling."

Bernard Katzenbach frowned mournfully down at the table. He was clearly being put on the spot, and he didn't like it. Discussing the merits and demerits of a painting or a piece of sculpture was one thing. After all, paintings and sculptures didn't have ears. But openly discussing a person's physical perfections and shortcomings, especially with that person present, horrified him. Yet what choice did he really have? He had the peculiar sensation that his business relationship with his best client hung precariously in the balance.

Katzenbach raised his eyes across the table to study Tamara. She was holding her breath, sitting as immobile as an ancient statue hewn from marble, her face in three-quarter profile, so beautiful it nearly hurt. Despite her extraordinary beauty, he began seeing flaws . . . serious flaws. If she were a work of art, he knew that he would have to reject her. She was not the perfect woman, not a masterpiece after all.

"I see a very beautiful woman," he said carefully, "but like all living creatures, and unlike art, she is far from perfect. She is neither skinny nor voluptuous . . . a little too much baby fat still there, I think."

Tamara flinched as if she had been slapped; the others nodded in solemn agreement, as if this were something they already knew.

"Go on," Skolnik said.

"Her upper teeth are crooked," Katzenbach pointed out. "Her nose angles off to one side . . ."

"Then you don't consider her a goddess," Skolnik pressed in a quiet voice.

A flush crept into Katzenbach's face and his usually gentle topaz eyes flashed fire and then dimmed. He wanted nothing more than to leap up and stalk out of this wretched house, never to return, but he was a cautious man not about to jeopardize future sales. "There is a difference between a goddess of art and a goddess of the cinema," he said tightly. "Surely you don't need me to point that out. In art, perfection is generally the highest achievable plane, at least in the opinion of the West. The Japenese consider perfection so commonplace that their artists often create a single flaw in an otherwise perfect masterpeice in order to make it *truly* perfect."

Tamara remained motionless, looking into Katzenbach's eyes. Quickly he shifted his gaze.

"But she has more than one flaw," Skolnik said. "You just got through saying so yourself."

Katzenbach hesitated. "I did. However, in the motion-picture industry there are tricks of lighting, makeup, who knows what? I am no cinematographer, so I don't really know. I have heard that the camera sees only what one wants it to see. However, as far as the excess weight, the teeth, and the nose go . . . I don't see how a camera can disguise those." He shrugged eloquently and shook his head sadly. "I fear close-ups would only exaggerate those flaws, magnifying them for all the world to see."

Skolnik nodded slowly. "You have been truthful," he said, "and I appreciate that. I also want to apologize for taking up so much of your time. It has been a pleasure having you with us."

Bernard Katzenbach recognized a cue when he heard one, and he pushed his chair back from the table. He dropped his damask napkin to the left of his dessert plate as he rose to his feet. "Ladies," he said with a bow of his head, pointedly avoiding Tamara's accusing eyes. He could see that she was breathing deeply, forcing back her tears. "Gentlemen. You must excuse me, it is getting late."

"Frédérique will show you out." Skolnik said smoothly, and the black butler appeared as if on a predetermined cue.

Katzenbach nodded and went to the door.

"Bernie . . ."

The art dealer turned and looked back at the table.

"Leave the Malevich." Skolnik allowed himself a faint smile. "A messenger will drop by your hotel in the morning with the check."

In the dining room, the tapers in the heavy sterling candelabra were burning low. Skolnik turned to Tamara, his face showing not the least remorse. "I think it's time we went to the screening room and watched your test," he said with an unrepentant smile.

She turned to face him and stared dumbly through him. She was suddenly exhausted, her entire body feeling as ravaged as if she had been drawn and quartered. The thrill of the evening was gone. She felt completely drained.

Like an automaton she somehow managed to push herself to her feet. For a moment she swayed unsteadily. She couldn't remember ever having felt less confident of herself.

She was devastated.

For the first time in her life she felt truly ugly.

She couldn't help thinking: If I'm that ugly, and he doesn't want me in his films, why should I sit through the test? Why make me suffer more?

In the center of the luxurious screening room Tamara found herself swallowed up in the suppleness of an overstuffed jade-green leather armchair. To her left, seated in an identical chair, was Skolnik; Ziolko sat on her right. The others sat on the proportionately smaller, armless chairs around them, the position of the chairs attesting to the pecking order at the studio. "All right, Sammy," Skolnik called out, "let it roll."

The screening room was abruptly dark and the film began to roll. Tamara held her breath while the giant black countdown numbers, trapped inside a swiftly moving one-handed clock face, flashed upon the flickering screen: 9, 8, 7, 6 . . .

. . .5, 4, 3, 2 . . . The numbers suddenly disappeared from the screen altogether, and then she emitted a startled, throaty sound. There she was in the identification shot, gazing directly out at herself. Her huge black-and-white face filled the screen, and she seemed so improbably huge, so . . . so unlike herself as she smiled tenuously, that she burrowed even further back into the refuge of the huge armchair. Never before had she realized that she smiled quite so horribly. That it was more a monstrous, toothy grimace than a smile.

A sickening feeling engulfed her. Worst of all, the sheer immensity of that ten-foot-high face seemed to magnify the trembling corners of her lips while her blank, unmoving eyes were focused straight ahead. She looked as stiff, as immobile, as un-movie-star-like as a police-department mug shot. Bernard Kazenbach's cruel critique of her beauty had been justified, she had to admit now. In fact, he had been tactful, all things considered. Her nose *did* curve unattractively off to one side, throwing the rest of her features slightly off balance. Her body was *not* perfectly proportioned. Also, she *was* far too heavy, dammit. And as for her teeth . . . Good Lord, could they really be *that* crooked? She shuddered, suddenly all too painfully aware of her physical shortcomings. Why hadn't she noticed them before?

Tamara was filled with an ugly sense of self-loathing. The tears were threatening to burst from her eyes in a violent cloudburst. As if to emphasize the mug-shot image, against her bodice she was holding the small white cardboard sign, die-cut in a wide spatula shape so that she could hold it by its short, squat handle. It shook in her trembling fingers like a paintbrush, the printed letters shaking violently with every anxious, magnified twitch. The blank spaces had been filled in with neat black letters.

NAME	*Boralevi Tamara*		DATE *1/24/30*
CHAR.	*Leila*		WRD. NO. *1*
PIC. NO. *B-112*	MKP. NO. *3*		HDR. NO. *2*

At last, to her immense relief, the long introductory shot with her hideously vapid smile faded, and a wooden clapper lettered *The Flappers* snapped shut like a zebra-striped jaw.

In the dark, Tamara's hand crept up to her face. She gnawed mutely at a crescent thumbnail, her eyes remaining steadily focused on the screen.

Then the dazzling miracle of Hollywood unexpectedly and shiningly occurred. It was the Creation of Eve, Columbus' first glimpse of the New World, the initial golden glint of the mother lode to a jaded prospector's weary eye. Like the proverbial ugly duckling metamorphosing into a stunning swan, so too Tamara had been transformed from that ungainly girl into a sleekly graceful young woman. The combined talents of Louis Ziolko, Pearl Dern, and the rest of the test crew had created a person who had not previously existed, except possibly in the uncharted reaches of a godly imagination.

Dazed, Tamara found herself flung by this exotic wizardry into another world, a new dimension. It was as if the screen test of the past and the screening room of the present were no more. She herself seemed to have disappeared as an entity.

Her eyes were wide with disbelief. No, it simply could *not* be. Magic and miracles were phenomena which happened, if at all, to others, not to her. But it *had* happened, and on the grandest scale imaginable. The film proved it. The woman on-screen did not appear to be acting, but actually living the role, thanks to Ziolko's shrewd and manipulative direction and editing. This radiant Tamara did not move gawkily like the real one, but gloriously. Sensually. And she looked dazzling. She enchanted and glittered, swept aside everything but her own beauty, personality, and sexuality.

Several fleeting scenes melted swiftly one into the other. Dumbfounded and numb with sudden pleasure, she watched her giant double moving with inborn effortlessness and grace. She heard her voice—low, husky, and purring. Or at least she thought it was her voice; it sounded strange and foreign to her ears, not at all like her voice sounded when she heard herself talk. She had had no idea that her voice could sound so alluringly husky, so smokily sexy.

And then came the final scene Ziolko had made her perform over and over until his exacting standards of perfection had been met. How simple and fluid, how perfectly *right* the scene seemed now, with her and Miles Gabriel doing a frenzied, sexually charged Charleston. Miles was exceedingly smooth and handsome in white tie and swallow-tails, his gleaming black hair combed back, his pencil-line mustache adding a lusty animalism to his sensuous lips, and she . . . *No, that simply cannot be me!* she thought in rapt astonishment.

She was shaking now, her heart working overtime and hammering against her rib cage as she finally saw that that wondrous, exquisitely costumed creature was indeed she. Slightly overweight, with a nose that definitely did not photograph straight in the close-ups—nor were her eyes perfectly matched, those same critical eyes told her. But none of it mattered. What did matter was the electricity sparking on the screen, the fact that she had somehow conquered that expanse of silver canvas, had drawn the focus of attention and through some magic forced it to remain on her, never letting go.

Enraptured, she stared at her new glossy self, dizzy with entrancement.

Suddenly she gave a start. Just as she was getting caught up in the miracle on-screen, the film finished rushing through the rattling projector and giant white dots flashed and flickered on a pale gray background.

The joy that had buoyed her spirits higher and higher suddenly evaporated. It was over. She felt sad, depleted. She wished it could have gone on forever.

"Lights, Sammy," Skolnik called out into the darkness. Then he leaned toward Tamara, lowering his voice confidentially. "Well, what do you think?"

The overhead lights clicked on and she blinked rapidly, her gaze still on the now-blank screen.

"Cat got your tongue?" Skolnik smiled smoothly. "You didn't like what you saw?"

She hesitated, trying to find an appropriate answer. It was futile. Now that the test was already a blur in the past, she no longer felt quite so sure of her rapturous opinions. After all, what did she know? Who was she to judge? "I . . . I don't know," she said uncertainly, turning to face him, her fingernails clawing into her thighs. "Wh-what do *you* think?"

"I think the test speaks for itself. You do have a certain quality," he admitted carefully, "and even your acting, though it could stand some improvement, is not half-bad. As things stand right this minute, I've little doubt that you'd be successful in quite a variety of pictures."

She waited, barely daring to believe her ears. There was a stupendous rushing inside her head now, as if someone was holding a giant seashell to her ear.

"I could, of course, sign you up for supporting roles immediately," he said. "However, that's like uncorking a fine wine prematurely, and I've never been a man to squander fine things. I can afford to wait until the time is right.

You see, I'm not looking for just another actress. We have plenty of those to choose from."

"Then what are you looking for?" she managed to ask softly, holding his gaze.

He stared at her. "The most elusive, highly prized commodity in this town."

She frowned slightly.

"A star, Tamara, that's what I'm looking for," he explained frankly. "Not just a great actress or another beautiful face, but a full-fledged, runaway, box-office *star*. We have Miles Gabriel, but he's our only major male star. We need others like him. What's more important, we don't even have one actress on a par with Gabriel." He paused. "I'm looking for a woman to become that star."

"And you think I . . ."

He half-smiled. "I don't think, I know. The only problem is, how far are you willing to go to reach that exalted status?"

She didn't speak, since she had no idea what he meant.

"There are, of course, your weight, your nose, your eyes, your teeth. All cinematic obstacles to consider."

She gave a low, husky laugh. "I'm afraid I was born this way. Unfortunately, I can't climb back inside the womb and come out differently."

He gave her a peculiar look. "Can't you?" His voice was hushed.

"Of course not. You know there's nothing I can do except lose some weight."

"That isn't entirely true. Your teeth are a simple matter," he said easily. "They can be capped right here in L.A."

"But what about my nose?" She stared at him broodingly. "My eyes?"

He continued smiling slightly, though she noticed his cheekbones had gained angular tautness, and she was alarmingly aware that he was no longer concealing the predatory expression of a tiger smelling blood. She realized then and there that this was a man who always got what he wanted. Beneath his handsome tanned skin was a skeleton of steel. A tingling chill of fear rippled up and down her back.

"There is a doctor in Italy," he told her, "a pioneer really. He is making remarkable progress in a relatively new field called reconstructive surgery."

"I've never even heard of it."

"I'm not surprised. Neither have most doctors."

"And this doctor . . . *he* can change my nose and eyes?" she asked in disbelief.

He nodded.

She turned away from him, staring blankly at the screen. "Would you consider it?"

Her voice took on a harried shrillness. "I don't even know what I'd be letting myself in for!" Tensely she bit down on her lip and then faced him again, her eyes slashing shards of brilliant green ice. "I take it it's called reconstructive surgery because there *is* surgery involved?"

He nodded expressionlessly.

She clenched her index finger and bit down on it. She was totally deflated, and frightened as well. *Surgery.* The very word filled her with dread. She had never heard of anyone healthy agreeing to undergo an operation. And just to improve your looks . . .

"I have your contracts drawn up," Skolnik said negligibly. He paused. "How does one thousand dollars a week for seven years sound? Guaranteed. You start getting paid as soon as you sign."

She was speechless. *One thousand dollars a week!* That was unheard-of. She sat bolt upright, her mind reeling in shock as she swiftly calculated astronomical figures. Why, that came to . . .

A fortune.

She cringed at a stomach spasm.

That was more than enough to secure her future forever. But at what a price.

Surgery.

He was waiting patiently. Only the occasional sound of creaking leather as he shifted in his chair reminded her that he was there.

After a while she found her voice. It was shaky and subdued. "I take it that these terms are all contingent upon whether or not I agree to the surgery?"

Skolnik nodded. "That they are."

"But how do you know the surgery will be successful?"

"Dr. Zatopek comes highly recommended." His face was solemn. "I am living proof."

"You!" She frowned deeply. "I don't understand."

"It's simple. I've personally tested all the new aircraft developed by Skolnik Aviation, and I've had more than my fair share of crashes. One in particular nearly did me in. You should have seen me before Dr. Zatopek patched me up. I looked monstrous enough to send little children running." He chuckled slightly. "As a rule, Dr. Zatopek restricts himself to accident victims, but with you he'll make an exception. You wouldn't believe the techniques he's developed. And, seeing as how you're almost perfect as is . . . well, I'll wager anything you'll be the most beautiful woman this town has ever seen." A broad smile cracked his usually unsmiling lips.

"You've already talked to the doctor?"

He nodded. "He's agreed to take you on. It's all been arranged. I just received word yesterday."

Suddenly everything fell neatly into place. She was annoyed. "So that's why I had to wait so long before you showed me the screen test," she accused bitterly. "Until you'd heard from him?"

"Guilty." He looked at her with new respect.

"All right." She took a deep breath and grasped the arms of her chair with trembling, splayed fingers. "But I want four hundred thousand dollars over the next eighty-four months. Guaranteed—whether the surgery is successful or not." She slid a sideways glance at him.

He looked at her expressionlessly and took his time relighting his pipe. "You drive a hard bargain, little lady," he said as he lit up. "What makes you think you're worth four hundred thousand?" His face was wreathed in blue smoke.

She smiled slightly. "The same thing that makes you think I'm worth three-sixty-four."

"Without the surgery, you know you're not worth a fraction of that. Why get greedy?"

"I'm not greedy," she retorted. "I want to be covered just in case . . ."

"The surgery fails," he finished for her.

She nodded. "That, or I'm left with worse complications than I started out with. If that happens, any career I might want will be finished before I start."

"Fair enough." It was his turn to nod. "Agreed." He signaled to Carol Anderegg. "Carol, you and Claude scare up a temporary wardrobe for Tamara, will you? Including a white mink coat. If this little lady's going to be a star, she'd better get used to looking the part. I want her to go first class all the way."

He turned back to Tamara, who had slumped limply in her chair. She looked emotionally drained. "Come to the studio at eight tomorrow morning to sign the contract," he told her. "At nine you'll report to wardrobe for measurements and whatever they'll have scrounged up for you. At eleven a car will take you to your first appointment at the dentist's. As soon as your teeth are fixed, I'll see to it that you and Louie are flown to Italy. It'll probably be a couple of weeks."

"Flown! A couple of weeks!" Tamara gasped. "But—"

Skolnik made a casual gesture. "Don't forget, I have an entire fleet of airplanes at my disposal. Why waste time on trains and ships when you don't have to? Time is money, after all. *My* money."

She shook her head blearily. She was completely overwhelmed now. After waiting this long for a break, she suddenly found herself swept up in a whirlwind. "Tomorrow!" she murmured weakly. "It's going to start tomorrow?"

He shrugged again. "Why shouldn't it? You'll be on my payroll as of eight o'clock in the morning, so we might as well get cracking." He sat back and grinned, contentedly puffing on his pipe.

"In that case, I'd better be going," she said, rising to her feet. "It seems I'll need all the beauty sleep I can get."

"You go do that. I'll see you tomorrow. Louie will drive you home."

She nodded numbly, said good night to the others, and followed Ziolko unsteadily out of the room. Her knees trembled. She felt anything but elated. A sudden depression had permeated her every limb.

She tightened her lips. Her dreams of success had been nothing like this. She didn't know why she felt so unhappy. Except that maybe she had made a deal with the devil.

It was dusk a little over a month and a half later when the stabbing yellow headlights of the Fiat Balilla crested the spruce-studded hill high in the Italian Alps. Snow crunched under the clattering snow chains as the chauffeur expertly negotiated the car up to the lamplit entrance of the four-story chalet, where it rolled to a smooth stop. Immediately he jumped out and held the rear door open.

Max Factor, makeup genius and cosmetologist extraordinaire, and Oscar Skolnik exited together. The March chill and the clear, thin mountain air sharpened Skolnik's senses. Even in the dusk, his vision seemed crystal clear as he inhaled the heady fragrance of fresh air. If air could have healing properties, then this was it, he thought. Abruptly he pulled his lips back across his teeth in a grin. His eyes were lively, dancing with unsuppressed excitement. In fact he looked far better rested than the well-rested Max Factor. On a lesser mortal the strain of the trip would have been all too evident, but Oscar Skolnik was a master at conserving his energies.

At the sound of the car pulling up, Louis Ziolko had hurried down the chalet's terraced stone steps, half his face in deep shadow. He was well bundled against the alpine cold in a thick loden coat and scarf. He had been restlessly prowling the foyer for this moment. "Have a good trip?" he greeted quietly, his breath a plume of vapor. "Your room and a hot bath are waiting." His cheeks were taut, and he seemed oddly subdued, as though he had been under an enormous strain.

Skolnik strode purposefully up the steps past him. "How's she faring?" he asked without preamble, never breaking his swift stride, and thereby causing Ziolko to turn around in surprise and hurry back up the steps after him. "The last time I spoke to her on the telephone, she sounded crotchety and annoyed."

"You can't really blame Tamara," Ziolko retorted with barely controlled anger. "The surgery she underwent was painful, and apparently the bandages cause a lot of itching. They've been on for over a week and a half."

Skolnik stopped on the top step and turned around. "But they're still on?"

Ziolko nodded and sighed. "She still looks like a mummy, if that's what you want to know," he grumbled. "Dr. Zatopek was anxious for them to come off two days ago, but he held off until you could be here."

"Good." Skolnik nodded with satisfaction. "I take it he's ready, then? I'll go straight up to her room. Have him meet me there at once."

Ziolko hesitated. "It's Dr. Zatopek's dinner hour, the only time of day he insists on not being disturbed. I think it wise if we wait half an hour or so."

Skolnik regarded Ziolko stolidly. "I traveled two whole days and nights and seven thousand miles to see this. If I could do that, then the good doctor can interrupt his dinner."

"Very well." Ziolko compressed his lips and nodded. He glanced down at the car. The chauffeur was unloading the luggage from the trunk, and a familiar figure he couldn't quite place was climbing the steps toward him.

"You've met Max Factor, of course," Skolnik said offhandedly. "He's been sworn to secrecy. We can trust him to take our little secret to the grave."

Curiously, Ziolko looked at the makeup creator. "Good to see you again, Max," he said equably, hiding his anger and shaking the man's hand. But inside, Ziolko seethed. Tamara had specifically asked for Pearl, a known quantity in her life, whom she trusted. Instead, she had gotten one of the world's foremost cosmeticians . . . but a stranger. Max Factor or no, she would be greatly disappointed.

Skolnik had caught Ziolko's brief flash of subdued anger. "I asked Max to come along so that he could personally do Tamara's makeup before she sees herself in a mirror. I want her to look her absolute best. I know this hasn't been easy on her."

Not easy! Ziolko wanted to shout with a new flare of anger. *If that was me under all those bandages, I'd sure as hell have ripped them off by now and found myself a mirror. And broken it and attacked Skolnik with the shards.*

For he remembered only too well the warning Dr. Zatopek had given him, but which both he and the doctor had carefully kept from Tamara: the operation might well be successful; then again, it might not. Facial surgery was in its infancy. Worse yet, she could even be disfigured for life.

With a heavy step, Ziolko followed Skolnik into the warm foyer, praying as he had for the last month that the series of operations had been successful.

Soon now, too soon, he would know if his prayers had been answered.

Which would she be? Beauty? Or the Beast?

Tamara's eyes.

They were all that was visible of her face. Snowy white bandages made the rest of her head a smooth, featureless mask. Her nostrils were mere slits. Her mouth, a gash of darkened, wet bandages.

She did not even look remotely human—unless one looked closely into her eyes.

They were human and wide and filled with fear. The fear was much more evident now than before because of the lights, a brilliant, blinding cluster of five-hundred-watt operating-room bulbs.

She sat stiffly erect in the hard, upright chair beside the operating table in her shapeless striped gown, eyes blinking against the glare, wary of the tray of gleaming surgical utensils beside her, awaiting Dr. Zatopek's imminent arrival. When, she asked herself, would it finally end?

First, her teeth had been straightened and capped in California, too fast and therefore too painfully. She had also begun to lose weight there through a daily exercise regimen and virtual starvation; at the weighing this morning, she had lost the last of the twelve pounds she had been striving to lose. She was now five-feet-nine and weighed 120 pounds. It had been no easy feat. For the last month and a half, she couldn't remember a night when she hadn't gone to bed hungry. Or hadn't had trouble sleeping because of excruciating physical pain. When she had first agreed to the surgery it had never occurred to her that it would be so painful or that she would be constantly humiliated. To date, the nose surgery had been the worst by far. In order to reshape it, her nose had been broken and then reset, packed with endless yards of fine, thin absorbent tape. Through the hazy fog of the local anesthetic she had heard her own delicate nose cartilage shattering, had heard the scalpel scraping. Even thinking about it now made her shudder. Then, when the packing had come out, she had been nauseated for two entire days and nights. Even that she had suffered in silence, and although Louis Ziolko had been at her side throughout this ordeal and they had grown quite close, she would have much preferred Pearl, or better yet, Inge, to whom she would not have hesitated to pour out her woes. But what she found most difficult of all to bear was that Dr. Zatopek had refused to let her have even the slightest fleeting glimpse of herself and her "new" nose. At the clinic, mirrors were a carefully guarded commodity, locked in closets and brought out only when the patient was deemed physically and psychologically ready; even her compact and the hand mirror she had packed in her luggage had been confiscated upon her arrival.

"There is still too much swelling and far too many bruises," Dr. Zatopek had informed her with his usual brusqueness. "When I think you are ready, then I shall let you see yourself. But not a moment before." And with that, the case was closed. Dr. Zatopek refused to hear any more arguments, and his nurses were stern and unbribable.

She could not remember when she had felt more frustrated.

Then there had been the delicate eye surgery; the top men at IA had agreed that her eyes did not quite match in shape, in the much-magnified close-ups on-screen it was much more evident than in person.

But now, at long last, the surgery was all over. The bandages were about to come off. She couldn't hear Dr. Zatopek's brisk heels approaching outside in the hall since her bandages muffled all but the loudest sounds, but she caught Ziolko, Skolnik, Max Factor, and the nurse turning expectantly toward the door.

She caught her breath and uttered a swift prayer as it opened and Dr. Zatopek stepped into the room. Her heart was pounding. A vise bound her head above her eyes. She dug the fingernails of one hand deep into the soft palm of the other, hoping that the pain would overpower her growing hysteria.

When she looked into a mirror from now on, whom would she see?
Herself? Or a stranger?

The itchy bandages were off less than ten minutes later, but it was another three full days before Tamara was finally allowed to see herself in a mirror. This time it was not the doctor, but Oscar Skolnik, who declined her request. "I don't want you to get the wrong idea," he said. "There's still your makeup and your hair to be done first. You've waited this long, what's a few more days?"

A lot, she discovered to her chagrin: the hours and days crawled by with interminable slowness. Time had come to a stop.

When the big moment finally came, Dr. Zatopek was not in attendance. He washed his hands of the entire affair. "I have better things to occupy myself with than this foolishness," he declared pointedly to Skolnik, who raised his eyebrows in surprise. "The sooner this room is vacated, the sooner someone who truly needs help can be moved in."

And with that, the door snapped abruptly shut behind him.

The doctor's cutting words and brash tone put a damper on Tamara's spirits. Mercifully, it was only temporary. There was little time for her to concentrate on the negative aspect of things—besides which, Oscar Skolnik was proving himself a rare magician, pulling surprise after surprise out of his hat. For the first time in six weeks, Tamara was almost faint from excitement. She thrived on all the bustling attention. A hairdresser had been sent for all the way from Rome to bleach, color, cut, and style her hair, and Max Factor had spent the last three days locked up creating the perfect makeup exclusively for her, which he now painstakingly and artfully applied, changed, corrected, and reapplied. Throughout, Oscar Skolnik paced in concentric circles like a predatory shark or a nervous father-to-be—Tamara couldn't decide which—constantly barking commands or giving advice on further improvements. Only Louis Ziolko was a silent bystander, sitting next to her, from time to time smiling reassuringly or taking her hand and giving it an encouraging squeeze.

Still more tedious hours dragged by before Skolnik finally nodded his tight-lipped approval. The nod was taken as a silent signal: Max Factor put his brushes, creams, lotions, and pencils away, and Ziolko emitted a sigh of relief, beamed, kissed her cheek, and got to his feet. Without having said a word, the men trouped out behind Skolnik like obedient ducks following their mother, and a plump, pleasant-faced maid came bustling in to help her get dressed. When the woman first caught sight of her, she stopped cold in her tracks and stared wide-eyed.

Tamara looked at her strangely. "Is something wrong?" she asked.

The woman shook her head swiftly but was silent for a moment. "*Scusi,*" she apologized in obvious embarrassment, her face coloring. "Please forgive me. I . . . I am unused to seeing such beauty."

Tamara stared at her. "Am I . . . beautiful, then?" she asked falteringly.

The woman laughed. "Are you—" Then she noticed Tamara's dead-serious look and the laughter died in her throat. She stepped closer. "You do not know?" she asked softly, her eyes searching Tamara's.

Tamara shook her head, the tears beginning to well up in her eyes. "No," she said hoarsely, swiftly turning away. "I haven't seen myself for weeks."

"You poor thing." The maid tilted her head to one side and smiled reassuringly. She nodded slowly. "You are very, very beautiful, signorina."

Tamara turned to look at her. Impulsively she reached out and pressed the woman's hand. "Thank you," she whispered fervently, her voice trembling with relief.

"For what? Speaking the truth?" The matronly woman was happy now, smiling. Humming cheerfully, she busied herself digging wordlessly through voluminous layers of rustling tissue paper in an enormous sleek cardboard box. After a moment she unfolded the Vionnet gown from Paris which Skolnik had ordered to Tamara's new measurements and had brought with him. The humming stopped suddenly. "*Mamma mia!*" the maid exclaimed with a gasp, holding it up, her dark topaz eyes dancing as she examined it closely, all the time making impressed little cooing sounds.

Tamara took a deep breath and drew closer to inspect the gown. "How pretty!" she exclaimed, instinctively reaching out to feel the luscious white silk taffeta. It was cool and regal.

"Ah, what a treasure, signorina! Just look! *Bellissima!*" the maid exclaimed, holding the gown against Tamara. She sounded breathless, like an excited child at Christmas.

Yes, it was indeed a treasure, Tamara had to agree. Even she, inexperienced as she was as far as good clothes were concerned, had at least been exposed to Hollywood's finest costumes through the magic of the motion pictures she had seen; now she had to admit wholeheartedly that genuine Paris couture was light-years ahead of the most splendid costume designer's most extravagant creation. This exquisite gown was designed to take one's breath away. As well as stand up to the most minute scrutiny. No mere costume, this.

The maid slid the gown reverentially off the padded velvet hanger and helped Tamara dress, her face beaming, her cheerful, bustling manner and constant stream of words never letting up. "*Mamma mia*, but you look like a *principessa, si*! A genuine *principessa*. Maybe you have Italian blood? I have heard all about you, of course. Everyone here gossips like magpies, but I truly had no idea how beautiful you are! And this gown . . . Now, turn around, please, and let me fasten . . ."

When Tamara was completely dressed, she moved tentatively this way and that, feeling the fabric's every elegant move, every billowing swirl. She looked down at herself, once again silently cursing the absence of a mirror. But she knew that the gown was a masterpiece of design and handwork. It reached to mid-calf in the front and down to the floor in the back, flaring gracefully from her shoulders to the small of her spine, where a series of tiny seed-pearl buttons held it snug. An attached sash from the front wrapped around to the back in a kind of massive sculptured-taffeta bow which fell to a six-inch-long train.

"You are a fairy-tale vision, signorina." The maid stepped back to study the effect, happily wringing her plump, short red hands as she beamed in pleasure. Then, wishing her the best, the maid left.

The men once again filed in, stepping forward to examine her more closely, then stepping back again as though they were studying their own reflections in a mirror or deciding upon the purchase of a particularly priceless object. In they leaned. Back they stepped. Over and over. Max Factor hurriedly made some fine adjustments with a pencil and a brush. Finally, wordlessly, they all looked at one another and nodded. Now there were smiles and handshakes all around. Congratulations for one another.

"That doctor's a magician if I've ever seen one," Skolnik said happily, lighting his pipe. "Can't see a stitch, can you, Max? He'd make a fortune in Hollywood."

And ". . . Can't believe what that platinum does to her hair. See if we can't bribe that hairdresser to come out to Hollywood. We sure could use her . . ."

And ". . . Makeup's good, Max. Real good. Nice definition around the eyes. Gives her a kind of . . . hmmm . . . haunted quality, wouldn't you say? But sexy. The women'll love her and try to copy her, and the men'll eat her up, fantasizing about her in the bedroom. A great job, Max."

And ". . . That Vionnet lady's something else. Just from the measurements, she came up with this gown. Tell you what, we'll have her make up an entire wardrobe, maybe even have her do some sketches for movie costumes."

Tamara bit down on her lip, disgusted with them all. *What about me!* she railed silently. *Didn't I have something to do with this? Isn't this me they're going on and on about? After all I've had to go through . . .*

She wanted to scream.

Instead, she glared at Skolnik and cleared her throat angrily.

Ignoring her, Oscar Skolnik snapped his fingers at Ziolko, who went out into the hall and signaled for two orderlies to carry in a draped three-panel dressing mirror. Tamara stared at it, her heart thumping. The moment of reckoning was at hand.

The anger seeped instantly out of her, replaced by a wave of dizzying excitement.

Skolnik smiled as he approached the mirror and flicked his wrist like a magician, flinging aside the sheet.

Tamara's excitement edged into panic. What would she see?

Trembling, she forced herself to walk slowly toward it, and then her body slid into her line of vision and was reflected threefold. She let out a gasp. Skolnik stopped behind her, his face half-hidden by her own, his one visible eye gleaming with Svengali satisfaction over her right shoulder.

She shook her head in disbelief, frowned, shook it again. The noble, high-cheekboned face staring back at her had a Slavic, almost otherworldly beauty. Lustrous platinum curls gleamed with an angel-hair whiteness. The figure was svelte, as perfect in its proportions as a finely chiseled Greek marble. The nose was thin, patrician, perfect. Indeed, everything about her was perfect. The arched brows, nothing short of magnificent. The teeth, luminous. Skin the translucent clarity of a very fine, very pale dessert wine. The eyes, perfectly balanced now, and heavily lidded and shadowed and outlined, enchanted and beguiled even herself.

"Do you recognize her?" Skolnik asked softly into her ear.

"I . . . I don't know," Tamara stammered, softly touching her new face with featherlike fingertips. "This . . . this isn't the old Tamara Boralevi."

335

His voice was even. "No, it isn't," he replied. "Tamara Boralevi is no more. Even that name ceases to exist. From now on, you will be known only as Tamara. No last name. Just Tamara. Throughout the world, everyone will be on a first-name basis with you."

"I . . . I just can't believe this is me!" She turned to face him, her moist lips parted, her teeth gleaming iridescently.

He shook his head and smiled slightly. "It isn't you. The Tamara you used to be has ceased to exist. The woman you see before you is flesh and blood, but she was born of no woman. I have had the opportunity to do that which many men have dreamt of doing, but none has ever achieved. I have played God. I have had you created. I have created an ideal. I have created perfection."

She nodded silently, gooseflesh breaking out on her arms. "Yes, yes, you have, Mr. Skolnik," she said huskily, turning back to the mirror.

"O.T.," he reminded her. "You're supposed to call me O.T." His face slid out of view.

"I'm . . . I'm *beautiful!*" she cried. "I'm truly, truly beautiful!" The tears flooded forth unchecked now, blurring her vision, running in mascara rivulets down flawless cheeks.

It was Louis Ziolko who stepped forward, reached for his handkerchief, and dabbed her eyes dry. " 'Beautiful' does not begin to describe you," he said softly. "I think you are now the most beautiful woman in the world."

She swallowed visibly and didn't know how to reply.

"Oh, by the way," Skolnik said almost negligibly, "you'd better take care of that face. I've got a big investment in it, you know. It's being insured with Lloyd's of London for one million dollars."

After he and Max left, she and Louis stared at the door for a long, long time.

Night had long since fallen. A brisk alpine wind rattled the windowpanes, relentlessly seeking cracks and crannies through which to invade the room. Under the feather-light eiderdown duvet, Tamara listened to the high-pitched keening of the wind. Somewhere out in the hall a clock chimed twelve times.

She sighed and stared blearily up at the dark ceiling. Midnight already, and still she lay awake. She had tried to go to sleep hours ago, but sleep had eluded her. So much had happened, and so quickly. Since coming here, she had become a woman who previously had not existed.

So many fears wrestled with her mind. Now that she

336

looked different, would she have to act different? More important, would people treat her differently? And if so, how was she to respond? There was no time to get used to the new Tamara, to grow comfortably into the character. She had been born virtually overnight.

Almost angrily she pounded her pillow with her hand, turned it around to the cool side, and shut her eyes again, determined to sleep and exorcise her demons, but she only tossed and turned sleeplessly. The clock in the hall chimed the half-hour. Twelve-thirty.

Resigned, she finally swung herself up into a sitting position and reached for her robe while her toes felt the chill floor for her slippers. Rising, she shrugged herself into the robe and walked to the door. For a long moment she stood there hesitantly, one hand poised on the brass handle. Then, before she could change her mind, she swiftly pulled it open. She glanced up and down the long, pine-paneled hall. It was dark, with only night-lights at the far ends to help illuminate the way. The chalet was quiet, creaking now and then as old buildings will. Ghostly shadows seemed to lurk everywhere, waiting to pounce. Across the hall, she noticed a sliver of bright light shining beneath Louis Ziolko's door. It seemed to beckon her. Throughout her entire nightmarish medical ordeal there had been but a single constant, a solitary anchor. Louis Ziolko.

She took three quick steps forward, held her breath, and rapped softly on his door.

Inside, she could hear a mattress squeaking. Bedcovers rustling. Dim footsteps slapping against the polished wooden floor.

Louis opened the door. He was wearing maroon silk pajamas.

She smiled hesitantly, clutching her robe together in the front. "I couldn't sleep," she said apologetically.

"Neither could I." He opened the door further. "Would you like to come in?"

She slipped inside and he closed the door behind her. "You're shivering," he said. He stared at her intently. "Are you cold?"

She shook her head. Her emerald-green eyes became two limpid pools. "I'm frightened."

He looked surprised. "Of what?"

"Me." She laughed humorlessly. "The new me."

"Millions of women would like to be in your shoes."

"I know." She looked away. "Hold me?" she whispered.

Then she could feel his strong arms wrapping around her. Slowly she turned to him, staring deep into his eyes.

337

"I know I'm being silly," she said huskily, "but I need someone."

His voice was hushed. "There comes a time when we all need someone."

She did not reply, but her eyes were tear-bright as his arms engulfed her and drew her toward him.

Time ceased to tick; the world had slipped into a silent dimension in which they were the only two people on earth. Even the chimes in the hall belonged to another time.

She clung trembling against him; he lowered his mouth to hers and his lips touched her lips, his tongue sought hers. Their gentle embrace grew more heated, their kisses more impassioned and deep. His fingers felt her tight body, groped along the raised ridge of her spine, and then moved slowly to the front of her robe. Then his hands slid inside, found her silky flesh, the perfect soft round breasts, then felt slowly, inexorably downward to her smooth hard belly. She moaned and tightened her grip on him as his fingers curved over the soft forest of hair on her mound. A tremor rippled through her body. Barely touching her, his hands feather light, he felt for the distended clitoris with its tonguelike protrusion and without warning, slipped two fingers inside her moistness.

Her body arched then and she gave a deep-throated cry. This was it. The promise and the passion. The other side of dying. The reason for having been born. As though possessed, her own hands fumbled inside his silk pajamas, and then she had her hands around his manhood. Power seemed to surge through it, and she could feel it pulsate. She could not believe how huge and hard it felt. She was at once frightened of it and desperate for it.

"I want you," she whispered hoarsely. "Louie, I want you. I need you." She began kissing him urgently, little moans escaping from her lips. "Please, I need it. Oh, God, how I need it."

He moved away from her, slid the robe from her shoulders, and watched it glide down the smoothness of her body. His breath caught in his throat. It was as though a drapery had slid away, exposing a priceless treasure. He had had no idea that her body was such perfection. The orbs of her breasts were tipped with strawberry areolae and jutting nipples, her waist was tiny, her hard abdomen rose and fell with each breath, and her hips had more curvature to them than he had thought possible when he saw her dressed. Between her muscular thighs he could see a glistening, almost oily sheen.

338

Wanton lust burned in his eyes. She had the face of an angel and the body of a whore. And she was his. His for the taking. His for loving.

Without taking his eyes off her, he slipped out of his pajamas and then stood straight and tall before her. She stared at him. Now it was her turn to catch her breath. He looked like a Greek god, more like the conception of a man than a real flesh-and-blood one. His shoulders were thickly muscled, his arms and chest powerful, his abdomen rippled. He was so lean. So tight. So muscular. Swirls of curly hair matted his chest and legs, softening the carved alabaster hardness of his chiseled physique. Slowly her eyes fell. And held. She was transfixed, and stared with breathless wonder. His engorged penis jutted out from the base of his abdomen, curving high, its purplish circumcised head appearing to be precariously balanced. A drop of clear nectar oozed from within and glistened like a dewdrop. Below, like ripe heavy fruits, hung succulent testicles.

Effortlessly he bent over and scooped her up like a prize. She snaked her arms around his neck as he padded over to the eiderdown softness of the bed. Solemnly, almost ritually, he gently laid her down on it and in one smooth, fluid move slipped on top of her. She stared up into his eyes, nervously licking her lips as she spread her legs. He knelt in a wide stance, bowed his head deeply, and reverently kissed her mound. Then as he lay forward, his penis found its home between her fleshy thighs, rubbing teasingly against her clitoris.

And he entered her.

Her jaw dropped, her lips parted without a sound. She thrashed her head from side to side on the pillow and closed her eyes. A mere touch, an infinitesimal slide forward inside her, and her nerve endings burst into full, glorious life. This was ecstasy.

Slowly he moved in her, centimeter by exquisite centimeter. Deeper. Deeper.

She gave a faint cry of disappointment as he hit the obstruction.

His eyes widened and she caught his look of surprise. Quickly she looked away.

"Why didn't you tell me?" he whispered gently.

She tightened her grip on his shoulders and turned her head so that she stared into his eyes. "Does it matter?" There was a weak tremor in her voice.

He bowed his head again and kissed a jutting nipple in reply, and then with one savage thrust he burst through. A white-hot kaleidoscope of pain exploded in front of her eyes.

She gave a violent jerk, and her sudden scream became a whimpering moan as he slid deeper and deeper inside her until his groin touched the very lips of her vulva. He was all the way inside, filling her completely, and she was shaking, waves of shuddering spasms coursing throughout her body.

Slowly his firm buttocks drew away as he pulled himself out, and then without warning, they contracted as he thrust himself in again. In. Out. In out in out in out. She jerked her legs up, gripping his buttocks as she forced him toward her, dug her fingers into his back, scratched her nails across his flesh. In out in out in out. She gasped and gasped again as he thrust away at her, and then he abruptly began moving his hips into a wide, circular grinding movement, and she wanted to cry out. He was massaging her womanhood, touching every inch of her being, manipulating her every sensation. She thought she was going to go completely out of her mind. His penis was hers, her vagina was his, their sweat mingled as one. She was no longer Tamara, and he was no longer Louis. They were one and the same, a gasping, moaning monster of savage fulfillment.

In and out he pumped frantically, faster and faster, and then, when he was afraid that he might burst prematurely, he slowed to fight off the impending climax, before continuing with a steady, relentless, ever-mounting rhythm. Like a horseman possessed, he rode her as her hips rose and fell to meet his every thrust. This was living. This was dying.

She twisted and writhed, greedily maneuvering her body to take advantage of his every thrust. The breath seemed to be pounded out of her. His cock seemed to skewer her all the way up to her throat. The world blistered and burned. Radiant orange suns burst in front of her shut eyes, searing her nerve endings, flashing and flaring with volcanic heat. And then, thunderously, the world seemed to black out completely for her and the cry burst from the depth of her being. She dug her nails into his shoulders, clamped his legs together in a scissor hold, and all her pent-up passions, her innermost dreams and hopes and desires, her very womanhood, seemed to burst into a soaring symphony as wave after wave of orgasm crashed through her. And still that purest ecstasy kept on coming, rolling over her and drawing her in its smashing surf. Gradually, as though a storm had spent itself, the waves of spasms stilled.

At her climax, he whipped himself to even greater fury. His thrusts became fierce, furious. "I'm coming!" he breathed hoarsely from a choked throat. "I'm commmmiiinnnggg . . ."

The assault upon her became more pitiless, and with one

last superhuman lunge he reared like a bronco and threw his entire body at her vagina and let out an earth-shattering bellow. Tamara hugged him tighter and then felt his body jerk. Inside her, his penis lunged and throbbed, and then a moist warmth stole through her.

His body went slack and he slowly drew himself out of her. He flung himself faceup alongside her. They were both swallowing huge, deep noisy gulps of sweet mountain air.

"God," she marveled between her pants, "that was . . . good." She turned sideways on her pillow to look at him. "Is it always this . . . good?"

"Or better."

"Or better. *God.*"

Her breathing had barely returned to normal when her hand drifted lazily down to her mound. She was still tingling deliciously inside. Idly she wondered at the miracle of lovemaking. She had never imagined it could be as heavenly as this.

Before she knew what she was doing, she parted her legs and started to massage herself. After a moment, her hips rose off the bed as her masturbation brought her to a second orgasm.

Louis slid alongside her. "You're wonderful," he whispered, playing with her mussed hair.

She smiled and made a little catlike mew as she snuggled into his warm arms. She had never felt quite so good, so totally content, so completely a woman.

Now at least she knew what her body was for. She had discovered the mystery of her passions.

For this night, at least, he had chased away her fears.

She let her eyes droop shut and her breathing suddenly became shallow. He raised himself on an elbow and looked down at her marvelous naked body. Very gently he tugged the duvet out from under her and covered her. She seemed to smile.

She was sound asleep.

The lovemaking might have blessed Tamara with silent sweet dreams, but Louis found he could not sleep. Nor did he want to. He spent all night staring at her serene sleeping form beside him, his heart filled with rhapsodies. *God, but she's beautiful. I want her like no woman I've ever met,* he thought with a lightning bolt of incisive knowledge. Sex had always been a driving, purely physical act for him, but this he recognized as something greater. Far greater. He had fallen in love, something which had never happened to him before, and to his surprise, his heart surged and he felt like he was floating on a puff-ball cloud. He had thought that there couldn't be a woman alive he'd want to share his life with, but here she was lying beside him, in the perfumed flesh. And ah, what superb flesh, what a sublimely magnificent face. She was his living, breathing golden goddess, the stuff of which movie dreams were made. And like a movie he had worked on and subsequently grown to love deeply because of his personal commitment and the life he had breathed into it, so too he had been more than a little responsible for molding Tamara into the awesome, nonpareil beauty she had become. Unbelievable as it still seemed to him, he had been the one to discover her. And she was his treasure.

Careful, so as not to wake her, he bent low over her face and kissed her marvelously sculptured lips ever so lightly. She smiled and murmured in her sleep, snuggled closer to him, and then her regular breathing continued.

Ah, what dazzling witchcraft could have wrought such an exquisite creature? he could only wonder in amazement. "You're mine," he whispered proprietarily, "all mine."

As though to reply, she shifted her head and smiled up at him in her sleep, her white-blond angel hair fanning out across the pillow like phosphorescence in a pacific sea.

Tamara, like many a prospective bride, looked forward to her first encounter with her future mother-in-law with the same enthusiasm the eighteenth-century French nobility had shown for the tumbrels which would transport them to the guillotine. Not knowing quite what to expect of Zelda Ziolko, but fearing the worst and knowing full well that first impressions were lasting ones, and thus of utmost importance, she was determined to win the woman over by sheer personality and a wholesome girl-next-door image, no easy feat for a woman whose hair was dyed spun-sugar platinum and who was already being hailed as "the most beautiful woman in the world." For once, Tamara believed that ordinary looks would have served her better. After all, Zelda was another woman and one who, herself, was enjoying a relatively exalted status as mother of "The Director." She wouldn't want her thunder stolen, and therefore Tamara must be prepared to be met by a very finely honed verbal ax. She enlisted Inge's aid to transform herself into as down-to-earth a girl-next-door as possible. The first step, rummaging through her vast new wardrobe—courtesy of IA—made it evident that there was nothing suitable for the look they were trying to achieve, not amid that sea of extravagant satins, chiffons, and silks that ranged from bright and showy white to ashes-of-roses.

"There's nothing I can wear!" Tamara lamented, flinging aside dress after dress. She stamped her feet in frustration. "Oh, Inge, what am I to do?"

"Don't worry, we find you something," Inge assured her in a calm and measured voice. "You have five days, no?"

"I suppose you're right," Tamara said broodingly. She pressed her hands against the sea of froth and hastily slammed the closet door shut. "Why is it that mothers-in-law are so notorious for being picky, anyway?" She scowled.

"Because they love their sons," Inge replied wisely, re-opening the closet door to release a wedge of chiffon pinched between the door and frame. "I would be no different myself."

"Yes, but you're no ogre. And you like Louie."

"Who says his mother will not like you?"

"Oh, slim chance she will." Tamara plopped herself down on the bed and sat there morosely.

Inge took a seat beside her and touched her arm. "Tell me, why do you worry so much about this?"

"Because . . . I love Louie." Tamara looked down at her slender, fidgeting fingers. "I don't want anything to go wrong."

Inge smiled reassuringly and drew her closer. "Then it will not, I assure you. Just calm down."

"How can I calm down?" Tamara cried. "Can't you see I'm nervous?"

"Have a sandwich."

"That'll make me fat," Tamara said morosely.

"Then think about pheasant things."

"Pleasant things," Tamara corrected humorlessly.

Inge ignored her. "If I were Mrs. Ziolko, I would be happy for my son to marry you."

"But you're not," Tamara pointed out with her typical, maddening sense of reality. "She'll think I'm a streetwalker, or worse. I mean, just look at me! This hair!" She grabbed a handful and yanked until she grimaced in pain. "It looks fine on film, but I feel like such a freak in public!"

"Stop worrying. Try to take one, two hours off work sometime this week and we go shopping and have lunch. We find the right thing to wear. It will be fun."

"Fun!" Tamara's eyes slid sideways with liquid green venom. "I hate shopping," she mumbled.

"Since when?" Inge looked at her in surprise. "You always like it."

"I *did*," Tamara admitted heavily with a sigh, "but that

was when I went shopping for myself and didn't have to please the whole country . . . or Louie's mother!"

"Ah, there is that," Inge said. "There is that."

The Sunday of the visit Tamara wore a minimum of makeup, brushed her hair casually back, and dressed in the slim-cut conservative tweed suit with near-ankle-length skirt and beautifully tailored green jacket she and Inge had picked out together. Her platinum hair looked hopelessly out of place with the nubby tweeds, but Inge had resolved that problem by the inspired act of knotting a silk scarf, which matched Tamara's hair color precisely, around her throat. When she heard the unmistakable honk of the Duesenberg from the curb, Tamara picked up the platter of fresh-baked apple strudel, Inge's specialty, swiftly blew Inge a good-bye kiss, and pushed her sunglasses onto her nose with her free hand.

"No, no. No classes," Inge said, waving her hand back and forth. "Makes you look too much like a moving star."

Tamara thrust the glasses at Inge, and on sudden impulse yanked the extravagant bouquet of white lilies out of the vase on the foyer table. Water dripped down from the long green stalks.

"What you do that for?" Inge demanded.

"I'll give them to Mrs. Ziolko," Tamara said.

"You take flowers to a woman?"

"Why not?"

"I thought only men brung flowers," Inge said.

"I'm desperate." Tamara grimaced more than smiled.

Louis, as was his custom when he visited his mother, forwent his chauffeur and drove the huge car himself. Seeing it, Tamara felt her pervading sense of doom brighten, as if the Duesenberg were a lucky charm. It had taken her to Oscar Skolnik's mansion, where it had been decided she was to become a star. Why shouldn't it portend good luck now as well?

She deposited her peace offerings on the back seat and climbed in up front, beside Louis. He kissed her and they drove off.

As they neared the neighborhood where Zelda Ziolko lived, Pasadena's large, pleasant houses with their generous lawns gave way to small cookie-cutter bungalows, each a carbon copy of the next except for the color of the stucco. Despite her attempts at dressing down, Tamara began to feel foolishly overdressed and acutely conspicuous, definitely a fish far from water. She would have felt far more confident among the worst tenements or the priciest mansions, but the sameness of these low-roofed bungalows lining both sides of the street on brownish postage-stamp lots depressed her. The Deusenberg attracted undue attention, as though it had washed up on a drab beach from some distant, wealthier continent.

"Here we are," Louis announced as he pulled up alongside the curb. "Mother's home, humble home." He smiled wryly.

Tamara turned to look at the neat little bungalow and saw the living-room curtains move. Quickly she snapped open her compact and repaired her windblown hair while Louis got out of the car. He opened her door and helped her down. She opened the back door, gathered up the strudel and flowers, and followed him up the tiny concrete walk.

The front door flew open before they reached it, and Zelda burst out, her plump hands outstretched. A tragedy seemed clearly in the making as she flung herself straight on a collision course with Louis, her thick legs with their swollen ankles carrying her as swiftly as they could, her heaving bosom jutting forward like the imposing prow of a ship, her every breath wheezing out of her lungs as if emerging from a giant bellows. "Louie!" she cried. "Louie! My *bubbale!*" Just as Tamara was about to shut her eyes in anticipation of her knocking Louis down, Zelda came to a sudden stop, hopped up on tiptoe the same moment that Louis bent down, tilted her crinkly-haired head way back, and deposited a resounding kiss on his lips.

"Hello, Mother." He embraced her, dutifully kissing her rouged cheek.

"'Hello Mother,'" Zelda scolded. "'That is all you can say? A peck on the cheek, that is a way to kiss your mother? That's what they teach you to do in that Hollywood?"

Oh-oh, Tamara thought, steeling herself. This is *not* going to be a bed of roses. She looked on as Louis, obviously embarrassed, kissed his mother dutifully on the lips.

"That's better," Zelda said, her eyes narrowing. "I missed you, Louie. You should visit your poor old mother more often!" She wagged an admonishing finger at him. "Everyone asks, when is that nogoodnik son of yours coming? What can I say? That I don't know? A fool you make me look!"

"Mother," he interrupted gently, "I'd like you to meet Tamara."

Tamara stepped forward and smiled shyly. "Hello, Mrs. Ziolko," she said softly. "It's a pleasure to meet you at last."

Zelda's eyes were appraising as they swept Tamara from

345

head to toe and back to her head again. For a moment she did not speak. "You're very pretty . . . in your way," she said finally in a grudging, almost accusatory voice.

"Mother," Louis said in exasperation, "is that any way to greet your future daughter-in-law?"

"*Nu*?" Zelda, arms akimbo, glared challengingly up at her son. "So she's pretty. I said she was pretty. Next I suppose you're going to tell your mother to her face that she tells lies?"

Tamara could see the muscles in his cheeks tightening as he held his anger in check, and her heart went out to him. No wonder he didn't come to visit her more often. "I brought you these flowers, Mrs. Ziolko," she said brightly to cover up the awkward pause. She thrust the bouquet at the woman.

"Lilies!" Zelda stared down at them malevolently. "And such a big bunch! You should have saved your money. A spendthrift my Louie doesn't need." She shook the lilies at Tamara. "You want I should tell you how many ways you can keep your money from being stolen on a bus?"

Tamara blinked. She was taken aback and slightly confused, but determined to be undeterred. "And I helped bake you this apple strudel." Smiling, she proffered the covered platter like a prize.

"Strudel!" Mrs. Ziolko scoffed, her eyes flashing dramatic shards of brittle ice. "You want strudel, you taste *my* strudel. It's baking in the oven right now. Two hours I took just to make the dough so it comes out so nice and flaky it melts on your tongue. I'm famous for my strudel." Eyebrows raised, Zelda Ziolko turned on her heel and marched into the bungalow. "Ha!" Tamara heard her mumble under her breath. "Strudel she brings. Strudel."

Louis smiled apologetically and gave an eloquent shrug of helplessness as he held the screen door open for Tamara. She smiled at him with a cheerfulness she did not feel. Her eyes were angry and her heart pounded with a fierce fury, but she arranged her face into an expressionless mask. She wasn't about to give this monster the pleasure of seeing her upset.

She's a dragon, Tamara thought with a sinking feeling. My God, she's even worse than anything I'd imagined.

It was getting dark out by the time they finished eating. Zelda suddenly pushed herself to her feet and switched on the small chandelier with its meager crystals. It threw a garish, surreal glare, and Tamara had to blink against the six sixty-watt bulbs.

"Louie, you go on into the living room," Zelda ordered

shortly. "Listen to the radio. Read the Sunday paper. Tamara here is going to help me to clean up."

He and Tamara exchanged quick glances. With her eyes and a smile of infinite patience, she managed to convey to him that it was all right with her. "Okay," he said, crumpling his napkin into a ball and getting to his feet. He came over to Tamara and kissed her. Then he turned to Zelda. "That was a fine meal, Mother."

"If you like my cooking so much, you could come visit your poor mother more often," Zelda complained.

He kissed her cheek and made himself scarce.

Zelda shut the kitchen door behind him, but Tamara could hear the low volume of the radio coming from the living room. She recognized the symphony. Mahler. Funereal and depressing, but somehow appropriate in this cheerless house. She wondered how Louis could bear to visit as often as he did.

Zelda washed while Tamara dried. For a while they worked in uncomfortable silence. Tamara couldn't get over the feeling that there was a greater purpose for her participation in this ancient female rite. She waited, knowing that Zelda would tell her in her own good time.

She didn't have long to wait.

"So you want to marry my Louie," Zelda said at last, and Tamara wondered whether the accompanying sigh was the result of their marriage plans or the recalcitrant dried crust on the bowl Zelda was scrubbing. "It goes without saying that I want my son to get married. I'm his mother, I want what's best for him. What mother doesn't want that, I ask you?"

Tamara remained silent, guessing that Zelda didn't really expect a reply.

"After all, Louie is thirty years old. It's time he gave me grandchildren." Zelda flicked a sideways glance at Tamara, suspicion evident in her sharp, piercing gaze. "So do you like children?"

Tamara's mind shifted gears, alerting to this unexpected course of conversation. "I . . . ah, yes . . . of course," she murmured.

"Humph." Zelda dipped the bowl into the steaming rinse water and handed it to Tamara. "Marriage is much more than playing house and making babies," she continued, stuffing the soapy washrag into a glass and twisting it around and around inside it. Then she pulled the rag back out, plunged the glass into the rinse water, and held it up to the light to check that it was clean. "Marriage is making a home. Run-

347

ning it smoothly. It takes dedication, and it's a full-time job, let me tell you. Louie tells me you want to continue working. So tell me, how do you expect to make a home, have babies, and be in the movies too?" She looked at Tamara searchingly. "I suppose you can do three times as much as anybody else?"

Tamara could feel herself flushing under the unwavering scrutiny, but she raised her chin stubbornly. "Louie and I love each other," she countered challengingly.

"Do you?" Zelda held her gaze. "Maybe you *think* you love each other—"

A brilliant kind of sureness flared in Tamara's eyes. "I know we do," she said definitely.

"You're so young," Zelda hissed impatiently. "So tell me, how old are you, child?"

"Eighteen."

Zelda's eyes blazed. "All of eighteen! *Oy!* And already she knows everything!" She shook her head and washed some plates in brooding silence. Then suddenly she flung her hands out of the dishwater and whirled on Tamara. "Let him go!" she demanded abruptly, her eyes dancing with a mad light. "Louis is only thirty. Already he's been divorced once. Don't let him make the same mistake twice. I beg of you—*leave* him!"

Tamara was so stunned that she was momentarily speechless.

Zelda sensed that she'd gained the upper hand and drew closer. For an instant she glanced over her shoulder at the door, making certain that Louis had not come in without her noticing. When she spoke again it was with such force and fury that Tamara had to wince against the spray of spittle. "I know what it is you want! You're like all the other women who try to throw themselves at him. Louie is a famous director, and you think he has a lot of money. You believe he can make you a star!" Self-righteous triumph blazed crazily in her eyes.

"That isn't true!" Tamara whispered vehemently. "I love him!" She felt suddenly dizzy as the kitchen seemed to turn slowly, tilting in carnival-ride revolutions around her. She grabbed hold of the counter to steady herself.

"Then prove it to me."

Tamara wiped her eyes. "How? By giving him up?" She gave a snort of mirthless laughter and turned away.

Zelda paused. "No," she said finally, taking Tamara by the arm and turning her around to face her. "There is another way."

Tamara raised her eyebrows.

"By signing a document my lawyer has drawn up."

Tamara regarded Zelda suspiciously. "What kind of document?"

"A marriage contract of sorts, only it is between me and you instead of you and Louie. It is very simple and states that should you get a divorce for any reason, or God forbid, Louie should die before you, you relinquish all rights to his estate. At least while I'm alive."

"In other words, you want to make sure that I get nothing . . . and you get everything."

Zelda frowned. "I didn't put it into those words, you did. But I guess in a way you're right. The thing to remember is that by signing, you will prove to me that you are not marrying my Louie for his money or influence."

"Does he know about this?"

"No!" Zelda emphasized. "And he does not need to. Why worry him, I ask you?"

Tamara stared at her in disbelief. "You're sick!" she whispered.

"Am I?"

"Perhaps I'm wrong. Maybe you're just a greedy criminal. You *are* trying to blackmail me."

Zelda's eyes were icy. "I see now that I might as well not have bothered with the contract. I was right about you all along. I should have known."

Tamara gaped at her. "You're serious about this, aren't you?"

Zelda raised her chin in certainty. "I am. I have the contract right here." She slid open a drawer and took out a two-page legal document stapled to a pale blue backing. She thrust it at Tamara.

Slowly Tamara took it and read through it, her lips silently mouthing each cruel word. There were a lot of whereases, theretofores, inasmuches, and hereunders, the precise, unemotional legal jargon maintaining a judicious distance from the emotions that had been the basis for it. Despite the strange nature of the contract, she didn't at all doubt that it was perfectly legal and would stand up in a court of law. She was certain Zelda had seen to that. She didn't strike her as the kind of woman who could make a mistake about something like that.

Tamara's voice was weak and strained. "And if I don't sign?"

"Then I will not give Louie my blessing to marry you. Oh, I know my Louie is headstrong and might go ahead and marry you anyway. But how long do you think your happiness will last after his own mother has disowned him?"

"You've had it all figured out from the start, haven't you?" Tamara said bitterly. "You went to your attorney and had this prepared"—she rattled the document—"before you even met me. You decided in advance not to like me." Tears stung in her eyes.

"Like or not like, you had nothing to do with it. Louie is my only child, and I intend to protect him at any cost. I would gladly die before I see another woman take advantage of him."

"That makes two of us."

"So." Zelda looked at Tamara evenly. "You will sign then, won't you?"

Tamara drew herself up with dignity. "Yes, I will sign," she said wearily. "And you need not worry." Her voice became choked with emotion. "I will never tell him about this. I would never want him to know just how heartless his mother really is. No son should have to know that."

For a brief moment the steel in Zelda seemed to soften. Then, before she became too pliable, she caught herself and hardened again, as tough and unbendable as ever.

She held out a pen. Tamara snatched it from her and signed.

"In triplicate," Zelda said, producing two more copies of the contract.

"There." Tamara slapped the contracts down on the counter. "And now, if you'll excuse me, I think it's time Louie took me home." Her voice was quivering as she fought to keep her rage under control. "Thank you for the dinner."

She went to the door, struggling to compose herself and, pushing it open, went out into the living room. The Mahler symphony sounded louder and more tragic. It reminded her of a dirge, the unseen instruments weeping in low, rhythmic mourning as a lone soprano wailed her way up the scale before plunging back down into the abyss of bleak darkness.

Tamara, eighteen years old, International Artists' much-publicized new discovery and, according to the press releases, the daughter of a brilliant Russian actress and a powerful prince, a displaced refugee, and would-have-been heiress to an awesome fortune, married Louis Frederic Ziolko on the set of *The Flappers* on Sunday, April 20, one day after the film's final scene had been shot. For Tamara, the wedding wasn't so much a ceremony of exchanging vows as a scene in a maddeningly overcrowded zoo. It turned into a national spectacle, as royal an occasion as there ever could be in a democracy. It was a civil rather than a religious ceremony, and if there was anything religious about it, it was the pomp and splendor of Hollywood idolatry.

Oscar Skolnik, ever the entrepreneur and never one to let a moneymaking scheme slip idly through his fingers, seized the opportunity to cash in on what he believed must surely be the most brilliant publicity stunt ever devised. Having pumped fifty thousand dollars into the ceremony, and beaming as brightly as any genuine father, he gave away the bride on soundstage twelve, amid the still-intact massive ballroom set of *The Flappers,* which had been specially decorated with fifteen thousand dollars' worth of snow-white flowers for the occasion.

Gossip columnists would report that there wasn't another white flower to be found as far north as San Francisco or as far south as the border.

While flashbulbs popped unceasingly, shutters clicked, and newsreel cameras rolled, Tamara, in a Jean Louis-designed gown of dazzling Valenciennes lace with a twenty-two-foot train and a diamond tiara borrowed from Tiffany, arrived as royally as any genuine princess in a regal, flower-festooned coach pulled by six matching white horses, thanks to IA's considerable back lot jammed with props. Page boys in medieval tunics announced her arrival with triumphant trumpet blasts. Sixteen bridesmaids, all major Hollywood stars, scattered white orchids in her path.

"Something old" was a treasured lace handkerchief given her by Garbo, "something new" was the pearl choker Oscar Skolnik presented her with, "something borrowed" was the Tiffany tiara, of course, and "something blue" was a garter belt courtesy of Mae West.

Holding a small bouquet of white cymbidiums as she exchanged vows with her exceedingly handsome director-husband, who slipped a twenty-carat (also borrowed) diamond on her finger, Tamara instantly became the consummate bride, ingrained in the public's consciousness as a vision in white. The picture of Louis lifting her veil and kissing her made the front pages of every newspaper from coast to coast.

ROYAL FILM STAR TAMARA MARRIES DIRECTOR.

FIFTY-THOUSAND-DOLLAR WEDDING STUNS COUNTRY— *Thousands Are Homeless as Hollywood Parties.*

RUSSIAN PRINCESS HAS STARS IN HER EYES.

TAMARA: *"I lost my country but won a husband."*

TAMARA'S STORY: *The Star They Call "Your Highness."*

Among the hundreds in attendance at the ceremony were

Hollywood's elite, as well as a flock of stars-to-be. Rival studio moguls called a truce for the occasion, shared gossip, and toasted the bride with glasses of fruit punch. All around them, dressed to the nines, was an eye-popping roster of their producers, directors, stars, and stars-to-be. Inge and Jewel, both sniffling happily and dabbing their eyes with handkerchiefs, sat in the first row. Zelda Ziolko was anything but the picture of the bridegroom's happy, proud mother. For her, this wedding, performed by a justice of the peace, was a mockery of both religion and the solemn vows of matrimony, with its hundreds of stars and celebrities vying for attention with the bride and groom. Her idea of a wedding was a sacred ritual presided over by a rabbi and performed under the *chuppa,* with a goblet of wine and lit tapers and shouts of *"Mazel tov!"* and the traditional Jewish dances. Much as she was secretly flattered by the stars that had come out for her son's wedding, the public spectacle was a shameful affair that she forced herself to endure in grim, uncharacteristic silence, or so she very vocally claimed.

Lily Pons, who made her American debut that year, sang two arias; there were also a choir, a thirty-seven-member orchestra, and fireworks at dusk. As party favors, every last one of the eight thousand oysters served to the guests came with a lustrous, carefully placed pearl. The vast publicity mills which had made the "newly discovered Russian princess, Tamara," into a household word even before filming of *The Flappers* had begun, now catapulted her into the lofty firmament to which she had always aspired—before the film was even edited. The Depression-weary public ate it all up. Poverty and despair were all too commonplace. What people wanted was a glimpse of lavishness, and in Tamara they were not to be disappointed. If glamour was a beacon of happier times ahead, then she was it.

There was little surprise when, two months later, *The Flappers* was released in IA's string of nationwide theaters and its box-office receipts earned it the distinction of being the highest-grossing motion picture made to date.

For Tamara, 1930 was a particularly wonderful year. So many dreams had come true. She had a handsome husband. She was a major Hollywood star. She had plenty of money. She was in love.

It seemed that nothing could go wrong.

For a long time, nothing did go wrong. Tamara and Louis' marriage was cementing nicely, their lovemaking was mutually satisfying and, overall, their lives were charmed if frenetic. Tamara found herself in the midst of such an exhilarating but hectic whirlwind that she was reminded of a queen bee around whom the swarm hummed and buzzed incessantly. She was in constant and glorious demand, and it felt good. Thanks to her instant celebrity status, she and Louis were Hollywood's most sought-after couple. So many invitations poured in daily that they had to sift through all of them, carefully paring them down to the two or three most advantageous for their careers, and with a thousand-odd pieces of fan mail pouring in each week, Tamara was forced to hire a full-time secretary in the person of Lorna Nichols, a formidable widow of forty-three who mothered her, jealously guarded her privacy as though it were her own, and adroitly juggled both of the Ziolkos' busy, ever-changing schedules.

With filming, researching her characters, perfecting her diction with the help of a dialogue coach and her acting at IA's on-lot acting school, memorizing her lines, and the little but therefore all-the-more precious home life she and Louis enjoyed, there was a multitude of obligations for Tamara to fulfill. A star, she was discovering, could not call her life her own. She was the property of a fickle, ravenous public which had to be kept appeased. Her moviegoing fans had made her; they could just as easily desert her for someone else. So there were whirlwinds of still-photography sessions, both for the studio and reporters, no end of interviews to conduct, film premieres to attend, products to endorse, and charity functions to host or support—all of which were shrewdly calculated to keep her in the public eye. The demands made on her were awesome, but she cheerfully complied. If she had any complaints, it was that she had been swept into the eye of a hurricane and had too little time to spend alone with Louis. Still, she wouldn't have had it any other way. Her public took precedence. Her own life had to take second place. And besides, being the queen bee was intoxicating. She basked in all the attention.

Rival studios were bidding unheard-of sums to borrow her for films of their own, but Skolnik wasn't having any of that, at least not yet. He was still smarting from not having had a major female star of his own for so long, and having been at the mercy of whomever the other studios could spare still rankled him deeply. Not that he was one to carry a grudge, especially if forgetting it could earn him money. It was just a matter of good business. Now that he was on a major winning streak with Tamara, he was anxious to take full advantage of it and ride it out. He didn't want to waste her. She was money in the bank.

The Flappers was followed by *Marie Antoinette,* a long, lavish costume drama with an enormous budget, dazzling costumes, and stupendous sets. Meanwhile, Rhoda Dorsey's reading department was under constant pressure to hurry up and find a new property that could be begun as soon as the filming of *Marie Antoinette* was wrapped up. The following year Skolnik was planning to use Tamara in four pictures, all in major starring roles, and all involving endless, grueling work.

Despite its obvious creature comforts and luxurious appointments, Tamara was getting weary of living in the bungalow at the Beverly Hills Hotel, which she and Louis had called home since exchanging vows. One evening as they sat out by the pool sipping a particularly fine bootlegged vintage wine, she broached the subject of their getting a real home of their own.

"What's the matter with this bungalow?" Louis asked in mild surprise. "Anything you could possibly want, they come running with at the drop of a hat. We'll never get such good service anywhere else."

"It isn't service I want," she emphasized softly. "I want us to have a home. A real home. Living out of suitcases just isn't enough."

He nodded silently. Tamara had a point, he had to admit. They couldn't live at the hotel forever. "I'll build us a house," he said. "I've wanted to ever since my old one slid down the hillside."

"But it'll be a long time before it's completed," she pointed out. "Meanwhile, Inge is living all the way across town."

"I asked Inge about moving into the bungalow next door when it becomes available. She said she likes the new apartment."

Tamara didn't doubt it. After Paterson's Mortuary, the worst hovel would have seemed like a palace. "I know that," she said patiently. "But I've got a duty to her. Louie, she's the only family I've got. She and I should be under the same roof."

"I tell you what, princess," he said, "tomorrow I'll call up a real-estate agent. As soon as we find something you like, we'll move in."

She wrapped her arms around him and placed her head on his chest. "You're too good to me," she murmured happily, fingering the curly chest hair which peeked out of his shirt.

"Damn right, princess," he said, "damn right."

A week later, they signed a lease on a large two-story pink stucco house on North Beverly Drive. It had three wings attached to the arched main building and a handsome corrugated orange tile roof. The rooms were spacious and it came furnished. Up front were the obligatory locked gates, and in back were a tennis court and a rectangular turquoise swimming pool. There was plenty of room for Inge, and the house came with a Mexican caretaker couple and a Japanese gardener, which simplified matters immensely.

On New Year's Eve, as 1931 was being ushered in, Tamara took stock of her life and counted her blessings. She basked in the sunshine and adulation, happily unmindful that fate could as easily dish out the bad as the good. After all, she had everything. Life was as near-perfect as it could possibly be.

"I think it's a mistake," Tamara insisted firmly, not bothering to disguise her disgust as she slapped the bound proposal facedown on the conference table. "This smacks too much of *Marie Antoinette*."

"It does not!" young, curly-headed Richard Sonnenthal, vice-president of creative projects, defended in a miffed tone. "*Affair of State* is about Madame de Pompadour, and in case you haven't noticed, it's done with a comic twist."

Tamara rolled her matchless emerald eyes and groaned. "Spare me the gruesome details," she said tightly, compressing her lips into a thin red line of annoyance. "*Marie Antoinette*'s not even completed and you already want to stick me in another one of those damn wigs! I mean, what do you want to do, recycle the costumes? Use the same sets, God forbid? Personally, I think you should shelve this idea and let it collect dust. It creaks."

"I suppose *you* have a better idea?" he snapped nastily.

She raised her chin with all the dignity she could muster. "As a matter of fact, I do. I was thinking more along the lines of something sophisticated. You know, light and witty, modern. Sort of a . . . a stylish comedy of manners."

"A stylish comedy of manners!" Sonnenthal sighed nastily with exasperation and tucked his chin into his chest. "So it's something sophisticated she wants," he said sarcastically, gesturing with theatrical helplessness. "You all heard the lady."

"I think Tamara has a point," Skolnik said unexpectedly.

They all turned to look at him in surprise. Without exception, they'd almost forgotten he was there. For the past half-hour he hadn't voiced a single opinion. He had seemed content to lounge back in his chair with deceptive laziness, puffing on his brier pipe with an expression of benign boredom while the debate had heated up around him.

Outside the French doors, the night was dark and chilly. The brainstorming session had been scheduled for seven o'clock, but Tamara and Louis had raced in forty minutes late, due to complications on the set. Besides them, Skolnik had summoned Sonnenthal, Claude de Chantilly-Siciles, Rhoda Dorsey, Carol Anderegg, and Bruce Slesin. Upon her tardy but breathless arrival, Tamara had been gratified to notice that the walls, which were hung with framed IA movie posters, had among them not only *The Flappers* but also, already in the place of honor, the poster of the soon-to-be-completed *Marie Antoinette*.

"Well, we can always fall back on *Joan of Arc*," Sonnenthal murmured.

"Joan of Arc? *Joan of Arc?*" Skolnik's voice suddenly bellowed and he banged a fist on the table in fury. Everyone jumped. "Christ, what do I pay you for?" He glared at Sonnenthal. "Are you blind? She's a woman, if you didn't notice. *All* woman! How's she going to look running around in a pageboy haircut and armor? We're trying to push her glamour image and you want her to play soldier. You want to ruin me?"

Sonnenthal flushed under the verbal onslaught and nervously tapped his pencil against his teeth.

There was a long, drawn-out silence, and the tension in the conference room was almost palpable.

"In case I need to remind you," Skolnik continued, "this is an emergency meeting. There's only a week's shooting to go on *Marie Antoinette*, and none of you've yet come up with a single viable vehicle for Tamara to star in." He looked around the table. "That's not what you're getting paid for."

The others remained prudently silent. From past experience, they knew he wasn't through speaking his mind. "Maybe I should simplify matters for you," he said softly. "As it is, you're all running around in circles, chasing your tails." He looked questioningly at Sonnenthal. "What's Tamara's background?"

"A Russian refugee." Sonnenthal smirked. "A princess." He looked around the room with smug laughter in his eyes.

"That's very good, Richard," Skolnik praised in the honey-eyed, sarcastic tones of a grade-school teacher. "However, I strongly advise you to wipe that shit-eating grin off your face at once," he added in a violent voice. "I said she's a princess, so by God she *is* a princess. If you don't agree, you can head straight for your office and clean out your desk." Skolnik's face darkened and his voice dropped. "I can also see to it that you'll never work in this business again. Do I make myself clear?"

"Yes, sir," Sonnenthal gulped, blushing so deeply that his face turned uniformly purple.

"Good. Just so that we understand each other." Skolnik glared around the table. "And the same goes for the rest of you." He paused. "Now, Richard, bearing in mind of course that you do agree that Tamara is a Russian princess, what is the most obvious thing to star her in?"

Sonnenthal's red cheeks quivered with the indignation he was fighting to control. "S-something Russian," he said uncomfortably.

"Ah!" Skolnik made a production of beaming. "Now you're on the right track. Suppose you use that imagination I'm paying you so handsomely for and think back to your school days. Throw a few titles at me."

"Catherine the Great."

"No, no, no, no, *no.*" Skolnik shook his head in disgust. "That isn't a title. Even if it were, it would be too eighteenth-century—it brings us right back to the Madame de Pompadour problem. I meant something later, straight from the pages of a classic novel. We barely have the time to work on a script, let alone the luxury of plotting an entire movie from scratch. We've got to rely on a book that's already been written."

"*War and Peace!*" Carol Anderegg cried.

Skolnik shook his head. "It's too long and much too sprawling. It would take half a year just to get all the sets built. And there's no way we can condense it properly into a ninety- to a hundred-and-twenty-minute film."

Tamara sat forward, her eyes suddenly gleaming. She felt a surge of pulsing excitement flow through her. "*Anna Karenina!*" she whispered, the gooseflesh breaking out on her arms.

Smiling, Skolnik sat back and made a flourishing gesture. "There it is folks, on a platter. *Anna Karenina* it is. My prediction is that it'll be the biggest picture of the year." Then his smile faded as swiftly as it had appeared. His tone became brusque and businesslike. "Richard, I want your writers to start on the script first thing tomorrow morning. You've got five days to produce the first draft."

Sonnenthal blanched. "Five days—"

"Five days," Skolnik repeated. "You can enlist all the writers you need, except those who're revising scripts for properties currently in production. Just break the book down into sections and fan out the work."

Sonnenthal relaxed slightly. "Well, now that you put it that way, it shouldn't be all that difficult."

"Good." Skolnik turned his attention to Carol Anderegg. "Carol, I want Miles Gabriel to play Count Vronsky. The public adored him and Tamara together in *The Flappers*, so let's hope history will repeat itself. Has he finished shooting his scenes for that war movie yet?"

"*The Front*?" Carol frowned. "I'll have to check, but offhand I'd say there are probably close to two more weeks of scenes left for him to shoot."

"Check it, then. I know it's behind schedule and over budget, but keep me informed. If need be, have the shooting sequence revised so that the scenes requiring his presence are shot first. I want him to be well-rested before he begins work on *Anna*, and he'll need plenty of time for rehearsal. Also, I want you to work closely with Richard's department so you can be kept abreast of the characters we'll use, and those we're going to cut from the story. Start rounding up talent immediately. The sooner we know who'll play who, the better. I don't believe I have to tell any of you that I expect each and every one of you to read *Anna Karenina*," Skolnik continued. "Not a condensed version, but the entire book as Tolstoy wrote it. The studio library's sure to have at least one copy, and tomorrow I'll have Miss Martinko get extra copies from the public libraries. If you've already read it, then reread it. That's an order. Claude . . ."

The art director raised his eyebrows.

"This gives you one hell of an opportunity to design one hell of a production. I want it very Russian in atmosphere, very elegant, and very, very slick. I don't think I need to tell you that I want the costumes to complement the set, and vice versa. Pull out all the stops."

"What kind of budget are we talking about here?" Roger Callas, the general manager and ever the financial pragmatist, asked worriedly.

"Whatever it takes," Skolnik said. "I want a projected financial breakdown from the various departments on my desk no later than a week from today, and we'll know then. Bruce, you start the publicity mills churning. I want a massive buildup. Also, you and Tamara sit down together and work out a more detailed Russian bio of her than the ones we've released to date. Add a lot of juicy new information. I want so much press coverage that the public will be panting for this picture to come out. Also, arrange for a newsreel to be made about it while it's being filmed." He paused. "Any questions?"

"Yes," Louis said. "When do we start filming?"

"Two weeks from tomorrow. In the meantime, I want work to proceed around the clock. And as far as Tamara's next movie after *Anna* is concerned, I like her idea of a witty, stylish comedy of manners. I don't want her typecast, and this is a good way to avoid that. Richard, get in touch with Somerset Maugham and see if he's interested in writing the screenplay." Skolnik tapped the contents of his brier pipe into a heavy crystal ashtray. "One last warning," he said sternly. "I want you all to bear in mind that we'll be dealing with Tolstoy, and not some local hack. Treat this project with some respect, eh? I don't want to see him butchered."

Tamara smiled inwardly. There was little fear of that. Louis was too good a director, and besides, she liked this project. Something about it just seemed to sit right. If problems manifested themselves during the filming, which they always did, well, she'd fight tooth and nail for whatever improvements she or Louis could come up with.

"That should about wrap it up for now," Skolnik said. "We might as well call it a night. It's late, and I know Tamara has an early wake-up call. Carol, scare up my chauffeur and tell him to drive Tamara home and then to come back for me. Louie, I want you and Bruce to stay awhile longer. There's some other business I want to discuss with both of you." Skolnik tapped his pipe against the ashtray and the crystal rang out true and clear. "This meeting is adjourned."

Because of the ungodly working hours required of a star, Tamara had recently become proficient at grabbing whatever rest she could. Normally she dozed while being driven to and from work; now, however, this recently developed talent deserted her. As Skolnik's three-year-old white-topped Mercedes Benz Model K convertible slid smoothly through the dark, empty streets of Hollywood, she was too wound up to close her eyes. The meeting in Skolnik's office had been more productive than she would have dreamed, and her energy level was running at an all-time high. She hoped she would be able to sleep once she got home, but she sincerely doubted it. She'd probably have to take a sleeping pill, maybe even two.

Smiling to herself in the cushioned leather seat, she was oblivious of the chauffeur as she hummed the theme song of *The Flappers* to herself. She could feel her adrenaline still pumping mightily. She was so swept up by *Anna Karenina* that she felt like she'd been drugged. *Now I know what it feels like to be at the top of the world*, she thought.

Even now, several miles from the studio, she could somehow *feel* things gaining more and more momentum. And half a year from now when the picture would be completed, her performance captured for posterity, and the reels of film fanned out to the network of IA theaters, the public would sit enthralled. She was sure of it.

How lucky she felt, having been able to sit in on the film's humble conception.

What a shame that she had to finish *Marie Antoinette* first.

Anna Karenina was more than a role. The very idea made something stir deep inside her bones. It was as if she were going to be transported back to her childhood, but as a woman.

"Either of you care for a drink?" Skolnik asked after the others had left.

"I'll take one," Bruce Slesin said immediately.

Skolnik looked questioningly at Ziolko.

"Why not?" Louis said, blinking the blur away from in front of his eyes. "It's been a hell of a long day."

It had been, too. He and Tamara had awakened at four-thirty in the morning, been on the set by six, worked thirteen and a half hours straight through with only a forty-five-minute lunch break in the commissary, attended the meeting, and it was now well past nine o'clock. Unless it was a Saturday night, he and Tamara were usually asleep by eight-thirty. In any case, he had little choice but to have a drink—Skolnik hadn't asked them to stay for nothing.

"Let's go into my office," Skolnik suggested, leading the way from the conference room to his adjoining office. He headed straight for the bar. Before she'd left, his secretary had seen to it that the sterling bucket was filled with ice and the cut-crystal tumblers stood in readiness. Using tongs, he plopped two cubes into each of the glasses, added a generous splash of Chivas Regal from a decanter, and handed them out. "Let's go sit."

Skolnik sank into the chair nearest the fireplace, placed his glass on the fender, and busied himself with the ritual of stuffing a meerschaum pipe with an English-blended tobacco while Ziolko and Slesin took the chairs facing his.

As soon as the pipe was drawing, Skolnik wasted no further time telling them what was on his mind. "The Academy Awards are becoming more and more important with every passing year. You've only got to look at the winners of

1930–31 to figure that out. Lionel Barrymore for *A Free Soul*, Marie Dressler for *Min and Bill*. And RKO for *Cimarron*." His cheeks tightened angrily. "As soon as those pictures were nominated, they enjoyed a new life. The public went in droves to see what was so special about them. And when they won . . . well, need I say more?"

"Why harp on the awards?" Slesin said curiously. "With *The Flappers* we've had the largest six-month box-office receipts in the history of this business."

"That's beside the point," Skolnik said darkly. "What I'm getting at is that the Academy Awards have captured the public's attention."

"Which means you want to get an award for *Anna Karenina*, I take it?" Louis asked. "That's what this conversation is leading up to?"

Skolnik sucked thoughtfully on his pipe. "Of course. *Anna Karenina* is our best chance at next year's award," he agreed, nodding. "And I want it badly." He paused, took the pipe out of his mouth, and when he spoke again his voice was hushed. "But what I want isn't just one award. I want the whole package. The Best Actor award. The Best Actress award. The Best Picture award. I want IA to come out a triple winner."

Louis let out a whistle. "You don't want much! Just the whole shebang! It hasn't happened so far. Not even two of them. What makes you think we can take all three awards for one picture?"

"With you as director, Tamara as actress, and Miles as actor—any way you look at it, that makes for one damn fine team. And don't forget *Anna Karenina* is one of the best stories ever written."

"Still, what you're after is a little unrealistic," Louis warned.

"Not from my perspective, it's not," Skolnik growled. "I think the awards are political, and they'll only get more so as the years go by."

"The awards are based on merit, and you damn well know it!" Louis said hotly. "This year's movie and performances deserved to win. So did last year's. And the year before that."

"Calm down," Slesin intervened pacifically. "O.T.'s not out to ruffle our feathers." He added softly, "I think he may have a point."

"I do at that." Oscar Skolnik gestured with his pipe as he spoke. "Since the first Academy Awards were given out for the 1927–28 season, studios've started keeping them in mind when making pictures, and who can blame them? Everybody likes to get an award. I sure as hell would." Skolnik sighed. "It takes a class act."

"And with *Anna Karenina* you think we have one?"

"I know we do. I want to make it into the best movie this studio, or any other, has ever produced. If we do that, and the performances are up to par, chances are we just might be able to swing all three awards. It's just a matter of time before one picture is so outstanding it'll grab all the awards. Why shouldn't it be us?"

"Because this is a small community out here, and all of us have friends at other studios. People like to spread their votes around. That way all the studios have a winner." Louis took a long sip of his Scotch.

Skolnik shook his head. "I don't really think so," he said slowly. "But even if that's what they like to do, we can influence their voting to the contrary."

"What!" Louis nearly choked on his drink. "You're not thinking of tampering with the votes or blackmailing anybody, are you?"

"Of course not!" Skolnik said irritably. "What do you take me for, anyway? I'm trying to suggest something simple: we manipulate the voters by influencing them, not by tampering with the ballots or their personal lives."

Slesin's interest was piqued. "How do you propose we do that?"

"By campaigning for the votes. By lobbying for them."

"You mean . . . blatantly?" Louis stared at him. "Surely you're not going to *ask* people for their votes."

"Not in so many words, no. It'll be done discreetly . . . through the power of suggestion. Needless to say, everything depends on the picture. So it'll have to be outstanding. There are lots of fine pictures released every year. Now, how do they qualify for the award?" He looked at Louis.

"First they've got to be nominated."

"By our peers, yes." Skolnik smiled. "And what in particular *gets* them nominated?"

"The quality of the picture."

"Aha. There you have it."

"I don't understand."

"Bruce will. Bruce, what, specifically, brings people to the movie theaters, besides wanting to be entertained?"

"The story. The title. The stars."

"Yes, yes, but outside of all that," Skolnik said impatiently.

"Gossip. Reviews. Adverti—" He stared at Skolnik. "*Advertising*," he whispered.

Skolnik smiled. "There you have it." He leaned forward

excitedly. "We've learned to tickle the public's interest and make them want to go and see our films. And I believe we can ignite the same kind of enthusiasm in our peers in order to get *Anna Karenina* nominated. That's the first step."

"We campaign for the awards!" Slesin said excitedly. "Starting tomorrow, we begin leaking the word that *Anna Karenina*'s only the greatest thing since *Birth of a Nation*. Once people have heard it often enough, they're going to start believing it. We'll harness the power of suggestion. We'll just be planting the seeds of an idea—*Anna Karenina* being so great—in their subconscious."

"We'll have to make certain it works," Skolnik said with finality. "I say we try it." He paused. "Is there any way we can cover our asses in case it should backfire?"

"Sure." Slesin grinned. "That's the beauty of it. We won't be the ones who'll have come out and said all those wonderful things. It'll be other people, at other studios. All we have to do is plant a few confidential rumors on a regular basis and then sit back and watch them spread. A well-calculated slip here, another there . . . in no time at all we'll set this town buzzing. And when people ask us outright for more information, we play it humble, cagey. If we play our cards right, nobody will be able to resist spreading what we've planted. And believing it."

"Rumors!" Louis scoffed. He looked at Slesin in disbelief. "You think we'll sweep the Academy Awards by virtue of rumors? What makes you think the information's even going to spread?"

"It will, because I'm counting on the dark side of human nature. Our enticing little droplets of information will be quote-secret-unquote. Nobody can resist that. I mean . . ." Bruce's voice was pointedly soft and he held Louis' gaze, his gray eyes intent. "No matter what you may like to believe, or how hard you work at keeping things private, how many people are there in this town who can really keep a secret?"

Tamara was blissfully unaware of the mounting offensive to secure the Academy Awards. Other, more immediate things occupied her mind, and Louis thought it best to say nothing regarding the conversation he had had with Skolnik and Slesin, as it might interfere with her concentration.

She had thrown herself into the role of Anna Karenina with a vengeance. The beautiful, sensual, rebellious central character seemed tailor-made for her, as though Tolstoy specifically had had her in mind when he created his tragic heroine in 1875. The stylish, wintry ice-palace sets and the emotional turmoil of a passionate, flamboyantly flaunted illicit love affair racing toward doom were the perfect ingredients for a film, and Louis' superb direction, magnificent camerawork, and chiaroscuro effects displayed her incredible beauty and virtuoso performance as deftly as a conductor leading his orchestra. He used her face and body like a pliable mask which could be molded to the precisely desired effect. If, over the course of her film career, she slipped completely—and seemingly effortlessly—into any one single role, then this was the one. Even she could not explain exactly why that happened. Perhaps it was her Russian background. Whatever the case, the only thing of which she could be absolutely certain was that despite Skolnik's best efforts, nothing on the soundstage itself, save Louis' directing and Tolstoy's story, transported her from Hollywood to nineteenth-century Russia.

There was really no way she could have slipped into the character by forgetting where she actually was. That was always too painfully apparent. Her performance happened in spite of a multitude of day-to-day disasters which took place during the filming. For one thing, the unheated soundstage was dark and cold and drafty. In the midst of filming a scene in which Count Vronsky and Anna live abroad in a neglected old Italian palazzo with frescoed walls, the roof of the soundstage began to leak, destroying the set and disrupting the filming, but Louis was not one to take defeat sitting down. He used the leaky roof to his ultimate advantage by continuing the filming. In the final print, it was the leaks, more than the genteel shabbiness of the palazzo interior, which set the mood for the scene. But the cost was stiff. Tamara had gotten drenched, and subsequently developed a ravaging flu. Her fever climbed to 103, and she was bedridden for six days. When she crawled prematurely out of bed and returned to work, Louis took one look at her gaunt, feverish face and juggled the shooting schedule to film the haunted, emotionally charged close-ups of the film's final scenes—those of a woman under emotional siege. The images would be hailed as cinematic classics for decades to come. What neither the critics nor filmgoers suspected was that these scenes were purely accidental. Tamara did not have to act the part of someone feeling miserable: she was in truth acutely miserable and still quite ill.

The tragedies mounted.

During the fifth week there was a fire on the set one day, and the next, a laboratory accident which ruined fifteen minutes of completed film.

But actors are actors first and foremost, by necessity an especially hardy species when it comes to survival, and the old adage held true: the show must go on. And go on it did, with remarkably few complaints, everything considered. If ever there were troupers who took everything in stride, the cast of *Anna Karenina* ranked among them. Despite the obstacles posed by rain, illness, accidents, and death, the film would be among the finest ever to come out of the Hollywood entertainment factories.

When the filming was completed without any further mishaps, everyone involved felt a deep sense of relief. In all, the filming had taken thirteen weeks—six longer than initially anticipated. The cast dispersed—Fay Bainter, Janet Gaynor, Dorothy Gish, Fredric March, and Charles Laughton to the studios from which they had been on loan, the bit players and others to whatever projects they were to do next. Tamara was given what would become her customary week off between pictures before she was thrust into *Razzmatazz*, a frothy, energetic farce of glittering Manhattan (actually soundstage eight), mistaken identities, and twin sisters (she played both the guileless, innocent Sabrina and the sophisticated Simone, a music-hall star who smoked Primrose cigarettes in a long ivory holder). Her costars were Billie Burke and, once again, Miles Gabriel.

After she had been immersed in *Razzmatazz* for one week, she felt so curiously detached from *Anna Karenina* that it was as if she had never been involved with the film at all. She threw herself into the dual roles with such abandon that it was as if she had slipped under the skins of the characters and lived flesh-and-blood roles. Even when she left the set each evening, she took part of the characters home with her. She lost all sense of time and reality, and it was almost as if things were happening to the characters she was portraying instead of to her. One Monday, when Louis announced that they had been invited to a formal dinner at Ciro's the following Sunday evening, she didn't give it a second thought. A dinner was, after all, just a dinner. Why shouldn't they be invited to a dinner? Weren't they Hollywood's acknowledged golden couple?

Inside and out, the restaurant was decked out as though for a festival. At the curb, a massive black doorman in a striped cotton djellaba opened the rear door of the Duesenberg, bowed low, and helped Tamara out while the chauffeur held open Louis' door. Louis joined her on the sidewalk under the domed kiosk that had been specially erected in front of the entrance for whatever occasion this was and straightened his lapels. He smiled at her. "You look sensational, as always," he said, taking her by the arm and leading her to the door.

"What's going on here?" she asked him in a low voice. "Why is that doorman dressed in that funny thing?"

"Well, I suppose it must be a theme party of some kind. The kiosk is probably part of it too." He smiled good-humoredly. "Don't worry, his outfit doesn't hold a candle to yours. You've never looked more beautiful." He stuck his tongue out comically and panted like a dog. "Come on, let's scandalize the whole town. Disrobe right here. You look so good I could eat you in public."

She clapped a gloved hand over her face and stifled a wild wave of laughter. She did look particularly dazzling in the resplendent silver sheath which hugged her body like a second skin. Her shoulders were bare, and the gown plunged daringly to her waist in the back, displaying an enormous area of ivory flesh and showing off the polished-bead necklace that was her spine. The ten-foot-long silver-fox boa she had draped around her like a stole added a regal touch, while the small diamond drop earrings he had given her for her last birthday flashed and jiggled from her ears. She looked every inch the star, from the top of her platinum hair to the tips of her silver sling-back heels.

She kept her eyes on Louis as they stepped over the threshold into Ciro's, and thought that his beautifully tailored evening clothes made him look even more handsome than usual. She felt an inordinate sense of pride and jealous possessiveness surging through her veins. How lucky I am, she thought, to have him for a husband. No other wife in the world could possibly be as treasured as I am.

Once inside the restaurant, she couldn't help wondering anew at the usually haughty maître d's tasseled red fez, but as usual he treated them with the deference reserved for Hollywood royalty. "Miss Tamara, Mr. Ziolko," he murmured, giving an obsequious bow.

Tamara flashed a brilliant smile. "Good evening, Jacques."

"If you would be so kind as to follow me . . ." He made a sweeping gesture and led the way.

They'd followed the maître d' for barely a few feet when Tamara stopped in her tracks. Her face registered her surprise.

She couldn't believe her eyes as her gaze swept the softly lit dining room. The kiosk outside, the doorman's strange garb, and the maître d's fez had been only the teasers for the sight which now greeted her. As though a magical genie had worked his wonders, the entire restaurant had been beautifully transformed into a Middle Eastern palace in some faraway oasis—a wonderland of magic and magnificence straight out of *A Thousand and One Nights*.

"Why, it . . . it's just like a harem!" Tamara exclaimed in astonishment. "Like in that Douglas Fairbanks movie!"

Louis only laughed. "Come on," he said, "the maître d's waiting to show us to our table."

They had no sooner started across the restaurant than a hidden orchestra struck up a tune and everyone seated at the tables began to applaud.

Now Tamara was confused. Still smiling entrancingly, she surreptitiously pinched Louis' arm. "There's something going on here," she growled out of the corner of her mouth, and looked at him sharply but said no more, for they had reached O.T.'s table. He was sandwiched between two extraordinarily beautiful identical twins with identically styled red tresses and identical low-cut white gowns with fake emerald shoulder straps. Tamara had never seen them before, but there was no doubt that they were intimate with O.T., judging from the way they clung to his arms. She noted also that this table, which would normally have seated eight, had only two empty chairs, signifying that there would be just the five of them. This was obviously the table of honor.

She searched her mind frantically. What on earth *was* the occasion?

Skolnik rose as he saw them approach and kissed Tamara's cheek as the maître d' pulled back her chair. "You are positively glowing," O.T. said with a smile. "I would say that marriage definitely agrees with you. Happy first anniversary." Then he held out his hand and shook Louis'.

Tamara's mouth fell open. She was stunned. "Oh, my God, it *is* our anniversary, isn't it?" she said with dawning horror. She looked at Louis for his nod of confirmation. "I'm so sorry, darling," she said quickly, touching his arm. "I was so caught up in work and . . . I can't imagine a year has already gone by . . ." She made a face and added meekly, "You *will* forgive me?"

"In time, perhaps," he said with a good-natured grin. "But you'll certainly have to work hard to assuage my hurt feelings." His eyes glittered with mock lasciviousness.

"Well, *this* is certainly a first," one of the twins piped up with a high-pitched giggle. "I thought it was wives who reminded husbands of things like birthdays and anniversaries, not vice versa."

"Tamara, let me introduce the Karan twins," O.T. said

easily, sitting back down. "On my left, here is Karla. And on my right, Kitty."

"You've got it wrong again, O.T.," the one introduced as Kitty said with a petulant, kittenish pout. From the way she pronounced "a-*gain*," Tamara could tell she was from the Pacific Northwest—Washington or Oregon, probably. "*I'm* Karla and *she's* Kitty."

"In any case, how do you do?" Tamara said smoothly.

"And this is Louis Ziolko, Tamara's husband, as you surely have guessed."

Louis inclined his head and bowed low over each of the twins' hands. They giggled and Tamara felt an ice-cold stab of irrational jealousy at his gallantry.

She slipped into her chair and the maître d' pushed it in for her, letting the fur boa slide over the back. She smiled at the nearest twin. "You'll have to forgive me if I get the two of you confused. It's amazing. You do look exactly alike." She turned to her husband. "Don't they, Louis?"

"That they do," he agreed, pulling his chair closer to hers.

The glasses of champagne arrived almost immediately, discreetly poured out of sight and still bubbling. O.T. raised his in a toast. "To many more happy years together."

"I'll drink to that." Tamara smiled, and she and Louis kissed.

They clinked their glasses and sipped.

After dinner, the lights were dimmed as the four-tiered anniversary cake was wheeled in on a trolley to great applause. A single sparkler burst radiantly from the top, sizzling and showering white sparks.

O.T. got to his feet, tapped a fork against a glass to get everyone's attention, and gradually the room fell silent.

His voice was firm and strong and rang out clearly. "I won't give a long speech, since I'm sure you'd all prefer to be dancing or talking rather than listening to me. However, just bear me out for a moment, and then I'll sit back down." He paused and his gaze swept the room. "This is a happy occasion for all of us who belong to the cinema family. In one year, Tamara and Louis have become Hollywood's First Couple, and I know there isn't a person here tonight who doesn't wish them all the best. God only knows, you'd better. I've got enough invested in them both."

There was assorted laughter and scattered applause.

Solemnly he raised his glass. "So, ladies and gentlemen, I propose a toast. To the most distinguished director and his wife, the most beautiful woman in the world. In honor of their wedding anniversary, let's hear it for IA's own Tamara and Louis Ziolko!"

There were good-natured shouts, some cries of "Hear! Hear!", and the roomful of celebrities raised their glasses and sipped.

O.T. gestured to Tamara and Louis. They rose to their feet and, linking hands like happy children, smiled out at the assembled guests. Tamara spoke first, projecting her voice so that people at the most distant corner tables could hear her clearly. Then Louis gave his short speech, and together they ceremoniously cut a slice off the anniversary cake, after which they sat down and let the waitresses continue cutting the slices.

O.T. got to his feet again. "In honor of the occasion, Louis and Tamara will lead the first dance. And I'll reserve the second," he added, smiling down at Tamara. "It isn't every day that even a studio head gets to dance with his favorite star."

Tamara glowed with happiness as Louis led her to the dance floor and began to swirl her gracefully around. True to his word, O.T. cut in for the second dance. It was a slow dance, and Tamara suspected that O.T. had arranged for that. She felt herself go rigid as O.T.'s fingers touched her bare back and pulled her close, and she made an effort to keep an obvious distance between him and herself. *Louie and I should be sharing this dance*, she couldn't help thinking.

"You're tense," O.T. reproached softly into her ear. "I'm not poison, you know. You don't have to pull so far away."

Rebuked, she closed the distance between them somewhat, and it was then that it occurred to her just how much she had changed over the past year. She was no longer young and guileless, no longer the innocent in a sea of sophisticates. A year of Hollywood parties and exposure had taught her more than she would have liked. Youth and beauty were not only commodities for the screen, she had learned, but brought out the worst in men. Some flirted harmlessly, others tried to cop a feel or make an effort to brush against her. There had even been times when she had been approached outright by men craving to sleep with her. True, O.T. had always been the perfect gentleman, but she had never given him any excuse to behave otherwise, and she wasn't about to start encouraging him now.

"You're pulling away again, Tamara," he said.

"That's because you've wrapped yourself around me."

"You're making it sound as though I'm making a pass at you."

She raised her chin. "Are you, O.T.?"

He clucked his tongue chidingly. "You have a dirty mind."

"And you're behaving like a dirty old man."

"I like to believe that nothing in life is unattainable. Especially a beautiful, exciting woman."

She looked into his eyes. "What do you need me for? You've got the Karan twins."

He laughed. "Those empty-headed scatterbrains? It's you I really want."

"I'm married, O.T."

"A fact I'm painfully aware of, believe me."

"Don't talk that way! You know this is my anniversary!"

"Ah, beneath that perfect exterior you've no heart, I can see that now. I've helped create the beauty by which all others are judged, but I forgot to see about giving her a heart."

"You make me sound like a robot."

"That's because you're cold and unfeeling."

"I'm faithful and monogamous. There's a difference."

He drew her close. "But you must agree there's no harm in trying." He smiled.

"On the contrary. I think it's very harmful."

He made a face. "Come on," he urged. "Let go. Live a little."

"What you're proposing isn't living. It's cheating."

"You'd only be cheating yourself by missing out on me."

"I'll gladly take that chance."

Despite her warnings, she could feel his arms tightening around her. Then she felt his hips pressing against hers, and for a moment she felt his solid warmth. One of his hands was at the base of her bare spine, tracing little circular motions with a finger. Despite herself, she could feel her nipples hardening, and then a warm wetness moistened her thighs.

A curious kind of confusion came into her eyes and her heart contracted. One part of her wanted to recoil while another craved his clever fingers. She looked into his eyes, and they seemed to glitter with a perverse triumph, as though he sensed that he'd pushed the right buttons.

It was precisely the look she'd seen when he'd unveiled her in front of the mirror in Italy. She was something he'd labored to create. He thought of her as something which had sprung from his fertile mind, something which he had breathed life into. Soberly she realized that he considered her his own personal Galatea.

Now she was becoming increasingly agitated and more

than a little annoyed by the unrelenting caressing of her back. The lusty hardness of his groin was barely contained by his trousers, and for a fleeting moment she felt a wave of panic. What if someone noticed O.T.'s advances . . . more important, what if Louie happened to notice? How was she to explain that she had done nothing to lead him on?

Silently she cursed the dampness of her mound. Her body's instinctive reaction to a masculine touch was like a slap in the face. *What was wrong with her*?

His hands slid down to her buttocks, and she felt his palms cupping her silver-sheathed cheeks, and then a thumb pressed the cleft between them.

Damn! He wouldn't stop!

Now her irritation was turning to red-hot anger, and she could feel the adrenaline rising inside her. Obviously, ignoring him or trying to reject him discreetly was getting her nowhere. Far more drastic measures were called for.

Tightening her lips, and smiling sweetly and never missing a beat, she adroitly kneed him in the groin.

It was the last thing he'd expected. His eyes bulged and he could barely stifle a cry. His face went white as a sheet and for a moment he looked confused, as though he didn't know what had hit him. "Je-sus!" he finally managed to gasp.

She looked suddenly contrite. "Oh, I *am* sorry, O.T. You've aroused so much passion in me that my body just went wild!" She clutched him like a vise with her lacquered talons. "You've got to understand one thing, O.T.," she said softly, her tone dead serious. "I love my husband. Nothing in the world is going to separate me from him. Nothing and no one. Not you or anyone else."

He looked at her with growing respect. "Louis is a lucky man."

"And I'm a lucky woman. I never forget that, not for a day." She smiled. "What's the matter? You've missed another step."

"Damn you." He gritted his teeth. "I'm going to sing soprano for a week."

She shook her head. "You'll never sing soprano, O.T.," she said definitely. "Your balls are too big."

And with that she turned her back on him and made her way back to the table.

He stared after her, ruefully shaking his head.

The house seemed especially quiet and seductive after the raucous noise of the party. Only the foyer lights were lit; the rest of the house was dark and asleep. She started to head straight up the curving staircase to the master suite, but Louis caught her hand and wordlessly led her into the living room instead. Then he let go of her and, to her surprise, went around switching on all the lamps.

She saw it immediately, on the wall over an end table so that the open top of the lampshade bathed it in a circle of light. It was an exquisite little Mattisse oil that suggested, rather than illustrated, a tabletop still life. Tears sparkled in her eyes and she couldn't speak. He took her hand and pressed his warm palm against hers. Clasping their fingers together, they stood there studying the painting for a long time.

Finally she turned to him, her eyes bright and shiny.

"Do you like it?" he asked softly.

She stood on tiptoe and brushed her lips against his. "I love it," she whispered huskily, her tongue tracing his lips. "And I love you even more. Today was the second-most-wonderful day of my life."

"What was the first?"

She smiled. "The day we got married."

"Well, there are a lot more to come," he promised.

And there were. Unknown to her, he had started a family tradition. They would celebrate their second anniversary in the Crystal Room, the Beverly Hills Hotel's principal ballroom, and afterward Louis would present her with a large Toulouse-Lautrec painting of a Moulin Rouge scene. After their third anniversary, which was held in tents on O.T.'s lawn, Louis gave her a vibrant, startling Van Gogh landscape that seemed to pulsate with a strange inner light.

Each time she looked at it, she could feel her own mind bridging the gap to the artist's fine madness and wished she could achieve the same kind of genius in her acting as Van Gogh had achieved in that painting.

But despite the more valuable paintings which joined their growing collection each year, it was the little Matisse, the first anniversary gift, that would always remain her personal favorite. Because it had been the first, it was the most treasured.

Anna Karenina, Tamara, and Miles Gabriel were all nominated for Academy Awards.

To celebrate her nomination, Louis gave Tamara a brand-new white Packard convertible with white-walled tires and red cowl.

"I'm going to buy you a new white convertible every time you're nominated for an Academy Award," he said expansively. "And if you win it, then we'll upgrade you to a Rolls."

But *Anna Karenina* went away empty-handed. Oscar Skolnik's best-laid plans had gone astray. A lot of great movies with a lot of great stars in them had been released during the past year. MGM's *Grand Hotel* won the Oscar for Best Picture, Helen Hayes for *The Sin of Madelon Claudet*, her very first film role, and Fredric March and Wallace Beery made history by tying for Best Actor, the former for *Dr. Jekyll and Mr. Hyde*, and the latter for *The Champ*. Walt Disney received a Special Award for Mickey Mouse.

Oscar Skolnik fumed. Miles smarted. Tamara, delighted at having been nominated at all, had never really believed she stood a chance to win, so she took losing with philosophical good humor. What mattered to her was that her peers thought highly enough of her to nominate her and that *Anna Karenina* was a resounding success, both artistically and at the box office. It did far better than *Marie Antoinette*, but admittedly less well than *The Flappers*, which still solidly held its position as the most successful box-office smash made to date. Nevertheless, she was one of the hottest celebrities in a town chock-full of celebrities, no mean feat by any standard. After having made only three movies, she was already one of the most recognizable stars in the industry. Her face appeared on the covers of so many magazines that she joked about it: "I could paper my living-room walls with the covers, and still have some left over for the den." IA's publicity department clipped so many articles about her, ranging from respectable reviews to the most outrageous fiction, that she could not possibly read them all. Five thousand fan letters a week were pouring in. She was at the very peak of nationwide popularity. Her platinum hair had become all the rage. If she changed her hairstyle, it was news, and hairdressers cross-country were obliged to copy the style. Nothing about her was sacred. It was strange, she often reflected wryly, that she didn't *feel* any differently at the pinnacle of success than she had before. The major differences in her life were the way others responded to her, the financial security which she enjoyed, and the detestable inconveniences, which she grew to hate. Whether at home or at the studio, she was like royalty or a cherished, particularly priceless gem, protected from the public by guards and gates. The begowned, bejeweled siren who could cause mass hysteria by simply being seen in public was, by necessity, turning into a virtual recluse.

Unless her presence was absolutely required somewhere,

Tamara preferred to keep herself isolated from the public. She had to think twice before leaving the house. Autograph hounds, photographers, and fans haunted her every step. Even her home was not spared—the curious, with an eye peeled for a glimpse of her, drove continually back and forth in front of the house. Fans went so far as to ring the doorbell and offer to help around the house free of charge; they were willing to do anything, as long as they could be close to their favorite star. Tamara-watching had become a national pastime. She was a superstar before there was such a word to describe her.

Still, there were some ordinary pleasures she did not have to sacrifice, and none pleased her more than doing absolutely nothing. What few idle hours she could call her own each week, she guarded jealously, and tried to spend either in the garden or at the poolside. There she felt safe from groping hands, screaming mouths, and prying eyes. The landscaped grounds provided both privacy and security, thanks to a ten-foot-high wall *and* a twelve-foot-high hedge. She had grown to love the big rambling house and its generous, protective grounds. Here she felt safe. Secure. And at home.

The walls kept the world at bay.

She would have been content to live here forever and never leave.

Louis sprang the surprise on her on a sunny Tuesday afternoon in late May 1932. It was an artist's dream day. The sky was clear, uniform blue with only the slightest edge of haze, the temperature had climbed into the high eighties, and the garden was in full, riotous bloom. Butterflies flitted soundlessly among the delphiniums, dutiful bees buzzed from flower to flower to collect their precious nectar, and an occasional hummingbird hovered delicately, its wings moving so swiftly that they were an almost invisible blur.

Tamara lay contented on the rattan chaise under her favorite jacaranda tree. The rattan table beside her held a half-full glass of iced tea and a sweating glass pitcher. She lazed luxuriantly, her lips half-smiling. She was reading *The Good Earth*, by Pearl Buck, which had been published the previous year but which she was only getting around to reading now, and she was engrossed in it. It was the perfect afternoon for reading, and for once she could relax completely. For this day, at least, she hadn't a worry in the world. Bifocals halfway down her nose, Inge was seated in the shade of a tilted, fringed parasol nearer the pool, catching up on her mending.

Turning a page, Tamara heard the quickening click of leather heels on the flagstone path and knew that Louis had returned from the mysterious mission he had departed on more than two hours earlier.

"I'm back!" he announced unnecessarily as he ducked beneath the jacaranda branches. He bowed low in front of her and with a flourish produced a long-stemmed day lily from behind his back. He proffered it formally. "Madam?" he said somberly.

She plucked the lily from between his fingers and held it to her nose, inhaling its fragrance, her eyes never leaving his. She wondered what her handsome husband had been up to. There was a gleam in his eyes, a barely subdued excitement which glowed on his face.

"Hi." She grinned, waggling her fingers lazily at him. Her nose still in the lily, she cast him one of those seductive up-and-over looks for which she was so famous on-screen. "What's up?"

"Come on, get dressed," he urged breathlessly. "We're going for a spin. I have a surprise to show you."

"Louie!" she protested, marking her place in *The Good Earth* with the lily stalk and putting the book down in the grass. "It's so peaceful here. Just listen for a moment." She paused. "What do you hear? Birds? Crickets? Leaves rustling in the breeze?" She opened her eyes and they were filled with a peculiar, pleading brightness. "Can't the surprise wait?" She reached out for his hand.

He stepped back obstinately and thrust his hands into his jacket pockets, his lips setting into a thin, strained line of annoyance.

She sighed and rolled her head sideways, away from him. Now she had upset him, but she felt that if anyone should have been upset, it was she. He knew how much this peace and quiet meant to her. She had just finished shooting *Razzmatazz* the previous Friday, and it was her customary week off between pictures—on this occasion a single week extended to a lavish, unheard-of three entire glorious weeks, twenty-one magnificent days in all, a well-deserved vacation she and Louis had had to fight tooth and nail to receive. Now, after she had looked forward to rejuvenating herself at home without ever having to be seen in public for any reason, Louis wanted her to leave her oasis. It wasn't fair.

"Louis, I'm enjoying myself," she explained quietly. "So is Inge. Why don't you grab a swimsuit and join us? You know, this is the first time I've managed to sit down and read a book in over a year. At least one that doesn't have something to do with making movies."

"This is important to me," he said softly. "It's something I've done for . . . us."

"Honey, I'm sorry," she said contritely. "You must think me a monstrous bitch, and with good reason. Of course I'll be glad to come." She reached out, tugged one of his hands out of his pocket, and held it. "I should be grateful for every opportunity we're together. Where are we going, anyway?"

He shook his head. "Can't tell you that."

"Because it's a surprise." She laughed.

"Because it's a surprise," he agreed.

And it was: twelve and a half acres of prime undeveloped hilltop overlooking Los Angeles and miles of coastline below to the west, and the rugged Santa Ana Mountains rising to the east.

"But . . . there's nothing here!" Tamara said in puzzlement as they got out of the car to wade through the dry, bur-infested, knee-high brush.

"That's the beauty of it," Louis said excitedly. "Don't you see? It's virgin land. Ours to do with as we damn please. Here's where we'll build our home." His eyes glowed with excitement. "Just think—it'll be *our* home, not a house that used to belong to someone else. It'll be everything that *we* want it to be. Isn't it beautiful?"

She gazed around, doing a complete turn, and nodded. They were standing on the flat two-acre crest of the hill, and the rest of the property rolled gently downhill before it dropped off sharply beyond the property line. There was a dry, rock-strewn creekbed which attested to heavy runoff during the rainy season, and Tamara was startled when a frightened hare burst out of the dry weeds and hopped away. Overhead, a large bird circled silently. The view was incredible, uninterrupted for 360 degrees all around. Looking in three directions, you actually felt you were in the middle of a wilderness—there wasn't a house as far as the eye could see—but the view of Los Angeles sprawling below in the fourth direction told you that you hadn't left civilization completely. It was the best of both worlds, and natural and unspoiled. Except for its treelessness, she loved the property on sight.

"Let me guess," she said slyly, kicking at a pebble in the creekbed. "You've already bought it?" Her head was tucked down and she peered sideways at him, her hands in her trouser pockets. A warm breeze lifted the platinum curls sticking out from under her sharply angled beret.

"Uh-huh. Got the deed right here." He flashed her a white grin and patted his breast pocket. "Signed, sealed, and delivered. Took three weeks of negotiation and I got the price down some, but it didn't come cheap because the owners didn't really need to sell. But it's worth every penny. Look at the location." He pointed down to the flat expanse of Los Angeles sprawling below. "With the city spreading further and further out all the time, there's no telling how valuable this property's going to be in the future. Another few years and we probably wouldn't be able to touch it for twenty times as much as we paid for it. Property values are going to skyrocket, you wait and see. The Depression can't go on forever."

"I suppose you're right." She paused and studied the terrain. "It's going to be expensive to build here," she mused aloud. "We'll have to start off by bringing a road in from the turnoff . . ."

"I know that. And we'll have to have the property walled in for privacy. And the house won't be cheap, either, but you'll be crazy about it. It already looks great on the blueprints."

"What!" She spun half-around, her eyes flashing silver. "Louie, do you mean to tell me that you went ahead and had a house designed without even consulting me?"

"Well, yes," he said, shifting uncomfortably. "I know what you need and like better than anyone. And I know what I need and like too. Listen, don't get upset. I know you like the house we're renting now, but I guarantee you'll love this one a whole lot more. You'll have a garden like you wouldn't believe. It'll make the Garden of Eden and the Hanging Gardens of Babylon look like weed patches by comparison." He grinned.

"You did all this behind my back," she said accusingly.

"Tamara, you're making this sound like some sort of Greek tragedy."

"Maybe it is."

"No, it's not. I wanted this to be a surprise, that's all. I only went behind your back because you're so busy that you don't have the time to do half the things you want. I just wanted to make things easier on you. If you want, we'll forget about the house and put the property up for sale. It's not worth having if it's going to come between us. I don't want us to fight."

"Neither do I," Tamara said quietly, melting at his words. "I'm sorry I reacted the way I did. It was just . . . a momentary shock." She attempted an awkward smile. "I behaved stupidly."

She raised her head and looked into his face. His eyes were bright in his strong tanned face. She felt a hypnotic pull in them, like the tide tugged at by the mysterious forces of the moon. He took her face in his hands and gently tilted it further upward. Then his lips descended.

His mouth was moist and soft and filled with a thousand warm promises. The last ragged bits of anger and frustration seeped out of her. She was suddenly weak. She could feel the moist beginnings of passion starting up between her thighs. She wanted him to kiss her forever, to take her right on the spot.

But she finally pulled away from him. "That's enough . . . for now," she whispered hoarsely with a low laugh. "There's no telling what I might do if we don't stop."

"We'll come back . . . often."

"Yes."

They walked silently along the dry creekbed to the car, holding hands like teenage lovers. Tamara felt a warm glow of satisfaction. They were always more like young lovers after they'd had a disagreement and made up, as though through some mysterious alchemy, anger became passion.

"What's the next step?" she asked as soon as they reached the car.

He leaned back against the warm hood of the Duesenberg. "You mean, about the house?"

She nodded.

"Well, it wouldn't hurt to consolidate our finances. The way things are set up, our paychecks are automatically deposited into our respective accounts. As far as the house goes, it would make things a lot easier if we paid everything out of one joint account.

"That makes sense to me."

He smiled slightly. "Only you're my wife, and I don't like the idea of having to use my wife's money for anything."

"Why, for heaven's sake? What's wrong with my money?"

He took a deep breath. "It's the way I was brought up. The man is supposed to be the provider."

"That's silly!" she scolded him. Then she looked at him closely. "You're serious, aren't you?"

He nodded. "Like I said, it's something that I'm just not comfortable with. I'm sure it'll pass."

She looked exasperated. "I should hope so."

"At any rate, what it boils down to now is cold hard cash. I paid for the property and the architect out of my own account, but I don't have nearly enough to pay for the house as well. A joint account would simplify a lot of things. If you

378

don't like the idea, and frankly *I* don't, I filled out a power of attorney for you. It's only temporary, and all you have to do is sign it. Then, until it's canceled, I can get to your money without any problem. This way I'll be able to divert funds from both our accounts into one separate checking account just for payments involving the house, but in essence we'll still have separate accounts."

"Couldn't I just sign checks as we need them?"

"I thought of that, but what if I need to get at money in a hurry and you're on a publicity tour?"

"I see your point." She thought for a moment. "How much will the house run, do you think?"

He watched her steadily. "Two hundred thousand dollars."

"Two hundred thousand!" she sputtered. A disbelieving look clouded her face. "What are we building here? Versailles?"

"Only a reasonable facsimile," he joked weakly. "Actually, it's not all that bad when you consider the overall picture. I looked around, and an average seven-room stucco house in Beverly Hills runs five thousand."

"A fortieth of what you're proposing."

"I know that. But you have to take into account that we need something better than average. Also, this property is totally unimproved. There are no roads. There's no electricity. We'll need to dig for water. Arrange for sewage. Wall the property in."

"How much was this property, anyway?" she asked.

"Twelve thousand."

She let out a gasp. "That's . . . that's pretty steep."

He gestured around the hill. "It's also twelve and a half *prime* acres. That's not exactly chickenfeed."

She looked up at him. "No, I suppose it isn't," she said hoarsely.

He looked at her with concern. "Now what's the matter? You look like you've seen a ghost."

"The specter of poverty's more like it," she said grimly.

"Princess! Get hold of yourself. We're talking about a house, not some plaything like a yacht or a car. Houses are bought and sold every day."

"They get repossessed every day too. You have only to read the statistics in the papers."

He shook his head. "Sometimes I don't understand you. You're intent on harboring this notion that a house is going to bankrupt us. How many people do you know that that's happened to? Name one."

"King Ludwig of Bavaria."

He burst into rich peals of laughter. "That you know personally," he spluttered. "Be serious."

"I am being serious," she said anxiously. "Louie, if we go ahead with a two-hundred-thousand-dollar house, we'll end up broke!"

He laughed. "No we won't. Besides, it's not like it's got to be paid for all at once. Hell, nobody does that."

Her face was still pinched. "But can we really afford it? I mean, we'll have more money going out than coming in . . ."

"With my three hundred a week and your thousand, we're raking in over fifty-two hundred every month! Of course we can afford it."

"It's not as easy as it sounds, and you know it," she protested, calculating swiftly. "We'll be skating on very thin ice. There are taxes to consider."

"Granted."

"And our expenses are astronomical. Louie, we can't just build a house and let it sit there empty; we'll have to furnish it. Where's all the money going to come from?"

"Oh, for God's sake, Princess," he said in exasperation, "we're rich. *Rich*. R-i-c-h rich. Can't you get that through your head? You're still thinking of yourself as the girl I met in the coffee shop."

"Maybe," she admitted. "But I never want to go back to that ever again."

"Trust me, you won't. Another five years and your contract's up for renegotiation. You'll be able to write your own ticket. The money'll just keep rolling in."

"Like magic, huh?"

"Well, close to it."

"Then why aren't we saving more than eight hundred dollars a month? Sometimes it's even less. I feel like we're on a perpetual treadmill."

"To make more, you have to spend more," he said equably. "We *can't* cut down on expenses. It's part of what keeps the public intrigued. They don't want their stars to be just like the girl next door."

"And what if," she said earnestly, her expression clouding, "something should happen to either one of us and the money *doesn't* keep rolling in?"

"Trust me," he said softly. "Would I steer you wrong?"

She looked up at him and saw the earnest expression in his eyes. "Of course you wouldn't," she said softly. "You know I trust you completely." She took a massive breath. "You said you've got the power of attorney on you?"

"Right here." He fished it out of his pocket with a flourish.

"Got a pen?" she asked, holding her hand out, palm up.

Grinning, he produced a fountain pen, unscrewed the cap, and handed it over.

As impassively as possible, she placed the paper on the hood of the car and scrawled her famous autograph across the document. She frowned down at her name. Her signature was not smooth, self-assured, and fluid, but rather shaky, crimped, and hesitant. Like a miser's signature, she thought. Or at least the signature of someone who had signed against her better judgment.

When the final figures were tallied a little over two years later, the total cost of the house had climbed to a staggering $440,000. They didn't own it. The bank did. Two weeks after it was completed, there was a second mortgage on it.

Much later, when she would reminisce upon the past, Tamara would pinpoint the moment she had scrawled her signature on the power of attorney as the precise point in time when the wheel of fortune stopped spinning in their favor, when their problems would start to mount, when the good life they enjoyed would begin to go bad.

In the meantime, there was the house. The publicity it generated made it worth every cent. The trouble was, she and Louis had to pay for it, not IA. It wasn't Versailles, but there was nothing humble about it. Members of the press trouped through it, dutifully "oohed" and "aahed," and went away impressed and anxious to enlighten their readers. And why shouldn't they have been impressed? Tamara asked herself wearily. Hell, she was impressed. After all, how many people ever really lost their fairy-tale fantasies completely? And that was what the house really was—a dream castle, a spun-sugar confection.

But she had never felt less comfortable in any other house she could remember. It wasn't a home. It was a daunting monstrosity.

For months she couldn't pick up a newspaper or magazine without running across some mention of the house Louis named "Tamahawk" in Tamara's honor.

Screen Story magazine devoted an entire eight-page spread to the house, complete with seven photographs. The acid-tinged article, written by the much-feared columnist Marilee Rice, was appropriately titled "Home Is Where the Castle Is." A smaller, catty subtitle read: "Eat and drink, Tamara we die," which set the tone for the article which followed.

* * *

"Cut and . . . *print!*" Louis' voice boomed out through the megaphone.

Everyone on the soundstage, from the director of photography to the best boy, broke into spontaneous applause. Tamara acknowledged her peers' esteem with a gracious bow, the high Viennese hat with its tight cluster of plum-colored bows and short plumes she wore slipping forward off her head. The wardrobe assistants were momentarily distracted, but Pearl came rushing to rescue it before it could topple to the floor.

"Thank God," Tamara gasped as Pearl's youthful assistant grabbed the ivory fan out of her hand, unsnapped it with a flick of her wrist, and began fanning her furiously. Now that the heavy hat was off, she felt curiously light-headed. Under her tight curls, her scalp was drenched and she could feel beads of sweat crawling relentlessly down her back. "I feel like I'm going to faint," she gasped. "How hot is it, anyway?"

"The radio predicted it would hit the mid-nineties," Pearl said.

"It feels more like a hundred and thirty in here," Tamara groaned. "These winter clothes are like a sauna! At least the real Baroness Maria Vetsera didn't have to suffer California heat waves."

"The real Baroness Vetsera had to suffer chilly palaces and icy hunting lodges in winter, and was shot to death by her crown-prince lover, which is a hell of a lot worse than putting up with our weather, if you ask me," Pearl retorted.

Tamara glared at her. "You know just how to cheer a person up, don't you?" she said irritably as she lowered herself into her director's chair, surely the only one of white silk in all of Hollywood. She had to perch precariously on the forward edge because of the ungainly bustle her costume required.

"I look at things optimistically," Pearl growled, striking a kitchen match on the wooden arm of Tamara's chair and lighting a Lucky Strike.

"Spare me your optimism. And would you *please* stop using my chair as a matchbox?" Tamara snapped.

"Ooooh," Pearl observed with raised eyebrows, "but aren't we getting touchy."

Tamara shut her eyes and let the fan cool her face. Louis came hurrying over, megaphone still in hand. "That was a magnificent scene!" he crowed jubilantly. He leaned down and kissed Tamara's cheek exuberantly. "If you don't watch it, princess, you *will* win the Oscar this time around."

Tamara opened one eye and glared malevolently up at

him. "For what?" she snapped, extending her arms straight out so that the two assistant dressers could unbutton the eighteen pearl buttons on her formal white kidskin gloves. "Enduring the hottest costume? The heaviest hats? The most deformed, unnatural figure, thanks to this hideous steel-wire bustle? I look like I'm pregnant in my backside!"

"You look beautiful and you know it."

"I look like a goddamn camel!"

He looked at her in surprise. "Hey," he said gently, "loosen up, will you? I know the costume's not the most comfortable thing under the sun."

"You're not kidding."

"Why don't you go and change into something comfortable? Then you and Pearl head on over to the commissary. I'll meet you there."

Tamara shook her head. "You both go on. Me, I just want to go to my dressing room, get undressed, and lie down stark naked. That's the only way to cool off in this heat."

"I'll have someone bring you a cold salad platter," Pearl offered.

"Thanks, but no," Tamara said firmly. The assistant dressers peeled off her gloves and she shooed them away with impatient flaps of her hands. "Right now, a few gallons of club soda and a tub full of ice'll do more for me than all the food in the world."

She grabbed a moist towel from a passing grip and pressed it against her forehead. "Ah, that's better," she moaned with relief. "This makeup just doesn't let my skin breathe. Well, I'm off." She dropped the towel, rose to her feet, and started struggling with the buttons of the restricting chin-high collar of the lapeled, plum-and-black-striped two-layered floor-length dress. "See you later," she called back over her shoulder. She continued struggling with the tiny buttons even as she staggered outside into the blinding sunlight on her way to her dressing room across the street. It was high noon, and hotter than ever. In anticipation of her four treasured electric fans, she ran so swiftly that by the time she hurried up the three steps, she was certain she was going to faint. She staggered into the first of her two rooms, unexpectedly colliding head-on with Inge.

Inge grabbed her by the arm to steady her. Tamara stared at her and drew back, her face suddenly going white. "Inge!" Her voice broke. "Something has happened."

"No," Inge assured her quickly.

"Tell me!" Tamara urged.

"Not to worry," Inge assured her. Something in the tim-

383

bre of her voice changed suddenly. "At home everything is fine."

"Then what is it?" Tamara asked. "It's not like you to show up here without calling first. You gave me quite a scare."

"I know this. I am sorry." Inge's somber eyes held Tamara's gaze directly. "Do you have some minutes?"

"I'm on lunch break. I've got a whole hour to kill. Are you hungry? Do you want me to send for something to eat?"

"Not for me, thank you." Inge tucked her shapeless gray dress under her buttocks and sat rather primly on the edge of the white couch.

Tamara felt a ripple of uneasiness stir within her. "Why are you staring at me like that?" she asked.

"I am sorry." Inge dropped her gaze and patted the couch cushion beside her. "Sit, and I will tell you why it is I come here." Tamara sat down next to her and Inge took a deep breath, steeling herself for what she had to say. "Ever since we arrive in Germany, I have try to raise you as best I could. Like you my own child, my own flesh and blood. Which is how I think of you, since I got no other family," Inge began, choosing her words carefully.

"I know that." Tamara smiled fondly. "We're more family than most people who are related."

Inge nodded. "And I think you know I never try to take your mother's place. I try to keep her . . . her memory living for you always, yes?"

Tamara gasped. "Then what are you trying to tell me?" Tamara cried. "Inge, you're frightening me!"

Inge looked upset. "Please, Tamara, let me tell you my own way. For me this is . . . very difficult."

"I'm sorry," Tamara said gently.

"Over the years, I told you as much about your mother and your childhood as I thought was . . ." Inge frowned, searching for the right word. ". . . appropriate. Some things were overlooked, of course. I did not see to your religious upbringing, because I do not know Jewish customs. Also, there was always confusion about you being Russian Orthodox. Is very confusing. Anyway, even your mother, *Gott* rest her soul, was not . . . well, the best when it come to religious matters. As for your father . . . well, I told you not much about him." Inge shut her eyes and held her forehead as if she suddenly had a severe headache. "I should tell you everything long ago, I can see that now. Only, I want to spare you." She sniffled and wiped her nose. "I did not want to see you hurt. You must believe this."

384

"Of course I do." Tamara smiled gently.

"Since you probably learn everything soon anyway, you might as well first hear it from me. You have right to know."

Tamara was apprehensive. "Go on . . ."

"Tamara . . ." Inge sat up straight and folded her hands in her lap. "It concern your father."

"My *father*? But . . . I barely knew him! For all we know, he's dead."

"No." Inge's voice was a strained whisper. "He is alive."

"Alive!" Tamara's eyes lit up and she clutched Inge eagerly. "Where? How do you know?"

Wordlessly Inge unfolded the newspaper she had been clutching and smoothed it on her lap. It was that morning's Los Angeles *Herald Express*.

Tamara snatched it away from her and stared at it, the paper rustling in her quivering hands. Her smooth brow furrowed as she mouthed the boldface headline to herself: DELEGATION OF JEWISH PALESTINIANS TO VISIT HERE ON U.S. TOUR. She wondered why on earth Inge had deemed this important enough to come rushing to the studio as if the world were on fire. Inge knew that although Tamara considered herself nominally Jewish, she was uninterested in practicing her religion.

Then her eyes dropped to the bank of smaller lines directly below, and she jerked as though she had been punched by an invisible fist. There, in black and white, was a name she couldn't help but recognize: EVICT BRITISH AND FORM A JEWISH NATION, BORALEVI URGES.

Boralevi. Thunderstruck, she sat paralyzed.

Boralevi.

She stared at the name as if in a trance. Was it possible? Could it be?

A small photograph of a man accompanied the article. She jumped to her feet, lunged to the makeup mirror across the room, and switched on its perimeter of glaring, highwattage bulbs.

Schmarya Boralevi, the caption under the photograph read. *His Goal Is a New Middle Eastern State.*

Tamara held the slightly blurred picture closer to her eyes and stared at it in wide-eyed silence. What a handsome man Schmarya Boralevi was. His face had been caught head-on by the camera, and there was something infinitely heroic about the proud facial bone structure, the aristocratic, noble nose, and the large eyes which burned with an intense, almost spiritual fervor. The effect was further heightened by the insolent set of his sensuous lips, the paleness of his thick, pale blond or white mane of hair, and the strong granite set of the cleft chin barely visible under his luxuriant pale beard. Tamara stared at the photograph for long minutes, trying in vain to recognize something—anything—which would match up with the hazy, long-forgotten memories of the Schmarya Boralevi she had once known—barely. Then, eyes darting from line to line, she greedily read the article.

SPECIAL TO THE HERALD EXPRESS

by John Fogel

A six-member Jewish delegation led by Schmarya Boralevi, an outspoken Palestine resident who is urging the British to surrender control of the eastern Mediterranean Mandate and turn it into a nation for the world's Jewish peoples, will stop here as part of a nationwide tour.

Boralevi, a Russian Jew by birth, who suffered devastating bodily injury at the hands of the Okhrana, the dread secret police of the late Czar, and immigrated to the Holy Land in 1918, said in a New York speech that he will attempt to hand-deliver a detailed report to President Roosevelt during his delegation's stopover in Washington, D.C. To date, there has been no response from the White House as to whether or not a meeting with the President will be granted.

"Palestine is the Holy Land for the world's Christians," an impassioned Boralevi told a packed synagogue on Manhattan's West Side, "but everyone forgets that it was the Israelites whom Moses led there in order to obtain freedom from the oppression of the Pharaoh. Now, through military, police, and immigration tactics, the British are keeping the rightful heirs of Moses from their Promised Land."

He denounced the British Mandate as "a yoke of slavery and oppression, which has more than outlasted its need or welcome." He also claims that he is "a fugitive of sorts" in his adopted land.

"I am a wanted man, constantly in transit," he said. "For years now, the authorities have been trying to arrest me." According to the British, Boralevi and a band of his supporters are wanted for smuggling hundreds of illegal immigrants into Palestine "by land and by sea." More recently, he claims to have been responsible for several air flights originating from Greece or Cyprus, landing in deserted areas of Palestine by night.

The problems in Palestine in general and with the British Mandate in particular are not new. As the Great War drew to a close, Dr. Chaim Weitzmann obtained the famous Balfour Declaration of November 2, 1917, from Great Britain, which pledged British support for the establishment of Palestine as a "national home" for the world's Jewish people.

However, as the *Aliyah*, or immigration, of Jewish pioneers to Palestine began, the British found themselves facing a greater wave of immigrants than they expected, as well as growing Arab unrest. Clashes between the new settlers and the old Arab inhabitants increasingly turned into bloody battles, with fatalities on both sides.

Giving in to mounting Arab pressure, the British exempted Trans-Jordan from the provisions of the Mandate, thereby in a single move barring most of the territory from both Jewish immigration and land development. In their struggle to be impartial to both Arabs and Jews, the British deemed it necessary to stem the flow of Jewish immigrants. Laws specifically aimed at discouraging Jewish settlement paved the way to higher taxes and set strict rules in the area of agriculture.

"First the government of Great Britain wants to help us set up a homeland," Boralevi thundered, "and simultaneously they try to make it impossible for our people to reach it, and if they do, to make carving out a decent living nearly impossible. If this criminal charade continues, Great Britain will have a lot to answer for in the years to come."

Sir Colin Bentley Plimmer, Great Britain's most outspoken critic of the Balfour Declaration, addressed a group of anti-Zionists recently in London, claiming: "They [the Zionists] want nothing more than to wage war and wrest Palestine from its rightful inhabitants, the Arabs."

Plimmer went on to denounce Boralevi as "a common criminal, a gunrunner, . . . and he should be branded as such. It is dangerous that he should be perceived as a hero. We have irrefutable proof that Mr. Boralevi and his small band of brigands are intent on attacking Arabs and British alike." Plimmer says he deeply regrets the "false sympathy" Mr. Boralevi is stirring up among Jews. "Under the guise of raising money to help immigration and create a Jewish nation, he is smuggling immigrants and arms into Palestine, slipping in and out of the borders to make his deals. He must be stopped."

During his speech in New York, Boralevi denounced

Plimmer's accusations as "ridiculous." "If Plimmer considers me a criminal, then so be it. I will continue, however, to do as I have been doing. Throughout history we, the Jewish people, have been attacked, captured, enslaved, and slaughtered. Let it not be on my conscience that we did not adequately protect our women and children. If our enemy is armed, then unfortunately, so we must be armed to repel them. If we must fight, then we must fight. I have lived through one pogrom. I do not intend to live through another, and if I have to, I will go down fighting."

Slowly Tamara turned and looked Inge imploringly in the face. "This . . . this is my . . . father?" she whispered. "You're absolutely certain?"

Inge met her eyes unwaveringly. "Yes," she replied definitely. She nodded her head. "That is him. I recognize him from the picture even without first reading name."

"It just seems so . . . so farfetched finding him through a newspaper article! I didn't think things like that could happen in real life. It's like something out of the movies."

"Often real life is stranger than make-believe," Inge agreed.

Tamara studied the photograph some more. She found it difficult to keep her eyes off it. Yes, her father was indeed very handsome, in a larger-than-life Biblical kind of way. She could well imagine why her mother had fallen in love with him. And this handsome man had been her very own father. He was a stranger to her. She couldn't even remember his ever having been there.

"Do you think he'll like the food?" Tamara fretted while pacing the room nervously, constantly rubbing her hands together. "Maybe he just eats kosher."

"He'll eat," Inge assured her, keeping at her needlepoint without looking up.

"What if he never arrives?" Tamara asked.

Inge looked irritably up over her bifocals. "Settle *down*," she said sharply. "You are acting like you are going to jump out of your skin."

Louis said softly, "Relax, princess, you look beautiful."

"How can I relax? Do you have any idea when I saw him last? Inge says I was four or five. If it weren't for the picture in the paper, I wouldn't even know what he looks like. I wish I could have gone and heard his speech. It would have made meeting him easier."

"You know that wasn't possible," Louis said. "O.T. was

justified in not letting you attend. The press was probably all over the place, and someone would have been certain to make the connection between the two of you. IA just couldn't afford to take that chance. You're supposed to be the daughter of a Russian prince, not a refugee fighting for a Jewish state. I'm sure your father will understand." All three of them looked up as the telephone jangled. Louis picked up the receiver, spoke quietly into it, and hung up. He nodded. "That was the front gate. They're letting him in now."

Heels clicking sharply, Tamara hurried out into the travertine-floored foyer, where every available wall surface was a sparkling sheet of mirror, and an ornately carved wood console held an enormous stone urn brimming with begonias.

The front doorbell rang suddenly, startling her so much that she jumped. As she heard the brisk footsteps of the maid approaching, she was filled with so much anxiety that she raced on tiptoe back into the living room, where Louis and Inge had already gotten to their feet. "He won't like me!" she fretted, twisting her wedding band nervously round and round her finger. "Louie, we should never have had him meet me here. It's so ostentatious!"

"It's too late to worry about that, and I shouldn't think it would matter where you meet." He reached for her hand and gave it a reassuring squeeze. She tried to smile.

They could hear the maid's disembodied voice coming from the foyer, and then another, deeper voice answering, and two distant sets of footsteps ringing out on the travertine, Esperanza's quick and steady and the other's heavy and uneven, as though from a severe limp.

"Thank you, Esperanza," Louis called out, "you can go now."

"*Sí, señor.*" Esperanza tucked her chins down into her chest, turned around, and waddled off flat-footed.

Louis crossed the room with long strides to greet Schmarya Boralevi. "I'm Louis Ziolko," he said, holding out his hand, "Tamara's husband."

The two men shook hands firmly. "I am pleased to meet you," Schmarya said in thickly accented English.

Tamara stood rooted to the spot, her eyes focused on the floor. "Go on," Inge whispered. "He's your father! Go to him!" Tamara took a deep breath and then felt Inge giving her a little push from the back. She went hesitantly forward, and when she had gone halfway, she looked up slowly. She stopped and stared at him, her heart beating unevenly, her silk skirt swaying around her ankles.

One look into her father's eyes and she knew immediately the man he was.

There are men who remain boys, those who mature, and a chosen few who embody the very essence of masculinity. Schmarya Boralevi was one of those few. There was something as unyielding as Gibraltar about him.

His intelligent pale blue eyes were at once both hard and soft, set into taut, scarred leathery skin that on close inspection saved him from mere handsomeness. His thick, curly hair had been bleached white from decades spent in the sun. The high ridges of his cheekbones could have been sculptured by an angry artist, and his towering body was thickly slabbed with muscles to offset the weakness of his wooden leg. And yet his eyelashes were thick and golden and his lips were sensuous, as though to soften the endurance-hardened man he had by necessity become.

He made her feel instantly safe and sheltered, somehow, as though he alone could keep the bad things of the world at bay.

He gazed back at her steadily. Finally he nodded and spoke. "My God, but you are very beautiful," he said in the kind of deep, resonant voice that belonged behind a pulpit. "You are just like your mother."

She smiled nervously and forced herself to walk the rest of the way toward him. Not once before in all her life had she felt this awkward or shy—not even when she had met O.T. Skolnik. "Hello, Father," she said guardedly, a lump blocking her throat. She held her hands out politely and he took them in his. She rose on tiptoe and kissed him on both cheeks.

He took a deep breath. "It is good to see you," he said softly, still holding on to her hands when she stepped back. "Let me take a good look at you."

She stood there silently, blushing under his gaze.

"It has not been easy for me to come here," he said, still looking down at her. "When I received your letter I was so ashamed of having abandoned you that I almost decided not to."

"And I was so nervous of meeting you," she confessed, holding his gaze, "that for the three days since I had it delivered to your hotel I haven't known whether to be here or go away and hide." She gave a low laugh. "It's silly, isn't it?"

"No, on the contrary. I can understand it." His voice cracked. "I should have never left you." His eyes were moist.

"But you came."

"Yes. I am glad."

She smiled. "So am I."

Inge advanced slowly from the living room and studied Schmarya over her bifocals. He and Tamara were still holding each other's hands. "You look well, Mr. Boralevi," she observed softly. "The years seem to have been kind."

He let go of Tamara's hand then and turned to Inge and frowned, clearly searching his memory for her.

"I am Inge Meier," she reminded him, holding out her hand. "I was the Danilovs' nurse."

"Ah, yes, I remember now," he said, taking her hand politely in his and giving a formal little bow over it. "Although you looked different then."

"It was twenty years ago. I was much younger."

"And you did not wear glasses then." He nodded. "You have been with Tamara all this time?"

Inge nodded. "We were all the family we thought we had. We escaped Russia together."

"And Senda? She is well?"

A veil seemed to slide down over Inge's eyes. "She died before she could leave Europe." She drew a deep breath and her voice quivered with thick emotion.

He was silent.

For a long moment they stood awkwardly in the foyer, staring at one another. Then Louis clapped his hands together. "Why don't we go into the living room?" he suggested. "I'm sure you all have a lot of catching up to do and it's more comfortable there."

Schmarya nodded and Tamara hooked an arm through his elbow. "This is a remarkable house," Schmarya said, looking around. "Why, this living room alone is much bigger than most houses! I have not seen anything quite like it."

"Neither have we," Tamara joked weakly. Then she looked concerned. "You are limping badly."

"I lost my leg in Russia." Schmarya shrugged. "I am used to it."

"I'm sorry. I didn't know."

"It was very long ago."

"I think this occasion calls for a celebration," Louis announced, going around to the bar. "Champagne?"

"That will be fine." Schmarya carefully lowered himself onto a couch and Tamara took a seat beside him. Crystal clinked in the background as Louis poured the drinks.

"After I got settled, I wrote many letters to you and your mother in Russia," Schmarya told Tamara.

She frowned. "As far as I know, we didn't receive any. But that's not surprising when you consider the state of things. I was too young to remember anything, but from what Inge told me, things in Russia were very confused. Everything broke down . . . communications, government, the postal system, transportation, food . . . everything. It took us a long time just to get here."

"That's not the reason you didn't get them," he said softly. "I wrote them, but . . . I never sent them. Part of me wanted to, but another part did not. I was young and brash in those days, and everything to me was black or white. At the time I left your mother and you, I blamed her for many things I now realize I probably had no right to blame her for at all." He stared at her intensely. "You are very like her, you know. But you are even more beautiful."

Tamara looked away suddenly.

"I am sorry. I did not mean to stare. Until I received your letter I had no idea that the great film star Tamara was my daughter." He smiled apologetically. "That will take some getting used to."

She was surprised. "Then you'd heard of me?"

He nodded. "You are famous even in Europe and Palestine. There are cinemas in every large city, and American films are considered the best. However, even in my wildest imaginings it never occurred to me to connect my daughter to the film star, despite the name. 'Tamara' is quite common in Russia; it would have been absurd to think it could be you. Or so I would have thought."

"Yes, it would have seemed rather unlikely," Tamara agreed.

Louis came to pass the glasses. "A toast," he said, remaining standing. "To old acquaintance, renewed acquaintance, and new acquaintance."

"I drink to that," Inge said.

"*Mazel tov!*" Schmarya added, leaning forward and clinking their glasses. The crystal rang true and clear and they sipped slowly.

"This tastes good," Schmarya said, savoring the smooth, bubbly taste on his tongue. "Not sweet, not sour . . . delicious. It is not often that I get the chance to drink champagne."

"It's Dom Perignon," Louis said, "the best. Thank God it's easier and cheaper to get again, now that Prohibition's finally over."

"Not that that ever stopped him," Tamara laughed. She explained for Schmarya's sake: "You wouldn't have believed our bootlegger's bills. Louie always said that next to your doctor, your bootlegger is the most important person in your life."

Over the next hours Tamara and Inge kept answering Schmarya's questions about St. Petersburg, Germany, and the movies. Tamara was surprised and pleased that he was so interested, and regaled him with anecdotes. Underneath her father's imposing, bigger-than-life physique and strength was a sensitive, gentle human. She could not imagine that this was the same man who had walked out on her mother and her.

They ate dinner outside on the football-field-size terrace overlooking the flat, twinkling expanse of Los Angeles below. Sitting there on the hilltop in the warm night air, Schmarya had the impression that he was floating in space, the lights stretching off into the distance on all three sides in that kind of grid-like pattern. Throughout the meal, he had a hard time keeping his eyes off his daughter. The flickering yellow light of the candles inside the hurricane shades seemed to heighten her bewitching features and animation.

"I've been talking nonstop about myself," Tamara said, leaning across the table toward him. "Now you must tell me about yourself. How did your speeches turn out? I wanted to attend one of the ones here, but it was impossible for me to do so. So I want to hear all about it. Did you get to see the President when you were in Washington?" She fixed her father with her famous gaze, her eyes glowing like liquid silver in the candlelight.

He shook his head. "I had to give the letter I wanted to hand-deliver to him to a sympathetic businessman who has connections with your White House." He gave a little self-effacing smile. "I would have liked to discuss our problems with him, but . . . well, it is not as though Jews are a major concern at the moment. I fear our struggle for true independence and freedom is not supported, let alone recognized, by any government with the exception of Great Britain. And Britain, unfortunately, treats us more like a colony than a territory bound for independence. Britain, our staunchest supporter and yet the greatest enemy of our freedom! It is ironic, no?" He fixed Tamara with a wry smile. "I will not pretend that I am not disappointed by President Roosevelt. A meeting with him might have proved very fruitful. However, we must not allow ourselves to think of what might have been."

She stared at him, her dessert spoon frozen halfway to her lips. "I don't understand it. President Roosevelt seems to be the champion of the underdog. I would surely have thought that if anyone would be supportive of your cause, it would be him, but since help from Roosevelt isn't forthcoming, isn't there some other way you can stir up support?" Tamara asked.

He sighed heavily. "I am trying. Believe me, I am trying. That is why I am here. To raise awareness and much-needed funds. But even many of the Jews consider me to be too . . . how do you say it? Inflexible? They like to believe you can accomplish everything quietly and with velvet gloves." He shook his head sadly. "If only that were true in this case."

"And in Palestine? Surely you are a hero to all the Jews there."

He made a disparaging gesture. "I am afraid I am not."

She stared at him. "I can't believe that! After all you're trying to do?"

"The people I represent are the minority even among the Jews in Palestine. For one thing, Jews comprise barely a fifth of our population. Of these, perhaps one in ten supports me. And of these, very few dare come out and do so publicly, for fear they will suffer Arab reprisals or that the British might use them to lay a trap for me." He smiled. "So you see, things are far more complicated than they seem."

"But you were successful in raising money and support while you were here?"

"Some, but hardly as much as we need. Everyone seems to like the idea of our creating a Jewish nation, but they do not wish to face the means needed to accomplish this. It all boils down to political pressure, money, and arms." He added wearily, "No nation was ever created without violence."

Tamara smiled. "Then you really are the swashbuckler the papers make you out to be!"

He laughed. "Like in your movies?"

"Well, something like that."

He sighed. "If only it was as simple as a movie. I hate violence, but only through guns and bullets can we survive. I do not mean we should go out and shoot Arabs. What I am saying is that when we are attacked, we must fight back. Even retaliate. In 1929, there was a massacre of Jews. We cannot let that happen again."

"But what about this fugitive business?" she asked. "Why should the British want you so badly? You're not doing anything wrong. Are you?"

"According to the existing British laws, yes, I am," Schmarya said. He smiled. "Morally, however, I believe I am doing the right thing." Seeing her startled expression, he said soothingly, "Believe me, I much prefer to live with my conscience, even if it means having a price on my head."

Tamara was shocked. "Do you? Have a price on your head?"

He laughed. "Not yet, but very soon I may well have."

There was a momentary silence around the table, which Louis broke. "But you believe Palestine has a real chance of becoming a Jewish nation?" he asked in a hushed tone. "You think it's more than just a pipe dream? That it will really happen?"

"It has to," Schmarya replied grimly. "Without it, the Jews of the world are doomed. With the situation in Europe being what it is, I cannot tell you how urgent it is that it happens very soon." He paused heavily and added softly, "Before it is too late."

"But why?" Inge asked. "What makes things now so much worse than they were at any other time? I thought there were always troubles for Jews."

Schmarya glanced around the table, holding each of their gazes for a full ten seconds. "You have all heard of Adolf Hitler, I presume?"

"Charlie Chaplin," Inge laughed. "*The Little Tramp*! He looks just like Chaplin."

Louis and Tamara laughed along with her.

"Do not laugh." Schmarya's face was grave. "There is nothing at all comic about the German Führer. No matter how ridiculous he may seem to you, the peoples of the world would be well advised to take him seriously. Do you not realize that the man is probably the greatest danger the twentieth century will have to face?"

"That clown!" Inge scoffed. "You cannot be serious!" She stared at Schmarya.

He nodded. "I am serious. If you know what is good for you, then you and the rest of the world had best begin to change your views of him before it is too late. Soon he will be unstoppable. Since he took office in January of last year, he has been given dictatorial power. Do you have any idea what that means? He now controls everything in Germany." His cheeks tightened and his eyes flashed. "*Everything*. And he has lost no time in consolidating that power. He has outlawed and disbanded all opposing political parties. Strikes have been banned. Everything, including culture and religion, has been brought under the aegis of the government." His voice dropped. "And Jews are disappearing every day. We must find out what is happening to them. If he is not stopped, more and more Jews will simply disappear."

A thin shiver, like a blade of fine steel, traced its way down Tamara's spine. Her voice was trembling. "He must be mad!" she whispered.

"Don't you think you're blowing Hitler slightly out of proportion?" Louis asked. "Surely you're giving a megalomaniac more credit than he's due."

"No," Schamrya said definitely. "If anything, even I am not taking his threats seriously enough. At first I did not want to believe what I was hearing either, but the stories I heard from the immigrants from Germany were all the same. Throughout Germany, entire Jewish families are rounded up and disappear."

Louis was silent.

"You have only to read *Mein Kampf*, Hitler's book, in which he outlined all his twisted beliefs and grievances," Schmarya said. "If it is up to him—and now that he is dictator, it may very well be—then there will not be a single Jew left alive on this planet. That is one reason—the most important reason—for the creation of a Jewish nation. Our people will be in desperate need of sanctuary. Germany is no longer safe for them. It will be worse than Russia ever was. There will be war as Hitler seeks to expand Germany, and everywhere the Nazis go, the Jews will disappear."

"You're frightening me," Tamara whispered.

"And well you should be frightened. Really. I am not exaggerating. Hitler intends to take over the world and kill off everyone who is not Nordic and blue-eyed and blond-haired. Aryan, at least."

"But that's . . . preposterous!" Tamara sputtered. "No one can do that!"

"If anyone can, it will be Hitler. And believe me, he will try."

Abruptly Tamara pushed back her chair and rose to her feet. "It seems to have gotten chilly suddenly," she said, rubbing her forearms briskly. "I suggest we have our after-dinner drinks indoors."

"If you do not mind, I will say good night and prepare for bed," Inge said, glancing at her wristwatch. "For me, it is far past my bedtime." She smiled at Schmarya and took his hands. "I am glad you have come," she said, looking directly up into his eyes. "You are a nice, brave man. Senda loved you, you know. Everything she did, she did because of that. I think now, if she were alive, she would be very proud of you."

"I should be going soon also," Schmarya said after Inge had left. "Tomorrow we take the train back to New York, and I still have to pack." He saw the protest in Tamara's eyes and smiled. "Well, perhaps I can stay a little longer. But, I do not wish to impose."

"I know that." Tamara grinned and squeezed Schmarya's arm. Then she took a deep breath. "You know, Inge was right."

He looked puzzled. "About what?"

"You *are* a very nice man. And I'm proud of you also."

He looked suddenly embarrassed, and then Louis asked, "Demitasse or brandy?"

"Brandy," Schmarya said quickly. "It is rare where I come from, and I might as well take advantage of civilization."

Louis splashed some Napoleon brandy into giant snifters and they sipped at them on the soft white leather chairs grouped around the circular fireplace with its copper hood and flue rising two stories to the glass-domed roof.

"Now tell me about Palestine," Tamara said, sitting up straight. "I want to know what it is about it that you love so much, that keeps you going and makes all the battles and hiding out, the struggles to survive . . . *everything*, so worthwhile."

"Palestine," Schmarya said softly, a faraway look in his eyes, "yes, I will tell you about the Promised Land. It is everything God promised it would be, and more."

Tamara was entranced, and even Louis had fallen under the spell. While Schmarya had spoken, they sat as though hypnotized, forgetting where they were. Through the sheer power of words, he had transported them thousands of miles eastward and into the past, centuries from the luxurious estate in Los Angeles to the ancient land of Deborah and Solomon and Jezebel and Elijah.

"I had no idea all that still existed!" Tamara cried when he stopped. "I always thought it was something in history books and the Bible. But you make it sound so real!"

"Ah, then you begin to understand," Schmarya said, nodding with satisfaction before continuing to sing the praises of his adopted land.

The hours slipped slyly by, and all too soon the time came for him to leave. It was well past midnight.

"I fear I really must leave now," Schmarya said, getting to his feet. "Let me call for a taxi."

"No," Tamara said adamantly. "Louis and I will drive you back to your hotel."

"But you must be tired. Surely you get up early."

"He's right, you know," Louis said. "You've got a makeup

call at six-thirty, which means you won't get more than four-and-a-half hours' sleep. You know how the camera picks up the slightest puffiness from lack of sleep. I don't have to be on the set until eight. You go on up to bed and I'll drive Schmarya downtown."

Tamara hesitated.

"Please," Schmarya said. He smiled slightly. "It would make me feel better."

After a moment she nodded. "In that case, how can I refuse?"

"Good." Schmarya smiled, and it occurred to Tamara that this was the first time in her memory that she'd had an opportunity to obey her father.

"I'll go get the car," Louis said, heading toward the foyer. "When I honk, meet me up front."

They watched him leave, and once he was gone, Tamara turned to her father. "I'm glad we found each other after all these years," she said warmly. She stared into his eyes. "My only regret is that we didn't have more time together."

"Mine also," he said. "You see how easy it is to get greedy?" He looked at her silently for a moment. "I should be grateful. After the way I ran out on you and your mother, I do not deserve the good fortune of having found my daughter again."

"I'm sure it wasn't all your fault. It can't have been."

"It was." He frowned to himself. "I was a brash young fool in those days, always out to change the world."

"Which you're still trying to do," she pointed out, but he did not laugh.

"Sometimes it seems remarkable that things have turned out as well as they have. It proves that life is not all bad."

"It doesn't do anyone any good for you to keep whipping yourself for something that happened so long ago," she said gently. "You're a fine man, in many ways much finer than I imagined my father ever to be."

Something like surprise showed in his eyes.

"You've even awakened me to the selfish life I've been leading. Here you are, doing so much for our people, for the world, and all I've been doing is thinking of myself. I'm rather ashamed. I never expected you to have such an impact on me. You seem to have a gift for helping others."

"You make films. You bring enjoyment to people all over the world. That too is a gift."

"Don't humor me. It's not the same thing, and you know it." She lowered her eyes. "I . . . I know I can't do much to help the cause you're fighting for. You see, my hands are tied. O.T.—he's the head of the studio—would have a fit if I opened my mouth and said anything political." She gave a low laugh but grimaced rather than smiled. "My contract specifically forbids me from making any public appearances and speeches except those sanctioned by the studio. And then they tell me what I can and cannot say. I suppose they all think I'm a child who needs constant baby-sitting." She sighed. "I wish I could do more to help, but . . . well, I want you to have this."

Almost furtively she pressed a folded piece of pink paper into his hand.

He looked down at it. "What is this?"

She made a negligible gesture. "Oh, just a little something to have made your tour a little more worthwhile. I know money can never take the place of personal involvement, but it must be necessary if you've had to come here on a fund-raising tour."

"You know you do not need to do this," he said quietly.

She raised her hand as though challenging him. "Oh yes I do. It's the only way I know of to help. Take it. Please," she urged. "There are no strings attached. Spend it on whatever you think is necessary, I don't care what. I left the bearer line blank since I didn't know how you would want it made out."

Slowly he unfolded the check and looked down at it. His eyebrows rose. "Twenty thousand dollars!" He met her gaze and shook his head. "This is out of the question. I cannot possibly accept this."

"I don't expect you to." She looked him straight in the eye. "I'm not giving it to you. I'm giving it to your cause, to help fight for a Jewish nation." She closed his fingers around the check. "Stop worrying, for heaven's sake, and just take it in the spirit it was given."

"Do you realize that this is the largest contribution we have received on the entire tour so far? You are certain you can afford it?"

"Look around you," she said lightly, gesturing at the room. "What does it look like?"

She was glad he did not reply to that. The twenty thousand was everything she had managed to tuck away during the past five years from her astronomical salary—an astronomical salary that seemed to vaporize as soon as she was paid. It was her secret emergency fund. A pathetic hoard, considering she'd earned close to a quarter of a million dollars and this was all she had to show for it.

From outside they could hear Louis honking the car horn,

and they both glanced toward the door. He leaned down and held her tightly as he kissed her cheek. "Did I tell you you have a very nice husband?" he said.

"No, but you didn't have to. I know."

"You will tell Inge for me that I enjoyed seeing her again?"

She nodded. "And I'll write often to the address you gave me," she promised.

"Do not be disappointed by the mail. Letter service is slow and sporadic in Palestine," he warned. "Often mail gets lost."

"Then I just may have to come in person."

"I would like that. If you do, and you write when you are coming and receive no letter from me in reply, do not worry. Come anyway and stay at the Rehot Dan Hotel in Tel Aviv. Check in under the name of Sarah Bernhardt."

"Sarah Bernhardt!" She laughed. "You've got to be joking!"

He permitted himself a slight smile. "It sounds rather obvious, but only to us. It will be our own private code, and no one else will suspect that it is a message to me." He smoothed her hair. "Sarah Bernhardt shall be a private joke between us."

"Sarah Bernhardt." She nodded solemnly.

"Then, after you check in, place a personal advertisement in the newspapers. It should read, 'U.S. passport lost vicinity Jericho. Contact Holy Land Pilgrimage Tours.' Do not add anything else. Then wait at the hotel until someone gets in touch with you. It may be me or someone else, and it could take several days, so try to be patient."

"It all sounds rather mysterious, like something worthy of Mata Hari. Are you sure all this subterfuge is necessary?"

"As long as I am committed to fight for a Jewish homeland, yes, I think it is."

" 'U.S. passport lost vicinity Jericho,' " she repeated. " 'Contact Holy Land Pilgrimage Tours.' I'll be able to remember that easily enough."

"Good, but it is all written down with the address I left you."

Louis honked again and Schmarya embraced her for one last time, enfolding her in the comforting paternal warmth of his arms.

"You'll see," she vowed with quiet conviction, "I'm going to visit you in Palestine. It might even be sooner than you think."

"Is Señor Harriman, señora," Esperanza announced from the door. "The man from the bank."

"Well, don't just stand there," Tamara said irritably. "Send him in."

Esperanza fixed her with a dark look. "Sí, señora," she said with resignation, and flapped back out, then led Clifford Harriman into the room and shut the door from outside.

"Miss Tamara," Harriman said, crossing the expanse of white carpeting to where Tamara was standing. "I hope I am not inconveniencing you."

"Not at all, Mr. Harriman. It's a pleasure to see you," she lied in a pleasant tone, holding out her hand for him to shake. His handshake was light and bony, almost brittle. She had the feeling that if she gripped him too hard, she would hear his bones breaking. "Please, won't you take a seat?" She waited until he put down his briefcase and was seated. "Can I get you a drink?"

"No, no, that isn't necessary." Harriman shook his head and the tremendous wattle at his neck trembled. He looked, Tamara thought, rather like a particularly bony, featherless, and ancient turkey. Even his sparse white hair looked like remnants of an imperfect plucking. But no turkey dressed in such a flawlessly tailored dark gray suit complete with white shirt, waistcoat, dark tie, and what was an obviously inherited and very fine antique gold watch.

"You wished to see me," Tamara said smoothly, tucking her skirt under her buttocks and taking a seat opposite him. She folded her hands in her lap and sat erect, her face composed in a clear, calm expression which gave no hint of the uneasiness she felt roiling around inside her. Ever since he had telephoned for an appointment two days previously, she had had the nagging feeling that something was amiss. Why else would the banker have asked to see her—alone? She had hardly ever dealt with him. "As a rule, my husband takes care of our finances, Mr. Harriman. Quite frankly, you should be speaking with him."

Harriman nodded at her from across the huge expanse of glass and chrome. "I have been dealing with Mr. Ziolko for some years now, but I felt it would be to your advantage to get you personally involved in your finances. It is no secret that your income is the larger of the two. Therefore, you have the most to lose."

She stared at him in confusion. There was a nervous tic in his left eye, and his almost translucent eyelid fluttered with tiny, rapid jerks, like a butterfly's wing. "Yes?" she said cautiously, her anxiety growing.

Harriman wasn't one to mince words or beat around the bush. He cupped a liver-spotted hand in front of his mouth, coughed discreetly, and came right to the point. "We at New West Bank are quite concerned about your assets, Miss Tamara. Or, I should say, your lack of them. Since the end of last year, all your accounts, and your husband's, have been consistently overdrawn. Also, it pains me to have to tell you this, but this is the second month in a row that your mortgage payments have . . . er . . ." He coughed again. ". . . have been insufficiently covered by the required funds."

She stared at him. "You mean the . . . the mortgage checks bounced?" she asked incredulously.

He nodded. "We covered them, but yes, they did."

"I . . . I had no idea," she said shakily, nervously reaching for a cigarette from the square cut-crystal box on the coffee table. She picked up a silver lighter and lit it with trembling hands. It was true. Long ago, she'd allowed Louis to take all their combined financial matters into his hands, and although they always seemed short of ready cash and lived from one day to the next, running up mountainous bills, she hadn't been aware that things were quite this bad. Perhaps Harriman was right. It might indeed be high time for her to get involved.

"Please, Mr. Harriman," she said softly, "don't spare me anything. I would appreciate it if you would put all the cards out on the table."

His look was one of growing respect. "Very well, I will be quite frank," he said, and she braced herself for the worst. "Between your income and your husband's, you are running into debt at slightly more than two thousand dollars each month. As of yesterday, you owed the bank just over sixty thousand dollars. That includes both secured and unsecured loans, but does *not* include the overdrafts."

"That much!" she exclaimed, staring directly at him.

"That much," he agreed, "with interest adding to the burden each day."

"But how could this happen?"

"I hope you do not think that I am speaking out of line, but you have expensive tastes, Miss Tamara. You have been living beyond your means for many years."

She nodded miserably. "What do you suggest I do?"

"Perhaps if you . . ." He coughed delicately again. "I do not know how to say this, Miss Tamara. You must believe me when I say I find it distasteful in the extreme to have to mention it."

She raised her chin. "Please say what is on your mind, Mr. Harriman."

He took a deep breath. "The major part of your problem

seems to stem from the power of attorney you gave your husband."

"Power of attorney? What power of attorney?" She searched her mind and then it came to her in a blinding flash. "But that was years ago!"

He inclined his head. "Yes, but it is still in effect. However, if you were to stop it, you might be able to gain better control of your own income, which is quite . . . well, shall we say, substantial?"

"But I don't see how that in itself would help any," she said. "Surely the only way to get things back on track and dig ourselves out of debt is to drastically cut back on our expenses."

"Then you haven't been going through your monthly statements and canceled checks, I take it?"

"N-no," she said carefully. "My husband has been doing all that. Is there some reason why I should?"

He reached for his briefcase, swung it onto his lap, and unlatched it. He took out a thin sheaf of papers that had been stapled together. "If you will be so kind as to glance through these . . . on the left of each you will find the check number, next to that the date it was written, then the payee, and finally the amount. The checks have been paid. Incidentally, they are on your checking account and were signed by your husband—which is legal, since he has your power of attorney." He passed them to her and she quickly glanced through them. Hundreds of dollars at a time, sometimes thousands, had been made out to a single payee. She let the papers fall to her lap and looked at him. "I . . . I don't understand. Could you explain this to me?"

He nodded. "Those checks were all made out to Persiani Enterprises."

"Yes, I can see that. But what is Persiani Enterprises?"

"You do not know, then."

"Know what? Please enlighten me."

"Persiani Enterprises is a local construction firm owned by one Carmine Persiani, who came to this city from New York some fifteen years ago."

"Then they must be payments still outstanding from building this house."

"No, Miss Tamara," he said softly. "I see that you do not understand. Persiani Enterprises is a well-known front. Oh, the construction firm exists, no doubt about it, but that is not where Carmine Persiani is said to earn his money. The construction firm is probably just a way of hiding illegal funds."

"I beg your pardon?"

"To put it bluntly, Persiani is an extremely unsavory man. He is suspected of being part of the underworld. Rumor has it that he runs all the illegal gambling in this town."

He watched the color drain from her face.

"Gambling? I don't understand! Louie doesn't gamble."

"Then how do you account for these checks?" he asked quietly.

She sat there completely devastated.

Louis was a secret gambler. Without her ever having suspected it, he had been gambling their hard-earned money away, pushing them further and further into debt. But when? And where?

She took a deep breath, forced herself to rally her strength, and pasted on a smile she did not feel. She rose to her feet in a studied, fluid motion. "I appreciate your having informed me, Mr. Harriman," she said with dignity, holding out her hand. "I know it cannot have been easy for you. Now, if there's nothing else . . ."

He hung back and lowered his eyes. "Well, there is one thing. Could I . . . My wife's sister . . ." he explained in disjointed embarrassment. "She is out here from Pittsburgh. It's her first visit and she asked if I knew . . . any film stars. Well . . . an autographed picture?"

A fan's request for an autograph was something Tamara was eminently equipped to deal with. She summoned her most dazzling smile. "Of course, Mr. Harriman," she said smoothly. "I'll have one delivered to the bank first thing in the morning."

"Her name is Charlotte. If you could . . . you know, write a little message for Charlotte . . ."

"It's as good as done. Esperanza will show you out."

As soon as he was gone, she sank numbly back down onto the couch, leaned her head back on the cushions, and stared blankly up at the glass-domed ceiling. Her entire body was shaking and she was physically and emotionally drained. She knew that she had no choice. She would have to face Louis about the gambling, and they would have to find a way for him to stop it. Such a financial drain could not continue. God only knew what other debts—to friends or merchants—he had run up on top of what they owed the bank. There was really no excuse for their being financially strapped all the time. None.

She shut her eyes. If only there was some miraculous way she could wish away the unpleasant scene she knew was going to result from all this.

But there could be no avoiding the issue. Like it or not, she had to face it and do something about it.

She sighed heavily.

Why, she asked herself, hadn't she shown any interest in their finances? And how could he have found the time for gambling? Above all, how could she have been so blind?

There were so many questions that needed answering. Oh, Louie, Louie, she prayed. Please prove to me that Clifford Harriman is wrong. But, she feared, too much evidence pointed to Harriman's suspicions being true.

"Señora."

Startled, Tamara opened her eyes and looked up. Esperanza was standing in the doorway again. Tamara felt an irrational surge of anger. The woman had the amazing ability, not unlike a cat's, to sneak up on you without making a sound. "What is it now, Esperanza?" she asked wearily.

"Miss Rice. She here to see you."

Tamara jerked upright as though she'd been electrocuted. "Oh, my God!" she exclaimed, slapping her forehead with the palm of her hand.

With all her worrying about Clifford Harriman's visit, she'd completely forgotten that Marilee Rice, the scourge of the stars, the same woman who had written the scathing article about the house for *Screen Story* several years ago, had been scheduled to interview her over tea again this afternoon. She felt a heaviness steal over her. She was in no mood to face Marilee. Certainly not now. There were enough problems to occupy her.

Still, wheedling out of it at this point would only raise the gossip's ire, which was something she didn't want. Marilee Rice had become more powerful than ever. For the last year, as her column continued to appear in newspapers and magazines cross-country, she had begun hosting her own weekly syndicated radio show as well. According to surveys, as many people tuned in to her *Hollywood Talk* as listened to FDR's "Fireside Chats." More than ever, Marilee Rice was a woman to be reckoned with. There was really no way Tamara could avoid the interview. Not this late. And she would have to be on her toes—the gossip didn't miss a trick.

Like a shark, if she smelled blood she closed in for the kill.

"Give me a minute," she told Esperanza. "Then show her in."

"*Darling!*"

The voice was a high trill.

The woman it belonged to came sweeping dramatically in

behind it, blowing noisy kisses past Tamara's cheeks. "Really, how well you look *today*," Marilee purred, emphasizing the present as she took a step backward and smiled, showing two rows of razor-sharp teeth.

Tamara squared her shoulders as though to do battle. She hated interviews. She hated Marilee. Careful, she cautioned herself. Simmer down and don't rise to the bait. Be kissy-kissy, even catty, but keep it all on those arch feminine terms.

"You look splendid yourself!" Tamara lied effusively, hooking her arm through Marilee's and leading her visitor outside to the sunny terrace.

In truth, there was no way Marilee could look anything remotely splendid. Her figure could have been drawn by a six-year-old: she was a stick figure with no breasts, buttocks, or curves. Despite its tailoring and cut, her exquisite silk dress, printed with magnified African violets, seemed to hang as though from a scarecrow, but she'd dressed carefully as always nonetheless: matching shoes on her pigeon-toed feet and one of her signature hats, for which she was justly famous, towering on her head. Marilee's face was also singularly unattractive and rather mannish, with a long straight nose and a lantern jaw. In a pathetic attempt at beautification, violet eye shadow shone thickly above her eyelids, and her mouth and nails were gashes of bright vermilion. One would have expected her voice to be deep and mannish as well, but it was high-pitched and feminine, each drawn-out vowel sugar-coated in that special way only true Southern ladies of breeding can confect the language.

Her pale eyes were sharp and alert—one could almost hear them click like a camera shutter.

Tamara steered her past the giant pool shaped like a five-pointed star, toward two cotton-upholstered easy chairs under a deep blue linen parasol. "Wasn't that Clifford Harriman, the banker, I saw pulling out just as I drove up?" Marilee asked in a honeyed, innocent voice.

Damn the woman. "Yes," Tamara said, "that was Mr. Harriman you saw. He's such a nice gentleman, isn't he? Imagine him taking the trouble to drive all the way up here just to give me some banking advice."

"Well, it must have been about saving," Marilee said archly, "since I don't think either you or Louis need any advice on how to spend."

The actress in Tamara knew a casual laugh was called for, and she gave it her all. "You do get away with saying the most outrageous things, Marilee."

"That's because everyone is frightened of me." Marilee took a seat, kicked off her shoes, and dug into her handbag for a notepad and pencil. She lifted an eyebrow archly. "Are *you* frightened of me, my dear?" she asked, holding Tamara's gaze.

"No, not frightened," Tamara said thoughtfully. "I respect you."

"They're often one and the same," Marilee said, deftly depositing a well-planted barb. "Now, before we begin . . . you probably know that my radio show has caught on extremely well?"

Tamara nodded. "I read somewhere that even FDR has been known to listen."

"Oh, that rumor." Marilee waved a deprecating hand. "I wouldn't go so far as to say that, but it *is* popular, and I *am* rather pleased with it. There's a kind of magic about listening to a star that people don't get just by reading about them. Last week I had Elsa Lanchester on, and the week before, Ruby Keeler. She even tap-danced in front of the microphone. It was a huge success."

Tamara nodded. "I listened to that one."

"It's done live, of course, which makes logistics a little difficult sometimes. Anyway"—Marilee smiled brightly—"I would like to have you on next week, dear. What do you say to that?"

"Me?" Tamara looked astonished. "I'd have to check with O.T. first, of course, but if he's amenable—"

"Oh, he is. I've already asked him."

Tamara looked at her in surprise. "He didn't tell me."

Marilee laughed, delighted to have scored one over Tamara. Then she got serious. "He agrees with me that this is a good time for the country to hear the real you. In fact, he was the one who called me about it."

Tamara looked thoughtful. "Do you know something you're not telling me?"

"Who, me?" Marilee asked innocently, placing a hand over her heart and trilling a laugh.

Esperanza flapped toward them and came to a stop beside the parasol. She looked at Tamara expressionlessly.

"Would you like a drink?" Tamara asked. "I'm having iced tea without sugar."

Marilee made a face. "How can you bear to drink that? Tell you what, I'd just looooove a mint julep. That is, if you have the makings."

"Of course we do. And Roberto's a whiz at bartending." Tamara smiled at the maid. "Esperanza, would you be so kind as to bring Miss Rice a mint julep? And a tall glass of iced tea for me? Lemon on the side, as usual."

"Sí, señora." Esperanza nodded. "I bring soon. Señora?"

"Yes, Esperanza?"

"The señor, he back. He ask see you."

For an instant Tamara shut her eyes. First she'd had to face the banker, then Marilee, and now Louis. It seemed as if the day itself were conspiring against her. She smiled apologetically at Marilee. "I'd better see what Louis wants. I really am sorry. Could you excuse me for a minute? I won't be long."

"Take your time," Marilee said magnanimously. "I'm in no rush. I've kept the entire afternoon open for you."

Tamara managed not to show her chagrin and hurried into the house.

She found Louis standing in the shade in front of the garages, his arms crossed, grinning like a Cheshire cat. A set of keys dangled from his fingers. He turned his head slowly, and following his gaze, Tamara let out a gasp.

There was a new car in the driveway—a huge Packard convertible, all streamlined curves and white lacquer outside and tawny fragrant calfskin inside—crisscrossed with a foot-wide white satin ribbon.

"What's this?" Tamara whispered.

"Yours," Louis said, grinning wider.

She felt a surge of elation. "The Oscar!" she cried, jumping up and down. "Don't tell me! *Fire and Blood* has been nominated!"

He picked her up and whirled her around in the air. "They say third time's a charm, princess. I just found out." He put her down and handed her the car keys.

"Louie . . ." She pushed herself away from him and frowned at the car.

He gave her a strange look. "Don't tell me you don't like the car?"

"No, no, of course I like it. It's a beauty."

"Then what's the matter?"

She turned to him, a pleading expression on her face. "Please, Louie, try to understand. Now's not the time for us to buy a new car."

"It's as good a time as any. Besides, we've made it a tradition. Remember, each time you're nominated for an Oscar, you get a new white convertible. And if you *win* the Oscar you get a brand-new Rolls."

"Louie."

Something in her voice stopped him and his grin faded.

She saw his disappointment and reached up to his neck, consoling him with an affectionate touch. "It's not that I don't appreciate it, Louie," she said softly. "It's just . . . we *have* to cut back. I just found out that there's no other choice."

"What did you find out?" he asked in a voice devoid of inflection.

She could see that he was starting to get angry. She could always tell when he got that stony look. "I can't talk about it now, Marilee's interviewing me and I have to get back to her. We'll talk later. Over dinner."

He gestured toward the car. "Then you're sure you don't want it."

She ran her fingertips lightly across the curvaceous fender. The metal felt sun-warmed. How curiously tempting a concoction of metal could be, she was thinking. Then she quickly snatched her hand away and thrust the keys at Louis. She shook her head. "We can't," she said quietly. "Please try to understand." She attempted a weak smile. "I'll always remember this car, since you went to the trouble to get it. But we can't keep it."

He turned away and she took his arm and turned him to face her.

"It's the thought that counts, Louie. Now please take it back." She rose on tiptoe and brushed a kiss against his cheek, but his stony expression didn't change.

"Have it your way," he said through tight lips, and tossed the keys on the car seat.

Tamara took a deep breath. "I know you're upset with me, and if the circumstances didn't warrant it, I wouldn't ask you to do this."

"Sure, I'll drive it back to the dealer. What the hell?" He began to tug at the wide satin ribbon. "My wife tells me to jump, I jump."

She flinched and stood there wordlessly, watching, hating herself for having burst his bubble, knowing how much he enjoyed giving her gifts. But there was no way they could afford a new car now. Not after what Clifford Harriman had told her. She wished there was something more she could say, some way to penetrate Louis' quiet anger, but there wasn't time. Tonight would come soon enough.

Sighing softly, she went back inside and got a pair of dark glasses. She slipped them on her nose. She should have thought of them earlier. At least she would be able to let her guard down somewhat, since Marilee surely didn't have X-ray vision.

As she walked back out to the terrace, Tamara could faintly hear the slam of a car door and the screeching of tires. The car was going back to the dealer. For a moment she lingered under the shady loggia, seeking strength and calm by inhaling deeply. It was a trick Louis had taught her when she'd first begun to act. Deep breaths. Filling the lungs completely, then letting the air out very slowly. One . . . Two . . . Three . . . There. She concentrated on her delicate facial muscles, relaxing them, and they seemed to change under the skin, creating a carefree expression. For the moment, at least, the unhappiness of the scene with Louis was shoved to the recesses of her mind. Armed with a serene expression, she could face Marilee again.

"Is everything all right on the home front?" The columnist asked Tamara as she sat back down.

"Yes, fine."

"Esperanza brought us the drinks. Yours is right there, beside your chair. You know, she's really quite a sweet, uncomplicated girl once you dig under that inscrutable passiveness of hers. We had a nice little chat."

Oh-oh, Tamara thought, her internal antennae going to full alert. "Did you learn anything interesting?"

"Actually, not as much as I would have liked." Marilee smiled.

Tamara reached for her glass of iced tea and took a sip. It was too strong and extremely bitter, and she hid her grimace. "You've been holding out on me, Marilee," she chided almost lazily as she put the glass down. "Why didn't you mention my Oscar nomination?"

"You heard?"

Tamara nodded. "Louie just got through telling me." She paused and smiled sweetly. "So that's why you want me on your show. As an Oscar nominee."

"Well, yes," Marilee admitted. "But more correctly, that's why O.T. wants you to do it. It's a great way to publicize the picture. Now . . ." She consulted her notes, poised her poison pencil, and looked Tamara squarely in the eye. "*Fire and Blood* is your first Technicolor movie. What did you think about seeing yourself in color for the very first time?"

The questions continued to come: "I know your husband directs all your films, but if he wasn't around, who would be your choice of director? . . . You always dress in white or pale colors. Tell me, is it your own style or did the studio decide it for you? . . . Which did you prefer to kiss, Clark Gable or Errol Flynn? . . . Do you really think Roosevelt is doing a good job in running this country?"

Tamara listened and thought quickly and replied as honestly as the questions allowed. They ranged from films to politics, an area O.T. had had her suitably tutored in from time to time so she could give concise middle-of-the-road views that would offend the least number of her fans. The barrage of questions was unrelenting, and when Esperanza came unhurriedly toward them in that flatfooted way of hers, Tamara actually welcomed the interruption.

Esperanza's face was as impassive as always. "There a policeman here to see you, señora."

"A *policeman*?" Tamara whipped off her sunglasses and frowned up at her. "Did he say what he wants?"

"No, señora." Esperanza shrugged. "He no tell me."

"I'd better see to this right away," Tamara told Marilee. "I'm sorry. Today it seems like we're doomed to be constantly interrupted. I'll be right back."

Marilee nodded and watched Tamara hurrying off. She was about to sit back, when her reporter's instinct made her get up and follow at a discreet distance.

Tamara found one of L.A.'s uniformed finest waiting just inside the sliding terrace doors, blue cap in hand. "You wished to see me?" she asked.

"Yes, ma'am. I'm Officer West of the LAPD. Are you the owner of a white Packard convertible?"

It was then that her heart began to beat like a sledgehammer on an anvil, but she forced herself to remain calm. "No . . . I mean, yes. I . . . I suppose so. You see, my husband just bought me one earlier today, and I didn't want it. He's gone to return it."

His face still looked straight at her, but his eyes shifted to the side, as though he was afraid to meet her gaze head-on. "I'm afraid there's been an accident."

She clutched his arm. "No!"

"I'm sorry, ma'am. According to eyewitness reports, there was the sound of a blowout just before a curve, and then the driver apparently lost control. The car overshot the road and . . . plunged down into the canyon."

"He's dead!" she screamed, her eyes widening in horror. "Oh, my God, he's dead!" She clapped her hands over her ears and started to scream.

And then the world seemed to screech and roar and tilt, whirling out of control and blasting her straight off the universe. Her eyes rolled and fluttered, and then her body went limp. Even before Officer West caught her and lowered her gently to the floor, Marilee Rice was dashing to her car. She knew a scoop when she heard one.

Louis' funeral was lavish. O.T. had put his chauffeured limousine at Tamara's disposal and rode to the synagogue with her and Inge. Once there, they were treated to a shock. Morbid curiosity seekers lined both sides of the street behind hastily erected police barricades; the press and hundreds of fans had turned out to catch a glimpse of the Hollywood notables come to pay their last respects. There was a carnival atmosphere in the air. An ice-cream vendor was doing a brisk business, and hand-held placards bobbed obscenely up and down, reading WE LOVE YOU, TAMARA or WE WEEP WITH YOU, and one young man was frantically waving one which read HOW ABOUT ME? The moment Tamara was helped out of the car, a single whisper flashed from person to person: "Tamara." Shutters started clicking and newsreel cameras rolled. And then the chant began: "Ta-ma-RA. Ta-ma-RA."

Reporters started shouting questions, and the crowd thrust the barricades aside, surging forward despite the phalanx of policemen trying to hold them back. One crazed woman managed to reach Tamara on the synagogue steps, waving an autograph book in front of her veiled face. While a policeman dragged the woman away, O.T. and Inge quickly hustled Tamara inside.

The synagogue was filled to overflowing. The film colony was a tight-knit community, and Louis had known almost everyone in it. Many of his friends and acquaintances, from studio heads on down to the grips, had shown up to pay their last respects. The floral tributes were mountainous, the service mercifully short, the eulogy, delivered by O.T., warm and inspiring. The casket was closed, so Tamara could take no comfort from seeing her loved one in peaceful, if cosmetic, repose, could kiss no chill lips good-bye before sending him on his final journey. There was nothing she could draw comfort from, not even the hope that death had been instantaneous. Louis had, in all likelihood, been aware of the car's plunge for several horrible seconds before it crashed into the canyon bed. She could only pray that death had then been immediate. The alternative was too gruesome to imagine. Louis had been pinned behind the steering wheel of the Packard and burned beyond recognition when the gas tank exploded.

Afterward, Tamara didn't know how she had managed to get through the ordeal, the single worst thing that had ever happened to her. Blessedly, most of it was a blur—she was still in a state of numb shock. Everyone remarked upon how dignified she was, how she kept herself in rigid control. In truth, she was closer to catatonia than life, and she simply let Inge lead her around like a zombie. All she had to do, really, was put one foot in front of the other. That was the only effort required of her.

It was at the cemetery plot, a stone's throw from Valentino's crypt, that the other nightmare occurred. As Louis' coffin was about to be lowered into the ground, Zelda Ziolko let out a shriek and rushed forward, flinging herself across it. "Louieee," she sobbed, beating her fists on her son's coffin. "Louieeee . . . don't you leave me here, Louieee . . ."

Friends of Zelda's who had accompanied her tried to pry her loose and managed to pull her back. It was then that Zelda pointed an accusing finger at Tamara. "You, you no-good bitch!" Zelda shrieked crazily. "*You* killed him! You killed my *bubbale*! I curse you, you bitch! May you never rest in peace!"

Inge swiftly placed herself between Zelda and Tamara, and then Zelda's friends pulled the hysterical woman back and hustled her off to a waiting limousine, her wails and accusations rupturing the otherwise dignified silence of the ceremony.

"Come, we must go," Inge said finally in a trembling voice that made it evident just how grief-stricken she was. She gestured at two workmen standing at a discreet distance, leaning on their shovels and smoking. "The gravediggers are waiting." Tears rolled down from her cornflower-blue eyes as she took Tamara's arm shakily and tried to steer her away. "It is all over now."

Tamara trembled slightly, her veil swaying in front of her face. "No, it's not over," she whispered in a thin, reedy voice. "Death is with you always. A part of me has died along with Louie."

When they arrived back at Tamahawk, they discovered that there would be no peace there either. Two men were waiting for Tamara in the living room. They rose to their feet as one the moment she entered.

"Mrs. Ziolko?" the taller of the two said, stepping forward. She lifted her veil slowly and frowned blankly at him, her puffy red eyes confused. "Who are you?" she asked in a shrill voice. "Who let you in? Get out this instant before I call the police!"

The man was undeterred. "I am David Fleischer and this is my associate Alan Salzberg," he said. "We are with the firm of Kasindorf, Steinberg, Rinaldi, and Fleischer, attorneys for Mrs. Zelda Ziolko."

"What does she have to do with you trespassing in my house?"

Fleischer held up a sheaf of folded documents. "We're sorry, Mrs. Ziolko, but we must ask you to vacate this house at once."

"What!" Tamara started to rush forward, and almost leapt at him, but Inge clung to her arm and held her back.

"According to a prenuptial agreement we prepared and you signed, you have voluntarily forfeited all claims to the estate of Louis Ziolko."

"Get out!" she whispered. "This is my house. I've been paying the mortgage on it! Get out! Get out! Get out!"

"According to the deed, both the house and the property are in Mr. Ziolko's name." He stepped forward and thrust the papers at her. She refused to hold them, and let them drop to the floor. "Pending a full investigation, we must insist that you do not remove anything except your personal clothes."

Tamara squirmed out of Inge's grip and raised her taloned hands threateningly. "Get out of my house!" she screamed, rushing at the lawyer. "Out! *Out!*"

The two lawyers departed swiftly. Like a blind woman, Tamara stumbled toward the nearest couch, felt it, and then carefully sank down into it. She was shaking so badly that her teeth were chattering. Would this nightmare never end? Was this the legacy she was to be left by her dead husband?

Tamara lowered her hands, raised her head, and sat there stiffly. "Inge, call the Beverly Hills Hotel," she said shakily. "See if they have a bungalow available for us. Then pack what we'll need. Two suitcases will do for now."

Inge stood her ground stubbornly. "You cannot let that witch get away with it!"

"Inge, please do as I say," Tamara breathed wearily. "I don't want to spend another night in this place." She glanced around the room and shuddered. "I never liked it much anyway. It reminds me too much of a mausoleum."

They were about to leave when Tamara took one more look back at the living room from the foyer. "We forgot something," she said, her grief finally turning to purposeful anger.

"What?" Inge wanted to know.

"Come on, I need your help." Heels clicking sharply, Tamara marched across the travertine and plopped herself down on one of the long white couches placed along the walls. She started to take off a shoe.

"What are you doing?" Inge asked, mystified.

Tamara looked at the sleek black pump in her hand and began to laugh mirthlessly. "You're right," she said, slipping it back on her foot. "They're not my smudges now, they're Zelda's. Let her get the cleaning bill." She climbed up on the soft white sofa cushions and signaled for Inge to climb up beside her. Still mystified, Inge did as she was told. When Tamara grabbed one side of the large gilt-framed Toulouse-Lautrec painting hanging over the sofa, she didn't have to be told any more. She grabbed the other side, and grunting, they managed to lift it off the hook and carry it out to the foyer. The ornate carved and gilded frame weighed a good sixty pounds.

"We can do this?" Inge, with her typical middle-class fear of courts and lawyers, asked in an astonished voice. "After what the man tell you?"

"Watch me do it," Tamara said grimly. "If Zelda tries to get her greedy little paws on these, she's got a fight on her hands. They're mine and I can prove it. Louie gave me one of these for each of our wedding anniversaries, six in all. All the columnists reported on the paintings I got from Louie as presents. As far as I'm concerned, that constitutes proof of ownership."

For the first time in three days, Inge almost smiled as they went methodically around the room, lifting the other five paintings off the walls.

"There," Tamara said after they'd leaned them against the walls in the foyer. She clapped the dust off her hands. "You're looking at money in the bank. Louie always said they were as good as cash. Now, get Esperanza and the chauffeur in here. They can help us lug these out to the car. Which reminds me. Don't let me forget to call those lawyers. All the cars except for the Duesenberg are registered to me."

Only later, in the limousine on the way to the hotel, did it occur to Tamara that when the lawyers had addressed her as "Mrs. Ziolko," it was the very first time since her marriage that she had been called by her married name.

Oscar Skolnik hit the roof. "Retire!" he thundered. "What do you mean, retire?" He glared malevolently at Tamara. "You're at the top of the world! Stars don't retire, dammit!"

The two of them were sitting alone amid the staggering luxury of his living room, the very room where she had first met him seven years earlier. This time the gleaming antiques, fine paintings, and glittering *objets* did not intimidate her in the least.

She drew a deep breath and her jaw tightened perceptibly. "I want out, O.T." she repeated firmly.

He threw himself back in his chair, the fingers of both hands working themselves up to a silent piano crescendo on the leather arms. He stared at her and puffed steadily on a carved ivory pipe, and when he spoke, he removed the pipe from between his lips. His voice was quiet. "What are you trying to pull?" His bright blue eyes stared into hers.

She raised her chin. "I'm not trying to *pull* anything. I told you, I'm finished with making movies. I've had it with Hollywood. Isn't that good enough for you?"

"No, it's not." He leaned forward. "What I want to know is, why isn't Morty Hirschbaum doing your bidding for you? He's your agent."

"I don't see what he's got to do with it. I'm not trying to renegotiate a contract. I just wanted to tell you in person what my plans are."

He smiled suddenly. "Now I get it. The little midget put you up to it. Thought he could put the squeeze on me by having you come waltzing in and frightening me with the announcement of your retirement." He shook his head. "Tell him no dice. If he wants to negotiate, he should come and see me instead of having his clients do the dirty work for him."

Tamara was getting exasperated. "O.T., you've got it all wrong. Morty has nothing to do with this. He doesn't even know I'm here."

"Clever." He shook his head admiringly. "I've got to hand it to you. You've got a lot more horse sense than I gave you credit for. You know, if you hadn't made it as an actress, you would've made one hell of an agent."

She stared at him. That he would refuse to accept the truth for what it was had never entered her mind.

"So who was it?" Skolnik asked. "Zanuck? Or L.B.? Or both?" His eyes glittered suspiciously. "What did they offer you to defect from IA?"

"Would you listen to me for once!" she yelled suddenly.

That did get through to him, she was gratified to see. His blue eyes blinked twice and he frowned slightly. "Okay. Let's stop tap-dancing circles around each other and get it over with." He paused. "Name your price."

Emitting a little growl of exasperation, she grabbed her purse and got to her feet. "I see that I've been wasting my time," she said angrily. "You can read all about it in Marilee's column tomorrow morning." She started stalking across the room to the door.

"Hey, hold on now!" He jumped out of his chair, caught up with her, and took her by the arm. "What are you getting so worked up for?" He turned her around to face him.

"You. You simply refuse to listen to me."

"I'm listening, I'm listening." He placed a friendly hand on each of her shoulders. "Shoot. Let me have it, barrels blazing." He smiled good-naturedly.

In spite of herself, Tamara found herself returning his smile. She couldn't stay angry with him for long, especially not when he smiled so ingenuously. She let herself be led back to her chair, and sat down.

"Now, why don't we start over again, shall we?"

She nodded, crossed one leg over the other, and reached for a cigarette. He picked up a table lighter and leaned forward to light it for her. She nodded her thanks and blew out a thin streamer of smoke. "I know I'm sounding like an ungrateful child," she said. "You were very nice to me after Louie died, and I appreciate the three weeks off you gave me so I could pull myself together again. I know how expensive it must have been to hold off filming my scenes, and I'll be forever grateful to you."

He made a negligible gesture. "Go on."

"Well, since then I've completed *Fast Company* and made *Contrary Pleasures*. I don't think I have to point out to you that there are only three weeks remaining on my contract. We both know that that's not enough time in which to make a movie."

"True enough." He nodded encouragingly.

"Then please hear me out," she said quietly. "I'm not playing any games with you. Nor am I trying to renegotiate a better contract or a higher salary. I have only one living relative left, my father, and I want to spend time with him in Palestine. He and I have a lifetime of catching up to do. And I want to travel, see something of the world."

"What it sounds like is you want a vacation."

She shook her head. "I don't want a vacation, I want out," she said stubbornly. "I've fulfilled my seven-year contract. Now I want to spend some years like ordinary people spend theirs."

"Tamara, Tamara." His smile was at once chiding and sad. "Don't you realize that you are far too talented to ever be ordinary? You're a fine actress and a spectacularly beautiful woman. No matter where you go or what you do, you'll always stand out from the crowd. You're blessed—or cursed. Take your choice. With special God-given talent. It would be a shame to let it go to waste."

417

"Be that as it may, I have to give it a try, O.T. I don't want to grow old with a crystal chandelier and a closet full of fur coats. I don't want to become an embittered old woman harping back on what I might have missed out on in life."

"You're obviously still hurting badly from what happened to Louie," he said gently. "Could it be you've gotten fed up with Hollywood because you somehow blame the city, or the industry, for his death?"

"No. At first I thought that's what it was too, but it isn't. Call me jaded, call me what you will, but I'm just plain tired of playing movie star. I can't do it anymore."

"You'll miss it," he warned. "Everyone who has once been a star misses it. Look at all the silent stars who couldn't make it because of their voices. They hate not being part of the industry anymore. They'd give anything—hell, both their legs—to be back where they once were."

"I won't." She shook her head. "I just want to be left alone."

He held his pipe and appeared to study it closely. "Tell me," he said slowly, "did you discuss these plans with anyone else?" He looked over at her. "A columnist? Someone else in the business? A friend even?"

She shook her head and stubbed out her cigarette in the crystal ashtray. "Only Inge knows, and if anyone can keep her mouth shut, believe me, it's Inge."

"Then do yourself and me a favor. Just one. That's all I ask."

She looked at him questioningly.

"Don't announce your retirement. Not formally or informally. Don't say anything to anybody. Just go away and have yourself a good time. For all practical purposes, I'll pretend it's a leave of absence. In the meantime, treat yourself to a nice vacation. God knows, you deserve one. Then, when you decide to return—"

"I won't return," she interrupted him.

He smiled tolerantly. "Then, *if* you should decide to return, all you need do is renegotiate a contract. You won't have burned any bridges you may need."

She looked at him. "O.T., can't you take what I'm telling you at face value? If you're hoping I'll return, you're only fooling yourself. I don't want to be Tamara-the-film-star anymore. I want to be Tamara Boralevi, the woman."

"You may feel strongly about that now, but what about six months from now? You can't know how you'll feel down the road." He paused for emphasis. "You've got nothing to lose doing it my way, and everything if you do it yours."

She let that sink in for a moment. "Perhaps you're right," she admitted. "I'll do it your way."

"Good. Then that's settled, at least." He smiled. "At the risk of sounding terribly pompous, I usually do tend to be right. You know, you're a young woman, Tamara, and young people need excitement. More important, the actress in you needs a creative outlet. Then again, I may be wrong and you may be right. Who can tell?" He shrugged. "Eventually time will prove one of us right."

"That it will, O.T." She smiled. "You know, I'm going to miss you."

"Not as much as I'll miss you. You were always my favorite, you know."

"Why, because I was your biggest moneymaker?" she asked shrewdly.

"That's part of it, but mainly because there's a rare quality about you that's . . ." Abruptly he changed the subject. "How are you fixed for money? Retirement, even leaves of absence"—he smiled—"can be expensive."

"I . . . I'll be all right. I've been liquidating my assets."

"And that mother of Louie's? Is she giving you any more trouble?"

She looked at him in surprise, wondering how he knew. "No, that's all settled," she said grimly.

He nodded. "It's a shame she got what she did. From now on, before you sign something, I hope you get some legal advice first." It seemed he had ears everywhere. "Isn't there anything I can do, then?"

"As a matter of fact, there is. Your friend, the art dealer . . ." She searched her memory and frowned. "I've forgotten his name."

"Bernard Katzenbach."

She nodded. "I've been meaning to get hold of him."

"He was in Chicago bidding at an auction for me. I believe he's supposed to return late tonight or early tomorrow."

"Tell him I'd appreciate it if he would call me. I want to sell the paintings."

"The Toulouse-Lautrec, Gauguin, and Renoir?"

She nodded. "Those and the others. I really have no use for them now, and the money will do me a lot more good."

For a moment she thought she caught an acquisitive glimmer in his eyes, and she held her breath, hoping for an offer. Oscar Skolnik was one of the biggest art collectors in the country, and the superb paintings Louis had given her would have made a fine addition to any collection.

He nodded finally. "I'll see to it that Bernie calls you as soon as I get hold of him."

"Well, that's all for now. I'd better be getting back home now. I've got to get up early tomorrow and start making definite plans. There's a lot I still have to do."

"When do you plan to leave?"

"As soon as the paintings and a few other things are sold."

"So soon?"

She nodded. "My mind is made up, so there's really no sense in delaying any further."

He nodded and walked her to the door. "Let me know when you leave, so I can come to say good-bye."

She kissed his cheek and then, without another word, hurried out into the unseasonably warm night.

A week later, Tamara was physically exhausted, mentally depleted, but despite the unpleasantness of it all, she felt rather pleased. It was almost over. The paintings were gone, even though Katzenbach's price was a huge disappointment. Inge had returned with the nine-thousand-dollar certified check from the furrier and had gone right back out to the jeweler's with a box tucked under her arm. Friendly Frank, the used-car salesman, had gone to Tamahawk and picked up the eight cars registered in her name. She had his certified check in hand too. After she'd tallied the money she had in the bank and the three weeks of pay she still had coming, and then deducted what she owed the hotel for the bungalow, she was gratified to discover that there would be a little over $115,000 if Inge managed to sell the jewelry for a third of its cost. And that was after the bank got paid off. All in all, it wasn't much, considering her retirement from the movies and the sobering fact that she would have no income. Still, it wasn't peanuts, not by a long shot. It would last, as long as she and Inge husbanded it carefully, and it was more than enough for a new start in life.

She tore up the paper on which she had done the figuring and tossed the pieces into the wastebasket. Then she pushed back her chair and rose from behind the little desk. For a long moment she stood in the center of the room and looked around. It seemed empty and colorless and depressing now that the paintings were gone. They had stamped the bungalow as her own, made it feel like home. Now it was just another hotel suite. The Matisse looked lonely and out of place by itself. Katzenbach hadn't wanted it.

She crossed over to the bar setup on the lowboy. She could use a stiff drink. Perhaps a neat Scotch.

She picked up the bottle and was about to pour, when she put it back down. She had a better idea. She picked up the phone and dialed room service.

After she ordered a bottle of 1928 Krug champagne chilled until frosty, she began to feel a lot better. The haggling had been exhausting, the money-grubbing distasteful. It reminded her all too much of the desperate months when they had been forced to live at Paterson's Mortuary. Now, at least, it was all finished. That was a reason to celebrate.

Besides, she and Inge deserved a premature farewell party, even if they would celebrate it by themselves. What better way to ring in the new, frugal chapter of their lives, she rationalized, than with one last bottle of hideously expensive champagne?

The next day, while Inge went to make the travel arrangements for the first leg of their journey, Tamara was already busy packing. O.T. watched her in silence, puffing on his ubiquitous pipe as he leaned in a corner, staying out of her way. "Now that you've slept on it a week, you're sure I can't dissuade you? Even for triple your current salary and unilateral approval over projects and script changes?"

She turned and stared at him. It was an unheard-of proposition, one any star would have jumped at, but she shook her head as she continued sorting through the closets. She was trying to pare clothes down to the necessities, in this case four suitcases and two steamer trunks full. She had originally opted for the bare minimum, but then prudence had won out. She didn't know what she would really need, and she would have to be careful with money from now on. Since there would be little to spend frivolously on clothes, and she could always give things away in the future, she thought it wisest to hang on to as much as possible now. "No, O.T.," she said wearily. "And do me a favor? Stop trying to convince me to stay. I thought we'd settled all this earlier."

"One last stab," he said. "A quarter of a million dollars per picture—will that change your mind?"

She drew a deep breath and met his eyes squarely. Turning that kind of money down was probably the hardest thing she'd done in her life. "O.T., I thought I'd made myself perfectly clear," she said shakily, "but at the risk of repeating myself, I'll tell you once again. It's not a matter of money." She tossed some dresses onto the bed. "I've spent seven years in this business and I've made eighteen films for you. I've let my face be carved up and changed the way you

421

wanted it. I dressed like you wanted, on the set and off. I acted in the films you wanted to make. I played roles on screen and off. I've lived a third of my life in a damn goldfish bowl, afraid to even breathe the wrong way. I was public property and belonged to everyone except myself. Now I think it's high time I became the person I really am—if I can find her again." She paused and added gently, "My mind is made up, O.T. If you care about me at all, you'll respect that." She continued packing in silence.

He didn't speak until a full minute had passed. "All right," he said finally. "You win. Contrary to my better judgment, I'll respect your decision. Just remember, if you ever do change your mind and decide to continue your career, come see me first. My door is always open to you, though I can't make any promises about how much you'll be worth then. The public's a fickle master, friend one day and foe the next. You know what they say: out of sight, out of mind. That's truer in this business than in anything else."

"I know." She smiled. "Thanks, O.T. It's nice of you to keep your door open despite the fact that I won't be coming back." She went over to the nightstand and picked up the small Matisse still life by the frame and held it at arm's length.

"Nobody controls color quite like Matisse," O.T. said admiringly, peering at it over her shoulder. "It's a beautiful painting."

"Yes, it is, isn't it?"

"You sold the others?"

She turned to him and nodded. "This one isn't worth what the others were. In a way, I'm glad—this way I won't be tempted to sell it. I think I'll keep it always. It'll be something I can hand down to my children." She gave a low, sad laugh. "If I ever have any."

He nodded. "It would be a shame if you didn't have one painting left. You had the beginnings of a fine collection."

She laid the painting down and padded it carefully with a blanket, then put it in one of the empty suitcases and tucked some clothes around it. "Just look at this. One entire suitcase reserved for this picture. Silly, isn't it?"

"On the contrary. I think it's wise. It's more than a painting. It's a treasure."

She smiled at a distant memory. "It was Louie's first-anniversary present to me." Her eyes took on a faraway look. "It seems a lifetime ago now, doesn't it?"

"The night we danced?"

"And you made that blatant pass at me."

422

"All I can remember is the pain after you kneed me in the groin."

She laughed. "You had it coming. But no one guessed. You sailed through the rest of that evening with a grin, if I remember correctly."

"A grimace."

"It never would have worked out between us," she said gently. "You know that."

He smiled sadly. "It's a shame it didn't. You were all woman. Still are."

"Only I was a one-man woman." She sat on the edge of the bed and was silent for a moment. "You know," she said slowly, her features furrowing into a frown, "life has never been the same for me since Louis died. Would you believe I haven't slept with a man since then?" She looked up at him.

He could only stare at her. "You don't mean to tell me that you've been celibate all this time?"

"I have," she said quietly. "Not that I couldn't have had my pick of men. It's open season on widows in this town. It's just that . . ." She paused and looked down at her hands. "I just never had the desire."

"I wish I had known."

She smiled wryly, "It was just as well that you didn't. I needed time to get myself functioning again."

"And are you?"

She shook her head. "Sometimes I think my body can no longer function in that way."

"You have to force it, then. You can't go through the rest of your life like a nun. You're a passionate woman, and celibacy doesn't suit you. It will only embitter you. I think it's time that we broke that cycle."

She shook her head. "I can't, O.T. Our going to bed together would be the worst mistake we could make. I just need to give myself more time, that's all."

"You've given yourself a year and a half already—a year and a half that should have been part of the best time of your life. That's far too long to live life as an incomplete woman."

"You don't understand. It's love I need, not *making* love."

"Sometimes the act itself can be as important as love. You have to free yourself of the shackles that link you to the past, and there's only one way of doing that."

She laughed. "I've got to hand it to you. That must be the wildest excuse I've ever heard for trying to take somebody to bed."

He didn't laugh. "I'm serious," he said gently. "Only by

making love can you be free again. Don't you understand that?"

She looked at him speechlessly. Inside her, she could feel something long-lost beginning to stir, like delicate humming-bird wings vibrating deep within her. Long-forgotten desires flickered distantly, began to uncoil slowly. Her eyes never left his, and the expression on her face was one of confusion.

He drew closer and his arms came up, wrapping them-selves around her. Then his face met hers and he kissed her, his tongue deep and probing as it swirled around hers. She didn't respond, but stood there statue-still, arms at her sides, unable to move. Like a figure carved of ice.

"No!" she whispered huskily. Suddenly she pushed him back and turned away. "I can't. I just *can't*."

"You can," he said softly, taking her chin in his hand and turning her around to face him. "You must. Don't you see that? Only this way can you go on truly living." She nodded hesitantly, and his fingers reached out for her blouse and he slowly began to unbutton it.

At his touch, her breath came in frightened, throaty little rasps, but this time she didn't try to move away. Nor did she push him away. She stood there, her body tense and trembling, and when at last she stood naked, he undressed without once taking his eyes off her. Her breasts rose and fell, and her skin felt cold.

His voice was low but there was no mistaking the com-mand in it. "Look at me."

She stared at him, and it was as though something was gripping her throat. His organ, free from the restraint of his trousers, was an angry serpent straining to lift its head. It looked very long, very thick, and very heavy. She had an impulse to flee, but her feet felt rooted to the floor.

Very gently, as if she were an extremely fragile blown-glass figurine, he lifted her and laid her down on the bed. As though in shame, she turned her head sideways on the pillow and shut her eyes.

"No. Don't look away. You must watch. You must be aware of everything we are doing."

She could feel his weight shifting on the mattress, and when she looked up at him, he was poised over her, his knees straddling her thighs. Her heart began to beat wildly. She stared at his body. The skin was stretched taut across his wiry shoulders, his waist seemed impossibly narrow, and his thighs were well-muscled and thick. To either side of the cleft, the two muscle slabs which were his chest sprouted curly dark hair and knoblike nipples. His belly was ribbed with a muscular shield, and his navel was a mere indentation in fleshy rock. The power he seemed to have over her frightened her. It made the long-forgotten moistness well up inside her and trickle down her thighs.

Slowly, carefully, he pushed himself inside her. She sucked in her breath and winced. Her body, having become unused to intrusion, clamped against the initial assault and tried to eject him, but he was patient and persevered. Soon she was filled with his warm thick hardness. Despite herself, a moan escaped her parted lips. Her smooth, silky skin turned electric, and her flesh began to crackle and rage and burn with ecstasy against her will. The moment his hips started to pump, the myriad nerve endings she thought had been dead suddenly came to sparkling life, sending delicious little shock waves down to the tips of her toes, up to her scalp, and all the way out through her arms to her fingertips.

It was like rediscovering a lost world. Or being reborn from a womb of desires.

Such a torrent of pent-up passion was being released that she felt herself shedding her old body and slipping into a new one. Reality receded, the world seemed to blur as if out of focus. She lost all track of time and being, of past and future, of the known and the given. It was as if he had pushed her over some mysterious threshold, through some magical, invisible doorway, and she found herself falling, falling, falling into a bottomless netherworld with no beginning and no end. It was as though she had become a hedonistic animal of carnal lusts awakened after a hundred-year hibernation. Thoughts were disjointed. Physical positions became fragmented. She had no idea of what was really happening or where she was. One moment her head rested on the pillow, the next it was between his taut, furry thighs, her mouth milking him relentlessly, and then her back was thrust against the carved headboard, her legs spread in midair as his mouth feasted noisily upon her. Passion defied logic, sent her caroming out into space and to galaxies beyond. Frantic gasps became animal growls, thrusts mingled with grunts and howls, and their moist tongues, her slick wetness, and the blunt scimitar plunging relentlessly into her groin were the only reality. She clutched him fiercely, as though he might vaporize into thin air if she let go. Visions burst in front of her eyes. Men from all the ages sprang up before her and merged into one while he thrust into her, and back out again, and into her again and again. And then, suddenly, it was Louis—Louis as he was that very first time they had made love at the clinic in Italy.

Her eyes were wide and dilated. "Louie," she whispered, digging her nails so deeply into O.T. that he cried out in pain. "You've come back to me, Louieee!"

And then, as suddenly as he had appeared, he faded from view, his face and body merging into O.T.'s.

"Louie!" she cried thickly, the tears streaming down her cheeks. "Don't leave me, Louie. Come backkkk . . ."

Then, as waves of orgasms crashed through her, O.T. let out a bellowing roar and thrust even more deeply, carrying her to the very vortex of the swirling whirlpool. Both their bodies convulsed, shuddered, shrieked, and plunged uncontrollably.

Suddenly everything was cast into a deathly silence. It was as if someone had thrown a master switch, turning the world off completely. Only the rapid beating of their hearts, the ticking of the alarm clock on the nightstand, and her quiet sobs were audible, those and the slowing rush of their blood.

The minutes ticked by and once again they joined the world of the living. At last he moved, and she stifled a cry as he slid limply out of her.

It was over.

O.T. leaned up on one elbow and smoothed the damp hair out of her eyes. "Are you okay?"

She sniffled and nodded. "For a moment, I could have sworn Louie was here," she said shakily. "And then he was gone." She stared at him. "Just like that."

"He'll be gone for good now," he replied. "You're free of him now. His memory can no longer hold you back."

She nodded.

"Strange, isn't it? I've wanted you for years, and it turns out we made love only to chase away the past."

"Was it . . . what you expected?"

"It was good. Hell, it was very good. But no, it wasn't what I expected. I though you'd be forever elusive. And you know what?"

Tamara shook her head.

"You still are—I know this won't happen again. But . . . I'm glad we did it."

She gave him a chaste kiss on the cheek. "So am I. I thought I was finished as far as making love was concerned."

"I'd say you've barely begun. You've got a whole lifetime of loving ahead of you."

She took his hand and pressed it warmly. "Thanks, O.T.— for giving me back my womanhood."

"I don't think you ever lost it. Maybe it just . . . went into hiding."

"Maybe . . ."

He sat up slowly and stretched, then heaved a sigh and looked around for his clothes. "Well, I'd better be going, or you'll never finish packing." He swung his legs over the edge of the bed, stood up, and started to dress.

She nodded and started dressing also. "And I'd better finish soon or I won't get a wink of sleep tonight. We're leaving first thing in the morning. Right now, Inge's out arranging for a sleeper on the train to New York."

He looked surprised. "Why don't you fly? It's a lot less tiring and a helluva lot quicker."

"It's a lot more expensive too. Besides, I'm in no rush." She smiled. "I've got all the time in the world now, and the train only takes five days."

"And once you reach New York?"

"We'll stay a week or so and then book a cabin on the next steamship for Europe. Then we'll probably have to change ships two more times. Palestine's not exactly on a direct trade route, you know."

"No, I don't suppose it is." He made a moue. "I tell you what. As a going-away present, I'll pay your fare—"

"O.T.—"

He raised a hand to ward off her protestations. "No, I want to do it. I can't bear the thought of you traveling steerage."

She laughed. "We're not exactly planning to go steerage. And besides, there are two of us. Inge and I are going to be traveling together. I can't afford to upgrade her fare, or expect you to pay it as well."

"Of course I will. It's my money, and I can do with it as I please. That's one of the nice things about being wealthy. No one can tell you how not to spend your money. You don't think I can sit back and let my biggest star travel anything but first class, do you?"

She sighed good-naturedly. "All right, you win. You always do come up with a good argument, I'll give you that."

"Good. I'll see to it that the tickets are delivered to you tomorrow morning. And you'll use them—that's final." He paused. "Don't get angry with me, but they'll be round-trip. The return dates will be left open."

She started to protest, but he silenced her. "If you don't come back, you can always cash them in after a year, no strings attached. Deal?" He held out his hand.

She smiled. He just wouldn't give up. "Deal," she said, shaking on it.

"If you ever get stuck in Timbuktu or need anything, call me. Okay?"

"Okay. First thing." She escorted him to the door.

"Good luck," he said. "I just hope you'll be happy."

Oscar Skolnik didn't try to sleep. Going to bed would have been useless. He never could sleep right after he'd made a major new acquisition. Something about the thrill of ownership kept his adrenaline pumping.

He sat in the darkened study of his mansion, his eyes never leaving the luminous colors of the paintings that had once hung on the living room walls at Tamahawk. They were flooded with light in the shadowy room. All five of them seemed to glow with an otherworldly life of their own.

He puffed contentedly on his pipe. He'd always wanted those paintings, and now they were his. Even after Bernard Katzenbach's ten-percent commission, he'd only paid a little over a third of their current market value, so they were also his single biggest art bargain to date. It only irked him that the Matisse had escaped his walls.

He heard a movement behind him and turned around as a beautiful face peered in at him around the door. "Aren't you coming to bed, O.T.?" the girl complained sleepily.

"Later," he said in a bored voice. "Go back to bed, Marissa. I want to be alone."

She pouted but withdrew obediently. When he heard the door close, he sighed to himself. She was just another of the thousands of hopefuls that comprised the vast pool of girls he could choose from. So many of them thought that sleeping with him would earn them a magic ticket to stardom, the little fools, when in reality all they got was a bit part, a part that invariably was the high point of their short, miserable careers. Meanwhile, they were his until he grew tired of them. Not one of them had what it took. None of them was like Tamara.

He turned his attention back to the paintings and stared at them until dawn lightened the east windows. Only then did the realization hit home that Tamara would never return. She would have never sold these master works of genius on a mere whim.

He could only continue to stare at them bleakly and console himself with the fact that he had profited immensely from her, right up until the very end.

"Ahead of us is the bay, which sweeps all the way from Haifa around to Akko, in a sort of wide, teacup kinda curve," Captain Dusty Goodhew told Tamara and Inge.

The three of them stood on the wraparound bridge in front of the wheelhouse of the ten-thousand-ton steamship *Lerwick*, and although the steady rumble from the ship's engine room could not be heard up here, it could be felt: the decks vibrated pleasantly beneath their feet.

The captain continued, "It's a deep, natural bay, among the finest in the entire Middle East. It's been dredged at Haifa by Her Majesty's government to accommodate deep-water vessels such as this one."

They were heading straight into the sunrise, and Tamara had to squint against the dazzling glare. At first, it seemed to her that the sun was rising directly from the sea, but then as it rose swiftly higher, sending out celestial beams to engulf them, she could make out the dark, narrow band of distant land silhouetted below the brightness like a long, thin, black-purple ribbon.

There it was at long, long last. Tamara's first glimpse of the strange, faraway land which until how had only evoked dreamy utopian visions. There it was, a very real band of terra firma at the easternmost shore of the Mediterranean. For this she had given six weeks and traveled some ten thousand miles by air and sea. And she hadn't reached it quite yet. It was just near enough to tantalize, yet too far to see distinctly. Miles of open Mediterranean with choppy blue three-foot-high waves stretched between it and the ship.

Captain Goodhew handed her his binoculars. "If you focus and look to yer right, mum, you ought to be able to catch yer first glimpse of Haifa harbor and the city risin' up the side o' the hill." He pointed with a stubby, callused forefinger.

She broke her reverie. "Thank you, Captain." She looped the thin leather straps around her neck and, holding the binoculars to her eyes, followed the direction of his finger. At first, everything seemed to swim in a hazy blur, but as she focused the little dial between the two lens tubes, the blur suddenly jumped into sharp focus.

She caught her breath. The hillside looked incredibly steep and green and was dotted with houses.

Captain Goodhew was saying, "If you look closely, you'll see that Haifa is actually three parts. The port and the main town are below. In the middle is the section called Hadar-ha-Carmel. And the top is ha-Carmel. Yer see it?"

She nodded. Sweeping the binoculars downward, she caught the panorama of the busy harbor with its clusters of ships. She felt vaguely disappointed. It resembled any other of the many Mediterranean harbors at which the ship had docked

429

over the past weeks. They were all interchangeable, right down to the army of antlike dockworkers swarming about while cargo booms swung from ship to dock and back to ship again in the never-ceasing ritual of loading and unloading. Between the tramp steamers and two small passenger ships, she could make out the distinctive gunmetal gray of Her Majesty's naval cruisers flying the Union Jack. Multitudes of gulls, attracted by a fleet of incoming fishing vessels, hovered overhead.

Beside Tamara, Inge was making impatient little noises, and Tamara reluctantly unlooped the binoculars from her neck and handed them to her. Then, clasping her hands, she leaned her forearms over the polished railing of the bridge, raised her head, and shut her eyes. She inhaled deeply.

So it was true what sailors claimed, she thought with an anticipatory little smile. You *could* smell land from out at sea.

Captain Goodhew interrupted her thoughts. "Yer goin' to be spendin' some time in Haifa?"

She opened her eyes and turned to him. She shook her head. "Not for the time being. As soon as we've docked, we're heading straight to Tel Aviv."

"You have friends there?"

She looked at him. "Just somebody . . . I know."

He smiled. "Best way to see this territory. From the insider's point of view. Just be real careful now. Can be a lot more violent in these parts than in Europe or America. Much as we've tried, it's still not what yer'd call civilized."

"I'll bear that in mind," she said, glad when he went inside to check the ship's bearings. He had gone out of his way to be nice to her, and she could only wonder what his reaction would have been had he known that she was the daughter of the single biggest thorn in the British Mandate's backside—the notorious Jewish gunrunner, Schmarya Boralevi. Would he have lectured her? Washed his hands of her completely? Alerted the authorities?

One thing she did know. From here on in, she would have to exercise extreme caution. One slip of the tongue, and the British authorities might follow her. She didn't doubt for an instant that they would try to use her to get to her father.

She felt a quiver of fear as the ribbon of land grew in size until she could see the individual houses on the steep green hillside with the naked eye. Well, here I am, she thought shakily. I'm no longer Tamara, the screen legend. I'm plain Tamara Boralevi from now on. There's no glamorous facade to hide behind now. I'm just like anybody else. A woman scared stiff of the future. Now I'll finally get to see if I've made the right choice—or the worst mistake of my life. She took a deep breath, making an effort to calm her nervous anticipation.

The captain returned to the deck, and Tamara turned to him. Her eyes were bright with a feverish impatience. *Palestine! At long, long last!* "Where will we be docking?" she asked, fighting to keep her rising excitement subdued.

"Over there, to the right," Goodhew replied. "Harbor's deepest there. Dredged again last year."

"Look! There's a boat coming out to meet us!" Inge cried

"Ah, the launch. That'll be one o' the harbor pilots and the British customs agents. They will help guide us into the harbor and begin the passport and visa checks. I radioed ahead that yer's onboard, and they agreed to let yer disembark here at sea. You ought to be able to skip most o' the formalities and be onshore long before anyone else. Yer're all packed now?"

Tamara nodded. "Our cases are in the cabin ready to go."

"Good." Captain Goodhew went inside the wheelhouse. When he came back out he smiled. "I've arranged for your luggage to be brought up on deck. Now, if yer'll be so kind as to excuse me, I must take over for the first mate." He extended his hand. "It's been a pleasure to have yer onboard, mum."

Tamara smiled and shook his hand warmly. "And the voyage has been a most pleasant one, Captain Goodhew. I thank you."

Another firm handshake and the captain was gone and Tamara and Inge hurriedly descended the embossed-metal companionway to their cabin, two decks below. Tamara found herself humming. Had it not been for the heat already streaming in through the two open portholes and the shabby gentility of the aging ship, she could have imagined herself on a dreamy yacht, hovering somewhere between ocean and heaven.

"I am glad to see you happy," Inge said cheerfully. "You did not sing to yourself for a long time."

"That's because one of my dreams is finally coming true." She took both of Inge's hands in hers and squeezed them. "Just think, Inge. We're almost there!"

"*Ja*, that we are."

They gathered up their purses and hats and checked the cabin to see if they might have left anything behind. Then Tamara sat in front of the little built-in vanity mirror and canted her hat rakishly over one eye. She smiled at her reflection. The hat matched her light silk dress, the big red polka dots on the white background looking at once chic and bright. It matched her mood.

They went back up on deck, where the purser awaited them. He formally handed them their passports, which, according to maritime custom, they had had to relinquish upon boarding.

Tamara snapped open her purse, took out a hundred dollars, and pressed it into his hand. "You will be so kind as to split this gratuity among the crew as is customary?"

"With pleasure, Miss Tamara." He gave a gracious bow. "And may I thank you for the pleasure of your company?"

The ship's engines slowed, the launch arrived, ropes were thrown down, and a gangplank lowered. The harbor pilot and two customs agents wearing khaki uniforms with sharply creased shorts and knee-high socks climbed easily up the rickety steps to the ship. The luggage was carefully carried down, and when the porters finished, Tamara and Inge carefully followed, clutching the rope banister on both sides. As soon as they were helped onboard the launch, they sat in the stern, the ropes were untied, and the engines sputtered to life. Bow high in the air, they raced toward shore, the hull slapping the water, sending showers of cool spray back.

As Tamara watched the distance close, warm excitement within her surged and built. Her newly found heritage . . . her faith . . . which had been buried for so long, could no longer be contained, manifesting itself through the sheer proximity of the Promised Land. Her spirits rose: just another half-mile to go now, and she would set foot on the soil of Palestine.

The small customs office was sweltering, despite the open windows and the lazy currents of air raised by the slowly revolving overhead fan.

Brigadier George Edward Diggins eyed them suspiciously from behind the desk, his fingers strumming the pages of their passports as if they were a deck of cards. His expression was the same as those of the customs officials in all the Mediterranean ports where the *Lerwick* had docked and she had gone ashore—except that he was British, and the British were notorious sticklers for exactitude. His assistant, Sergeant Carne, was stationed by the door.

As if we're criminals intent upon escape, Tamara couldn't help thinking.

The brigadier stared thoughtfully at her passport picture

and then at her, and Tamara stared right back at him, glad at least that her hat hid one eye so that she felt that much less vulnerable. She didn't chat or volunteer any information. Customs men were like policemen; one let them do the questioning.

She considered Diggins, who lifted a brow and pursed his lips as he studied her photograph. He was a slim, pale-eyed Englishman with sandy, sun-bleached hair, a pockmarked face, gaps between yellowing teeth, and a pencil-thin mustache. There was something self-important about him, more than a little of the strutting martinet. Clearly he was a dyed-in-the-wool career officer who considered civilians, no matter what their exalted status, far less than his equal.

She was becoming annoyed. "I was under the impression that I was taken ashore by the launch so that the usual formalities would be sped up," she said, placing her elbows on the arms of the chair.

"Sometimes that is the case." He spoke with slow deliberation and frowned, his fingers idly fanning the pages of the passports. "Oftentimes it's not."

"Such as?" She held his gaze.

"There might be questions which need answering before we allow certain visitors to remain ashore." He pushed his chair back on its squeaky casters and leaned back, eyeing her stonily. "You used a one-way ticket to get here. Does that mean you intend to emigrate?"

"I'm a visitor. In case you haven't noticed, I have another ticket with me, a round-trip ticket. I changed my travel plans and took the *Lerwick* only because it was the first ship leaving Marseilles for here."

"A visitor." He nodded to himself. "A pilgrim? A tourist?"

"A tourist."

"And your destination?"

She laughed softly. "Why here, of course. Palestine. Isn't that obvious?"

His voice was quiet. "I meant specifically."

She shrugged. "There's a lot to see. I decided to begin with Tel Aviv."

"That's a curious choice. Most people go to Jerusalem first. Why Tel Aviv?"

"Why *not* Tel Aviv? I hear it's cooler by the shore, and besides, it's centrally located. From there I can travel north to Lake Tiberias, south to Jerusalem or the Dead Sea . . . it's convenient."

"I see. Do you have hotel reservations?"

She shook her head.

A glimmer of interest brightened his eyes. "Then you will be staying with friends?"

"No." She was becoming more annoyed. "Why are you asking me all these questions?"

"Then with whom are you planning to stay?"

"It was my intention to stay at the Rehot Dan Hotel. It came highly recommended."

"The Rehot Dan?" He frowned and sat slowly forward. "That's not exactly the kind of accommodations I would have expected such a distinguished visitor as yourself to take."

"What would you have expected?" She looked deep into his pale eyes, almost as though she were challenging him.

"And the . . . ahem . . . purpose of your visit?"

"Just that," she replied calmly. "A visit."

He drummed his fingers on the scarred desktop. "And how long do you intend to stay?"

She shrugged. "That all depends upon how we like it here. A few days, a few weeks . . . perhaps even a few months. This is my first vacation in years, and I intend to take full advantage of it."

"I see." He pursed his lips and frowned. "It says in here that your name is Tamara Boralevi," he said softly. He held up her passport and waved it.

"That's my maiden name. Professionally I'm know as Tamara, but since even film stars cannot go around with just a single name on documents, I reverted to using my maiden name after my husband died. I do not see a problem with that."

"Normally, we would have whisked a star of your obvious stature through without formalities of any sort, but seeing that your last name is what it is . . . well, it changes things, what?" His eyes seemed to glare.

Tamara looked at him expressionlessly, crossed one knee casually over the other, and clasped her hands over it. She waited patiently.

"What I need to ascertain," Diggins said sharply, "is whether you are, or are not, a relation of one Schmarya Boralevi."

Tamara barely contained the wave of panic she felt at hearing her father's name, but she was unable to subdue the crimson flush that flooded her face. "My God, but it's hot in here," she murmured. She reached for a thin folder on Diggins' desk and fanned herself briskly with it. "Please, if we can cut this short before I pass out from heat prostration?"

"A glass of water." Diggins snapped his fingers and the sergeant hurried off to get it. He brought one glass for

Tamara and one for Inge. Tamara sipped hers and Diggins continued. "This is a potentially explosive land. The influx of Jewish refugees has made the Arabs very angry and protective and it's taking all our efforts to keep some semblance of peace. Believe me, Miss . . . ah, Boralevi, we do not wish Palestine to turn into a war zone, what?"

"Nor do I. But what has all that to do with me?" Her mind whirled: I should have expected something like this. How stupid of me. Why didn't I go by my married name? Now I'm liable to lead them straight to my father. Damn.

"Your name is the same as that of the most notorious arms smuggler in the territory," the brigadier was saying. "Our official policy is that the fewer weapons are in the hands of the civilian population, the more peaceful Palestine is apt to be."

"Very noble, I'm sure," she said mildly. "However, with all due respect, I don't understand the meaning of this. What could my name possibly have to do with this interrogation? I am not an arms smuggler."

"I did not say you were, Miss Boralevi," he said patiently. "You are merely being questioned as to your relationship, if any, with a man wanted for fomenting violence and smuggling arms. Those are very serious charges."

"Brigadier Diggins," she intoned emphatically, "you have searched our luggage minutely and found that we are not carrying contraband of any kind. I really cannot sit here and tolerate your accusations—"

"My dear Miss Boralevi. You are not being accused of anything. Please, try to understand our position. The name Boralevi is red-flagged. As soon as it crops up, we are required to investigate. I am not allowed to make any exception."

"Then let me tell you a few things about myself." Her face was grim and her anger was barely controlled. "I barely remember my mother and I cannot recall my father at all. Being a displaced person, I was raised by Miss Meier." She gestured at Inge. "I have lived most of my life in the United States and spent the past seven years making movies. For your information, I have no family. This is my first, and undoubtedly my last, visit here. I have no idea what has been going on in this place. Indeed, I know next to nothing about the Middle East in general, but I must tell you that this place is beginning to appeal to me less and less. If I am not welcome here because of my last name, I should think you would be so good as to help me make swift travel arrangements to Greece or wherever the next boat is headed."

"I didn't mean to imply—"

"Please," she interrupted him. "Spare me. I do not wish to stay where I am unwelcome."

Summoning all her talent, she raised her head so that she could focus an intense gaze upon him and play to him as if he were a camera. "I should also like to inform you, and this is off the record"—she lowered her voice—"that when I was in London a couple of months ago, your king invited me to return to see him on my way back and give him my opinions about Palestine. Now I'm afraid there will be precious little to tell him, other than my being traumatized and humiliated by one of his loyal subjects."

He stared at her as she rose to her feet.

"Come, Inge, let's leave this hellish oven and see if Captain Goodhew will be so kind as to take us back aboard the *Lerwick*." She turned and made for the door, and Inge, gaping in disbelief, shrugged in confusion and stumbled after her in silence.

Diggins watched them leave, studying Tamara's moves to see if she was bluffing. She had to be. Didn't she?

Soon she would reach the door. He suppressed a cry of anger and resentment and shot to his feet with such speed that he reached the door before her. "P-please, Miss Boralevi, d-do not be so hasty," he stammered quickly, barring her way with his body. "I did not mean to offend you. I was only asking the questions I'm required to ask." He cleared his throat and his Adam's apple bobbed visibly. "It would be a pity to get off on such bad footing so quickly, what?" His attempt at a confident grin came off feebly.

She stared at him as though torn between decisions. She could see the beads of nervous perspiration on his forehead and staining the armpits of his short-sleeved khaki shirt. She felt shame stealing over her. How easily crafty lies and manufactured emotions sprang to her lips and face; this must be her Hollywood legacy. But her father had to be protected. At any cost.

At last she raised her chin and a frosty smile slid across her lips. "Very well, Brigadier," she said abruptly. "I take that to mean we're free to go?"

He nodded quickly. "And don't forget your passports. This isn't America. You're supposed to carry identification at all times."

She nodded, took the passports from him, and slid them into her purse.

"And, Miss Boralevi, I am sure our district commissioner, Sir William Hippisley, will be delighted to meet you. He and

436

Lady Juliet hold open-house parties for English-speaking visitors each Saturday afternoon."

"How very nice. However, my intention is to travel incognito while here. I don't even want to register into the hotel under my own name. I would appreciate it if my privacy is respected."

He shrugged. "As you wish, Miss Boralevi, but Sir William and Lady Juliet will be disappointed, to say the very least."

"The disappointment will be mine, I'm sure. But I have no desire to be treated as a film star while I'm here. I wish only to melt into the crowd and lead a very ordinary tourist's existence. Good day, Brigadier."

"Good day, Miss Boralevi." Diggins turned and scowled at Carne. "Sergeant!" he barked. "See that Miss Boralevi's luggage is brought out to one of our cars. Have her driven wherever she wants, courtesy of this department. And step to it!"

"Yessir!" The sergeant's body went rigid and he saluted smartly. Then he pirouetted, stamped his feet, and marched briskly out.

Tamara stared. "That really isn't necessary, you know. Tel Aviv is much too far to accept a lift."

"It is nothing."

Alarm bells shrilled in her head. By insisting that one of his men drive her, he was regaining the upper hand and would be in a firmly entrenched position to keep tabs on her movements. Sooner or later, this could very well lead him to her father. She had to think of a way to decline firmly and graciously—and get out of his clutches fast.

"Really, I couldn't accept your generous offer. Surely your men have better things to do than escort me about."

"On the contrary. I can't think of a single man who wouldn't give his right arm for such delightful duty."

"I only need help in arranging for a hired car," she protested. "If you'd be so kind as to—"

"I won't hear of it. Please, accept the ride in the spirit of my trying to make amends."

She felt suddenly sick. She had been outmaneuvered, and it was time for her to back down. "How can I refuse?" she said smoothly.

"It's little enough to offer you for having put you through this . . . this trauma." He smiled slightly, but his narrowed eyes surveyed her shrewdly. "And considering that I've permitted you entry into this territory, I'm ultimately responsible for your well-being. You don't mind if I check up on you every now and then?" He paused and held his slight smile. "To make certain you've come to no harm?"

She looked surprised. "Who on earth would wish to harm me?"

"Who knows? This is a strange country, and violence is a way of life."

"You don't trust me, do you?" She forced a weak smile.

"On the contrary. I simply wouldn't want anything to happen to you. Especially since your friend the King might hold me personally responsible."

She nodded. "Thank you," she said tartly. "I'm sure Miss Meier and I will sleep more easily knowing we are under your protection." She extended her slender white hand and he shook it. Politely he held open the door for her. Crossing the threshold, she hesitated and turned around. "Brigadier Diggins . . ."

He looked at her questioningly.

"This . . . this Simon Boralevi."

"Schmarya Boralevi," he corrected with a half-smile.

"Whoever." She waved her hand airily. "Does this mean he's still at large?"

"I'm afraid it does."

"Then you'd do well to double your efforts to catch him, I would think," she told him solemnly.

"I'm in the process of doing just that." He smiled crookedly, and despite the roasting heat, she felt an arctic chill.

She didn't like playing cat and mouse, especially not when her father was the mouse and she was being used as bait. She would have to stay on her toes; this wasn't at all like making movies.

Two hours before sunset. A Wednesday. Thirteen days had gone by since she had placed the ad in the *Davar* and *Haaretz*, Tel-Aviv's two dailies. She and Inge were sitting under the vine-shaded arbor in the back of the small hotel, the remains of their dinners on their plates. The temperature was dropping, and a delicious cool breeze fluttered past, rustling the leaves overhead and rippling the checkered tablecloths. Tamara sat in silence, tapping a thumbnail against her teeth as she stared out at the sea and the relentless, crashing breakers spending themselves against the shore. She was a million miles away, lost in thought.

Inge was about to eat a forkful of leek-and-potato-pie when she noticed Tamara's blank look. She laid her fork down and pushed her chair closer to Tamara's. Smiling gently, she said, "You will hear from him soon. I know you will."

"It's been almost two weeks. Something's wrong or he would have gotten in touch with me by now."

"Maybe he has gone away somewhere. Or he is very busy. It could be that he is not even aware of your message yet. It may take time for him to see it. You must be patient. I think maybe the problem is that you have been waiting too anxiously."

"How do you mean?"

"Well, the longer we sit here doing nothing but waiting for him, the longer it will seem to take," Inge said with philosophical directness. "There are many things to do and see. I do not say waiting is wrong, but concentrating on only that will drive you crazy."

"But we did go and see some things," Tamara protested defensively. "We went to Tiberias and saw the Sea of Galilee, which was nothing more than a fair-size lake, and we went to Jerusalem—"

"That is exactly what I mean!" Inge said. "Two little trips in two weeks. You call that sightseeing?"

"I know there's a lot more to see, but do you really expect me to trudge around ruins and churches while I'm dying to hear from my father?"

"It would be better than to climb walls."

"I'm not climbing walls yet," Tamara contended halfheartedly. "I'm just . . . a little anxious." She picked up her wineglass and drained it in one swallow.

Inge narrowed her eyes. "If you were a cat you would be walking back and forth on the roof." Her expression suddenly softened and she tilted her head. "Tamara, you know I only want what's best for you. I only want to make things easier."

Tamara leaned one elbow on the table and cupped her hand on her chin. She looked at Inge and said slowly, "I'm starting to hate this place. It's awful and boring and filthy. I can't image anyone wanting to live here. As far as I'm concerned, the Arabs can keep it."

Inge looked startled. "That is because you are not giving it a chance. Myself, I rather like it."

"Who asked you?" Tamara hissed in a voice that was like a blade of steel. "Why can't you just shut up?"

Inge could only stare at her in disbelief. When she finally spoke, her voice was crisp and distant. "Tamara. Do not be like this."

"Like what?"

Inge leaned across the table and waved her fork angrily in the air. "You know like what! Like a spoiled child. It is not becoming. You have not behaved in this way since you were two or three, at the Danilov Palace in St. Petersburg. I will never forget how furious you were when you could no longer play in the palace's toy room and had to be content with your own few toys. I spanked you then."

Tamara looked at her in surprise. "You did? I don't remember you ever spanking me."

"I did." Inge nodded emphatically. "And you deserve it again."

Suddenly Tamara felt a smothering guilt. She was sorry for having spoken so harshly, sorry for having taken her anger out on Inge. Through thick and thin, Inge had mothered her, cared for her, uprooted her own life over and over again. "I'm sorry, Inge," Tamara apologized huskily. "I didn't mean to be nasty. I don't know what's gotten into me." She shook her head. "My nerves are so frazzled that I didn't even realize how impossible I was getting."

"Well, now that you do, you can do something about it. And trust me." Inge wagged an admonishing finger in the air. "Yesterday my ears are ringing and that means somebody was thinking and talking about us, and that somebody will show up. Go ahead. Be skeptical. I am right, you will see."

At that very moment the sun was suddenly blocked out and a long purplish shadow fell across the table. "Could it be that your ears were ringing because *I* was coming to see you?" said a silky British voice.

Tamara looked up with a startled expression. The man had appeared so soundlessly, so stealthily, that neither she nor Inge had heard his approach, and she was momentarily thrown, and dismayed as well, for she hadn't expected Brigadier Diggins to materialize virtually out of thin air. From his expression, it was impossible to tell if he had overheard anything important.

He clicked his heels together and gave a slight bow. "Good evening, ladies," he said pleasantly, tapping his riding crop against one thigh. "I trust you are enjoying your stay?"

He had positioned himself cleverly, Tamara noticed, so that the sun shone from behind him, and his face, under the tilted visor of his peaked tan cap, was in shadow, while hers was bathed in sunlight, every expression and nuance exposed. No, she must never, never underestimate him. He was very sly.

Raising her thinly plucked eyebrows, she said, "Why, Brigadier Diggins! How *nice* to see you." She favored him with her best false smile. "At last, someone who speaks

English. As I was just telling Miss Meier, all this Hebrew and Arabic jabber has been driving me up the wall." She gestured to an empty chair. "Won't you join us for a glass of wine?"

"I'm sorry, but I can't stay. I was just passing through when it occurred to me how derelict I've been in my duty."

"Derelict? I don't believe I understand."

"I haven't been checking up on you as I had promised I would."

She thought: *Have I only imagined that someone has constantly been spying on us?* "You're a busy man," she said. "One can't expect you to be everywhere at once." *But that's exactly what I will expect from now on.* Clearly, he has eyes everywhere.

He turned to Inge. "And how are you enjoying your stay, Miss Meier?"

Inge gave him a bland smile. "I rather like it here. More so than Tamara does, I am afraid."

"I see." He turned his attention back upon Tamara. "Then that must be the reason you are staying on despite the fact that you're not totally enchanted? For Miss Meier's sake?"

Tamara forced herself to hold his gaze, knowing that if she lowered it she could not give credence to her words. "Well, yes and no," she said slowly. "You see, I've been overworked for so long, and then the weeks it took traveling to get here have only exhausted me further. I'm afraid it's recuperation time for me. I really have little choice. Hopefully, the sea and the sun will revive me."

"Ah. Then that will explain why you have not been going on more outings."

He has had people spying on us. "I am gratified to see that although you couldn't personally be beside us all this time, we have indeed been under your protection, Brigadier," she said dryly.

"As I believe I told you when you first arrived, you are a very important visitor."

Is he sneering at me? "I see that I am indeed fortunate, Brigadier. Everywhere I go, I seem to have a guardian angel. In Hollywood, the head of my studio was very protective of me, and here I have you. What more could a person ask for?"

"Caution," he suggested. "You have exercised it so far, and I am glad that nothing bad has befallen you. I hope the rest of your stay will be as uneventful." He touched the gleaming visor of his cap and a gave a little bow. "Well, I really must be off. I hope I see you again soon."

Tamara inclined her head. "I'm sure you will."

"And may I suggest you do try to do a little more sight-seeing? It would be a pity if you didn't see more of Palestine. This is rugged but beautiful terrain. Ladies?" And with that, he spun around and marched off.

They watched him disappear around the corner of the hotel. Tamara picked up a teaspoon and toyed with it. Inge had been right. They really needed to go on more outings. Brigadier Diggins' sudden appearance had proved that they hadn't played tourist well enough to convince him that that was what they really were. If she wanted to throw him off her father's scent, they'd better throw themselves into the role, and with a vengeance. Maybe it *would* make time pass more quickly. Anything was better than this interminable waiting. Also, if they kept moving around, they would make things more difficult for Brigadier Diggins.

She felt Inge touch her arm, and she looked up.

"Are you all right?"

Tamara nodded. "I'm fine," she assured her, "but I don't want to eat anything else. If we're going to start sightseeing, we'd best get to bed early."

The sound.

Like a pebble tossed into a placid pond, it sent out widening ripples that radiated outward until it reached down, down, down into the slowly swirling depths of her dream. Against her will, she found herself drifting up, through its successive layers of lulling tranquillity. She lay motionless on her side, one hand flat on the pillow, under the right cheek of her face. Her forehead furrowed with anxiety; her eyelids fluttered.

Crrr-eak, the sound encroached again.

Her eyes flew open, but the primeval instinct which had alerted her to possible danger immediately made her close them to mere slits and kept her from sitting up. A smothering fear grasped her and cut off her breathing as effectively as a pair of strangulating hands wrapped tightly around her throat. With a supreme effort she pushed the fear back far enough to keep it from suffocating her.

Crrr-eeeak.

From somewhere behind her, she thought. Her heart rose in her throat. It was definitely not part of the dream. It was the very real, very furtive creaking of a floorboard and the shallow exhalation of a human breath. Someone was trying to sneak up on her.

She lay motionless, terrified, and held her breath, waiting.

442

When the sound came again, it was closer . . . much closer. Just then, a gust of wind came up. It stirred the curtains and they suddenly billowed toward her like two surging plump white ghosts. She nearly fainted from terror.

She slowed her breathing, giving herself a moment to try to pinpoint the exact location of whoever was in the room with her. That way, when she leapt out of bed, she would know exactly which way to run.

For escape she must: it was a matter of self-preservation. The sooner she was out of this room, the safer she would be. At least she did not have far to go. Inge's room was right across the hall. Just twenty short steps.

Shakily she bit down on her lip. She had waited long enough. Her hands crept to the covers. *Now!*

Taking a deep, slow breath, buoyed by the steady rise of her adrenaline, she flung aside the covers and leapt from the bed.

The moment her left foot hit the floor, she put her entire weight on it; before the other could find purchase, her body was already spinning in a 180-degree pirouette. She skirted the bed and, oblivious of anything in her path, flung herself straight for the door—and into the arms of a shadowy apparition. He jerked her backward.

She started to scream, but a rough hand clapped over her mouth, cutting off her breath and the sound with it. Her eyes were wild and her body twisted violently. For a moment she struggled against him, her nails clawing frantically at the arm in front of her, but it was futile. He was much too strong for her. Her shoulders slumped in resignation.

"I will remove my hand only if you promise not to scream," a strongly accented voice whispered harshly. She cringed. She could smell his perspiration, and each word he spoke was a puff of warm breath against her neck. "Do you understand? One sound, and I will be forced to gag you, yes?" His English was fluent, but as was the case with many multilingual people, he ended the declarative sentence with a question.

For an instant a challenge flared in her eyes, then died. Slowly, she nodded.

He removed his hand, but kept it poised in front of her mouth.

Her eyes, long adjusted to the darkness, did not need the help of light to see that he was over six feet in height. She could make out little of his face, other than the whiteness of determined eyes. His features were hidden in the shadows.

Who was he?

Before she could gather the courage and ask, he answered the question for her.

"My name is Dani ben Yaacov. I have been sent to take you to your father."

Once he was convinced that she wouldn't scream, he stepped away from her, crossed soundlessly to the window, pulled closed the wooden shutters, and drew the curtains quietly. For a moment the room was thrown into a pitch-black void. Then he switched on the glaring overhead light.

She realized with a start that she was wearing only a filmy nightgown. Snatching the blanket off the bed, she clutched it in front of her, her breasts heaving, her breathing labored. Her eyes were wide with surprise and her disheveled hair hung limply over her face. Adrenaline still pumped with a pulsating roar through her veins. It made her feel she could slay giants.

Without warning, the shrew in her whirled on him, her eyes shooting lethal daggers. "How dare you!" she hissed furiously, advancing threateningly toward him. She flung an arm in the air. "Sneaking into my room without warning while I'm asleep! You very nearly frightened me to death! I thought someone was coming to—"

"—ravish you." He seemed to find her discomfiture amusing. "Perhaps another time, when we are not so rushed."

Her temper was like an explosive charge. "You . . . you s-sneaking snake!" she stammered shakily. "You f-furtive, cowardly, yellow-bellied, skulking—"

"Ah, such colorful adjectives. You show an artful command of the language. Your father was right—you really are a fine actress."

She flushed under his calmly contemplating gaze. "Is that all you have to say for yourself? You give me the fright of my life and—"

"You look so beautiful when you are angry. Yes, it really does suit you. It brings out the emerald fieriness in your eyes and darkens the freckles on your nose."

"F-freckles . . ." she managed hoarsely. She could only stare at him. He lounged against the wall with such casual ease and looked at her so calmly through indolent, half-lowered eyelids dark with bristly lashes that her rage simply died. The fight seemed to go out of her—almost of its own volition—and her gesturing arm dropped futilely to her side. But her eyes were still locked to his.

Why am I staring at him? I can't tear my eyes away from him.

Whatever it was, something about him had disarmed her completely. His lopsided, gleaming smile that showed off his lupine incisors and dimpled his chin along with his cheeks? Or that catlike sparkle in this tawny eyes while he stared so deeply, so acutely, into her that for a moment she felt his gaze actually reaching into her soul? Whatever it was, some omnipotent force had reached out, cast a spell, and taken charge of her emotions. She was entirely helpless against it.

There was nothing studied about him; he was the real thing, the man the movie idols sought to emulate. She guessed him to be twenty-eight. His sun-darkened face was all cheekbones and angles, and his chin was strong and cleft, like a well-designed piece of structural architecture. His hair was thick and black, curly and unruly. His mouth was sensuous and cruel, and only his nose saved him from arrogant handsomeness; it was superbly sculptured, aquiline without quite being Roman, and so high-bridged it seemed to begin between his dark eyebrows. For all the sparkling, mischievous humor of his big eyes, a sadness lurked behind them—a vulnerability that seemed at odds with his inborn self-assurance. She sensed that he was a man of many layers, that one had to peel them back, one by one, in order to extricate, far beneath the surface, his true being.

She was completely nonplussed. There was something about him that picked at her heartstrings as sharply, as seductively, and as effectively as a fingertip plucking a perfectly pitched harp string. The thrilling vibrations coursed through her with tuning-fork precision, rippling up and down her spine, unearthing long-buried desires, and arousing passions she had not felt even when she had first met Louis.

She tried to tear her eyes away, but they were locked to his. And she knew he was as keenly aware of her as she was of him. Despite his casual demeanor, he was mesmerized with her. His eyes looked lazy, but the pupils were aware that their lives had somehow changed.

"We do not have time to waste." His voice was muted by the roaring in her head. "The sooner you are dressed, the sooner we can leave."

She kept the blanket pressed in front of her, knowing she was acting coy, ridiculously modest. She *was* wearing a nightgown, after all.

She didn't let go of the blanket, but she found the strength to speak. "You'll have to wait somewhere else if you want me to get dressed."

He shook his head. "I took a big risk just coming here. I do not think it wise for me to wait outside. It would attract too much attention, yes?"

Oh, but he was sly, with an answer for everything.

"The bathroom!" Damn her voice! It was shrill, sharp, reedy. "It's . . . it's only two doors down, on the left. Lock the door and no one will see you in there."

His smile widened and he did not move.

"I'll be ready in five minutes," she said quickly. "Now, go.. *Go*!" The words were a groan of torment.

He hooked his thumbs in this trouser belt. "I think you are trying to get rid of me. You are frightened of me, yes? Or just shy?"

"Shy. I'm very shy." She took a deep breath. "As soon as I'm ready, I'll go across the hall and tell my friend Inge I'll be gone. Then I'll tap on the bathroom door and get you." She tried to sever the gaze between them. But it held. She counted silently to herself, and with an effort wrenched her eyes away from his on "three." She turned away, stepped toward the wardrobe. "Where are we going, by the way?"

"A little ways from here, to a kibbutz named Ein Shmona. But please, do not tell your friend. The fewer people who know—"

"The safer my father will be. How long will I be gone?"

"A day or two. Three at most."

"What do you suggest I take?"

"Pack a small case with essentials. Only what is necessary, and dress casually. It is rough terrain."

She nodded, focusing her eyes safely, far above his. "Now, go . . ." She hurried toward the door and opened it. For a moment he did not move, as though challenging her to throw him out. She waited, color flooding her face, but she did not move either. Then he puckered his lips, tossed her a silent kiss, and slipped soundlessly down the hall.

She closed the door and leaned back against it, heaving a deep sigh of bewilderment. She felt curiously unsteady, at once exhilarated, agonized, and drained.

She shut her eyes and shook her head as if to rid it of his image; but something told her that the mind pictures would continue to appear of their own accord, no matter how hard she tried to erase them or how far away from him she tried to flee.

"We are approaching Ein Shmona now," Dani said finally as they crested a particularly steep incline after an exhausting all-night drive. Tamara sat forward to catch her first glimpse of the desert community her father had helped found. In her mind's eye she could already imagine it. Dusty, sparse, and deserted, like some frontier town in a western movie.

But then the narrow road curved through one last cleft in the neolithic cliffs and they came out of the mountains. Below, arid hills dipped to the almost flat stony desert.

"There it is!" Dani said, and Tamara followed the direction of his finger. She caught her breath. Any doubts she had been entertaining were dispelled forever. This was a far cry from the frontier town of her imaginings. Seen from the hills above, Ein Shmona was carefully laid out in a perfect circle, with a cluster of gleaming houses in its center and a lush patchwork of fields of various hues of green radiating outward in a cartwheel pattern.

It cannot be, she told herself. It goes against all the laws of nature. This lush agricultural community simply can't exist in the middle of the desert. It's a mirage, or my imagination, or some trick.

But as they approached closer, she realized Dani had been right: life really *had* been breathed into the desert. It was blooming riotously.

He dropped her off at her father's house. It was on the outermost rim of the circularly laid-out community, at the edge of a field of butter lettuce and green beans. She noticed that the buildings out here were much farther apart than those in the center of the wheel. Obviously this house, like the others edging the perimeter of the community, was part of the first line of defense. The nearer one got to the center of the kibbutz, the more protection would be afforded from hostile Arab raids. That was where the school, child-care center, community hall, infirmary, and livestock sheds were located.

The house was a flat-roofed, unpretentious cottage built of pinkish-white rough-hewn stone blocks. The front door was thick and heavy, unlocked, and Dani held it open for her. He made a point of staying outside.

"Please wait inside," he said, handing over her small Vuitton overnight bag. "Your father should be arriving shortly."

Inside, despite the scorching heat outside, the house was deliciously cool, like a shadowy cave. The thick stone walls did a good job of insulating it. Sunlight slanted in through the closed wooden shutters over the small windows, throwing thin railroad ties of brightness across the floor and up the opposite wall.

This was where her father lived.

She hesitated for just the barest fraction of a second. Then, despite harsh admonishing from her conscience, she snooped.

447

Ever since meeting him in California, she had wondered how her father lived: whether he was comfortable or lived Spartanly; what colors he liked; what books he read; from what he derived his strengths and his pleasures. He was still a vast mystery to her, and she was determined to learn everything about him. And what better way to know a man than to investigate his lair?

There were two rooms, the larger of which she had entered upon coming in. To one side of the front door was a coatrack from which hung various hats, and on the other, a little age-speckled mirror. Directly above the threshold was a small silver mezzuzah.

Eyes roving, she turned a few slow circles, not wanting to miss anything. The rough stone walls had been smoothly stuccoed and then washed with a hint of the palest pink, and the overhead timbers were exposed and white, giving the low ceiling an airiness it would otherwise not have had. A dried garland of grapevines hung along the central crossbeam.

Underfoot, the stone-flagged floor was softened by several small Oriental prayer rugs that added a note of luxury, and at the far end of the room a massive ebonized Victorian dresser topped with a matching ornately carved mirror stood against the outside wall. To either side of it were bookcases packed with volumes; where possible, books had been slid horizontally atop the neat vertical rows. She crouched in front of one of the bookcases, rippling an index finger along the book spines on the shelf. She read off the titles to herself. *Self-Emancipation*, by Judah Pinsker; *Der Judenstaat*, by Theodor Herzl; and *Old New-Land*, also by Herzl. There were a ratty, ancient copy of the Old Testament, several dictionaries, and political tomes in Hebrew, German, Russian, and English.

A round table stood in the center of the room, surrounded by six Victorian parlor chairs, the seats and backs of which had recently been upholstered in blue-and-white-checkered cotton. She circled the table slowly, reaching out and fingering the roughly cast bronze menorah which stood as its centerpiece. It felt cool and smooth.

She noted with special delight that art was not lacking. On one wall, two watercolors of flower samples hung one above the other, and over each bookcase was a large framed engraving of Jerusalem. On table surfaces and on shelves and displayed inside a glass-fronted breakfront which matched the Victorian dresser were carefully mounted shards of ancient pottery and little figurines from antiquity, which she guessed had been unearthed nearby.

A second door led to a very small bedroom, hardly bigger than the brass bedstead and painted cupboard which dominated it. The first thing that caught her eye was a framed photograph of her on the small nightstand beside the bed.

She felt a glow of warmth as she walked over and picked it up. It had been clipped from a magazine. In it she stared into the camera, lips pouting, one hand drawing mink lapels close to her throat. She recognized it instantly as one of the standard publicity shots the studio used to send out to the press.

Suddenly she knew what she had to do. She slid the picture out of the frame and pulled open the top drawer of the nightstand. Taking out a pen, she angled a personal message across the bottom: *For my father, with all my love, his daughter, Tamara.*

She blew on the ink to speed its drying. There. For now, at least, that was a little better.

She slid the picture back into the frame, replaced it on the nightstand, and headed back out. At the foot of the bed she tripped on a prayer rug. Straightening it, she felt the floor give a little under her feet. Frowning, she squatted on her haunches and flipped the rug aside. Set into the floor was a heavy wooden trapdoor with a recessed handle. She was about to grasp it when a little voice insider her piped up: *You've no business prying. Haven't you poked around enough in someone else's life?*

She debated for mere moments.

With a shriek of its hinges, the trapdoor flipped aside, hitting the stone floor with a bang. Tamara leaned over the hole. The door had been deceptively small for such a huge . . . She gasped and drew back in horror. Inge had been right: spies never did find anything good. A veritable arsenal was deposited in there—dark, malevolently gleaming guns, oiled rifles, several machine guns, a box of bayonets, two crates of dynamite.

She slammed the trapdoor shut and slapped the rug back down over it. Lurching backward, she gnawed at her nails. There were more than enough explosives down there to blow her to kingdom come, of that she was certain.

Shakily she walked back out to the living room, opened the door, and stared out at the lush green fields. People were bent over the crops, like gleaners in a Millet landscape, and far in the distance, on a rise, she saw a shadowy sentinel standing guard, the butt of a rifle resting on a hip.

She sat down on the stoop to wait. Despite the blast of ovenlike heat, she felt chilled and rubbed her arms briskly.

449

She tried to occupy her mind with more pleasant thoughts, and mulled over what she had learned about him.

He was neat, and very clean. The house was pristine. He read more for knowledge than pleasure; she'd seen no novels or escapist fare. He spent very little time at the house. However, even if he could visit it only sporadically, it obviously meant a lot to him. It was not a house, it was a home. The mezzuzah, menorah, and Jewish literature suggested that his religion and heritage meant everything to him.

Yet despite the hominess, there was the underlying atmosphere of a fortress: the windows were small, the front door heavy. Even the neatness had a military precision about it. And the arsenal . . .

Was such a cache of arms *really* necessary?

She hoped she didn't have to find out for herself.

Tamara heard the truck before she saw it. She lifted her head and her eyes scanned the fields. Then she saw it, half-hidden by the lush crops. It appeared to float atop the greenery.

She leapt up from the stoop and watched it turn in the dirt track that criss-crossed the fields and led to the house. Moments later, it headed straight toward her. Playfully she ducked into the house and hid behind the door. Peering out, she watched the truck grow bigger and bigger until it swelled to full size. Breaks squealed as it rumbled to a stop. The crunch of the hand brake rang out loud and clear.

She held her breath, barely able to contain her excitement. Then the door on the driver's side jerked open and her father ducked out. He was about to climb down when she stepped out from behind the door. He caught sight of her and froze, his good foot casually poised on the running board, one hand resting on the door for support. His mouth broke into a smile of pure joy.

"I always knew this place was very special," he called out. "But I did not realize it was such an attraction that it would become a tourist stop like Jerusalem or Bethlehem!"

"Father!" she cried softly. "Oh, Father!"

Then he swung himself down and she flew forward into his arms, her face pressing against his chest, her tears of joy mingling with the salty-smelling shirt that clung wetly to his hard-packed muscles.

It was a time of self-discovery, a time of strengthening and affirming the faith that Tamara felt had always lain dormant within her. From the moment she had set foot in Ein Shmona, she found herself immersed in the Jewish experience. For the first time in her life, she began to understand what it meant to be a Jew, and it struck a deep emotional chord within her. Everywhere she turned, she found herself face-to-face with more and more evidence of the faith which was her heritage, but which was as foreign to her as Buddhism or archaeology or physics—but, she had to admit, much more fascinating than any of those subjects could ever be. The agricultural pioneers of Ein Shmona did not only farm the land, she found, but also lived a utopian ideal which blended politics, day-to-day living, and religion into a unique life that was both physically comfortable and spiritually rewarding. She found herself being constantly surprised and impressed.

Schmarya was seated across the table from her in the community dining hall. Despite his urging her to eat, she was too excited to have much of an appetite. To please him, she took a few bites of her chicken and then pushed the rest of the food around on her plate. Her eyes scanned the other casually dressed diners, and she listened to the exotic musical sounds of mingling languages, trying to absorb it all. Hebrew, Yiddish, Russian, German, and Polish all competed with the music coming over the radio. It was like sitting in a large, simply furnished restaurant which served delicious, hearty home-cooked specialties and drew an international clientele of diners. But unlike any restaurant she had ever frequented, there was an air of informal good cheer and undisguised camaraderie such as she had never known. The camaraderie on the movie sets was closest to it.

"I like it here," she said, looking around. "Is everyone always this friendly?"

Schmarya glanced about also. "Oh, now and then we have arguments and feuds, but generally, yes." He motioned reproachfully with his fork. "You are not eating."

Dutifully she took another bite of chicken. "Is the food always this good?"

"Always." He smiled. "It should be getting even better in six months or so."

"Oh?" She sipped her wine. "Why's that?"

"A few months ago a German family escaping Nazi persecution emigrated here and joined our kibbutz."

She set her glass down. "And the wife's a great cook," she guessed, laughing.

"No, the husband, actually. It so happens that Herr Zimmermann is a chef of world renown. He used to be head chef at the Hotel Kempinski in Berlin. Germany's loss will be our gain."

"But I don't understand." She took another sip of her wine. "You said they're already here. Why isn't he cooking? Why does he have to wait six months? Is he ill?"

"No, no." Schmarya laughed. "It is the way we do things here on the kibbutz. All newcomers must first work in the fields. You see, they have to *earn* the privilege of changing to a job of their choosing."

Tamara stared at him. "You mean . . . he's not *allowed* to work at his trade?"

"No one is, until after they have toiled in the fields for a specified period of time. It is that way with everyone who comes here."

"But what if their skills are exceptional? Surely you make exceptions in certain cases?"

He shook his head. "I'm afraid not." Seeing her incredulous look, he added softly, "Can you think of a single more important skill than growing food?"

"In other words," she said, "even if I wanted to join the kibbutz, you'd toss me a hoe and send me straight out into the fields?"

"At the risk of ruining your pretty, manicured fingernails, yes." He smiled. "Though you would not have to hoe right away. The first job is clearing rocks and stones out of new fields."

"But isn't that being a little tough on people?"

He shrugged. "It is a tough country. To survive in it, we must also be tough, each one of us willing to pull his fair share and work for the common good. You see, the kibbutz is not a democracy. That form of government would never work here. So we practice socialism, though ours is tempered with justice, equality, and liberty. However much we love liberty, the freedom of the individual is secondary to the needs of the commune as a whole. Since the fields are our livelihood, they necessarily take first priority."

"Well, I can tell you one thing," Tamara declared. "If I were Herr Zimmermann, I'd probably be glad to plow and harvest instead of slaving over a hot stove! Speaking of which, I noticed your house doesn't have a kitchen."

"That is because I do not need one. We all dine here, in the communal dining hall. It is much more economical than having individual kitchens."

"I see. But to backtrack, I have a question. What happens if, say, the Zimmermanns don't like it here?"

"Then they have no obligation whatsoever to stay. They are free to leave, and may do so if and when they choose."

"Do many people who move here end up leaving?"

"Some. There have been those who find the life too regimented for their individual tastes, but for the most part, the people who move here enjoy it. The work is hard, but the rewards are satisfying. Perhaps not as far as personal gain is concerned, but for the community as a whole. It is as though each one of us works for something greater, a more noble ideal than just ourselves."

She narrowed her eyes. "Isn't that like communism?"

"Yes, in a way. But in a communist country people do not enjoy freedom and justice. We do. Our socialism is only for the common good, and as long as a person's interests are so inclined, his every need is provided for. The education of the children, legal costs, medical care . . . everything is borne by the kibbutz. Even food. No one has to do without. You might say we have a cradle-to-the-grave responsibility to each other. And don't forget, anyone is free to leave here at any time."

She was impressed. "It's amazing. And *you* thought all this up?"

"Good heavens, no," he laughed. "It is hardly an original idea. We are merely carrying on where others left off. There have been agricultural settlements like this one for over fifty years already. But what distinguishes us from them is that ours is the first community in the desert. The rest are in the north, where the land is richer. Most of them are in the Galilee."

Tamara was fascinated, and couldn't hear enough. From the pride in his voice, she could tell that she had hit upon his favorite subject. Even after leaving the dining hall, they talked about the kibbutz long into the night.

"If you like, I will arrange for you to have a tour of the kibbutz and all its facilities."

"I would like that."

"Unfortunately, I must be gone for most of the day tomorrow, but I know that Dani will be happy to show you around."

"D-Dani ben Yaacov?" She could not keep the fluster out of her voice.

"Yes. Do you not like him? He is very bright. Also he is fearless and inventive. I depend on him for many things. You might say he is my right-hand man. Believe me, you could not be in better hands. You can trust him with your life."

Yes, she thought soberly, but can I trust him with my emotions?

Tamara slept well that night. She awoke early the next

453

morning refreshed and filled with a sense of well-being. Her father had left already, but he'd thoughtfully left a bowl full of cool, sparkling clear water for her to wash with.

She dressed casually and ate a particularly hearty breakfast in the dining hall. Her appetite had returned with a vengeance, and she had to force herself to curb it. She nursed two cups of unsweetened black coffee while she waited for Dani.

When he arrived, he was all business. She was both relieved and annoyed to discover that she had no reason to fear his intentions. He was so well-prepared, had so many facts and figures at his fingertips, and deported himself in such a professional manner that she guessed he was an old hand at this.

They started the tour in the very center of the settlement and worked their way outward. Ein Shmona, she came to discover, did not have to rely on outside sources for anything other than the water which flowed in four thick pipes from its source somewhere in the nearby mountains. The place was a city in microcosm. Dani showed her the infirmary, the general store, the school, the electric generating plant, and even several private homes. When she balked at entering a house whose residents were out working, he laughed. "We have no crime here," he told her, "and front doors are always unlocked. We have no need for locks and keys. I hope it will always stay that way."

Tamara turned to Dani, "Do you think there will ever be a Jewish state? I know my father hopes so, but . . ."

"It will happen." He spoke with confidence and his eyes flashed with fervor. "In the words of Theodor Herzl, '*If* you wish, it will not be only a dream.' I believe that in my heart, and so do many others."

"You sound so confident."

"You should hear David Ben-Gurion on the subject! He is worse than your father and me combined!" Abruptly he changed the subject. "Would you like to have a look at our plan for the future?"

"I'd love to!"

He took her to the temple. In the back of it was what had originally been intended as a large storeroom. "We're running out of space," Dani explained apologetically as he turning on the overhead light, "so we use this as our planning office."

She expected to see rough plans marked on paper; blueprints at the most. What greeted her eyes was a ten-by-twelve-foot table that took up most of the room. Artfully recreated on its top was a detailed papier-mâché relief map of the immediate area, including the nearby mountains. It was a colorful scale model of a town, each building faithfully reproduced in miniature, like some extremely lucky boy's tablescape for his electric trains. What amazed Tamara was the size and scope of the community in front of her. It comprised some five or six hundred buildings, some of which looked like four-story apartment blocks with little balconies. And whereas the center of the town was still laid out circularly, as it was now, the future plan was to spread out around it in a grid, so that the perimeter of the two was in an L, belted by a four-lane road. It was all there in miniature: parking lots, residential areas, an industrial hub, a swimming pool, a park, even a distant small airfield.

"This?" she whispered. "You want to . . . to create *this*?" She turned to him. "Here?"

He looked at her levelly. "Why not?"

"It's . . . it's just . . ." She gestured agitatedly. "I mean, it's just so *big*. So . . . ambitious!"

"And why should it not be? If we continue to grow at the rate we have been, even what you see before you will be too small in twenty years' time. In the last five years alone, our population has more than tripled."

"Will it be self-sustaining? Agriculturally? Even that big?"

He nodded. "The fields will be pushed outward, to surround it all. At the moment, we have three thousand acres of flatland to work with, purchased through the Jewish Foundation Fund and the National Fund. We use only twenty-two of them now. We have been trying to negotiate the purchase of more, but the Arabs no longer want to sell us more land. In the beginning, it was easy to buy larger acreage cheaply. As a rule, the Arabs have traditionally preferred hilltop villages or, like al-Najaf nearby, an oasis. They were eager to sell plains, swamps, and especially desert land to Jews, since no one else was interested. Then, after the swamps were drained, the plains planted and tended to, and the desert irrigated, the Arabs began to become jealous, yes?" He paused and shook his head mournfully. "I fear it has made for much animosity."

She remembered the cache of weapons hidden in her father's house. "Is there much violence?"

He flapped his hand back and forth. "It comes and goes in waves, but the potential is always there. We must never forget that. In a moment of weakness, we could all easily be annihilated."

It was a sobering thought.

"Now," he said, leading her to the door, "I want you to see the general store . . ."

He turned off the light and they left the way they had come in, through the synagogue.

Her initial thrill and delight were rapidly turning to fear. It seemed so peaceful here, so quiet. But underneath it all was the ever-present threat of violence. Yet despite it, the people who lived here did so by choice. She didn't think she could, not if she had to be ever-alert to the signs of danger. Not if she had to look constantly over her shoulder.

The tour took up the better part of the morning and overlapped into the afternoon. Dani saved the fields and irrigation system for last. Before they headed out there, he stopped off at the single men's dormitory to get his rifle.

Wordlessly Tamara watched him sling it over his shoulder in the kind of casual manner that told of his having done it many hundreds of times before. As they walked through the fields, Dani pointed out the armed sentries keeping guard while the kibbutzim toiled. Tamara was more than a little disconcerted to find that every fieldhand had not only farming tools at hand but also a loaded rifle within easy reach.

She struggled to keep up with Dani's pace. He was fit and used to the heat, but she was beginning to tire. Small as the kibbutz was, the sun was overwhelming and she felt hot, wilted. Her feet hurt and her shoes pinched; sturdy as they were, they hadn't been made for walking in such rugged terrain, and she'd been on her feet for hours. Her head was spinning from all the information Dani threw at her.

She was relieved when the tour was finally over and they headed back to the dim coolness of her father's house. Schmarya had not yet returned, and this time Dani came inside. They sat facing each other across the round parlor table. He'd pushed the menorah off to one side so they could look at each other without obstruction, and poured two glasses of wine. Tamara was so parched that she had to gulp two full glasses of water before taking cautious sips of the wine.

Even so, because of her sudden tiredness, it went straight to her head.

Dani's deceptively lazy eyes studied her openly from across the table. She felt a stirring of fear. They were too intent for her comfort, those eyes. Their tawniness seemed both to leap out at her and to stretch back into endless smoldering depths. There was something unsettling about them, as if they could see into places her eyes could not.

He caught her look. "Is something the matter?"

She shook her head and quickly lowered her eyes as though the wine glass she cupped in her hands was worthy of study.

"You are beautiful," he said softly, startling her. "Even more beautiful than on film."

She felt a rush of emotion and looked up. "You saw some of my films?" Quickly she raised her glass and drained it, hoping the wine would clear away her awkwardness.

"I have seen one. *Anna Karenina*, at the cinema in Jerusalem. I enjoyed it very much. I never liked Tolstoy until then." He smiled.

She returned the smile, feeling silly at how important his approval suddenly was to her.

He picked up the wine bottle and refilled her glass without once taking his eyes off her. "Are you still planning to return to Tel Aviv on Friday?"

She nodded. "That's when I told Inge I would be back. If I don't show up, she'll worry herself sick."

"Why do you not invite her to come here?"

She looked startled. "Can I?"

"Of course."

"But . . . Brigadier Diggins. He's been having his men follow us. Surely sooner or later he's bound to find both of us here."

Dani suddenly laughed. "Your father is an old fox. He has outwitted the brigadier for years. What makes you think the brigadier can catch him now?"

"I don't know. Me?"

Dani shook his head. "Your father is like a phantom. He has been known to appear and disappear at will. Once the brigadier actually caught him, and he escaped right from under his nose." He paused and grinned, but his voice was low. "Does that change your mind about staying?"

"Yes," she said a little too quickly. Giddily, she felt both disturbed and immensely pleased. She wondered if he were aware of the power he held over her. "Yes," she repeated more slowly, huskily.

"I am glad that is settled, then. I shall send a message to Tel Aviv so your friend need not worry about you. On Monday, someone will go fetch the rest of your luggage and drive your friend here."

She stared at him. "You seem to have it all worked out."

"I like to think so." He smiled rakishly. "You see, I enjoy your company. You are not like any woman I have ever known."

She felt an irrational pinch of jealousy. He was extraordinarily handsome. Extremely masculine. There must have been plenty of women.

He seemed to sense her thoughts and reached across the table to take her hand in his. "So, it is all set then, yes?"

She nodded dumbly.

"Good. I, for one, hope you like it here." He flashed her that lopsided grin that had been so evident yesterday but had been lacking throughout the seriously conducted tour. "You see, it is very important to me that you do."

"And why should that be?"

He leaned closer and held her gaze. "Because I do not want to move. I like it here."

"Why should you have to move?"

"Because I intend to marry you."

But they didn't marry until more than a year had passed. She wanted to make certain first that she was really in love with Dani and that she could live happily on the kibbutz. Meanwhile, she lived in her father's house so that she wouldn't have to move into the single women's dormitory, something both she and Dani agreed would cloud her view of communal living. It turned out to be a favorable arrangement, since Schmarya was gone most of the time and she usually had the house to herself.

"If we were married, we could have a home of our own," Dani told her during one of his daily visits.

"I know," she replied, "but I'm not ready for that yet."

"I love you."

"I love you too. But if I find I go crazy living here, I don't want that to ruin a marriage. This place is your life, Dani. Your soul is here. We both know that you wouldn't be happy anyplace else. So please, don't rush me. I just need more time." She curled the chest hair which poked out of the V of his half-open shirt around a finger.

"If that is all it is," he said doubtfully.

"That's *all* it is," she assured him.

And it was true. She simply wasn't ready to be rushed into marriage. So far, the siren's call of Hollywood hadn't tempted her at all. Making movies wasn't glamorous, it was hard work. Nor did she miss Los Angeles. Here, away from the jangle of city life, she could enjoy calm and introspection. Fans weren't all over her wherever she went, screaming and clawing at her and shoving autograph books in her face. Above all, here there were no reminders of the painful past. At Ein Shmona, every newcomer arrived with a clean slate and could have a fresh start in life. For the time being, at least, she liked the feeling of being removed from the rest of the world and felt at home. And why shouldn't I? she often asked herself. This was the rugged chosen land of her father, and tracing her lineage back two or three thousand years to her forebears would surely have led her to this same merciless terrain which had been the chosen land of Moses and Esther and King David as well. Although she couldn't have explained it, just being here felt somehow *right*. The Biblical past seemed to come alive for her.

For the first time in her life she felt Jewish, and she liked it.

Here was her past, and here, she hoped, would be her future.

Meanwhile, there was more than enough to keep her busy. She didn't want to be a burden, so she insisted upon doing her share by working in the fields. Not content with her ignorance of Judaism, she set out to embrace and practice her faith wholeheartedly. She read books, went to temple, asked endless questions. Three evenings a week she attended classes in Hebrew. After six months she was proficient enough to teach drama and English classes in the school.

Everything was new and exotic and fascinating. She loved the sabbath, with the solemn ritual of lighting the *Shabbas nacht lichten*, the traditional foods, the stories of the Old Testament which were far more exciting than anything Hollywood screenwriters had ever come up with. But she loved the holidays best of all. That was when she really felt the gap between the present and the ancient days closing, so that the centuries seemed merged into one.

Of course, there were heartaches too. Inge hated the kibbutz. She stayed for three months, but then she couldn't take it any longer. She loathed the constant heat, the lack of seasons, the perpetual drought. She complained about the scarcity of commonplace items she had always taken for granted, and about the demands communal living made upon her. Being Catholic, she felt like a perpetual outsider. "It is a nice place to visit," she said, "but I do not think I could stay here forever."

One evening when Tamara came back after toiling in the fields, she found Inge packing her bags. For a moment she could only stare in shock. "Inge! What are you doing?"

Inge did not look up. "What does it look like I'm doing? I am packing."

"But you're not leaving already! Maybe if you give it a little more time . . ."

Inge shoved the last stack of neatly folded blouses into a suitcase and pressed down firmly on the lid with one hand. With the other she snapped the latches shut and then straightened, clapping her hands as though to rid them of dust. She turned to Tamara. "There. I believe that is everything."

Tamara came over and stood in front of her. "But you can't go!" Desperation was strong in her voice.

"*Liebchen,* I must."

"But how will I live without you?" Tamara asked wretchedly. "We've been together ever since I was a baby!"

"You love Dani."

Tamara nodded. "Yes, I do."

"Then I think you will live very happily without me," Inge said gently.

"But what are you going to do?"

"Remember the days I spent alone at the hotel in Tel Aviv when you first came here?"

Tamara nodded.

"Well, then you will remember the people I told you I had met, the Steinbergs."

"The ones from Boston," Tamara said glumly.

Inge nodded. "They have written to me and want me to come to Boston. The children's governess has quit her job, and they want me to fill the position. Linda and Marty Steinberg are lovely children, and they need me. Mrs. Steinberg wrote that I was the only person they ever took to so well."

"I should never have left you alone at the hotel."

Inge stood silent for a moment. "Sooner or later, we would have had to part, you know. The two of us could not live together for the rest of our lives. All little birds need to fly and make their own nests. Now that you have found yours, be happy!"

"But are you really, really sure you don't want to stay? We can make a whole new life for ourselves here, Inge! There's so much to be done! For the first time ever, I feel as though I'm really needed."

"What you are feeling is good." Inge nodded. "Knowing that makes it much easier for me to leave."

Tamara paced agitated little circles. "There's so much good you could do here too."

Inge smiled. "I am sure there is, and I will come back and visit you from time to time. It is not as if we had a fight and are parting enemies, never to see each other again." She walked around the bed and took Tamara's hands and held them. "This is a nice place to visit, *Liebchen,* but I prefer something greener, with seasons." She gave a wan little smile. "I am a little old to play pioneer, you know."

"But you're not old!"

Inge regarded her with a tilted head and then stroked her cheek. "Tamara," she said softly, "everything is working out for the best. Can you not see that? You have found a place for yourself here, and I have found a place for myself." She gave Tamara's hands an affectionate squeeze. "You have a whole new life ahead of you, and so do I. What more could we ask for?"

"To be together," Tamara said glumly.

"Tamara." Inge sighed, let go of her hands, pulled up a chair, and pushed Tamara down into it. She pulled up a chair opposite. "You have found your father, plus a handsome man you love, and even an exciting new world. Be satisfied with that! You know I cannot be with you forever."

Tamara looked across the room at the pieces of luggage. There was something so infinitely sad about packed bags.

"Now do me a favor," Inge said. "Since I am leaving in the morning, and have finished packing, let us spend the rest of the evening together, drinking wine and reminiscing. I want our last hours to be happy ones."

Tamara forced a smile. "All right."

"Good. And who knows? Someday, perhaps, we will be together again."

"Someday, perhaps . . . I feel like I've deserted you!" Tamara blurted.

"No, no!" Inge said harshly. "Do not speak like that. You are certainly not deserting me."

"But it just won't be the same without you."

"I should hope not!" Inge said with comic gruffness.

Schmarya and Tamara looked up expectantly as Dani came in and slipped into one of the parlor chairs. He was agitated, his face grim.

"Is it official, then?" Schmarya asked heavily.

Dani nodded angrily. "Yes," he said tightly, "I have just returned from Jerusalem. It is official. God help us all." He clenched his fist and suddenly slammed it down on the table with such force that the menorah teetered precariously. None of them made a move to steady it. "You know what this means," he added miserably.

Schmarya sighed. "This damn White Paper." He shook his head sadly. "Sometimes I think Jews were put on this earth only to suffer."

"Isn't there anything we can do?" Tamara asked.

461

"We are doing everything we can," Schmarya replied wearily, "which is not enough. No, my children, not nearly enough. We are at the mercy of Great Britain, and we are powerless. With the White Paper reducing immigration to seventy-five thousand Jews over the next five years, the British have cut it to a mere trickle. They have, in effect, nearly stopped it."

"But *why*?" Tamara wanted to know.

"Why?" Her father laughed humorlessly. "Because the British are afraid that war with Germany is inevitable, and they are taking no chances. Britain is terrified that Hitler will win the Arabs to his side." He sighed again. "So the British government has sold us down the river in exchange for barrels of crude oil. They are more concerned about commerce than about Jews." He smiled wryly. "It was to be expected, I suppose. We should have known in our hearts that something like this would happen."

Tamara was pale. "So in other words, the German Jews who wish to emigrate—"

"—will be slaughtered," her father finished for her. He rubbed his weary face with his fingertips. "They are as good as dead already."

"How can we let—"

"Wait." Dani held up a hand. "There is more."

They stared at him.

"Although it is not yet law, a proposal has also been made giving the high commissioner the power to keep Jews from moving around in certain regions within this country."

Everything inside Tamara stood still. "They can't be serious!"

"Let me assure you, they are dead serious," Dani said.

"It will be like Russia all over again." Schmarya was perturbed, but not in the least bit surprised. "We should have seen that coming also," he murmured, nodding slowly. "It would close off half of all Palestine to Jews. It is the answer to all the Arab prayers."

"And two more things . . ." Dani began.

Tamara's voice was a strained whisper. "You mean there's still *more*?"

"I am afraid so. They want to put heavy restrictions on the sale of land currently owned by non-Jews. In other words, the Jewish Agency would find it nearly impossible to purchase more land—"

"But that's preposterous!" Tamara interrupted.

"That is reality," Dani said. "Now for the last item, the biggest slap in the face of them all. The British want to establish Palestinian self-government within ten years' time. One based on Palestine's present population, needless to say. In other words—"

"Since Palestine is two-thirds Arab, and the Jewish population cannot increase much more, it would be an Arab government," Tamara murmured.

"Exactly."

Schmarya scraped his chair back and stretched his legs in front of him. "The way I see it, there is only one thing we can do," he said flatly.

They both looked at him.

Schmarya's face was as hard as granite. "Since we cannot afford to let what the British propose take place, we must step up our efforts to win our freedom from the British. I shall go and speak with David Ben-Gurion tomorrow. He will call a meeting of the Community Council, and perhaps we can come up with a strategy."

"Do you really think you stand a chance?" Tamara asked. "I mean, Great Britain is so strong. Surely—"

A faint smile touched her father's lips. "Did not David slay Goliath?" he asked her softly.

She reflected on his words and then she made her decision. "I want to help in any way I can. Count me in on whatever you plan to do."

Both men stared at her in surprise.

She looked from one to the other. "What's the matter?"

"I . . . I guess you caught us a little off-guard," Schmarya said mildly.

"Why should I have?" she asked. "This is my country too, you know." She tossed her head. "My mind is made up. I intend to stay here for good." Her smile across the table at Dani was glorious. "Would you set a date for the wedding, darling?"

They married two weeks later.

There was no justice of the peace, no media-attended circus. They were married by a rabbi under a *chuppa*. The ceremony would have done Zelda Ziolko proud.

They spent a blissful honeymoon at Eilat, and for two weeks left the cares of the world behind. All they had eyes for was each other, as if they were the only two people alive on earth. They walked the palm-lined beaches hand in hand, dived in the cool, transparent Red Sea, and chased the colorful, fleeting schools of fish along the spectacular shoals of the rainbow reefs. They joked, cuddled, and shrieked like carefree children, chasing each other with spiny crabs, threatening to slip them into each other's bathing suits. When he scraped his foot on the treacherous coral, she bathed the wound, kissed it solemnly, and made it well. As if such a thing were possible, each day seemed better than the last and brought contentedness on an ever-higher scale. Tamara had never been happier in her life. The memories of Louis became hazier, and the sharp twinges of pain she felt whenever she thought of him were becoming more and more subdued. She truly believed that Louis would have been happy for her.

Even in their happiness they kept to a schedule—or sorts. Mornings and nights—and sometimes afternoons—they explored one another's bodies and made passionate love with an ecstatic, almost primitive abandon. In between, they found time to weave glorious dreams and make heady plans for the future. In those tranquil fourteen days, nothing seemed impossible, no difficulties insurmountable. It was as though they both understood that as long as they were together, they could move mountains if they so chose.

"I'll fight as long as I have to to help Palestine become the state of Israel, just like Theodor Herzl dreamed," Dani declared passionately. "I'll be satisfied with nothing less."

Tamara was as fervent as he about a homeland for the Jews, but couldn't help thinking: I only want whatever you want, my love. The only things that are important to me are the things that are important to you.

The days flew past in a blur, and when the time came to leave the tranquil shore, they left without regret, for they knew that their lives were just beginning. Both of them looked eagerly forward to making the glorious dreams and heady plans they spoke of into concrete reality. They not only returned to Ein Shmona loving each other more deeply than before, if that were possible, but they understood each other perfectly and had gained a healthy respect for one another as well. They had left for their honeymoon a married couple, but returned as friends and lovers too.

A surprise awaited them—a newly built house miraculously erected while they were gone. It had four spacious rooms, and was the first private residence with indoor plumbing. "Everyone pitched in overtime to get it put up in time," Schmarya told them proudly.

Tamara loved it more than any of the mansions she had lived in in Hollywood.

However, the real miracle that had been wrought at Eilat was soon to become evident. Sometime during those magical weeks, she had become pregnant. When Dr. Saperstein confirmed it, she wept for joy. It was as though Dani's very touch had made her body bloom and bear fruit.

The joy she felt was indescribable.

Nine months later, Dani was at her bedside while she gave birth in the infirmary. It was the happiest day of their lives. They had been doubly blessed.

He rocked the blanket cradling the infant twins in his arms. "Two beautiful sons," he whispered proudly, shaking his head in disbelief. "And they are not even crying."

"That is because they take after their father," she said loyally from the cot where her head was propped up by four thick pillows.

He examined their faces closely. "They look more like their mother."

She couldn't help smiling. "All babies look alike. Give them time to grow into their faces."

"What are we going to call them?"

"I thought we'd already decided on Ari if it's a boy and Daliah if it's a girl."

"But they're two boys. We hadn't planned for that."

"No, we hadn't." She thought for a moment, and then smiled brilliantly. "How about Asa? Ari and Asa?"

"Ari and Asa it is." *We have each other and our children, and ours will be a family rich in love and peace and purpose. We will move mountains, just as we've planned, and we'll do it as a family. Nothing can part us, and nothing can stop us.*

But the combined forces of history and fate had other plans in store for them.

There was turmoil at home.

As they had feared, over half the territory of Palestine was closed off to Jews, and the heavy restrictions imposed upon the acquiring of land by the Jewish Agency was put into effect. Jews were condemned to a minority status, and the White Paper effectively curtailed immigration. Although it was denounced in Britain's Parliament by Winston Churchill, other Conservatives, and every leader of the Labor party, it stayed in effect.

And abroad, the world was even more in turmoil.

In March 1938, Adolf Hitler had annexed Austria, and then, six months later, Great Britain and France stepped aside and allowed Germany to dismember Czechoslovakia as well. The ravenous Third Reich had gobbled up two entire countries while the rest of the world stood by and watched.

Isolated though they were, the inhabitants of Ein Shmona

followed the Nazi exploits more closely, and with greater dread, than most people in the major capitals of the world. The people of Ein Shmona, better than most, knew that the terror which had been unleashed upon the world could easily destroy them all. Word trickling down from Europe was unthinkably horrifying, and their fears were very real, considering the harsh experiences of the past. They were the latter-day children of Moses and, like their forebears, had come to Palestine to escape pogroms and persecution. Now, it seemed, the very dangers from which they had fled might well catch up with them, overwhelm them, obliterate them.

To them, Hitler was no Chaplinesque buffoon. He was another pharaoh, another Herod—the dark Angel of Death.

"Why doesn't someone stop that madman?" Tamara cried passionately one evening while they were all gathered around the radio in the community hall, listening to the latest depressing news of Hitler's victories. "Before we know it, the entire world will be German!"

"Except for our people," Schmarya corrected her grimly, looking at each of them so resolutely that his own fears merged with theirs, creating a great collective terror. "We'll all be dead. There won't be a single Jew left on the face of this earth if Hitler gets his way."

In 1939 Germany and Russia signed a nonaggression pact which freed Hitler to attack Poland without fear of Russian reprisals. France and Great Britain, having guaranteed Poland's independence, declared war on Germany. During the blitzkrieg of April through June of 1940, Germany conquered Denmark, Norway, the Low Countries, and France—in one fell swoop, with hardly any resistance.

Then the Battle of Britain began.

Hitler amassed his troops on the French coast, preparing to cross the English Channel, but those few miles of open water were to be his albatross. He was stopped in his tracks. No matter how many bomber squadrons bombarded London, the British hung on with ferocious tenacity and fought back doggedly. But the endless bombs were taking their toll on Great Britain even though air superiority over the British eluded the Nazis. Day after day and night after night, the relentless Nazi squadrons filled the skies and the bombs whistled down upon British soil. Many feared that it was only a matter of time before the British would have to surrender.

It was on July 5, 1940, that Dani broke the news to her.

Over the past several days, Tamara had sensed that he was inwardly struggling with himself over something momentous, but she had come to know him well enough not to press him. She knew that he would tell her when he was ready.

That night, after dinner, he proposed that they take a stroll, and from the tone of his voice she knew that he intended to tell her what had been on his mind. They walked in silence, but even before he said anything, she felt a rising dread beginning to choke her. When they reached their favorite spot, a ridge that afforded a view of the entire community, he sat on a smooth boulder and patted it. She sat next to him and took his hand in hers.

The distant cries of the children at play in the supervised playground drifted up to them. Soon, she thought, the twins would be old enough to join them. The white plumes of the irrigation jets made water fountains of spray in the lush, geometrically laid-out fields which would soon yield the third of the four annual vegetable harvests. How tranquil everything looked! she couldn't help thinking. How deceptively peaceful the world seemed! Sitting here now, she could scarcely believe that, a mere few days' journey away, Europe had exploded into a massive battlefield of blood and death and gore.

"I've decided to join the British forces," Dani announced quietly, without preamble.

She jerked as if punched by an invisible fist. She turned to him. "The *British* army?" she asked incredulously.

"Well, the air force, actually."

She turned away and stared out into space for several minutes, seeing and hearing nothing other than his shadowy announcement, as if a damaged tape recorder played it over and over in her mind until it became such high-pitched, garbled gibberish that she thought she would go crazy and scream.

"Tamara," he pleaded softly, "please do not be upset with me. Let me explain."

He reached up and with a finger traced a gentle line from her forehead down to her lips. Usually it made her smile and look at him with a special loving expression. "Tamara . . ."

She sat there numbly, neither moving nor looking at him. He was leaving her to don a uniform, march off to war on some distant battlefield where artillery shells burst, bombs whistled down, and bullets whizzed. He would eat cold rations and bleed and . . . and . . .

She turned slowly to him then, and stared into his face. A sorrowful shadow had slid down over his eyes and they seemed to have lost their tawny luster. "Tamara."

"Yes." Her voice was dull.

"Tamara, you must try and understand."

Her eyes flared and she slapped her thigh. "Dani! The British are our enemies! They've proved that time and again! Ever since that idiotic White Paper, they've been keeping a lot of Jews from coming here." She gestured wildly. "Even Jews from Germany, whose only hope of survival is to come here! And since they're not allowed to emigrate, you know where they're ending up." Her voice was thick with emotion. "You told me so yourself."

"I know that," he said gently, "but I have no choice. I'm not the first Palestinian Jew to join the British forces and I won't be the last. Don't you see? For now our differences with the British must be set aside. A far greater evil is loose in the world."

She gave a wild, discordant laugh. "Hitler. Everything lately always boils down to Adolf Hitler."

"Yes, Hitler." He sighed heavily and looked very tired.

For a long time she could not trust herself to speak. "When are you leaving?" she asked at last.

"The first of next week."

"Four days from now." She pressed his hand. "So soon."

"Yes."

She watched the blood-red sun sliding silently behind the dark distant cliffs. For a heart-stopping moment everything looked blood-red—the ground, the sky, even Dani.

Her fears pressed in claustrophobically. She moved her arm protectively around him and clung to his side. Terrifying visions of war flickered through her mind like a speeding film, frame after frame filled with mounting horrors. Only now did she realize how much she had taken her newfound happiness for granted, when it was a blessing she should have given thanks for every day.

He was looking at her so gently that she felt he had been reading her mind. "We all have to do our part, Tamara," he said softly. "Don't you see? The only thing keeping Hitler from swallowing up more of the world is England. So far, his troops haven't gotten across the channel. If they do, the Nazis are liable to arrive on our doorstep next. And then what?" He shook his head sorrowfully, the weight of the world slumping his shoulders. "We're Jews, Tamara. We wouldn't last a week."

She stared at him as though in a trance.

We're Jews. Jews.

And suddenly the ugliest terror of all reared its monstrous head: What if he was wounded and fell into enemy hands and made a prisoner of war . . . and the Germans found out he was Jewish!

The thought made her head spin so crazily out of orbit she was certain she was going to throw up. It took every ounce of willpower to swallow the bile and keep it down.

Dani said, "Only if enough of us stand up and fight can we hope to survive. You can see that, can't you?"

She fought to be brave and found the courage to give a slight nod. He was right, of course; deep down inside, she knew that as clearly as she knew that death followed birth, that night followed day. His mind was made up. It was in his eyes. She could only agree with him, and hopefully strengthen his courage and resolve even further. It was hard enough for him to march off and do battle against Hitler's seemingly invincible forces without her reminding him of the hazards involved.

Whatever she did, she must not undermine his confidence, for that could prove fatal.

"Ye—" she started, then swallowed to moisten her mouth, and with a supreme effort tried again. "Yes, darling," she said simply, pressing the soft warmth of her body against him. "You must join the British forces. I . . . I understand."

He stared at her speechlessly.

"I'm so proud of you," she whispered. "I love you so much."

He shook his head wonderingly. "It is I who should be proud," he said as he pulled her closer to kiss her. "A lesser woman would have tried to talk me out of it." He smiled at her. "You know, you really are your father's daughter."

Suddenly tears sprang into her eyes. "My father's daughter wasn't speaking," she said thickly. "That was your wife."

"I know." He smiled more widely now and dabbed her eyes with his fingertips. "Don't I know."

"Dani . . ." There was a frightened look on her face. "Hmmm?"

"You'll be careful? You won't do anything foolish?"

He laughed. "How could I? I must come back, mustn't I? There are mountains to move, babies to make. We need every man, woman, and child to make Herzl's dream of a Jewish homeland a reality." He grinned confidently, his strong white teeth gleaming. "Nothing will happen to me until we have a houseful of children."

She felt a pang in her heart. When he smiled, he looked so young, so fragile, making her aware, not of his strengths, but of his fragility. Bones, muscles, organs, skin—they were all so damageable.

That night, and the three remaining nights they had together before he sailed, they made furious, savage love, as if they had to prove they were strong, potent, and very much alive.

Four days later he drove to Haifa to board the British frigate to take him to England, and she and the children went along. It was the most miserable ride of her life. Their time together was down to mere hours, the meter running. Even the twins seemed to sense her fears and were uncharacteristically subdued.

At the wharf, she was surprised by the sight which greeted her eyes. There was a contingent of at least two hundred other young Jewish volunteers waiting to set sail aboard the same ship. From the carnival merriment it was obvious that the men were going off gladly. Women and men of all ages were on hand to see them off, handing out flowers and glasses of Semillon wine. Musicians played traditional songs, and some particularly lively couples linked hands to dance an impromptu *hora* under the relentless sun. Tamara could only stare. Despite the knowledge that many of the men might not return, their enthusiasm was not dampened.

Her heart swelled with pride. She looked at Dani. Much as the settlers had struggled to win their freedom from the yoke of the British, many were willing to set aside their differences and send the flower of their youth off to fight Hitler alongside the English. They knew what was important to them.

This rousing sight brought a lump to her throat and made her proud to be Jewish.

The time came for Dani to board the ship, and she had to bite down on her lip and fight against the tears, but it was a losing battle. *As soon as that ship casts off, he'll be gone, at the mercy of faceless generals and nameless tacticians, fodder for an arsenal of bullets and bombs and God only knows what other horrors, and he might never come back. I might never hold him in my arms again.*

Tears slid in unchecked rivulets down her cheeks as they stood locked in their final embrace, a gust of warm sea wind rippling through their hair. "I'll pray for you, Dani," she whispered. She stared into his eyes and stroked his face, as if to memorize it by touch as well as sight. "Do what you have to, but don't make me a widow," she pleaded softly in Hebrew.

Unexpectedly, he threw back his head and laughed. "I'll be back in one piece, and soon. Wait and see. One good Jew is worth ten thousand Nazis. We'll show those Germans. Hitler won't know what hit him. The war will end in no time."

*　*　*

The war dragged on and on, with no end in sight. The days were long and the nights unbearably empty. Tamara felt like a widow. With Dani gone, there was a void in her life that was like that terrible loneliness after Louis had died. Had it not been for the unceasing daily work the kibbutz demanded, she would have gone out of her mind. As it was, the hours of drudgery weren't nearly enough to keep her busy. She cared for the twins, played with them, cleaned the house until it shone, organized theatrical events for the settlement's children, polished her Hebrew, devoured all the books she could get her hands on, kept a diary, wrote long weekly letters to Dani, and made herself available to any of the other families who could use her help. She was content to do anything as long as it occupied her mind so that she could forget the constant ache of emptiness for a while.

When more of the men went off to join the British forces, she and the other women learned to clean, oil, load, and practice firing Ein Shmona's hidden arsenal of weapons, so that in case of an attack they could defend themselves. To the surprise of the men, the women were no less marksmen than they. Their touch on the trigger was often more delicate, and they showed more patience lining up the targets in their sights.

The highlights of Tamara's life became those infrequent but exhilarating moments when Dani's letters arrived. She read them over and over. They were invariably censored, and she never knew exactly what he was up to or what his missions really were, but just hearing from him was enough. She knew he was a navigator on an airplane, out there amid all the violence and chaos, still alive.

Those letters were her lifeline, her salvation from madness. Months, then years, passed, and still there was no end in sight. Europe and the Pacific became two massive chessboards, and while victories had initially belonged to Germany and the Axis powers, U.S. involvement brought about a turning point. Slowly the tides of war started to favor the Allies in their relentless drive to push back the Axis powers. Now England no longer had to depend on her deteriorating defensive position. Thanks to American technology and massive infusions of aid, including men, armaments, and ammunition, Allied bombers began nightly retaliatory sweeps over Germany—missions in which Dani ben Yaacov was taking part.

Knowing that much from his letters, life became a living hell for Tamara. Each day dawned as a waiting game, and only long past nightfall, after no one arrived to proclaim her

471

a widow, did she fall into nightmarish, uneasy sleep. Her nerves became ragged, on edge. She was so cross, so crotchety, her neighbors began to tread with special care around her.

Then, during a scorching, deceptively peaceful-dawning Tuesday in August of 1942, Tamara's world short-circuited completely. In the morning, an irrigation pump feeding water to the fields and the settlement overheated and exploded. Around noon there was an Arab attack from the hills which took more than two hours to repel. In the early afternoon, the twins got into a wretched fight, and she'd had to punish them. And early that evening, just as she was certain her world had settled back into sanity, a British Land Rover screeched to a halt in front of her house and a British officer knocked on her door.

"Mrs. ben Yaacov?" he asked in a raspy voice.

"Y-yes?"

"Mrs. Dani ben Yaacov?"

A sudden fear swept through her and she clapped a hand over her mouth to stifle the scream. It was as if she were frozen to the door, unable to speak, or nod, or move.

Slowly she let her hand drop from her mouth. But a ghastly smile that could not thaw was frozen on her face.

"I am Major Winwood." The British officer peered at her closely with concern. "Are you quite all right, madam?"

"O-of course I am, Major," she said, holding the door to the living room wider. "Won't you come in? It's a beastly day, in the mid-nineties, I think. Surely you could use some refreshment?"

"Mrs. ben Yaacov, if you'd please sit down . . ." His breathing was labored, wheezy from a lifetime of smoking.

"I'm fine!" she said too quickly, with too much fierce chirpiness. "Please make yourself comfortable." She gestured to a chair and then paced the room, wringing her hands nervously. "I'm afraid the house is in such a mess. To tell you the truth, I really wasn't expecting visitors. If I'd know you were coming, I'd . . ." Her voice trailed off, as she found it difficult to continue with the niceties.

He remained standing, his feet planted wide apart. "Please understand that I find it very difficult to have to break this news to you, Mrs. ben Yaacov. Saturday last your husband was on a nighttime bombing mission over Germany . . ." His voice trailed off.

She whirled around, her face alabaster white. "G-go on."

He avoided her eyes. "I regret that it is my duty to have to inform you that his plane was shot down somewhere over the Ruhr."

She shut her eyes and the world seemed to tilt and scratch and shriek. Interminable minutes passed before she could trust herself to speak. "P-please . . . what happened?"

"From eyewitness accounts, all we know is that his plane sustained a direct hit."

Her mind reached out, found a straw, and grasped at it with all its might. "The crew parachuted to safety, I take it."

"The plane exploded in midair. I'm afraid there wasn't time for the crew to evacuate. There . . . there are no remains. I'm sorry."

She was thrown into a sudden tailspin. She swayed, stumbled, and then her body seemed to cave in on itself. He reached out to catch her before she fell, but before she collapsed she pulled herself together and her swaying lost momentum.

She shut her eyes and gripped the table.

The major was telling her that Dani was dead. That he was forever lost to her.

A midair explosion.

With no remains.

"Mrs. ben Yaacov . . ."

She took a deep breath, her face shining as brightly as polished steel. "I'm fine, Major. For a moment I . . . I felt a little weak. You must forgive me." She made a fluttering gesture with her hand. "I'm all right now, really I am. Won't you invite your driver in for something cool to drink?"

"I'm afraid we really must be going. I'll get one of your neighbors to sit with you."

She shook her head. "That's very kind of you, Major Winwood, but it really isn't necessary. There are a lot of things I must do. It's been so long since I sent my husband a package. Just ordinary things, you know, but touches of home."

"Mrs. ben Yaacov, I realize this is a shock . . ."

"Shock!" She glared at him.

"He's dead," he said gently. "You must come to terms with it. Your husband was killed."

"Oh, but you're mistaken, Major. You see, he isn't dead. He's very much alive."

He stared at her in silence. Her face had become even more radiant, even more like polished steel. He could almost imagine shards of light glancing off it.

Even before she heard his Land Rover drive off, she was already at her little desk writing Dani a letter. Her features furrowed into a frown. *What is all this nonsense about Dani's being dead. Dani isn't dead. He's alive somewhere. I can feel it in my bones.*

473

"Dani, my love, my precious sweet . . ." she wrote.

She didn't make a single reference to the major's visit. She clung desperately to her belief that Dani wasn't dead, that he would receive her letter or at least know it had been written. And three weeks later, when the last letter he had written to her before he'd been shot down arrived, she took it as a sign that she was right. Somewhere out there, he was alive.

Mentally she entrenched herself, doggedly waiting for him to return. Never once did she give up and admit defeat.

The war continued and the Allies continued to make headway.

After three winter counterthrusts, Russia began driving the Axis powers from all of Eastern Europe and the Balkans; British and American forces invaded North Africa, Italy, and Norway.

In the Pacific, the Battle of Midway turned back the Japanese advance, and successive island-hopping culminated in the decisive but costly victories at Guadalcanal, Leyte Gulf, Iwo Jima, and Okinawa. Massive bombing raids on the Japanese homeland began to wear down the Japanese defenses.

It became clear that an Allied victory would be assured.

Then 1944 crept into 1945.

Finally, on May 7, 1945, Germany surrendered and the war in Europe at last ground to a halt. In the Pacific, peace took longer to achieve, but three months and two atomic bombs later, Japan surrendered on August 14.

When the final tally was made, the war's death toll would stand at a staggering 45 million, more than one-seventh of them Jews who had perished in the Nazi death camps.

Slowly the Jewish Palestinians who had fought with the English were discharged from the armed forces and trickled home. Some came back wounded, some came back fit in body, but none had come through the war unscathed.

Tamara waited and waited, but Dani did not return.

During the painful days and weeks and months and then years, Tamara had staunchly refused to believe that Dani was dead. Something inside her—some vague intuition, a psychic notion, perhaps, or a wife's unflagging belief that her husband's living presence could travel on some mysterious wavelength back to her—simply refused to let her give him up for dead. She was well aware that others took it as a sign that she was unable to face the truth or that she was so shattered she was becoming mentally weak. Her friends and neighbors had long since given up trying to reason with her. Tamara herself couldn't explain why she felt as she did, but the feeling wouldn't go away.

It was the First Eve of Rosh Hashanah, the Jewish New Year, and since it was past sunset, Tamara had to light the holiday candles from a preexisting flame.

Solemnly she checked the twins to make sure they were still wearing their yarmulkes, covered her head with the prayer shawl, and went to the kitchen to get the thick, long-burning candle she had lit well before the sun had gone down. Carefully she tilted its flame to the candles she had lined up in little glass containers on the table. One by one, their wicks caught fire, flared with a slight hiss and crackle, flickered, and then settled into silent, brightening aureoles of steady light. She took the long-burning candle back to the kitchen. It was to burn continuously through the Second Eve, when, after sunset the following day, she would use it to light the holiday candles once again. According to religious tradition, a fire could not be struck during the holiday, so the preexisting flame had to be kept lit. Throughout the procedure, she couldn't help but be reminded of how much she had already learned of her faith, of how much she still had to learn. But unlike the previous Rosh Hashanahs, she no longer needed to read the prayers. She had memorized them all, and Hebrew had become such second nature to her that at times she surprised herself by actually thinking in that once-exotic language.

Now, bowing her head, she began to recite the benediction by heart: "*Boruch atoh adonoi,*" she began. She glanced down at the children.

"*Boruch atoh adonoi,*" they said obediently, and continued repeating each phrase after her.

"*. . . Yom hazikoron.*"

"*. . . Yom hazikoron.*"

She smiled at them proudly. "That was very good," she said in English. She was a firm believer in mixing Hebrew with judicious dollops of English so that they would be bilingual.

Alone with the twins, a glass of sweet red wine, and the flickering candles, she could almost feel Dani's presence. She bowed her head again and continued to pray, the twins echoing every word. "*Boruch atoh adonoi eloheinu melech hoolom shehehcheyohnu bikiyemcnu—*"

Abruptly the prayer was interrupted by a knocking at the

475

door. Tamara felt a stab of annoyance. She didn't *want* company. Hadn't she made that perfectly clear? Why did everyone have to be so well-meaning at times like this?

The knocks came again, louder this time.

"Mama, aren't you going to answer it?" Asa demanded.

". . . *Vehegeonu legman hazeh.*" Hurriedly she finished the remaining words of the prayer, and then, placing one hand flat on top of her head to keep the prayer shawl from sliding off, went to the door and yanked it open.

Her face registered little surprise. "Come in, Major," she said, recognizing the British officer at once. He was the same man who had come to deliver the news that Dani had been shot down. His breathing was as wheezy as it had been then. "Major Winfield, if memory serves me correctly."

"Winwood, madam," he corrected.

She opened the door wider and stepped aside. "Do come in."

He took off his hat, held it awkwardly in front of him, and stepped into the room. She closed the door quietly behind him. He looked at the flickering candles on the table and turned to her. "I hope I'm not interrupting something?"

"Only a little holiday celebration which shouldn't be celebrated alone," she said, unaware that the prayer shawl had slipped down over her shoulders. "Children, this is Major Winwood. Major Winwood, Ari and Asa."

"How do you do?" the twins said in chorus.

Tamara looked at the major. "Can I get you something?"

"In a moment, perhaps. First, I would like to inform you—"

"That my husband is alive and well," she finished for him, "and that he will return home shortly."

He stared at her in surprise. "How did you know that?"

"I always knew," she said simply. "I felt it in my heart all along."

He cleared his throat and looked embarrassed. "On behalf of the Royal Air Force and myself, I must apologize for having upset you unduly when I last came to see you. We really believed that there was no chance for his survival."

"But you *didn't* upset me unduly, Major," she answered him. "I didn't believe for a moment that Dani was dead. Now, would you join me in a glass of wine? This is, after all, the occasion of the Jewish New Year. And it will be a happy new year, I can see that already."

"Please, I don't mind if I do, madam." Again she could hear him wheezing heavily. She went to get another glass, poured wine for both of them, and they sat down facing each other across the table. He lifted his glass. "Cheers," he said, extending his glass over the candles.

"*L'Chaim,*" she replied.

They clinked glasses and drank.

"Now," she said, putting her wine down and lifting her chin. "I would appreciate it if you could fill me in on some of the details."

"They're a bit sketchy, I'm afraid. Apparently, when your husband's plane was shot down he parachuted to safety, but was severely wounded, and the years he spent in the detention camp didn't help him any. When the camp was liberated, he had no identification on him, and could barely speak. He was very sick and emaciated. In fact, if it hadn't been for some fellow prisoners, we wouldn't even have known that he'd been with the RAF. Last April he was transferred to a military hospital in Surrey. He only recently recovered enough to remember who he was."

"Then I must go to him at once!"

"There's no need for that, madam. As soon as he's debriefed, he will be on his way here, possibly within the week."

"In that case," she said, leaning over the table and blowing out the candles, "I think it would be appropriate to celebrate Rosh Hashanah a little later than usual this year."

For Tamara, the war was finally over.

Tamara was sure that Dani's return home would be the single happiest day of her entire life, but she was unprepared for the bittersweetness of the occasion. She barely recognized him when he came off the ship, and could only stare at him in a state of shock. He was not the same man who had marched off healthy and fit and tan to do battle with the Nazis. He was but a shadow of the Dani she had once known. His eyes were sunken into concave hollows and their expression ranged from weary and unfocused to hunted and suspicious, as though they had seen more horrors than they could endure. His cheeks were hollow as well, and his once-tan complexion was sallow and sickly. His uniform hung from a skeletal body.

She nearly let out a scream of horror. *What had they done to him?*

She took him into her arms and held him close, the tears streaming from both their eyes.

It was obvious to Tamara that what he needed was rest, and a good diet, and no end of loving care. She dropped everything she had been involved in, packed some suitcases, and the four of them went immediately to Eilat, where they had spent their honeymoon. For three months they did nothing but catch up on the years, draw strength and comfort from each other, and after the twins had been put to bed, make love.

Tamara dedicated herself completely to Dani. She cooked for him, cared for him, and nursed him back to health. Although he would never divulge the horrors he had been forced to witness and endure, often he awoke from nightmares screaming and drenched in cold sweat, and she would hold him and comfort him as best she could.

Slowly, she, the sun, the sea, and the boys worked their wonders.

Dani began putting on weight, and the regimen of daily exercise she prescribed for him, as well as the games the twins forced him to endure, fleshed out his muscles. His sickly, sallow complexion took on the darkness of a healthy, glowing tan. But the single most important thing with which she infused him over those first crucial months was a sense of stability, of normalcy and family life, of a nightmare turned right. Instead of famine, there were feasts; in place of abuse there was tender love, and Tamara managed to allay and then banish his fears. But it was also during his convalescence that she realized how wrong she had been. The war was far from over. Its grisly residue would haunt them all for a lifetime to come, lurking just behind the facade of happiness.

"I've been licking my wounds and feeling sorry for myself long enough now," Dani announced unexpectedly over breakfast one morning. He and Tamara sat alone, as the boys had gone fishing with another family. "It's time to go home."

She looked at him silently, tears of happiness blurring her vision.

He smiled. "Well, aren't you going to start packing?"

She could barely speak. "You mean you're . . . you're ready to leave now?"

"We've idled long enough. It's time we got going and started to move those mountains we used to speak of."

She wanted to applaud. The Dani she loved so fiercely had returned.

They sealed their happiness with a kiss. But his was no mere loving kiss. It became urgent, prolonged, a resurrection of body and soul, a reawakening to life and all its pleasures, a celebration of life over death. The savagery of it brought tears to her eyes. She was so overcome by her happiness for him—and for *them*—that there was something dreamlike, almost mystical about the lovemaking that followed. Before his tongue found her breasts, and long before he entered her, her mind and body had merged as one with his.

On that morning, their breakfasts abandoned on their plates, they conceived their third and last child.

At the oasis of al-Najaf, Jehan, the wife of Naemuddin al-Ameer, cleared away the last vestiges of the morning meal and then tied back the curtain which divided the one-room house into two separate living areas. She draped her head with the thick black veil she always wore when she went out-of-doors, paused to adjust it, and glanced out the open door. From nearby came the shouts and shrieks of Iffat and Najib, her grandchildren, happily at play.

How innocent the sounds of childhood! she thought, shaking her head mournfully. And how short that time of innocence was. Already Iffat was six, Najib twelve. How soon before they would be grown and discovered the world for what it really was—harsh and cruel and unfeeling?

Suppressing a shiver, she looked over at her husband. He was seated in his usual spot, a cushioned carpet at the far end of the room. Flutters of nervous apprehension ran through her. He had not touched his breakfast, and now he was letting his sweet mint tea get cold. She could tell that he was deeply troubled. His head was bowed forward, his wide brow deeply furrowed with worry; he was far away, lost in thought.

Soundlessly she walked toward him and dropped to her knees in front of him. "What troubles you, my husband?" she asked softly. She took his hands in hers and looked down at them. They were rough and gnarled, just as hers were, only larger. "There is nothing to worry about, is there?"

Naemuddin raised his head. At sixty-four he was still tall and imposing, but the strain he was under was showing. The proud, flowing black beard and mustache surrounding his hawk's beak of a nose were shot with gray, and in his gaunt face the bones were becoming more and more pronounced. His eyes, once sharp and canny, had become increasingly sad and confused.

"I fear there is much to worry about, my wife," he said gently. "For two days now, my half-brother's men have been oiling and cleaning their weapons. Now they are preparing to sharpen the knives in their scabbards. Do you think they do that in order to feast and celebrate?"

"Abdullah always feasts at the expense of others!" she spat in disgust. "Because he refuses to labor honestly, tending the sheep and goats, and he will not soil his hands with the crops." Then her voice grew softer. "But he is young. In time, perhaps he will see the er—"

"No! He wants only to play at death and destruction." His hands trembled and she clung to them. "But it is no game. He and the others will not be satisfied until the desert runs red with the blood of the Jews. You will see, my wife. Before the sun sets on three more days, their guns will be empty and their knives will drip red with blood."

"You have only to speak to make them see the folly of their ways!" she urged.

Naemuddin grunted. "You know I have done so many times. It is useless."

She tightened her grip on his hands. "Then speak to them again! You are their leader! They will follow you as the sheep follows the shepherd."

He shook his head. "It is too late. Their ears are deaf to all reason."

"Perhaps if you show them your strength," Jehan suggested, and then she felt the blood rush to her head. She was amazed at her own audacity: the words seemed to have burst forth of their own accord. Swiftly she looked away from him in shame.

Naemuddin regarded her sadly. "I have tried, my wife, but they refuse to listen to words which they no longer wish to hear. They think me weak because I urge peace, and they think Abdullah strong because he rages for blood." Again he shook his head, "They do not understand that bloodshed will only beget more bloodshed."

"But they still come to seek your advice," she said stubbornly. "Surely you can see that. Why else would they come here, as they will again in a half-hour's time?"

He shook his head. "The only reason they come now is out of courtesy and respect for a weak old man. Do not fool yourself, my good wife. I am no longer the leader of our tribe." His cracked lips trembled and his voice took on a bitter self-loathing. "It is time my young half-brother wore the distinguished headgear of the leader. It is no longer mine to wear."

"Naemuddin!" She looked shocked. "You know that Abdullah only wants power and war! You cannot seriously hand him the headdress of chieftain!"

"I will. I must." He nodded gravely, and she could not bear the depths of torture she saw in his eyes.

"Nae—"

"Do not try to dissuade me. What good is a leader if he

leads his people in name only, or splits their loyalty in two?" He paused, but she had no reply, as he knew she would not. "No, my wife, my time of abdication has come. There is nothing more I can do. Abdullah has gained the respect of everyone. Now everything is in the hands of Allah."

Jehan squeezed his hands to let him know that she shared in his pain and humiliation. Her eyes shone brightly with tears.

What her husband said was true, she thought. Abdullah had become the true leader of the tribe. Subtly at first, and then with increasing boldness, he had undermined her husband's authority until his power had steadily diminished to uselessness. Abdullah's rousing, feverish speeches against the Jews had inflamed the men's passions and won them over. His image as fearless warrior was respected by young and old alike, and, regrettably, was even being emulated by the children in their games. His ability to procure weapons and ammunition and to raid armories had astounded them all. And his teaching the men to use them had sparked off a bloodthirst which went back to primitive times and made them hold their heads high and walk tall. Yes, Abdullah had given them something her peace-loving Naemuddin had not been able to provide—a feeling of confidence and pride, a fighting spirit in a new age. Through sheer strength and willpower, Abdullah had molded the men of the tribe into a cohesive militant group with a purpose, and his cries against the Jews had been taken up until there was hardly a man other than Naemuddin who did not echo it.

How like men, she thought grimly, as soon as they had guns in their hands they immediately became fierce warriors.

For that, she knew, was Abdullah's appeal. He fed upon and nurtured the Arabs' fear and hatred of the Jews, a fear which was increasing with every passing year. Although she had never left the oasis since she and Naemuddin had returned from their holy pilgrimage to Mecca nearly thirty years before, how many countless travelers passing through had told story after story of the Jews taking over, pushing the Arabs from their lands? Even from a distance, they said, one could immediately differentiate a Jewish settlement from an Arab one. The Jewish settlements were always green and lush, the Arabs' invariably dun brown or yellow.

Was this not irrefutable proof, they argued—and none with more passion than Abdullah—that the Jews were draining the land of its precious resources, just as they were draining al-Najaf of its precious water?

She thought suddenly of the first Jew she had ever met.

How many years had passed since then? She couldn't remember exactly, but it seemed only yesterday that the injured one-legged stranger had been a guest in this very room, had been nursed back to health by Jehan herself. Since then, the community of the Jews was said to have thrived beyond comprehension while their own had fallen upon bleak and fruitless times. It was as if the Jew she had nursed had been sent to al-Najaf as a portent heralding changing fortunes and bitter times and, yes, ultimate doom.

Yet, was this not the very same Jew who visited on occasion, who honored her husband with the Arab-like gestures of obeisance which, as leader of the tribe, were Naemuddin's due, who brought them gifts of green crops and sometimes even a whole lamb, and who talked with him far into the night, discussing peaceful cohabitation? Was this not the same Jew who brought word of the far lands beyond the seas, of cities where magic boxes whisked people to rooms high in the sky, of a land so huge that part of it was sleeping while part of it was awake and strange rainbow jewels hung in icy skies?

She could only shake her head and wonder. Sometimes it was all too much, even for an intelligent woman like her, to comprehend. Like Naemuddin, she was confused by how the world was shrinking; how al-Najaf was no longer a secluded little community surrounded by rock and sand. Jews and all sorts of Europeans . . . from everywhere, strangers were crawling across the sands, strangers who, Abdullah roared, were infidels and must be slaughtered . . . and strangers who, Naemuddin argued, they must live peacefully beside.

But she felt no fear for herself or her husband. They were both aged and had lived contented lives; their remaining years were in the hands of Allah. But what of Najib and Iffat? Her precious grandchildren had their entire lives ahead of them. What would this shrinking, violent world do to them?

When he spoke again, Naemuddin's voice was weary. "Now, go, my wife," he told Jehan, "and join the women. We have talked enough. I wish to have a little time alone to pray. Soon the men will be here, and I must formulate my thoughts before they come, or else I shall be as stupid as the goats we tend."

Jehan nodded. "I shall do as you wish, my dear husband," she said with automatic obedience. She let go of his hands and rose to her feet. But she did not leave. She hesitated, lowering her eyes demurely. "No matter what happens, I am proud of you, my husband," she said softly. "Few men know that only through peace and without bloodshed can we be fruitful and multiply. To me, you will always be a great leader."

He regarded her fondly. Despite her age, Jehan was still a handsome woman, broad of shoulder and square of face. If anything, the passing years had only ennobled her features, and there was a strength behind her intelligent eyes that shone clean and bright and sure. In many ways he found her even more attractive now than he had during her more youthful years.

"And no matter what happens," he replied gently, "you will always be my beloved wife, Jehan."

"If it is the will of Allah," she replied quickly.

He nodded. "May he be merciful and beneficent." Then he glared up at her, his eyes suddenly flashing like heat lightning, and his voice rose to a thunderous roar. "Now, go and join the other women so that I can enjoy some peace from your jabbering tongue, woman! Or *Wallah!* By God! I will toss your useless carcass out into the desert where the birds will feast upon you and your bones will turn white under the sun!"

"Dani!" Tamara called out in a pleased voice when she heard him come in. "You're back so soon!"

She tried to hurry toward him, but her movements were slow and clumsy. The size of her stomach and the weight of the baby made her walk like a duck.

He took her in his arms and kissed her. Then he pulled away and looked down at her belly. "How's the little kicker?" he asked in Hebrew.

"Kicking," she laughed, also speaking Hebrew, which was now second nature to her. "Whatever it is, it's sure impatient to get out."

"I can't really blame it, with such a radiant mother to look forward to."

She couldn't help smiling. Why was it that everyone always had to refer to pregnant women as "radiant"? "Darling, I thank you," she said, "even though you're obviously biased."

She led the way through the living room out to the large stone-flagged porch Dani had added to the house the previous year, and which she had lined with terra-cotta tubs filled with bright red geraniums. Gently she lowered herself into one of the white wicker armchairs she had ordered from London and waited until he pulled one up and sat down also.

"When do you have to leave again?" she asked.

"Not until Monday afternoon. There's another boat coming in Tuesday night sometime," he said.

She nodded. He was referring to the *Aliyah Beth*, the illegal boatlift which was bringing Jews, mostly survivors of the Nazi concentration camps, into the country by the thousands. Since the unrelenting British still kept enforcing the White Paper, the only way to enter the country was on the overcrowded ships which dared run the British blockade, usually under cover of darkness. The immigrants then were either ferried in or in some cases had to wade ashore, holding their children and few precious personal possessions above their heads so they wouldn't get soaked. Dani and many others had formed groups who met the ships and helped the immigrants ashore and disperse to shelters. It was a highly dangerous undertaking, with thousands of potential accidents waiting to happen.

"About the ship coming in on Tuesday," Tamara prodded. "You don't expect something to go wrong, do you?"

"I'll be there to meet it, as usual, but I think you should talk your father out of coming along this time. He won't listen to me—maybe he will to you."

"Why?" She looked at him sharply. "Do you anticipate any special trouble?"

"I always anticipate trouble, you know that," he said, lighting a cigarette, and she nodded. "That's why we've been so lucky thus far. Not a one of us in my group has ever been caught."

"But Tuesday. Why are you so worried about Tuesday?"

"It's that other boat, the *Philadelphie*."

"The French one that's tried to unload twice already?"

"That's right. Both times it was chased off after the Royal Navy fired warning shots over the bow." He dragged nervously on his cigarette. "Right now it's in Cyprus. It's the worst-kept secret in the Mediterranean that they're just waiting to try again."

"So there might actually be two boats, not just one?"

"Not only that, but the British are on full alert because of the one in Cyprus."

"Damn." She looked out at the distant mountains, so jagged and purplish and crystal clear. Then she turned to him again. "How many people do you think are on each boat?"

He sighed and shrugged expressively. "Who can begin to guess?" He flicked a length of ash into the ashtray on the glass-topped wicker table. "From what we could see from

484

the shore before the *Philadelphie* was chased off, the decks were teeming."

She was worriedly silent.

"And that last rust bucket that made it through, a week and a half ago, couldn't have been more than fifteen hundred tons, but it had over nine hundred people crammed aboard. Nine hundred." He shook his head. "If one of those overloaded tubs happens to sink, it would make for a catastrophe like nobody's ever seen. There aren't nearly enough lifeboats to go around. A lot of those people are old and sick, and there are quite a few kids too. They're not exactly aquatic athletes, not after what they've been through in the camps."

"So what do you suggest we do?" she asked.

"Do? We can't do anything, that's what makes me so damn furious. Until the British lift the immigration restrictions, there's only one way in, and that's through the *Aliyah Beth*. All we can do is to have as many people as possible stationed ashore to help them."

"Well, that's better than doing nothing." She smiled. "You know, I'm so proud of you. I've never known a man who's more unselfish."

"Me?" He gave a short laugh. "No, not me. Your father— now, he's another story altogether. No matter what goes on in this country, you can bet that he's always in the thick of it, artificial leg and all."

"Dani . . ."

He looked at her, caught by her change of tone.

"About my father. I've been meaning to talk to you."

"So talk."

She sighed softly. "Isn't he getting . . . well, a little long in the tooth for these Errol Flynn heroics?"

"Old? The Wily Fox of the Desert?"

"He's almost fifty-two."

He nodded.

"I worry about him. I worry a lot."

"Rest assured, if anyone can take care of himself, it's your father."

"I know that. But can he take care of so many other people as well?"

"You know that this is his life. What do you expect him to do, sit in the shade and read? He's not that type of man."

"But you yourself are worried about Tuesday."

"That's right." He nodded, took one last drag on his cigarette, and stubbed it out. "That's because, on Tuesday, you can bet that every British patrol on the coast is going to be on full-force alert. The Navy intends to make an example of the *Philadelphie.*"

"One of your spies told you that?"

"One of our British sympathizers," he corrected her with a little smile which faded the instant it touched his lips. "Thank God there are as many of those as there are." He paused. "What I'm trying to say is, your father could be walking into a trap."

A cold dread left her speechless.

"You know we can't afford to let him get caught. He's one of the seven or eight men who're keeping all the Jews fighting for freedom as a cohesive group. It would be tragic if he were arrested." He added gravely, "That's why I want you to try to keep him from being on the beach Tuesday."

"I'll try." Sighing, she laced her fingers across her belly and stared out at the sawtooth mountains. They always reminded her of her father; they were as inflexible and unmovable as he. After a moment she turned back to her husband. "I'll do what I can, Dani, but you know my father as well as I do. Once his mind is made up about something, there's no changing it. He's as stubborn as you are."

"Then use your wiles. They work on me, so why shouldn't they work on him?"

"Because I'm his daughter, and feminine wiles can't be used on fathers."

"Ah, but daughters' wiles can. Use whatever weapons you must. Use . . . the baby."

"The baby!" She stared at him.

"Tell him you're developing pregnancy difficulties. Dr. Saperstein will back you up. Explain to your father that since I'll be needed when the *Philadelphie* makes her run through the blockade, you need him to stay here with you."

"I'll try my best," she repeated with little hope.

"Good." He smiled. "Just make sure you talk with Dr. Saperstein first, so your stories match up." He got up from the chair, leaned down, and kissed her cheek. "Don't look so worried. Everything is going to be fine."

She nodded absently. She wasn't so sure. Her father had been taking chances for years now . . . decades, surely. Only his wits, and sometimes good luck, had kept him from getting caught. She wondered how many lives he had used up already; she could only hope that he had more than a cat.

While the men met in her house, Jehan and the other women gathered at the house of her daughter, Tawfiq. Although they were well aware of the men's reason for meeting, the women, in keeping with womanly propriety, did not so much as mention the subject. Instead, over sweet date cakes and tiny cups of thick, syrupy coffee, they chattered like magpies, exchanging gossip and recipes, admiring each other's clothes, and discussing such heady topics as child-rearing and marriage contracts.

Just as Naemuddin kept himself removed from the men, so too Jehan maintained a distance from the women. She sat near the open front door where she could keep an eye on her own door, a hundred paces away. She did not join in the women's conversation, nor did she care to. Her mind was too preoccupied with what was transpiring in her own house, but every now and then fragments of what the women were saying filtered through to her consciousness: ". . . I think it is scandalous. Her parents are asking *twice* as much as that Diab girl's parents. I always say, deal with your relatives. Distant cousins are much cheaper . . ." As she waited, Jehan became inceasingly agitated. A half-hour passed, then one, then one and half, and still the men were in her house. ". . . Yes, but with the price of brides, who can afford a divorce . . ." Jehan's heart began to beat rapidly, unevenly. ". . . He is a good son, my Salam. Two years now have gone by since he went to Suez to work, and he sends us money every three months . . ." Jehan drummed her fingers on her draped knees, her eyes never leaving her door. She gave a start when Tawfiq touched her arm and leaned down.

"Your thoughts are not with us, Mother," she whispered reproachfully. "You know that if you continue to stare out the door and do not soon say something, the others will gossip about you. By the way they glare at you, I know they find your behavior strange."

"Let them gossip, if they have nothing better to do," Jehan said irritably. "They are a bunch of silly goats."

"Shhh!" Tawfiq sneaked a glance behind her to see if any of the others had heard. Relieved that they hadn't, she let out a little breath. Her voice took on a pleading tone. "Please, Mother, can you not at least feign some interest?"

Suddenly Jehan caught sight of Abdullah strutting out of her house. With a pang, she noticed that he wore the elaborate headgear which had adorned her husband's head for so many years. The other men poured out behind him, hurrying to keep pace with his cocksure gait. Her heart sank. She did not need to be told what had happened. The headgear and the men's obvious excitement said it all. Without answering her daughter, and leaving her standing there open-mouthed, Jehan leapt to her feet and hurried to her house.

She sensed that now, more than at any other time in their lives, her husband needed her.

The last of the men were coming out when she got to the house. She waited with her head slightly bowed, and then looked around the door.

What she saw made her catch her breath. Her husband stood near the door, not five paces in front of her, and the bright sunlight, driving a wedge of light inside, spotlighted him against the dimness as if he were standing on a stage. He was staring directly at her but made no sign of seeing her.

A sudden chill came over her. No, he was not looking at her, she realized with a start. He was staring *through* her, as though she wasn't there.

In the brightness of the shaft of light, his defeat was magnified and piteous to see. His shoulders were slumped and narrowed, his face was slack, and for the first time in all the years they had been together, he looked old and frail and, yes, impotent. It was as if he had crumpled in on himself.

Taking a deep breath and offering up a swift prayer for Allah to give her courage, she stepped inside. Going to him, she placed an arm around his shoulders. She staggered as he collapsed limply against her, but she was a strong woman, and held her own. His body trembled uncontrollably.

"They want to fight!" he whispered, as if in a daze. "They want to wound and maim. To kill!" His voice cracked. "In two days' time, they intend to attack the Jews' settlement."

"I know," she replied gently. "I watched them come out and knew from looking at their faces. They are fools."

"I have failed," he wept, shaking his head miserably. "I tried one last time to make them see the light, but they would not listen. They do not care that many among them will die."

"You have done all you can," she murmured soothingly, but her voice was touched with fear. She sighed thinly. "Their fates are now in the hands of Allah."

At that moment, just outside the open door, her twelve-year-old grandson, Najib, skidded on bare feet, oblivious of the pain inflicted on the soles of his feet. Jehan turned to look. As if by design, he stopped precisely in the center of the bright rectangle of sunlight. He was in profile and he brandished a stick. A moment later, little Iffat staggered toward him and let out a girlish shriek.

"I see a Jew!" Najib yelled. Pretending the stick was a rifle, he held it as he had seen the men do, the make-believe stock pressing into his shoulder. He squinted along it. "Bang!" he shouted. "Bang! Whhhiit! I killed one!" he yelled, and Iffat clapped her hands.

"Jew!" Iffat shrieked. "Bang! Jew!" She reached up, trying to tug the stick away from her brother. "I want it! I want to shoot too!"

Jehan turned silently to her husband. Naemuddin had raised his head and was staring at the children. Tears streaked down his parchment cheeks. "Just listen to them!" he wept, shaking his head in immense sorrow. "How have I allowed this to happen?"

Tamara had walked along the edge of the fields a third of the way around the settlement to her father's new house. When she got there, she knocked her *rap . . . rap-rap . . . rap-rap-rap* code on the front door, waited half a minute in case she'd caught him unawares, and then pressed down on the door handle. She stuck her head inside the living room. "Father?"

"I'm in here," he called back.

She crossed the living room and headed straight for his study. She found him seated behind his desk, his back to the open windows which looked out onto the small cobbled courtyard with its dazzling, chalky whitewashed walls.

He took off his reading glasses and pushed some papers aside as she came around the desk, bent down, and deposited a warm kiss on his cheek. "Hello, Father," she said. She could smell the faint, familiar smell of his sweat; he must have been laboring earlier and had not yet had a chance to shower. She put her hands on his shoulders and leaned over him, nodding at the papers strewn all over the desktop. "Am I interrupting something?"

He twisted around and looked up at her. "You, you can interrupt me anytime, Tamara." He smiled. "You know that."

She went to the other side of the desk and sat down heavily. After making herself comfortable, she said, "Are you ready to go over the housing problems? Or should I come back a little later?"

"Not so fast, slow down a little." He eyed her belly solemnly. "I take it the baby's coming along normally?"

She hesitated, the lie she had arranged with Dr. Saperstein burning at the tip of her tongue. "Of course," Dr. Saperstein had said to her, "if Dani thinks there's a trap your father might walk into, then he has good reason to fear it. So I'll stretch the truth just a little. I tell you what—pretend you have premature labor pains. That should keep him here. After all, we can't allow anything to happen to him."

How easy it would be, she thought now. In her head she could already hear herself telling him about painful cramps and suggesting that he stay close by; she would only have to say the word, and she knew he would. But now, she could tell that even her hesitation brought immediate concern to his eyes and a frown to his brow.

The lie dissolved unsaid. She just couldn't go through with it. He would worry himself sick. She couldn't do that to him.

"Everything's fine," she assured him, "really, it is. Dr. Saperstein thinks the baby will come right on time. Everything's A-okay," she added, switching to English.

"Good." He looked relieved, and then beamed paternally at her. "You just take care." He gestured at her belly. "That's important cargo you're carrying in there."

"I know." She smiled. "Which will it be, do you think? A boy or a girl?"

"Oh, a girl, definitely."

"That's because you want a granddaughter," she accused good-naturedly.

"Every grandfather wants a granddaughter."

"And if it's a son?"

"We'll just have to leave it on a hillside then, won't we?"

"Father!" she scolded.

"Just joking. Just joking." He held up both hands as though to fend off her protestations. Then his face grew serious. "You know, every time I see Asa and Ari, they seem to have shot up a few more inches." He shook his head. "I don't see half as much of my grandchildren as I would like."

"Is that why you keep moving further and further away from us? It took me nearly twenty minutes to get here. Your old house was a lot closer."

"But I felt hemmed in. What's the use of living in the desert when you have houses on all four sides, and your only view is of your neighbor's windows? At the rate Ein Shmona is growing, it looks like I'll have to move again soon. Another year or two, and the settlement's going to push way past here, and I'll be surrounded once again."

"Which brings me to the reason I came here," she said. "We've got to discuss the housing problem. In three days' time we've got to report our findings to the kibbutz committee and make our recommendations. I want to be prepared. There are some logistics we need to have worked out."

"Logistics," he sighed. "Committees. It was all so much simpler a few years ago."

"We were much smaller a few years ago," she pointed out. "Now we have over three thousand inhabitants, and more arriving all the time. More people makes for more responsibilities."

His expression was pained. "You're beginning to sound like a politician."

She laughed. "I hope not, but the fact of the matter remains. We've got a serious housing shortage. Out of every boat that runs the blockade, we get anywhere from ten to forty new inhabitants. And there are two boats coming in next week. That means we have to count on putting up twenty to eighty people. Father, where are we going to put them all? Already people are doubling up in the dormitories."

"What do you suggest we do?" he asked, his voice stern but not unkind. "You can't expect us to help them ashore and then disappear. They have to eat and sleep. To live. Somewhere. Someone's got to give them a new start in life. That's what makes them risk their lives to get here in the first place."

"Then we'd best make new housing our number-one aim. As it is, we might have to start putting up new arrivals in tents."

"If we must pitch tents, then we will pitch them."

"The point I am trying to make, Father, is that we're not building fast enough. To speed up the process, we're going to have to bend the rules a little. Right now, six recent arrivals—three builders, two carpenters, and a stonemason—are spending all their time out in the fields, picking up rocks and plowing and hoeing and weeding. While I understand the idea behind all newcomers' starting out by working in the fields, we've got to make exceptions in their cases. We have to. We need buildings more desperately than we need new fields."

"We need both."

"But those men are wasted in the fields! Right now we've got more than enough of a labor force for clearing and planting and harvesting, especially with the new arrivals swelling our size. If it were up to me, I'd get the trained builders out of the fields and get them building immediately. It's either that or . . . ." She halted and held his gaze.

"Or what?" he asked softly.

"Or we have to cut down on accepting new residents."

He tightened his lips. "Newcomers are our greatest strength, for only in numbers can we become strong." He drummed his fingernails on the desktop. "All right," he said at last. "You win. We'll recommend that we must be flexible and that exceptions should be made. But for the builders only."

She smiled. "And that they start immediately?"

He nodded.

"Good. I don't think we'll have any trouble getting that

past the committee, not if we're both agreed. But it's only a temporary solution, mind you. To keep up with the influx, we're going to have to find a way to build a lot faster. Just think what we'll be up against if the White Paper's revoked. We'll have to be ready for a flood of immigrants."

"Prefabricated housing," he said.

"What?" She frowned at him, her eyebrows knit.

"Prefabricated housing," he repeated. "An engineer in Haifa recently told me about it. What it is, is building in sections and then putting the sections together. Since we've got to find a way to come up with a lot of units fast and cheap, the way I see it, prefabrication is the only answer. It's like an assembly line. Whole walls are built, with windows, door, and all, four of them are stuck on a foundation, and a roof is put up over them. The same goes for the interior."

"You know we can't build walls like that. That takes wood, the only resource other than water that we have a constant shortage of."

"So? For now we can use metal. Or poured concrete." He shrugged. "For the time being, looks and longevity aren't half as important as having the available housing."

"Give me the name of the engineer you spoke with and I'll start on it right away," she promised.

"His name's Peter Highton, and he's with Rosdine Engineering. They've got a big warehouse and office at Haifa harbor."

"Good. I'll go see him and work my charms to see if I can enlist his help." Her green eyes locked into his. "There's just one more thing," she said quietly.

Alerted to her tone, he raised his eyebrows and waited.

"It's about the *Philadelphie*. Father, I'm begging you not to be onshore when she comes in."

"You're worried I'll get caught?" He looked surprised. "After all these years of eluding the authorities, you're afraid I'll get caught now?"

"Yes." She nodded. "You know very well that the British intend to make an example of the *Philadelphie*. They're going to try their damnedest to keep her from coming in and unloading the passengers. They'll probably even try to round up all the volunteers onshore as well."

"The more important I be there," he said staunchly.

"You're crazy!" She stared at him, blinking back a rush of tears. "Father, I could tell you that you shouldn't be there for the sake of the twins and the baby I'm carrying, and because I'm worried for you. But I won't. The point I *will* make, though, is that you're indispensable. If something should happen to you, everything here would fall apart. Can't you see that?"

Schmarya kept looking at her. "First of all," he said softly, "make no mistake. Everyone, including me, is dispensable. There is no such thing as an indispensable person. Not anywhere." She started to protest, but he cut her off. "And second, you and Dani and the others are doing such a fine job that I really wouldn't be missed. In the short run, perhaps. But in the long run?" He shook his head. "In the long run the kibbutz would do fine."

"Don't talk that way!" she said sharply. "You know that you're the glue that holds everything together! There isn't a man, woman, or child here who would dream of hinting to an outsider that you're here. That's why you haven't been caught yet. It's because everyone's so devoted to you that their lips are forever sealed. So you see, you don't owe it to me, or to Dani, but to *everyone* not to take such a chance." She rose from her chair and looked down at him, a pleading expression on her face. "Please, Father, I'm begging you to stay away when the *Philadelphia* makes a run for it. Don't tempt fate."

"Tamara," he said calmly, "don't get yourself so worked up. Stress isn't good for you right now."

"Dammit, why do you insist on avoiding the issue?"

"I'm not avoiding it. I'll keep in mind what you've said," he told her mildly. "At any rate, today's only Friday. The weather report has predicted calm and clear skies through the entire weekend. The *Philadelphia*'s not going to try until there's either fog or rain to use as cover for sneaking in." He smiled. "So you see, it's not a matter requiring an immediate decision. We'll sleep on it, all right? Who knows what might happen between now and the time the ship runs the blockade?"

The Arabs came without warning, in the hour preceding false dawn, when sleep is the deepest. By the time the alarm was sounded, they had already fanned out deep into the heart of the kibbutz. "Arbs!" Asa shrieked from the other room as the warning bell tolled simultaneously with the first cracks of gunfire. Asa's terror condensed the two syllables into one.

In the master bedroom, Tamara jerked upright out of her sleep. Before the second burst of gunfire cracked nearby, she was already wide-awake. Instinctively she flung the covers aside and groped to switch on the bedside lamp.

The bulb glowed reassuringly.

"Turn it off!" Dani yelled. With his honed reflexes, he was already halfway to the boys' room.

493

Startled, she fumbled with the switch and knocked the lamp over. She reached out to catch it, but it rolled away on its shade and went crashing to the floor. The bulb shattered and the room was cast back into blackness.

"I'm getting the boys," Dani yelled from the other room. "Get out of bed, and for God's sake, stay down!"

She did as told, crawling over the edge of the bed and letting herself drop to the floor. She landed with a clumsy thump and let out a cry. She had misjudged the extra weight of the baby, and a sharp pain knifed through her left knee-cap. Her hands went down on crunching shards of curved thin glass.

She sucked in her breath and cursed. The bulb. She'd embedded glass from the shattered bulb in the palms of her hands.

Damn.

Dani called out to her: "Are you dressed?"

"No."

"What are you waiting for! Put something on!"

She struggled in the dark with her voluminous maternity dress, got tangled up in the sleeves, forced herself to slow down, and finally managed to slip it over her head. She groped desperately around for her shoes and embedded more bulb shards in her hand before she found them.

Now all hell was breaking loose outside. A woman's high-pitched scream from somewhere nearby was abruptly cut off. Then suddenly there was an explosion and the room brightened, the walls flickering. She glanced up. The window was a roaring sheet of bright orange; the house next door was on fire.

Dani crawled noisily on his belly toward her, the boys slithering behind him. "You're dressed?"

"Yes." She looked at him. She could make out his face clearly now; it was grim and, like everything else in the room, tinged orange. Orange and pulsating.

"Mama!" Asa said, scooting over next to Tamara. "I'm afraid." His blue eyes were huge with fear and he was shaking. "Are you afraid?"

"Yes," Tamara said softly, touching his face. "I'm afraid too, darling. But everything's going to be all right. Your papa's here, and he'll take care of us." She forced herself to smile reassuringly.

Asa turned to Dani. "You'll take care of us, won't you, Papa? You'll see that the Arabs won't hurt us?"

"That's enough!" Dani said harshly. "We're wasting time. You'll all do exactly as we've rehearsed countless times already." He nodded to Tamara. "Here."

He thrust something into her hand. It felt heavy and cold and oily. She looked down. It was the American revolver, the .44 with the inordinately long, evil barrel.

She looked at him speechlessly.

"Now follow me," he ordered. "We have to get out of here before we're all trapped."

Like crabs in a speeded-up film, he and the boys scuttled effortlessly into the next room on their bellies, but with her own giant belly in the way, and being careful so as not to jar the unborn baby, Tamara could only crawl on her hands and knees, and at half-speed at that. At the front door Dani waited for her to catch up. Then, signaling for her and the boys to keep down, he leapt up, flattened himself against the wall beside the door, and gingerly reached for the door handle. He flung the door wide and it banged against the opposite side of the wall. The air smelled acrid now, heavy with smoke and cordite.

He slid his head around the doorframe for the merest fraction of a second and then flattened himself against the wall again. He was holding his rifle upright with one hand. The crackling of the flames was loud and hellish.

"Now!" he screamed. "Asa, Ari—go!"

The boys went out just as they'd practiced it during the weekly drills. On their bellies, their elbows flapping like seals' fins, they dashed for the stoop, dived and went flying while Dani covered them with bursts of gunfire. When they hit the ground, they rolled over twice and waited.

Dani peered around the door again, got off two more shots, and brought his free hand slashing down. "Tamara—go!"

She clenched her teeth and crawled like mad. The three steps were concrete and murderous on her bleeding hands and knees. When she reached the boys, she looked back at the house. Dani was coming out in a running crouch, the carbine blazing. He dived to the ground beside her. "Keep down," he whispered fiercely between clenched teeth.

"I'm trying," she hissed, "but I can't mash the baby!"

"Now, listen carefully, all of you," he said, his words quick but his voice calm. "Don't panic. Pretend this is a drill. Head for the community hall and stay there. You'll be safe; it's the best-protected building we have. Now, go! All of you!"

The boys wiggled away like tadpoles, digging their elbows into the hard ground and pulling themselves along while flinging themselves from side to side as they gained extra speed with their knees. Tamara hesitated. "What are you going to do?"

"Forget about me!" Dani hissed harshly, his eyes flashing. "I'll stay behind to cover you. Get moving!" He gave her such a painful shove that she cried out. Then she lifted her head to get her bearings. Bullets whined so close by that she swore she could feel their wind. The dirt beside her exploded into a cloud of dust.

That got her crawling. Scampering on her hands and knees, her heavy belly nearly grazing the ground, she zigzagged her way, trying to minimize herself as a target. There was chaos all around.

It was like a scene out of Armageddon. Bullets whistled in every direction. Explosions rocked the ground and blasted soil sky-high. She could hear the high-pitched screaming of children somewhere in the distance and prayed to God that they were not her own. Like shadow puppets gone wild, silhouettes darted madly back and forth in front of the burning house next door, the orange flames licking and leaping out of the windows and casting shadows of enormous malevolent demons. Then someone threw something through one of the windows and there was a *whoosh!* as the frenzy of flames was fed. A screaming man, his blazing clothes turning him into a human torch, staggered out of the front door, turned three slow-motion circles, and then fell facedown in silence, not eight feet from Tamara.

Her nose caught the stench of burning flesh and she almost retched.

It's like pork, she thought hysterically. Human flesh smells like roasting pork.

She scuttled away, past one house and then another, heading toward the center of the kibbutz. The buildings were built closer together now, affording more protection. She staggered to her feet and, keeping her torso bent forward, scrambled for the safety of the nearest thick stone wall. She slid around it and straightened. She was gasping for breath, and inside her she could feel the baby kicking. She put her hands on her belly and massaged gently. Despite the chill of the night, she was hot and drenched with sweat.

Finally she began to breathe more easily. She peered cautiously around the corner of the wall, back the way she had come.

It was too late to wish she hadn't.

Dark, long-robed figures were leaping in dervish dances. Knife blades caught the sheen of the fire and reflected orange slivers. She could hear cries of *"Allahu Akbar!"* as they rushed forward. A machine gun atop the blazing house mowed down a row off them, as though cutting their legs out from under them. There was a chorus of screams as they fell forward, their rifles catapulting in midair. Arabs.

She watched, frozen with morbid fascination, as one of the figures leapt up and an arm arced gracefully, as if lobbing a football. Instinctively she drew her head back and flattened herself against the wall. The ground shook mightily and the night seemed to explode in a split-second fireball. The machine-gun chatter stopped abruptly. Her ears were ringing.

She peered around the corner again. The Arabs had gained. They were closer now. Much closer. And then, suddenly, men without robes jumped out in front of them. Rifle bursts flashed and exploded. One of the Arabs shrieked and fell to his knees, clutching his belly before he fell headfirst to the ground. Arabs and Jews were face-to-face now. Bayonets stabbed; rifle stocks became clubs.

She had to get to the center of the kibbutz. To safety.

Ducking, she zigzagged from house to house, trying to put as many walls between herself and the bullets as possible. She cursed her belly. It was slowing her down. Without it, she could have crawled off as swiftly as the boys.

Suddenly she sucked in her breath. An Arab had leapt from around the corner of the next house, his carbine leveled at her.

She froze in her tracks, and time ceased to exist. The world slowed to half-speed, like a film in slow motion. Curiously, she felt no fear, only surprise. She could see the fanatical eyes flashing wild hatred; she could sense him lining her up in his sights and squeezing the trigger. Even the shot, when it came, seemed to happen in slow motion.

And then Dani came racing toward her, and everything sped up once again. "Tamara!" he bellowed, leaping to tackle her in order to shove her to safety while his own carbine blasted the Arab off his feet.

But the Arab had already fired, and Dani was too late.

Tamara's mouth gaped open and her eyes widened as something exploded in her abdomen. She found herself flying backward, off her feet, as if a massive gust of wind had sent her sprawling. Then she crumpled and fell heavily on her back, rocked forward on her buttocks, and fell back one last time, her arms spreading out as though she'd been crucified.

Dani didn't bother crawling to her; he dived the six feet to where she'd fallen.

She tried to raise her head, but it wouldn't lift. She stared up at him, her eyes wide and confused. "Dani," she whispered, "what's happened?"

"You were shot, darling. Shushhhh . . ." His voice was muffled, as if her ears were filled with cotton.

"The baby," she whispered, her words slurred. One arm moved and she gripped Dani's shirt so fiercely he nearly choked. "Our baby!" Tears formed in her eyes. "The baaabbbyyy . .." Her hand loosened from his collar and fell, and then she was still.

There was no moon to light their way, but it was a blessing in disguise; neither was there a moon to give them away.

Now that the time was nearing, the men began to prepare their weapons. They had slept all day, hidden in the shadows of the sawtooth mountains, which had soaked up the heat of the sun and trapped the simmering air, and then, when the temperature had plunged, they had waited patiently through most of the chilly night. The desert was eerily disturbing in its intense and utter silence.

The oasis was less silent, but no less disturbing: overhead, date palms scratched frond against frond; below, the herd of goats rustled uneasily in sleep and a single dog growled every now and then, its nose sniffing the air. Three times Dani had left his men to slip silently into the night, invisible in the darkness, and reconnoitered the perimeter of the oasis, the last time, an hour ago, actually slipping unnoticed into its very heart. What he found did not gladden him, but eased his tension. There were three men on guard; two were asleep and the third was smoking carelessly.

He nodded to himself: retaliation was not seriously expected, or else the guards would have been more aware.

He returned to his group of handpicked men and materialized out of the darkness. "We wait until after morning prayers," he said softly with the patience of the hunter.

The men understood. They were going to wait for the dawn, when the muezzin would call the Muslim faithful to morning prayer. Dani was bitter and there was no mercy in his heart, just as there was none in theirs. The attack would begin after the prayers were said: the people of al-Najaf would need the opportunity to make peace with God.

When dawn lightened the sky in the east, Dani gathered the men around him. "An eye for an eye," he said grimly. "One house burned, three dead, and six wounded. No more, no less." He looked at Schmarya.

"So be it," Schmarya pronounced.

They fanned out soundlessly, surrounding the oasis and moving into their predetermined positions. There they waited, hidden and silent, while the oasis was coming awake. Doors opened, and people came outside, going about their morning business. Women fetched pitchers of water. Smoke began to curl from chimneys. Then the muezzin climbed the steps to the minaret of the tiny stone mosque and called them to morning prayer, his singsong words echoing monotonously. Everyone, the guards included, stopped what he was doing, cleansed himself ritually, and turned southeast toward Mecca. Everyone dropped to his knees and prayed. All was peaceful at al-Najaf. All was well.

The twelve men from Ein Shmona double-checked their weapons. Dani peered out from behind a rock, waiting to fire off the first shot, which would sound the signal for the attack to begin twenty seconds later. Moishe Karavan, who was positioned nearest the houses, transferred gasoline from a can into a bottle, stuffed a gasoline-soaked rag into its neck, and held matches at the ready. Schmarya, catching sight of Naemuddin, felt a wave of guilt and anguish and bent his head in silent prayer. He was glad that Dani had decided to wait until after morning prayer to attack. The families of those who would die would at least be assured that their loved ones would enter Paradise.

Prayers over, the people of al-Najaf went about their daily affairs, happily ignorant of the attack in store for them. The three guards shouldered their rifles, smoking and chattering in a group, unknowingly calling attention to themselves as easy targets.

"They have prayed," Dani told himself through clenched teeth. "Now we shall see if they are ready to die." He fired once into the air to give fair warning for the women and children to seek safety, and then he counted to twenty. Shrieks of terror rent the quiet as mothers snatched up their children and scattered in panic while the men dashed indoors to fetch weapons. Caught by surprise, the three guards fired blindly, foolishly staying together in a tight group. They were felled instantly by a fusillade of shots that hit true. Dani nodded to himself with satisfaction. It was going exactly as planned: the dead guards were the revenge for the dead of Ein Shmona; that left one house to destroy and four men to wound.

He covered Moishe while his friend made a mad dash with the flaming bottle. Moishe had kept his eye peeled for a house into which none of the women and children had fled, presuming it to be empty. Reaching it, he chucked the bottle inside, and there was an immediate explosion. An orange fireball burst out the door as if to chase him away, and the house became a roaring inferno.

Dani covered Moishe with a spray of bullets, aiming to wound, not kill. The shrieks and screams coming from the women and children were cries of terror, not pain, of that Dani was certain. He had given the men explicit instructions: harming women and children was to be avoided at all costs.

By this time the men of al-Najaf had had time to snatch up their weapons, and there was heated return fire, puffballs marking the positions of resistance. Moishe let out a scream as a bullet felled him, but it was a minor injury and he painfully low-crawled to safety.

There were no firearms in the house of peace-loving Naemuddin and Jehan, his wife, and so they returned no fire. At the sound of the first shot, Naemuddin had pulled his wife down to the floor and instructed her to stay put. His face was contorted with anguish and his voice was filled with rage. "Abdullah has brought this upon us!" he roared, and then hurried outside to try to put a stop to the madness. Moments later a stray bullet smashed into his shoulder and whirled him around. He fell heavily. Jehan, hearing his cry of pain, disregarded his instructions and ran outside to pull him to safety. She offered up a prayer of thanks that it was only a flesh wound, not fatal, and immediately put water on the stove to boil.

Abdullah was enraged. He had been hoping for a retaliatory attack, knowing that nothing would fuel the fires of hatred quite as powerfully as the deaths of innocents. Armed as always, he had been prepared and had dived for shelter behind a low wall, and had been the first to return fire. He had warned the guards to be alert, but they had failed. Seeing them fall, he cursed them: they deserved to die. They had been lax, and he hoped they went straight to hell.

But the retaliatory attack was not going as Abdullah had hoped. The Jews were careful shots. From what he could see, not one woman or child had been hit. He cursed again. Already the sounds of gunfire were slowing.

It was then that he caught sight of little Iffat, his half-niece. She was crouched behind a stone wall not twenty-five feet in front of him. He looked around furtively. No one could see; everyone was hiding or busy shooting. She would be a worthy sacrifice, a sacrifice necessary to catapult the mourning of the dead men and the hatred of the Jews to extreme, feverish pitch.

He trained his sights on her and pulled the trigger.

He lowered his rifle and smiled, satisfied. Her death would be blamed on the Jews.

* * *

Dani had kept tabs; the moment he counted three killing shots, four wounded men, and the fire, he gave the signal for his men to retreat. Two of them grabbed Moishe under his armpits and dragged him with them. They left as suddenly as they had come.

The attack had taken less than two minutes.

Schmarya had not fired a single shot.

The moment the men returned from the retaliatory raid, Dani headed straight for the infirmary.

"She's stable," Dr. Saperstein told him.

"Can I see her now?"

"Against my better judgment, I will give you five minutes with her." The doctor wagged an admonishing finger. "Not one minute longer. I don't want you to tire her."

"Right now, even five minutes is the gift of a lifetime," Dani said.

He went into her room and pulled a chair close to the bedside. He sank down on it, hating the heavy medicinal odor and the way Tamara was laid out so still and straight, with her head precisely centered on the pillow. His heart stopped beating and he was afraid she was dead. It was too corpselike a pose, the white sheet too smooth and shroudlike. For the first time he noticed isolated strands of silver here and there in her silky white-blond hair. Her skin was drawn and like chalk, so curiously translucent that he could make out every ridge of her facial bones.

She looks old, he thought, a coming attraction of what she will look like at sixty-five . . . seventy. Still beautiful, but extremely fragile and bony.

On their honeymoon, she had teased, "Will you still love me when I'm old and ugly?" They had both laughed.

A tear formed in one eye, trickled slowly down his cheek. Yes, yes I will, he swore in his mind.

He reached under the sheet and took her hand gently, feeling pain at its rubbery limpness, but immense relief at its warmth. She was alive.

"Tamara." His voice came out a choked croak, barely more than a whisper.

She lay motionless, her breathing so soundless that he had to strain to make certain her lungs were still working.

Wake up, my darling, he willed her silently. Come out of it, please. Without you, life is nothing. Nothing.

"Darling. Darling!" He pressed her fingers, desperately seeking a response.

Tamara's eyelids quivered and then, ever so slowly, opened.

"Darling, can you hear me?"

She felt so weak, so disoriented. She tried to lift her head, but moving was too much of an effort, too taxing . . . impossible. She shifted her eyes—even that taking an immense amount of concentration—trying to catch as much within her field of vision as possible. But everything looked murky, lost in a gray fog. She could hear . . . voices. No, one voice, distant, distorted, and disjointed. That was what had reached down, down into her sleep, that voice and . . . and a touch.

She concentrated deeply, trying to will the fog away, but it only darkened and shifted, taking on a vague face like the faces children imagine they can see in puffy clouds.

Her lips parted a crack but barely moved. "Da . . . ni?" It was a mere hint of a whisper, the barest exhalation of breath.

"Tamara, yes, darling. It's me." It sounded muffled, like words uttered from a face buried deep in a pillow. She sensed more than heard them. Why didn't he speak up?

"Da . . . ni," she repeated with supreme effort, slightly louder this time.

It was so hard to speak. The words and thoughts formed in her mind, but her lips would barely move to let them out. It took such effort to get anything out at all. *Where am I? Why can't I move? Things aren't usually in this kind of a fog. What's the matter with me?*

"Thank God, Tamara." His voice seemed a little clearer to her now. "Oh, thank God." She felt him lift her hand, holding it against . . . yes, against his lips. She attempted a smile, but her feeble lips merely shifted a fraction of an emotion.

Still, it was a ghost of a smile, and he didn't miss it. He felt like jumping for joy.

"Don't worry, darling. Everything is fine," he said, the tears running down both cheeks now. "Dr. Saperstein says you're going to be all right. You're over the worst of it. Thank God!"

She was tired. So very tired. Eyelids so heavy . . .

Another thought wiggled toward her, and this time she snatched it before it could get away. She forced her lips to form the words.

"The . . . baby."

"The baby's fine, darling! Just fine!" His words tumbled out in such an exuberant rush that most of them flew past her in a blur. "It's what we wanted, darling. A girl." He squeezed her fingers again. "Oh, she's premature, yes, but hanging on. Tough. A real trouper. Like you."

She stared at him, annoyed that his features were starting to shift again, becoming an indistinguishable cloud. She wished someone would stop the wind from blowing the cloud apart.

"G—girl?" she whispered.

"Yes, a girl!"

"N—not dead?"

"No, darling, no. She's very much alive! As soon as you're stronger I'll bring her in so you can hold her! Dr. Saperstein had to . . . Nevermind."

Operate, he'd almost said, *cut her out of you because your womb was punctured by a bullet, and your colon too.*

"She's gorgeous, darling," he went on, "a real angel. Dark-haired, though."

"Dark?"

He nodded, grinning with joy, the tears still streaming down from his eyes. "She's raven-haired—just a few wisps, of course."

Her eyelids could no longer stay open. They were heavy . . . oh, so heavy, and the fog was turning back into darkness, and what he had told her slipped away, out of reach. She tried to remember what it was he'd said, but it all evaporated.

But her sleep was now contented, a Mona Lisa smile on her lips.

Dani felt a tap on his shoulder. He looked up. It was Dr. Saperstein. "Your five minutes are up."

Carefully Dani put Tamara's arm back down and tucked it under the sheet. "She's going to be all right," he said softly. "Isn't she?" He searched the doctor's face for confirmation.

Dr. Saperstein nodded. "Yes, she's going to be all right." He clapped a hand on Dani's back. "Now, let's go into the other room. It's time you gave your daughter some attention."

Suddenly a frightening thought jumped through Dani's head. "I'm not dreaming, Doctor, am I?"

Dr. Saperstein laughed. "I hope not, because if you are, then we're both dreaming."

"Do you know what, doctor?"

The doctor shook his head.

"You're beautiful!" Dani clapped his hands on both of Dr. Saperstein's cheeks, pulled his face close, and planted a noisy kiss on his lips. "I love you!" Then he danced out of the room in a little shuffle-off-to-Buffalo.

Some days, nothing could go wrong.

Interlude: 1956

The year 1946 brought about the beginning of a new era in the Middle East. Both the Arabs and the Jews revolted against the yoke of the British Mandate, and violence and terrorism burst out from both sides. Because they were unable to control the bloodshed, the British finally asked the United Nations to help solve the problem.

In 1948, as the British left Palestine, David Ben-Gurion proudly declared the birth of the independent State of Israel. The announcement caused the worst outbreak of violence ever seen in the Middle East. The day after the birth of Israel, Arab forces, which had opposed the UN's decision all along, swarmed into Israel and soon captured the Old City of Jerusalem, threatening to drive the Jews to the sea.

The short but bloody battle that followed the invasion was a miracle of modern history and was to be repeated time and again. Against overwhelming odds, the Jews drove the Arab army first from Jerusalem, then Tel Aviv, Haifa, Jaffa, and Galilee. And, finally, the Negev as well.

By 1949 the State of Israel had opened its arms to offer a homeland to Jews from all over the world.

—Contrucci and Sullins, *The Mideast Today: Strategies to Cope with the Seeds of Yesteryear*

It was past two o'clock in the afternoon when the petite MEA stewardess came up the aisle. A faint cloud of Chanel Number Five followed behind her.

She stopped at the fourteenth row and leaned across the two empty seats. "We'll be landing in about half an hour," she said in soft Middle-Eastern-accented English. She flashed a white enamel smile at the black-haired young man with the honey skin and the hungry mouth who sat beside the window. "We lost nearly forty-five minutes bypassing the storm front. Could I get you a drink or a cup of coffee?"

He nodded. "I'll have a whiskey. Neat."

She smiled, genuinely this time, and went to get it. Approvingly, he watched her move. She walked elegantly, on low heels, her lacquered fingernails touching the seat backs as she smiled professionally to the left and the right.

When she returned, she handed him the plastic glass and a little square paper napkin. "Here you are." She smiled again.

"Thank you." He took it from her and held it, not bothering to fold down the tray table.

She lingered, half-sitting on the armrest of the aisle seat. "Where in England are you from?" she asked.

He shook his head. "I'm not English." He smiled slightly, showing wolfish incisors. "I'm Palestinian."

"Oh." She looked surprised. "I would have taken you for British from your accent."

"Many people do."

She eyed the drink she had just brought him. "I could get you some juice, if you prefer."

He laughed shortly and took a sip of the whiskey. "I've spent the last four years at Harvard University, and the six years before that in English schools. Until we land I might as well take advantage of the liquor." He looked down at the glass. "It doesn't look like I'll be seeing much of this for a long time to come."

She nodded. That meant he almost certainly wasn't from

Beirut, where there were plenty of nightclubs and glittering hotels and liquor and a thousand other temptations for the asking. "Are you planning to spend some time in Beirut?" she asked softly, her dark liquid eyes probing his.

"I'm afraid not." He smiled apologetically.

The professional smile went back on her face, but she couldn't hide the disappointment from her voice. "I see. Well, if you need anything, just press the call button."

He nodded, tilting his seat back as far as it would go, and nursed his drink. She had made her overture, as he'd guessed she would, and he had rejected it politely. Inwardly he shrugged. Even at his age he had had more than his share of women already. They were there for the picking. Always throwing themselves at him. What was it that Revlon model in New York had told him? "You're too damn good-looking for your own good, Najib al-Ameer. All you do is take and take, but you never want to give!" He smiled, remembering her anger when he wouldn't take her a second time.

Forgetting women for the moment, he shut his eyes.

Nearly ten years had passed since he had left al-Najaf, and he had returned to the Middle East only once in all that time. That had been four years earlier, right after he had graduated from Eton. Now it seemed a lifetime and a world ago.

July 12, 1952. The day the real horror had begun.

He would never forget it as long as he lived.

It had taken him nearly three weeks of travel to reach that fateful rendezvous with the twelfth of July in the middle of Negev. Happily unaware of what awaited him, he felt jubilant, and with good reason. He had done his people proud. Soon he would be home in the village of his birth, a graduate of an exclusive English school with a crisp new diploma in his possession to prove it. He could imagine how it would be passed around from person to person, solemnly fingered with awe and respect, for never before had a villager attended so many years of school, let alone such an important one. There would be much celebrating, for this was a momentous occasion. A holiday would be proclaimed; there would be a week of feasting on succulent lamb and music and dancing. For six long years he had been gone . . . six years during which he, the village's most gifted son, had been provided with an education fit for a prince. It was as much their victory as his. And he had done them proud, graduating at the top of his class. The only thing that made him uneasy was that he hadn't received a letter from the village for the past six months.

The journey through the familiar Negev brought back memories, and he felt exhilarated but enervated: it was July, one of the hottest months of the Middle Eastern year, and the years he had spent in the English countryside had almost made him forget the brooding oppressiveness of the gritty desert heat which lay in stifling blanket layers. Now, at the height of summer noon, it hit him full force, and he sweltered unbearably despite the flowing desert robes he had changed into.

He was unprepared to meet tragedy. The peaceful ivy-clad halls of learning had protected him from the harsh realities that were the mainstay of Middle Eastern life, had sheltered him from the ever-present lurking dangers, had made him forget the potential violence which, he was to discover, had shattered the peaceful tranquillity of his birthplace while he had been away enjoying peaceful study in blissful ignorance.

For the remainder of his life, the memory of that day would remain crystal clear.

The desert had been unearthly still, even for the sun-baked Negev. No living creature moved or breathed. Under the great vast bowl of the cloudless sky and the blazing white sun, the silence was eerie and unearthly. It chilled him to the bone, that mute otherworldly soundlessness that somehow held a portent of bleached bones and destruction. It was the kind of ultimate, deathlike quiet that heralds a ghost town which even the scavenging bugs and ubiquitous flies have long since deserted.

When he stumbled out of the car he had hired in Haifa, he could only stare in disbelief. He dared not believe his eyes, certain that they were deceiving him. Maybe what he was seeing in the shimmering heat waves was really a mirage.

But he knew deep down inside that it was no mirage, and it sickened him. He had expected a noisy reception, and had pictured the village just as it had been before he left it: abuzz with activity, the proud walnut-hued men wearing their flowing *bishts*; the prematurely aged women their dark, dusty *abbeyas* and headcloths as they patiently hoed the fields or prepared the traditional meals; the children shrieking at play under the tall, graceful date palms heavy with clusters of ripening fruit; the fields all around lush from irrigation; the lake which gave succor to all, gleaming silvery with the precious water provided by Allah the Munificent— such a beautiful, bountiful oasis, demanding lives of grueling work but good, happy lives nevertheless.

But something bad had swept through—a scythe of annihilating terror. It was as if a plague had visited al-Najaf.

The grove where date palms had once risen proudly was now a wasteland of parched dead trunks completely denuded of fruit and fronds, and the desert had reclaimed the fields. Where once the small neat houses had dotted the oasis were piles of rubble, blackened, bullet-riddled, jagged fingers of ruin. The charred carcass of an overturned automobile was a rusty sculpture of despair under the merciless sun. The little lake which had nurtured life was completely dry, its concave hollow filled with rippled waves of golden sand. The perpetually creaking water wheel he had known since his earliest days was silent, its precious wood either buried in the sand or burned in whatever holocaust had visited.

He blinked back salty tears. This couldn't be his beloved village! he thought wildly. Except for the time the Jews had attacked, just before he'd left for England, his village had been peaceful, had thrived. He must have come to the wrong place!

But the imposing neolithic rock formations in the distance were all too familiar. They were the very ones he had grown up with, embedded in his memory forever as the shapes of giant animals and people. Now the benign fantasy figures had undergone a metamorphosis, had become leering, malevolent, mocking hulks. This was his village, all right, and he had no choice but to face that it was gone. Only an extinct ghost town remained to mark its place, only rubble gave evidence of what was once a thriving, happy hub of life in the Negev. His eyes wet with tears, he dropped to his knees, threw back his head, and keened a cry of rage, an eerie, ululating wail of mourning and despair for that which was no more.

It was then that he caught sight of Abdullah. He stood atop a pile of rubble in phantomlike silence in flowing robes of intense blackness. His waist was circled with a cartridge belt, and a second, longer bandolier crisscrossed from shoulder to waist like a badge of authority. The *ghutra* he wore for protection from the sun was of the same depthless black.

Najib stumbled to his feet and stared at him, speechless.

Abdullah's voice was soft but mesmerizing. "Welcome, half-nephew, grandson of my half-brother."

Najib remained silent, as Abdullah came down from the pile of rubble and walked toward him.

Abdullah's powerful body was lean, all steel and springs, and his physical strength seemed to emanate from him like a malevolent aura. Yet his hands were slim and elongated, almost feminine in their delicacy. But it was his gaunt face which arrested. His forehead was high and noble, his cheekbones broad slashes, and his scimitar mouth wide and sensuous and cruel. His nose was magnificent; he had inherited the same stately hawk's beak as Naemuddin, testimony to the mother they had shared. But Najib remembered Naemuddin's eyes as wise and kind, and Abdullah's, under majestic black brows, were messianic, pitch black, and liquid as simmering oil. His skin was smooth and tawny, light for that of an Arab, and was as yet unweathered and unlined: he had yet to turn thirty-five. Like all predatory beasts, he appeared to be both relaxed and alert and gifted with an inborn sixth sense which made him sensitive to the presence of danger, no matter how distant it might be.

When they were face-to-face, Abdullah extended his hand and Najib took it and pressed it to his lips.

"So," Abdullah said softly, "you have not forgotten the traditional gesture of respect. That is good. I had feared that perhaps you had become too Westernized to remember it." Then he embraced Najib within the batlike folds of his robes and kissed both his cheeks, as was customary. "You have been gone a long time," he said, drawing back and touching Najib's elbow. "Come. We have much to discuss."

Najib stayed rooted to the spot, unable to move. "What happened here?" He gestured round at the surreal ruins. "What in the name of infernal hell has caused all this?"

A strange vampirical light came into Abdullah's face, his cheek hollows seemed to grow deeper, the skin of his face stretching so tautly that Najib had the crazy sensation he was staring at a skull. "The plague is come."

Najib stared at him. "What plague, my half-uncle?"

"The plague of Jews!" The words ripped odiously from between the knife blades of Abdullah's lips. "The Jewish swine who stole our water and our lands, and who now multiply like locusts!"

Najib was blinded by a searing rage. "And our people?" he asked tightly. "Where are they?"

"Gone," Abdullah replied, "as though scattered by the four winds. The weak who survived are in refugee camps in Lebanon and Syria. The strong fight at my side."

A vise clutched Najib's heart and seemed to tear it from his chest. "And my parents? My grandparents?"

"They are safe and well."

"Praise be to Allah," Najib said fervently. His brows knit together. "Are they in camps also?"

"No. Your father is brave and fights by my side, and your mother and grandparents live in a small house outside Beirut."

Najib looked angrily at Abdullah. "Why did not somebody write and tell me of this?"

Abdullah's eyes were hard and cruel. "Better that you should see for yourself what the Jews have done to us," he said harshly. "This way you shall never be tempted to become weak and forget."

"I will never forget!" Najib's eyes glittered feverishly. "I will not rest until their blood drips from my knife or their flesh is torn to shreds by the bullet of my gun!" He saw Abdullah's mocking smile, and his anger and purpose grew to dizzying proportions. His lean, handsome face took on a rapacious intensity. "You have always been a leader, Abdullah. For as long as I can remember, you fought against the British and the Jews."

Abdullah did not speak.

The anger burst inside of Najib and the words came out in a rush: "I wish to join the men you lead! I wish to train in your camp and fight in your army—"

Abdullah's arms blurred with the speed of light and he grabbed hold of Najib, his eyes shining with a kind of maniacal inner fire. "What have you heard?" he demanded, shaking him. "Tell me! What is this about a camp of mine?"

Najib was suddenly stricken with fear. "I . . . I heard nothing! But I remember—"

"Memories are best forgotten." Abdullah let go of him and turned around, his black robes swaying about him, and he stared at the distant mountains.

"Please, let me join you!" Najib begged. "You will have reason to be proud of me!"

When Abdullah turned around, his mouth was twisted in a smile. "Are you certain you have the stomach for it, my young falcon?"

"I have."

"And what of peace?" Abdullah said with a cynical laugh. "Have not the blood and the thinking of your weak grandfather tainted your veins?"

"My blood is not weak!" Najib's face was set and he no longer felt any fear. "Will you accept me within your group, or must I seek vengeance on my own? Is everything I have heard about you the creation of storytellers?"

Without warning Abdullah's hand slashed through the air and his open palm cracked against Najib's cheek with such force that Najib staggered backward. His hand flew up to his face, where a handprint shone whitely. He looked at Abdullah with surprise.

"That is a warning," Adbullah said softly. "Speak that way to me again and you will regret it for as long as you live."

"You have not yet answered me," Najib said stubbornly. "Will you accept me into your group?"

Abdullah stared at him and then nodded.

"When?" Najib pressed eagerly.

"When you receive word. Until then, you do nothing. Is that understood?"

And with that, Abdullah's black robes billowed and he strode off in the direction from which he had come.

He had turned so quickly that Najib had not seen the look of triumph glowing in his normally bleak eyes.

A week passed before Abdullah arranged for Najib to be taken to his hidden camp. It was in a small valley in the mountains of Syria, and everywhere Najib looked there was evidence that this was some kind of military training facility. The men were all heavily armed; he could see a distant watchtower and hear the gunfire from a firing range. Small tents had been pitched, and smoke rising from a campfire smelled of roasting lamb.

Abdullah no longer wore his black robes, and was dressed in green fatigues and combat boots, but on his head he wore the traditional Arab headgear. He stayed outside his tent and waited for Najib to come up to him.

Najib walked proud and locked eyes with him. "I have come," he said simply, wondering if his half-uncle could hear his heart pounding. "I am ready to swear my oath."

Abdullah stared at him and then raised his hand in a signal. Immediately a small crowd of men pressed around them both. "My half-nephew, Najib al-Ameer, has asked to join our Palestinian Freedom Army," he announced to them all. "He wishes to become your brother. If any of you have reason to doubt his intentions, now is the time to speak your piece."

There were murmurs and Najib felt two dozen hard, appraising sets of eyes on him. A few of the men he recognized from the oasis, but most were strangers.

Abdullah placed his hand on Najib's shoulders. "I have your word, then? You will obey all orders I give you, whether you like them or not and whether you agree with them or not? You will accept each of these men and others who join us as your true and only brothers?"

"By Allah I swear."

"I advise you to think well before you swear, half-nephew," Abdullah said softly. "If you are treasonous, or we so much as suspect you of being unfaithful to us, death will come not only to you and your immediate family but also to all generations thereof. Your entire bloodline will cease. Do you understand?"

Najib drew a deep breath, astonished at the harshness of the threat. He took a deep breath and nodded. "I understand," he said tightly.

"Then let it be done. These men will be witness." Abdullah slid his knife from its scabbard. "Hold out your hand."

Najib held out his right hand. He did not make a sound as the knife flashed and its blade slid softly into his flesh. Immediately he could see his warm blood spurting forth in a thick spray.

Without hesitation, Abdullah then held up his own wrist. Najib saw that it was heavily crisscrossed with thick raised scars from a multitude of other such oaths. Then Abdullah sliced it open, his bleak eyes dancing with an unholy joy as he held Najib's gaze. "Do you swear, by almighty Allah, to champion the Cause of the Palestinian Freedom Army, to accept me as your absolute leader, and count each one of my men as your true brothers, till the moment after your death?"

Najib held himself proudly. "I swear so by Allah," he whispered, his eyes aglow.

Abdullah rubbed his wrist against Najib's, kissed him on both cheeks, and drew back. "Our blood is merged!" he announced for all to hear. "Now we are truly brothers."

Najib glanced down at his blood-smeared wrist and then looked around at the other men. He felt the swelling of pride come up within him. He was one of them. He would fight at their side. Now he could at last avenge the death of Iffat and seek vengeance for the ruination of al-Najaf. He turned back to Abdullah. "I thirst for blood."

Abdullah shook his head. "You will wait until permission is granted," he told him impassively. With another gesture he dismissed the other men, and they went about their business. He looked at Najib. "Come, let us walk while I give you your first orders."

Najib fell into step beside him.

"You will spend two weeks in training here," Abdullah told him, "during which time you will be forged into a man and learn to be a soldier. Then, at the end of the summer, you shall leave again, this time for America."

"No!" Najib grasped Abdullah's arm. "I must stay to avenge the dishonor brought upon us! I must fight!"

Abdullah's voice left no room for argument. "You will do as you are told!" he said coldly. "Mere minutes ago I warned you of the punishment for treason! Do you have such a death wish that you wish to die already?"

Najib was silent.

"You need to complete your education," Abdullah said briskly. "You will attend a fine university. Harvard."

Najib stared at him. "Harvard!"

"It is one of the finest schools in America. Now, I want you to listen carefully. Most of our men are . . . impressionable. Uneducated. They tend to see only the short-term gain: the next skirmish, an attack on a schoolyard, a few sniper shots at a kibbutz, the bombing of a synagogue." Abdullah made an irritated gesture. "They are fools! They do not realize that we are in for a lifelong battle, and that it can only be won on the economic battlefield." He slid a sideways glance at Najib.

Despite himself, Najib's interest was aroused. "Go on," he said slowly.

"My plan is twofold," explained Abdullah, the quiet in his voice belying his own excitement. "The short-term part of it will be the constant harassment of this so-called nation which calls itself Israel. That will appease our people's immediate bloodthirsty need for revenge, and it should also keep the Jews from getting too comfortable—a little tension now and then, and they will constantly have to look over their shoulders."

Najib took a deep breath. "And the long-term part of it?"

"The long-term plan." Abdullah nodded. "It is far more important and complicated, and I have been planning it for many years now. That is why I diverted funds donated for the procurement of weapons and used them to finance your education at Eton instead."

"You!" Najib stared at him. "You paid for Eton?"

Abdullah nodded.

"But I thought my grandfather—"

"With what?" Abdullah's mouth became a sneer. "You know Naemuddin has no money."

Najib found himself nodding. He realized that he should have known. But even in his wildest dreams he had never suspected that Abdullah had any plans in store for him. Especially since he had hardly ever given him the time of day.

"But how does my education fit into your plans?" Najib asked, curious.

"It is said that to Westerners an education at a fine university is like gaining entry into an exclusive club."

Najib couldn't help show his surprise. He would never have suspected that Abdullah was so knowledgeable about such things as education. The only thing that he had ever seemed interested in was weapons and violence.

"The plan is this," Abdullah continued. "At Harvard you will make friends with people you would otherwise never have an opportunity to meet—friendships that will serve us well in the far-distant future. You will meet the young men who will eventually become powerful forces in business and occupy the highest seats in government, and eventually may whisper important secrets in your ear. And you, in turn, will on certain occasions be able to help swing their thinking in a certain direction. Ours."

Najib stared at him, impressed by the boldness and far-reaching consequences of the plan.

Abdullah smiled and his lean face regarded Najib thoughtfully. "So you see, your part in this is quite indispensable. It is not easy to befriend our enemies and know them intimately, or to understand the way their minds work, or to be able to influence them and gain their trust and respect. But only by doing that can we truly exploit the Westerners to our purposes. Think of the vast possibilities! If you start a business, a legitimate business that is successful and respected, but is actually a cover for our activities, the Western banks, and even Jews"—he gave a low laugh—"can unknowingly finance our cause, and we can then buy all the weapons and politicians we need. Their factories can even supply us, however indirectly, with bombs! Their ships can bring them to us! We will be able to undermine the very foundation of Israel and, if it so behooves us, the countries of the smug Westerners as well."

"There is only one problem," Najib pointed out. "From my experience at Eton, I have found that Westerners do not like Arabs. They are contemptuous of us and consider us beneath them."

"Then it is up to you to change their way of thinking. You will be a rich student and therefore a popular one. You will become even richer afterward and thus even more popular. The Westerners worship the money in their banking temples more than they do their god in the churches. They are dazzled by riches. There comes a point when they are ready to forgive someone anything—murder even—as long as millions of dollars are involved."

"It is not easy to come up with millions," Najib cautioned.

"With seed money, a fortune can grow as long as it is tended carefully and the right people guide its growth."

"But we do not have money."

"We have. I will provide it, as I have provided for your education. There are many rich Arabs who dare not speak out publicly for fear of losing American investments, but who have offered to help finance this. And you, Najib al-Ameer, will be at the head of it all. You will keep this secret and tell no one. You will report only to me. Just think! With true power—economic power—we can accomplish more than with all the guns and knives in the world combined! Eventually . . . Who knows?" He shrugged and smiled slightly. "We might even become a world force to be reckoned with."

Najib looked at Abdullah with rising respect. "It's . . . awesome. Brilliant."

"Yes, it is." Abdullah paused. "So you will do as I bid you to do?"

Najib hesitated. Abdullah seemed to have it all worked out—except for one thing. "But the Jews from the settlement. The ones who murdered my sister and stole our water. Will I never be able to avenge what they have done?"

Abdullah's face darkened with fury. "My plans for you are far too important to let simple vengeance interfere with them!" he said coldly. "Get the sand out of your eyes and be not so blinded! You will make them, and a million others, pay a thousandfold! Do you not see that?"

"But I have vowed vengeance," Najib said stubbornly.

"So you have." Abdullah looked at him. He could see the hungry unforgiving face, the dark liquid eyes turning cold as ice, and the intractability in the set jaw. But he saw far beyond that; the young man was his most potent weapon. The future depended upon him, and nothing could be allowed to get in the way of that. If Najib did something foolish now, it could ruin all the years of careful planning. "We will discuss your personal vendetta when the time is right," he said flatly, intending to put an end to the subject for the time being.

But Najib smiled. He was sure of himself now. Abdullah had let him know that he was indispensable. "I will do as you wish, half-uncle," he said quietly, "but one thing you must promise me. I will wait for my vengeance until the time is ripe, and I will do nothing which might jeopardize your plans. But when the time comes that the Jewish settlement and its leaders and families are destroyed, I want to be part of it. In person. I intend to fulfill the vow I made."

"Very well." Abdullah nodded. "That can be arranged." He was pleased, but made a point of not showing it. "Just remember one thing," he warned, "and never forget it, half-nephew. You will have one foot in the Western world and the other in ours. You will grow rich and powerful, but do not let it seduce you. Never forget for a moment where your allegiances lie. For if you should . . ." He left the threat dangling.

I will be destroyed and so will my immediate family, and all generations thereof, Najib thought. *My entire bloodline, those born and yet to be born.*

The last week in August Najib again exchanged his *ghutra* and his robe for his Western suit and left for the United States. He remained there for the entire four years until he graduated from Harvard. When he left, his address book was filled with the names of friends—names which brought to mind former and current presidents, ambassadors, Supreme Court justices, bankers, law firms, corporations, and countless millionaires from all arteries of business.

In the meantime Abdullah had grown stronger and his band of guerrilla terrorists began to make such a reputation for themselves that they were mentioned in Western news broadcasts with regularity.

The runway raced forward to meet the DC-4, and then the tires touched down on the concrete, sending puffs of friction smoke squealing up from the rubber. A shudder passed through the fuselage. Najib tore himself away from the memories and came back to the present as the plane taxied up to the terminal, the propellers spinning slowly now.

The stewardess was standing atop the mobile stairs when he got off. She smiled her professional smile at him. "Goodbye," she said. "We hope you have a pleasant stay in Beirut."

Najib winced at the almost visible blast of heat as he hurried down the steps. Once again he had forgotten just how furnacelike this climate was, and how blinding the light. Silently he cursed the constricting, sweat-soaked seersucker suit he wore. He hated Western clothes. They did not let him breathe. He much preferred the long, cool, flowing robes of his people, which made far more sense in this arid climate.

He smiled to himself. He had been gone far too long. It was good to be back.

He wondered what plans Abdullah would have in store for him.

"Mr. Najib al-Ameer . . . MEA passenger Mr. Najib al-Ameer. Please come to the information desk," a disembodied female voice called out over the paging system.

Karim Hassad's eyes scanned the customs area. When Najib came breezing through, suitcase in hand, and headed for the information desk, he moved forward to intercept him. He fell neatly into step beside him, matching his stride. "Was there fog in London?" Karim asked softly.

Najib missed a step. Slowly, he eyed the man curiously. "London was sunny," he murmured carefully, replying to the elaborate password which Abdullah had arranged for him four years earlier.

"And Barcelona?"

"I did not visit Barcelona, though I was once in Lisbon."

"And the Portuguese ladies, are they as beautiful as the Spanish?"

"If they are without their *dueñas*, they are."

"Greetings," Karim said solemnly, acknowledging Najib's correct replies. "There is no need to go to Information. It was only so I could identify you. Let me take your suitcase. The car is waiting outside."

Najib handed the suitcase over and followed him through the terminal and outside into the white glare of sunshine. Karim was a huge man, over six feet tall, and he had extraordinarily wide shoulders and thick, powerful legs. Even his neck was massive. Although he was dressed in the Western fashion, he wore a short white headcloth with a shiny black coil. His pockmarked olive face sported a drooping bushy mustache. He looked like a bodyguard.

The car, a dented black Mercedes dressed as a taxi, was waiting at the curb. Karim tossed the suitcase into the trunk and Najib started around to the front passenger door. Karim shook his head and unlocked the rear door for him. He held it open. "It is best if you look like an ordinary passenger. I hope it does not inconvenience you, but our mutual friend would like to see you before you are driven to the house of your parents," Karim told him as he switched on the ignition and pulled out into the traffic.

Najib nodded and let himself relax, looking out at the passing scenery. Everywhere, there were signs of a booming economy. A lot of construction had gone on during the four years since he had been here last. Modern balconied apartment blocks and glittering new high-rise hotels made Beirut look far more European than Middle Eastern. And every-where, more big buildings were under construction. Western and Arab women were dressed in the latest Paris fashions. He could almost smell the prosperity in the air.

They headed to the north, past the city limits to an exclusive residential suburb. Here, high walls enclosed quiet villas, and the urban hubbub seemed far away. Birds chirped happily from hidden gardens.

Karim turned off into a driveway and came to a stop in front of a pair of tall, imposing gates. They were topped with lethal spikes which even the elaborate Oriental motif of the wrought iron could not hide. He honked the horn twice and waited.

At armed sentry in traditional robes and headgear appeared, Karim signaled, and the gates swung open electronically, and a pair of rust-colored Dobermans came galloping to meet the car. They split up, one taking the left side of the car, the other the right, and they ran silently beside it all the way up to the house. The security precautions seemed to be formidable.

Najib couldn't help but feel a pang of envy. It was a small but beautifully tended estate. To either side of the patterned tile drive were young palm trees, hedges of cacti, stands of sisal plants and, sheathing the inside of the walls which completely surrounded the estate, lush bright cascades of fuchsia bougainvillea. The sprinklered lawn was almost blue-green and sparkled from a recent watering. The drive ended in a circular sweep around a water fountain in front of a big white stucco villa with large arched windows and a gently sloping tile roof.

Karim stopped the car and got out slowly, allowing the Dobermans to sniff him. Then he held Najib's door open. "Come out slowly and stand still so the dogs can smell you," he said.

Najib did as he was told; after a moment, the dogs loped off.

"I will wait here," Karim said. "Just knock on the front door and you will be taken to see our mutual friend."

Najib nodded and went up to the glossy door. Before he could lift the brass gazelle's-head knocker, the door swung open. He froze; another guard in robes and headcloth stood in front of him, a semiautomatic rifle aimed directly at his midsection.

Without moving his weapon the guard took four steps backward and gestured with his head for Najib to come in. Najib stepped in slowly, cautious to make no sudden moves.

"Close the door," the guard said. "Slowly."

Without taking his eyes off the weapon, Najib reached back and pushed the door shut. Then, while the guard still covered him, a second guard, also in traditional dress, patted him down expertly, checking him thoroughly for weapons. When the hands felt around his crotch, Najib's eyes narrowed. "Let's not get personal," he growled.

The guard ignored the gibe and continued the search. Finally satisfied that Najib was unarmed, he announced, "He is clean."

To Najib's relief, the semiautomatic was moved aside.

"Take off your shoes," the guard told him. "Then follow me." Najib did as he was told, noticing that both guards were barefoot. He left his shoes beside the door and followed the man through an apricot-silk-draped doorway into an immense sybaritic living room. Low couches with cylindrical tasseled cushions made up four separate white-silk seating areas on the expanse of pink marble flooring. Tufted throw pillows of metallic silver fabric shone richly. Floor lamps—eight-foot-tall silver palms with glowing, opaque globes as their coconuts—provided muted lighting. It was a Spartan room, cool and luxurious and impersonal. Along two walls, Moorish-arched windows with diagonal latticed panes looked out on the gardens. From somewhere nearby came the luxurious sounds of a gurgling fountain and the cooing of turtle doves.

Abdullah was lying naked facedown on one of the couches, his eyes half-shut. Kneeling on the floor beside him, her breasts and hips draped only by diaphanous pink silk scarves, was a beautiful young Arab woman.

She saw Najib before Abdullah did. Her expert kneading fingers stopped in mid-massage and Abdullah's eyes opened all the way. He nodded to Najib and then twisted around to look at the girl. "Wait outside until I call for you," he said.

She obeyed at once, rising fluidly and running gracefully toward an arched doorway leading out to the gardens, her bare feet slapping softly against the marble.

Najib watched her, feeling an exquisite ache in his loins. He had forgotten how beautiful Arab girls could be. Then he turned to Abdullah. His half-uncle was rearranging himself into a sitting position. "It looks like you know how to live, half-uncle."

Abdullah grunted. "The house belongs to a businessman who is vacationing in Paris with his family, and the girl comes with the place." He shrugged. "At least the guards are mine."

Najib made the usual show of respect and Abdullah motioned him to a facing couch. It was low and soft, and as he sank back he couldn't help comparing it to the hard high couches he'd gotten used to in America.

Abdullah clapped his hands once, and a serving girl materialized, flat-footed and modest, brass tray in hand. She placed it on a low table, poured two cups of savory fresh mint tea, and handed one to Abdullah and one to Najib. She placed a flaky golden pastry shaped like a gazelle's horn on each of two plates and handed them each one. Then she hurried away, her scarves floating.

"This tea is good," Najib said, sipping from his tiny handleless cup. "What I missed most in America was the tea and the pastries."

Abdullah picked up a gazelle-horn pastry and bit delicately into it. He smacked his lips. "These are filled with almond paste. Try yours."

"I had better not. Otherwise I will get fat."

Abdullah finished his pastry without speaking and then licked his fingers, one by one.

"I gather you have new instructions for me?" Najib asked, bluntly bringing the subject around to what was foremost in his mind.

"I have." Abdullah nodded. "But first, an update on the subject I believe is closest to your heart."

"Schmarya Boralevi! The Jew my grandfather nursed back to health so many years ago—"

"—and who was the leader of the settlement which attacked us when your sister Iffat was killed." Abdullah nodded again.

Najib sat up straighter. "What about him?" he asked softly.

"It seems he has been making quite a name for himself, and currently holds a high leadership position in the Israeli Ministry of Defense. Of course, his having helped create the modern Israeli army in 1948 out of such diverse groups as the Palmach, the Haganah, the Irgun, and the Stern factions has not hindered his career any. Neither have his friendships with Ben-Gurion, Dayan, and Meir. Many political analysts have gone so far as to speculate that he is next in line to become Israel's minister of defense."

"I see." Najib paused thoughtfully. "I take that to mean he no longer lives at . . . What was the name of that kibbutz?"

"Ein Shmona." Abdullah shook his head. "My intelligence sources report that he spends most of his time in Jerusalem now. His daughter, the former film star, and his son-in-law and grandchildren still spend some time there, but even they live most of the time in Tel Aviv."

Najib was silent for a moment. "And Ein Shmona . . . it is thriving more than ever." It was a glum statement, not a question.

Abdullah nodded. "You would not even recognize it. There is a population of nearly sixty thousand people, and its irrigated farmlands stretch out in all directions. In fact, it's hard to think of it any longer as a kibbutz. It has become a full-fledged town."

"In other words, it will be more difficult than ever for me to seek vengeance."

"Have no fear. I have people watching the entire family. Vengeance will avail itself in due time. Suspecting that you would be anxious to keep track of them, I have been keeping a current active file on them all." He picked up three sheets of single-spaced typed paper from the low table and handed them to Najib, who quickly scanned the pages on Schmarya Boralevi, his daughter, and his son-in-law.

His face furrowed in a frown. "It seems the longer we wait, the more powerful and untouchable they all become. I should have avenged myself four years ago."

"Vengeance is like wine," said Abdullah, "it improves with age. For the time being, there are far more important things to accomplish which your personal vendettas must not get in the way of. When the time comes, it will be so much sweeter." He held Najib's gaze. "Your grades were excellent, and I am pleased. Now that your education is completed, it is time for you to start your legitimate business. I trust the Harvard business courses have prepared you well."

"Yes."

"Good. Have you decided what kind of business you would be best suited for?"

"To begin with, I was thinking of starting an import-export firm, which would be based in New York but have branch offices in London, Hong Kong, Stuttgart, and here."

"Excellent!" Abdullah smiled, steepled his fingers, and placed them against his lips. "That would certainly open up a conduit between the capitalist West and our Palestinian Freedom Army. Also, it will be a way for us to disburse funds to our sympathizers in Europe. There are groups of youths in Italy and Germany who champion our cause and could use some help. While you were gone, we trained four Germans and two Italians in terrorist tactics. Two were women." He paused and brought the subject back to the business at hand. "How much money do you think an import-export firm would require?"

"I am not sure yet. I will have to do some more calculations first, but I should know within a week."

"Good. Remember to overestimate rather than underestimate. It is said that many businesses go bankrupt during the first year because they are undercapitalized. Now, to another matter." Abdullah sipped his tea delicately. He was silent for a moment, staring over his cup, past Najib and out through one of the arched doors to the gardens. When he spoke, his face was expressionless, but his voice was gentle. "Two weeks from tomorrow you are to attend a wedding."

"Western or Arab?" Najib smiled. "I have to know so I can decide how to dress."

Abdullah did not return his smile. "Arab, I would suppose. Of course, that depends on the bridegroom."

"And who is the lucky man? Anyone I would know?"

"The lucky man, as you so aptly put it, Najib, is you."

"Me!" Najib stared across at him, his eyes wide in disbelief. "Surely you are joking!"

Abdullah shook his head. "I have never been more serious in my entire life."

From Abdullah's tone Najib suddenly knew that it had already been arranged. The only thing left to do was to exchange vows. "I think you have gone too far."

Abdullah's voice left no room for argument. "You will do as you are told!"

Shakily Najib got to his feet and clenched his fists at his side. He was fighting to keep control. "Now, unless you have more unpleasant surprises in store for me," he said angrily, "I think it is time for me to leave! Do not bother to show me out. I know the way." He headed across the room, but before he could reach the curtained doorway one of the guards slipped through and blocked his way.

"You have not yet been dismissed," Abdullah said mildly from the couch.

Najib stared at the guard. His semiautomatic made it difficult to argue. Wearily, he retraced his steps to the couch. He remained standing and looked down at Abdullah, his eyes flashing. "Do all your dealings have to be done from the other end of a gun?"

"Only when obedience is questionable." Abdullah gestured to the couch. "Sit down!" he barked sharply.

"All right," Najib said wearily, and sat back down. He sighed deeply. "Tell me about her."

"There is not much to tell. Her name is Yasmin Fazir, and

524

she is quite beautiful, if you like the independent Western type of woman. Her father is a very wealthy Lebanese banker, and her mother's side of the family is highly respected and also quite wealthy. They are carpet merchants in Damascus."

"Then what's wrong with her? Beautiful, rich daughters aren't generally passed out to poor young men like alms to a beggar. Is she crippled? Does she wear braces on her teeth?"

"She is cursed with none of those things," Abdullah said irritably. "And you forget, with your education you are not exactly a beggar. You have become quite an eligible young bachelor."

"Then give me one good reason why I should marry her."

"Her father is willing to put up one hundred thousand dollars for you to get your start in business," Abdullah said quietly, watching Najib's reaction. "That is one good reason."

Najib whistled softly. "He must want to get rid of her pretty badly."

"You could do much worse," Abdullah said sharply. "Remember, you will need a beautiful wife if our plan is to succeed."

"I am sorry, but I do not quite follow your reasoning."

Abdullah gestured irritably. "A wife is necessary for entertaining . . . to add gloss and respectability to your image. Yasmin will serve those purposes quite well. As far as her family is concerned, their uses are multifold. Her father is a generous supporter of our cause. And as for her mother's family, you might want to consider exporting their carpets overseas. We shall have to wait and see. Meanwhile, you will meet Yasmin tomorrow. You and your parents are invited to the Fazirs' for dinner. They are Westernized, so you can wear what you like. I was going to make it for this evening, but Yasmin, like so many of the silly Western women she idolizes, insists on holding a job. She flies often between here and Europe."

"You make her sound like a bird."

"Be serious!" Abdullah said sharply. "This is no laughing matter. There is much money at stake."

"It appears to me that my entire life is at stake," Najib reminded him.

"What is at stake is the future of the Palestinian Freedom Army! That is far more important than your life."

Najib sighed. "It does not sound like you are leaving me much choice."

Abdullah smiled coldly in reply and got to his feet. Najib rose also. "She'd better not be a dog," he growled morosely as Abdullah put his arm around his shoulder and walked him to the doorway.

As it turned out, he was in for a surprise. Yasmin Fazir was quite beautiful, and he recognized her at once. She was the petite MEA stewardess.

She was beautiful and she was rich and she looked like a lady. But there was one thing he knew she was not. And that was a virgin.

Consequently, her father deposited ten times more in Najib's bank account than the originally agreed-upon hundred thousand dollars.

Yasmin was, after all, damaged goods.

III
Daliah
1977–1978

ISRAEL'S BEST-KNOWN EXPORT
WAS KIBBUTZ-RAISED
BUT SHE'S NO VEGETABLE

Actress Daliah Boralevi pops vitamin pills like they're going out of style, and her idea of a rush is B12 injections. "I've got more needle tracks than a junkie," she confides. "Sometimes I look like a pincushion. I mean, just *look*." Unself-consciously she hikes up the little something designer Yves St. Laurent ran up for her, gives a tug at her tiger-print panties, and displays the needle tracks. "I always tell the doctor, 'There . . .'" She points to a tiny spot. "'You can only stick me there, in those two square inches.' I don't want holes punched all over me."

The way her life has been moving along lately, it's small wonder she needs vitamin boosts. During a single week recently she finished location shooting in Ireland, zipped to Paris to be fitted for a new fall wardrobe, and flew to New York, where she signed on for the next Woody Allen movie and popped in on Liza Minelli's party. She shot a commercial for Maybelline, managed an entire day at home for herself, participated in preliminary discussions with Avon regarding a possible perfume line bearing her name, and packed her bags to go to Cannes for the film festival where . . .

—cover story, People

Nine-twenty-two in the morning.

The first day of the two-week film festival.

As happened every year at this time, Cannes was swept up in an orgy of madness. The lobby of the Carlton Hotel was a shantytown of trade-fair booths, with giant overhead banners advertising films, and showcard posters on easels creating a maze, while outside the flags of all nations flapped along the Croisette and thousands of people crowded the sidewalks. Standstill traffic was backed up on the broad palm-lined Corniche for miles, furious horns blaring a symphony of Manhattanish frustrations. The celluloid peddlers were in town, and for the next two weeks Cannes would be a marketplace of high-stakes selling, buying, bartering, and financing. The air was balmy and the sky a perfect powder blue with a regatta of puffball clouds headed for Italy racing across it.

On the breakfast terrace of the Carlton Hotel, Daliah was cornered by a whirring, clicking swarm of cameras that was steadily advancing on her like some hundred-eyed beast. The lunging microphones waving at the end of tentacle arms were coming so near that another inch and she feared the enamel would be scraped off her front teeth. Behind the expensive Rolleis and Leicas and Nikons and shouldered video cams, the photographers and reporters were one impatient, inhuman mass.

She raked her fingers through her hair and shook her head. Her gleaming raven mane was brushed to either side of her face from a central part and flowed naturally to below her shoulders, where it frizzed out in baroque magnificence like the Madonna's in a Bartolomé Murillo oil. But her exquisite oval face was lively, with a decidedly un-Madonna-like spark in her eyes, and a flash of indignation highlighted her features with photogenic animation. She was wearing a dress with a skintight beaded sea-green bodice which had been appliquéd with bright, oversize glass jewels. The full scarlet leather skirt with the huge bustle bow matched her

529

loose hand-stitched Tartar boots, the inordinately high chippy heels only adding to her already impressive height.

Although she emanated the very essence of chic and control, she was inwardly fighting to keep herself from exploding. At the moment, Daliah Boralevi was a very angry, very annoyed, and very steamy star.

It had been hard enough for her to agree to the press conference in the first place, harder yet to actually subject herself to it at that hour of the morning, without so much as a crumb of brioche in her stomach. The Visine she had dripped into her emerald eyes only half an hour earlier had gotten the jet-lag redness out, but had not done a thing for the stinging, and the one demitasse of decaffeinated black coffee she had foolishly allowed herself was now burning in the pit of her stomach. But it was especially hard because Jerome St.-Tessier—may he rot in hell for eternity, the putz, because he should have been here at her side to keep the press reasonably at bay and the conference in some semblance of order—had simply not shown up. No telephone call, no message—nothing. After having kept the press waiting twenty minutes for him to show, she hadn't been able to hold them off a minute longer, and she could sense their hostility and impatience growing by the second. Not that she could really blame them. The town was filled with an international army of more famous, beautiful faces to interview and photograph than there was time to do it in. Without Jerome, it was left up to her alone to appease the press and provide fodder for their columns and empty air time, thereby hopefully getting as much free exposure for *Red Satin* as was humanly possible.

At this thought, another surge of anger colored her creamy complexion. Whatever the hell Jerome was up to, or wherever he might be trapped, the schmuck should at least have managed to oil his way out of it and been here at her side where she belonged. As both producer and director of *Red Satin, he* had called the press conference in the first place!

Finally, despite the two last-minute disasters she'd discovered—runs in her green lace stockings, and one of the bright glass jewels missing from her bodice—she had flung her raven mane back, raised her chin, and marched resolutely out to face the press.

They had set upon her like wolves, reveling in the noisy brashness of newshounds who have flown halfway around the world for the occasion and are only exercising their God-given rights. Their questions were a shouting match she had to struggle through in order to pick out a single voice from among the barrage, the motor drives of the cameras only adding to the general confusion, and the curious on-lookers on the terrace, pressing closer to see what the excitement was all about, not helping alleviate the circus atmopshere.

Daliah pointed at the loudest shouter of them all, and the others immediately fell silent to catch her every word.

"Renate Schlaak, *Der Spiegel*," the tall, mannish woman called out in a guttural German accent. "Miss Boralevi, you were born Daliah ben Yaacov. Why, then, are you using the name Boralevi?"

"Determination, I suppose." Daliah's voice was loud and clear, and she spoke slowly so that her reply could be scribbled down into notepads. "It was the name of my grandmother, who was an actress in czarist Russia, but she shortened it and simply used 'Bora,' since it sounded less . . . well, less Jewish, to put it bluntly. It was my mother's name also, but she did away with the surname altogether at the insistence of Oscar Skolnik, who owned IA studios. When I started in show business, I was determined that the name finally be used rather than sweeping it under the carpet. Also, it's a well-known fact that my mother is Tamara ben Yaacov. When I started in show business, I wanted to do it all on my own. If I had gone by the name ben Yaacov, people would have put two and two together and come up with the fact that I'm Tamara's daughter. I didn't want that at the time. I wanted my own talent to speak for itself. Next." Daliah looked around at the frantically waving hands and pointed to a young curly-haired woman in the back.

"Tosca Lidell, the *Tatler*. Speaking of your mother, I hear Tamara is not only your country's cultural minister but has become quite heavily involved in the theater in Israel as well. Could you expand on that?"

"Yes, I can. My mother believes that Israel's theaters, even though they're young, have a large pool of talent to draw from, and she is dedicated to helping make them a major force in entertainment. Lately she has also been busy trying to expand Israel's fledgling film industry. But she insists upon working behind the scenes, and not onstage or in front of the cameras. Next."

"Irith Cohen, *The Hollywood Reporter*. Does your mother plan on coming out of retirement?"

"My mother has never been retired, Miss Cohen. She's not stopped working for a day. But if you mean, will she ever return to Hollywood and act in films—I'm afraid she's never made any mention of that to me. She's very happy with what she's doing behind the scenes. Next."

"John Carter, *Time* magazine. Getting back to your most recently released film, Miss Boralevi, *Red Satin* has received all sorts of notorious reviews, and not only has the Vatican denounced it, but now preachers from many fundamentalist churches are up in arms about it too. Do you think the notoriety will help or harm the overseas sales?"

"There is really no way to answer that until the box-office receipts are in, but I would venture to guess that the denouncement won't harm the film's success. If anything, it's probably aroused that much more interest in it. Next . . . the lady in yellow over there—"

"Tina Smith, *Variety*. Miss Boralevi, would you say there's ever a chance, however remote, that you and your mother would make a film together? If the right project came along?"

"I can't really answer that because the right project hasn't come along yet. But offhand, I'd have to say no. As I said before, my mother just isn't interested in making films anymore. Next."

"Lorraine Asnes, Fairchild Publications. How did your parents, especially your mother, react when you first told them you wanted to go into show business? Were they supportive, or did they try to dissuade you?"

"I remember the first time I wanted to be an actress. I was eight years old at the time, and I had just seen *Roman Holiday* with Audrey Hepburn. After that, I wanted to *be* Audrey Hepburn. I tried to do everything I could to look like her, even wearing my hair up and starving myself, which was ridiculous, of course. But the acting bug never left me. My mother tried to talk me out of it, like so many show-business parents do, but after I did my military training in Israel, my mind was made up. I was determined to go to New York or Hollywood, and my father, seeing that I couldn't be talked out of it, gave me five thousand dollars and a one-way ticket to New York. Next."

"Isabelle Retzki, *Paris Match*. My question is twofold, Miss Boralevi. You have now made six movies with Jerome St.-Tessier. First, are you planning on making more films with him, or do you think you might work with another director in the future? And second, it is no secret that you and Mr. St.-Tessier have been sharing a personal relationship for some years. Does his absence here this morning indicate a rift in that relationship?"

Bitch! Daliah thought. *Hyena!* She had never been able to come to grips with reporters who made a career out of digging into someone's most private life and trying to come

532

up with dirt. A rotten, underhanded way to make a living if ever there was one.

On and on, the questions hurled at her were endless. Finally, after more than half an hour, she put an end to the madness and headed upstairs to the suite which Jerome had engaged but neither of them actually stayed in—the hotel was too much a circus during the film festival to allow them a decent amount of privacy. He used the suite as an office where he could discuss financing and distribution deals with anybody who might be interested.

Restlessly she prowled the suite, every so often going to the window and glaring out at the flags flapping along the Croisette. The beach itself was curiously empty, but the sidewalks were packed and the traffic snarls even worse than before. Her anger was mounting steadily. They had planned to spend last night together at the villa they'd rented at Antibes, but just before dinner he'd begged off, claiming he had to meet with some important potential backers. She'd dined alone, and waited up for him, finally giving in to jet lag and going to bed by herself. This morning, when the alarm clock shrilled her awake at seven, he was still gone, his side of the bed unslept-in, his pillow fluffed and untouched. And not a word on paper or over the telephone.

Now she still waited. Waited and waited. Finally, feeling her temper reaching the boiling point and her blood pressure rising alarmingly, she kicked off her boots and knelt on the carpet, spreading her knees as far apart as they would go. It was time to channel her energy, or else she would have an imbalance in her system, and that would cause a severe emotional disturbance.

She shut her eyes and breathed deeply, frowning in concentration until she could feel her mind clearing, bit by bit. First came the exercise, which would limber her body, then the meditation, which would relax her mind and lead up to the finale of the therapy—her touching the various pressure points on her body the way Toshi Ishagi, her Japanese stress therapist, had taught her during his Ishagiatsu classes. Upon completion of the exercise, the negative energy which had been blocked would be released, thus ridding her of everything extraneous fouling her emotionally, and so cleansing her of stress.

She leaned to one side, placed one hand behind her head, and rested the other palm against her forehead, her fingers reaching to the back of her skull. Slowly, ever so slowly, she felt her heartbeat slowing to normal, the tenseness seeping out of her pores. For a while, at least, she almost, but not quite, forgot about Jerome and his leaving her in the lurch.

*   *   *

They had met eight years earlier in New York. It had been at a little hole-in-the-wall movie theater on East Seventh Street which showed two classic black-and-white films for the price of one. It had been her first visit to the nostalgia theater, and she had been drawn there by the ad she had seen in the *Village Voice*. They were having a Tamara Film Festival that week, showing two Tamara films each day—on that particular Sunday afternoon, *The Flappers* and *Anna Karenina*. She had sat through them both, spellbound and misty-eyed, not at all able to reconcile herself with the fact that Tamara, the exquisite creature on the screen, could be the same Tamara who was her no-nonsense mother.

She'd cried and sniffled throughout the last ten minutes of *Anna Karenina*, and when the lights finally came up she'd hurried outside so that no one could see her tears. It was then that she ran into him. The tall tousle-haired young man with the round wire-rimmed glasses. They both tried squeezing out through the one open door at the same time. That being impossible, he had stepped aside like a gentleman to let her through first. She stumbled out into the bright winter sunshine, a tall, deceptively waiflike bundle of gleaming straight black hair and puffy army field jacket, all giant pockets and military patches, and mascara-streaked cheeks. She dabbed her eyes ineffectually with her fingertips.

The very sight of her touched the Gallic cavalier in him, and he came up beside her and solemnly held out a clean, folded handkerchief. Wordlessly she snatched it from him, turned away, and blew her nose in a noisy honk.

"Do you always cry at the end of tearjerkers?" he asked with a strong French accent, his S and Th sounds coming out as buzz-saw Z's.

She turned around slowly and blinked. "I only cry at weddings and funerals," she sniffed. And then smiled slightly. "And unhappy endings."

"And that was one of the grandest unhappy endings of them all." He touched her cheek. "You have another streak there."

"Oh." Quickly she wet the handkerchief with her mouth and smeared the spot under her eye some more. "There." She raised her smudged face. "Now am I presentable?" She looked at him, her eyes still moist.

"Eminently." He grinned, finding the black smear terribly attractive. "Did you come for all the last five days of movies?"

She shook her head. "I just found out about them today. Did you see them all?"

He nodded.

"I suppose you're a . . . a Tamara fan."

"Oh, I can take her films or leave them."

"Then you don't like them?"

"They're interesting historically, but I think they're overplayed. Like Garbo and Dietrich. Too much mugging."

"That was the style of the time," she said loyally, jumping to her mother's defense. "If she made movies now, they'd be different. More natural."

"At any rate, that's academic, wouldn't you say? The point is, she is not making any more films. Perhaps it is for the best. Better to create an aura of mystery than to fall flat on her face with failure, eh?"

"She wouldn't fail!" Daliah cried staunchly, her emerald eyes flashing gemlike sparks. "She would never fail!"

He laughed. "It seems I have found her most loyal and devoted fan." He paused. "How would you like to have a cup of coffee?"

She looked at him dubiously. "How do I know I can trust you?"

"Because we'll go to a restaurant or a coffee shop and not my home. You can always scream for help or go running out. What do you say?"

She nodded.

"I know a nice little Polish restaurant over on First, where babushkas serve strong tea and homemade pirogis."

"Sounds too ethnic . . . too *serious*. Do you know what I'm *really* in the mood for? What my greatest weakness on earth is?"

He smiled slightly. "I haven't the faintest idea, although I would like to find out."

"McDonald's or Burger King french fries! Tons and tons of those air-filled greasy french fries accompanied by loads and loads of salt. Once I start on them, I can't stop till I burst."

"Is there anything else I should know about you? Such as your putting chocolate syrup on rice, or mixing crême de menthe with catsup and pouring it over green beans?"

She made a face. "Really, you are quite abominable!" But she smiled and locked her arm through his. "Where is the nearest junk-food franchise?"

"Over on Third, near Sixth Avenue."

"Well, what are you waiting for? Steer me there at once."

"Do you mind if we walk?"

"I'd love to walk." She tossed her head in that peculiar way she had so that her hair whipped around, and when they turned the corner, she tucked her chin down into her chest against the bitter gusts of the buffeting November wind.

They sat on the plastic chairs on the second level of the overheated McDonald's for over an hour and went Dutch on six cups of coffee and four orders of fries. She finger-fed him his across the table.

"I think the girl behind the counter downstairs is taking pity on us," Daliah laughed when she came back upstairs with yet another tray of coffee and fries. "She tried to sneak me a couple of burgers on the sly."

"Did you tell her you have a weakness for their fries?"

"I did, but I don't think she believed me. She probably thinks fries is all we can afford." Daliah uncapped the plastic lids off the two containers of coffee and settled back. "Now, tell me about yourself," she ordered. "You know, the things I don't already know."

"You don't know anything about me. We've only just met."

"Oh, but I do." She got busy tearing open the tiny paper containers of salt in order to make a pile to dunk the fries into. "You're obviously French, and your English is so good it tells me you've been living here for quite a few years. Your jeans are tattered, but that doesn't tell me anything, since it's chic to wear jeans that are coming apart all over. Your ancient scuffed black motorcycle jacket with the waist belt hanging loose may be a favorite jacket, but your scarf is coming apart and the heels of your shoes are worn down. The sole on the left one is starting to come apart, which I gather means you're rather financially strapped, and that cable-knit sweater, which is made of the best Irish wool, was obviously a gift, since a man would never think of buying himself an expensive sweater like that one. It was probably given to you by a well-heeled girlfriend. Also, long hair is stylish, but yours hasn't been styled, so you obviously don't have to look your best at whatever it is you do. And those little round Heinrich Himmler glasses you insist upon wearing give me the feeling that you don't really care how you look. They're ugly but functional." She sat back, smiled sweetly at him, and stirred her coffee with a plastic stick. "How am I doing?"

He looked startled. "You should be a detective. All that shows, huh?"

"It definitely does." She nodded, reached for another fry, dipped it in the pile of salt, and munched it thoughtfully.

"Sodium is bad for you." He gestured at the salt.

"I never eat salt," she declared.

"You are eating it now."

"I only eat salt when I have fries. Then I can't seem to get enough." She made it sound like a confession. "Most times I eat very, very healthily." She eyed him curiously and then nodded to herself. "Let me see . . . you're an unemployed actor?"

He laughed, showing his strong white teeth. "Close, but not quite. I studied filmmaking at NYU until I discovered I could learn more, as well as earn a decent living, by working for film companies rather than studying. So you see, I'm rather employed."

"That explains your rattiness, then. Theater trash." She nodded solemnly to herself. "Are you working now?" She reached across the table and proffered a fry.

Dutifully he opened his mouth to accept it. "I'm production assistant for a German movie company that's filming here," he said, chewing and swallowing. "Eventually, though, I want to direct. And you? What are you?" He held her gaze. "An unemployed actress?"

"Semi-employed. I'm with an Off-Off Broadway repertory group, but right now we're between shows. We don't go into rehearsal for another three weeks."

"What is the group called?"

"The Actors Outlet Ensemble. We're on MacDougal Street." She looked at him hopefully. "Maybe you've heard of us?"

"Let me see, the last play was *Wilde Night*, loosely adapted from the essays of Oscar Wilde?" She nodded exuberantly, her eyes shining, and he looked at her more closely. "*You*! Now I recognize you! You were one of the reciters in white face and dressed all in black so only your face could be seen! You were the one at the far end who stole the show!"

There was a pleased look on her face and she stopped munching for a glorious moment. Then, pretending nonchalance, she slowly continued chewing on a fry. She thought it tasted extraordinarily good, better than a fry had ever tasted before. She adored rave reviews.

Suddenly he leaned excitedly across the little table. "Tell you what. How would you like to be in a film?"

She stared at him, at first not knowing whether she should take him seriously or not, and then burst out laughing. "Oh, come on!" she said. "If that's a variation on the old 'Come up and see my etchings' routine, it's hardly original."

He looked slightly hurt. "I don't have to resort to such cheap routines," he sniffed. "For your information, women tend to find me very attractive."

537

She adjusted her facial muscles into an expression of contrition. "I'm sorry."

He looked at her earnestly. "I'm serious about the film. I wrote the script three years ago, and have been waiting for the right person to come along. I think you could do it. I know you could, after the way you performed onstage!"

"What's it about?"

"Well, originally I wrote it for the stage as a one-woman monologue in three acts. Then, after I became more interested in films, I rewrote it for the screen and added a few characters. Basically, it's a tour de force about a German woman in Berlin at ages eighteen, forty-two, and seventy-nine. It starts out in the present, when the old lady tells her life story to her grandson, and then flashes back to her past. The way the story comes out is that she is despicably cruel and anti-Semitic. Only at the end do we find that she is really Jewish and suffering from overwhelming guilt because by pretending to be Aryan she survived the horrors in which most of her friends and a lot of her family died."

Her eyes glowed with interest. "It sounds marvelous!"

"It is," he said. "But it won't be easy to film."

"Why not?"

"Well, we'd have to rehearse and film nights, after my regular shooting day is over, and I can't afford to pay you. But the hardest thing of all is that we all have to keep very, very quiet about it since we'll all be moonlighting. We can't afford to let the unions find out what we're up to. They'll shut us down and take away our union cards if they do." He paused, holding her gaze. "Now that all the cards are on the table, are you still interested? You'd play the old lady, of course."

"Well, I suppose . . . *yes*! But, you know, I don't even know your name."

"Jerome St.-Tessier." He extended his hand formally across the table and grinned. "And yours?"

"Daliah. Daliah Boralevi."

They shook hands firmly, as though shaking on a secret pact, and then he found a pen and hastily scribbled something on a napkin. He slid it across the table at her. "Meet me at this address at seven-thirty in the evening exactly one week from today. It's the second doorbell from the top. After you ring, wait for me to lower a basket on a string. It will have the keys to the front door and the freight elevator in it."

She couldn't help laughing. "All right, Jerome St.-Tessier. I'll be there a week from this evening. But if we decide to follow through with this, I think you'd better get a spare key made."

It was a loft on Bond Street, just off Lafayette, and it took up the entire fifth floor of what had originally been a warehouse. As was the case with almost all the loft buildings, the poorly maintained exterior of Jerome's grimy industrial building and the steep wooden warehouse stairs with baby strollers and bicycles parked on the dingy landings belied the awesome spaciousness within each loft. Jerome's was high-ceilinged and had over four thousand square feet of unobstructed space. It was all gleaming polyurethaned wooden floors and window-lined walls interspersed with two rows of cast-iron Corinthian columns. It was almost like being in an empty cathedral.

He met her at the elevator door, which opened right into the loft. "You're early," he said. Smiling like the Cheshire cat.

"I'm punctual," she corrected, laughing. "I always am. It has something to do with defective genes, I think."

He looked delighted to see her and watched as she reached back and pulled her waist-length hair from inside the collar of her field jacket and shook it loose. Below the shapeless utilitarian olive green, her legs were encased in a second skin of outrageously expensive French jeans which were tucked into a pair of gleaming high-heeled fuchsia cowboy boots. He looked at her approvingly. "You are a sight for sore eyes. Come in."

"Said the spider to the fly?" she asked softly as she breezed across the threshold and shrugged off her glove-leather fuchsia shoulder bag. She watched as he rolled the heavy, riveted metal door shut and latched it with a heavy iron bar. Then she followed him across the wooden floor, shiny as the floor of a gym, to the distant seating area where thriving tall ficus trees were spotlighted by can lamps, creating a dappled, leafy shadow effect on the ceiling. Four sofas, each draped with rich, shimmering throws of silvery fabric, faced one another across a shipping pallet which had been pressed into service as a coffee table. Enormous abstracts, bold slashes of color, hung on the exposed-brick walls. The view north looked out at the distant Empire State Building and the glittering office towers of midtown. Janis Joplin wailed softly over the turned-down powerful stereo. Daliah liked the place at once. There was something exceedingly stylish and eminently luxurious about all that barren, empty space in the middle of one of the most crowded cities in the world.

"This place is nice," she said, parking her huge bag on one of the couches.

"I'm glad you like it. Why don't you have a seat while I get you a copy of the script. Then I'll explain my overall idea to you. Would you like some wine? I happen to have a decent Bordeaux uncorked."

She shook her head. "I'm purging today. A glass of plain water will suit me just fine."

"I'll be right back with it. Make yourself comfortable."

She took a seat on one of the couches. The fabric felt luxurious. She ran her hands over it. It was antique Fortuny. "You have good taste," she said.

He handed her a glass of Perrier on ice. "More taste than money, I'm afraid," he said with a smile. "Right now, even if I had the money, I wouldn't spend it on any more furnishings. God only knows what location I'll be sent to next month."

She heard some pounding and scraping noises and turned around. "Is that someone hammering?"

He followed her gaze to where a white linen curtain hung down from the ceiling, neatly dividing the 150-foot loft in half. "Why don't you go and see for yourself," he suggested softly. The Cheshire cat smiled wider now.

Obediently she rose, put her glass down on the pallet, and walked the fifty-odd feet to the curtain. She hesitated, and then pulled it swiftly aside. She caught her breath. For a moment she could only stare in amazement. Two young men and a stringy-haired blond in coveralls were busy putting the finishing touches on what was obviously a three-sided movie set.

She moved closer to it, her eyes everywhere at once. It looked amazingly authentic, as though a musty, stuffy middle-class parlor had been scooped up from prewar Berlin and set down right here in Manhattan. Everything looked historically correct, right down to the fussy pattern of the wallpaper, the faded, tattered Oriental rug, the Biedermeier secretary, the Bechstein piano with its clutter of old photographs and bibelots, and the overstuffed armchairs complete with yellowed lace antimacassars. And facing all that were the high-tech implements of a much more recent decade—flood lights on trolleys, an overhead microphone boom, and a professional thirty-five-millimeter camera, as well as all the other expensive paraphernalia and accoutrements of the professional filmmaker. A jumble of thick black electrical cables snaked across the floor.

"Oh, glad you're there, Jer," the blond girl called out.

She moved a chair a few inches to her left. "You want the piano the way it's there now, or you want it on the other side, by the window?"

"Where it is now is fine, Marie. But the backdrop outside the window is still too garish. Soften it up with some more tree branches. I want an effect of very hazy, dappled sunlight once the floods are switched on."

"Will do, boss." She grinned and saluted. "That lady our star?" She indicated Daliah.

"It is. Why don't you stop what you're doing for a minute and come meet her. And you guys too."

Marie and the two men dropped what they were doing and came on over.

"This is Marie," Jerome said. "Marie, meet Daliah."

Marie gave her the once-over and grinned. "Pleased to meetcha." She stepped forward, popped a giant pink chewing-gum bubble, and pumped Daliah's hand vigorously.

"Marie is our set designer," Jerome explained. "And this is Tim Fawcett, and Ian Potter. From their names they might sound like a plumbing company, but believe me they're first-rate engineers. Tim works the sound and Ian the lighting."

"Fawcett and Potter at your service," Ian and Tim said in a chorus.

Daliah laughed "Nice to meet you both." She shook their hands and nodded at the set. "You've been busy. I must say it looks impressive. Up to now I've been calm and collected, but just seeing the set and all that equipment is making me weak-kneed."

"I've got just the thing to mellow you out," Marie said. She went to get her bag, rummaged through it, and came up with a Marlboro box stuffed full of rolled joints. She extracted one, stuck it in her mouth, and scratched a match. She took a couple of tokes and handed it to Daliah.

Daliah held it delicately between two fingers and looked at it for a moment. "I've never done this before," she confessed sheepishly.

"There's no time like a first time." Marie smiled brightly. "Just inhale deeply, hold it, and let it out slowly. It'll make you into a new person. I guarantee it."

Daliah took a deep toke, held the smoke in, and broke out in a coughing fit. Then it subsided and a sense of well-being flooded through her. She passed the joint to Jerome, who took two tokes and passed it on.

"Good pot," Jerome said. He looked at Marie. "Got any more I can buy off you?"

Marie shook her head. "One of my boyfriends was making a film on the West Coast and brought it back with him. He only gave me half an ounce."

Tim passed the joint back to Marie. "Well, we'd better get back to work." He made a little gesture for Daliah's benefit. "Jerome's a slave driver and wants us ready to roll by the weekend."

Daliah turned to Jerome. "So soon?"

"And why not?" he asked. "We have the script, we have the equipment, and now we have the actress. The other members of the technical crew and the supporting actors will come and go on an as-needed basis." He glanced around. "Where's Cleo?"

"She was working on the costume sketches just a minute ago," Ian said. "Maybe she jumped into the bathroom."

"Cleo!" Jerome called out.

"Comin', White Bwana," a muffled voice called back cheerfully. There was a distant flush and a moment later a young, thin black woman with an urchin's face and glowing, intelligent, but naughty eyes and the build and poise of a model stepped out of the bathroom and came toward them. Her hair was corn-rolled, her face had a lively expression, and she was dressed in baggy army fatigue pants and a tight-fitting camouflage T-shirt. Yet despite all the man-tailored military green, there was something decidedly feminine about her, and the perfectly shaped apple-sized breasts tipped with aggressively jutting nipples made it clear that T-shirts were not for men only. "What's the matter?" she asked. "Can't a girl have her period in pea—" She came to an abrupt halt. Slowly she bent forward, her eyes widening to saucers. "Daliah?" she asked incredulously under her breath. "White Woman, is that you?"

Daliah leaned toward the black woman and blinked her own eyes in disbelief. Her voice was just as incredulous. "Miss Cleopatra, honey?" she asked softly. "Is that you?"

Cleo's wide mouth curved into a huge white grin. "Well, I'll be damned!"

And then they were both laughing happily and flew into each other's arms, embracing warmly. After a minute they drew back, each holding the other at arm's length.

"Jesus, it's been years!" Cleo exclaimed, laughing and crying at the same time.

"Seven years, to be exact."

"Wrong. Six years, ten months, and let me see . . . twenty-four days." Then they hugged each other again. "Jesus! After we lost touch Ah never thought I'd see you again. What are you doin' here?"

542

"Haven't you heard?" Daliah said. "I'm the star of Jerome's movie."

Hearing his name, Jerome cleared his throat noisily and both Daliah and Cleo looked at him. Only now were they aware of the perplexed looks the others were giving them.

"I take it you two know each other?" Jerome said at last.

"Shore do." Cleo nodded happily. "I was an exchange student in my sophomore year, and Ah spent it in Israel. Then we sorta got out of touch." She turned to Daliah. "Well, we ain't gonna let that happen again, are we?"

Daliah shook her head. Her eyes were shining.

"What I want to know," Cleo asked Jerome succinctly, "is how the hell did you ever talk her into starring in this shoestring movie, anyway?"

"I asked her. Why?"

"Don't you know she could be in anything she wanted?"

Now it was Jerome's turn to be puzzled. For once he looked out of his depth. "I don't understand."

Cleo shook her head in disbelief. "White Bwana," she declared, placing her hands on her hips and arching her back, "you mean you don't know who she is?"

He looked at her blankly and then peered at Daliah closely. "No. Should I?"

" 'Course you should." Cleo placed an affectionate arm around Daliah's shoulders. "This here is the daughter of one of the movie greats of all time. Just so you find it out sooner instead o' later, her mother happens to be your number-one screen idol!"

He stared at Daliah. "You mean—"

"Thas right." Cleo nodded. "White Woman here, she the daughter of the one and only Tamara. But what *Ah* wanna know is, what's she doin' in a hick production like ours!"

Daliah heard the key turning in the lock, and then the door of the suite opened and shut. Still in her Ishagiatsu pressure-point pose, she opened her eyes and twisted her head around. Jerome was standing just inside the door. His wire-rims reflected a shaft of sunlight, and he was holding a bottle of Cristal champagne by the neck in each hand. A crystal champagne glass was tucked under each of his armpits. He grinned wickedly.

She lowered her arms from her head and wrenched her knees together. Now that he was back, the calm the Ishagiatsu had inspired was all for nothing. Just seeing him made her temper return in spades. "Welcome back, stranger," she said sarcastically. "What's the matter? The party finally over?"

Ignoring her, he strutted wordlessly over to the desk by the window. He set the bottles and glasses down and with a flourish began peeling the foil off one of the bottles.

She climbed to her feet and thumped over to him. Angrily she grabbed his forearm just as he popped the cork. It went flying across the room.

"Don't ignore me, dammit!" she yelled, pulling him around to face her. "Where were you all this time while the sharks were having me for breakfast?"

One corner of his mouth twisted into a grin. "While the sharks were having you for breakfast," he said, maddeningly unfazed by her outburst, "I was out shaking the money tree, chérie. And guess what fell?"

"Obviously something hard and near-lethal, but not hard enough to kill you, which is what you deserve and what I'm going to do to you in a second. You are a skunk and a prick and a dildo and a piece of scum! Eat shit and die!"

"Said like a true lady," he said with a good-humored bow. "How does seventeen-million-five sound to you?" He waved the bottle in front of her. "Care to celebrate?"

She was suddenly speechless and all she could do was stare. Seventeen million, five hundred thousand dollars was the exact amount of money he'd budgeted as necessary for their next film!

"Well?" he said slowly, leaning into her face. "Has the cat got your tongue? Meow? Meeeowww?"

She couldn't trust herself to speak. "You . . . you mean to say you managed to raise it *all*?" she said shakily. "Already? On the very first day?"

"Every penny. Every last shekel and shilling and yen and sou. Every buck and pound and beautiful drachma. My name isn't skunk and prick and dildo for nothing. Now all we have to do is push the foreign sales of *Red Satin*, and then we're flying!" He rubbed her with his nose and leered at her. "I don't have to meet with the backers until lunch. What do you say we kill a couple of hours in bed?"

"Did you think you had to ask?" she said seductively, and with one fluid movement snatched up the unopened bottle and waltzed into the bedroom.

Jerome hung the DO NOT DISTURB sign outside the door, took the phone off the hook, and shut out the world behind closed windows and thick, heavy curtains. The noise from the traffic jam was muted now, and the room was a dim, sensuous womb. Bright slivers of sunlight leaked through the chinks between the curtains, each beam a spotlight alive with dust motes dancing suspended in the air. Leontyne Price warbled Samuel Barber's *Knoxville: Summer of 1915* on the big portable tape deck. The second bottle of champagne was half-empty on the nightstand, and the air smelled pungently of marijuana.

They were lying side by side on the big double bed, looking dreamily up at the ceiling as they passed a joint back and forth. After a few more tokes, Jerome pinched it out and placed it carefully in the ashtray. Then he slid around, got to his knees, and looked down at her.

Her arms were stretched lazily above her head, the pillow entirely hidden by the glossy blanket of her fanned-out hair. She had one knee casually bent, and the other leg stretched out straight, her toes languorously playing with the corner of a sheet. Even in a languid pose, there was something of the jungle cat about her, at once tauntingly feline, yet almost virilely powerful. Naked, she always looked charged, ready for sex. Her brownish nipples jutted like small hard cones from the dusty-rose areolae of her conical breasts, and her lean, hard body looked ready to pounce. There wasn't an ounce of superfluous flesh on her. From her neat lattice of ribs down to her forward-thrusting pelvic bones and sleek, coltish legs, her entire body seemed as streamlined as a Deco statue. Her smooth, muscular belly dipped smoothly inward, so that her hairless mound seemed to rise aggressively outward, a firm pink hill.

As always, the mere sight of her nakedness and the mellow high of the pot had aroused him. His swollen penis was slender and pink, and swooped upward at a rakish curve. His testicles were two tight little fists taut against their nest of mat dark pubic hair. His eyes gleamed devilishly.

She looked up at him in anticipation, her lips slightly parted, the tip of her pink tongue visible between her straight glossy white teeth.

Slowly he reached down and strummed his fingertips lightly back and forth across her nipples so that each fingertip brushed them ever so slightly. The ticklish sensation made her catch her breath, and she began to grind her pelvis obscenely into the sheet. From the heavy way she breathed, he could tell that she was ready.

But for him it was too soon. The game had barely begun.

He dipped two fingers into the open jar of Vick's Vap-O-Rub he had handy on the nightstand and scooped some out. Deftly he smeared a little dab on each of her nipples and slowly worked it in. Instantly she could smell the eucalyptus and, as the menthol made her nipples start to tingle, they jutted out more aggressively than before. Cruelly he slid a glob of Vick's inside her vagina and another up her anus. In a moment her back arched in such a spasm of agony that her pelvis lifted up off the bed and she seemed to levitate. He probed some more and she squeezed her eyes shut and thrashed her head back and forth in ecstasy. Suddenly he slid his fingers back out, kneaded her nipples, and squeezed. She went crazy, the burning and tingling inside and out making her writhe like a cat in heat.

It was exactly how he wanted her.

"You thirsty?" he asked.

She nodded.

Grabbing the champagne, he swigged straight from the bottle, filling his mouth. Then he held her face between his hands and pressed his lips against hers. She parted them, and slowly he fed her little spurts of champagne from his mouth. At first she looked surprised and then her throat worked hungrily. It tasted warm and tingly.

He drew his head back and watched, pleased by the way she licked her lips lewdly. Then he lowered himself gently atop her. A moment later she could feel his penis sliding between her warm, wet thighs. She braced herself, squirming into position, parting her legs wide and relaxing her muscles to make the entry easier. Little by little he prodded himself into her. When his hardness filled her completely, she felt impaled. "Oh, God, God!" she cried out at the exquisite sensation. With grim determination she scissored her legs tightly around his waist and clutched him close.

Slowly he began to ease in and out with steadily mounting thrusts.

Everything inside her burst into glorious, sparkling life. Every thrust and retreat hit a raw nerve and sent delicious ripples of passion through her entire body. The movement inside her slid and throbbed, and her face shone eagerly as she gazed up at him. His tempo built as his need became more urgent, and still clamping her legs tightly to hold him close, she began to grind her hips, thrashing and rolling and lifting herself halfway off the bed as she responded with a wild abandon, pushing her hips up and forward to meet his thrusts. Her face became controted into a grim mask of concentration; purring sounds rasped from deep within her throat.

Quickening his ramming thrusts, he dug his fingers into her buttocks and rode her for all he was worth, throwing himself aggressively into her. His face was grotesque with an unholy joy. His muscles gleamed as they strained. And still he triphammered, pounding in and out of her, faster and faster and faster. The blood was roaring through her and a rushing sound rose in her ears. Liquid fire erupted within the depths of her womanhood. Soon he had to explode; surely he couldn't continue on this way much longer.

But he had incredible staying power.

His frenzy only kept increasing. His assault was that of one possessed, his thrashing that of an animal gone wild. The power of his sex dug deeper, and his hips swung sideways every few strokes, rolling his testicles over her.

She felt as if she were drowning, swirling ever deeper and deeper, ever downward into a delicious maelstrom of madness. Her cries became muffled, and soon she was beyond the point of crying out. She felt she was going out of her mind, had ceased to exist as a person, had been turned inside out, entering her own womb and becoming a creature of pure sensations. And then a ululating wail rose slowly in her throat and issued forth from her lips like the scream of death. Jerome dug ever deeper into her in a final, furious lunge, and exploded into his climax, every part of his body ramming, thrusting, and pitching.

His breath rushed out of him in an explosive scream which merged with hers and he bucked against her spasms as they both burst over the finish line and together went flying off the edge of sanity.

They clung together as long minutes ticked by, waiting for their shudders to subside and their breathing to calm. Finally he slid out of her. Her insides ached mightily but exquisitely.

She looked at him dreamily. "Wow," she exclaimed softly. She shook her head as though to clear it. "That was something else. For a while, I wasn't even here."

He reached for the champagne, took another swig, and spotted the alarm clock on the nightstand. He swore under his breath and swung his legs out over the edge of the bed. "Damn! It's almost noon." His penis was still semihard and a pearl of semen glistened at its tip.

With one catlike movement she tucked her legs under her, closed her hands around his penis, and brought it to her lips. Her eyes glanced up at him as she flicked off the drop of semen with her tongue. "Are you sure the lunch won't wait?"

"I told you." He went around the room, retrieving his clothes from the floor. "I've got to meet the backers at two."

She made a face. "Can't they wait until tomorrow? Then we could spend the whole day in bed."

"They're just here for the day," he said casually. "They're leaving for Riyadh in the morning."

She blinked, her brows furrowing. Then she gave a throaty laugh. "I didn't quite catch that. For a moment, I could have sworn you said Riyadh."

"That's right, I did."

Her voice dropped. "You mean you're making a deal with *Arabs*?"

"They're an Arab investment consortium," he said stiffly. "Their money's the same color as anybody else's. Only they have more of it."

"You fucking creep!" Without warning, she sprang from the bed like a cat and her arm blurred through the air. Before he knew what was happening, her open palm caught him across the face and cracked like gunfire. He swayed unsteadily for a moment before he regained his balance. His hand flew up to his burning cheek and he touched the white welt and stared at her. "What in hell did you do that for?" he asked angrily. "Now I'll probably have a bruise."

"Good." She raised her head so high that the cords stood out boldly on her neck. "I did that because you deserve it. I should do a lot more, but I see now that you're not worth it. I was a fool to ever get involved with you."

He stared at her coldly. "Don't say something you might regret later on."

Spinning around, she grabbed the receiver off the phone. He grabbed it out of her hand and slammed it down. It gave a shrill half-ring. "Do you mind explaining what has suddenly gotten into you?" he demanded.

She stared at him. "You mean to tell me you don't know?"

"No, goddammit!" he roared. "What am I supposed to be? A goddamn clairvoyant?"

"Well, try this on for size." She squared her shoulders and the tendons on her neck made a deep V. "If you so much as touch a penny of Arab money, we're through. For good. I mean it. I'll leave you."

He let out an exasperated sigh. "Simmer down and try to let me explain." He reached out to touch her, but she shrank back.

"I only want to know one thing," she said. "Do you really intend to use Arab financing?"

"It's there, isn't it? And for your information, it's not all that easy to raise seventeen and a half million dollars."

"Thank you." She smiled hideously and her voice trembled. "Now get your goddamn paws away from the phone. I'm calling the concierge to book me a seat on the next flight out."

"Don't you think you're carrying this Arab vendetta of yours a little far?"

"Why should you care?" she retorted. "It's over between us."

He looked at her in disbelief. "You mean to tell me you're going to throw eight good years down the drain? Just like that?"

She held his gaze, her green eyes burning right through his. "Damn right I am. Or hasn't anyone told you? Jews and Arabs are like oil and water. They just don't mix."

"Daliah," he pleaded, "please be reasonable. This isn't political, it's moviemaking." He stepped toward her, but she tore herself away from him and fled to the bathroom. She slammed the door shut and locked it.

She stepped back as he tried the door handle.

"Daliah!" he called out, shaking the door. "Come out of there." He started hammering at it with his fists. "Daliah! You can't just leave, dammit! We have a contract!"

"Then sue me!" she barked. Her eyes stinging with tears, she turned on the bidet and began washing herself furiously. She couldn't stand the thought of having any of him in her any longer.

She wept quietly, oblivious now of Jerome's knocks and pleadings, oblivious of the swift-swirling warm water beneath her, oblivious of the steady *glugging* noises of the plumbing. All she could think about was the day she had learned to hate Arabs—all Arabs. That terrible day in June when tragedy had laid the foundation of the hatred which would be with her always.

She had been a little over six years old on that bright hot Sunday, and the whole family was spending the day on the Tel Aviv beach. They had just moved from Ein Shmona to the new seaside apartment house in Hayarkon Street a few weeks earlier, and this was a very special day since it was the first one in over a month that her father could spend it with them. They had packed a big picnic lunch, and Dani had stuck a striped umbrella in the sand and sat beside Tamara in the shade on low canvas folding chairs they had lugged over from the new apartment. She could see their fifth-floor balcony whenever she looked up from where she was playing. It was right across Independence Park, which divided the beach from the first street of buildings along this edge of the city. The huge expanse of golden sand, stretching out in both directions, was noisy and crowded. Everyone was out enjoying the sun and sand and surf. Out beyond the breakers, a regatta of little sailboats raced across the water like gulls. Somewhere behind her, Ari and Asa played with a group of agile boys, yelling excitedly as they kicked a soccer ball back and forth along the edge of the water. They sounded like they were having a lot more fun than she was.

Suddenly she was bored with the sand molds she was making. Even when she used moist sand, it dried out quickly in the sun and the molds would start to crumble. Frustrated, she mashed all of them with her little red shovel and then flung it down in the sand. She looked up with a pout. Her mother's head was way back, a wide straw hat and big dark glasses hiding her face. Her skin was bronze and gleamed from lotion, and the life-size glossy head of a cover girl looked up from the fashion magazine she had placed, tentlike, on her belly.

"Mama," Daliah said, "I'm thirsty."

Her mother raised her head. "But you just had a glass of juice with your lunch, sweetheart."

"I know, but that was *hours* ago."

Tamara lifted her wrist and glanced pointedly at her watch. "Not even half an hour ago. I thought you wanted to keep your stomach empty so you could go play in the water."

"That was before. Now I want a Co-Cola."

Her mother smiled. "But you know we didn't bring any. We just brought juice and bottled citrus drinks."

Daliah looked at her shrewdly. "Papa's got money, and that man up there is selling Co-Colas," she said with the irrefutable logic of a six-year-old. She pointed up toward the street, where a pushcart vendor was doing a brisk business.

Tamara sighed and looked sideways. "Dani?"

Daliah focused her eyes on her father now and gave him The Look. That was what he called it when she made her eyes big and round and helpless. Her father laughed. "All right, angel, but just this once. You know Cokes aren't good for you."

She watched intently as he dug a bill out of the shirt he'd folded up neatly under his chair. She grabbed for it, but he held it out of her reach. "I don't want you going up to the street. There's too much traffic and it's dangerous. Get one of your brothers to go for you, and have him bring back a Coke for each of us."

Laughing happily, she took the money, kissed him sloppily, and ran off to break up the soccer game.

Ari was annoyed with her intrusion and tried to ignore her. Turning his back on her, he crouched down, effortlessly deflected the black-and-white ball with a head butt, and snapped, "Can't you see we're in the middle of a game?"

She stood there clutching the bill in front of her. "Come on, Ari," she begged. "I can't get it myself. Papa won't let me." She turned to her other brother. "Asa!"

"Oh, all right." Asa ran over to her, swooped the bill out of her hand, and dashed off up the embankment. "Be right back," he called over his shoulder to Ari. "Time out."

Happily, Daliah watched him jogging up to the vendor's pushcart. Several children and adults were crowded around it and Asa had to wait his turn. While she watched, a swarthy man with sunglasses and a hat pulled way down over his face sauntered casually by and dumped something into the wire trash basket next to the pushcart and strode quickly off to a waiting car. Before he could jump all the way in and slam the door, the car took off with a squeal of tires.

She waited impatiently, twisting her body from left to right, while Asa awaited his turn. She licked her lips in anticipation. She loved Coca-Cola. It was sweet and cold and bubbly.

Finally it was Asa's turn. She watched him hand over the money, and the vendor give him an armful of bottles

That was when the bomb in the trash basket went off.

And blew Asa, the vendor, and four others to bits.

Time and again, Cleo had proved herself. Whenever Daliah had a crisis, she was there to hold her hand and help her through it. And she was there now at Kennedy Airport for that very reason, waiting for the Air France passengers to start straggling through customs.

Daliah was one of the first ones through. Having flown first class with no more than a Vuitton handbag and giant matching bag which had been constructed expressly to fit under a first-class seat, she sailed through customs in record time. To avoid recognition, her telltale hair was completely hidden by an Hermès scarf, her travel-durable outfit was simple and nondescript, and she wore huge butterfly-shaped sunglasses which rendered her so featureless that she could have been any one of three hundred instantly recognizable famous faces traveling incognito, from Jackie O to Charlotte Ford. Even Cleo, long used to her various disguises, had to look closely to recognize her.

Cleo held out her long cinnamon arms invitingly and embraced Daliah warmly. "White Woman, *baby*," she said softly. "I know you're hurtin'."

Daliah's lips were pinched. "I don't know which I feel more strongly," she sniffled. "Hurt or anger."

"Come on, the car's waitin' outside. We can talk about it

later." Cleo, ever practical, slipped the bag off Daliah's shoulder, coiled a reassuring arm around her waist, and steered her expertly through the crowded terminal toward the glass exit doors. Her face was set in a worried look. "Are you all right?"

Daliah started to nod, but then shook her head. "No, I'm not all right," she said, her low, hoarse voice heavy with pain.

Cleo looked sharply sideways, and she could see that behind the huge black glasses Daliah's matchless eyes were swollen and red from crying, and that there were dark hollows beneath them.

Daliah turned to her. "Why," she asked in a quivering voice, "did I ever have to get involved with that miserable schmuck in the first place. Why, of all the billions of men out there, did it have to be that prick Jerome?"

"White Woman," Cleo sighed, "if I knew the answer to that one, I wouldn't only be rich, I'd be happily married and surrounded by fifteen screamin' kids too. But I know one thing for sure, and that's not to try an' analyze what we feel and why we feel it. Once we start doin' that, the curtain comes down and all the fun's gone outta life."

"Life's never fun," Daliah said glumly. "How can fun go out of something it's never been in?"

Prudently Cleo clamped her lips together and shut up. She knew better than to argue. Daliah was barely holding herself together. Despite the independent air Daliah projected to the world, deep down inside she was one of the most sensitive people Cleo had ever known. It had taken her a long time to find that out.

They went out into a day that had turned angry and gray. A warm wind had started to blow, trash and papers taking flight and dust and grit swirling in little eddies. It looked like it would start pouring at any minute.

Cleo peered up and down the sidewalk. "Damn! The cops musta chased the car away. He's probably had to circle."

They waited, and a minute later a white Eldorado convertible, overloaded with sparkling chrome and flying coon tails like proud pennants from the antenna, nosed toward the curb. The whitewalls gleamed, the dice dangling from the rearview mirror were fuzzy, and James Brown was throbbing with ear-splitting volume over the stereo speakers.

"Here he is," Cleo shouted above the din. She grabbed Daliah's arm. "Come on."

Daliah's lips parted and she hung back. "This . . . *this* is our ride?" She eyed the driver suspiciously. He was ebony-skinned, with hooded eyes, a scraggly goatee, and wore a lime-green, brilliantly plumed hat which matched his elaborately tailored suit.

"That's him," Cleo affirmed lightly. Cheerfully she waved him to remain seated, pulled the passenger door open, and despite his protestations, leaned inside and switched the stereo off. From the expressions on the faces of the people nearby, the sudden silence was a godsend.

Cleo flipped the front seat toward the dash and made a sweeping gesture for Daliah to climb into the back.

For a moment Daliah could only stare. "Cleo . . ." she began haltingly, "what if we cabbed it?"

Cleo made a gesture which silenced her. "No, I haven't started hookin', if'n that's what you were gonna ask," she said in a low voice. "Coyote here's all right, long as you don't have to work for 'im. 'Member that William Friedkin movie I did the costumes for?"

Daliah nodded.

"Well, I arranged for Coyote and some of his girls to have bit parts in one o' the scenes. It made him the big struttin' man on the block and he owes me a few favors for that, so I call 'em in whenever I need wheels at my beck and call. Like he's a private limousine service, you know, 'cept that this here's a free ride and that's a *lot* cheaper than any taxi or limo anytime. Get in. It'll be fun."

Seeing it was futile to argue, Daliah climbed obediently into the back and settled onto the chinchilla-covered seat. Cleo got in beside her. Then Coyote flipped the seat back and reached over to the passenger door and swung it shut.

"An' put up the roof," Cleo ordered like a queen from the back of the car.

"Say *what*?" Coyote turned around and stared at her, his hooded eyes widening to surprised white orbs.

"You heard me. Put the top up."

"Hey, baby." Coyote's voice rose to a falsetto. "Wha's the use o' havin' a convertible if'n the top's up? It ain't rainin' yet."

"That's right," Cleo agreed. "But Daliah, she need a little peace and privacy. Everyone stares at this here pimpmobile anyway, and if there's one thing she don't need right now, it's bein' recognzied and stared at." Her voice sharpened, leaving no room for argument. "Put it up, nigger."

Coyote just about choked, and Daliah was ready to die, but the convertible canopy whirred and unfolded itself overhead. And not a moment too soon. The first angry splats of rain suddenly drummed heavily on the black cloth top.

They rode most of the way in silence, Daliah staring blankly out the rain-streaked windows at the traffic. Going into Manhattan wasn't too bad, but by the time they drove past Queens Plaza, traffic in the oncoming lanes was practically at a standstill, with both lanes already backed up all the way to the Midtown Tunnel. The clock was just inching toward four, but rush hour was already well under way.

"I don't know what your plans are," Cleo told Daliah. "I can have Coyote drop you off at your place or you can come home and stay with me. It's your choice."

Daliah turned away from the window and looked at her. "I'd really prefer not to go home," she said quickly. "If I'm not imposing, that is."

"Imposin'? Shit, you ain't never imposin', White Woman," Cleo assured her cheerfully. "My place it is." She leaned forward and raised her voice. "Coyote, make it Hamilton Terrace."

The pimp's sloe eyes glanced back at her in the rearview mirror. "Yes, ma'am."

Cleo giggled. "Did I hear right?" she asked Daliah. "That nigger call me 'ma'am'?"

"C'mon, Cleo," Coyote begged. "You're gonna' ruin my reputation. If word gets round that I'm soft on you, how you 'spect my girls to do like they s'posed to?"

"Don't worry, Coyote," Cleo said with a laugh. "I'll try to show more respect when your girls are around."

"One fuckin' bit-part walk-on," he moaned, "and she think she owns me. How much longer am I gonna have to pay for it?"

"Well, if you want another walk-on in a new Kurt Russell movie," Cleo said slowly for maximum effect, "I'd say you'll be enslaved a good while longer."

"Another part?" Coyote's eyes flickered back at Cleo from the rearview mirror with such interest she knew she had him hooked. "Which movie's this?"

"I'll tell you all 'bout it when I have more information to give you. Meanwhile, Daliah's feelin' a little down, and I'm not at my greatest either. Up the windows all the way and pass the goods on back here."

Coyote gladly handed her a small glass vial with a tiny silver spoon attached. Cleo unscrewed the cap, quickly took a snort up each nostril, and handed it to Daliah.

Daliah shook her head.

"C'mon," Cleo urged. "It's pure coke. One hit, and I guarantee you'll feel a lot better."

Daliah lifted the spoon carefully to her nose. She snorted

deeply. Then her eyes brightened and she passed the vial back. Cleo was right. The moment the coke hit her system, she felt a hundred percent better. "What is this, a wake?" she asked suddenly. "Let's have some music. Turn on the stereo!"

"All *right*!" Coyote exclaimed happily, his hand already reaching to punch James Brown back on.

Cleo lived in one of those tenement railroad flats, a series of six dark narrow rooms stretching from the front of her building all the way to the back. The bathtub was in the middle of the kitchen, and Cleo's bed was surrounded by mousetraps, but the front door of the building was secure, the intercom usually worked, the boiler broke down only once or twice each winter, and best of all, it was that rare New York phenomenon—a rent-controlled apartment handed down to Cleo from a relative who'd lived there for nearly thirty years so that the rent was a minuscule eighty-three dollars a month. Besides being such a good deal financially, the apartment also let Cleo keep one foot in black culture, so that no matter how far or wide her job might take her, she always came back to Harlem and never completely lost contact with her origins.

The last two hours had passed by quickly. Daliah had unloaded her heart to Cleo, not leaving out a thing, and once she'd gotten everything off her chest, she began to feel a little better. Not great, to be sure, but just talking things out and having someone listen seemed to have helped.

Cleo was an attentive audience; she was also the only logical ear for Daliah to turn to. Cleo knew Jerome well enough to understand how his mind worked, and being Daliah's closest friend, she could sympathize with what her friend was going through. Also, being in the movie business herself, and having worked on and off with both of them, Cleo had a good understanding of the problems inherent in film financing and production. The business being the frenetic zoo that it was, for a long time she had marveled at Daliah and Jerome's being able to both live and work together, and she'd wondered how such obvious professional strains could not affect their personal relationship. Now she wondered no more about it. The strain had obviously reached the breaking point.

"Well, at least there's a bright side to all this," Daliah murmured. She looked morosely down into her drink. It was Cleo's special, a quart-sized screwdriver with just enough ice to cool it but not enough to dilute the alcohol. The initial sense of well-being she had felt from the coke had long since worn off, but she'd refused another snort. She looked back up and held Cleo's questioning gaze. "Jerome and I aren't married, and we don't have any children," she said softly. "There's that for a bright side."

Cleo considered that, and then she shook her head. "White Woman, that's like sayin' you're glad you didn't get treated for lung cancer because you've died of a heart attack. That don't make any sense at all."

"You're right, of course." Daliah nodded and compressed her lips. "But children or marriage *would* have made it more difficult to break up."

"Relationships." Cleo shook her head. "Why can't they ever be perfect?" She paused and looked at Daliah. "I take it you're not planning to go back to him?"

"Not unless he refuses the Arab financing, no."

"Still, you should have stayed on in Cannes. You're up for an award. I wouldn't have missed out on that if I were you."

"Cannes," Daliah said succinctly, "is too small for both Jerome and me." She traced her index finger around the rim of her glass.

"So what are you planning on doing now?"

Daliah shrugged. "Well, for the first time in over two years I have three weeks to myself. We were going to spend two of those weeks in Cannes, but now I can add that to my vacation time." She gave a low laugh. "It's been so long since I've had nothing to do that I'm not sure I know what to do with all that time. But first, I think, I'm going to find an apartment of my own here."

"You mean you're gonna move out of the loft?"

"That's right." Daliah nodded. "It was Jerome's loft to start with, so I can't really throw *him* out. I figure it'll take me a week to find a place and get my things moved in. Then I think I'll go up to Cape Cod and stay with Inge for a few days."

Inge's employers, the Steinbergs, had died and left Inge a respectable inheritance, which she had used to purchase a motel on the beach, and Daliah had a standing invitation to visit.

"And then, of course," Daliah continued, "there's Ari's wedding. I was planning to fly to Israel for it anyway, and that hasn't changed. It's been too long since I've been back home. Eleven years is a lifetime, and I've been neglecting my family for that long."

Cleo nodded. "When it comes down to it, family's sometimes the only thing you can depend on." She grinned suddenly. "Family *an'* me, that is."

Daliah set her drink down, leaned forward, and took Cleo's hand in her own. She smiled. "Yes, you've been a true friend," she said, "and I know I'm lucky to have you."

"An' that goes vice versa too," Cleo declared staunchly. "We're each other's sob sisters." She gestured at the end table. "C'mon, hand me that dirnk. It's all water by now an' it's time I freshened it up. I mean, what's the use of bein' miserable if you can't at least tie one on, huh?"

Three afternoons later, after having scouted nine different rental apartments and four fixtured living lofts, Daliah found a suitable two-bedroom corner apartment on Central Park West. It was on a high floor and had four living-room windows along one wall, which looked out over the park, and another two windows looking over at the steep green Gothic roofs of the Dakota. It was available for immediate occupancy and she signed a one-year lease. Then she got on the horn and found a moving company that could take care of her the following day. Two more phone calls proved it would be three days before the telephone company could hook her up, and eight days before the cable people could come, but she didn't care. Moving her things out of Jerome's loft as quickly as possible meant severing yet another tie with him, and she felt that the sooner that was done, the easier things would be for her in the long run.

She and Cleo spent all that Tuesday night packing cartons, getting ready for the movers in the morning. It had been years since she'd moved last, and she'd almost forgotten what it entailed. How things accumulated when one lived in the same place for years and had the luxury of endless space to store it all in! There was the gleaming 1820's Biedermeier furniture she collected, with the burled veneers and layers upon layers of lacquer—a very serious luxury for a person who hailed from a country which had been denuded of wood over the centuries and where every twig counted. Then there were the wardrobes full of clothes, the mementos she had collected during her travels to location shoots, and silver-framed photographs by the dozens. Why did it take a move to make one see just how much one had accumulated? Not that she minded getting rid of things for which there was no longer any space or use, but right now she just didn't have the time or the patience to sort through it all and start editing out the useless things. For the moment, at least, it was simplest just to pack it all and have it moved.

Closing off her mind to the size of the chore at hand, she

separated what clearly belonged to her and what was Jerome's, and when ownership was in doubt, she settled upon leaving it behind.

She and Cleo packed, folded, wrapped, taped, and labeled, and it became clear to them that if they wanted to be finished by the time the movers arrived, they would be at it all night long.

"How on earth did I acquire so much junk?" Daliah moaned at one point. She flopped down into a chair and stared at Cleo through bleary eyes. "The new place is going to look like a warehouse."

"Don't worry, we'll get it all unpacked and put away within a couple of days," Cleo assured her. "We don't have to do it all by ourselves. I can always call in some favors."

"Like Coyote?" Daliah laughed.

It was then that the telephone rang.

Daliah jerked upright as though she had been struck. She looked over at Cleo, sudden panic flashing in her eyes. "Will you get it, Miss Cleopatra, honey?" she asked shakily. "I've got a feeling that that's Jerome."

"And if it is?"

"I don't care how much he yells, threatens, or tries to sweet-talk you, I don't want to talk to him. Period."

"Consider it done." Cleo squared her shoulders and marched off to answer it. A few minutes later: "He says to tell you you've got to talk to him!" she called out grimly across the loft. She was holding her hand over the mouthpiece. "He says you're contractually bound to him."

"Maybe he doesn't know it yet, but contracts are made to be broken."

After Cleo hung up, Daliah asked, "Did you tell him I'm packing my things?"

"Should I?"

"Next time he calls, you might as well. Maybe then he'll finally get the message that I'm dead serious."

Cleo raised her eyebrows. "White Woman, honey, from the way he sounds, I think he already knows that."

Daliah packed in silence.

Thirty minutes passed and then the phone rang again. Daliah gritted her teeth. "Why doesn't the prick just leave me alone?" she growled angrily.

"You can't 'spect people to do that when you're beautiful, smart, and one o' the biggest box-office stars in the world," Cleo said reasonably.

"BS," Daliah mumbled. She felt her pent-up tears beginning to spill down her cheeks, and struggled to keep them back. "Don't *you* start giving me that shit," she said in mock anger.

This time after Cleo hung up, she came back grinning. "There!" she said triumphantly, clapping imaginary dust off her hands. "Ah think that's done it. We won't be hearin' from *him* again tonight." Her big dark eyes glowed with satisfaction.

Daliah was mystified. "Why, what did you tell him?"

"Oh, a l'il bit o' this, and a l'il bit o' that," Cleo said vaguely. "This time I decided to let him have it. Now we'll be able to enjoy some peace and quiet."

But Cleo was wrong. It wasn't even an hour after she'd hung up on him for the third time that the door buzzer gave off the shrill, steady blast of someone leaning on it.

Daliah froze and her face went white. "That can't be him!" she exclaimed. "He's in France."

" 'Course it ain't him," Cleo reassured her. "Takes six or seven hours to fly here." She strode over to the intercom and pressed the "talk" button. "Who's there?" she said into it.

"It's Patsy Lipschitz," a disembodied voice squawked back. "Let me in. I've got to see Daliah."

"Just a moment," Cleo said patiently.

Instantly the unrelenting buzzer sounded again. And again.

Cleo punched the "talk" button once more. "Hold your horses. I'm gonna see if Daliah's in."

"She's in," the voice accused brashly. "Now let me in."

Cleo looked questioningly at Daliah.

"Shit." Daliah flung some packing paper on the floor in disgust.

"Can I let her up?"

"Might as well," Daliah shrugged. "If I know Patsy, she'll keep leaning on that buzzer all night long, or until we let her up. Better yet, take the freight elevator down. She's liable to have a heart attack if she's got to climb the stairs."

Patsy Lipschitz was Daliah's agent, a gargantuan woman who wore voluminous muumuus and whose sweetly puffy features hid a brain which was the envy of financial computers; moreover, she was blessed with a bazaari's natural gift for tough negotiations as well. The rumor mills had it that she was a notorious lesbian, but as far as her relationship with Daliah was concerned, she was all business.

"Will do, White Woman." Cleo saluted smartly, slid the freight elevator cage door aside, got in, and rattled the door shut again. A moment later Daliah heard the rheumatic whirring and clanking of the elevator as it descended, as well as Cleo's cheerful calls as she passed each floor: "Lingerie . . . Better Dresses . . . Bargain Basement!" Then the whole process was repeated as it rose back up, Cleo continuing to chant imaginary store departments. ". . . Notions . . . Menswear . . . *Credit Department!*"

Patsy didn't even wait until Cleo slid the cage door completely aside. She caught sight of Daliah from inside the elevator and started right in on her.

"Whaddya mean, you're refusing to have anything more to do with Jerome?" she yelled out. "He called and said you've left him and are packing your bags!"

Patsy was bicoastal and shuttled between New York and Hollywood with the ease that other people commuted between Manhattan and Westchester, but she had come to show business via Brooklyn, and the world of Erasmus Hall High ran deep in her blood. She was loud, brash, and obnoxious, and Daliah often wondered why someone hadn't sent her to charm school; more often, how she had survived so long without having been shot. Right now she wondered about the latter. Obviously Cleo did too, for she made herself scarce.

"You heard correctly," Daliah replied calmly as the enormous hennaed redhead bore heavily down on her. She stepped adroitly aside; when Patsy was riled up, she was like a charging rhinoceros. "Everything's over between Jerome and me."

Patsy wouldn't hear of it and waved a fat multiringed hand negligibly. Clusters of diamonds gave off rainbow flashes. "Dollcake, nothing in this town or this business is ever completely finished. You and I know it's like one big, unhappy, incestuous family." Patsy groped around in her giant woven handbag, came up with a thin cigar, stuck it in her mouth, and lit it with a chrome Zippo lighter. Clicking it shut, she squinted at Daliah through a cloud of bilious blue smoke. "Take my advice and stop packing. Give yourself a few days to sleep on it."

"I've made up my mind," Daliah said stubbornly.

Patsy headed for the seating area and parked herself on one of the four big sofas. She kicked off her shoes and put her feet up on the shipping-pallet coffee table. "I think it's just a phase you're going through. You and Jerome have known each other what now? About seven years?" She glanced at Daliah for confirmation.

"More like eight."

"Then you're obviously experiencing the eight-year-itch," Patsy said definitely. "It's nothing that a little extramarital affair won't cure."

"Jerome and I aren't married," Daliah reminded her as she took a seat on a facing couch. "Remember?"

"But you've been living together all this time," Patsy said emphatically. "Except for semantics, living together for eight years and being married are basically the same."

"There's more to it than that."

"Well, if you feel so strongly about it, move out of his personal life, but keep making movies together." Patsy's voice was loud and grating.

Daliah didn't reply. She sat in stunned silence, and despite her best efforts, a tear slid out of each eye and trickled down her cheeks. She should have known that Patsy wouldn't understand.

"Oh, shit," Patsy said disgustedly. "Now you're going emotional on me. You can't allow your personal feelings to get in the way of business."

"I can't help it."

"You'd better. I don't have to remind you how quickly today's box-office draw can become tomorrow's box-office poison. Jerome gave you your start in this business. He made you into the star that you are."

"I helped him," Daliah pointed out. "I did his first picture for nothing, and that was the one that put him on the map."

"Yeah, but now you're getting one-point-five mil from him and everybody else. That ain't exactly bubkas."

Daliah sniffed. "I never said it was."

"Good. Just so you know it." Patsy puffed away in silence for a moment. "Look at it this way, dollcake," she said at last. "This year you've got the Woody Allen movie as well as Jerome's new one. Plus CBS video's paying you two hundred thou for the exercise tape, and Jhirmack wants to put you on a half-mil-a-year retainer for pushing their hair conditioner—"

"Which I don't use."

"Never mind that. With hair like yours, they could peddle panda piss and the public would snap it up, 'cause there isn't a woman alive who wouldn't give ten years of her life to have a mane like yours." She shook her head slowly. "No matter how you look at it, dollcake, money's money." Patsy looked over at Daliah through narrowed eyes. "That brings your income to three and three quarters of a mil for just this year alone. Add the Bob Hope special, and guest-starring for two weeks in that new Broadway show, and you've got a cool four mil. Don't piss it away."

"I'm not pissing anything away," Daliah said indignantly.

"You will, if you walk out on Jerome." Patsy nodded

emphatically. "You'll lose a million and a half. And if that ain't pissing money away, I don't know what is."

"Patsy," Daliah said wearily, "the only difference between making four million and two and a half is that I have to pay more taxes on four than I do on two."

"Taxes, schmaxes, it's your reputation I'm worried about, not Uncle Sam." Patsy stabbed her cigar toward Daliah to make her point. "Listen, dollcake, you're under contract to St.-Tessier Productions, and that means you're obligated, period. If you don't hold up your end of the bargain, word will get out that you're difficult to work with, and you know how fast news like that can spread in this business."

"It doesn't have to spread at all, unless someone leaks it."

"Even if all three of us clam up, news like that still has a habit of getting out. And then, before you know it, other producers are going to think twice before hiring you. You wouldn't want that to happen, would you?" Patsy paused a moment for dramatic effect and then lowered her voice to a grandmotherly tone, and she even smiled. "When Jerome called me, we had a nice long chat. He still loves you a lot, you know."

Daliah didn't say anything.

"Believe me, you could do worse in a relationship," Patsy continued. "He's good-looking, hardworking, and honest as they come. That's rare in any relationship, and even rarer in this cutthroat business. What more could you ask for?"

"Someone who understands where I come from and where I'm going. Someone who takes *me* into account, and not just so many dollars and so many thousands of feet of film."

"There isn't anyone else in your life, is there?"

Daliah shook her head. "No," she said miserably.

"Then that proves it," Patsy said triumphantly. "You still love him. Now, take my advice and pick up the phone and call him. He's really quite reasonable, you know. He told me he's willing to forgive you your . . . your tantrum, if you will—"

"Now, wait a minute, Patsy," Daliah growled. "This isn't exactly something I want to be forgiven for." She leaned forward and narrowed her eyes into dangerous green slits. "What kind of song and dance did Jerome give you, anyway?"

"None at all." Patsy puffed nonchalantly on her cigar. "Oh, he said that you'd had a little spat, sure. But he assured me that it really wasn't anything serious."

Daliah's voice cut in, sharp as a newly honed knife. "Did he tell you what it was about?"

"Well, he did say it had something to do with financing the picture."

"That's right." Daliah nodded. "He wants to take Arab money, and I refuse to let myself be tainted by it."

"Arab, schmarab." Patsy waved her cigar expansively. "This is business, dollcake, so try to keep this and your highfalutin personal standards separate. In this business, it's your professionalism that counts, and no one cares where money's been, only where it's going. Besides, this movie of Jerome's is going to be a classic."

"Then it will have to be a classic without me." Daliah raised her chin resolutely. "I will not be in an Arab-backed film. This discussion is closed." She sat back, folded her arms in front of her, and looked at Patsy coldly. "I would have thought that you, of all people, would have understood that. Or have you forgotten that you're Jewish?" she added softly.

Patsy bristled. "Just because you were born in Israel doesn't give you the right to be any more Jewish than me!" she said hotly. "You sabras haven't exactly cornered the market on Judaism, you know."

"I never said that; you just did. But I've grown up closer to the Arab problem than you have. It was my brother they blew up with a bomb, not yours."

Patsy's voice was soothing. "I know all that, dollcake—"

Daliah bristled. "And for God's sake, stop calling me 'dollcake'!" she shouted angrily. "I'm *not* your dollcake. My name happens to be Daliah." She tossed her head in that peculiar way that indicated she was very upset.

Patsy stared at her. She knew when she'd gone too far, and she started to back down. "Daliah, then," she said quickly, and urged, "Daliah, please try to be reasonable—"

"No, *you* try to be reasonable," Daliah snapped. "Go home and think about what Ive just told you. For once, try to put yourself in my shoes. Better yet, take a couple of months off and go live in Israel. Then, when you come back, *then* you can tell me what I should or should not do for my faith."

"Then why aren't you there now?" Patsy countered sharply. "If memory serves me correctly, you've been living the cushy life in this country for years now. If you're so pro-Israel, why don't you go back and live there full-time? Or aren't you really cut out for the tough life?"

"Why am I not there?" Daliah said softly, more to herself than to Patsy. Her eyes took on a distant look. "You know, that's a very good question." She nodded slowly to herself. "It gives *me* something to think about as well." She rose to her feet. "Please, go home, Patsy," she said wearily. "Go back to bed. I've still got a lot of packing to do."

"Daliah—"

"The case is closed," Daliah said coldly. "Or must I remind you that as my agent, you're supposed to be supportive of me, and working exclusively for *me*? I don't recall your ever having been hired to represent Jerome St.-Tessier."

Patsy stared at her. "I . . . I can see that you're upset," she said quickly. "Tell you what, doll . . . Daliah. I think I'd better let you sleep on this." She bent over to retrieve her shoes and struggled to get them on over her swollen feet. She attempted a smile, but it came off ghastly. "Whaddya say we talk again in a couple of days, after we've both simmered down?"

When Patsy disappeared as abruptly as she'd arrived, Daliah almost had to smile. She knew good and well why Patsy had left in such a hurry. It all came down to the lowest common denominator—dollars and cents. Patsy's commission on two and a half million dollars would come to a respectable quarter of a million, and Jerome or no, Patsy knew where her priorities lay. She wasn't about to sacrifice the goose that was laying her golden eggs—and certainly not over any arguments about religion or politics.

Done like a true agent, Daliah thought. She shook her head and sighed. That was the one thing about agents. You could trust them to do cartwheels, light firecrackers, or sell their mothers if that was what it took for them to get their commissions. And that was exactly what Patsy had just done. She had backed down only because her commission was in jeopardy, not because of any ideals about Israel or Judaism.

The sun had slid below the Palisades of New Jersey two hours earlier, and the large half-million-dollar media room was dim, with the electronically controlled champagne-colored raw-silk drapes closed across the glittering Manhattanscape. Najib al-Ameer never ceased to be dazzled by the view, and this was one of the very few times he could remember that he'd been in New York and shut out the shimmering backdrop of city lights. He was watching the videotape of *To Have and To Hold*, one of Daliah Boralevi's earliest films, on the big Sony projection TV, and other than the three concurrently running tapes on the three built-in regular televisions beside it, he didn't want anything, least of all the expensive view, to tempt his hawklike eyes from the screens for even a moment.

One of the smaller televisions showed a videotape compiled of black-and-white close-ups from all of Tamara's old movies.

On the set right beneath that one, a succession of news photo stills, videotaped interviews, and news footage showed image after image of Dani ben Yaacov.

The third and lowermost set endlessly repeated the few times Schmarya Boralevi had ever been photographed or filmed. Most of these images were grainy and blurry, having been shot by distant telephoto lenses.

The multiple images fueled Najib's hatred. Fanned his waning thirst for vengeance sworn long, long ago.

He stared at the screens in the intense silence.

The push of a button on the gold-plated control panel built into the bone-colored leather couch on which he sat had cast the soundproofed media room into a hushed, unearthly quiet. He did not need sound. The images were enough.

Daliah, dominating his vision on the big screen. Her beauty was almost magical. Those extraordinary cheekbones and fathomless eyes, which she had inherited from her famous mother, and the determined, aggressive cast of her jaw, as well as that proud way she had of holding her head high, which obviously came from her father.

Tamara, queen of the thirties, possessed of an unnatural, haunting beauty with her candy-floss white angel's hair. And those eyes, those famous pale eyes which, coupled with her extraordinarily high Slavic cheekbones, had made her the most fabulous face of them all.

Dani, her husband, former ambassador to Germany and Great Britain, his handsomely rugged features and smooth demeanor a casting agent's dream for the part. And rumored to be involved in Mossad activities. Handsome, powerful, and dangerous, a disquieting combination.

And finally, the old man. Camera-shy. So unassuming and casual that he could have been mistaken for a lone tourist wherever he went. The man his own grandfather had once saved from certain death. Who for a time had visited the oasis regularly and brought them gifts and won their friendship. Who was leader of that accursed infidel community which had raided his village and killed his sister.

His sister. Iffat.

He attempted to conjure up a mental image of her, but try as he might, too many intervening years had passed, and she remained but an elusive, faceless blur. With each passing year, she had faded more and more from his memory until she was but a recollection without a face.

And all because of those Jews. If they hadn't killed her, she would be alive today.

His face was drawn. His jaw muscles quivered tensely.

The past twenty-one years had been extremely kind to Najib al-Ameer: the handsome son of the oasis had turned into a sleek, imposing man with an inborn regal bearing that left no doubt of his commanding presence or the extraordinary wealth he had accumulated. His face was craggy and proud, with liquid black eyes which missed nothing, and his olive skin was smooth and as yet unlined, thanks to the comforts and care his fortune had helped provide. His one sign of aging was his thick hair; the black was graying at the temples now. He wore it swept back in the same style as the Shah of Iran; his silk lounging pajamas and matching dressing gown, as well as his socks and slippers, from Sulka, custom-made, would likewise not have been out of place gracing a Pahlavi. Nor would his fortune. The most recent estimate of his personal wealth hovered, incredibly, somewhere between the four- and five-hundred-million-dollar mark and, more importantly, he actually controlled billions more, thanks to his uncanny business acumen, his strong ties to his Arab friends, the power Abdullah held over the movers and shakers of Islam, and the rich oil reserves hidden beneath the sands of the Middle East.

At the still relatively young age of forty-two, Najib had become that twentieth-century phenomenon, a pirate of the international financial world, with billions of petrodollars at his disposal at any given time. Consequently, he had to change time zones with the ease that other men commuted four miles to work. This he could do as swiftly or as leisurely as he liked, with an arrogant disregard for airline schedules. Not for nothing did he own a private Boeing 727-100, equipped with long-range fuel tanks, which functioned as his business command center. This cross between a flying palace and a multimedia discotheque was so full of luxuries that Aladdin would have blushed. It boasted a huge bedroom complete with a king-size bed (equipped with seat belts in case of a bumpy flight), a compact gourmet kitchen, a living room which could seat twenty in comfort, as well as a carefully ballasted Jacuzzi which sat three; cruising along at thirty-five thousand feet with the Jacuzzi jets blasting, while the view out the Perspex windows was of a sea of clouds, was the ultimate way to travel. And then, of course, there were the two Lear jets, the fleet of helicopters, and the two-hundred-and-sixty-foot yacht complete with swimming pool and helipad, which he kept in the Mediterranean.

Then there was his country house high in the cool flower-fragrant hills of Lebanon, the Moorish palace in Tangier, his twenty-thousand-acre game preserve in Kenya, his private island off the coast of Turkey, two adjoining villas in the South of France, the mansion in Beverly Hills which had once belonged to Tamara and which, out of a sense of perverseness, he had bought for himself, and the apartments in Tokyo and on Maui. And then there was his city palace: the quadruplex atop the Trump Tower, where he was ensconced at the moment, one of Manhattan's, and perhaps the world's, most ostentatious, prestigious, and unabashedly luxurious addresses—with all of New York City glittering at his feet on all four floors and all four sides. If the in-flight Jacuzzi would have made Aladdin blush, then the indoor swimming pool, high above Central Park, would have made him choke with envy.

In the beginning, these visible perks of wealth had been slow in coming, but after Najib had made his first million he soon discovered the magic of money and its dizzying geometric progression. One million easily became ten million, and ten million almost effortlessly mushroomed into a hundred million. And though he was gifted with the Midas touch, luck had had more than a little to do with it. Never before in history had the time been so ripe for building a fortune as during the late 1950's to the mid-1970's. The silicon-chip, state-of-the-art communications systems, and the world's ravenous demand for ever more oil, had opened up a plethora of international trading opportunities. Men were hurtling through space every few weeks, and science was undergoing quantum leaps. And suddenly, the world was within reach: the jet plane had shrunk a transcontinental flight down to five hours, and a single ordinary telephone could dial any other telephone anywhere in the world, so that multimillion-dollar deals could be negotiated by simply letting one's fingers do the walking.

Nothing seemed impossible for Najib al-Ameer.

Gifted with extraordinary foresight and an uncanny ability to pick winners, he was the acknowledged highest roller in the high-stakes game of making megabucks. He was among the first to invest in aerospace and Silicon Valley; he foresaw the Japanese high-tech industries before they came into being; he seemed to know precisely when to buy oil tankers and when to sell them. No matter what he did, his timing was always impeccable.

It was in 1963 that he made the first of the deals which would become his trademark and enable him to leapfrog his way to his first hundred million dollars. After arranging to control exclusive oil-export rights for two minor but oil-rich emirates, he then flew to New York and approached the staid WASP bankers for a loan. Armed with his oil contracts, he easily borrowed forty million dollars and used it to purchase a fleet of oil tankers; two years later, he was building the world's largest-ever supertanker in a shipyard—of which he was part owner—in Japan. And then he hit the real jackpot.

The oil sheiks were a withdrawn lot, suspicious of foreigners who came to curry favor and pump their oil. Ever cunning, Najib placed himself between the sheiks and the corporate representatives. When Great Britain and America's most powerful oil companies wanted to arrange business deals with the Arab nations, they found they had to come to him. Thus, he found the largest single source of his income, and his true calling. Simply by arranging these deals—without investing a single cent of his own capital—his commissions amounted to countless millions every year and earned him the nickname "Mr. Five Percent." And those millions he invested, and then reinvested. Money begat more money. And enough money made for true power. Soon his power was such that he was wooed by the ultimate power brokers, and he hobnobbed with leaders of the Kremlin as easily as he brushed shoulders with the movers and shakers of Washington, D.C. At one point he owned no fewer than forty small to mid-size companies, all carefully diversified, and then he began to shape them into a single powerful conglomerate.

By 1965 he had made his first quarter-billion and was well on his way to the half-billion-dollar mark. By 1970 he was the world's most-celebrated Arab, and was constantly written about in the columns. His smiling visage became as familiar a face as the shah's or the Saudi king's. His flying palace with its gold-plated faucets, Lucite shower, and priceless Persian carpets became famous for swooping down at a different airport every few hours while he consummated one business deal or another, after which he would take off for halfway around the world and celebrate his successes on board his luxurious yacht. His life seemed to be an open book. When he divorced Yasmin, his wife of twelve years, her fifty-million-dollar divorce settlement made the headlines in New York, Sydney, London, and, as if to prove non-Soviet decadence, even Moscow. So did his affairs with some of the world's most glamorous and desirable women.

But there was an awesome price to pay for all this wealth and position, and his life, in reality, was open only to the pages he wanted the world to see. Those who came into contact with him saw only the suave charm of the high-living hedonist or the cold efficiency of the ruthless corporate raider. But there was a third side to him, the dark one, the part he had worked as hard to keep hidden as he had slaved to amass his riches. Despite his own staggering fortune and the billions of dollars at his disposal, he was not his own man.

Around the globe, millions of people envied him his power and fortune, but no one knew that he was merely a puppet. Najib al-Ameer, the womanizer who seemingly answered to no one, who billed himself as one of the five richest men in the world, was in fact completely under the control of Abdullah, the most feared authority of them all. More and more, Najib had become only too aware that in the shark-infested waters of big business, he, one of the biggest sharks of them all, could all too easily be harpooned. All it would take was a single public proclamation from Abdullah. If ever he incurred Abdullah's wrath, his entire empire would crumble, and everything he had worked for would become but a heap of ashes.

It was a shaky foundation for any empire, especially one where half a billion dollars was at stake, and he had grown to curse the devil's bargain he had made with Abdullah, from which he saw no way to extricate himself. The blood oath he had sworn so eagerly in his youth was binding.

Admittedly, his secret association with Abdullah had served him well. It had provided the seeds he'd needed to get started, and the business training and contacts he had made at Harvard, thanks again to Abdullah, had opened all the right doors, just as his half-uncle had foreseen. But Abdullah had not only sown the seeds for financing a dark empire; he also reaped part of the harvest, and a grimmer reaper did not exist. More and more often lately, Abdullah's hunger for creating senseless violence and chaos frightened Najib. It was almost as if the terrorist leader's power had gone to his head. Abdullah had begun to revel in bloodshed and in taking stupid chances. Small though it was, Abdullah's PLF was a powerful, monstrous instrument, and Abdullah a force to be reckoned with.

Najib steepled his elongated fingers and tapped them thoughtfully against his lips. His mind had been wandering for a full ten minutes now, and he had become oblivious of the scenes unfolding on the television screens. With a jerk, he pulled himself together and made himself concentrate.

The twilight of the Boralevis and ben Yaacovs was at hand.

Finally everything was falling into place. After three decades of waiting to fulfill his long-ago vow of vengeance against the family of Schmarya Boralevi, the time to do so had come. Just as he had begun to believe that Abdullah had forgotten all about it, the message to proceed had arrived.

One by one, the family of Schmarya Boralevi was to be picked off and destroyed.

And, as though fate had conspired to bring it about, the telephone had rung just a few hours ago. He had been in the big dressing room off the master bedroom, dressing for a dinner party. Looking at the flashing light on the multiline telephone, he had immediately noticed that it was his most private line. Only a handful of people had that particular number, and it was the best-kept secret in an empire replete with them.

He punched the flashing button, switched on the scrambler, and lifted the receiver to his ear. "Yes?" he answered curtly.

"I've got news," a familiar Brooklynese voice said.

He felt the sudden dizzying rush of adrenaline and quickly looked out into the bedroom to make sure none of the servants was about; the special scrambler system he had had hooked up would keep anyone who happened to pick up an extension elsewhere in the apartment from listening in. All an eavesdropper would hear was garbled gibberish. "Is your scrambler activated?" he asked softly.

"Yeah."

"What is the news, then?"

"Daliah Boralevi's moved out of the Bond Street loft. She lives on Central Park West now."

"And?"

"She drove off this afternoon. One of my men followed her. She's gone to a motel on Cape Cod."

Najib was suddenly angry. "You call that news?" he snapped. He took a deep breath and fought to keep his anger under control. "I thought your instructions were to let me know of any *special* travel or vacation arrangements. Especially overseas."

"That's why I called." The voice at the other end of the phone sounded hurt. "She's flyin' to Israel in a week."

Najib was suddenly alert. "Israel, you say?" Surprise edged his voice.

"That's right. She's goin' there for her brother's weddin'. It seems it'll be a big family occasion. I . . . I've got her travel timetable, if you're interested."

"I am," Najib said. He listened for a little while, and although the man at the other end of the line could not see him, he nodded from time to time. "How did you get news of this?" he asked.

"From her agent's secretary. She's pretty much of a dog, but you'd be surprised how that type will tell a man anything if he pushes the right buttons."

Najib was immediately on guard. "What did you tell her?"

"Nothin', actually." The man laughed coarsely. "I didn't have to. The broad thinks I'm a reporter for one of those supermarket scandal rags."

"Good." Najib nodded again. "If anything else should come up, give me a call and keep me posted. I trust you received last month's check for your services?"

"Yeah, I did."

"This month you will get a bonus."

And with that, Najib hung up.

That had been several hours ago, and he had called his dinner hosts and apologized profusely for canceling at the last minute. Then he had come up here to the media room on the third floor of the quadruplex, and watched the videotapes. He had spent nearly two hours deep in thought, wrestling with the pros and cons of vengeance.

What surprised him most was that now, with the time for vengeance at hand, he felt peculiarly remote from it all. He had always thought that when the time came he would feel heady with triumph. For decades the thought of vengeance alone had kept him going, had fueled his ambitions and dictated his every action. But now? Now he wasn't quite sure how he really felt about it anymore. The past suddenly seemed far away, part of another person's lifetime entirely, as distant as the elusive features of Iffat whenever he tried to conjure them up.

Strange, how the passing of time played games with one's mind. Things that had once seemed important faded to inconsequence, while other matters of new import moved forward to take their place. There was a time when he had believed that revenge would be with him always and motivate his every action, but that had not been the case. His perspective had changed. It was his empire, social position, and power which mattered most to him now. And yet he was locked into his vow of vengeance and his oath to Abdullah, and knew he was neatly and inextricably trapped.

As though on cue, the telephone shrilled again. He glanced at the control panel built into the couch. It was his private line again, the same line his detective had called on. He raised the receiver to his ear and activated the scrambler. "Yes?"

"Allah Akbar," a distant voice greeted curtly. "God is great." Abdullah's voice echoed above the rushing static of the long-distance lines, the scrambler distorting his voice even further.

Najib suddenly felt icy fingers stealing over him. Abdullah calling him so quickly after he had spoken to the detective was surely no coincidence.

"You do not sound pleased to hear from me," Abdullah said reproachfully after a long pause.

"It is always a pleasure to hear from you, half-uncle," Najib replied automatically. "What can I do for you?"

"I was surprised you had not contacted me already. I had the feeling you had news to tell me."

Najib stared at the silent, flickering bank of video screens. Now he was certain what Abdullah was getting at. Somehow, through spies or otherwise, he had already learned about the detective's call. "Y-yes," he said slowly. "In fact, I was about to call you."

"I hope so. I do not like to think that you are getting soft after all these years."

"How did you hear?"

"I have my sources," Abdullah replied vaguely. He paused and asked pointedly, "You have not changed your mind?"

"N-no. Of course not."

"I am pleased to hear that. I do not care for men who disregard their blood oaths. I believe you have not forgotten what happens to those who desert me?" He left the implied threat dangling, and then the telephone went dead in Najib's hand. Without looking at the control panel, he slowly put the receiver down. He stared blankly at the television sets.

On the screens, the faces he had familiarized himself with so often seemed to be mocking him.

Najib al-Ameer, the man whose very name was synonymous with wealth, who could cause tremors on Wall Street, the man who entertained presidents and prime ministers aboard his four-deck yacht, whose power was such that a single nod of his head could cause international repercussions, had broken out in a cold sweat. He had more than just a healthy respect for Abdullah.

More and more, his involvement with his half-uncle frightened him.

She was car-lagged and bleary-eyed by the time she hit the Cape. She had driven straight through, stopping only once, and that was to tank up at Groton; on impulse she made a second stop a few miles from Inge's at an all-night convenience store located between Truro and North Truro along Route 6. She grabbed two bottles of Moët out of the cooler and waited for the clerk to tear himself away from a portable typewriter he was pecking away at behind the counter. She smiled automatically when he got up, and pushed the bottles toward him.

He rang them up and looked at her. "That'll be—" The words suddenly failed him as realization dawned on his face. "Jesus H. Christ!" he exclaimed softly under his breath. "You're Daliah Boralevi, the actress!"

Daliah nodded. "That's right." She tossed her head, shaking her hair back over her shoulder.

"Well, I'll be goddamned." He shook his head in disbelief. "I just watched the rerun of *To Have and To Hold* on the Sunday-night movie. Must've been the tenth time I've seen it. The crash scene at the end never fails to choke me up." He seemed awkward for a moment. "You know, that shot of you getting whiplashed as your car crashes through the police barricades? It's something else."

"You really saw it ten times?"

"At least." He grinned disarmingly. "The first time was right after it came out, but to tell you the truth, I lost count after the seventh." He chuckled to himself. "You wouldn't believe the crush I used to have on you. Remember your swimsuit poster?"

She nodded.

"Well, I bought one and hung it up in the fraternity house. The girl I was going with at the time didn't appreciate it one bit."

She smiled at him. He would have been in a fraternity, she thought. He had the big build and squeaky-clean look of a campus jock. "You're a quarterback for Harvard," she guessed.

He shook his head. "I *was* a fullback at Brown. Then my kneecap got smashed, and bye-bye team, my brilliant career in sports was over." He snapped his fingers. "Just like that." Then he shrugged and smiled. "Since all I really wanted to do besides play ball was write novels, I found myself looking around campus one day and wondering what the hell I was doing there. That's why I'm here now, pecking away on a dead-end job. I dropped out to write the great American novel."

She eyed him more closely. He didn't look like a writer or a shop clerk—whatever they were supposed to look like. With his thick curly blond hair, toothpaste-ad teeth, and freckled tan he could have been a California surfer gone three thousand miles astray.

"You staying here on the Cape?" he asked.

She nodded.

"I tell you what. I get off in about forty-five minutes. What do you say you step down off the pedestal and hobnob with us common folk? I know the greatest little dive the tourists haven't discovered yet where the lobsters weigh three pounds each."

"I'm sorry, but I've been on the road for half a day." She shook her head. "It sounds tempting, though."

"Tomorrow, maybe?"

She surprised herself by actually considering his offer. Normally, it would have been unthinkable. A star just didn't mingle with her fans; it was begging for trouble. The world was full of crazies. But he did seem genuinely nice, and he was good to look at, in that surfer kind of way. With a tan like that, a good square chin, and big wide baby-blues, he couldn't be all bad. Besides, other than Inge, she really knew no one up here. It occurred to her that having a man around might not be such a bad idea after all. Just possibly, the best way to get over Jerome might be to fight fire with fire.

She smiled. "I'll think about it."

A smile wrinkled his eyes. "I'll give you a call."

What the hell, she thought, and nodded. "I'm staying at the Sou'westerner Motel. It's listed. Just ask for me."

He grinned. "By the way, my name's Clyde. Clyde Woolery." He extended his hand across the counter and she shook it. His grip was strong and firm.

She watched as he stuffed the two green bottles into a brown paper bag and slid a piece of cardboard between them so they wouldn't knock against each other. He handed it to her and smiled.

"I haven't paid you for the bubbly yet." She looked at the cash register. "How much do I owe you?"

He laughed and flapped a hand. "Forget it. I'll ring it up as a mistake. When inventory time rolls around, it'll be listed under breakage. It's no skin off my back."

She indicated the bag by hoisting it a few inches. "Many thanks, Clyde Woolery. I owe you."

He shrugged. "It's nothing. I'll call you tomorrow afternoon sometime."

"Okay." She waggled her fingers. "Bye-bye."

As she walked back outside to her car, the night air felt cool and smelled tangy with salt, and in the distance she could hear the muted crashing of the surf. It felt good to be away from the rat race. A week away from it all would work wonders.

She placed the bag on the front seat beside her and glanced one last time at the store as she started the engine. Behind the well-lit expanse of plate glass, she could see that Clyde was already bent over his little Smith Corona, and that made her feel good. Maybe she really would go out with him, even if it was only for drinks. After all, he wasn't ogling her from the door like she was some sort of creature set down by a UFO, which was usually the case when she was recognized. Nor, thank God, had he been silly enough to ask for her autograph.

He looked up then and waved to her. She waved back, put the car in reverse, and backed out neatly with a showy squeal of the tires.

She grinned devilishly to herself. What the hell, it was her vacation. She might as well enjoy herself.

She looked both ways. There wasn't a headlight or taillight as far as the eye could see. Then she slammed her foot down on the accelerator and took off as though a man with a checkered flag was waiting two miles down the road at the motel.

Daliah nosed the rented Cutlass into the parking lot just as the bright white moon broke through the clouds and plated the weathered motel cottages in its silver glow. The motel was modest, the individual units gray-shingled and sagging, but it more than made up for its size and sad state of disrepair by occupying eight full acres of prime oceanfront land.

The moment she pulled in, she could see Inge lifting the checkered print curtain and peering out the window. Within seconds the front door of the manager's cabin was thrown wide and Inge came flying out, a huge golden retriever bounding alongside her. Daliah had to smile. Despite her age, Inge could still move like a whippet when she wanted, and seemed taller and much younger than she was, her snow-white hair braided and coiled in a crown of concentric circles atop her head like links of sausages at the butcher's in her native Germany. She wore a loose cotton print housedress and low white canvas sneakers.

The instant Daliah ducked out of the car, Inge flung herself at her, throwing her arms around her in a stranglehold.

Inge's energy was in contradiction to her age. She was the antithesis of an eighty-four-year-old. Those who met her were instantly thrown off guard and tended to forget at once her advanced years and her diminutive size. There was a robust, energetic spark of life and an inner glow to her that most people a fraction of her age did not possess. Her face was lined and creased with a network of fine wrinkles, but her skin glowed with a rich, healthy pink sheen and her eyes were still porcelain white, the irises the same cheerful bright cornflower blue they had always been. They could have been the eyes of a child. She was quick of both foot and mind, with a salty, witty retort to anyone's comments ready on her tongue, yet her feistiness was tempered with a warm sense of humor and a loving heart. Clearly, neither age nor the fact that she had lived on three continents and had had to start life over twice from scratch could put as much as a dent in Inge's indomitability. She was more than just a survivor; no matter where she was, she seemed to be able to adapt magnificently.

"Daliah! *Liebchen!*" Inge cried, clinging to her as tightly as a Siamese twin. "I'm so glad you could come! It has been so, so long!"

Not to be outdone, the dog jumped up and was all over them, his huge paws resting on Daliah's shoulders while he happily licked both women's faces with drooly slurps.

Daliah tried to hide her face. "Down, Happy," she laughed. "Down, boy, down!"

Happy obediently let go and sat down next to their feet. He looked up worshipfully, a huge openmouthed grin on his face.

Inge gripped Daliah's forearms. "Is everything all right?" she asked worriedly. "You sounded upset over the telephone."

"It's nothing serious, Inge."

Inge looked up at her with anxious eyes. "I can always tell by your voice when things are not quite right."

"It's nothing earth-shattering," Daliah assured her. "Really."

"It does not have to be earth-shattering. Sometimes things can be just as upsetting that they might as well be."

"I promise to tell you all about it later." Daliah gave Inge a kiss on the lips. "You look marvelous!" she said, drawing back to arm's length. "Let me look at you! This place really must be the fountain of youth! You haven't aged a day!"

"Daliah, you lie through your teeth," Inge declared. "You know I am seventy-nine and look every day of it." But she looked pleased.

"Now you're the one who's lying through her teeth," Daliah accused with good-humored badinage. "I happen to have it on good authority that you're eighty-four, and that you'll be eighty-five on September third."

Inge stuck her nose in the air. "That just goes to prove you have been snooping around where you have no business snooping."

"Why should I have to snoop? I've got everyone's birth-date written in my calendar book," Daliah said. "My mother gave me the information, and she's never wrong about these things."

Inge's eyes slid shiftily sideways. "Daliah, even your mother can get dates mixed up," she said testily.

Daliah was distracted from retorting by Happy's impatient whine. When she didn't react, he gave two deep barks to get her attention. She looked down at him. His quill tail was sweeping back and forth, creating a curved furrow in the gravel.

"Okay, okay!" she said affectionately. She squatted down in front of him and gave him a big hug. He smelled of dog and perfumed flea powder. "Have you been taking good care of Inge?" she asked him softly.

The dog cocked his head to listen and offered her a huge paw. Solemnly she shook it. Then she got up, yanked her giant Vuitton shoulder bag out of the car, and slammed the door shut.

Inge had prudently dropped the subject of age. "Your usual cabin is available," she told Daliah as they walked toward the manager's office. "I make it a point never to rent it out."

"You know you don't need to do that."

"Of course I don't *need* to," Inge said irritably, "but I want to. I like to keep it available in case you should visit unexpectedly. I just had it repainted, and sewed some nice new curtains and slipcovers. It's all blue, just the way you like it."

Daliah looked up and down the row of moonlit cottages. Each one, except for the one she always stayed in, at the farther end, had a car parked in front of it. It wasn't Memorial Day yet, but a lot of tourists had obviously jumped the gun. "You shouldn't keep it empty just for me, Inge," she scolded. "I know you could have rented it. I would be just as happy sleeping on the convertible sofa in the back of the office."

Inge shrugged. "What's the difference if I rent every unit or keep one empty for you? I am an old woman, and I don't need the extra money. I've got more than I can ever spend."

"Nobody has more than she can spend," Daliah said.

Inge looked at her sternly. "When you get to be my age, believe me, you do. What is there to buy? Clothes? They are

577

all designed for younger women. Appliances? I have got so many they do not even fit in the kitchen. Jewelry? I never wear any except for what you give me. A new car? I cannot drive anymore, anyway. They wouldn't renew my driver's license." Inge opened first the screen door and then the inner door of the manager's cabin.

Daliah followed her inside. She held open the door for Happy, but he wanted to stay outside. He was ecstatically lifting his leg against his favorite yew branch.

"I'll just give you your key, and then I'll let you go off to your bungalow," Inge said. "Everything should be just the way you left it. Otha was in and cleaned it earlier today." She headed behind the counter and fished a key out of one of the little cubbyholes against the back wall. "I know you will want to freshen up. By the time you have done that, I will have something ready for you to eat."

Idly Daliah twirled a postcard rack, watching the glossy Cape Cod scenes spin around. She shook her head. "Don't go to any trouble. It's late, and I don't want to keep you from going to bed."

"It isn't any trouble," Inge declared. "Besides, I like staying up late. The trouble is, there usually is no reason to. The tourists are at the restaurants or have gone dancing, and there is no one to talk to. If I turn on the TV, all the movies they show on the late show are ones I have already seen." She handed Daliah the key. "Go clean up. In half an hour I'll have fixed you a nice Kaiserschmarnn."

"My favorite." Daliah smiled and hugged her. "You always remember."

"Of course I remember," Inge said with exasperation, her eyes flashing vivid sapphire shards. "I may be old, but my brain has yet to retire."

Daliah luxuriated dreamily in the shower. Sheets of pulsating hot water sluiced off her body. Clouds of steam rose to envelop her. She sighed with an almost beatific rapture. After all those hours cramped in the car, the throbbing massage of the water was invigorating and cleansing.

After a good fifteen minutes, her fingertips were so wrinkled that she looked like she'd been washing dishes all day, and she knew it was best she get a move on. Water invariably made her lose all track of time.

Steeling herself for the shock, she twisted off the hot water and nearly cried aloud at the sudden plunge from hot to ice cold. She forced herself to endure the frigid extreme for a full two minutes. When she turned it off, her teeth were chattering but she felt completely rejuvenated and wide-awake. It always worked wonders and fooled the body. She felt as though she'd just awakened from a long, marvelous nap.

She slid the plastic shower curtain aside and reached for a giant blue-striped terry-cloth towel. Briskly she rubbed herself dry and tucked it around her like a sarong. Expertly she wrapped a second striped towel around her streaming hair in a towering turban. Her hair could wait. She'd work on it later, tomorrow even. Now that she was wide-awake she was keen on only one thing, and that was spending some time with Inge.

She glanced over at the Hermès alarm clock that went with her wherever she traveled. Incredibly, it showed the time was already eleven-thirty.

That got her moving. She slipped into a pair of baggy pants made of parachute silk, buttoned a matching blouse over her shapely torso, and slid her feet into her favorite huaraches. Then, her hair still wrapped in the turban, she made a dash for the manager's cabin, stopping at the car to retrieve the two bottles of champagne she'd nearly forgotten about.

Inge had already finished setting the table, and the sugary smells of baking mingled with the fruity aroma of boiling raspberry syrup. Happy was on alert, sitting a respectable distance from the oven, but eyeing it covetously. Steady dribbles of saliva dripped from the corners of his jowls.

Inge turned from the stove and waved a raspberry-coated wooden spoon. "You are just in time," she called out. "I already made the Kaiserschmarrn and it's warming in the oven."

"I brought champagne." Daliah went over to Inge and handed her the bag. "I forgot all about it and left it in the car. It's probably gotten warm in the meantime."

Inge felt inside the bag and shook her head. "The bottles still feel cold, but I will put them in a bucket of ice water right away." Smilingly she shook her head. "Champagne to go with the Kaiserschmarrn. You spoil me, Daliah. Every time you come here you make me feel like an empress."

While they were eating, Daliah filled Inge in on her split with Jerome. Her spirits had plunged. She picked at the food desultorily, barely touching the shredded, raisin-studded omelet Inge had prepared to perfection. It was sweet and fluffy, dusted with a snowy layer of sifted confectioner's sugar and served along with Inge's thick homemade raspberry syrup. Piece by piece, she fed it to Happy, who wolfed it down.

Even Inge ignored the food. There was a dead, mournful look on her usually lively face, and she looked like she was about ready to cry.

After a while, Daliah couldn't bear the expression on Inge's face any longer. "You look like the world's collapsed," she said. "Please don't look so sad."

"I cannot help it." Inge blinked her eyes rapidly. "I can tell you are hurting, and that makes me feel terrible."

"Like Patsy would say, 'This is but a moment in time,' " Daliah said lightly, but her smile was bleak. "And it'll take time, but eventually I'll bounce back."

"I only want for you to be happy." Inge sniffled. "That is not asking for so much, is it?"

"I'm afraid that sometimes it is." Daliah's eyes were glassy. "But don't worry, I'll get over it. Being Jewish helps." She gave a low laugh. "No matter what's dished out to us, we always keep right on going."

"Sooner or later, I know you will meet the right man."

"Maybe." Daliah's voice rose slightly and she looked over into Inge's eyes. "And then again, maybe not. There are many women who have, but there are also a lot of old maids out there—"

She saw Inge flinch as though she had been slapped, and her voice came to an abrupt halt. She was suddenly stricken. A long moment dragged out to what seemed an eternity. Daliah bit down on her lip. "I'm sorry, Inge," she said miserably, a heavy feeling of guilt taking up residence inside her. She frowned angrily and shook her head. "I didn't mean to imply . . ."

There was another awkward pause. After a moment Inge gave a sad smile and fingered the stem of her champagne glass. "I know you didn't," she said gently. "Let's forget it was ever mentioned, shall we?"

Daliah nodded. She was only too happy to. But unspoken though the subject remained, it had been raised like a malevolent spirit at a séance, and it hung there over the table like a cloud.

Inge had never found the right man; for that matter, she hadn't even found the wrong one. Some people were doomed to go through life alone, and Inge was one of them. She had never complained about it, and had kept all her thoughts regarding it to herself, but now Daliah, in her own tortured misery, had inadvertently brought it up.

Damn, Daliah thought miserably. What did I have to go

and blurt that out for? I love Inge. Hurting her was the farthest thing from my mind.

"It is getting late," Inge said finally. She pushed her chair back from the table and got up. "Run along, now, and get some sleep. We can talk more tomorrow."

Daliah nodded, kissed her wretchedly, and then fled guiltily to her cabin.

In the morning, Otha took over in the office, and Daliah and Inge walked along the beach. Clyde Woolery rang in the afternoon, just after they'd eaten lunch.

"Remember me?" he asked after Inge handed Daliah the receiver. "The lowly store clerk?"

"The budding author, sure," she said warmly. "How is life?"

"Dull, dull, dull. I was hoping you'd be able to pull me out of the doldrums."

"The writing can't be going that badly," she laughed. "And it's quiet up here, not dull."

"Sometimes I wonder," he said. "Are we still on for a date?"

She had to laugh. "You make it sound like we're innocent schoolchildren. But yes, I would like it."

"Seven o'clock all right with you? Don't forget, this isn't New York. Up here, they roll up the sidewalks at eleven P.M."

"Seven will be fine."

"And don't dress up. Be as casual as you like."

She laughed. "You'll be sorry."

"I doubt it." He laughed also. "I'll come by and pick you up on the dot. And don't worry, the place I have in mind is so backward that it'd be a miracle if anybody recognized you."

Daliah smiled into the receiver. He sounded almost too good to be true.

From across the room Inge watched her hang up the phone. She had moved deliberately out of earshot, but curiosity was killing her. "He sounded like a very nice young man," she prompted. "Very polite."

"If this is your way of trying to fish for information, then I might as well warn you that I'm onto your methods, Inge."

"You do not have to get nasty, Daliah," Inge said virtuously. "If you want to keep secrets from me, that is quite all right. For your information, I have plenty of other things to keep me occupied." She made a show of busying herself with some pots and pans at the sink.

Daliah went over and watched Inge rubbing Twinkle onto the copper bottoms of some barely tarnished frying pans. Inge pretended not to notice her, but after a while she began giving Daliah some inquisitive sidelong glances.

"All right, Inge," Daliah laughed, "I'll tell you what you want to know. You won't have to fix dinner for me because he's coming to take me out on a date."

Inge looked slightly mollified. She abandoned the copper cleaning and began to put the pots away again. "It will do you good to go out," she said, nodding.

"I think so too. You don't have to wait up for me, though."

"I was not going to," Inge sniffed.

"And you don't have to worry if I stay out late. It's only an innocent date."

Inge looked at her severely. "You are a big girl now, Daliah. I cannot tell you what you can and cannot do."

Daliah spent the rest of the afternoon giving Happy a bath, helping Inge in the manager's office, and drinking a Campari and champagne while she got ready to go out. She took her cue from Clyde and brought new meaning to the term "casual." She had done nothing to her hair, other than pulling it to one side and securing it with several barrettes; it stuck out dramatically like a wavy black ponytail growing out the right side of her head. She wore her most treasured pair of washed-out Levi's, the disreputable ones with the ragged holes worn through in the knees, a too-large man's lumberjack shirt in a rich, brilliant tartan pattern of red, blue, and yellow, and as she heard Clyde pull up punctually outside and lean on the horn, she grabbed the first accessories which came to hand. Flying out the door as she secured them, she barely noticed the incongruity of her choices—a tooled mock-western belt with an eighteen-karat-gold buckle, which she slung casually over her hips, and a pair of fifty-thousand-dollar teardrop ruby earrings, set with choice pavé diamonds in yellow gold, which Jerome had bought her at Bulgari more than three and a half years previously.

Catching sight of her, Clyde jumped out of his vehicle and went around to the passenger side. It was an old army-surplus jeep, and even several new coats of olive-drab paint could not completely hide where the white stars and military markings had been. They hadn't been sanded off, and showed slightly in relief.

She twirled around once in the gravel. "How do I look?"

He grinned. "Gorgeous," he said. Then he let out a whistle. "Those real rubies?"

Daliah flashed him one of her "get real" looks as she jumped up and swung herself expertly into the jeep.

"You did that like you've spent a lifetime in a jeep."

"Well, not a lifetime, exactly. Just my tour of duty in the Israeli army." She waited for him to climb in. "So where're we going?"

"Depends what you're in the mood for." He fiddled with the stick shift. "How's steak and lobster sound to you?" He looked at her questioningly.

She smiled. "It sounds fine."

"Good." He stepped down on the accelerator and turned the jeep around, practically on a dime. "I bought two fillets, two jumbo lobsters, and stole a magnum of champagne. I also collected some driftwood. Since it's an unusually balmy evening, what do you say to a picnic on the beach?"

She grinned at him. "I say that sounds just fine."

The jangling of the telephone reached down through the layers of her sleep and startled her awake. Eyes closed, she felt blindly for the receiver, finally located it after knocking the alarm clock over, and mumbled, " 'Lo?"

"Lunch is ready in half an hour!" It was Inge, and her voice sounded so loud and cheerful that it would have awakened Dracula in broad daylight.

Daliah cringed and held the receiver away from her ear. Then she frowned. "You mean breakfast, don't you?" she grumbled.

"I mean lunch," Inge said definitely. "We generally eat lunch at one-thirty in the afternoon, not breakfast. And it is one o'clock now."

"One in the . . ." Daliah's eyes snapped suddenly open and she sat up wide-awake. She righted the alarm clock and stared at it closely. Inge wasn't kidding. It was one o'clock, all right, right on the button. And behind the drawn curtains the sun pulsated like floodlights.

"All I want to know," Inge said, "is should I bring your lunch over on a tray, or do you want it here?"

"I'll have it there," Daliah said, swinging her legs out of bed. "Just give me five." She hung up and got up too suddenly. She groaned and touched her forehead gingerly. It felt like someone was stabbing it with a handful of ice picks. What Clyde hadn't told her was that he had *two* magnums of Taittinger—*and* a thermos of ready-made margaritas on ice. And somehow, between them both, they'd managed to put away every last drop.

She stumbled into the little bathroom, stared into the

mirror with disbelief, and quickly gulped four aspirin. After slapping handfuls of cold water on her face and gargling furiously with Listerine, she managed to slip into some clothes and staggered outside. The sunlight was so blinding that she had to shield her eyes with her arm.

Inge was bustling around her kitchen, cheerful as a dwarf in a Disney cartoon. "I put on a fresh pot of coffee for you, but you can have tea instead, if you like. Lunch isn't quite ready."

"I'll wait." Inge slid a cup of steaming coffee in front of her. One hand on a hip, she stood there for a moment, waiting, looking down at Daliah, but Daliah pointedly ignored her and poured a scant teaspoon of cream into the coffee. She knew Inge was waiting to hear all about her date, and she wasn't in any mood to talk, at least not until the pounding in her head abated.

"By the way, you had a phone call," Inge said conversationally as she went back to the sink. "It was Jerome, and he insisted on talking to you. I told him not to bother, but he said he would call back."

Daliah gritted her teeth. "Why doesn't he just give up and leave me be!"

"If you want, I can put him off," Inge said, "but maybe it would be best for you to tell him that you don't want to talk to him. He won't listen to me; maybe he will listen to you."

"I doubt it." Daliah blew on her coffee, but before she could take the first sip, the telephone shrilled again. The sound went straight through her head.

Inge went to answer it. "Daliah, it is Jerome," she said, holding her hand over the receiver.

Daliah twisted around, her face quivering with anger. "Oh, all *right*!" she said truculently.

Inge brought the phone over to her, and she lifted the receiver slowly. "Yes," she said warily.

"Daliah!" He sounded cheerful and relieved both. "It's nice to hear your voice."

"I wish I could say the same," she said.

There was a pause, and when he spoke again there was reproach in his voice. "I wish you didn't try to avoid me so obviously. I tried calling all over town to get your new number, but no one would give it to me. I'm still in France, and you don't know how much trouble that put me through. If I hadn't figured you'd gone to Inge's, I'd never have found you. You didn't have to go into hiding, you know."

"Who said I'm in hiding? You found me, didn't you?"

"There you go again! I really don't know what's gotten into you. You're behaving very strangely, you know that?"

"How do you expect me to behave?" she said with a touch of asperity. "Do you want me to tell you everything is okay, and act kissy-kissy?"

"I wish you wouldn't be this way, that's all." Exasperation crept into his voice. "I don't know you like this, Daliah."

"I don't know myself like this either," Daliah replied. "Leaving myself open to get hurt is entirely new to me. I haven't quite got the hang of coping with it just yet." Her voice turned suddenly brisk. "Now, the sun's shining here and the dog wants to go for a walk along the beach. Why don't you just get whatever it is on your chest off it? That way we won't have to argue about it all day long."

He didn't seem to have heard her. "You know, you put me in an embarrassing bind, running back to the States the way you did. I didn't know what to tell people. It wouldn't have been half so bad if *Red Satin* hadn't walked away with the Palme d'Or, but since it did, your absence was only that much more obvious. But I guess you know that already."

"As a matter of fact, I was out of touch. I didn't know *Red Satin* won." She added dryly, "Congratulations are in order, I suppose."

"No, you should be the one being congratulated. It was your performance that did it. I wasn't at all surprised that you won for best actress too. Since you weren't here, I accepted your prize for you, but now I don't even know where to bring it."

"Sending it would be the easiest. Airmail has gotten quite reliable."

"Daliah." He paused and added gently, "We have to talk."

"We're talking now," she pointed out.

"You know what I mean."

"No, I don't. I thought I'd made myself perfectly clear. You use Arab money, you lose me. Period. It's cut-and-dried."

He couldn't keep the ugly edge out of his voice. "You're a tough bitch, you know that?"

"Thank you very much. I'll take that as a compliment."

"Look, I really need to see you so we can talk. In person." He paused to emphasize that point. "I'm sure if we sat down together, we could work this thing out like adults."

"I've made my position crystal clear, Jerome."

His voice rose three octaves. "Will you listen to me, goddammit? I haven't accepted a dime or even signed a single contract yet. I had the backers eating out of the palm of my hand, but after you split, I put them on hold while I scrambled to find alternative financing."

She raised her eyebrows and blinked. This was news indeed. For the first time, she could feel herself thawing a bit. "But you haven't turned them down, either," she said cautiously. "Have you?"

"Oh, for God's sake, Daliah," he retorted. "Do you have to be so smug and sanctimonious?"

"I'm not being either of those things." She was silent for a moment. "And calling me names isn't going to get either of us anywhere."

"All right, all right," he said finally, and from the testy resignation in his voice she could tell he was fighting to keep himself under control. Jerome was worse than most people when he was backed into a corner. "Look, you rushed off so fast you never gave me a chance to explain who the backers were."

"Does it make any difference? You told me it was Arabs. That tells me all I need to know."

"Daliah, it's the Almoayyed brothers," he said, aggrieved and struggling to be patient.

"So?"

"So? They're accepted everywhere! I mean, they even race their horses at Ascot and are always welcome in the Royal Enclosure! Queen Elizabeth even invited them to Windsor Castle."

"I know who they are," she said wearily.

And who didn't? she asked herself gloomily. The flamboyant Almoayyed brothers—Ali, Mohammed, Abdlatif, and Saeed—had appeared practically out of nowhere during the oil boom of 1973, and had taken the world by storm. It was said that their family, the ruling family of one of the six United Arab Emirates, was among the most powerful in the Persian Gulf. Lately, the four brothers, who were inseparable, had become as famous for their impressive string of thoroughbred horses as for their multibillions. Recently, Desert Star, their prize horse, had won both the Kentucky Derby and the Ascot Group 1 Gold Cup.

Jerome's voice dropped to a confidential tone, but he couldn't keep the excitement out of it. "Well, the Almoayyed brothers don't know it yet, but B. Lawrence Craik expressed interest that he might be willing to back the film, and I put feelers out to Giò Monti too."

She was genuinely surprised. This was more news, yet. Jerome had certainly been keeping busy.

The recently knighted Sir B. Lawrence Craik owned

Timberlake Studios in London, where many independent producers shot their soundstage footage and had their films processed; he was also sole owner of Craik Films, a family-held company which financed, produced, and released ten middle-of-the-market pictures a year.

Giò Monti, on the other hand, was much more famous and flamboyant. He was the undisputed King of Cinecittà, Rome's answer to Hollywood. As well-known for the B movies that had made him a multimillionaire as for his years of living in sin with and subsequently marrying Daniela Zanini, Italy's big-breasted bombshell, he was, now that his fortune was secure, trying to branch out into important first-rate films. And, more important, he was willing to exchange financial backing for sweetheart distribution deals.

"So you see, I've got Craik and Monti on the sidelines, and the Almoayyed brothers in the middle," Jerome explained with mounting excitement. "If I have to, I can play them against each other."

"That's playing with fire, and you know it," Daliah said.

"I'm doing it for you."

"Jerome, you're full of shit, you know that? If you were doing it for me, you'd drop the Almoayyed brothers completely."

"Listen, all I'm asking is to talk it over with you in person. That isn't asking for so much, is it?"

"It's asking for a great deal, Jerome."

"So I'm asking for a great deal. Okay. I know it's a great deal." He paused. "Are you still planning to fly to Israel for your brother's wedding?"

"That's right. I'm flying over six days from now."

"You'll be at Inge's until then?"

"I'm heading back to the City the day before I take off."

"Tell you what. Why don't you change your flight and stop off in Paris? Just for a day? That way we can meet and discuss all this."

"I don't want to stop off in Paris. If you're so anxious to meet, then you come over here."

There was a long pause. "All right," he growled. "I'll see what I can do. But it'll depend on whether or not I can sew up the *Red Satin* distribution deals by then. But I'll try."

Perhaps he tried; then again, perhaps he did not. She couldn't be sure. The way things worked out, the *Red Satin* deals kept him busy for the next two days; the two days after that he spent in London trying to entice Sir B. Lawrence Craik, who was lukewarm to the size of the projected budget. Then it was on to Rome, where Giò Monti listened to his proposal and decided to think it over before coming to a decision. Finally, deciding that a bird in the hand was certainly worth a flock in the bush, he flew to Saudi Arabia, and back into the good graces of the Almoayyed brothers.

Time had a habit of slipping through one's fingers. By the time the sixth day rolled around, he was still in Riyadh.

And Daliah planned on leaving the Cape in the wee hours of the following morning.

Inge was already up by the time Daliah was set to leave. She had a thermos of hot coffee waiting. "For the drive," she said.

"You're a jewel, you know that?" Daliah said fondly, stooping to give the tiny figure in the quilted bathrobe a warm hug.

Inge shrugged and followed her outside to the gravel parking lot up front. Happy pranced ecstatically at her side.

Despite her jacket, Daliah shivered. It was still dark out, and chilly. The damp sea fog hung in the air, and the porch lanterns to either side of the front door gave off little halos of fuzzy light. The air smelled of salt. On the other side of the big sand dunes, the breakers made crashing noises as they spent themselves upon the beach.

"I'm going to miss you," Daliah said when they reached the car. She unlocked the door and opened it a few inches so that the little overhead lamp inside could click on and give them some more light. She turned to Inge and smiled. "As soon as I'm back, I'll try to come up and visit for a few more days."

Inge looked pleased. "I would like that." Her eyes glinted moistly in the weak light, and she pulled the driver's door wider open so that Daliah could get in. "I hope you have a good flight."

"Oh, I'm sure I will. Patsy's secretary made all the arrangements, and she even bought the seat next to mine. That way I won't have anyone beside me, and I'll be able to enjoy complete privacy."

"That is good." Inge nodded and fussed with the zipper on Daliah's jacket. "I worry about you all the time, you know. You are very famous, and there are a lot of crazy people out there. Every time I pick up a newspaper or turn on the TV, all I hear about are murders and violence."

"Don't worry so much," Daliah said with a smile. "I'm very well-insulated from the rest of humanity. I don't even have to sit in airport waiting rooms anymore. As soon as I get to an airport, I'm always whisked away to the VIP lounges. No matter where I go, there are always special airline representatives who take good care of me.

"Besides which," she added, "I know how to take care of myself. All Israeli girls do. During my military training I learned hand-to-hand combat." Playfully she flattened her hands and took a classic fighting stance.

Inge looked up at her without amusement. She shook her head. "I still worry," she insisted stubbornly.

"That's all I need," Daliah laughed. "Two mothers."

"Well, one mother and maybe a grandmother. Of sorts."

"What do you mean, 'grandmother of sorts'?" Daliah embraced Inge again and kissed both her cheeks. "I've always considered you my real grandmother," she said huskily. "You know that."

"I know." Inge smiled, got up on tiptoe, and kissed Daliah on both cheeks.

Daliah kissed her back. "I promise that next time I'll try to stay even longer. Maybe I'll even spend two whole weeks."

Inge nodded and let go of her. "We will see. I know you are very busy, and even a day or two is enough to satisfy me. When you get old, you would be surprised how far a little visit can go." She tilted her head to one side. "You will give your mother my love?"

"I will," Daliah promised as Happy trotted over to her. She squatted down and he licked her face. She grabbed hold of him and gave him an affectionate squeeze. "You take good care of Inge, Happy, hear?"

Daliah slid into the car and looked up at Inge. "Thanks again for the hospitality. And don't look at me like that." She slammed the door shut, rolled down the window, and switched on the engine. She raised her voice so she could be heard above the roar of the motor. "I'll be fine."

"It's not that, Daliah. You know, you still didn't tell me anything about your date. You went out two times with him, and you still didn't tell me a thing."

"What's there to tell?" Daliah shrugged. "He was very nice, we talked about lots of unimportant things, and we never went to bed, if that's what you're getting at."

"I didn't mean it that way at all, Daliah," Inge said severely. "I don't know why you young people can only think about sex."

Which was, Daliah thought, the perfect exit line.

With a wide white grin and a cheerful wave of her hand, she gunned the motor and the car leapt out of the parking lot onto the highway. At this early hour there was no traffic. Faster, faster! The needle on the speedometer swept inexorably to the right, and the view out the side windows blurred as the tires gobbled up the leaping yellow divider lines. Faster, faster, faster. Hurry, hurry, hurry!

The giant jet engines changed pitch, the wheel hydraulics whined, and the plane seemed to slow to a halt and hang there in midair. For one gut-wrenching moment Daliah felt stricken with terror. She hated flying, and on the other side of the square of Perspex, the Mediterranean looked so near that she had the sensation the belly of the jet was floating on the water and that if the plane didn't gain some more speed right away, it was going to sink to the bottom of the sea like a giant bomb.

She felt one ear pop, and then the other. She dry-swallowed hard a couple of times and licked her lips. Then she grimaced. Her mouth felt dehydrated and stale, as full of cotton as though she'd spent a night drinking. Pressurized cabins never failed to do that to her.

She strained against the seat belt and shifted uncomfortably in her seat. Once again, she was conscious of a prickly rash. Her mound had started itching again, and it took more willpower than she would have liked to admit not to reach down and scratch it surreptitiously. The hair which Jerome had always insisted on shaving was growing back in.

And that was another thing, she thought, her lips tightening, her mind happily clutching any thought but that of flying. From now on, she would let her pubic hair grow and blossom into an extravagant, luxuriant bush. Even if she had to set it in curlers and coif it, she was going to have the pubic bush to end all pubic bushes.

Fuck Jerome's perversities. That hair was hers, and hers alone, and she would keep it that way. If nothing else, keeping her mound unshaved would symbolize a measure of newfound independence, of not needing men, and certainly not men like Jerome.

Her eyes flickered to the window again. Impossible as it seemed, the plane was *still* descending; the water seemed close enough for her to touch the tops of the waves. Then, mercifully, the gray concrete runway rushed to meet the plane, the wheels bounced twice, then held. She let out a deep sigh of relief. Israel. She was back at long last.

And quite suddenly, for no apparent reason, she had the peculiar sensation of time compressing, that she'd really left here only yesterday and was returning a bare day later. But of course, that was silly. Even the plane belied that illusion.

She'd left on a battered old DC-3 and was returning by sleek jumbo jet. A lot of years had sped by in between.

He could see that they were all in position, scattered at strategic intervals throughout Ben-Gurion Airport. As he passed the familiar faces while hurrying to keep pace with the handsome young El Al VIP representative, Khalid Khazzan's eyes did not so much as give a flicker of recognition, nor did they seem to notice him. They were there merely as backups, and nothing about any of them could tie them all together. If one fell, he or she wouldn't be taking the rest of them down too.

Striding through the busy terminal, Khalid could feel the VIP representative's occasional sidelong glances, but he felt no undue cause for alarm. They were merely curious appraisals, he thought; all first-class passengers probably got them.

But something was bothering the VIP representative; something did not sit right, and kept gnawing elusively at his mind. There's something about that man that seems curiously familiar, Elie Levin couldn't help thinking. I could swear I've seen his face before, somewhere. But where? And why can't I place him?

Elie's dark eyes slid sideways again. The businessman had a slightly olive complexion; perhaps he was of Italian, Arab, or Jewish descent, though it was difficult to guess. Especially with Americans, which the man's passport proclaimed him to be. But he was definitely a businessman, and a successful one at that, judging from his self-assured swagger, first-class ticket, and well-tailored brand-new suit.

Now that he thought about it, Elie realized that everything the man was wearing or carrying was brand-new: his gleaming shoes, his shirt, even the molded gray Samsonite carry-on which had ridden through the X-ray machine with total innocence. It was almost as if everything he had on had just been unwrapped.

Is that what bothers me about him? Elie asked himself. Because everything is *too* new?

Elie laughed to himself. This surely proved that his job was starting to get to him. The airport's elaborate security precautions and his own antiterrorist training were beginning to spook him, he decided. It made him look constantly over his shoulders and eye everyone with suspicion. He was starting to see ghosts everywhere. His mother always did say he had a vivid imagination.

But why, then, he asked himself, are my hands so clammy?

Why do I feel those ripples of static raising the hairs at the nape of my neck?

Because you've got an overactive imagination, he answered himself.

Elie Levin would have no time to regret ignoring the warning bells that jangled in his mind. A group of tourists was headed their way, strategically blocking their path. He and the businessman had to skirt them, brushing the wall with their shoulders.

And another thing, Elie thought suddenly. When the businessman had walked through the finely tuned metal detector, possibly the most finely tuned metal detector in the world, nothing had set it off. Not even loose change, a stainless watch, or a bunch of keys.

Then, in front of him, another obstacle loomed in his path. A woman he didn't recognize, wearing a blue El Al uniform, stood smiling professionally beside a door marked AUTHORIZED PERSONNEL ONLY. They would have to squeeze past her in order to get around the horde of tourists.

Just as he and the businessman reached her, the woman's gracious smile widened and she pushed down on the door handle. The door yawned wide in front of him.

Elie was trapped, sandwiched neatly between the half-open door in front of him and the businessman behind him.

Quicker than the eye could catch it, the businessman elbowed him savagely and thrust him expertly sideways into the dark little room. Elie's breath was knocked out of him. He let out a grunt and doubled over. The door shut with a snap of finality.

A moment later, the overhead fluorescents flickered on.

"Khalid!" Recognition suddenly dawned on Elie. In that split second he knew where he had seen that face before: countless times, but never clean-shaven. In all the blurry photographs, the terrorist had been bearded, dressed in army fatigues and the traditional Arab headgear.

But it was too late. That split-second recognition, and that one fearfully whispered name, were the last things Elie Levin ever experienced. Khalid's blurring palm, expertly chopping his throat, cut off any further sound, and then a powerful elbow scissored around his neck. Elie's eyes widened, and he wanted to scream his terror. But then his bones crackled and snapped, and he slid, limp as a rag doll, lifelessly to the floor.

Death had been instantaneous.

Three minutes later, dressed in Elie's spotless uniform, Khalid stepped casually back out into the terminal, adjusted his tie, and remembered just in time to unpin Elie's name tag. He slipped it into his pocket and strode confidently toward the arrivals section.

He glanced up at the overhead monitors and smiled with satisfaction. Trust the Israelis, he thought. Flight 1002 from New York had put down right on the button.

Daliah was the first passenger off the plane, and she was gratified to see that, just as Patsy's secretary had arranged, a VIP representative was waiting at the door. She favored him with a warm, grateful smile.

He smiled pleasantly enough back at her, but she was aware of curiously cool, appraising eyes. "If you'll give me your passport and baggage claims, Miss Boralevi," he said, "we can skip the usual formalities."

She nodded, dug into her bag, and handed over her ticket folder and the Israeli passport in the thin Mark Cross leather sheath with gold corners, a Christmas present from Jerome, and yet another reminder of him she would have to pack away and hide.

The VIP representative was the model of efficiency; she had to hurry to keep pace with him as he marched her swiftly past the backed-up line of passengers from an Athens flight. He flashed her open passport to an official behind the counter and then guided her through the noisy terminal, making a beeline for the exits.

The big terminal was crowded with arriving and departing passengers. Daliah glanced around. The signs in Hebrew brought a lump to her throat.

Home. Home at long last.

The sliding exit doors were approaching, and she fell back from the VIP representative.

"Wait!" Her voice stopped him.

He was sliding her passport and the ticket folder with the stapled-on luggage claims inside his jacket pocket.

"What about my luggage?" she asked. "And I need my passport!"

His smile was cemented in place. "I'll have the baggage delivered to you by special courier within the hour," he said reasonably. "The same goes for your passport. Our first consideration is you. We have to be very security-conscious, and you, Miss Boralevi, are a very important national treasure. El Al does not like for highly visible celebrities, especially one such as yourself who hails from a prominent family, to be unnecessarily exposed to possible danger in public areas." His smile never left his face, that unsettling scimitar smile which held no warmth. Also, there was something about the way he looked at her, something mocking and unpleasant.

"Surely there's a VIP lounge," she said. "I can wait there while you get the luggage, and save you a lot of trouble. Besides, I can't walk around without my passport. If I remember right, it's against the law here not to carry identification papers on you at all times."

"Don't worry. I have strict orders, and your safety is our sole concern. The car is waiting outside."

The car filled with her family, come to welcome her home! Without further delay, she rushed forward and burst outside.

The VIP representative was right behind her, guiding her toward a shiny old Chrysler limousine at the curb. Still smiling, he gripped the chrome handle and yanked open the rear door.

Daliah ducked inside the big car. Then she froze, half in, half out, staring into the barrel of a .44 Magnum revolver.

The stranger holding the gun gave her a ghastly smile. "Welcome to Israel, Miss Boralevi."

Finally she realized what was happening.

If Daliah's beauty and talent could be attributed to her mother, then it was from her father, Dani, that she had inherited her almost Germanic streak of obsessive, stopwatch punctuality. Never once, in all the years she had lived at home, had she ever known him to miss a single flight or a train, or arrive late for any appointment. It wasn't his fault today that he and Tamara got to the airport late. They had left with plenty of time to spare, and there were just the two of them. Dani was driving the big black Cadillac de Ville, borrowed from the State Department, and Tamara sat up front on the bone-colored leather seat beside him. At the breakfast table, Ari and his fiancée, Sissi Herschritt, had communicated something between themselves with their eyes, and had begged off.

"There are some more things we've got to hang up," Ari explained.

"We forgot an entire bagful of decorations," Sissi added.

Tamara looked around the apartment and frowned. The living and dining rooms had been festively decorated the night before with balloons, crepe-paper streamers, and confetti; it looked rather like a goyische New Year's celebration was about to take place. A string arced between the widest walls, hung with bright cut-out letters: WELCOME HOME, DALIAH.

"I see," she said dryly. She did, too. It was merely a ruse for Ari and Sissi to take advantage of having the empty apartment to themselves for an hour or so. She'd suspected that they'd been sleeping together, and now she was certain. Wisely, she didn't pursue the subject.

Then, just as she, Schmarya, and Dani were going out the door, a call from the Defense Ministry deducted Schmarya from the group as well.

"Just my luck," the old man muttered grumpily. "The day my granddaughter returns, I'm called to Jerusalem for an emergency meeting."

"It isn't anything serious, is it?" Tamara had asked.

Even after decades of living through late-night calls and early-morning summonses for Dani or Schmarya, she had still never gotten quite used to sudden emergencies. After all the wars and skirmishes and attacks, every time the phone rang she was certain it was a portent of tragedy.

"No, no," Schmarya assured her with a cantankerous wave of his hand. "Some gonif at the ministry's probably gotten a bug up his tuchkas, that's all." He smiled to reassure her. "I have called the airport and checked. The plane is on time." He smiled. "Give Daliah a kiss for me. Tell her I will be back this afternoon."

She nodded absently and turned a cheek for him to kiss; then he clapped Dani on the back and strode out.

So Tamara and Dani drove off to the airport by themselves. Nine minutes later, it became apparent that they wouldn't get there on time. They were driving down a narrow one-way street when the accident happened. Dani let out a shout of warning and slammed on the brakes so suddenly that if Tamara hadn't been wearing her seat belt, her head would have gone crashing against the windshield. As it was, the Cadillac fishtailed, but the brakes did the folks at General Motors proud. The big car skidded safely to a stop with several feet to spare. But directly in front of them, at the intersection, a van collided with a tractor-trailer. The big rig jackknifed and, in seeming slow motion, overturned and went crashing over on its side.

Dani turned to Tamara. He was white-faced and obviously shaken. "Are you all right?"

"Yes, I think so." She nodded. "And you?"

"Idiots!" He shook his head. "Did you see what happened? The van had the right of way, and the tractor-trailer kept right on going!"

"I . . . I didn't see anything." Her voice was low; she was trying to get her thumping heart out of her throat and back to her chest, where it belonged. "It all seemed to happen so fast."

Dani had his seat belt off in an instant. He jumped out of the Cadillac. "I better go and see if anyone got hurt," he said grimly. "Stay here. I don't want you to have to see anything ugly." He ran off, squeezed around the sprawled trailer, and Tamara sat there and waited uneasily. A minute later he was back. She looked at him worriedly.

"No one seems to have suffered any injuries, but since I'm a witness, the driver of the van wants us to wait around for the police. They shouldn't be too long. The driver of the tractor-trailer went to phone them." He turned around. Already, impatient commuters behind them were leaning on their horns, creating a raucous symphony.

Well, let them honk all they want, he thought angrily. Couldn't they see that he couldn't go forward, since the tractor-trailer barred the way, and that he couldn't go backward either, with them wedging him in from behind? His car was trapped.

He slid back into the driver's seat. "Damn," he cursed. "Today, of all days!" He hit the steering wheel with the open palm of his hand. "Double damn!"

Tamara reached over and touched his hand. "You know that getting upset isn't going to help anything," she said calmly. "It's not your fault that that accident occurred. You should thank God no one got hurt."

He lifted his arm and glanced at his watch. "By the time the police come, and we give our account of what happened, and that truck gets towed, the plane will have long since landed." He slumped glumly back in the seat. "Daliah's going to think we've forgotten."

"No, she won't," Tamara told him. "If she doesn't see us, she'll wait for us in the VIP lounge."

He turned to her. "I suppose you're right. I'm probably just overreacting."

"No, you're not. You're making noises like a father."

He smiled suddenly, then leaned toward her and brushed her soft cheek with his lips. "And you, little mother, are growing more beautiful with every passing day," he declared.

"Dani!" She laughed and pushed him away. Playfully. "What's gotten into you?"

"Nothing. But it's true."

And to him, she *was* as beautiful as ever. At sixty-five, she could still make heads turn; he'd seen it happen, and there wasn't a younger woman he'd ever laid eyes on who could hold a candle to her. The years had been very kind.

She didn't look a day over fifty, and her body was as perfect as it had ever been, thanks to her active life. Nor did she carry as much as a superfluous ounce of flesh on it. She had metamorphosed into a mature, natural beauty. Well, not totally natural, he amended. He knew that by looking at her vanity table, at the bottles of creams and lotions, and in the medicine cabinet, at the boxes of hair dye. The candy-floss white angel's hair, her cinematic trademark, was no more, but was instead dyed the exact shade of honey blond she had been born with. He thought it suited her far better. Her skin was smooth and unblemished, but not the pale alabaster people admired in her old movies; it had become richly tanned from the relentless Israeli sun. Her teeth, capped on Oscar Skolnik's orders back in 1930, were as perfect as they had ever been. And her eyes—those beguiling emerald eyes, which, with her extraordinarily high Slavic cheekbones, had made her the most fabulous face of them all—were, despite the lack of false lashes and with only a hint of mascara and shadow, still as theatrically expressive as they had ever been.

Now, her famous gaze fixed unblinkingly on the tractor-trailer lying on its side, Tamara sat, still as a statue, her mind on Daliah.

She was smiling to herself with satisfaction, commending herself on a job well done. She had raised Daliah right, she thought. Her daughter was a credit to both the Boralevis and the ben Yaacovs. Daliah had never sacrificed herself as just another pretty slab of Hollywood meat. Far from it. She was as famous for her off-screen campaigns, for sticking up for her rights and the rights of others, as she was for the roles she played so superbly. She championed causes, no matter how unpopular they might be, if she believed in them wholeheartedly, and always resolutely stood her ground and stuck by her commitments. And for that Tamara was immensely proud. From an early age, she had tried to imbue in Daliah a sense of what was important in life, and what was not, and Daliah had learned her lessons well.

Tamara could sense Dani still staring at her, and then she felt his hand covering one of her hands. She closed her fingers around it and clasped it.

She and Dani had been married for nearly forty years now, and their love for each other had only grown stronger with each passing day. He was two years older than she was, but how incredibly handsome he still looked with his craggy face, thick gray hair, and authoritative manner! With him she had created the three most momentous and poignant gifts of their lives—poor Asa, and Ari, who was about to be married, and Daliah—and her role as mother had been the most fulfilling part she had ever played.

"A shekel?" he teased her softly.

"For my thoughts? They're not that cheap!" She laughed, that tinkling silver-chime laugh he so adored. Then her expression sobered and grew pensive. "I was thinking of Daliah, that's all. How much she's done, and how fast."

"You miss it, don't you?" Dani asked suddenly.

"Miss it?" She blinked.

"You know, the excitement. The glamour. Being where she is now."

Being a star, he meant.

She shrugged. It was a simple, yet entirely eloquent movement, the kind the camera had always picked up so well. "Sometimes . . . well, sometimes I still miss it a little, I suppose. I would be lying if I said otherwise. But it has been forty years, Dani! Retiring was *my* decision. And it was the *right* decision." She smiled and her gaze held his. "I'm not sorry I did it. I've never been sorry, not for a moment."

He gave her hand an affectionate squeeze. "I just want you to be happy. You know that."

"I *am* happy! You, better than anyone, should know that! I've been happy for close to forty years, and that's a lot more happiness than most people in Hollywood can boast, believe me."

"You could always go back," he said. "You know, come out of retirement and do a picture or two."

"Dani," she said. Her look was one he knew so well—one part theatrical chiding, one part humorous warmth. "Not only don't I want to, but even if I did, too much time has passed. Acting styles have changed. I'm afraid I'd only make a fool of myself."

"You could never do that." Dani shook his head. "Besides, your fans are legion. I mean, today there's a whole new generation of young people out there discovering your movies. You were the best. You still are the best."

Tamara smiled. "You're so terribly sweet and so terribly loyal. But I'm not that good. I never was. Now, Daliah—she's far better than I *ever* was. With her, acting is a natural talent. It's in her blood."

"You're a natural too!" he said staunchly.

She shook her head slowly. "Noooo . . . I was a technician."

"What's the difference? You were always one hell of a fine actress."

"But there *is* a difference, don't you see? I had to learn. I had to study, and watch people, imitating them so I could make audiences believe I had slipped under a character's skin. You see, Dani, I *acted*. But Daliah . . . well, I don't know how she does it, but she *becomes* her characters, quick as you can snap your fingers. She's got what I think Inge meant when she always said my mother was a natural. You either have it or you don't."

"You have it," he said loyally. "Don't try to tell me otherwise."

She was about to tell him otherwise, when the wailing sirens of a squad car and an ambulance rose in the distance. "There," she said. "You see? Help's already on the way."

He opened the car door again and got out. "Don't go away," he teased. "I'll be right back."

But he wasn't. She sat in the car, counting the minutes. Five. Fifteen. Twenty. When he finally returned, he was walking slowly, shaking his head and scratching it. "How strange," he said as he slipped into the driver's seat. "It just doesn't make sense."

She looked at him, puzzled. "What doesn't?"

"Both the driver of the van and the driver of the rig . . . well, they seem to have disappeared. Poof! Just like that."

She frowned. "You mean they left the scene of the accident?"

He nodded. "And not only that. When the police radioed in the license numbers, it turned out that the rig and the van both have been reported stolen."

"A tractor-trailer like that? Stolen here, in Israel?" she asked. "That doesn't make sense. Not in a tiny country like this. It would be discovered in no time." She added slowly, "Unless, of course, it was filled with a valuable cargo. If they wanted to unload it fast—"

"But it wasn't loaded. It was stolen empty, and it's still empty. The same goes for the van."

"Well, maybe the thieves didn't know that."

"Could be," he said. "But I doubt it. Something just doesn't sit right about this accident. It's almost as if . . ." His voice trailed off.

"As if what?"

"As if it had been planned." He shrugged. "It sounds silly, I know." He glanced at his watch. "Anyway, we'd best hurry. If the plane came in on time, it's already been on the ground for five minutes."

When they reached the airport, Tamara and Dani split up. She checked out the VIP lounge, the various waiting areas, bars, restaurant, and ladies' rooms while he went to inquire about Daliah in the customs hall.

Avraham Goshen, the inspector in charge of the customs officials, was an ugly beak-nosed man with a shiny bald pate and a ring of short black hair curving around his head from the back of one ear to the other. Beside him stood Micha Horev, who was everything his superior was not. Horev was a youthful sabra, all vibrant tan and flashing white teeth. They were both facing Dani. Behind them, Daliah's Vuitton cases were going round and round, solitary orphans on the otherwise empty luggage carousel. "Of course I recognized her," Horev was saying. "She came through about twenty minutes ago. One of our VIP representatives whisked her through."

"Which representative?" Goshen, a solidly competent inspector who had worked at the airport for the last fifteen years, asked.

"I don't know," Horev replied.

"You don't *know*?" Goshen thundered. "You've worked here for four years, and you don't know? Surely you know everyone."

"He was new. I'd never seen him before today."

Goshen was frowning as he marched off to the nearest wall telephone and punched out a number. After a few minutes he returned, shaking his head slowly. "No new VIP representative was on duty," he said softly. "Elie Levin was scheduled to meet her at the plane."

"It wasn't Elie," Horev said definitely.

Avraham Goshen was no man's fool. His beak nose was famous for sniffing out trouble, often long before it happened. It had never failed him yet, and he smelled trouble through those massive nostrils now. "Call airport security," he said without a pause. "Get them over here right away. On the double."

Horev, his tan gone suddenly white, sprang into action.

Tamara pushed her way through the crowds with such furious impatience that people snapped at her left and right, but she was oblivious of all the snarls of "Watch it, lady," and "Can't you look where you're going!" She was too tense to notice anything but her own growing fears. Her body felt weak, as though an invisible leech had depleted her of all energy, and yet her pulse was racing and her heart was hammering ferociously. When she met up with Dani in the customs hall, they both looked at each other hopefully, and when both their eyes dimmed, neither had to speak in order to communicate.

Blindly Tamara felt for the contoured plastic chair behind

600

her and lowered herself listlessly down onto it. Her shoulders slumped and her face was strained. "She . . . she's just not here!" Her voice came out a quivering, hoarse whisper. She stared up at him, her eyes wild, and he knew that the memory of Asa had exploded into her mind. "Dani, she's not here! I've searched everywhere!"

"Don't worry. She might have gone home on her own."

"Don't be silly! Her luggage is still here. Daliah wouldn't just abandon it! And I . . . I called home twice. Ari answered both times, and she hasn't arrived there."

They had her paged while teams of airport security men methodically searched the terminal from one end to the other.

Tamara's head was spinning. *Daliah has to be all right. She has to be.* As they waited, she kept her hand glued to Dani's, seeking his comfort and reassurance, knowing that his presence was the only thing between her and instant madness.

Finally Inspector Goshen sent for Dani.

"You stay here," he told Tamara.

She jumped to her feet. "No! I'm going with you."

"You will do as I say!" he said with such cold firmness that she stared at him in surprise. "Sit back down!" Then, his face somber, he followed the inspector's messenger and strode off.

He was back almost immediately. As soon as he came in, Tamara jumped to her feet and grabbed him by the arm. "Dani, what is it?" she asked, seeing his bewildered expression. "Is she . . . is she . . . ?"

He shook his head. "No, it's . . . it's one of the airline employees. He's been killed."

"Oh, Dani! How awful!" But he saw the relief in her eyes, just as it had been in his, and he hated seeing it there at the expense of someone else's misery.

He let out a brittle sigh, and for the first time, he looked every year of his age. "He's an El Al VIP representative," he told her, "Elie Levin, the one scheduled to meet Daliah's plane."

She shivered as though ice ran through her veins. "Dani?" she said slowly in rising hysteria. "First the accident with that tractor-trailer, as though it had been set up deliberately to delay us, then Daliah's disappearance, and now *this*." She stared at him, her eyes huge. "Dani? What the hell is going on?"

*   *   *

Daliah was filled with a thousand terrors, too much in a state of shock to be more than numbly aware that they were still at the airport, driving in inconspicuous leisure around to the cargo terminals at the far end. She felt engulfed by a heightened sense of unreality, and two hitherto foreign emotions held her in their ugly grip. She felt dominated. Totally dominated and exceedingly demoralized. She didn't have to look down to see if the revolver barrels were still aimed at her sides; she could feel them digging through her clothes, pressing into her flesh. She was terrified that the sudden jolt of a pothole, or an abrupt stop, or even her own acute trembling would accidentally cause one of the men to squeeze the trigger. She didn't dare try to escape, at least not while the guns were pressing into her sides. These men seemed to have no compunctions. They were inhuman, and would kill her on the spot and think nothing of it.

The car passed some chain-link gates and then slowed as it headed into the gaping maw of a dark, deserted hangar. It was like going from day into night. For a moment she could not see, and the terror was overwhelming. When the car came to a stop, the driver clicked on the overhead light. Even then she felt no relief.

The driver turned around, and when she saw what was in his hand, she sucked in her breath. It was a hypodermic syringe, and his thumb depressed the plunger, releasing a thin arc of clear liquid.

Eyes wide, she tried to squirm further back in her seat, but it was futile. There was no getting away from it. Not with guns pressing into her flesh. Abruptly the driver reached out, grabbed one of her arms, and yanked it forward.

"Wh-what are you doing?" she whispered. Her lips and throat were so dry from fear that her voice came out a croak.

He held the needle poised in the crook of her elbow. "Pleasant dreams, actress," he said with an ugly sneer, and at that moment, without bothering to roll up her sleeve or dab her arm with alcohol, he stabbed the needle deep into her flesh.

It stung sharply, and she let out a scream. Then she could feel a sleepy sensation streaming into her arm and spreading outward through her body. Suddenly everything seemed to slow down and become fuzzy. She was vaguely aware of the car doors opening . . . of slumping forward and being tugged outside. Her legs were too limp to support her, and the men had to hold her up.

"I worry about you all the time," Inge's voice echoed

somewhere in the back of her mind, and that was her last thought. Then her expression slackened and her eyelids drooped shut. The world blurred and went black.

Najib al-Ameer's study on the top floor of the Trump Tower was book-lined and exceedingly luxurious. Armless suede couches, signed tan-leather-covered French chairs, tole lamps, and a lacquered bronze-embellished desk made by *maître* Philippe-Claude Montigny for Louis XV himself could barely hold their own among the tortoiseshell-finished bookcases lined in brass and the warmth of books, books, and more books.

But there was more to this library than mere beautifully bound books and shelves upon shelves of first editions. Huge shallow drawers held a king's ransom of ancient Persian script fragments, sheafs of historical documents and treaties signed by kings, queens, presidents, and prime ministers, three thousand-year-old Egyptian papyri, seventeen-thousand-year-old painted rock fragments plundered from a cave in Lascaux, France, and the world's largest private collection of ancient maritime maps. The jewels of Najib al-Ameer's priceless treasures were Christian: the first a Gutenberg Bible, the second a complete illuminated manuscript of the *Book of Hours* from the fourteenth century.

At the moment, Najib, who usually found solace, peace, and immense joy in this, his sanctum, was finding that for once even his precious study could not divert either his gloom or his feeling of impending doom. The instant the telephone shrilled, he pounced on it, by habit activating the scrambler before the caller had a chance to speak.

"It is done," a distorted voice told him over the rushing static in Arabic. "The product is in our hands."

Najib's hand began shaking so hard that the receiver knocked against his ear. After three decades of waiting patiently for this moment, the reality of the situation suddenly left him feeling stupefied: weak and depleted. For a moment he found it difficult to speak.

"Are you there?" the voice asked after a long pause.

He pulled himself together. "Yes, I am still here. Did everything go smoothly?"

"Like clockwork. Shall we deliver the product to the destination agreed upon?"

"Yes," Najib replied. "I will be awaiting delivery."

Slowly he lowered the receiver and let it drop back in its cradle. Then, loath to taint his sanctum with his gloom, he went out into the adjoining reading room and stared out the wall of tinted floor-to-ceiling windows. The sky looked phlegmy; it was one of those hot, muggy gray days, a preview of the oppressive summer to come, and the gray glass only made everything look muggier and more polluted than it really was. For a moment his mind pictured the Mideastern desert, so clear, so pure, so unspoiled. So clean and dry, with rippled mountains of sandy dunes, lengthening purple shadows, and blast-furnace heat.

Hands clasped behind his back, he paced, once again wondering whether it was all worth it . . . or whether it wouldn't have been better to just forget about the past and let it be.

But Abdullah wouldn't let it go, had let him know as much in no uncertain terms.

His hands still shaking, Najib picked up the telephone receiver and punched a number. Newark answered almost immediately.

His voice was resigned. "Prepare the plane for takeoff," he said in English. "No, not the Lear. The 727. You'll have to file an overseas flight plan." When he hung up, he went to get his two briefcases, one filled with work, the other with travel documents and more work. Everything else he might need, including a complete change of wardrobe, was on the plane.

The Bell Jet Ranger helicopter with Daliah aboard finally received control-tower clearance and rose shakily up into the air. It nosed swiftly higher, higher, into the bright, cloudless blue of the sky, and then headed due east, over Samaria, then straight south along the Jordan River to Jericho.

Trust the Israelis, Khalid was thinking with a smirk. Smuggling the actress into Jordan would be easy enough. She would simply go over the Allenby Bridge in a truckload of fruit or vegetables bound for Amman. Even during the Yom Kippur War, this economic link held up; despite the fighting, West Bank fruits and vegetables kept being trucked over.

He grinned. Those Jews would never learn.

When Daliah came to, her first thought was that she was being cremated alive. Then came the realization that she had been trussed. She raised her head and tried to move her arms, but that wasn't possible because her wrists had been securely tied behind her back. For a moment she struggled to free herself, but the cleverly tied knot was out of reach, and the more she struggled, the more she caused the bonds to dig into her flesh and chafe her skin. If she continued this for much longer, she'd succeed only in rubbing her wrists raw.

With a grunt, she let her head slump back. She closed her eyes for a moment, trying to deal rationally with the situation. But thoughts came sluggishly, and it was difficult to hold on to them for long. Between the narcotic still in her system and the debilitating heat, she felt impotent.

The heat was the worst. It was unbearable: oppressive, deadening. Her lungs burned from it and her skin prickled with a heat rash; it was so hot that it was impossible for her to take one really full, deep breath. All she was capable of were short, shallow gasps of stifling air, and the lack of a refreshing lungful brought on the beginnings of galloping panic.

She fought to regain control of herself. Giving in to panic, she warned herself, would only make everything that much worse. She knew she should be grateful for just being alive.

Then she became aware of her thirst. It was a thirst without dimension. There didn't seem to be an ounce of moisture anywhere in her body; every square inch of her flesh felt squeezed dry and hydrogenized. *I've been freeze-dried!* She opened her mouth to laugh like a lunatic, but her throat was so dry that not a sound could be voiced.

She knew then that unless she got hold of herself she was going to go certifiably mad. Slowly a burgeoning anger rose within her and kept the impending madness at bay It was still within sight, still temptingly close, but for the time being she'd managed to shove it away.

I have to keep my anger fed. Only that way can I stoke my will to live, and hope to survive. Think, dammit. Think!

She raised her head again, this time taking stock of her surroundings. She had been lying on her side, and the hard ground beneath her was spread with a heavy, scratchy, dirt-encrusted black goat-hair cloth. Grit was everywhere. Sandy grit. She could feel it in her nose, taste its crunch in her mouth. She could feel it, scratchy and abrasive, beneath her.

She was alone inside a stuffy black tent. A mere cloth prison, but an effective one. She also realized that she was stark naked. Well, there was nothing she could do about that. If they had done that to humiliate her, then they had another think coming. She almost had to smile. Here they had miscalculated. She found nothing humiliating about being nude. She had been raised to be proud of her body, and whether it was sunbathing nude on the beaches of St.-Tropez or being filmed in the nude for all the world to see, she found it natural and was not in the least bit inhibited.

Another tiny victory won.

Her satisfaction was short-lived, for gradually she became aware of her heartbeat. It seemed to be getting louder and louder all the time, until it throbbed so noisily she became frightened. Then she understood. It was the silence—the kind of intense, awesome silence one can find only in the middle of the desert at high noon. A silence so powerful and penetrating, so all-enveloping, that it was like an awesome physical presence.

She had been dumped in the middle of nowhere and left to die!

A new thought flashed out of nowhere: *Where there was a tent, there had to be people! Perhaps if she called for help . . .*

She swallowed several times to lubricate her throat, and then she began to yell for help. She yelled "Help" in English and Hebrew and Arabic so often and so loud that her ears began to ring with her cries. Even after she fell quiet, she had the sensation that the air still echoed with her voice.

She held her breath and listened carefully above the *thump-thump . . . thump-thump* of her heartbeat for a response. But there was none, and her hope evaporated as swiftly as the moisture had seeped from her body. She'd succeeded only in straining her vocal cords and working herself up to an even greater thirst.

Water. She had always loved water. She had taken glass-fuls and tubfuls and poolfuls for granted, had soaked in it, luxuriated in it, and loved it so much she half-believed herself to be a Pisces changeling. But now there suddenly was no water, not a single drop, and the stratospheric temperature seemed to climb higher and higher. Water. Water. She was almost delirious with her need for it.

In a sudden flash of enlightenment it hit her.

If there wasn't any real water, perhaps she could slake the worst of her immediate thirst with *imaginary* water. After all, wasn't she an accomplished actress? Couldn't she imagine almost anything, and actually believe it for a while? If she could pretend a three-sided set was a real place, an actor a real character, and a gun loaded with blanks capable of killing, why couldn't she do that now with water? Why couldn't she ease the worst of her thirst by acting as if it were there?

She shut her eyes, conjuring up a dripping faucet, and then lavishly sprinklered lawns, cool foggy morning mists, refreshing drizzles, and violent rainstorms. She imagined pools, lakes, oceans and oceans of glorious, cool, clear water.

And then, imagining her trussed arms were free, she raised them gracefully above her head and dived neatly as the dancing smoothie holding his umbrella aloft sang "Singin' in the Rain."

Before she hit the water, she plunged into the safe, welcoming blankness that was sleep.

At four thousand feet, the pilot rolled the 727–100 gently to port and then banked the plane in a wide sweeping curve. Najib was seated in the living-room section on a leather couch specially fitted with seat belts. In anticipation for landing, he had changed from his Western clothes into the traditional Arab robes and headgear, and he was staring unseeingly out the little square window at the tilting desert below.

It was the Rub' al-Khali, the "Empty Quarter" in the Saudi Arabian southeast, and its name fit it perfectly. All there was, as far as the eye could see, was desolate wilderness. Alternately golden sand and dung-colored rocks, it was a place where nothing grew and where it never rained, where, aside from a sprinkling of oil wells and refineries, there was nothing, and the only signs of life were the airplanes flying high in the sky and very rarely a tribe of bedouins crossing the desert on their camels, heading to or from Mecca the same way their forefathers and their forebears' forebears had crossed it before them. It was a cruel wilderness, harsh and unforgiving, and was avoided by all but the most foolhardy and the bedouins who knew how to survive it.

A stewardess in a red St. Laurent shift came soundlessly up behind him. "We're coming in for the final approach now, Mr. al-Ameer," she said in a breathy little voice.

He looked up at her and nodded. She was one of the two handpicked stewardesses: Elke, the blond Austrian Valkyrie who, except for her too-large bosom, looked like she had just stepped straight off the cover of *Vogue*.

She leaned closer, enveloping him in a heady cloud of perfume and musk. Her smooth, manicured fingers reached for his seat belt and clicked it together around his waist, her clever fingertips grazing his groin. Her pale gray eyes held his gaze. "Will we be stopping over, or are you planning to send us back, Mr. al-Ameer?" she asked huskily.

He looked surprised. "Captain Childs has forgotten his instructions?"

She shook her head, her eyes lowering obviously to his groin and then back up again. "I would like to know," she said, her voice heavy with promises.

He gave a rueful little smile. "I'm afraid I will be staying on alone. The plane is returning to Newark right away."

"Oh. I see." She tried to hide her disappointment and moved away.

He turned back to the window and stared out. At first, all he could see was desert, desert, and more desert. And then suddenly, like a mirage, there was the palace, sliding into view a few miles ahead. It was a huge sprawling modern building built on a manmade hill, and looked like a cross between a terminal at Kennedy Airport and a flying saucer. Massive concrete buttresses crisscrossed in arcs above it, giving the illusion that the palace was actually suspended from them. The entire perimeter of the eight-acre compound was surrounded by thick protective walls, inside of which were also some scattered outbuildings with satellite dishes and revolving radar antennae on their rooftops, lush emerald-green lawns, clay tennis courts, a sparkling turquoise swimming pool, and two tall water towers disguised as postmodern minarets.

He looked straight down as they flew over it. He could see armed guards patrolling the grounds, the rooftops, and the walks atop the walls. At the moment, their attention was on the plane; they all had their faces upturned. He smiled twistedly to himself. He could tell from their paramilitary green field uniforms and white Arab headcloths that they were Abdullah's men. Then his eye caught the distant flash of silver. Twin gleaming lifelines, one a pipeline for fuel, the other for water, stretched from the house for 180 miles to the desalinization plant on the coast. And beyond the far side of the compound, the private airstrip was a shimmering water mirage, a ribbon of concrete writhing amid the sands. A small Cessna and a twin-engine Beechcraft were parked at the far end. A windsock hung limply.

It certainly looked as though the Almoayyed brothers had built themselves the ultimate hideaway, even if every pound of soil had had to be flown in and every fluid ounce of water pumped across the desert. Abdullah, requiring all the secrecy and privacy he could get his hands on, had been wise in borrowing it from them. With its sophisticated communications systems, state-of-the-art electronics, and remotest of remote locations, its nearest neighbor eighty miles away, the Almoayyed palace was a formidable fortress, and virtually impregnable. One could come and go and do whatever one wished without anyone knowing about it. But he wondered idly, as he often did when it came to the palatial homes of Arab millionaires, sheiks, and oil ministers, why, when money was no object, they insisted upon buildings which looked and felt, inside and out, like expensive modern public terminals or high-rise hotel lobbies.

That thought slid out of his mind as the palace slid out of view. The fuselage shuddered as the landing gear lowered and locked into place. The desert seemed to rise to meet the plane. Then the golden sands rushed past in a blur and the plane touched down smoothly, the engines whined in reverse, and the instant the captain applied the brakes, Najib felt himself thrust backward in the couch. Even before the plane taxied completely to a halt, he could already see the boarding ramp being towed forward by a tractor, and an elongated shocking-pink Daimler limousine with black-tinted windows coming behind it.

He unhooked the seat belt, got up, and walked forward. Elke was already pushing the door open to oppressive heat.

The pilot ducked his head out from the cockpit. "You still want us to take off and leave you here, Mr. al-Ameer?"

Najib nodded. "I do, Captain Childs. Take the plane back to Newark and wait there for further instructions. I'll let you know when to pick me up. You can refuel in Riyadh."

"Will do, Mr. al-Ameer." The pilot gave a casual half-salute. "Hope you enjoyed your flight."

"It was smooth and right on time, thank you," Najib said, already on his way down the ramp, Elke and the other stewardess following with the two briefcases and a suitcase.

The Daimler had just pulled up and the driver got out to hold the rear door open. Najib nodded to him in greeting, recognizing him as Hamid, a Lebanese Shiite and one of Abdullah's most trusted lieutenants. He ducked quickly into the back of the car, and Hamid slammed the door from the outside and put the luggage in the trunk.

The air conditioning was like ice, and so was the woman on the back seat.

Najib hadn't expected company, and he eyed her with a mixture of surprise and curiosity. She would have been quite attractive under normal circumstances, he thought, but her blond hair had been shorn to little more than a crew cut, and she was dressed in unflattering baggy men's battle fatigues: tunic, bloused trousers, jump boots, and webbed belt. It was obvious that she had done everything in her power to defeminize herself, right down to the bitter, down-turned corners of her mouth and the hard, unrelenting set of her jaw. From the slightly mad feverishness in her Aryan-blue eyes, he took her to be a fanatic, probably a European terrorist in training. On her lap lay an American-made M16 A-1, pointed in his direction.

He reached over and moved the barrel carefully aside. "I get slightly nervous when those things are pointed straight at me," he said in English. He gestured at the ammunition clip. "Especially when they are loaded."

She gave him a look of pure steel. "I know who you are," she accused harshly with a heavy German accent. "I recognize you from the pictures in the newspapers and magazines." Her jaw tightened perceptibly. "Someday, all capitalist pigs will have guns trained on them, and the world will belong to the people."

He raised his eyebrows. "Is that so?" Despite himself, he couldn't help but smile. She was so serious, he thought. So humorless and repressed. "I am not your enemy, young lady," he said in a stern voice. "It would serve you well to remember that."

Her eyes flashed with rabid passion. "All capitalists are our enemies," she said, "especially those who are bedfellows of the American pigs and pretend to be our friends!"

Hamid's eyes flickered back at them through the rearview mirror. "I would not pay her too much attention," he said easily. "Monika's heart lusts for blood, but her head is warped by the Marxist propaganda. She is with the Baader-Meinhof gang and came to learn how to set off bombs correctly." He chuckled. "I hear she needs the training. She almost blew three of her friends to Paradise when she set off a bomb at a U.S. Army base in Kaiserslauten."

Najib glanced at her. She sat there tight-lipped and seething, so angry that he wouldn't have been at all surprised if she had emptied her cartridge clip into Hamid's back right then and there.

Hamid chuckled again and shook his head as he put the big car into gear. "You should see her in action. She can outshoot, outfight, and outcurse any of our men. The only thing she will never learn is making bombs and throwing grenades. Those things are still best left to men."

Monika swore. "You sexist pig! You men think you know it all." She tossed her head. "One of these days you'll awaken to the fact that we women are equal to any of you. You won't be able to keep your women subdued forever, you know!" Her voice had risen with such feverish triumph that Najib realized she was probably mentally disturbed. He didn't like the idea of her walking around armed.

"Her trouble," Hamid said, lighting a cigarette and grinning over his shoulder, "is that she is so butch no man wants to even try to fuck her. It is said she keeps razors in her garden of earthly delights. Her anger, Allah help her, comes from being sexually repressed."

"Sex!" Monika scoffed contemptuously. "That is all you can ever think about!" She turned to Najib. "I suppose you are just like him."

Najib thought it wise to ignore her. "Has Abdullah arrived yet?" he asked Hamid. He had to talk very loud to make himself heard above the screams of the jets as his plane hurtled down the runway and swooped up into the air directly above them.

Hamid nodded. "He is here, but he has to go to Tripoli tomorrow night." He glanced back intermittently, cigarette dangling from his lips. "He is looking forward to seeing you."

"And the woman?"

"The actress, you mean?"

"Yes." Najib nodded. "Her."

"Khalid, Mustafa, and Muharrem are with her. They have already smuggled her into Jordan. Tomorrow they will cross the Saudi border near Dhat al Hajj with a group of bedouins headed for Mecca."

Najib tightened his lips. "That means they still have a thousand miles to go. I should have waited some more days before coming."

"Once they have crossed the border they will be here in a matter of hours," Hamid assured him. "Abdullah has arranged for air transit for them."

Najib nodded and kept his face bland. They were approaching the palace compound, and to his astonishment he saw that the walls were not only concrete but also sloped up in a cresting, overhanging curve to make scaling them nearly impossible. They were fifteen feet high, and the top edges were embedded with lethal broken-glass shards. And if that were not enough to discourage intruders, five feet of high-voltage fencing rose even higher. Twenty feet, with walkways along the parapets. It was overkill, he thought to himself, and wondered what it was the Almoayyed brothers feared so much to have built such a prison for themselves.

The car had reached the main gates of the palace compound and crept to a halt. It took a full minute for the gates to slide open. They were electronically controlled from inside and weighed tons. "Two-foot-thick steel!" Monika boasted. "Abdullah told me they were made by a bank-vault company, and it would take a tank to blast through them!"

They drove on, past the green lawns and perfumed gardens. All around, water sprinklers twirled lavishly, throwing out scintillating rainbow sprays and keeping everything lush and moist. Water fountains plashed and leapt.

Najib glanced around, noting electric eyes attached to statuary, walls, and posts. He guessed that there was probably a network of laser-activated alarms as well.

It was a luxurious prison, one which was infinitely peaceful, but formidable. One from which there would be no escape.

One by one, the Boralevis were going to be snatched up, brought here, and made to suffer until they slowly died.

Hamid swung the big car up the gently sloping drive to the main entrance of the palace and parked it in front of the sweeping marble steps. Getting out, Najib felt dwarfed. It was a huge edifice, much bigger than it had looked from the air, and it was all polished beige-mottled marble and sheets of green mirrored glass. Close up, he could see that it had been exquisitely finished, the telling details hinting at highly skilled craftsmen. Looking around, it was difficult to believe that beyond the encircling walls lay a desert wasteland. Water seemed to gurgle extravagantly from all sides; fountain jets leapt into the air and came crashing back down, only to leap again moments later.

Monika waited in the car while he and Hamid went up the marble steps. To either side of the front doors stood two guards, automatic rifles at the ready, black wraparound sunglasses rendering their expressions featureless. A third guard, armed to the teeth and grenades hanging from his web belt, opened the heroically scaled hammered-bronze doors from inside.

The palace air conditioning was working overtime; it was as cold as the interior of the Daimler had been. Najib looked around, surveying the octagonal foyer. It would have done a Miami high-rise proud, and was done up in that peculiar fusion of futuristic Italian modern and traditional Arab design which the nouveau riche of the Persian Gulf all seemed to go in for. Las Vegas Araby, he thought uncharitably. Anywhere else in the world it would have been considered tasteless and brazen and gauche, but as with the pink Daimler, it seemed somehow to fit in this hot, rainless climate with its stark, blinding light. There was a sunken octagonal fountain in the exact center of the floor, where four entwining plumes of spume danced gracefully up into the air and fell crashing back into the octagonal basin in silvery sheets of crystal water. Chandeliers of thin vertical crystal rods covered the entire ceiling. Two sweeping white marble staircases with glass railings and brass banisters curved up to a second-floor gallery. The seating banquettes were long and low and futuristic, and the predominant colors were white, silver, and turquoise.

"Everything has been prepared for your visit," Hamid said. "I think you will find things to your satisfaction. I will have your briefcases and suitcase brought upstairs. You are to stay in one of the brothers' suites."

Najib nodded. "And the Almoayyeds' servants?"

"For the time being, they have all been dispatched to the brothers' main palace in Abu Dhabi. Abdullah saw to it that we will have absolute privacy."

Najib nodded. "I would like to speak to him immediately if that is possible."

"He has asked me to bring you to him the moment you arrive." Hamid gestured. "He is in the *majlis*. Come with me."

Najib followed him up one of the staircases, along the mezzanine gallery, which completely encircled the foyer, and past a three-story waterfall which began near the ceiling and rippled down an angular wall of smoothly polished purple-striated white *pavonazzetto* marble, to disappear into the recessed, coved edges of the white floor below.

They came to an intersection of four identical corridors. Hamid unerringly chose the correct turnoff and led Najib down the wide expanse of cool marble to the *majlis*. Now priceless Oriental rugs softened the marble floors underfoot, and modern sculptures stood in careful placement under specially designed skylights which bathed them in floods of natural light.

Eventually Hamid knocked on a set of imposing sculptured bronze doors which looked as if they had been designed by Louise Nevelson. Without waiting for a reply, he pulled them open.

The *majlis*, or reception room, seemed to stretch from the doors to infinity. Najib guessed it to comprise a generous quarter of an acre, and its domed ceiling rose to a height of three stories. Through its stained-glass panels, colorful dappled light streamed down and glowed a radiant circle on the floor. Abdullah was standing by the curving wall of tinted windows, looking down upon the velvet lawns, his paramilitary green-and-black-banded, checkered headgear thoroughly out of place amid all that stunning luxury. His hands clasped behind his back, he turned around as Najib approached, and raised his chin. As usual, he held out his hand imperiously, waiting for Najib to take it and press it to his lips. "So," Abdullah said, "the time has finally come." He watched Najib's reaction closely through his hooded, cunning eyes. "You did not sound pleased over the telephone."

"The news was unexpected." Najib kept his voice purposely bland. "After so many years, it seemed quite anticlimactic. Almost as though it was not worth the bother."

"Ah, but she is most definitely worth the bother. Do sit while I explain why she is more than worth her weight in gold." They took a seat on facing turquoise-upholstered, white-framed bergères. Abdullah gestured to an antique silver coffee service on a silver tray mounted on cabriole legs. "Would you like some refreshment?"

Najib looked at the coffee service and shook his head. "No, thank you, half-uncle. I would prefer something cooler."

"Cooler? Or stronger?" Abdullah's liquid black eyes squinted shrewdly. "Perhaps something alcoholic is more to your liking?"

Najib shook his head, some deep instinct warning him off. "No. Actually I would like some sparkling water with ice, if that is not too much bother."

A fleeting look of disappointment flicked across Abdullah's face, and was gone so swiftly that Najib almost missed it. But he, too, had been watching closely, and he realized that his instinct had paid off: his half-uncle was trying either to test him somehow or to entrap him. The drinking of alcohol was, after all, a major vice. Good Muslims did not drink, and the imbibing of spirits was punishable by law, though it was common-enough knowledge that many Arabs drank up a storm when they went abroad, and many even went so far as to have secret stashes of alcohol and wines in their homes. Najib would have willingly bet half his fortune that somewhere within the palace compound, the Almoayyeds had a wine cellar that would have rivaled that of half the châteaux in Bordeaux.

"Over there." Abdullah gestured to a white armoire which had been lacquered in so many layers that it shone with the same smooth richness as the body of a Rolls-Royce. "Inside that is what I believe the infidels call a . . . 'wet bar'?" Under his thin, pointy salt-and-pepper beard, his thick vulpine lips twisted in distaste at the very words.

Najib rose to his feet, went over to the armoire, and pulled open the double doors. He had to smile. He would have won his bet without even having left the room. The specially designed armoire, outfitted with a small built-in sink, refrigerator, and icemaker, was fitted with beveled glass shelves holding a bartender's ransom in spirits—everything from amaretto to zinfandel.

He took a cut-crystal highball glass, some ice, and squirted some soda from a siphon, then crossed back over to Abdullah, looking abstracted.

He was glad of the distance he had to walk; it gave him time to think, to ponder his half-uncle's attitude toward him. Abdullah's goading had recently become downright hectoring, as if he had found unimpeachable reason to suspect that Najib was traitorously working against him—a suspicion that was ridiculous, since it was groundless, but which to Abdullah's twisted mind was probably very real. Perhaps paranoia was the fate of all rebels who rebelled for too long, Najib considered; Abdullah had become his own worst enemy. Once he had at least been able to shoulder the blame for shoddily planned disasters which were his fault, but now he blamed his men; once he had delegated authority, but now he listened to no one; once he had been trusting, but he now regarded even his closest lieutenants and most faithful associates with distrust, and once his actions had burned with righteous fervor, but now they were all planned with but one thing in mind—the glorification of his own infamy. Though he still kept his pulse on the problems of the Mideast, and saw himself as the only possible savior for the Palestinians in the refugee camps, the people were now merely the means toward an end, and his own power-hungry schemes took precedence.

Abdullah had come to revel in power. He delighted in it, used it indiscriminately.

Najib sipped at his iced soda and decided to try to keep the conversation neutral: one had to dance circumspectly around Abdullah, gauging his every change of mood. He sat back down and looked at his half-uncle. "How did you come across this palace?" He gestured with his tinkling glass.

Abdullah followed Najib's gesture with his eyes and then looked back at him. "For many years the Almoayyed brothers have been lax in supporting our cause," he said smugly. "Now, it seems, they wish to make amends for their past slights. They have put this palace at my disposal whenever I so wish." He gave a thin smile. "You would be surprised at how amenable they have become."

Keeping his voice mild, Najib said conversationally, "Hamid said he expects the Boralevi woman to be brought here tomorrow."

Abdullah nodded. "She will be coming on the same plane on which I am flying out." He seemed to puff up visibly with self-importance. "Muammar has invited me to Tripoli for a week. A great supporter of mine, Muammar is. And I of him, of course. The colonel is the one leader who has backed me from the moment he came into office."

Najib was starting to get angry. "I wish you could have forewarned me that you will be gone." He couldn't help the note of asperity in his voice. "What am I supposed to do while she is held captive here? Sit around and kill time until you return?" He looked down at his glass and rattled the ice cubes. Then he looked up again. "In case you have forgotten, I have businesses to run. I cannot see the point of having to wait around."

"Ah." Abdullah held up an index finger. "But there is a point." He smiled with malice.

Najib waited in silence.

"It is a test. You do see that."

Najib felt a stab of pain in his bowels, and the moistness shone on his forehead. But otherwise he appeared outwardly calm. He shook his head. "I am sorry, but I do not see. Perhaps you will be so kind as to explain."

Abdullah looked at him craftily and placed his hands on the carved white arms of the chair. "I want to see whether you still have it in you."

Najib was suitably outraged. "Have it in me? Have what in me?"

"Najib, please." Abdullah flapped a hand in a pacific gesture. "Why do you insist we play these games? We both know very well of what I speak. Your Westernization. The softness which I suspect your life of wealth and position has lulled you into." He smiled mockingly, the sharp lower teeth showing in front. "It is time for me to see if the injustices of the past still rage like the fires of hell within you."

Somewhere deep within himself Najib found a reservoir of careless fury. "The past, the past!" His harsh voice tore up out of his throat. Suddenly he did not care what the consequences of an outburst might be. He had had enough. "You always bring up the past," he said grimly. "You forget, perhaps, that it was my sister—*my* sister—they killed, and not yours." He glared at Abdullah.

"We are all brothers and sisters in the eyes of Allah," Abdullah quoted stiffly.

"Why is it that whenever things get difficult, you always use Allah to hide behind?" Najib demanded. "When things need an excuse or an explanation, it is always Allah this, Allah that."

Abdullah's dark face went white with trembling rage, and he was barely able to control himself. "You are not only treading the quicksands of treachery," he screamed, "but you blaspheme as well! I have had men executed for less!"

Najib tightened his lips across his teeth in a kind of grim grin, "Execute me, then." His soft voice reflected a controlled contempt. "Kill off all your supporters, and one day you will look around and find yourself alone, wondering what has happened to all your friends." He got to his feet, surprised to find himself suddenly calm, and not really caring one way or another what the consequences for this outburst might be. He looked down at Abdullah. "I have had enough. I will be in my room. You can send for me when you have come to your senses."

"Sit down," Abdullah said gloomily. His eyes had dimmed, the maniacal light going out of them.

Najib stared at him, amazed. It was as if by standing up to Abdullah, he had somehow managed to defuse his half-uncle's temper. It was something he would have to remember. Silently he sat back down.

"I did not send for you to argue with you," Abdullah said wearily. "There are too many important things to discuss."

"Nor did I come here in order to waste time," Najib countered flatly. "You know I have a business empire to run. I cannot wait around forever until you decide to return from Libya or whatever. Time is money, and I do not intend to waste either. Now that you have the woman, either finish her off immediately and get it over with, or let her go. There is no need to pull the wings off the insect when killing it swiftly and cleanly is safer for all concerned."

Abdullah gave him an oblique look. "I hope you do not think I went through all the trouble of capturing her only to kill her? That could easily have been done at the airport. Or even more easily abroad."

Najib frowned. "Then what is it that you want?"

"Money, for one thing."

"Why get greedy? You know that we have millions at our disposal."

"More millions will not hurt," Abdullah pointed out practically. "However, financial gain is not my real aim."

"What is?" Najib asked economically. He lifted the glass to his lips, but only ice cubes remained. He sucked one into his mouth and kept it there, letting it melt slowly.

Abdullah rose to his feet and paced the flokati. "Twelve of

our men are currently being held in Israeli prisons. Three men are jailed in Greece because of that airline hijacking. I want their unconditional release." He ticked that point off on one finger. "I also want to gain the release of all Al Fatah, Fedayeen, and PLO prisoners." He ticked those three points off on his hand also. "And then, of course, there is a small matter of fifty or sixty million dollars, to be distributed among the refugees in the camps." He folded his thumb down. "That is what I want." He splayed his fingers. "Five things."

Najib could only stare. His mind was reeling. Abdullah's mad ambition was even greater than he had imagined. He swallowed the half-melted ice cube. "The Israelis won't stand for it," he said quietly. "They have steadfastly refused to deal with any and all ransom demands in the past."

"Ransom!" Abdullah snorted. "You make us sound like common kidnappers."

Najib let his silence speak for itself.

"In the past," Abdullah said, "we have never had a hostage of her caliber. Just think of the pressure we can exert through holding her." He clenched his hand and shook it. "She is one of the most famous women in the world; there will be an outcry from millions of fans worldwide. Half the governments of the Western world will pressure Israel to relent. I would not even be surprised if they debated her fate in the United Nations." His black eyes glittered like coal. "And then, my half-nephew, just think! Think of the vast, limitless power which shall be mine if I gain the release of the prisoners! Even Arafat will not have a single supporter left, nor will the leaders of any of his splinter groups. They will all join me! *Me!*" He pounded his chest with his fist. "*I* will be the most powerful leader in all of Islam!"

He's mad. This proves it beyond any remnant of a doubt.

Abdullah continued his pacing, working himself into a frenzied excitement.

"Have you given any consideration to where we are?" Najib asked him softly.

"What do mean?" Abdullah was so caught up in his vision of grandeur that he barely gave him a glance.

"We happen to be in Saudi Arabia," Najib reminded him unnecessarily, "and the Saudis enjoy excellent relations with the United States. They depend upon America for oil dollars, technical know-how, and military hardware. At the moment, negotiations for an entire new fleet of American fighter planes are in progress. The Saudis will not do anything to jeopardize that. They would hand us over on a platter to the Americans if the sale of the fighter jets hangs in the balance."

"You worry too much," Abdullah said with a negligible grunt. But he had stopped his pacing.

A sudden revelation came to Najib. "The Saudis . . . I take it they do not know you are here?"

Abdullah's lips drew back in a chill smile. He continued his pacing. "Why should they? What they do not know will not hurt them. There are many ways to cross the border undetected."

Najib leaned his head back and shut his eyes for a moment. He was almost too dumbstruck to think. Abdullah's madness-hatched plot could easily bring outright war to the entire Middle East. As if there were not enough sparks to set off the powderkeg, now Abdullah was adding more. It went beyond madness. Wearily he opened his eyes and sat forward. "And if what you propose should work," he said carefully, "what happens to the Boralevi woman then?"

"As long as she is a bargaining tool, we will keep her alive," Abdullah said flatly. "Once our use for her is over, we will kill her."

"Even if—and I repeat, *if*, since it's such a long shot—the prisoners should be released?"

Abdullah blinked. "I do not see why that should make any difference."

"But if her release is part of a deal—"

"Deal!" Abdullah scoffed, his voice hard and knifelike. "You have grown too soft, half-nephew. One doesn't deal with one's enemies. I see now that it will do you good to stay with us for a while. It will make a man out of you all over again."

Najib flushed, but chose to ignore the insult. There were more important things to do than spend the time fighting. For one thing, he had to give himself leeway; he must not be trapped here. He, too, could all too easily become Abdullah's prisoner; all it would take was his half-uncle's displeasure. Anything was possible: Abdullah had lost all sense of reality.

"It sounds like this is a lengthy proposition," Najib said. "I cannot stay here for such a long period of time, you know that. Without me constantly staying on top of things, my entire business empire could collapse." He paused, frowned, and drummed his fingertips on the arms of his chair. "But with the jet, I suppose I *could* juggle my schedule and commute between here and New York."

Abdullah's lips also turned down into a frown. After a

while he nodded. "Then juggle things," he said with finality. "But be here when I return from Tripoli. I have something important I need to talk over with both you and Khalid."

"Can we not discuss it tomorrow, after Khalid and the woman arrive?"

Abdullah shook his head. "There will not be enough time tomorrow. Also, much of what I will propose depends upon my meetings with Colonel Qaddafi."

"Very well," Najib said with resignation. "I shall be here when you return."

"I hope so." Abdullah gave him a half-smile. "I guarantee that what I will propose to you will shake the world to its very foundations."

Soft giggles and ghostly whispers roused her from her sleep, while rough-skinned hands propped her up into a sitting position.

Opening her eyes, Daliah shrank back in horror. She struggled with her bonds, but the ropes around her wrists held tight.

In the light of an upheld kerosene lamp, three apparitions in black robes seemed to be dancing devilishly around her. Gnarled fingertips touched her tentatively, and muffled voices chattered and giggled. Elongated witchlike shadows twisted and writhed monstrously on the drooping walls of the tent.

A sudden chill dread came over her, and her eyes darted around as she turned to keep up with all three of the ghostly figures. They were robed in black from head to toe, and only their glowing eyes were visible. They were eyes without faces, like doctors masked for surgery or burglars dressed for break-ins.

One of the masked heads leaned in close to her. She could hear the sounds of breathing and smell the sour odor of sweat. The eyes in front of hers were dark and luminous and surprisingly gentle.

She let out a deep breath and began to shake with relief. These were no nightmarish ghosts or masked bandits, she realized. They were merely flesh-and-blood bedouin women, and the reason they had looked so threatening was that veils covered the lower halves of their faces—veils decorated with colorful embroidery and hung with rows of clinking gold coins, symbols of their husbands' wealth.

She was almost faint with relief.

Unexpectedly, the woman beside her reached out and ran her hand gently through Daliah's hair, fingering its fine, silky texture. The other two giggled and sighed and fussed at her feet: they had caught sight of her pearly toenail polish and were examining her toenails closely, feeling the lacquer and exclaiming aloud with delight. That was when she first realized that her feet were sticking out from under a heavy scratchy blanket. Night had fallen and the temperature had plunged, but someone had been thoughtful enough to cover her while she had been asleep.

"We have brought you water," the woman who had fingered her hair told her in Arabic. "You must be thirsty. Fadya!" She clicked her fingers and gestured to one of the other women. "*Myeh!*"

The woman tore herself away from Daliah's toes and sprang into action. She knelt beside Daliah and held up a goatskin bladder, the nozzle just an inch from Daliah's lips. "*Min Fedlak,*" she said. "Please."

Daliah made a face. She could smell the bladder: it reeked sourly of decayed filth, and in the light of the lantern she could see that the nozzle was encrusted with dirt. For an instant she felt a wave of revulsion, but managed to stifle the onslaught of nausea before it could grab hold of her completely. Throwing up was the last thing on earth she needed. Her body had no more moisture it could spare.

"*Min Fedlak,*" the woman said again, gesturing with the bladder. Water sloshed around inside it. "*Myeh.*"

Obediently Daliah opened her mouth. The woman expertly squirted a stream of water into it, without spilling a precious drop. Daliah closed her lips, sloshed the water around in her mouth, and swallowed it slowly. She almost sighed with pleasure. It was warm and silty and tasted stale, but it was water. Wonderful, precious, life-giving water. It tasted better than any expensive bottled water or mountain stream she had ever drunk from.

She opened her mouth for a second squirt, but the woman shook her head and put the bladder down. Swiftly Daliah lowered her eyes. She was suddenly embarrassed by her obvious greed: she knew she should have been grateful for a mouthful, and that she should have waited to see if more would be offered before asking. To bedouins, water was more precious even than gold.

"*Shukkran,*" she said hoarsely, raising her eyes and thanking the woman.

The nut-brown laugh lines around the woman's eyes crinkled with pleasure at Daliah's use of Arabic.

"*Min Fedlak,*" Daliah begged in the language she'd learned so long ago and remembered only haltingly. "Please, kind friend. The ropes hurt me. Could you untie me?"

The woman's voice was soft and sympathetic and muffled by the veil. "No, no, we cannot do that, Excellency!" she said.

Daliah's eyes were imploring. "Then can you at least tell me where we are?"

"No, no. So sorry, Excellency, so sorry." A look of fear grew in the woman's eyes, and she shook her head and made Daliah lie back down, tucking the scratchy blanket gently around her. "So sorry," she repeated sincerely. "We will bring you more water and lamb stew soon. So sorry . . ."

Then the woman scooped up the kerosene lamp, and the three of them backed off as one and scurried to the tent flaps. Lifting them, they slipped soundlessly out into the blackness of the night.

Daliah shivered. She wished she hadn't caught sight of the night. It was completely dark out, and the darkness was of an intensity such as she had never before encountered.

Wearily she let her head drop back down to the goat-hair floor covering. She closed her eyes.

She might as well try to go back to sleep.

Eighteen hours had passed.

In the Hayarkon Street apartment, the festive decorations were still up; no one had bothered to take them down, and the drooping WELCOME HOME, DALIAH letters were mocking reminders of her absence. They moved with each current of stirred-up air as Dani paced restlessly beneath them.

Tamara, her face gray, sat in a wing chair, crumpled and tearful. Sissi and Ari held hands, sitting white-faced side by side on the floral chintz couch, their faces strained and tortured. Schmarya, having worked himself up into a fury of Biblical proportions, stamped about, his artificial leg thumping heavily on the floor with each second step.

"It's our own damn fault, by God!" the old man was thundering. He brought his fist crashing down on a sideboard, and everyone jumped; their nerves, already worn thin, were so frazzled by tension and lack of sleep that they were all at the snapping point. "We've become so complacent during the lulls between wars that we're shocked when something like this happens! I tell you, we deserve every bomb and bullet and kidnapping if we don't protect ourselves better! And yet, how can we expect to do that," he went on, now launching into his favorite subject, "when the Neturei Karta, damn their Orthodox souls, do not even recognize the State of Israel? I ask you! They want to live here as Jews and have the best of it, but will they live as

Israelis? No! They won't even recognize Israel as a sovereign state! How on earth can we expect to survive our enemies' attacks from without if we tear ourselves apart from within?" He shook his head and slammed his fist again and again on the sideboard.

The three strangers in the room, two of them men from the Shin Bet, the General Security Services, Israel's equivalent of the FBI, and the third, a certain Mr. Kahn, who, perhaps because of his imperturbability and soft-spoken manner, Ari and Sissi suspected was Mossad, ignored the old man's tirade and calmly continued hooking up the tape recorders to the telephone lines, adding two extensions to listen in on.

Once started, Schmarya found it difficult to stop. "How many times have I tried to make those thick-headed fools in the Knesset see that unless we constantly maintain a united—"

"Oh, Father, do shut up!" Tamara cried wretchedly. Her hands were in her lap and she was fidgeting constantly. "We're nervous enough as it is, without your going on and *on*! We don't need any lectures now as to what we could and should have done to avoid this! If you go on ranting and raving and slamming your fists around, I'm going to start screaming in a minute!" Suddenly her voice began to crack. "I don't know why anyone would want to do anything to dear, dear Daliah, and all I know is that she's disappeared and I want her." She repeated, "I *want* her," and bit down so hard on her lip that she drew blood. Then she clapped her hands over her eyes and began to sob violently. She dabbed at her eyes with a handkerchief. "It's just that . . . if only we'd heard something already, some sort of ransom demand . . . something . . . if only we'd heard *something*! That's what usually happens, isn't it?" She turned her head sideways and directed this last question, instinctively and guilelessly, though she couldn't have said why she had chosen him in particular, at Mr. Kahn.

Sensing that she was speaking to him, he raised his eyes from the wires he was hooking up. "In usual kidnapping cases, yes, that is what normally happens," Mr. Kahn said with a nod.

"Well, it's been over eighteen hours," Tamara fretted. "We should have heard something by now, don't you think? I mean . . . Oh my God!" Suddenly her mouth dropped open and she sat bolt upright, turning in the opposite direction. Her hand shot out and caught Dani in mid-stride. She shook his arm violently. "Our telephone number's not listed!

Perhaps that's it! Oh, good Lord, Dani! They might have tried to call and—"

"Mrs. ben Yaacov." It was Mr. Kahn, still unperturbed and unemotional. "If your daughter has been kidnapped for ransom, the kidnappers will surely find a way to make their demands known to you. Perhaps they already have your number. Or they can get it from your daughter. Or a message may be delivered by mail." He shrugged. "There are countless ways they might go about it. But in case they do not have the number, and call information, this new telephone line has been listed in your name."

Instead of calming Tamara, his words had the exact opposite effect. "You keep referring to 'usual cases' and say 'if she's been kidnapped for ransom'!" Tamara's voice became shrill and piercingly raw. With every passing hour the dignity with which she'd held herself for the first few hours had crumbled away, bit by bit, until she'd become the mass of raw, naked nerves she was now. The emotional toll was showing in her face as well: for once she looked old and caved-in. "Of course it's a usual kidnapping," she snapped. "What else would it be? Someone kidnapped Daliah and is holding her because he wants something."

"True," Mr. Kahn said. "But I must caution you, it may not be money."

"Dani!" She twisted back around in her husband's direction. "What does he mean by that? Of course it's money. Shouldn't we already be trying to raise it?"

Dani looked at her with compassion. "Mr. Kahn may be right, darling," he said quietly. "It's no use raising any money until we know the specific demands." His features tightened into a hideous expression and he looked away. "If there are any demands."

"Dani!" She paused. "What are you trying to say?"

"This is Israel, darling. Kidnappings for money are extremely rare. Almost unheard-of."

"You mean," she said shakily, her voice dropping, "it might be . . . political?"

"Look, darling, it's past midnight. Let's try to get some sleep. All incoming phone calls will be monitored. Someone from the Shin Bet will be here at all times. If there's a call, they'll wake us up." He drew closer to her chair and placed his hands on her shoulders. "All we can do is wait."

"Wait," she repeated dully, and sighed. "Oh, God." She reached up, seized his wrists, and tilted her head back so that she could look up at him. "I'm so frightened, Dani.

They won't hurt her, will they?" And when he didn't reply, she dug her fingers deeper into his wrists. *"Will they?"*

They were constantly on the move, it seemed, and now they were moving on once again.

For breakfast, the women had fed her broken bits of dry, unleavened bread, two meager strips of tough, dried lamb, three mouthfuls of tepid water, and a tiny cup of bitter hot strong black coffee. Then they had dressed her in bedouin clothes, in a heavy black *abbeya*, and a veil with only a rectangular meshed eye opening through which she could see out hazily, but no one could see her. She recognized it as the most extreme of the various Muslim women's veils, and any hopes she had entertained to be recognized and freed were dashed the moment she saw the outfit. Even her parents, if they had been standing right in front of her, could not have been faulted for not recognizing her. She had been rendered utterly sexless and shapeless, a walking bundle of faceless rags.

She shuddered to think of the ghostly figure she cut.

To avert suspicion, two of the other women wore the exact same extreme outfits.

Daliah noticed that, herself included, there were sixteen in the party. Twelve were bedouins; the other tour included herself and the three men who had captured her. They too had changed from Western clothing into bedouin gear. She would have been hard-pressed to recognize them, the change was so drastic.

The one named Khalid was in charge. It was he who, from his perch high atop one of the six camels, checked and rechecked their course constantly on a small German compass, and it was he, too, who decided when and where they would stop to rest or eat, and for how long. He paced them so that they neither slowed nor rushed, but kept going at a steady speed.

They had started while it was still cool and pitch dark out, and the sky was blanketed with enormous stars. Khalid had sat her atop one of the camels, her wrists still tied, and had lashed her feet to the saddle. To avoid any danger of the camel breaking away and running off into the night with her, one of his men rode alongside on another camel, holding her camel's ropes.

She supposed she should have been grateful for not having to walk, but the saddle was uncomfortable, and the constant sideways swaying motions made her feel seasick. Her arms, from the shoulder sockets all the way down to her wrists, ached and cramped without letting up, and her legs, tied immovably to the saddle, soon grew numb and started going to sleep. Before long, her entire body was tingling with numbness. She shut her eyes and let her mind drift, pretending that the swaying motions of the camel were the rocking of a boat. Anything was preferable to facing harsh reality.

The rest of the group walked ahead or alongside on foot.

When the sun came up and she couldn't run off into the dark unnoticed, they brought her camel to its knees and untied her legs. Then they pulled her to her feet, and she felt so dizzy and unused to standing that she fell to her knees.

One of the women instinctively rushed forward to help.

"*La!*" Khalid's sharp command stopped her in her tracks.

"*Samahni*," the woman murmured obediently, turning around and going away.

Khalid pulled Daliah to her feet. "You will walk," he told her roughly in English. "If you try to escape, we will tie you up again. Do you understand?"

"Yes," she said shakily, and nodded, wondering if he could hear her through her prison of thick, muffling robes. He must have because he cut through her wrist ropes with a sharp dagger, and her arms were free at long last. But she could not feel her hands. They were totally without sensation. She tried to clasp them together, but she couldn't get her fingers to move. She could barely even curl them. She guessed it would be a while before the blood would circulate properly through her hands.

In a way, walking felt good. She had been tied up for so long, unable to move, that the exercise slowly restored her circulation and made her feel alive. On the other hand, walking was treacherous. She kept tripping and stumbling. The ground was never flat; it was either uphill or downhill, or slanted sideways. Rocks and pebbles constantly gave way beneath her feet; at other times, she sank up to her ankles in thick sand, which made walking sluggish.

They kept her separate from the bedouin women, who from time to time turned around and cast her sympathetic glances. Unless it was absolutely necessary, they did not allow her to speak to anyone. When she had to go to the toilet, it was the woman named Fedya who took her aside, dug a hole in the sand, and helped her raise the robes so she could squat. The indignity of it all both shamed and angered her.

From the position of the sun, Daliah guessed that they were headed southward, but from where they had started, or where they were headed, or where they were now, she had no idea.

The bare, dry, bleached hills all around glowed with an incandescent haze of dust, and the dun-colored desert was a belt of sand and rocks. They avoided all roads, tracks, and known paths, and stuck to the wilderness, being careful to skirt any villages or places of habitation. Every now and then, Khalid and one of the bedouins would go on ahead, climb each hill that afforded a view, and scout out what lay ahead. From time to time Daliah turned around in a complete circle, but all she could ever see were the monotonous sun-baked hills, jagged boulders, and barren stretches of sand. All under the towering blue of the sun-scorched sky. There was no way she could begin to guess the location—it could have been the Sinai, the Negev, or any of the surrounding countries. The brown mounds were featureless and entirely unmemorable.

Before noon, they stopped to rest, and the women prepared a lunch of more bits of unleavened bread, a cup of sour goat's milk, and two more stringy strips of dried lamb. Then they moved on again, but this time she could sense a tension, an obvious wariness. The group's sudden change in behavior she took to mean that something important was about to happen. She looked up at the sky. From the position of the sun, she guessed it to be about two o'clock. Everyone was quiet, looking around constantly, searching the distant horizon.

Then the tension was suddenly gone. Khalid even went so far as to change Daliah's headgear to a normal veil, so that her eyes were free. She guessed that they must have sneaked across a border, or come close to civilization, but when she asked, no one would reply to her questions.

Several hours later they stopped again, this time for tea. Khalid checked the sun, a map, and his compass. Then he dug a shortwave radio out of one of the camel's packs, raised the antenna, and had a short conversation. After that, he checked his compass bearings, consulted his map, and they moved on again. Less than thirty more minutes passed and they suddenly came upon a neglected airstrip, where a yellow twin-engine Beechcraft was waiting.

Khalid and his two men put her aboard, climbed in, and the pilot, who had been waiting for them, started the engines. Dust, stirred up by the propellers, boiled in a cloud.

Minutes later they were airborne and heading south. To the west, a sunset begging for a camera heralded the coming of night.

627

*   *   *

Najib looked out the big wall of windows in Saeed Almoayyed's third-floor suite. He had seen the bright runway lights outside the palace compound click on. Where there had been darkness an instant before, a dazzling two-strand white pearl necklace now stretched half a mile across the desert.

He hit the rheostat so that the room was plunged into darkness, slid aside one of the expanses of glass, and waited to catch sight of the plane. If the landing approach was the same as his, the plane would come from somewhere behind the palace and then fly directly overhead at no more than three hundred feet, drifting into view as it made its final descent to the runway beyond.

He cocked his head as his ears picked up the sound of a distant buzz-saw whine. It grew steadily louder, and then suddenly blinking wing-tip lights swooped overhead in a blur and seemed to slow as they dropped into full view and filled the entire window. He could faintly make out the Beechcraft's underbelly, and then its thin elevator fin topped with a flashing light came into view and the plane drifted over the compound wall, growing smaller and smaller as it descended to a perfect three-point landing. In the distant glare of the runway lights he could just make out the boxy shape of the waiting Daimler.

He walked away from the window and turned the lights back up. His lips tightened into a mirthless smile.

So. Time had done its quantum leap and the past had finally merged with the present. The decades had condensed. The time was come. Daliah Boralevi had dropped out of the skies for a date destiny had scheduled long, long ago. At this very moment she was probably leaving the aircraft; it would immediately refuel, and then Abdullah would be gone to Libya.

Frowning to himself, Najib went over to Saeed Almoayyed's built-in bar and poured himself two generous fingers of bourbon. Raising the glass in a silent salute to Daliah Boralevi, he swallowed it in a single gulp.

How quickly one's perspective could change, he was thinking. Until this very moment he would have been happy to wash his hands of the entire affair and forget it all. Now he was suddenly glad that he had come. He understood that his presence here was as predestined as hers. If nothing else, perhaps by seeing this vendetta through he would finally be able to make his own peace with the past and thus be liberated from the shackles that reached across all those years.

Preparing to meet her, he donned a fresh robe and his formal black-and-gold-banded white headgear. Before going out, he stopped to look at his reflection in the endless wall of mirrors. He nodded to himself in approval, satisfied with the figure he cut. The robes made him look suitably impressive and authoritative, like a true son of the desert.

He went through the big Nevelson doors and out into the sculpture-lined hall. Without hurrying, he made his way to the mezzanine of the octagonal foyer, and when he reached it, he did not descend either set of sweeping staircases. He would wait up here, and watch her being led in from below.

Slowly he paced along the waist-high glass railing and polished brass banisters, his robes swishing and rustling about his feet. The palace was so hushed that he had the illusion he was the only living person in it; all he could hear was the splashing of water as it spilled and rippled down the pink marble wall. Vaguely he wondered if, forever after, he would equate the sound of running water with this wasteful palace in the desert.

He had to wait some fifteen minutes before they came in. One moment there was silence, and the next a sudden flurry of activity as the tall bronze doors below crashed open and Khalid, Hamid, and the German girl roughly pushed a stumbling black bundle in ahead of them.

"Move!" Monika shouted harshly from below. "*Schnell!*" There was the sound of hasty footsteps as she pushed the figure in the black *abbeya* and veil forward. "That way!" she ordered sharply, pointing with her rifle. "Through that door."

"Leave her be." Najib's voice echoed sternly down from above.

Startled, they all looked up to the mezzanine. The two men obeyed and withdrew immediately, but Monika stood her ground, her left hand clutching tightly to the shapeless black bundle.

He took his time coming down the sweeping staircase; after all these years of waiting, he saw no need to hurry now. Head raised, he advanced toward the two women.

He gestured for the German terrorist to move away.

Monika resolutely stood her ground. She thrust out her chest, drew herself up with importance, and her words were clipped with that peculiar military bark. "Abdullah gave me clear orders! I am to guard her with my life!"

"I believe I can handle this myself," he told her coldly.

There was no mistaking the authority in his voice. "Get out."

Monika's face flushed redly. Abruptly she did an about-face and marched to the door.

The heavy bronze portals banged shut with a hollow echo. They were alone.

The world was reduced to the foyer.

He turned to Daliah, and the instant he laid eyes on her a sudden tightness seemed to clench inside his gut. Everything he had felt up to now drained swiftly away. The foyer spun dizzily.

For a long moment he could not trust himself to speak.

All he could do was stare.

Daliah's eyes.

One look into them and he felt himself reeling.

There have been faces that launched a thousand ships, lips that caused the fall of empires, but for him, all it took was a pair of eyes. The moment he looked into their depths, he knew he'd tasted of forbidden fruit and that nothing else would ever taste quite the same again.

They were arresting eyes, the kind of twin jewels maharajas and kings throughout the centuries had killed to possess, and were all the more beguiling since they were all of her that he could see.

For the first time in his life he was utterly mesmerized, as though an enchanted spell had been woven around him. Wispy trills of gooseflesh rippled up and down his body.

Those eyes.

They were the eyes of the purest emerald green flecked with darker slivers of rich Siberian malachite and highlights of paler jade, two luminescent matched cabochons. Their shape was slightly almond, rounded near the nose and tilted upward at the outside ends at an exotic, almost feline slant, and the lashes were black and long, of perfect sable softness, made of black velvet, of spun-sugar dreams.

He nearly groaned aloud.

He'd been dealt the queen of hearts. The ace of spades. A royal flush.

Like two dueling titans they stood squaring off in that cool octagonal foyer, he in whitest white and she in blackest black. Beneath her veil, he was positive, her chin was jutting with the same indignation he saw in the light-fractured flashes of her eyes.

An eternity seemed to pass. Then he caught the sudden movement of her *abbeya* as she drew a deep, startled breath.

Her eyelashes fluttered rapidly in a blink of recognition and, unexpectedly, he heard a ripple of taunting laughter rising from beneath the veil.

It was like a physical assault. He took an anguished step backward; the laughter had reduced his self-possession to nothing, had hurt as intensely as a knife stab straight through the heart. Then the cynical amusement reached her eyes as well and glowed there like yet another harsh slap: potent, painful, utterly humiliating.

He stared confusedly at her.

It was then that she spoke.

"Well, well, *well*!" Her voice, as taunting as her laugh, was throaty and mature, almost smoky in its alluring richness. "Who would have thought that the famous Najib al-Ameer had to resort to white slavery to get women!"

"You recognize me." He looked slightly startled, and then cursed himself for showing it. Of course she would recognize him! It was a fool thing not to have thought of it before. His face had appeared with more regularity than he liked in newspapers and magazines and on television on five continents.

"Even in that silly Rudolf Valentino get-up," she said astringently.

"You are surprised."

"Why shouldn't I be? I didn't expect it to be you I would find at the end of the line." Her voice took on the ugliness of mimicry. "Not Najib al-Ameer, the richest man in the world!" She laughed tauntingly again.

His cheeks trembled from the effort of trying to keep himself under control, but his voice remained steady. "I am not the richest man in the world," he said stiffly. "Nor have I ever claimed to be."

She gestured with her arm. "The richest. The second-richest. The tenth-richest. What does it matter?"

He did not speak.

The laughter drained out of her eyes and they narrowed to lynx slits. "What do you want of me?" The words hissed venomously forth.

He did not reply.

"Why have you brought me here?" she demanded again, more sharply this time. "Answer me, dammit! Are you playing some sort of perverse sexual game?"

He flinched at the angry words. "I would watch my tongue if I were you," he advised with more calm than he felt.

It was then that he noticed her hands. She was holding them up in front of her, as though unaware that she was gently massaging her wrists. He stifled a wince when he caught sight of the ugly chafed skin and the deeply embedded pattern left from too-tight ropes. Quickly he averted his eyes.

Nothing was working out right. Nothing. Never in his wildest dreams had he imagined he would feel such pangs of guilt and responsibility, such immediate remorse. Whenever he'd imagined this moment, it had seemed so clear-cut, so well-defined and simple. Nothing at all like this, so complicated and confusing, so rife with boiling emotional turmoil.

It was all turning out wrong.

Curse the veil and the *abbeya*! Instead of rendering her sexless, they lent her an exquisite, painful aura of timeless mystery which reached down into his loins, and deeper still, into his very being.

He was seized with the mad impulse to rip the offending veil away and reduce her to something human that he could hate and lash out at.

"I am sorry that we are forced to meet under these regrettable circumstances," he finally said for lack of anything better. "If there is anything I can do to make this stay—"

"You bet your sweet ass you can do something!" she snarled with shrewish magnificence. She waved her arms and flapped her robes in righteous anger. "You can release me at once and arrange for my transportation out of this godforsaken hellhole, that's what you can do!"

He shut his eyes and tried to cast her from his mind, his memory. He had made a terrible mistake. He should never have come down here to see her. She was supposed to be everything that he had taught himself to hate, everything he had dedicated his lifetime to destroying. So why shouldn't he have wanted to see her, just once?

But he hadn't counted on drowning in the spell of her eyes and his own torment. He was not surprised by her anger and her spirit, but he found himself totally thrown by them.

What a fool he was making of himself!

He opened his eyes and managed to find his voice. "I will take you to your room." He reached out to take her by the arm.

"Don't touch me!" Angrily she shook him off.

"Very well. If you prefer the German girl to me . . ."

If looks could have murdered, he would have been dead. "I prefer anyone to you, Arab pig!"

Faster than the speed of light, his hand shot toward her, grabbed hold of the veil, and yanked it savagely from her face. The wild light blazed wilder in her eyes.

He pulled his lips back across his teeth. "Jew bitch!"

She drew up her head, hawked deeply, and spat a globule of saliva into his face.

He did not bother to wipe the dripping spittle away. For long moments he could only stare.

An unholy look changed his face completely, turning his black eyes to mercury, so silvery that she could see herself reflected in them. Without warning, one of his hands clamped around the back of her head and thrust it forward to meet his, and the other unerringly found a breast through the thick cloth. He squeezed it cruelly.

The pain tore through her and tears formed in the corners of her eyes, but she refused him the satisfaction of crying out. Then his savage lips forced themselves hungrily upon hers.

It was as if someone had thrown a switch. She went stiff as a marble statue; even her lips seemed to have turned suddenly to stone. But her eyes were alight. They seemed to burn with hell's own fury.

He squeezed her even more cruelly, still staring into her face. She had gone pale, and moisture beads stood out on her forehead, but the taunting expression in her eyes refused to die.

Savagely he shoved her away. His voice was ugly but touched with a grudging respect. "You make a lousy whore," he said.

Her taunting expression changed to one of wild triumph.

Hamid and Monika escorted Daliah upstairs, still in a daze of confusion; if she hadn't known it to be impossible, she would have said that Najib al-Ameer had been attracted to her. Why else would he have stared at her so intensely, and then forced himself on her the way he had? But she decided that that had not been desire, but hate—undiluted hate. That was why he had tried to hurt her.

Vaguely she was aware of endless enormous halls and giant pieces of modern sculpture. Finally Hamid opened a massive door.

"You can thank that Arab capitalist for this," Monika growled. "I don't know why he should have a soft spot for you. If it were up to me, I would lock you in a dark cellar."

Daliah didn't know what she meant by that until she'd been shoved inside a room and the door slammed and locked from the outside. She stared around her in disbelief at the palatial pink suite.

Why not a dark cellar?
Why this gilded prison?

* * *

Every city in Europe has its one world-famous café where local inhabitants and tourists alike are drawn, and the tables and chairs spill out onto the sidewalks, where one can sit and watch the world parading by. They are places where one goes both to see and to be seen, where life is unhurried and newspapers can be read over leisurely cups of coffee or cool drinks nursed, where the intellectuals gather and spend hours arguing the important topics of the day. In Tel Aviv, such is the Kassit Café on Dizengoff Street.

Schmarya had chosen it specifically because it was so public and obvious a place; he suspected, correctly, that no one in his right mind would expect murky business to be conducted so out in the open. The few people who might possibly have recognized the secretive man he was with would no doubt think that the two of them had run into each other by chance on the street and had decided to sit down and enjoy a cup of coffee together before parting again.

Chaim Golan was the head of the Mossad, Israel's world-envied secret service.

An unassuming man, Golan could have been mistaken for anyone's favorite grandfather: behind his dark sunglasses his twinkling eyes were bright blue, the laugh lines around them ran deep and crinkled constantly, and his eyebrows were snowy white. He had a merry Karl Malden bulb of a sun-burned nose, and unruly thick white hair. Few people would have suspected the ice water that ran in his veins, or the streak of stubborn toughness that lay just underneath his twinkling countenance. For behind the facade he was all raw guts and pure steel.

Now Chaim Golan's eyes, hidden behind black glasses, twinkled and crinkled in deceptive grandfatherly humor. "Look at them," he said gruffly. He gestured at the sidewalk crowds passing by—the euphoric shoppers, sweethearts walking hand in hand, friends who had run into each other and were stopping to chat. "Like children they go about. Without a care in the world. Like this was Paris or Rome, they act. Always schlepping their purchases, always seeing stars in each other's eyes." He shook his head slowly. "Do they have any idea, these merrymakers, that at this very instant a bomb could go off and blow them all away? Poof! Like that." He had stopped smiling, but his naturally curved lips seemed unaware of that.

"Of course they know that." Schmarya nodded. "It's always there, in the back of their thoughts, hidden just below their laughter. That is why they are so carefree—because they know this moment of joy might be their last."

Golan turned to Schmarya and looked over his glasses with respect. "The trouble with the two of us," he said, "is we're jaded." He sighed deeply. "Both of us, we have lived through too much. Seen more tragedy than any human being ought to be exposed to."

"And yet, neither you nor I am prepared when something happens." Schmarya frowned and was silent for a moment. "When it does, we are as surprised and shocked as the rest of them."

"True, true." Golan nodded, patted his pockets, and came up with a cigar. He stuck it in his mouth, and patted himself down for matches. "Now, to the subject on your mind. So far, we have dug up nothing. It is as if she disappeared into thin air, your Daliah." He smiled slightly. "But we both know better."

Schmarya grunted. "The borders?"

"As far as we know, no one has tried to take her across. That does not rule out the possibility, of course, that she could have been smuggled across one of them before we doubled our manpower and cracked down on every outgoing vehicle." He found his matches, scratched one, and lit his cigar.

"Any word on the street?"

Again Golan shook his head. "None."

"Then what about word from our informers across the borders? You did approach them, didn't you?"

Golan looked disgusted. "Of course we did. But so far . . . *bupkes.*" He pointed with his cigar. "I can tell you one thing. Amateurs these people aren't, that's for sure. A bloodhound couldn't sniff the trail they've left."

"Nothing? Not even about the murdered airline employee?"

"*Bupkes.* The trouble with crimes committed in public terminals like the airport is that potential witnesses have all flown the coop before we could track them down to question."

Schmarya frowned and toyed with his coffee cup. It was half-empty, and had grown cold. He heaved a noisy sigh. "So what do we do?" he asked at last.

"Time. These things take time." Golan nodded compassionately. "With no clues, unless we hear from the kidnappers it will be virtually impossible to find her. We can trace her only if they contact us. Otherwise . . ." He shrugged expressively, not needing to put the unspoken into words.

Schmarya felt a sudden surge of helpless anger. "This is

my granddaughter we're talking about!" he said forcefully. "Israel's most famous celebrity!"

"Believe me, my friend, I understand the way you feel," Golan commiserated. "The more the victim is loved, like your Daliah, the more the family suffers. For their sake, the best thing you can do is make a show of a strong front. Also, my friend, remember that the lack of communication isn't necessarily all bad."

"Not all bad!" Schmarya exclaimed so explosively that the people at the surrounding tables turned to stare. Shocked at his own outburst, he dropped his voice to a near-whisper. "I want to kill whoever it is that's responsible for this!" he hissed. "I could murder them in cold blood!"

"So why am I here?"

Schmarya frowned and toyed with the cup. His fingers were trembling so badly that he nearly knocked it over. He looked up, his eyes sunken with pain. "There has got to be some way we can push them into playing their hand!"

"Well, my friend," Golan asked conversationally, "how are you at press conferences these days?"

Schmarya was glum. "I'm okay, but my daughter's terrific. A pro."

"That's it, then. You just be there, and Tamara, let her do all the talking."

Schmarya swallowed. "A press conference? You think that could maybe smoke them out?"

"It might encourage them to make a move; then again, it might not. Who can predict? Obviously they are in no hurry to get in touch with you, otherwise they would have leaked word of what they've done. To the press, somebody. But if you announce what happened . . ." He nodded. "Yes, why not? After all, so far no one has claimed responsibility, and this might get them to do so. Also, it will encourage anyone to come forward who might have seen anything."

"What do we say?"

Golan puckered his merry lips and considered. "Whatever comes from the heart."

"And then we wait."

"And then we wait." Golan sat back, his expression deceptively cheerful. "Remember, at least we have every reason to hope that she is still very much unharmed and very much alive. And that, my friend, is more than the families of most kidnap victims can say. I keep asking myself, *why* did they kidnap her? These crimes are not done for the thrill. There has to be a reason."

Schmarya nodded bitterly. "Day and night, I have been asking myself that same question."

"And?"

Schmarya shrugged. "I've come to the conclusion that they'll want a special ransom. And not money, either, I'm afraid."

"That could be." Golan sat back, and puffed on his cigar. "That is sound reasoning, I think. Especially since . . ." He cleared his throat. "Since there's you and Dani to consider."

Schmarya looked up sharply. "What are you trying to get at?"

Golan shrugged. "Maybe I'm barking up the wrong tree, and then again, maybe not. But it could very well be that they plan to use her as some sort of leverage against one of you. Maybe both of you. Need I remind you that you and Dani hold important, highly sensitive posts within the government? That you're both at the highest decision-making level in the cabinet?"

Schmarya stared at him. The very same fears had gnawed at him, only he had been afraid to voice them aloud, as if that might have given them extra credence somehow. But now that Chaim had brought it up, he could no longer avoid the issue. "So, keeping that in mind, how do you suggest we proceed?"

"The only way we can, under the circumstances. Everything we have been doing, we continue to do. We turn the country upside down. Leave no stone unturned." Golan sighed. "We wait. We hope. We pray."

"And what do we do when the kidnappers get in touch?"

Golan looked surprised. "Why, we do what we always do in these cases. You know the procedure. We try to stall them. We negotiate. Try to bring the price down, if there is one, and meanwhile search high and low for her. Try to free her before their demands can be met—or at any rate, before we have to tell them they can't be met."

"Yes, Chaim, but what if . . ." Schmarya paused and tightened his lips. "What if she isn't being held here, in Israel?"

Golan put his finger on the nose piece of his glasses and slid them down an inch. He stared at Schmarya narrowly. "If you're asking me what we do if she's held outside Israel, the answer, which already you know, is that we can't mount a rescue attempt without prior government approval." He stared over his glasses. "Lawfully, at least. You know that as well as I, so why ask?"

"Chaim." Schmarya quickly glanced over both his shoulders, then sat forward and hunched over the tiny table. His voice dropped to a murmur. "Look, what I'm saying is completely off the record, all right?" He waited for Golan's nod, and then continued. "We both know that there are certain men in our armed forces who willingly go beyond the call of duty. Israelis who don't listen to all the dissenting voices and the namby-pambies our government's become filled with. You know the men of whom I speak."

Golan slid the glasses back up and neither nodded, nor shook his head, nor spoke.

"All I'm asking is, should the situation come down to it, can I count on you to help mount a rescue attempt? By at least getting me in touch with the men who would be willing to do it. Unofficially, of course."

"You're suggesting we might take matters into our own hands?"

"If it comes down to that, yes." Schmarya spread his hands helplessly. "For my granddaughter," he added quietly, "I would do anything. Even commit murder."

"These thoughts I would keep to myself if I were you," Golan warned.

Schmarya was undeterred. "But what if she is in Libya? Or Jordan? Or worse, even somewhere slightly friendlier? How can we guarantee that there'll be an outright rescue attempt if it's a country our government's trying to talk peace with?"

"It's politics you're talking now, Schmarya." Golan downed the remainder of his coffee and rose from his bentwood chair. "That question, I can't answer, Schmarya. You know that. It's purely hypothetical. We'll have to wait until the time comes, and God willing, it won't. But if it should, then we'll discuss it. Go, get things set up for the press conference. Meanwhile, I will forget we ever discussed this. And you I advise to do the same."

Schmarya smiled weakly. "Fair enough. And thank you, Chaim. I know you didn't have to come. *Toda raba*."

"*B'vakasha*, Schmarya. If you hear anything, you let me know."

"You'll be the first," Schmarya promised. "*L'hitra'ot*."

Golan gave a half-wave. "*L'hitra'ot*."

Schmarya watched him leave and melt into the sidewalk crowds. Then, spying a passing waiter, he raised his hand to attract his attention. "Waiter!" he called. "*Ha'hesbon*!"

Restlessly Daliah prowled from one room to the next. Everything about the rooms was engraved in her mind, and she feared that if she managed to get out of this alive, she would never be able to forget this place for as long as she lived. She knew the dimensions by heart. Not counting the sixteen-foot-square foyer alcove, the living room of her prison measured twenty-one moderate steps in width, and the length thirty; in other words, it was thirty-eight feet wide by forty-six feet long. The bedroom was another thirty-eight by twenty-four feet. And the two enormous marble-sheathed bathrooms—one clearly "his" and one "hers"—both equipped with beauty-parlor chairs, carved marble pedestal sinks in the shapes of shells, and whirlpool tubs set with mosaic tiles, would each have made respectable studio apartments in New York City. There were two walk-in closets, seventy-six running feet of closet space in all, and a forty-six-foot length of floor-to-ceiling sliding glass windows—but despite all that glass, as a prison it was highly effective. The electronically controlled steel security shutters were down and locked into place, making escape impossible; the electronic controls for them had been disconnected. So had all eleven telephones, including the two in each bathroom, one mounted above the sink and the other built right into the side of the Jacuzzi.

As she stalked about like a caged tiger, the richness of everything only succeeded in making her crosser and crosser. She felt like she'd stumbled onto some stupid set and was trapped in a ludicrous skit. What kind of a prison was this, anyway, with its tons of veined pink marble, acres of quilted pink-suede-upholstered walls, and soft pink silk fabrics? It was farcical. Ridiculous. An Alice-in-Wonderland prison that succeeded in unnerving her more than any tiny six-by-six-foot cell ever could, because of its unexpected luxury.

Abruptly bored with her pacing, she threw herself down into a pink suede couch, sinking slowly deeper and deeper into the overstuffed down-filled cushions. How much longer were they going to keep her here, anyway? Two days had now passed since she had been brought here, and she knew every corner and bibelot. Once again, for the twenty-fourth time in the space of one hour, she glanced over at the desktop clock. That was another thing about being imprisoned. Although time had become academic, she was constantly aware of its passing and leaving her behind. No matter where she looked, clocks ticking away were all around her. Curiously, her captors hadn't tried to confuse her about the passage of time, something she'd once read all kidnappers tended to do, and she wondered whether she should infer anything significant from that. She wondered, too, if putting the clocks away, out of sight, would make any difference psychologically, and decided it really wouldn't. Every eight hours, she would know exactly what the time was, since they brought her her meals so regularly that she could have set the clocks by them: each meal was dictated by the beginning of a new guard shift and thereby spaced eight hours apart. Breakfast was brought promptly at eight A.M., lunch at four P.M., and dinner at midnight. It played havoc with her sleep and general functions. But she guessed that it had nothing to do with her discomfort: it was simply more convenient that way. From the quality of the cooking, she guessed that the cook—as well as the other servants—was not currently in residence.

From listening at the door, she knew that there were at least two guards stationed outside her door at all times. She also gathered that two more guards were stationed below her shuttered windows at all times. Sometimes, if she opened the sliding glass panels, she could hear voices below her windows, and could catch the smell of pungent cigarette smoke drifting in through the hairline cracks between the metal slats. Three people took turns bringing her the trays of food and checking up on her every now and then: two men, Ahmed and Haluk, and the German girl, Monika.

Monika was the cruelest because she was the most truculent and hate-filled of them all. For some reason, Daliah suspected the German girl resented her; whatever the reason, she made that fact painfully clear in as many little ways as she could. When there was soup, she made a point of having spilled most of it on the way; the same went for coffee. Or she would carry a food tray so that the plate was positioned just right for her thumb to poke into the main course. Once, sliding her cold, bleak eyes in one of her sidelong glances, Monika had muttered, "I didn't spit or piss in it. Not *this* time." Her lips had scarcely moved, but the vitriol was potent.

Daliah pretended to be unfazed by the German. She knew better than to argue with her. Monika, she knew, was spoiling for a fight, and it was important that she do everything to prevent one. Each time Monika baited her, she forced herself to remember the first rule of hand-to-hand combat. It seemed a million years since she'd worn her olive-green uniform and done her stint in the Israeli army, but her combat instructor's lessons stayed with her. "If your adversary is armed and you're not," the burly sergeant had barked, "avoiding confrontation may be your most effective combat tactic." At the time, she'd never thought that the lesson would sometime serve her well.

Monika was armed to the teeth.

Most of the men, on the other hand, weren't too bad, except for the little one named Ahmed. He had a nervous manner and never seemed to be able to keep completely still. He was always dangerously wound up; always bouncing up and down, as though dancing to some beat only he could hear. He also kept one hand in a pocket, blatantly playing with himself as he leered at her. Every time he grinned at her, his silent message was like a screamed threat: One of these times, I'm going to come in and stick it in you! Instead of checking up on her every hour or two, when he was on duty he kept popping in every fifteen or twenty minutes.

Ahmed frightened her even more than Monika did, because she sensed he was genuinely crazy.

The rest of them tended to ignore her, looking in on her at regular one- or two-hour intervals. Sometimes she could hear them swapping ribald jokes on the other side of the door or below her windows. Other times they played radios or tape recorders, and the music filtered in.

Of one thing she was unarguably certain: she was being guarded around the clock. They were taking no chances that she'd escape.

Not that she hadn't tried. Immediately upon her arrival, she'd gotten the bright notion to use her dinner fork to pry the security shutters loose. She'd received a rude awakening. The shutters were electrified: the shock hadn't been powerful enough to kill her, but she'd felt her hair stand straight up; then she'd been flung backward a good ten feet.

The most obvious means of escape, those well-guarded Nevelson doors, were like the doors of bank safes: thick, impenetrable, and unyielding.

Wearily she let her head drop to the back of the couch and gingerly felt her forehead with her fingertips. From the base of her temples all the way around the crown to the back of her skull, her head was beginning to pulsate and throb. There was nothing, she thought, quite like mental depression for manifesting itself into a very real physical pain. If your mind was fouled up with garbage, and things were beyond your control, the body picked up on the negative rhythms and never failed to get in on the act. She could feel a whopper of a headache coming on.

She slid to the floor, knelt with her knees planted wide apart, and leaned her head back as far as it could go. But still the feeling persisted that, for once, her spirits were at such an all-time low that even the Ishagiatsu pressure-point exercises wouldn't help.

*　　*　　*

One of Najib's earliest memories was of a time when he found himself alone in the little house at al-Najaf after his mother had sped to his grandparents' house across the way on an errand, giving him the opportunity to experiment with matches. He had become so entranced with lighting them and throwing the little flares around the room that he never even heard his mother return. The shock and horror she felt made themselves known in a punishing lesson: instead of spanking him, she simply lit a match, grabbed his hand, and grimly held it to his fingers until they blistered. After that, she never had to worry again. Having gotten his fingers burned once, he had gained a healthy respect for matches and was cured from playing with fire—forever, he'd thought.

He was reminded of that incident now as he sprawled white-robed on an enormous low L-shaped couch. Was he begging to get his hands burned once again? he wondered. Had he not, after all, learned his lesson painfully enough when his mother had shown him what playing with fire could do?

But this new fire to which he was drawn burned too alluringly for him to ignore. Najib knew he couldn't stay away.

As inexorably as a moth drawn to a flame, he was drawn to Daliah. He couldn't explain it. All he knew was that something quite extraordinary was happening to him. No matter how he tried to shut his mind against it, Daliah's presence was a siren's call which stole after him wherever he went, and reached even to the furthermost reaches of the palace. He had the unnerving impression that he could have been halfway around the world and it would have followed him still.

For two nights now, he hadn't been able to get more than a few scattered catnaps. As soon as he went to bed and shut his eyes, then *her* eyes, luminescent and full of wild magnificence, would spring up before him. Every waking minute, and every minute he tried in vain to go to sleep, all he had was Daliah on his mind. Daliah's eyes. Daliah's voice. Daliah's spirit. She was everywhere. She had him twisted up in knots. After thirty-seven hours of not having seen her, he was convinced that if he didn't go and see her immediately he was liable to go berserk. Finally, deciding that not seeing her would only compound his misery, he did the only sensible thing possible under the circumstances. He went to see her.

As usual, two guards were posted in front of her door. As was also usual, they had pulled up chairs, propped their weapons against the wall, and were listening to music on a tape deck while leafing through dog-eared back issues of *Playboy*. On duty were Haluk, a big pockmarked Egyptian, and Ahmed, the tense, wired little Syrian who looked like he'd really gotten into the music and was clicking his fingers crazily to the beat.

They looked up at him warily.

"Has she been giving you any problems?" Najib asked, maintaining a noncommittal tone.

Haluk, his eyes still on the unfolded centerfold, shrugged disinterestedly. Ahmed grinned at Najib, wiggled his eyebrows, and winked lewdly.

Najib's hand caught Ahmed's fatigue shirt and half-lifted him out of the chair. The little Arab lost the musical rhythm, his eyes glazed and fearful. He tried to grin ingratiatingly, but it came off unconvincingly.

"Do you want the key?" The slow-speaking, deliberate voice belonged to Haluk.

It defused the tension. Najib felt the mad anger rushing out of him. He flung Ahmed back and let him slide down into the chair. Nodding, he took the key from Haluk and inserted it in the keyhole. For the barest moment he hesitated, his hand pressing down on the huge sculptured handle. Then swiftly, as though he wanted to get it over with before he could change his mind, he turned the key and pushed the door open.

The first thing that hit him was the chill. She had the air conditioning turned up high, but otherwise, all was warmly feminine. The pink silk taffeta curtains were drawn tightly across the shuttered windows, relieving the bleak, dark view of the shutters, and the lamps were all lit, spilling soft pools of yellow light.

He could almost feel her nearness. The air was electrified with her presence. His blood rushed crazily through him, and beneath his robes his penis grew rock hard.

She was not in the living room.

He went into the bedroom.

The bed looked unslept-in; it was still flawlessly made, covered with the quilted pink silk spread. Quickly he looked around the room, at once feeling both alarm and wild hope that she had somehow managed to escape.

Then he saw her.

She looked anything but a hostage, slumped as she was casually in the fur-lined cocoon of a giant spherical fiberglass chair which looked like a hollowed-out pearlized pink egg. Her feet were bare, and she sat with one of them tucked under her. Her hair was loose and spilled down in a thick tangle over her shoulders, nearly to her waist, and her hands were tucked into the pockets of one of the Almoayyed wives' best Barguzinski sables. Of course, he thought; that was why the air conditioning was on full blast. To freeze her visitors out while she, wrapped up in fur, didn't feel a hint of discomfort.

Catching sight of him, Daliah raised her head aggressively. For an instant her face shone with a look of such pure steel that it could have killed; then, shrugging eloquently, as though he was not really worth the bother, she casually swiveled the chair around in the opposite direction, so that all he faced was the shiny pink fiberglass globe of the back of the egg-chair.

He felt the color rising to his face, and his cheeks prickled hotly. The unmitigated impudence! No woman had treated him so dismissively. Not ever!

The need to lash out prompted his tongue. "You bitch!" he said in an intense whisper.

A staccato laugh trilled from the other side of the chair. Angrily he strode toward it. Then, as though through a miracle of theatrical timing, she whirled the chair back around just as he was about to touch it. She stared up, and he had the sensation that her pupils expanded and her green eyes glowed pitch black. Then she laughed again, and they receded to green.

He took a deep breath. "I do not see anything to laugh at," he said with wounded dignity. "Perhaps if you find something funny, you would care to share the joke with me."

"Hmmm."

Finger poised on her lips, she twisted the well-oiled chair lazily back and forth in silent little arcs, so that he found himself alternately looking left, then right, then left again, like a spectator at a tennis match.

"You look tired." There was not a hint of sincere regret in her voice. "This little adventure seems to be wearying you." She eyed him slyly. "Maybe you should try to get some sleep."

He gestured at the chair, finding it impossible to focus his words at a constantly shifting target. "In the name of Allah," he said irritably. "Can you not be still for an instant?"

She raised her eyebrows. "Why?"

"This is not a game," he snapped. "It might be well for you to take this seriously."

"Of course this isn't a game," she sighed. "In case you've

forgotten, it wasn't *my* idea to be here. I didn't ask to come. Did I?" Still she swayed back and forth. "What do you expect me to do? Plead with you to let me go? Burst into tears? Beg for mercy on my knees?" She smiled. "You would like that, wouldn't you?"

He shook his head. "As a matter of fact, no," he said softly. "I wouldn't." His fists quivered at his sides, and he felt as awkward as he had felt two days earlier when he had first seen her downstairs in the foyer. Just as he had then, he was again convinced that it would have been better—far better all around—had he been able to shut his ears to that siren's call and stayed away. For some reason, she had the knack of reducing him to something gangly and all thumbs.

Her eyes never strayed from his. "Then let me ask you this: why are you here?"

"I only came by to see if you were comfortable," he said inadequately.

The chair stopped moving abruptly and she stared, her head tilted sideways, her eyebrows arched. "Would you care to repeat that?" She blinked rapidly. "You want to know if . . . if I am *comfortable*?"

He did not reply.

She began to roar with laughter. "I suppose the next thing you're going to ask is how I like it here." She swallowed her laughter. "But to answer your question, of course I'm comfortable. Any idiot could see that. Who wouldn't be in a cage of spun gold? I feel like the Queen of Sheba. The Maharani of Jaipur. The Begum Khan." She gestured expansively around the room. "Not happy, mind you, but comfortable. Now are you pleased?"

"If you need anything," he said stiffly, "just tell the guards and they will let me know."

She extended one splendid creamy leg and twisted her foot back and forth as though admiring her toenail polish from afar. She glanced up at him. "I suppose my telling you that what I need is my freedom won't cut any ice, will it?"

He smiled sadly. "I am afraid not. This is entirely beyond my control."

"Pity. I was always under the impression that you were so powerful." She made a face and then shrugged diffidently. "Oh, well, you can't win them all, I suppose. I know you would hate having to see me go. You see, I've been doing some thinking." She knit her brows together. "When you're locked up the way I have been, you have time to do nothing *but* think. And you end up thinking the craziest things." She paused. "Anyway, what I was thinking was . . . well, that I wish I had gone to the university and studied some psychology."

He raised his eyebrows. "Indeed?"

"Uh-huh. Because you see," she said in a serious tone, although her eyes were alight with laughter, "maybe then I could figure out why you can't stay away from me. Maybe then I'd know why you kissed me so savagely two days ago. It may come as a rude awakening to your overblown ego, but I'd really much rather be left alone. If I need you, I'll whistle."

"Then I shall leave you alone." He turned and began to stride toward the living-room door. He had almost reached it when she called out coyly in sugared tones, "Oh, Mr. al-Ameer?"

He turned around. She had uncoiled herself and gotten up out of the chair and was standing, her legs planted in a wide stance.

"Yes?" he said.

"Look."

She whipped off the fur.

He started. She was stark naked, and her body was astonishingly sleek, as streamlined as an Art Deco statuette. Her physical perfection was almost painful. Long coltish legs, generously curved hips, flat, taut stomach, conical breasts with dusty-rose areolae, as though color-coordinated to fit this apartment. From head to toe, she had all the makings of a thoroughbred.

Now the battle to keep himself under control began in earnest. "If I were you," he advised coldly, "I would think carefully before I did something like that. You are only asking for trouble. Do not forget where you are. In this country, for such behavior you could be stoned to death."

"Indeed." Her lips were bared across her teeth. "Well, then, why don't you stone me and get it over with?"

"Hurting women is not my habit."

"What is? Capturing them?"

Her taunts were starting to grate on him, and for a moment his anger was so overpowering that he almost lost control. Only through sheer willpower did he keep his rage subdued. "You may soon wish it were," he said darkly.

Then he sucked in his breath. She sashayed salaciously toward him, swinging her hips in a parody of Mae West.

He shut his eyes against the sight. It was not that he minded her nudity. What he found so offending was the inspired ugliness of the parody. The outrageousness of its obscenity. The way it reduced her exceptional one-in-a-billion quality to a level of the lowest street trash.

When she reached him, she stood before him, her hands resting on her cocked hips. "Am I embarrassing you?" she purred with a pout. "Hmmm?"

His eyes snapped open and the explosiveness within him ignited and flared. Suddenly he could stand it no longer. He stared at her with a crazed wildness. Explosions were shattering all around him.

As though in slow motion, the tip of her tongue licked her lips.

"Harlot!" he shouted, his hand flashing in a blur.

If she saw it coming, she made no move to avoid it. His palm cracked like a gunshot across her left cheek.

Wild things danced dervishes in his head as he watched her spin sideways, stagger backward, and fall to her knees. She deserved to suffer. Deserved to hurt.

She knelt there and slowly raised her head, looking straight up at him, not with anger, or loathing, or even surprise. The way she looked at him, despite her awkward position, was the way a woman looked when she owned the world.

"You know what?" she said softly, her voice suddenly devoid of mockery. "I pity you."

The genuine gentleness of her voice had the effect of oil tossed upon stormy waters. The explosions in his head stilled, and he could feel himself tremble as the world turned back to normal. For a long moment he did not move. Then, when the last shards of insanity evaporated, he reached down and pulled her to her feet.

He shook his head. "Perhaps you are right," he said tightly, holding on to her arm. "Perhaps I should be pitied."

She averted her gaze and started to pull away, but he held her fast.

His face was mere inches from hers. "You have every reason to hate me," he said. "I can accept that. What I cannot accept is your stupid game-playing."

"Who said they're games?" Now she raised her eyes to his, and before he knew what was happening, she brushed feathery fingertips across his face. He drew in his breath sharply. Her touch seared like a blowtorch, sent jolts of fire all the way down to his feet. Now it was he who wanted to pull away, but it was she who was holding tight. Her eyelids were half-lowered. "Am I making you nervous?"

"No!" he whispered fiercely, taking a staggering step backward. When she moved her hand up to his face again, he swiftly turned away. "Do not do that!" His voice was agonized, and a kind of torture glazed in his eyes.

She looked at him with genuine surprise. "You are afraid of me," she said softly. "What do you have to fear from me? What could I do to you?"

"Nothing . . ." Then his tortured voice cracked and he shook her off.

"Why do you look away? Are you afraid to look at me?" she said softly.

But he had already turned on his heel and was striding out, his white robes flowing. Before he could even shut the door, her reckless, taunting laughter followed him outside to the hall. Angrily he thrust the key at Haluk. "Lock it!" he ordered tightly.

Haluk stared at him, and Ahmed quickly averted his face to hide his grin. "I think the hellfire bitch has a soft spot," he murmured to Haluk out of the corner of his mouth.

Najib heard him and whirled. "Shut your camel's ass of a mouth before I stuff it full of dung!" he whispered. Then he hurried off blindly.

When he was around the corner and out of sight, he slumped against the marble wall and closed his eyes. Despite everything—her taunts, her mocking performance, even the way she had crashed through his defenses and fired his temper—despite all that, he could still feel the aching hardness beneath his robes.

He rubbed his eyes wearily. He didn't understand what was happening to him. It was almost as if their roles had reversed. Who, he asked himself, was really whose prisoner?

When he was gone, the real Daliah took over. She sank weakly down into the nearest chair and buried her face in her hands. She was emotionally drained. It had all been a performance—the most difficult performance she had ever given.

The bravado, the taunts, the laughter—they had all been one hell of an act.

In truth, she had never felt so scared and helpless in her life.

Long hours after he'd gone to bed, Najib stared blearily up at the dark ceiling. He was still awake. He'd tried everything—sleeping on his back, sleeping stretched out on his side, sleeping curled up in the fetal position, and finally, in desperation, even sleeping on his belly.

But nothing helped. Dead tired though he was, as soon as he shut his eyes, all he could picture were Daliah's eyes.

Cursing, he finally switched on the bedside lamp, got up, splashed some Napoleon brandy into a glass, and prowled the carpet restlessly, his body naked, the drink in hand.

He sipped and thought, sat and paced. He knew very well what his problem was, although he kept pushing it away, unwilling to admit it.

It was because of her. No matter how hard he tried, he just couldn't exorcise Daliah from his mind. Whether he was trying to sleep or moving about, all he could think of, hour in and hour out, the only thing that seemed significant to him anymore was her. Her. Her. Her. Daliah Boralevi had taken control of his life; she haunted his every hour and suddenly took precedence over all else.

Her old films, which he used to play and replay countless hundreds of times in order to nurture his hatred, and which he had memorized, scene by scene, were now having the exact opposite effect he'd intended. Each time he shut his eyes, the same thing would happen. Long-memorized scenes from her films would come rushing headlong toward him and flash past with a *whoosh!* like the headlights of traffic in an oncoming lane. They were Technicolor mental videos, and seemed even more vivid and real than they had on film. One after the other, the scenes rushed and jumped crazily: a flash of curved elbow; a curtain of ebony silk hair; shiny, moist teeth.

A rage of helplessness rushed through him, and crying out in despair, he flung his drink across the room and watched the silk-clad wall explode in a wet stain and the glass shatter and burst and rain down. Then he whirled around and pounded his fists against the wall again and again. "It's not fair!" he moaned. "It cannot *be!*" Then, his fists slowing in futility, he flattened himself, his forehead pressed against the wall, his raised hands slowly uncoiling, his fingers raking the silk. He was breathing heavily. Streaks of sweat were running down his forehead.

And still the Daliah scenes keep flashing in front of him. Daliah Boralevi was Helen of Troy, Cleopatra, and the Mona Lisa, all rolled into one.

She was also the spawn of the butchers who had slaughtered Iffat, one of the greedy hordes who had stolen Palestine from his people. Even worse, she was an infidel.

So? a tiny voice whispered in his mind. *She didn't kill Iffat, did she? She never hurt anybody. Did she?*

Shut up.

He clamped his mind shut against the persistent voice, but it kept creeping back in, whispering and taunting. *How could she have stolen Palestine? She was a baby back then. Babies are innocent.*

Shut up! Shut up!

She's an infidel only by Muslim standards, the sneaky little voice continued. *Sure, you're a Muslim, so it's easy to say she's an infidel. But Jews believe in only one God too. And according to both your religions, there is but one God—*

As if his anguish was not enough, he had that infernal voice attacking him now too, like a hammer chiseling away at the very bedrock of his foundation.

You want her.

You need her.

Shut up shut up shut up! his mind screamed silently.

The tortured hours crawled by interminably. The truth, when he finally gave in to it, seemed to cut off his oxygen, as though the air had been sucked out of the suite. *You've fallen for her,* the tiny voice in the back of his head whispered, *and you might as well come to terms with it.*

Violently he shook his head, damning that insistent tiny voice, and thrust the truth away. No, it simply could not be! Not her, anybody but her. How was it possible? What devious witchcraft had been played on him? But yes, *oh Allah be merciful*—he was in *love.*

He groaned aloud, clapped a hand to his forehead, and reeled drunkenly. *He was in love with his archenemy.*

He was in love with *her!* Of all the billions of women in the world, it was Daliah Boralevi—his sworn enemy.

He was in love with a Jew, a love that could never be.

The knowledge hit him like a physical blow; the force of it jerked his head with such overwhelming physical force that he flinched. For a moment he paced wildly, first in one direction, then the other. Finally he staggered over to the windows and yanked aside the white silk curtains.

His view faced east, and outside, the first gray of dawn was just beginning to pale the sky. As he watched, the sun began to do daily battle with the night. Then, suddenly, as can happen only in the desert, it slid victoriously up from under the edge of the world and its lemon-yellow explosion blasted the night to pieces with such intense speed and power that he had to shield his eyes against it.

And with the coming of light, his anguish melted away and a kind of wonderment came over his face. As suddenly as that desert sunrise, it came to him in a flash—*kaboom!* Out of the clear blue, lightning had struck—unfried his brains and thrown open the doors. The simplicity of the situation dazzled him.

Screw everything! He was in love, and love made its own rules, did it not? So she was Jewish. So he was supposed to hate her and her family. So Abdullah would try to squash him. So what?

For it was her that he loved, and if it had initially taken the seeds of hatred for love to germinate, it only went to show how powerful love could be. Even more important, if love could rise out of the embers of bleakness and destruction, then surely the poets were right and it could conquer all.

Nothing else mattered; he knew that now. What mattered was Daliah; her and nothing else. Even if it killed him, even if she would never be able to find it in her heart to forgive him for her imprisonment, even if she never spoke to him again, he would still show his love for her by extricating her from Abdullah's clutches.

He would let her go!

His eyes glowed. Everything inside him began to sing. For the first time in his life he was filled with a surge of pure, undiluted joy. It was so overpowering that he felt as if his feet had left the ground and he was floating upright in midair.

And to think he had never even known such a feeling could exist!

Then his burgeoning euphoria began to deflate.

What rot these emotions were! he thought, as gathering clouds of depression closed in. What use was love? In reality, he and she were worlds apart. Not only were they not compatible religiously and ethnically, but even if those gaps could be closed, that still left Abdullah to deal with. His half-uncle would never hear of such a union, let alone allow it to take place. Heads would roll—the heads of Najib al-Ameer and Daliah Boralevi, specifically.

He could feel the walls moving and closing in.

Abdullah's long-ago threat still echoed loud and clear. Should he ever be treacherous, not only would he die, but all his generations, past and present and future. He, his aging parents, who lived in the outskirts of Beirut, perhaps even Yasmin, the loveless wife he had once been married to. Everyone, every last man, woman, and child who shared his blood, all nieces and nephews and uncles and aunts—everyone, of course, but Abdullah himself!

He stared at the blinding sun, and like a thunderclap, another door was thrown wide open to dazzling light.

A world without the madness of Abdullah, a safer, saner world where his long-ago rash pledge of allegiance no longer held. . . .

The vision flashed and seized hold, and he could feel his excitement growing.

The storm clouds of depression were fleeing now. He knew what he had to do, and it was so simple, so elementary. It wasn't murder: it was a surgical procedure to cut out the deadliest and most dangerous cancer of them all, and if he had to be the surgeon, then so be it. The world would be a better place for it—the nerve center of a deadly terrorist cell would be removed once and for all; financial and armament conduits to terrorists worldwide would be plugged; there would be less killing, far fewer innocents wounded, fewer bombs and snipers and hijackings. Peace would be given, if not a real chance, then at least a better one.

A life free of the dark specter of his mad half-uncle.

A life with just slightly less hatred and violence.

Above all, a life in which he could live and love as he pleased, no puppet strings attached, no allegiances to a madman.

He took a deep breath and held it, the awesome scope of his vision just starting to sink in. The sun no longer seemed to scorch; it seemed to shine gloriously. For the first time in his life he had a warm feeling, however slight, that he had touched upon something good and greater than himself, something even possibly heroic.

Of course, it would require intricate planning, and he would have to be twice as cautious and crafty as he normally would be. Fingers trembling with excitement, he punched out a call to Newark, oblivious of the time difference, and caught Captain Childs just after he'd gone to sleep. "Bring the jet to Riyadh," Najib ordered, his excitement mounting steadily.

He was pacing again, but his steps had quickened and were purposeful.

Now that he had at last awakened from blindness to dazzling vision, his creative thoughts knew no bounds. Ideas, plans, and plots crowded his mind.

He would need the yacht, because it was equipped with a helipad and—more important—a long-range Bell Jet Ranger helicopter.

He eyed the telephone thoughtfully, and then made another call, this time to Monte Carlo, where his yacht occupied the prime berth just inside the stony arm of the breakwater.

Now he awakened Captain Delcroix from the middle of *his* sleep.

"Start the engines at daylight," Najib instructed the groggy man. "Bring the *Najah* at full steam through the Suez Canal, and anchor her along the coast of Oman."

From the coast to this palace was one hundred and eighty miles by air. Three hundred and sixty miles round trip would leave just enough range for the helicopter, which had been specially outfitted with long-range fuel tanks. The helicopter, he suspected, would come in handy.

But he wouldn't tell Daliah, he thought. Not yet. Not until everything was set to go and there was no turning back.

He flopped down on the sun-washed bed, put his arms under his head, and shut his eyes. He basked in the warmth and smiled. He had made up his mind and felt wonderful.

For that matter, he felt better than he remembered ever feeling.

He was going to help her escape, and would fight to overcome whatever odds stood in their way.

Perhaps by doing this he would prove to her that he truly loved her. Perhaps this way, too, he would find redemption for the pain and terror he had caused her.

It was then, at long, long last, with sunlight flooding the bed, that for the first time in days he drifted off into a deep, nourishing, and completely untortured sleep.

Like the pleasure dome of a latter-day odalisque, the enormous bed was piled high with as many books and magazines as Daliah had been able to find, the nightstand lamp glowed softly, a glass of water and the TV remote control were within easy reach, and the stereo played soft string music. "A Man and a Woman." "Lara's Theme." "Moon River."

Daliah lay there amid it all, the quilted pink silk covers pulled up to her chin, a black velvet sleep mask covering her eyes. She was still as a statue, but her breathing was irregular. She was wide-awake.

She'd tried counting sheep, counting backward from a hundred, chanting a silent mantra, and mentally numbing her body from the toes upward, just the way Toshi Ishagi had taught her. She'd leafed through the magazines and tried to start a book. Then she lay back, convinced that if nothing else worked, at least Mantovani would lullaby her to dreamland.

Well, he hadn't. All she had done for the last two hours was toss and turn and keep fluffing the down-filled pillows.

She sat up, whipped off the sleep mask, and flung it aside. She pounded the bed with a fist.

It was just . . . no . . . good. None of the sleep remedies worked. No matter how she yearned to blank out her mind and welcome sleep, the maddeningly persistent images of Najib al-Ameer—of all people—kept jumping into her mind. Najib al-Ameer, the prick to end all pricks, the schmuck who outschmucked all the world's greatest schmucks, the A-rab criminal who she *knew* had gotten her into this life-threatening situation in the first place—*may he be drawn and quartered, and then rot and fry slowly in hell for eternity!*—she'd tried everything to banish him from her mind. She had even gone so far as to fantasize suitable fates for him—dismemberment in a horrible accident; crippling spinal-cord injuries; advanced leprosy; castration, which sounded especially appealing. When that still didn't put him out of her mind, she tried to kill him mentally, imagining herself as some kind of mad operatic Medea. In her mind she stabbed him, shot him, clubbed him, electrocuted him—she tried every method of murder she could think of, the more macabre the better—including the use of an electric knife, a steam iron, and a blowtorch. But the vision of him survived all these mental onslaughts intact, and persisted as a healthy whole—which only made her crosser and crosser.

Finally, her nerves still strung as taut as steel springs, she abruptly flung back the covers, swung her legs out over the bed, and jumped to her feet. Her nerves were so shredded that her hands were actually shaking. Then she sank down onto the edge of the bed and rubbed her eyes with the palm of her hand. She had to get control of herself. Otherwise, if she wasn't careful, she was soon going to find herself going off the deep end. Her mood swings had been fluctuating too radically, from deepest despair all the way up to the peaks of anger.

It was so unlike her. So disturbing.

What was happening to her?

The night crawled on and on.

Sleep, she thought yearningly. If only she could sleep, then she would at least stop thinking about him for a few blessed hours! How marvelous that would be.

She climbed back into bed, pulled the covers up over her, and shut her eyes.

But she remained awake for hours longer.

She had never felt such torture, such anger, such extreme helplessness.

He, her enemy, had taken up residence in her mind and wouldn't let himself be evicted.

Damn!

As if she were not in enough trouble with the kidnapping, now she had to deal with the voices of her heart as well—voices of emotional turmoil and anguish-causing confusion. Hour in, hour out, there he was, springing up before her, his predatory eyes staring hotly, probing, always probing deeper within her, as though trying to penetrate to some secret spot.

She was in—

Hastily she slammed a door in her mind.

That was one thing she couldn't face. Not the misguided desires she felt for him. It was too perverse to even consider. Perhaps, she thought hopefully, once she got out of this wretched place and far away from him, then he would be not only out of sight but also out of her mind. Maybe then she would be able to forget him. He couldn't, after all, have really reached that far down inside her, all the way to the center of her soul?

Could he?

Finally, just before dawn, she drifted into a shallow, uneasy doze.

And dreamed, of course, of him—who else? In the dream he had captured her in his arms and was holding her in a steel-and-sinew embrace, such a real embrace of supercharged flesh that she felt his heat and could hear the rapid beating of his heart.

He felt hot and hard and deliciously moist—

With a start, she awoke in a cold sweat. Her forehead pounded. Her pulse raced. She lay there confused and shaking, filled with shame and bitter self-loathing. The dream had seemed all too real, and she felt soiled by it, as though she'd been violated, somehow raped. How could she even dream such a thing?

But why, the little voice in her mind whispered slyly, why, if she really hated him so much, did her heart burn with the treasonous flames of desire?

She raked a hand wildly through her hair. *Why him? Oh damn damn damn, why him?*

She struggled to sit up and it was then that she was truly appalled with herself. The dream had seemed so real, so passion-filled, that she had actually reacted physically.

Her thighs were sticky.

Dumbly she reached down and felt the seeping moistness between her legs. For an instant she was frozen with horror. Then she lunged wildly from the bed and looked around like a madwoman. The first object to come to hand was a heavy crystal cigarette box.

Her pulse tripped furiously. Her blood boiled so wildly she could hear it crashing in her ears.

In a rage of overpowering frustration, and needing to hurt someone—him . . . *anything*—she aimed it at a priceless Venetian mirror which gleamed, one of a pair, frostily on a pink suede wall.

She flung it with all her might.

The instant it hit, the mottled antique mirror exploded into a cobweb of cracks, and a corner of the baroque frame broke off as though in slow motion and fell soundlessly to the carpet.

Then, for the first time since her capture, she sank to her knees, bowed her head to the carpet as though in supplication, and wept.

Fifteen hours later and 375 miles to the north, Najib's Boeing 727–100 touched down in Riyadh.

The prospect of holding a press conference was daunting for all of them, but for Tamara in particular it had all the makings of a nightmare. Because of Daliah's fame, she knew that even without her own presence it would be a worldwide event; with it, it would become a three-ring circus. Dani told her she didn't really have to attend, but she disagreed. "I'm Daliah's mother," she'd told him flatly. "I have to be there, Dani. You know it, and I know it." And she had seen the relief deep in Dani's eyes, and knew why it was there. In order to get the kind of news coverage they sought, the long-retired platinum-blond box-office star of the 1930's was the carrot being dangled in front of the press.

She knew this was every journalist's dream story. It had all the ingredients necessary for selling papers and filling airtime—crime, mystery, and no less than *two* famous movie stars, one of whom was a virtual recluse. From this day forward until long after the kidnapping was over, the media were going to have a field day, and for as long as they could, the press lords would keep this story alive, fanning it furiously until every last ember winked out. It didn't take much imagination to visualize the sensational headlines that would roll off the presses that evening:

FAMOUS MOVIE STAR KIDNAPPED. FILM-STAR RECLUSE FACES CAMERAS AFTER 40 YEARS. ISRAELI HERO'S GRANDDAUGHTER MISSING. FAMOUS FAMILY IN SHOCK.

That in itself would have been bad enough to have to deal with, but even more reprehensible to Tamara than the publicity was the idea of having to share the family's grief with the public. After retiring from Hollywood, she had struggled fiercely to surround herself and her family with a virtually impenetrable wall of privacy, but now the defenses would come tumbling down, with friends, neighbors, acquaintances, costars of both Daliah and herself, and forgotten people from over the years crawling out of the woodwork to be interviewed. Not a single aspect of their private lives was going to be left untouched.

The conference was to be held out front, in the sealed-off parking lot of the big apartment building, and was scheduled for eleven o'clock in the morning. By seven-thirty, when Tamara first went out on the balcony with a cup of coffee, she was shocked to find that the media people were already gathering like a flock of hungry vultures, and from eight o'clock on, the cluster of microphones being set up outside just grew and grew. It took three policemen and one agent from the Shin Bet to keep the reporters from entering the building, and even so, three of them managed to sneak in by pretending to be tenants. Finally, all four entrances to the building were blocked off by uniformed police.

By nine o'clock the news media's vans and cars were double-parked up and down Hayarkon Street, and more were arriving by the minute. To make matters worse, sidewalk vendors, attracted by the prospect of doing a brisk business, were pushing their carts into position.

It had all the air of a festive carnival. The only thing missing was the band. By then, Tamara had resigned herself. Before long, she knew, crowds of passersby and people from the neighboring buildings would be drawn by curiosity and the crowd would swell enormously.

Tamara paced the long living room, which they'd created four years earlier by buying the apartment next door and knocking through the walls, tracing and retracing the same steps over and over, from the country French pine table above which hung her treasured jewellike Matisse, to the far alcove, with its book-lined shelves, her hands clasped in front of her waist, her head bowed and furrowed.

She kept thinking about Daliah. Though she claimed to love Ari equally, deep in her heart she knew better. Daliah had always been her favorite. Much as she loved Ari, he took after Dani. But Daliah had inherited that dangerous spark of independence which had once been her own hallmark, and had gone out into the world, prepared to take it by storm, just as she herself had once done. Everything that had burned within her now burned within Daliah. All Tamara had ever wanted for her children was to protect them from the terrors of the world. It was such a useless wish; what had happened to Asa and Daliah proved that. Wishes were fairy tales, and reality could always be counted upon to shatter them.

Dani went over to her and she slipped into his arms and stood on tiptoe to embrace him. "Don't look so frightened," he said gently.

She looked up at him wide-eyed, and then nodded toward the window. "It's a circus down there, Dani," she whispered shakily.

"They're only here to help."

"Are they?" she asked sharply, hysteria creeping into her voice.

The doorbell rang just then, shrill and shocking, and they jerked apart and turned toward the foyer. "They're getting impatient," she said worriedly.

Schmarya came out of the kitchen, for once limping noticeably. The ordeal was taking its toll on them all, Tamara thought.

"I'll go downstairs," the old man said gruffly, "and tell them to hold their horses." He limped out and snap-locked the door behind him.

She stared after him. It was the first time she'd seen him wearing his yarmulke around the house. She had been wondering what he was doing in the kitchen, and now she knew. He'd been praying.

She moved over to the windows and parted the curtains a crack. Four stories below, Schmarya was raising his hands for silence and shaking his head. After a moment he turned to a policeman, had a brief conversation during which he gesticulated a lot, and then pointed to the lobby doors. After more gesticulating, he went inside the building again.

When Tamara heard him unlock the door, she advanced toward him, a questioning look on her face.

"They're impatient," Schmarya grumbled, "but I got them to wait. We said eleven o'clock, and eleven o'clock it will be. I don't think they'll be ringing the bell again," he said with a touch of satisfaction, and lumbered back into the kitchen, his limp even more pronounced.

At a quarter to eleven, Tamara went into the bedroom. Dani stopped her. He looked at her with concern. "Where are you going?"

She looked surprised. "Why, to put on some makeup and change, of course." She gestured at herself. "I can't face the cameras looking like this."

He had to smile. "Like Swanson in *Sunset Boulevard*? Facing the cameras again at long last?"

658

She didn't attempt even a ghost of a smile, and he realized his mistake at once; this was no time for jokes. "I'm sorry," he said lamely.

"Don't be," she said. "I'm only getting dolled up to get the reporters on our side. I think they and the public will take more interest in this case if I give them what they want."

He looked at her with renewed respect. Always, her instincts were right on the mark.

He kissed her cheek. "Go put on a drop-dead face," he said gently.

She nodded. "I shan't be long."

And she wasn't. When she came back out, she looked like a new person. Her wrinkles were smooth, filled with expensive creams and lotions, and her pallor was hidden by a thin, unnoticeable layer of blusher. Of course, the strain still showed, but it was controlled and toned down, and that was not only the result of cosmetics. The Tamara who had gone into the bedroom had looked defeated and disheveled, but the one who came out ten minutes later was groomed, composed, and dignified. She had put on her best suit for the occasion a cream-colored Chanel with navy piping, three strands of giant faux pearls, and an elegant white straw hat.

"You look beautiful," Dani said.

She was carrying his good summer-suit jacket, and she held it as he slipped his arms into the sleeves. Then, turning, she fastened the middle button and adjusted the handkerchief in the breast pocket. "There." Her smile was strained but generous. "You look very debon—"

Startled, she broke off and raised her eyebrows: the clock had started to chime eleven o'clock.

Schmarya limped out of the kitchen, mumbling gruffly under his breath.

"Ready?" Dani looked from one of them to the other.

Tamara looked at Schmarya. "Father?"

"I'm as ready as I'll ever be."

Tamara looked at Dani questioningly. "The prepared statement?"

"I have it right here." He felt the inside pocket of his jacket. "A box of copies to hand out is downstairs by the front door."

She thrust her chin out determinedly, but there was a feverish glitter in her eyes. "Well, then," she said with forced lightness, "let's go break a leg. And remember, no tears, no show of misery. We're going to come off dignified and controlled . . ." Her voice wobbled and she whispered, "Let's get it over with."

They went out into the stairwell and hooked arms, so that she was in the center, and they went downstairs that way, showing a united front and drawing strength from one another.

As soon as they made their appearance, the camera shutters clicked in unison and the reporters surged forward. Dani felt Tamara going rigid, but he and Schmarya managed to shield her as they pushed through the crush. Focusing a blank stare just above the crowd's heads and ignoring the babble of shouted questions, they headed toward the forest of microphones in the parking lot. The police linked arms, holding everyone back.

It's like a damn premiere, Tamara thought. If someone thrusts an autograph book at me, I'm going to scream.

Dani leaned into the microphones. "First, I would like to read a prepared statement," he said levelly. "Afterward there will be time to answer your individual questions. If you'll please hold them until then . . ."

He looked down at the paper and read it verbatim, his voice never wavering. "Ladies and gentlemen of the press. It is with heavy hearts that we inform you that our daughter, the actress Daliah Boralevi, is missing, and presumed kidnapped." There was a flurry of movements and gasps, and he held up a hand to silence them. "She arrived at Ben-Gurion Airport two days ago on El Al flight 1002, and was intercepted by a person or persons unknown. There have been no ransom demands, and the police and the Shin Bet are investigating. It is believed that her disappearance may be tied into the murder of Elie Levin, an El Al customer-service representative. . . ."

Tamara looked at him as he continued to give out the prepared bits and pieces of information, along with the new listed telephone number and the number of the police. She marveled that he seemed so in control. It was impossible to guess that he was a man near the breaking point. He had pulled himself together for the cameras and was giving it his all.

"Thank you, ladies and gentlemen," Dani was saying. "Before you leave, the policeman in the lobby has copies of this statement, which he will distribute to all of you. Now, if you have any questions—"

He got that far before pandemonium set in. The barrage of hurled questions was such an incoherent babble that it was impossible to hear a single one.

Dani looked at Tamara, and she nodded. Drawing a deep

breath, she stepped forward. Miraculously, the reporters fell silent.

"Ladies and gentlemen," she said softly in that unforgettable screen voice, "I don't think I need to introduce myself."

She looked around, and there were appreciative chuckles. Her own wry smile let them know that she appreciated their response.

"All I have to add is that I am not here as an ex-film star. I am here as an ordinary mother. Daliah is my daughter," she continued, her voice quivering with controlled emotion, "and as any mother would be under these circumstances, I am worried sick. I beg of you, ask your readers and television watchers, if any of them has any information, anything at all, no matter how trivial it might seem, to please, *please* contact us or the police. Our telephone is manned around the clock, and anything anyone can tell us will be held in strictest confidence. We have put up a reward of fifty thousand U.S. dollars to anyone who can give us information leading to Daliah's release, no questions asked." She paused. "We'll be forever grateful for your help in disseminating this message." Her lips trembled and she dabbed at an eye with her fingertips. "Thank you."

And then the questions began anew. As expected, they were all directed at Tamara.

Fighting to keep her voice steady, she answered as best she could:

"No, I'm afraid we have no idea who could have done this. . . . No, she has no enemies as far as we know. . . . Yes, sometimes I do worry about the price of fame. There are a lot of unstable people out there, and being so recognizable . . . But I don't honestly think it could have been a demented fan. Fans would never . . . No, we have no idea at all . . ."

As Dani watched her, a feeling of amazement held him in thrall. The flush of her nervousness had brought a glowing color to her face, and her constantly shifting eyes caused them to gleam with the lively brightness he knew would be caught so well on film. Even in distress and advancing age, during this, what was probably the single most painful moment in her entire life, she shone as photogenically as she had at the height of her fame.

"Of course, we never expected anything like this, otherwise we would have had bodyguards. But they're such a violation of one's privacy. And as I said, we truly never expected anything like this to happen. But then, who does?"

Dani's amazement grew. Tamara was still obviously under

severe stress, but some of her tension was melting away. The reporters and photographers were actually respectfully giving her time to think before replying to their questions. They even began to behave more civilly to each other. A lot of their pushing and shoving had stopped.

TAMARA TAMES THE PRESS, Dani mentally headlined it.

"It goes without saying that we'll do everything within our power for Daliah's return," Tamara was saying. "They could even trade her for me, although I'm not so sure they'd be crazy about an old woman."

Dani exchanged glances with Schmarya, and it was then that he knew he was not imagining it. Tamara was wrapping the reporters around her little finger.

"Once she's back?" Tamara asked. "I couldn't advise her to stay out of the public eye, could I? I mean, that's her job, just as it was once mine. Is there a reporter among you who would refuse a job simply on the grounds that it was dangerous?" Her eyes roved over them. "No, I expect not. So, yes, I'd advise her to live her life as she has been doing."

Tamara kept up her dignified monologue, making sure every last reporter got to ask a question. She spoke to them as though they were friends. The hysteria which had crept into her voice upstairs was completely gone.

By God, Dani thought wonderingly, she's playing a role! Creating the character as she improvises the script.

"What advice would I give her if she watches this broadcast?" Tamara paused, waited for two inaudible drumbeats, and with flawless theatrical timing grinned and said, "If you can't think of any other way to get away, then kick 'em where it really hurts!" She gave a little nod of a bow. "Thank you, ladies and gentlemen."

There was absolute silence.

Lowering her head, Tamara stepped back from the microphones, hooked her arms swiftly through Dani's and Schmarya's, and together they made a hasty but dignified exit.

Once they were indoors, Dani shook his head in disbelief. He stared at his wife. She had been magnificent. Instead of presenting the usual teary-eyed, sniffling visage of a worried mother, Tamara had seemed as strong as the proverbial rock. And yet there hadn't been a person out there who couldn't see that beneath the veneer of wan humor and dignity, the fear and worry were all-consuming.

Through sheer acting, she had brought it off.

Her star quality had shone through.

Only after they got upstairs did the veneer crack. It was as though the press conference had removed any vestige of hope that the kidnapping was only a nightmare.

Tamara sank into a chair and wept.

The Almoayyed palace was equipped with all the latest in telecommunications technology, and television programs from around the world could be snatched from the airwaves via the satellite dish perched atop one of the outbuildings.

Ever since his arrival, Najib had made it a point to catch the news broadcasts several times each day, and depending on the time of day, he watched the German, Israeli, American, British, and Saudi reports. He knew it would be only a matter of time before Daliah's kidnapping would be reported, and when it was, he wanted to know immediately—and exactly—what was being said about it.

In truth, he had been both relieved and disappointed when, two days after the event, there had still been no word of it. Surely, he thought, she must have been reported missing already. A person of her public stature could not disappear into thin air without a hue and cry. The authorities had to be out scouring Israel for her. Of course, they could be searching clandestinely, and since no one had stepped forward to claim responsibility, and no ransom had yet been demanded, perhaps a quiet, unpublicized search was preferable.

In a way, he himself preferred the lack of news. At least this way Abdullah was not going to be pressured into making any rash, regrettable decisions.

But now all that suddenly changed.

Although Najib had been prepared for it to happen sooner or later, the announcement of Daliah's kidnapping, when it came, gave him a shock. The story broke first on one of the American networks.

One moment, the New York CBS TV News lead-in had filled the screen, and the next, the picture abruptly switched to the anchor desk and the camera came in for a tight close-up of the handsome, boyish-faced anchorman.

"Good evening," the professional clipped voice began. "This is the CBS evening news, Norb Severt reporting. Is it more terrorism, or is it private criminal elements at work? That is the puzzle facing Israeli police as the presumed kidnapping of actress Daliah Boralevi—"

It was as if Najib had been zapped. His face went rigid and he could feel the hair at the nape of his neck standing out. There was something so surreal about hearing the news of her kidnapping—especially with her being held at the other end of the palace—that he missed most of the first portion of the broadcast. It seemed to rush in one ear and back out the other without making any sense.

"Miss Boralevi's mother, the film star Tamara, broke her customary silence to the press and pleaded for help on her daughter's behalf."

The videotape of the Tel Aviv press conference was blurry and slightly jumpy. Najib sat forward, his eyes glued to the screen. The film showed the former film queen, flanked by two men, being hurried toward a cluster of microphones. The next picture was a close-up of her face in front of the microphones. He noticed just the faintest shadows under her eyes, and her hair wasn't as dazzling as it had been during her movie days, but other than that, she looked much the same. More mature, of course, but there was do denying her beauty. She wasn't smiling, but a kind of radiance lit her face from within. Her voice was deceptively gentle and controlled.

"No, there have been no demands yet," Tamara was saying carefully, enunciating each word clearly. "We're worried sick, all of us. We're also saddened for the family of Elie Levin."

Abruptly the picture changed to a black-and-white still of a clean-cut man in his early thirties, and the anchorman's voice-over explained, "Elie Levin was the El Al VIP employee scheduled to meet Miss Boralevi's flight."

The picture then changed to a black-and-white police photo of a sprawled body.

"According to Israeli police, the autopsy shows that Mr. Levin suffered a broken neck. Apparently one of Miss Boralevi's abductors then met her at the gate. Here in New York, Patsy Lipschitz, Miss Boralevi's agent, perhaps best summed up the anger and frustration of the friends and families of all kidnap victims."

The face of a huge Shelley Winters lookalike, with the same brownish-blond tight curls, filled the screen. "It's an outrage, you know? One moment the world's fine and the sun's shining, and the next you don't know what the hell's going on!"

The camera switched back to the anchorman. "To repeat, at the head of the news tonight, Daliah Boralevi, world-famous screen star, is presumed kidnapped in Israel. . . . In other world events, the military government in—"

Najib pointed the remote control at the television set and flicked the Off button.

For once, he felt curiously ambivalent, as though not

quite certain what to think. Good, bad; he had no inkling what effect the broadcast would have. On the one hand, the press conference had been a brilliant concept. He didn't doubt that summer tourists who had been at Ben-Gurion Airport the day Daliah had been kidnapped were going to start remembering little things they had seen and given no heed, and connect them with the kidnapping. The police were soon going to start getting definite leads. In that way, the press conference had probably been a very smart move.

On the other hand, he was afraid that it could have dire consequences for Daliah. It was just possible that the news might frighten Abdullah into moving her to another spot—a place perhaps even Najib himself wouldn't know of. Or his half-uncle might work himself up into one of his famous rages and order her killed on the spot.

But worst of all, the press conference could easily throw a wrench into his own plan for Daliah's escape.

He stood in the center of the room, his face stony, his hands on his hips.

For once, he just didn't know what to think.

Some twelve hundred miles northwest, the telephones were starting to ring off the hook.

"I strongly advise against answering the phones yourselves," Dov Cohen of the Shin Bet had told them emphatically. He was a big man of about forty, with shoulders too wide for his suit jacket, and a face of chiseled granite. There was something eminently comforting about his massive size and intelligent eyes. "Our men are trained to handle situations such as this. While I can understand your wanting to—"

"Please, Mr. Cohen," Tamara had interrupted smoothly, rising fluidly from the wing chair. "It's important to us that we do something."

He gave her a long look. "You'll wish you hadn't," he warned her. "There's no telling the kind of creeps who are liable to call. Just in case you change your mind, I'll leave two men on duty here, and another shift will take over in the morning. Meanwhile, I'll stay on a few more hours myself."

"Thank you." Tamara tried to smile, and watched him sit down and slide a pair of headphones over his ears. Just then the telephone shrilled. "Wait!" she called out. She raced to the extension just as Dani pressed the Record button to activate the tape deck of the main line. Holding his hand on the vibrating receiver, he nodded across the room to her. She nodded back and they both lifted their receivers in unison.

"Hello," Dani said, forcing his voice to sound normal. "This is Dani ben Yaacov speaking."

"I'm calling about the ransom," a rough voice growled.

Dani's heart seemed to check, miss a beat, and then race furiously. He caught Tamara's eye. She was staring across the room at him.

"Who are you?" she asked tightly.

"Never mind who I am!" The voice was threatening. "Just listen carefully. I want one million U.S. dollars in twenties. Got that?"

"Yes." Dani gripped the receiver with both hands.

"Put the money in a suitcase and take it to the General Post Office. Just inside the Jaffa Road entrance there's a garbage can. You can't miss it. Put the suitcase in the can and leave. You have until noon tomorrow!"

"How do we know she's—"

"Just do it!" the voice snarled. "And come alone. If we see policemen, she'll be killed."

"How do I— Hello! *Hello!*" Desperately Dani rattled the cradle, but the connection was broken.

With shaking hands he replaced the receiver and turned to Dov Cohen.

"I don't know," the big man said dubiously with a shrug. "It could well be a crank."

Dani's face burned angrily. "Don't you think we should be collecting the money alrea—"

"No. We wait." Dov Cohen's expression was grim and his eyes flinty. "You can't hand over a million dollars to any Abe, Dave, or Moishe who calls. If they're for real, they'll call back. When they do, they'll have to prove they've got Daliah, and that she's alive. Otherwise, it's a no go."

"Hello. This is Dani ben Yaacov speaking."

"You're the ones looking for Daliah Boralevi?" a stranger's voice asked.

Dani could feel a steel band constricting his chest. "Yes," he said tightly. "Do you have any information?"

"I know where she is."

Dani's hands tightened on the receiver. "Can you tell me where?"

"They've got her."

"They? Who is 'they'?"

The voice turned whispery. "You know, the green men. The ones in the UFO. They've taken her away to their planet."

He heard the crackle and click as the connection was broken.

The caller had hung up.

"Damn!" Dani shut his eyes and flung the receiver into the cradle.

Dov Cohen stretched out his hands, palms up, and looked beseechingly up at the ceiling. "God help us," he muttered. "This should never have been publicized. It was begging to hear from all the crazies."

"Hello. This is Dani ben Yaacov speaking."

"I saw the press conference on television," a woman's voice gushed with barely suppressed excitement. "Is this the right number to call?"

"Yes, do you have any information?"

"I have to talk to Tamara. I won't tell it to anyone else."

"I'm sorry, but she isn't available. Can I take your information?"

"No! I will only tell her."

He sighed and looked questioningly across the room. Tamara nodded.

"Hello," she said pleasantly. "This is Tamara."

The gushing voice turned into a shrill, thunderous shriek. *Just because you're rich and famous you can beg for help on TV! Well, what about us regular people? When my daughter was sick and I had no money, the doctors didn't give me the time of day, and she died! I hope Daliah dies too! If she doesn't, I'm going to kill her myself!"*

Tamara dropped the receiver and shrank back in wide-eyed horror. The room was spinning wildly around her.

"Darling, darling." Dani was at her side, cradling her head and rocking her back and forth. "Forget it, darling, try to forget . . ."

"Oh, Dani, Dani," she moaned. Suddenly she felt overwhelmingly tired and defeated. "How can people be so awful?" She looked searchingly up at him. "Maybe Mr. Cohen is right. Maybe it's best if we let the Shin Bet answer the calls." She shuddered and clung to him. "Let's go to bed, Dani. It's been a long day."

He nodded and pulled her to her feet. "Too long," he sighed, holding her tightly. His cheeks tensed. "I have a feeling that the only thing the news conference has accomplished has been to open Pandora's box."

The water sluiced off him as Najib pulled himself out of the swimming pool and threw himself down on the umbrella-

667

shaded chaise. The heat already felt as if the sun had sucked all the oxygen from the air, even though it was not yet nine-thirty in the morning. He was filled with a pantherlike tenseness and a need to flex his muscles, and yet he was weary; he felt heady with the excitement of outmaneuvering Abdullah and causing his downfall, and yet he felt curiously remote from Abdullah already. He was as thrilled as a chess player who has made a series of moves, each one brilliant in and of itself, that he believes good enough to determine the final outcome of the game. The battle for which he was preparing still loomed distantly, and there were many problems to work out before the first salvo was fired.

One of them in particular seemed insurmountable.

He had to get through to Schmarya Boralevi or Dani ben Yaacov, but he couldn't do it through ordinary channels. Certainly he couldn't simply pick up the phone and dial long distance from the palace; he wouldn't put it past Abdullah to have all telephone calls, both incoming and outgoing, monitored or taped. Nor could he fly to Israel without arousing undue attention. His arrivals and departures anywhere in the world were invariably reported in the press. Fame had its advantages, but it had severe disadvantages too.

He mulled over the problem. He *could*, of course, call them from elsewhere—even from his plane in midair. But since the press conference, Daliah's family was probably being buried under an avalanche of crank calls, and every call would require careful scrutiny—a process too slow and dangerous to suit him. He had to cut through all the red tape. What he needed was something of Daliah's which they would instantly recognize, irrefutable proof that his was a serious call. Furthermore, since he couldn't meet them in Israel and he had to speak to one of them in person, whatever he used to lure their attention had to be something impressive enough to get them to leave Israel and meet him elsewhere—a remote spot in Greece perhaps, or someplace on Cyprus.

If only he had something of hers! A driver's license or a passport . . . even an identifiable piece of jewelry.

But she had arrived in bedouin clothes, empty-handed, and everything had been taken from her. He couldn't just walk up to Khalid and ask to borrow a ring of hers, or her passport.

There had to be *something. . . .*

And then an idea came to him. Grabbing his towel and staying as much as possible in the cooling shadows, he made his way back uphill to the palace and went straight to his suite. He searched the various closets and drawers for twenty minutes before he found what he was looking for.

A Polaroid camera.

He would simply take her picture. Then he would summon his jet, give the picture to Captain Childs, and have him deliver it personally. Meanwhile, he needed to find some film.

It took another fifteen minutes of searching.

He loaded the camera, tested it, and smiled.

It's strange how everything's working out, he thought. Each time I run across a problem, the solution pops up. Now, if only that keeps up . . .

After slipping on a pair of slacks and a shirt, and steeling himself for a confrontation of fire and ice, he headed straight to her suite.

"Where are your robes?"

Najib looked at her and blinked in surprise. Her words and expressions were absolutely level, normal, and without spite. There was no fire and no ice, and even her slight frown seemed absolutely genuine.

"In certain classes of Arab society, the men often wear Western dress," he explained, "and the women even Paris couture. Behind closed doors, of course. I thought you knew that."

She glanced at his beautifully tailored Sulka shirt, open at the collar, and his dark Milan-tailored slacks. "In other words, the last two times when you wore your sheik get-up . . . that was for my benefit."

He smiled slightly. "Those were no sheik's robes, I'm afraid. They were very average."

"I see." She looked at him doubtfully and then, catching sight of the peculiarly gentle look in his eyes, she swiftly turned away in agitation and focused her attention on the expensive bric-a-brac on a sideboard. She rearranged the circular Japanese ivory boxes, nine amber glass balls, Indian ivory goblets, barley-twist candlesticks, and miniature globes. "I . . . I wish you'd go away now." Her voice quivered huskily.

His expression was almost loving, but inside, his heartbeats came in quick succession. He felt the overwhelming need to try to explain everything to her, to make her understand that he had no wish to see her come to harm, that he had not wanted to go through with this mad scheme; that the vow of vengeance he had sworn so long ago had ceased to be of any importance to him, and that he, like her, was a prisoner trapped in the webs of the past. Above all, he felt the surging urge to let her know that somehow, even if he had to move heaven and hell to achieve it, he was going to get her out of this mess.

He actually opened his mouth to speak, but the words would not come, and he was glad they hadn't. They would have sounded so inadequate in light of what she was going through.

He watched her with a growing sadness as she kept moving the *objets* around. She was so close—just a few steps away. And yet they might as well have been light-years apart.

If only she would understand . . .

"I need your help," he said softly.

She stopped her aimless rearranging and stood stock-still.

"Please, I'm not going to hurt you." He took a step toward her and then checked himself. If he got too close, he might frighten or anger her. There were too many barricades between them as it was; the last thing they needed was another. "Please," he said again in a low voice.

He could see her unfreeze and sigh, the striped cotton caftan moving slightly with each deep intake of breath.

"Daliah," he began, "if you ju—" Abruptly he clamped his mouth shut with an audible snap. He had never called her by her first name, and the fact that it had slipped out so unexpectedly and unconsciously startled him as much as it did her. He could see her jerk painfully at the sound of her name, and then her shoulders squared under the caftan. She whirled around so swiftly that a curtain of hair swung across her face. She raked it apart with slashes of her talons, and he took an involuntary step backward. She was the hellfire bitch again, and her rage was monstrous.

It was demonic, this rage, all the more so as it had come without warning. For a moment he had almost believed that she was human and rational, that he could reason with her. The next, the she-devil within her had taken control.

Her mouth curled down with loathing and her eyes blazed with white fire. "Get *out*!" she shouted.

He drew back slightly. "This will take but a minute," he said quietly. He lifted the camera to his eye and peered through the view finder.

"Don't you understand?" she roared. "I don't want to see you!"

He stepped closer to frame her in the picture, pressed the button, and waited for the built-in light meter to adjust to the room's dimness. Suddenly the flash exploded in blue and the mechanism whirred, feeding out the blank, milky picture.

"You bastard!" She flung herself at him, her fingernails slashing wildly. "How dare you do that?" Her slaps rained against his left cheek, his right, his left again. "Leave me alone leave me alone leave me *alone!*"

"Daliah . . ."

"How *dare* you call me by my first name! Filth! *Pig!*" She smacked him again and again.

Najib did not move. He stood there frozen, stoically holding the camera in one hand, the undeveloped picture in the other, while his head swiveled from side to side with each stinging slap.

"Hurt, dammit!" she panted. "*Hurt!* Why don't you cry or moan or at least try to defend yourself, you *bastard!*" Her mouth sprayed spittle, the tears streaked down her face, and her slaps grew even wilder.

"Stop it."

The deceptively soft note in his voice held such an undercurrent of menace that her hand froze in midair, and the slap for which it was poised never came. She stared at him with a sudden stab of cold fear. His face, which had been a stiff, immovable mask, seemed to have changed expression and darkened, as though a powerful storm was flashing and rolling just beneath his skin.

The fight drained out of her as his charged sexual tension transferred itself to her. Her raised arm dropped weakly to her side.

Under the caftan, she felt her sticky wetness trickling down the inside of her thighs. Her brow furrowed in confusion. A moment before, all she had felt was anger, and now it was replaced by an overt sexuality of such force that she could barely control it.

Danger signals clanged in her head, and the air was hot and alive, crackling with peril, as though a thousand lethal rattlers were coiled on the carpet all around her.

She felt her legs begin to tremble. What was wrong with her? She couldn't understand what was happening. Never before had such a torrent risen within her. It wasn't as if she consciously wanted him. Why, then, had her awareness of him as a man become so overwhelmingly heightened? She stared at him. He was tall and strong and stood proud, and she could sense the rippling of his muscles beneath his shirt and the swelling of his manhood within his trousers. The room seemed to tilt and recede. The strength and power of him was all that she noticed, and a hunger of wanting such as she had never before known surged up in her. The heat within her was almost unbearable. Her heart pounded like wildly hammering jungle drums. A building pressure clogged her ears, muffling all sounds except her own heartbeat. Without realizing it, she had held her breath. Although her lungs were ready to burst, she was almost afraid to breathe, as if that would somehow convey her needs.

Tears of self-loathing squeezed out the corners of her eyes and she shook her head violently. She *couldn't* want him!

She swallowed hard.

Anybody but him!

But she had sensed the male essence of him, and her body, heedless of all her mind's railings, was already preparing itself by lubricating her for him. She recalled, suddenly, how long it had been since she had last made love—in Cannes, with Jerome. But even then she had not felt such an overpowering need.

God help me!

She stood there for a moment, frozen and indecisive, all too aware of the muscular lines of his body and the heat emanating from him. Moistness. As though to infuriate her further, ever more sticky moistness trickled from within her, coating her thighs. The scratchiness of the nubby cotton seemed pronounced as her nipples thrust against the caftan.

No! No! No!

He locked eyes with her, communicating his intentions without words. From a primeval knowledge handed down through the millennia, she understood. She knew exactly how he would drain off his rage. She was to be the outlet for the strong pressures bursting within him.

She took a deep breath. He was undressing her with his eyes.

"No!" she gasped, shaking her head. Sensing the purpose within him, she took an involuntary step backward, then another, and yet another.

He advanced with threatening deliberation, and she truly feared for herself now. Deep in his eyes she saw a savage hunger grow, and a cold, barely suppressed cruelty touched the corners of his mouth.

"So. You are in the mood for physical assault," he said slowly, the words tripping softly from between barely moving lips. "I wonder . . . how strongly will you resist me now?"

"Stay away from me!" she warned in a quivering whisper, and hated herself for the thick sound of fear.

"And if I don't?"

She kept retreating, taking another wary step. With her hands, she groped behind her back, feeling for obstacles. She wasn't about to turn around to look where she was going, because she didn't dare take her eyes off him. "Wh what do you want from me?" she asked shakily.

"You know very well what I want. You." With every step she took backward, he was taking one forward. "Do you think I am blind? I can see the passion in your eyes as clearly as if you spoke of it. Of course, you may pretend to fight me off. That is part of the game, isn't it?" She could hear the jeering humor in his voice.

"Keep away!" A redness crept up from her breasts to her throat and then up her face. Her mouth trembled. "I . . . I'm warning you. I . . . I'll kill you if you touch me!"

"Kill me, then." A fierce black fire flared in his eyes and seemed to leap out at her. There was potent desire mixed with contempt in his blazing gaze, and it seared her like a glowing brand. She nearly cried aloud, and took another quick step backward.

And then her hands felt the lacquered edge of a piece of furniture. She stifled a high-pitched cry. Unwittingly she had let him maneuver her into a corner. She was trapped.

Obviously relishing her predicament, Najib laughed derisively.

Humiliation slashed at her as savagely as animal fangs. She trembled with a killing rage. He was *laughing* at her!

"It seems that I've got you," he said, a diabolical gleam in his eyes.

Her eyes darted about in desperation. Then her breath caught in her throat. The bedroom door to the left of her was open! Perhaps . . . if she could reach it and lock herself inside . . . Yes! She would find sanctuary there. Warily she looked at Najib, trying to gauge his moves. As though he sensed her panic, a cruel smile played on his lips. For a brief moment she was reminded of a cartoon cat at the instant before it makes its move on the mouse.

Now! she thought.

She feinted to the right but lunged abruptly in the opposite direction, diving for the bedroom. The moment she was through the doorway, she slammed the door shut and pressed all her weight against it. With a sob, she realized there was no key. No latch. No lock.

Uttering an incoherent cry, she looked around wildly for something to block it with.

It was too late. With a crash, the door burst inward, sending her sprawling to the carpet. She scrambled to her feet, but his hands shot out and caught her roughly. Her hair whipped around and the air burst from her lungs in a gasp as he whirled her around to face him, jerked her closer, and pressed his mouth hungrily down on hers. It was more an attack than a kiss, and she recoiled as his tongue pried her contorted lips apart and slid into her mouth.

Daliah struggled against him like a madwoman, bending, twisting, and jackknifing every way to free herself from the steel of his arms, but he had one hand at the back of her head and held it in an iron grip, and the other, centered on her spine, crushed her against him so tightly, so roughly, that it hurt. She could feel the unyielding muscles of his rock-hard body. The strength with which he had planted himself firmly in a wide stance. The rapid tripping of his pulse. The angry, bulging tumescence of his groin.

"Let . . . go . . . of . . . me!" she gasped when she finally managed to pull her face away. She eyed him with loathing. "You're an animal!" she hissed hoarsely.

His jaw tightened to squareness, and his eyes went silver. Something flickered within them and, gripping her head even tighter, he forced his mouth back on hers, cutting her curse short. In desperation, she clamped her teeth down on his tongue and locked her jaw.

An unholy joy filled her eyes as she tasted his coppery blood and heard his wounded grunt of pain.

Suddenly he retaliated, and with merciless strength wrenched a handful of her hair and nearly lifted her off her feet by it. Instantly her jaw loosened and her teeth let go of his tongue. Then her eyes widened and she screamed as she felt his hands tearing savagely at her caftan. The ticking-striped cotton ripped noisily and her breasts, full and strong, leapt free, the nipples jutting forward from the dusty-rose areolae in conical points.

Almost in slow motion, the caftan slid down her body and lay on the floor around her feet.

She was naked, and her humiliation was complete. And yet the wetness still flooded her loins. *Why won't my body repulse him? It isn't as if I want him! I* hate *him!*

And then she was possessed of a force she could not control. Letting out a shrill scream, she curved her fingers into talons and slashed like a panther. He ducked, clamped his steely hands around her wrists, and slowly forced her arms down to her sides.

In desperation she spat into his face. He jerked his head stiffly backward, and she drew satisfaction from at least seeing him flinch.

Without looking, he kicked the bedroom door shut.

Her head jerked at the sound. There was so much finality in it.

He scooped her up, one arm under her knees, the other around her back, and swooped her high against his chest. Like a conqueror, he carried his struggling prize toward the altar that was the bed. She fought, kicked, and clawed to get loose, but to no avail. His arms were like vises.

With barely any effort, he flung her onto the bed. She landed on her back, bouncing on the mattress, one of her outstretched arms knocking the nightstand lamp to the floor. The bulb went dark.

Now in half-light, he towered over her, one side of his face glowing golden, the other in purplish shadows. His lips were drawn tightly across his even white teeth, and she was suddenly aware of how tall he was. How potent and powerful he looked. His eyes flashed down on her, and the angles of his face seemed heightened. She let out a muffled groan when she saw what he was doing. His deft fingers were working at his shirt buttons and loosening his belt.

In a last ditch attempt, Daliah scrambled across the bed, but he caught her by one ankle and heaved her back, her breasts sliding across the satin cover, her face hidden by her curtain of silky black hair. Hanging on to her ankle with one hand, he slid out of one shirt sleeve and let his trousers fall. Then, when he changed hands to slip his other arm out of his shirt sleeve, he rolled her over. Her breasts were heaving, and the taut convex of her belly rose and fell with every quick breath.

She stared up into his eyes. They were heavy-lidded and hazy. Then, as her eyes fell, she sucked in her breath. He had a sleek, elongated body, a sculptured chest and abdomen topped with flat brown nipples. Sinewy long brown legs. She stared at his manhood as though hypnotized. The angry monster phallus looked too big to be real.

"Please," she begged in a throaty whisper. "Don't. It's wrong." She glanced back up at him. "Don't you see? It's all *wrong*!"

He was deaf to her pleas. He had eyes only for her flesh, smooth and tan and satin, and her arrowhead mound, prickly with regrowing hair. An anguished moan escaped from deep in his throat.

She tried to crawl backward, but he flung himself down on top of her, one knee brutally parting her thighs, his hands seizing hers and holding them down above her head. Her breasts rose and fell. She could see the red pulse throbbing in his temples. Time came to a standstill. She lay there paralyzed. "N-no," she begged for the last time, more weakly than before. "No . . ."

And then, without warning, he lowered himself atop her. The smooth warmth of his body made her gasp. For an instant her blinding hatred receded, and then his tender kisses brought out a sweet agony in her.

He kissed her lips and her neck, her shoulders, her nipples. He drew the cup of one breast into his mouth and sucked savagely.

Her body throbbed.

Moist threads of saliva were creeping down, tickling her warm breasts.

She clenched her teeth, torn between struggling anew and submitting quietly.

He forced his head into the cleft of her bosom and his tongue traveled ever so slowly down her body, darting moistly between her breasts, then encircling the areola of each nipple. He slid further down, licking at her belly, rimming her navel, then tonguing little circles on her shaved mound. She parted her legs in a V, and his head lowered into it, his tongue pushing through her opening until it was up inside. He rolled her clitoris very gently between his teeth.

She moaned and shuddered at the delicious sensations that darted through her like arrows of passion. Her fury was gone, replaced by a passionate urgency.

This—this is what making love must really be, she thought suddenly. Not playing perverse little games like Jerome, but this—an act which can soothe savagery and tame the hatreds of centuries.

She scissored her legs around his neck, trapping him as he ate his way up inside her, all his being intent on but one purpose. This time he was tasting of her, giving her pleasure as he took his own. He fingered her anus and she moaned again and rolled her hips. Then he slid around like an acrobat, all his weight on one hand as his legs moved lithely out from under him and his groin was above her face. She watched his penis lowering to her lips, and she opened her mouth. It entered smoothly, and at the same time, his head was between her legs. He kept his hips poised above her, and the only sounds in the room were those of his tongue and hers. The world was forgotten; the centuries-old barriers between Arab and Jew meant nothing now: nothing could touch them. They were invincible and one. All their concentration was on each other's fulfillment, on giving and taking and giving and taking again.

He balanced himself on his toes and, defying gravity,

wedged the rest of his weight on his shoulders, then bent his head inward while at the same time he lifted her buttocks slightly off the bed. She let out a cry as his tongue momentarily brushed her anus. Then he was off her.

In a fleeting moment he was on his knees straddling her. For a split second he was poised, his monstrous penis smooth and glistening wet, and then he smoothly swooped down inside her. She thrust her own hips up off the bed to meet him, and her legs dug into his sides. It seemed as if he was filling her completely.

She clutched him and then moaned, rolling left and right, rising upward to meet his thrusts head-on, and their rhythm became syncopated. As he moved faster, so did she, perfectly in tune until the hammering became a frenzy and both of them clenched their teeth as they grunted purposefully, striving to achieve that which joined them, searching for ever-higher plateaus of pleasure. For a moment, he slowed, his hips making circular grinding motions, his penis circling inside her; then he bent from side to side, sliding in and out of her at every possible angle. He slowed down as he felt his juices rising dangerously, then he continued to hammer. He leaned forward over her, his lips sucking on her nipples, kneading them with his lips, flicking them with his tongue. Then once again he would smoothly plummet in, ever more easily as she became wetter and wetter and the torrents of passion threatened to burst from within them like thunder.

Then without warning, her screams reverberated through the bedroom and bounced off the walls like infinite echoes of ecstasy. The heat within her was bursting, a sun flaring its delicious tongues of flame outward from the very core of her body. She was crazed with passion, and the orgasms were exquisite, washing over her, one after the other, while he smoothly slammed himself all the way up insider her, then all the way out again, then all the way up. His pounding was relentless, like the rhythm of her heart.

Frantically, like an animal, he settled down to his task and began to hammer purposefully at her, his thighs slapping noisily against hers, his breaths coming in quick, heavy pants. Gone completely now were the last remnants of hatred. She clenched her teeth, dug her fingers into his flesh with the frenzy of the moment. Her face grimaced determinedly, her body perspired deliriously as it shuddered and shuddered. She felt herself floating, and through closed eyes, lacy arabesques burst and receded like starbursts until she could bear it no more. Her lungs felt as if they were bursting. Drops of his perspiration rained down on her like liquid flames. She felt them sizzle on her flesh. She forgot where she was, who she was, what she was doing and with whom.

And then his convulsions merged into hers as his engorged penis thrust so deeply inside her that for a moment she was afraid she couldn't breathe. He let out a cry and savagely dug in as far as he could. Then he clung to her and shuddered uncontrollably as his juices burst forth. She felt his penis contract against the warm soft walls of her vagina, then expand, and the explosion was complete. Her insides seemed to rock, then go fluid and slack. His body slowed and he lowered himself on top of her, his breathing coming in gasps. He hung on to her until she could feel him growing limp inside her.

She opened her eyes, her breathing as labored as his. For a moment she looked surprised, as though she did not know where she was. She let out a weak cry and drew back. "Oh, damn!" she said softly. Her eyes were helpless. "I didn't mean for this . . ." She shook her head to clear it.

His breathing was still rapid; she could feel his pulse racing. "It was beautiful," he whispered. He curled a tendril of her hair around his index finger. "It was very, very beautiful." He leaned forward to kiss her lips, but she drew back.

She shook her head again. It *was* good. God, was it ever good! The best ever. But still . . .

Still, it could not be.

"Please," she said huskily. "Go now. Get dressed and go!"

"Why? I love you, Daliah."

"You . . . l-love me? You . . . cannot say things like that." Her voice trembled and she clenched her teeth. "You can . . . *not*!"

"Why can't I?" he asked gently. He drew up closer to her so that his face was level with hers. "If it's the truth—"

"The truth!" Her voice was a plaintive wail, and she turned her face away as the tears rolled silently from her beautiful eyes.

"Do you not feel the same way about me that I do about you? Daliah . . . look at me!" When she refused, he reached out and turned her face back to his. "Can you look me in the eye and tell me you do not love me back?" he whispered. "After what we have just done?"

She heard his voice, but it sounded far away, muffled. "Can you be impervious to the voice of your heart?" he was asking. "You have every right to despise me. If I were you, I would probably want to kill me, and with all rights." He gave a mirthless little laugh. "But, Daliah"—his voice dropped to a whisper—"despite the nightmare you have been thrust into here, please, I beg of you: do not turn a deaf ear to your heart!"

Her eyes were like those of a somnambulist, curiously vacant and listlessly remote. *I am not getting through to her. Something inside her has snapped, and she has switched off.*

"I want you to listen to me, Daliah. I need for you to understand . . ." His heart pounded quicker inside him, but he forced himself to speak slowly. "Then, afterward, when I have told you what I must, only then should you decide whether you should still hate me or love me. Are you willing to give me that?" He reached for her hand.

Her touch was cold and unwilling.

"It began long ago," he started, speaking slowly and thoughtfully; then, gradually, the pictures of the past became clearer. His voice began to quicken with the events, his words sketching swift, lucid explanations. "It was before either of us was born, you see. Our grandparents knew each other, Daliah. There was a time when they were *friends.*"

It was probably the longest monologue he had ever recited, and certainly the most emotional and tortured. He told her everything he knew—about his grandparents, Naemuddin al-Ameer and his wife, nursing Schmarya Boralevi back to health, the drain of Ein Shmona on the oasis' water supply, resulting in the slow but steady parching of al-Najaf. He told her of what he knew about Abdullah's long-ago attack on the kibbutz, and of the counterattack upon al-Najaf in which Iffat had been killed. He told of Abdullah's sending him away to England to boarding school, and then to Harvard. He tried to explain, as forthrightly as he could, the vows which bound him to Abdullah, and the hold his half-uncle had over him. He left nothing out—not his previous loveless marriage, nor even the plot for vengeance he had become embroiled in. He tried neither to soften anything nor to paint himself better than he was. He was brutal in his frankness. He told her how Abdullah had gone a step beyond their planned vengeance, using her capture to increase his power. And last of all, as much as it hurt him to say the words, he told her, too, that Abdullah would never release her alive.

When he was finished, the silence was intense.

"Now you know everything," he said at long last. He felt suddenly drained and yet exhilarated. The pain of laying open the truth was immense, and at the same time, he felt oddly at peace for the first time in his life. It was as though he'd been to confession and a great burden was lifted from his shoulders.

He took her hands in his, bent his head in a kind of bow, as though her fingers were something holy, murmuring, "Now that you know it all, you can judge. If you still hate me . . ." He looked pained, but shrugged. "Well, that is up to you. But *if* you love me, as I suspect you do . . ." He let go of her hands and rose to his feet.

Daliah had heard it all without moving. Her face had been totally devoid of expression, but her mind had been a frenzy of emotions, alternately surging with outraged anger, recoiling in shock, and burning with pity. But outwardly, no matter what he'd told her, she hadn't shown any reaction. Not even at the end, when he admitted that Abdullah would never release her.

Peculiarly, at the moment her own doom didn't seem to matter all that much to her. At any rate, there was little she could do about it. What *did* impress her was the candor, the unvarnished truth. Slowly she looked at him and thought: No man, ever, has been this frank. It took more than mere courage—it took guts. How many men like that could there be? One in a billion? Not even that?

She shut her eyes. It had been so easy to hate and want to hurt him while he had been a stranger. Why couldn't he have stayed one? It would have been so much simpler and less painful. But with the unburdening of his heart and his quiet explanations, she had felt him evolving more and more into a real person of dimensions, one with feelings as intense as hers, one alive with passions and tortured with recriminations—a man teetering at the edge of two worlds.

Why couldn't he have stayed the heartless stranger he had been? *And he loves me. He told me he loves me . . .*

I do love you! she almost cried aloud. *I need you and want you!* But she bit it back. Another part of her mind, the part dominated by common sense and learned behavior, held her in check. She sat rigid and silent, the conflicts roaring and pounding and thrashing.

"Daliah . . ." he said softly.

And she looked up, no longer listless, but in lively confusion. She shook her head. "It cannot be. Please—don't make this any harder than it already is," she sighed. "Whatever we may feel . . . it doesn't matter."

He stared at her, his bleak face aging in front of her eyes. "How can you say such a thing?" he whispered.

"I only know what must be and what must never be." She looked into his face and saw him flinch, saw the muscles below his skin sag, and such pain came into his eyes that she felt as if she had struck him.

Swiftly she looked away, unable to face the hurt.

"Oh, Daliah, are we forever going to be trapped in a cage of someone else's making? Will you not wake up and joyfully take what is rightfully ours?"

"Ours?" Despite herself, she sounded quite calm. "We came from opposing worlds!"

His face became earnest, and she knew that within himself he had grappled with this problem already, and had worked it out for himself.

But for her it was no use. She had not come to terms with it, nor did she think she ever could. The gulf between them was too great. She was Jewish. Israeli. And whether or not she practiced her faith, and whether or not she spent time in Israel anymore, being Israeli was still a state of mind.

"Please," she begged softly, "just go. For both our sakes . . ." She swallowed and shut her eyes for an instant. "Forget about me and . . . and don't come back."

"Daliah. Listen to me!" He sat on the arm of her chair and put a hand on her shoulder.

She drew away. "Najib—" She halted suddenly, cursing herself for saying his first name. For even thinking of him in such intimate terms. *What is happening to me?*

He hadn't missed it. The sound of her soft voice intoning his name—two syllables that had jumped unbidden off her tongue—only proved to him that she felt the same way he felt, but was trying to evade him. Her not allowing herself the pleasures of her heart—that, more than her struggle to turn him down, tormented him. Would she live her life like this? Unhappy? Afraid? He couldn't bear to think that she would.

"Just listen a little longer," he begged. "It won't take long . . ." He swallowed, then continued. "I understand the way you feel. Your being held hostage, no future to think of—perhaps that is why you will not allow yourself to be happy. But I'll get us out of this." He lowered his voice to a forceful whisper. "Don't you understand? I've been working on your escape . . ."

Despite her surge of excitement, whispers of suspicion lingered. She looked at him doubtfully. "Escape?" she repeated absently. Then, when it sank in, she breathed in sharply. She blinked and gave her head a little shake. "You're going to help me to escape?"

"Yes," he said.

She sat in perfect stillness.

"Why?" she asked at last. "Why do you want to do this?"

"Because I love you. Also because . . ."

"Yes?" She was staring at him.

". . . because it will redeem me from what I have helped cause," he said softly. His expression was nakedly unguarded.

That touched something within her, for she laid a gentle hand on his cheek.

For the time being, that touch was more than he had hoped for. It made him feel instantly, immoderately happy.

Then, afraid that his continued presence would only cause her more anguish, he got up, hurriedly dressed, and left.

But not before brushing her lips with his. And feeling hers respond.

She watched him walk to the door. "Najib . . ."

He stopped and turned around slowly.

She took a deep breath. "If only . . ." she began, and then sighed painfully. "Go," she whispered, shutting her eyes as though in immense pain. "Go."

The *Najah*, Najib's sleek, Italian-built yacht, had taken two and a half days to reach Oman, and dropped anchor off Khāluf in the Arabian Sea. Captain Delcroix immediately telephoned Najib for further instructions, and to report that the helicopter was tuned up, topped off, and ready to fly.

"Stay anchored there until you receive further notice from me personally," Najib instructed him.

As he slowly replaced the receiver, Najib's lips were compressed into a thin, grim line. Slowly but surely, the logistics were all falling into place. Allah willing, the press conference would have no serious repercussions as far as Abdullah was concerned.

It was time to have Daliah's Polaroid delivered.

Six hours later, Abdullah returned from Tripoli and summoned Najib and Khalid to the *majlis*. As they approached, he held his hand out imperiously.

Was the gesture more arrogant this time? Najib wondered. Or had it always been that disdainful?

He took the dry callused hand in his, raised it perfunctorily to his lips, and embraced his half-uncle.

"Najib, my half-nephew." Abdullah's eyes glittered with feverish excitement.

"Half-uncle." Najib pulled away and held Abdullah's gaze. "I trust from the sound of your voice that things went satisfactorily in Tripoli?"

Abdullah smiled, but his voice was reproving. "You should

know better than to hazard guesses. Things are not always as they appear."

"Indeed," Najib allowed, "often they are not." He felt the beginnings of anger stirring within him, but he hid it well. Anger, as well as a myriad of other emotions and truths, could be superbly disguised with the expansive, flowery use of Arabic. But what rankled was the way his half-uncle always toyed with him. If Najib said the sky was blue, Abdullah was bound to say it was green. What he wanted to know was *why*. Why did Abdullah keep needling him? Ever since he could remember, Abdullah's choice of words and tone reflected an undisguised contempt for him.

He stepped aside so that Abdullah could greet Khalid. As he watched them, Najib felt that something had changed. There was something different in Abdullah's bearing. He was more self-assured. His chest was puffed out further. He seemed to hold his head higher. They were not great changes, and much too subtle to notice unless one had known Abdullah for a long time; but he knew Abdullah well—far too well, he often thought. And there *was* a change.

"Things went well. Very well indeed." Abdullah allowed himself a smile and clasped his hands in front of him.

Then Najib knew what it was that bothered him. Abdullah seemed younger and more excited than he had before Tripoli. The trip had seemingly rejuvenated him, had given him a burst of vitality and impetus. Even his green fatigues were different. They were no longer soft and they no longer sagged; they were more tightly tailored—starched stiff as cardboard, pressed, and creased. Qaddafi's influence, no doubt.

"Muammar and I found much common ground," Abdullah continued. "And we had several highly inspirational discussions." He looked from Najib to Khalid. "I want you both to see what he has given me." Smiling like a smug magician, he raised a hand and clicked his fingers once.

From somewhere in the shadows behind him, two big men suddenly appeared and advanced soundlessly. They took up positions to either side of him. Both were armed and looked eminently capable, and beneath their headcloths, both had eyes hidden behind black wraparound sunglasses. And both, Najib noted, had that peculiarly expressionless robot air about them that he had noticed in other elite fighting forces. Zombies. For all practical purposes, that was what they were: Abdullah's zombies.

He felt a chill, sharp as a breath of arctic wind.

"Let me introduce Colonel Qaddafi's gift to me. Surour

and Ghazi. My Praetorian guards." Abdullah seemed to swell with pride as he looked from Khalid to Najib. "Muammar fears that there are elements around me who might wish to do me harm." He smiled at Najib. "The possibility exists, do you not think?"

Najib nodded. "There is always such a possibility," he said moderately, while inside him a sudden alertness started shrieking and shrilling: *He suspects! He knows! You've fallen in love with Daliah Boralevi and told her you'd help her escape. And somehow he's found out!*

"Surour and Ghazi are sworn to protect me, and they will never leave my side. They will travel with me, eat with me, bathe with me, and sleep with me. One of them will always be awake, at my side, so I can sleep without fear." Abdullah's eyes narrowed. "They will do anything I ask of them. *Anything!* Let me demonstrate." Excitedly Abdullah gestured for the four of them to follow him to a French card table set up in front of the windows. On it was an ordinary butcher-block carving board. Four ice picks and a felt pen were lined up on it.

Abdullah's eyes searched Najib's, and then Khalid's. "Long ago, you both swore allegiance to me," he murmured. "Do you remember?"

Najib nodded and swallowed. He was starting to feel peculiarly queasy. How well he remembered that afternoon in the mountains of Syria when his wrist had been sliced open and his blood had merged with Abdullah's. Ever since, he had been in his half-uncle's clutches. How could he forget?

Abdullah picked up the felt pen and uncapped it with a flourish. "I want each of you to hold out your right hand, palm-up."

Surour and Ghazi didn't hesitate. They pulled back their sleeves and held out their hands. Najib exchanged glances with Khalid, but Khalid's expression was guarded and unreadable. Slowly they both extended their hands also.

One by one, Abdullah felt their hands with his fingers and carefully marked an X at a certain spot on the palm of each.

"Notice how carefully I have marked those X's," he pointed out. "If your hands were to be X-rayed, you would discover that in the precise center, where the two lines of the X cross each other, there is a small boneless spot. A mere hollow of flesh."

Najib felt himself reeling. *Mere flesh? What did he mean by "boneless" and "mere flesh"? And what in all damnation were those grisly picks doing out?*

Seemingly unaware of Najib's horror, Abdullah picked up the ice picks by their thin long points and passed one to each man. When he was handed his, Najib almost dropped it. He glanced at Khalid. Khalid had been Abdullah's second-in-command for as long as he could remember, and he had always proved himself fearless. But like many a fearless man, the sight of his own blood—even the prospect of a hypodermic needle piercing his skin—was enough to send him into a dead faint. Najib noticed that Khalid was now hanging on by sheer willpower. His swarthy skin had turned pasty yellow, and his eyes seemed to roll up and flicker in their sockets. Another moment, Najib thought, and Khalid would be out cold on the floor.

"I want to demonstrate just how dedicated Surour and Ghazi are to me," Abdullah said. "Then perhaps you will understand just how well they will guard me." He nodded at the nearest man. "Ghazi, you are first. Place your hand, palm-up, on the cutting board. Then stab the pick through the precise center of the X and impale your hand."

Najib stared at Ghazi. If the big Libyan felt any emotion, he did not show it. He bent over the table, laid his hand, palm-up, on the cutting board, and poised the pick six inches above it. For an instant the long thin shaft of steel caught the light and gleamed. It wasn't even quivering. His hands were perfectly still.

Then, with the speed of lightning, and without as much as a gasp of pain, he slammed it down through his hand.

Najib turned swiftly away, but even though he didn't look, he could hear it. Abdullah either hadn't marked the X properly or Ghazi hadn't taken the time to line up the point exactly. the snapping crunch of breaking bone was unmistakable.

Najib thought he might vomit.

"I want you to look closely," Abdullah said, a satisfied note in his voice. "See what Ghazi has done to himself with not a moment's hesitation! Now do you understand his devotion? I give him but the word, and his life shall be mine!"

Allah be merciful! And to think I helped that madman all these years!

"I said—*look*!" Abdullah hissed so fiercely that Najib could feel the sour spray of spittle on his face.

He forced himself to turn around and stare at that impaled hand with its wriggling fingers. His eyes kept trying to slide away, but somehow he held his gaze on that hand.

"*Shukkram*, Ghazi," Abdullah said. "That is enough."

Najib watched in morbid fascination as Ghazi grasped the

685

handle of the pick and, in one swift movement, and once again completely devoid of any emotion, pulled the pick free. A thin spray of blood squirted up and fell back like a silent red fountain. Then the spray stopped and the blood leaked out thickly, as if from a stigmata.

The cutting board was a shiny pool of gleaming blood.

Abdullah handed Ghazi a damask napkin, and the big Libyan wrapped it around his hand and stepped back.

"Surour," Abdullah said. "You are next."

Najib turned away. He could not bear witness to this self-mutilation any longer. It was sick. No, it was worse than that. It was insane.

"Half-uncle, please," Najib said weakly. "Enough is enough. We get your point."

Abdullah ignored him. "Surour!" he commanded. "Impale your hand."

Surour's pick flashed, but without the sickening crunch of bone.

Then it was Khalid's turn.

Shaking and white-faced, Khalid poised the pick above his palm. Then, before he could bring it down, he swayed on his feet, his eyes rolled inside their sockets, his eyelids fluttered like butterflies, and he dropped the pick as he fainted dead away.

Abdullah turned to Najib triumphantly. "Now perhaps you can see why I need my personal guards. Obviously, the men about me cannot be relied upon." With his jump boot he rolled Khalid over in disgust. "He has the heart of a chicken and the courage of a woman!" he spat contemptuously. "How can I count on him to protect me in times of danger?"

Najib's head was spinning out of control and he was weak-kneed from horror. He felt he should point out to Abdullah how devoted Khalid had always been, and how often he had put his life on the line, but his mouth was dry and bilious. It was all he could do to nod dumbly.

"And now," Abdullah said with a little taunting smile, "it is your turn, Najib."

Najib went stone cold and time seemed to screech to a stop. He stared at Abdullah and then at the butcher block. Ghazi and Surour's blood was already coagulating, becoming a pool of thick red gelatin.

"Najib?" Abdullah's voice was deceptively mild.

Najib stared at him, then down at his palm. Slowly he raised his hand to his eyes. He stared at his palm. The X was smearing from the sudden sweat he had broken out in, and what was left of the mark seemed to pulsate and throb, becoming bigger and smaller, bigger and smaller, as though coming closer and receding again. As though it were a beating heart.

Sweat was beginning to drip down his forehead too, and his lips were twisted into a moist grimace. He stared at that pulsating X with such concentration that the tears stood out in his eyes and a silver thread of saliva drooled out of the corner of his lips.

"Well?" Abdullah said softly. He placed a hand on Najib's forearm and forced his hand down on the bloodied board. He looked into Najib's eyes.

Najib took a deep breath and held it. He poised the point of the pick an inch above the center of the X. He was shaking so hard that the point kept wavering back and forth.

He couldn't. *He just couldn't!*

But he knew he had to. If he didn't, Allah alone knew what Abdullah might do to him. Have him assassinated? And then what would happen to Daliah?

She would be at the mercy of that merciless madman, with no one in the world to turn to for help. If he refused to impale his hand, he might very well be signing her death warrant.

"Must I doubt your allegiance?" Abdullah's voice turned hard.

The sweat was pouring off Najib in a sheet now, dripping down on the butcher block, glistening on the blood. Gritting his teeth, he clutched the ice pick with all his might and let out a grunt. In a single surge of blinding strength, and imagining her face, her *eyes*—those hypnotic green striated jewels—he let out a scream that came out "Aaah!" and with all his might slammed the pick down through the air, through his hand, and into the thick block of wood underneath it.

The pain was like a burst of lightning as the ice pick's silvery steel shaft punched through his flesh. Abruptly he let go and stared at his impaled hand in horror. The handle quivered back and forth and . . . and he could even move his *fingers*. He wiggled them, then clenched them halfway. A sense of ridiculous triumph filled him to bursting. He had managed to do it. Because of Daliah, he had been able to, and he felt a savage joy. Surprisingly, there was very little blood.

"Very good." Abdullah nodded, his eyes gleaming. "That is enough," he said gently. "Pull it back out."

For some reason, it seemed to take more effort to pull the pick out than it had taken to plunge it in. Grabbing hold of the shaft, Najib squeezed his eyes shut and in a massive single pull yanked it out of his hand.

The blood spurted now, raining all around in thick droplets.

Abdullah handed him another heavy damask napkin. With his left hand, Najib gave it a shake to unfold it, and wrapped it tenderly around his injured hand.

Abdullah smiled suddenly. "Now that that is done," he said with all the politeness of a Beverly Hills hostess, "let us transfer to the dining room. The food should have been prepared by now."

As though, Najib thought weakly, his stomach churning, any of us has an appetite left after this.

He held up his injured hand. "I will be back momentarily to join you in the dining room. First, I want to wash this."

He hurried up to his suite, found a bottle of alcohol in the bathroom, and poured half of it over his hand. He had to bite down on a towel to keep from screaming. The alcohol burned like liquid fire, and both his palm and the back of the hand were swelling so tenderly that when he wrapped a bandage gingerly around the wound, he screamed momentarily.

Just to make it through dinner, he swigged a half-pint of bourbon straight out of the bottle.

Abdullah presided over the dinner as if nothing out of the ordinary had occurred. The food was tasteless, greasy and gray and rubbery, and had been prepared by one of Abdullah's men.

Like footmen, the Libyan zombies were stationed just steps behind Abdullah's chair.

Najib pushed the fatty lamb around on his plate with distaste. With all the refrigerated and frozen gourmet delights in the kitchen, he found it difficult to believe that such slop could be served. Not that it mattered, really. It could have been oysters and caviar, and he still wouldn't have had any appetite. The bandage he'd wrapped around his right hand was stiff and dark brown with blood, and he could barely hold his fork for the bolts of pain which shot through his hand and sliced all the way up to his elbow.

Like some mad medieval monarch, Abdullah waited a full twenty minutes before he would touch his food. The zombies had to taste it first. The week his half-uncle had spent in Libya, Najib noticed, had unleashed his paranoia to new, previously unparalleled heights.

"Mecca, the Wailing Wall, and St. Peter's Square in Rome," Abdullah was saying conversationally as he chewed a piece of long-cold lamb. "A three-pronged attack occurring over a period of three days. It will be a multiple explosion heard round the world." He smacked his lips and took a long sip of water.

Khalid dropped his fork with a clatter and Najib stared at his half-uncle in stunned shock.

"Mecca!" Khalid was the first to find his voice. "Why . . . Mecca is the most holy shrine in all Islam! In all the world! It . . . it would be desecration!"

Abdullah stared at him sternly. "Sometimes," he said darkly, gesturing with his fork, "it is necessary to tear down the old before rebuilding it for the better."

"It's folly!" Khalid whispered. He pushed his plate aside. "The Wailing Wall and St. Peter's . . . I don't like those targets either, but they, at least, are infidel shrines. But Mecca—"

"It must be done!" Abdullah said sharply. He, too, pushed his plate away. "The holy war must be started at once. The sooner it begins, the sooner it will be over, and then the entire world shall be Islamic. Consider for a moment." He drummed his fingernails on the marble. "First, Mecca will be destroyed. Bombs placed strategically will bring the walls tumbling down. Muslims the world over—Muslims in India and the Far East, Muslims in the four corners of the world will be outraged and rise up as one! A day after that explosion, the infidels' Wailing Wall will be but a pile of Jerusalem rubble, and the third day . . . Ah! On the third day, St. Peter's will come tumbling down. But Mecca must be the first! The outrage of that act will, of course, be blamed on the infidels. It is very simple, you see." From the rising excitement in his voice it was clear that he was warming to the theme. "The Christians and Jews will be blamed for the destruction of Mecca, and in turn, the destruction of their infidel shrines will be blamed on us Muslims. It will spark a holy war of such magnitude that the Crusades will pale in comparison! We will rewrite the world's history, my brothers, and in the centuries to come we will be almost as revered as the Prophet. All three of the world's major religions—and thus their armed forces—are going to battle to the death! And Islam will win!"

He sat back with the satisfied air of one having delivered a bombshell.

There was a stunned silence.

A sense of passionate and just outrage overrode the pain of Najib's wound. He shook his head slowly and chose his words carefully.

"An attack on Mecca has been tried before," he reminded Abdullah quietly. "The men who invaded the shrine were executed."

Abdullah made an irritated gesture. "Those men were fools! They took Mecca and tried to hold it. We will merely destroy the shrine. Not one of our men will be within a hundred-mile radius when the bombs explode. No one will be able to blame us." He paused. "Muammar will provide extra manpower, as well as explosives. Although he will not admit any involvement in this either, he sees the necessity behind it. Look at the dazzling possibilities! Islam will, at last, not only be united, but will be a world strength to be reckoned with. All the countries of the Middle East—and India and Pakistan too, every country in which there are Muslims—may end up being reshaped into one massive religious state."

"I fear this is begging for the fires of eternal hell," Najib said flatly.

"On the contrary." Abdullah permitted himself a faint smile. "As Allah's warriors, I believe this will ensure us a spot in Paradise forever."

It was after two o'clock in the morning when something awakened him. He sat up in bed, his heart beating wildly, and held his breath, listening. But other than the hum of the reverse-cycle air-conditioning/heating unit, he could not hear anything. The suite was pitch black. So far as he could tell, nothing moved or breathed.

But that could not be true. Why else would he have the overpowering feeling that he was not alone? Why else were tingling breaths of caution dancing like electric currents at the back of his neck? His bandaged hand throbbed and stung.

With a growing fear he reached for the bedside lamp and switched it on. He gave a start and sat up straight. Khalid and Hamid were standing, still as statues, at the foot of his bed. He stared at them. "What are you doing here?" he asked angrily.

"Ssssh!" Khalid held a cautioning finger to his lips. "Not so loud," he whispered. "Keep your voice down." He turned to the other man. "Hamid, check to make sure the door is locked."

Soundless as a furtive night creature, Hamid went back out into the living room, and neither Najib nor Khalid spoke until he returned. When he came back and nodded, the two men lowered themselves into chairs and Khalid lit a thin black cigar. After taking a few puffs to get it going, he sat back, crossed one leg over the other, and slid the cigar from his mouth. He studied it reflectively. "I thought it was time the three of us had a little talk," he said in a soft conversational tone.

Najib wasn't fooled for a minute. He knew that when Khalid's eyes drooped in the deceptive way they were drooping now, it really meant that he was sharply alert.

"You know," Khalid said, "I have been watching you for quite a long time now."

Najib was silent.

"You are a strange man," Khalid continued, his eyes sliding from the cigar over to Najib. "You, more than any of us, have tried to maintain a certain distance from Abdullah. Also, you are the one among us who is the most indispensable to him. Yet you permit him to treat you no better than the lowliest new recruit. I have often wondered why."

"Abdullah treats all men alike," Najib murmured dismissively.

"Does he?" Khalid's gaze became sharp and silvery. "Do you really believe he treats Qaddafi like he treats us?"

Najib shrugged and his reply was simple. "I would not know that, would I, because I was not there."

"But from the way he spoke of Qaddafi this evening," Khalid said shrewdly, "what do you infer from that?"

"Do you mean is he friends with Qaddafi?" Najib asked noncommittally, and then answered himself, "Yes, he is. Does he respect him? The answer to that is yes also. He looks up to the Colonel. He is a nation's leader, after all, and whether you like the Colonel or not, you would feel no less pride if a ruler gave you so much attention. Nor, for that matter," he added, "would I."

"That is not my point." Khalid gestured with the cigar. "To Abdullah, Qaddafi has become some sort of holy prophet. I would not doubt that this mad scheme of a holy war was Qaddafi's idea originally, and that he has recruited Abdullah to pull it off."

"Then what are you saying?" Najib asked quietly, feeling his way cautiously through a potentially lethal minefield. Soon, now, he would have to decide whether what the two men were telling him was genuine, or if they had been sent by Abdullah to trap him.

"Abdullah has changed." It was Hamid speaking.

Najib looked at him now. "Changed? In what way?"

"You know what way!" Hamid's voice was low but impassioned. "Over the years, he has become a different man from the one he once was. It is almost as if someone else has slipped into his skin. There was a time when he did things to help our people. When he fought for the things which they could not fight for themselves. But now?" Hamid's voice became bitter. "Now he revels in his own glory! Now he is even willing to sell us out, and has become Qaddafi's slave in order to forge new paths to glory! He has become blinded to the issues for which we have always fought."

"I feel you are both dancing around the issue," Najib said. "Surely you did not creep into my room in the middle of the night only in order for us to chase one another round and round the palm tree?"

"No, we did not." Khalid frowned and paused, as though gathering his thoughts. Then he sat up straighter. Tilting his head back and exhaling a cloud of blue smoke, he said softly, "We cannot allow Abdullah to destroy Mecca."

He lowered his gaze and continued in the same level tone. "That is why we have come to you. We wish to enlist your help to keep this sacrilege from happening."

"You speak of treason to Abdullah!" Najib reminded him coldly. "Do you not realize that were I to repeat as much as a word of this to Abdullah, he would not hesitate to have you killed?"

Hamid jumped to his feet so quickly that his chair fell over backward. A long-barreled pistol, like a writhing blue-black snake, was aimed at Najib at point-blank range.

"Put the gun away, Hamid," Khalid said wearily. "Can you not see that he is already on our side?"

The pistol wavered, but Hamid's expression was doubtful.

Najib ignored the pistol and stared at Khalid. "How can you be so certain that I am on your side?"

Hamid's smile was expressionless. "You have proved it on at least two occasions already."

Najib frowned silently, but did not speak.

Khalid blew a smoke ring. "The first time was a test."

A sudden memory flashed through Najib's mind. "My overhearing you both talk. That night in the Jordanian hills!"

"After we lost the six men in that foolish raid on Zefat." Khalid nodded. "Yes, that was the test. We held that conversation for your benefit." He smiled easily. "If you had wanted to report us to Abdullah, you would have done it then. When you did not, we knew for certain that you could be trusted."

The gun disappeared back inside Hamid's holster.

"You said there were two times," Najib said.

"The second occurred this past week." Khalid squinted at him. "Your visits to the Jewish woman did not go unnoticed."

692

Najib waited, his expression blank, but his thoughts were flying. What could they know about his visits to Daliah? How closely had they been spying on him?

Khalid's lips formed into a mirthless smile. "Some of your conversations were overheard," he said in a voice which was all the more powerful for its mild tone. "You are in love with her. You plan on helping her escape." He puffed contentedly.

Najib did not say anything.

"Would you like to hear some of the specifics, perhaps? The names she called you? The things she muttered to herself each time you left?"

"You were eavesdropping." Najib's voice was a whisper, but its edge was ice.

Khalid shrugged easily. "On Abdullah's orders, yes. However, therein lies the irony." He smiled that mirthless smile again. "Eavesdropping is only as trustworthy a source of information as the eavesdropper."

Suddenly Najib had heard enough. "You are trying to blackmail me for your own purposes," he said grimly. Oblivious of his nakedness, he got out of bed and stood in front of Khalid. "This discussion is finished," he said contemptuously. "I have never dealt with blackmailers in the past, nor will I begin to do so now. You will be glad to know that this conversation will go no further than this room." He paused. "Now, get out."

Khalid remained seated and puffed on his cigar with slow deliberation. "What would you call being tied to Abdullah for all these years? Was that not a form of blackmail? Or perhaps I read you wrong, and for all your power and alleged courage, inside of you beats the heart of a chicken?"

Najib's eyes flashed. *"Get out."*

Khalid did not move. "Do you think you can help her escape on your own?" He waited for a reply, and getting none, added, "No, I did not think so." He gestured at the bed. "Please, do sit back down. This could well be our last opportunity to meet like this. It would be a crime to waste it."

Najib hesitated. Khalid was right, he knew. It would be folly for the three of them not to ally themselves. Basically, they each wanted the same thing. More important, he would need help in order to set Daliah free. After a moment, he nodded and sat down on the edge of the bed.

Khalid nodded approval and flicked a length of ash into the crystal block on his knee. "The three of us share enough common goals and problems that we cannot afford the luxury of fighting among ourselves. There is safety in numbers, and in order to be strong, we must be friends." His eyes held Najib's in their lazy way. "Well, if not friends exactly, then at least temporary allies."

Najib nodded. "Very well, then. Obviously you already know what it is that I want. Now it is my turn. What is it that you want?"

Khalid's voice was soft. "I want this nonsense about a holy war dropped. I care neither one way nor the other for the Jews' Wailing Wall or the Christians' St. Peter's Square, but I care deeply for our people and for Mecca. I refuse to allow thousands of innocents to die needlessly, or our most holy shrine to be destroyed. In order to do this, as well as to ensure the continued survival of the PFA, Abdullah must go. Otherwise, it is only a matter of time before this organization is destroyed."

"And then, after Abdullah?" Najib asked quietly. "What will happen then?"

"Then I shall be the leader of the Palestinian Freedom Army," Khalid said, surprised that Najib should have asked.

Najib held his gaze. "And that will change things?"

"For the better, I hope. However, if you do not believe that, then you could at least draw comfort by considering me the lesser of two evils." He gave a wry little smile. "Are we agreed, then? We can count you in?"

"Not so fast." Najib made a gesture. "Back up a little. You said Abdullah must go. What exactly do you mean by that? Abdullah will not voluntarily relinquish any of his power."

Khalid nodded. "He must be killed. He leaves us no other choice."

"And what about the men who are loyal to him?"

Khalid was silent.

"Then let me put it this way. Besides yourself and Hamid, how many more men can you count on to help us?"

"There are but the three of us," Khalid said softly.

Najib stared at him. "Are you mad? Abdullah has the support of hundreds. Of *thousands*."

"At the moment, he has the support of ninety-seven men here at this palace. It goes without saying that if we are to succeed, we stand our best chance of eliminating him here."

"And the two Libyans? Did you count them?"

"No. But they will die also."

"And the German girl makes one hundred." Najib shook his head. "There are not enough of us," he said with finality. "It would never work."

Khalid was undeterred. "We would enjoy the element of surprise," he said doggedly.

"There are not enough of us! We cannot even get to him while he sleeps. You heard him tell us. One of the Libyans is always awake guarding him."

Khalid looked at Najib shrewdly. "How were you going to get the Jewish girl out?"

Najib stared at him.

"Why do you look at me like that? As long as we work together, in the end we can both succeed and get what we set out to achieve."

Najib pondered that before he answered. He wondered how Khalid would react when he told him. "Are you willing to fight at the side of the Israelis?" he asked.

Khalid sucked in his breath and stared.

"Are you?" Najib repeated.

Khalid looked instinctively toward the door. His voice was a whisper. "What makes you think the infidels will want to help?"

"The return of Daliah Boralevi and the prospect of cutting down Abdullah say they will. They cannot afford to let him begin his holy war. They stand to lose more than anyone else."

Khalid remained silent.

"Well?" Najib was waiting.

Khalid frowned. "Who will have to know of their involvement?" he asked at last. The moment he said it, Najib knew he nearly had him snared.

"The two of you," Najib said after a moment. He frowned thoughtfully. "Me. The girl. And the Israelis, of course. I don't think you have to worry about that, though. It is to their advantage to make Abdullah's death look like a power struggle within the PFA. Otherwise, if the Saudis know the truth, they are likely to consider the rescue attempt an invasion. The Israelis don't dare let that happen. It could spell war."

There was a silence as each of them worked out the potential consequences in their heads. The risks were steep. But then, so were the rewards. All three of them knew that there was no such thing in life as major rewards for minor risks: risk and reward were always proportionate.

Najib glanced from one of them to the other. He could almost hear their gears turning. Now that they were nibbling, he knew better than to rush them. They had to make up their own minds.

"I have one question," Khalid said tightly. "We know that

Abdullah must be killed. Possibly the two Libyans, and the German girl also. But we cannot massacre everyone in the palace." He paused, his eyes searching Najib's. "What I want to know is: how am I guaranteed that no one will connect Hamid and me with the Israelis? If they do, you know we wouldn't last the first night."

Najib nodded. "I've already thought of that. It's simple, really. No one will know they're Israelis because they won't be in uniform, and I'll make sure they carry an assortment of Russian and American weapons. As long as they keep their mouths shut throughout the operation, and leave no wounded behind, you're covered."

Khalid took a deep breath. After a while he chuckled. "In a strange way, it would be poetic justice, don't you think? The Israelis helping me into a position of terrorist power?"

Najib did not reply.

Khalid looked at Hamid, and a silent signal seemed to pass between the two of them.

Najib looked at Khalid questioningly.

"You can count us in," Khalid said definitely.

Najib sprang it on them then. "First, I want three guarantees," he said flatly. "Without them, you are on your own."

Khalid's voice was edgy. "And what are those?"

Najib ticked the points off on his fingers. "First, after this mission is finished and done with, I am out of this organization completely. I want nothing more to do with the PFA. Second, I want to ensure my safety and the girl's, and that goes for as long as we live. And third, the same goes for her family. The Boralevis and ben Yaacovs are never to be touched by violence from this organization again."

He could feel Khalid tightening up. Guarantees that went years down the road weren't easy ones to make. "Those are my terms. Take them or leave them."

The minutes ticked soundlessly by. Again Najib did not press for a rushed answer. He didn't want a quick yes that wouldn't be honored.

Khalid finally nodded. "I will guarantee that," he said slowly. "But only from the PFA. As far as the PLO and the Fedayeen, and the other groups are concerned . . ." He shrugged helplessly. "I cannot be held accountable for them."

"I do not expect you to be responsible for the actions of other groups. Only for your own."

Khalid began to smile. "It is agreed, then."

"Good." Najib nodded. "And now, since we have only a few hours left for planning our strategy, we had better get busy. In the morning, I am flying to Riyadh, ostensibly to

have this"—he raised his bandaged hand and smiled grimly—
"taken care of. As they say in the westerns, when I return, it
will be with the cavalry."

"Then we have no more time to lose. When are you
planning on returning?"

Najib met his eyes straight on. "Two nights from now.
Waiting any longer wouldn't do us any good. It'll either
work or . . ."

Khalid finished the sentence: "Or it won't."

Famagusta, Cyprus, was an ordinary seaside city with
grandiose pretensions of becoming a kind of Mediterranean
Miami Beach. Although balconied hotels and modern apartment blocks of concrete and glass lined the length of the
shore, it hadn't yet reached the exalted status to which it
aspired, nor was there a likelihood that it ever would. Overall, it looked more like one of those Spanish resorts on the
Costa Brava which had gone slightly to seed, and as the day
waned, a curious phenomenon occurred. The Famagusta beach
faced east, and as the sun began to move behind the tall
buildings, the sunbathers had to move out of the giant blocks
of creeping purple shadow and arrange themselves in regimented
rows along the narrow, sunlit strips between the buildings.

The glass-walled suite was fourteen floors above the shadow-
darkened beach, and Najib, facing the windows from the
couch at the far end of the room, saw only a panorama of
vast blue sky. A distant speck of airplane flashed bright
silver as the sun reflected off it.

He lowered his eyes from the window and focused them
on Schmarya. The old man was in an armchair and faced
him squarely across the coffee table; Dani's swivel armchair
was angled toward them both.

No one spoke. For over a minute already, they had been
sitting in such intense silence they could have heard a pin
drop.

Najib slowly switched his gaze over to Dani. Dani's face
was a carbon copy of Schmarya's—white and tense—and
Najib could see shock in both men's eyes. Their disbelief
was nearly palpable; Najib could almost hear them wrestling
with themselves, and he knew that they were trying to find
loopholes in his story.

Najib pushed himself to his feet, went soundlessly over to
the sideboard, and splashed three glasses half-full of brandy.
He carried them back to the coffee table, set one down in
front of each of them, and lowered himself onto the couch
again.

He could well understand what the men were going through. Their minds would be numbed with shock and incomprehension. During the last half-hour, they had learned enough from him to be stupefied by the immense undertaking Daliah's freedom would require. Najib could tell by their looks that both of them had believed that the worst scenario would involve a half-dozen kidnappers at most—not a virtually impregnable desert compound teeming with a hundred well-armed, well-trained terrorists.

The drinks stood untouched and unwanted on the coffee table. Hands shaking, Dani lit a rare cigarette and drew in the smoke nervously, and Najib, still waiting, sat back, pinched the crease of his trousers, and crossed one leg over his knee; it was a while before any of them spoke.

It was Schmarya who finally broke the silence.

Najib knew what was coming before he even opened his mouth. The old man was going to pick holes in his story.

"Mr. al-Ameer," Schmarya said quietly. "Let me get this straight. You had the picture of Daliah delivered to us so that we could meet together here in private and arrange her release?" He looked at Najib. "Am I correct in that assumption?"

Najib met his eyes and shook his head. "Not quite, Mr. Boralevi. As I told you, I am afraid she will never be released. What we need to plan is her *escape*."

There was a short silence, and then the swivel of Dani's chair squeaked as he shifted his weight and sat forward. He frowned deeply. "With all due respect, Mr. al-Ameer," he said skeptically, "you are an Arab. You have just gotten through telling us that you have been involved with Abdullah and the PFA for the better part of your lifetime." His frown deepened. "Surely you realize that that makes us enemies."

Najib was unruffled. "Sometimes, Mr. ben Yaacov," he said in a hushed voice, "two enemies must form an alliance in the face of an even greater danger." He shook his head sadly. "Such is the case now. Our only choice is to unite forces. It is perhaps one of the ironies of life."

Dani was silent for a moment. "Tell me. Why should we believe that you really intend to turn against Abdullah? What guarantee do we have that you really want to effect Daliah's release?"

Najib spread his hands and pointed out the obvious. "I am here, am I not?"

Dani leaned even further forward and mashed his half-smoked cigarette in the glass ashtray. Then he sat back again. The swivel of his chair squeaked once more. "It could be a trap," he persisted.

Najib inclined his head slightly, a position which made his face look hawklike. "You will have to trust me that it is not."

"In ordinary circumstances, trust must be earned," Dani said bluntly.

Najib nodded. "We both know there is not time for that. In this instance you will have to trust me blindly."

"I know," Dani said tightly, "and I don't like it a bit."

Najib allowed himself a wry little smile. He couldn't blame Dani. If their roles were reversed, he would feel exactly the same way. "What you would really like," he speculated, "is some indication that her release would . . . ah . . . profit me. You would tend to trust me more if there were something in it for me. Is that it?"

"To put it bluntly, yes."

Najib got up from the couch. "I could give you countless reasons, such as: Abdullah must be stopped before he and Qaddafi begin the holy war I warned you they are plotting. Or because he wants to destroy Mecca, our most holy shrine. Or because I wish to extricate myself from him once and for all, and this is my only way out. Those are all valid reasons, but they are not the real reason why I came to you." He paused and added softly, "The reason is more basic than any of those: I am in love with your daughter."

Dani jerked as though he had been struck. Then his face twisted with rage. "You are *what*?" He stared up at Najib.

"I said," Najib repeated calmly, "that I am in love with Daliah."

Dani's lips made a hiss that sounded like air being expelled from a balloon. He blinked rapidly and exchanged glances with his father-in-law. "Impossible," he said in a horrified voice.

"Listen to him, Dani," Schmarya advised gently. "About such a thing he should lie?"

Dani propelled himself to his feet so swiftly that for a second Najib prepared for a fist to come slamming, but then Dani walked across the room. He stood trembling at the windows, staring unseeingly down at the deep blue sea. "Impossible," he muttered to himself shakily. He shook his head. "Impossible," he repeated in a whisper.

Schmarya twisted around. "When you live as long as I have, you find out everything is possible," he said to Dani's back. "Why shouldn't we believe it?"

For a long while Dani did not reply. Finally he crossed the

room and returned to his chair. He sat down heavily and sized up Najib more warily now. "I suppose what I have read about you is true," he said. "You really are most unpredictable." His smile held no warmth.

Najib sat down and waited.

"But then, Daliah is unpredictable too." His voice was trembling. "I suppose I never really understood her choice of men. First that medical student, and then that director she's lived with all those years . . ." Dani shook his head and made an agitated little gesture. "And now *you*." His expression became a cold, pained mask. "It seems she has a talent for choosing the . . . the unpredictable, shall we say."

Najib tightened his lips at that. If only Daliah *had* chosen him, he thought. But all she'd done was try her best to repel him. He wondered if her father would believe that.

Wearily Dani pinched the bridge of his nose, then let his hand drop to his lap. "I am sorry," he said stiffly, and reassembled his face into a mask of composure. "I know this is not the time to discuss your relationship. It just came as such a shock . . ."

Najib nodded. "It was not a good time to tell you, but I wanted you to understand why I want to help her escape, and why I have come to you. I need your help. The way I see it, Daliah's only chance is that you and I join forces. You have military resources available to you, and I have the inside knowledge of how to pull it off. Even so, it is a ticklish situation and will require utmost secrecy."

Schmarya looked thoughtful. "Tell me . . . are the Saudis aware that she is being held in their country?" He looked at Najib.

Najib shook his head. "I seriously doubt it," he replied, "because if they were, they would not stand for it. As you probably know, they are treading a fine tightrope at the moment. They need the new American fighter jets they are negotiating for, and thus cannot afford to anger the United States. And on the other hand, the United States cannot get too tough with them, because they depend upon Saudi oil. It did occur to me to appeal to the government of either Saudi Arabia or the United States to apply pressure on Abdullah—"

"And?" Schmarya interrupted.

Najib shook his head. "I'm afraid it would only have negative results. The Saudis do not want to anger the United States, but they cannot afford to anger Abdullah either. And can you blame them? Allah only knows where Abdullah's next bombs might be planted. Riyadh? Al Madinah?"

"*Mecca!*" the old man said. "If they were told—"

"No!" Najib cut down that suggestion at once. "That is out of the question. Abdullah is too crazed to listen to reason. If the Saudis pressured him, it might force him to do one of two things: either to kill Daliah right away or to move her elsewhere." He smiled grimly. "The way things stand now, at least we know she is alive, and we know where she is."

Schmarya took a deep breath. "So. What do we do? Right now, my own government is trying to hold out the olive branch and talk peace accords with our Arab neighbors. Because of that, Israel will not dare use military force to rush across the borders and rescue Daliah, or else all our efforts at gaining peace will be destroyed. There could even be war in the Gulf." He frowned and looked at Najib. "You were right. Without the permission of my country and the Saudi government, it is a very ticklish situation indeed." He paused and his eyes took on a kind of shrewdness. "I take it you have worked it out already?"

"I have." Najib leaned forward excitedly, but his voice was soft. "What is to stop a group of us from going in and releasing her? Unofficially, of course."

"You mean . . . use mercenaries?" Dani asked, perking up.

"No, no." Najib shook his head. "We do not have the time for that. It would take far too long to recruit a highly trained force. What we need—immediately—is the best commando team we can get hold of."

"Israelis." Schmarya grunted it as a statement, not a question.

Najib nodded. "Israelis. But dressed in civilian clothes, not uniforms. And they must not carry any identification on them. It goes without saying that if they are caught, your country would have to disavow any knowledge of our attempt."

Schmarya gave a snort. "You are not asking for much! Only our best boys to lay down their lives for an unsanctioned private invasion!" He narrowed his eyes at Najib.

"I realize that," Najib said. "But we have no other choice. It is that or nothing."

"I was afraid it would come down to something like this." Schmarya sat back heavily. "It will be very difficult. Very difficult."

"I cannot overemphasize how little time we have," Najib warned quietly. "A week ago, Daliah was important to Abdullah. He had plans for her. But since then, things have changed markedly. Now that he's gotten this idea for a holy war, I am afraid he'll soon find himself saddled with her—and have no reason for keeping her alive any longer. Already she is a liability to him."

Schmarya sighed painfully. "So speed is of the essence. When is it not?" He frowned thoughtfully and then got briskly down to business. "What, exactly, other than manpower, do we need for mounting a rescue attempt?"

"Weapons," Najib said immediately. "Under the circumstances, preferably as few Israeli weapons as possible. The rest is all in place. My yacht carries a helicopter, and I have had it moved into position off the coast of Oman. The palace has an airstrip, and I have a large private jet. Also, there are two of Abdullah's top men inside the palace right now whom we can depend on."

He paused and added softly, "We have already planned the mission for tomorrow night."

"Tomorrow!" Schmarya was shocked.

"Tomorrow." Najib nodded. "Except for the commandos, everything is set to go. I have sketched plans of the palace layout, and the two inside men will do what they must at the appointed hour. You must understand, we have no choice. The mission *must* be accomplished tomorrow, or never at all. It is too late to change the timetable now."

"It is crazy." Schmarya rolled his eyes.

"Perhaps. But it is necessary." Najib caught his look. "Then I can count on your help?" he asked.

"We'll see what we can do," Schmarya grunted gruffly. "I'll get on it right away."

"Two-forty-five A.M., solar time," Najib warned. "This is the hour it must take place tomorrow. If you cannot round up the men in time for that mission, there is nothing else I can do."

"I understand," the old man said, the deep lines of his face settling into taut grim crevices. "I only hope to God that my contact understands it too."

"In that case, we had better waste no more time." Dani looked at his watch and rose to his feet. "I will call the airport and see when the next flight leaves for Tel Aviv. The sooner we get back, the sooner we may be able to arrange something."

"There is no need to call the airlines," Najib said. "I have taken the liberty of chartering a jet for you. Right now, it is waiting at Nicosia International, and is prepared to take off the moment you board. The pilot has instructions to remain in Tel Aviv until you give him further instructions. When you have rounded up the men—and I am working on the

702

assumption that you will—the jet will fly them all here. My own jet, which we will be using for the escape attempt, will be at an abandoned military airfield on the Karpas Peninsula. It is suitably deserted, and if there is time, we can perhaps hold a drill. Your pilot knows where it is."

Schmarya frowned. "And the men's weapons? How will we get them past Cyprian customs?"

"That has already been arranged." Najib allowed himself a slight smile. "The authorities will look the other way."

"But if your customs agent should come down sick, or be—"

Najib shook his head. "It will not matter who is on duty. I chose Cyprus specifically because of my relationship with the Cypriot government. For some time now, they have been negotiating with me to build a waste-processing plant, wineries, and an airport addition here." He smiled wryly and his voice was unconcerned. "They will look the other way. I have spoken with someone at the highest level of the government, and it was a condition I insisted upon before I agreed to their terms." He smiled again. "It seems they will have gotten the buildings with less negotiating than they expected."

Schmarya was impressed. "You have apparently thought of everything."

Najib's brow furrowed. "I only fear that there must be many things I have overlooked."

For the first time, Schmarya permitted himself a smile. He rose from his chair. "I think we understand each other, Mr. al Ameer," he said warmly. "You are a man who cuts swiftly to the heart of the matter. Who knows? Maybe—just maybe—we stand a chance." His voice became thick with emotion. "Your grandfather must be very proud of you."

Najib got to his feet and turned away quickly. "My grandfather died last winter," he said quietly. "He had never been quite the same since Abdullah took over the leadership of our village. It was then, many years ago, that he began to die. After that, he was but a living shell."

"I am truly sorry," Schmarya said. He stood there a moment, silent, and then tears filled his eyes and his voice grew husky. "There was a time when he and I were close friends."

"I know," Najib said softly. "He spoke of you often."

"It is a pity that our religious beliefs and politics pulled us apart. I owed him my life, you know." Schmarya shook his head. "And now, it seems, Daliah may well owe you hers."

The words stirred Najib. He shook his head. "She will owe

me nothing, Mr. Boralevi. It is as I told you. I love her." He extended his hand. "Thank you for coming to see me. I will be anxiously awaiting word from you."

The old man's grip was dry and firm. "Let us only hope that I can cut through red tape as swiftly as you."

Najib turned to Dani and held out his hand, but Dani made no move to shake it. After a moment Najib let it drop to his side. "I cannot expect you to like me, Mr. ben Yaacov," he said, seeing them to the door. "I hope, however, that, given time, we may perhaps become friends."

He stood in the open doorway. "A car is waiting for you downstairs. You have my number. I will wait here for your call."

When they were out of earshot, he added softly in Hebrew, *"Shalom."*

"You," Schmarya said pointedly as the chauffered car pulled to a stop on the tarmac beside the chartered 737, "have been abnormally quiet." He closed his mouth as the chauffeur came around and held the rear door open. Waving away the solicitous hands and grunting, the old man ducked out on his own. Dani emerged behind him, and together they climbed the boarding steps. The sun was slipping down and the magenta-and-orange sky painted the silver wings in a soft pastel glow.

"You look like a man for whom the world has come to an end," Schmarya said with a touch of asperity.

Dani glared at him. "Hasn't it?"

Schmarya sighed. Dani had become like a simmering volcano. He'd spoken hardly a word during the entire ride from Famagusta.

"I know it's too early to celebrate, Dani," he said quietly, "but you should be happy that Daliah at least stands a chance now. Without Mr. al-Ameer, we would surely never see her again. Did you give that any thought?"

"You've always had a soft spot for the al-Ameers, haven't you?" Dani snapped savagely, and pushed his way past a smiling stewardess into the plane.

Schmarya nodded apologetically at the woman and sighed again. No matter what he said or did, Dani was in no mood to be cheered up. He could put his finger on the precise moment something inside his son-in-law had snapped—the moment Najib al-Ameer had announced his love for Daliah.

"Would he prefer the man wasn't in love with her, and wouldn't help her?" he mumbled under his breath as he went inside the plane and sank into a big leather armchair facing Dani's. Despite himself, as he glanced around, he had to raise his eyebrows in surprise. Someone had done a major overhaul on the interior of the jet. This was nothing like a commercial airliner. It was all high style: sleek, sparkling, and sophisticated.

Schmarya tightened his lips. It rankled that the one time in his life he was surrounded by luxury, he couldn't even sit back and enjoy it. Opposite him, Dani had already strapped himself in and was glowering out at the sunset.

The lithe stewardess approached, smile in place. "We will be taking off immediately. Shall I get you gentlemen a drink?"

Dani shook his head without removing his gaze from the window.

The stewardess looked at Schmarya. "And you, sir?"

Schmarya shook his head. "Nothing, thank you." As she started to turn away, he cleared his throat. She glanced questioningly over her shoulder. "Tell me, miss. Is it possible to make a telephone call from this plane?"

"Of course. The moment we are airborne, I will bring you a telephone." She smiled nicely. "If you'll give me the number now, I will be able to place the call without delay."

Ten minutes later, as the coast of Cyprus was dropping away below them, Schmarya listened to the strangely distorted ringing tone. It sounded tinny and weak and far away.

"*Ken,*" a voice answered curtly after the fourth ring. "Yes."

"My friend," Schmarya said cautiously. "What would you say to a cup of coffee at the same place where we met last time?"

There was a long pause at the other end of the line. Finally Chaim Golan spoke. "So. It has come to that, has it?"

"I will tell you all about it. Could you make it in an hour and a half?"

Golan grunted. "Where are you? It sounds like the bottom of a garbage can."

Schmarya laughed. "I'm in-flight. An hour and a half, then."

"In-flight." Chaim sounded impressed. "Fancy schmancy. If we don't watch it, you will soon get too grand for the rest of us, Schmarya." And with that, he rang off.

Schmarya signaled to the stewardess and handed her the phone. Then he, too, stared out the window. As he watched, the light drained completely from the sky and everything became dark velvet.

It was really not much of a flight: a steep ascent followed by a steep descent. Up and down. But between Dani's sulky mood and his own worries over the outcome of his upcoming meeting with Chaim Golan, it was the longest forty-five minutes Schmarya had ever endured.

He was glad when the plane put down at Ben-Gurion.

"You go on home," he told Dani when they climbed into a cab. "Just drop me off on Dizengoff Street."

Dani nodded. He was still in no mood to speak. He was hoping it wasn't true that Daliah and Najib al-Ameer were in love with each other.

Now that the sweltering day had become a cool, breezy night, Dizengoff Street teemed even more than it had during the day. It seemed that everyone was out taking advantage of the breezes, and at the Kassit Café and its rival, the Rowal, every tiny table was occupied. Sounds of intense conversation and the metallic chimes of cutlery on china merged with the ever-present tinkling of glasses. Headlights and taillights, streetlights and neons, bicycle lamps and flood-lit marquees—it was a perpetual kaleidoscope of patterns and colors. Schmarya took a sip of his rosé wine and listened. From somewhere behind him he could hear impassioned youthful voices rising as someone formulated a petition that had to do with Soviet Jewry.

It seemed to him that he and Chaim had sat in silence amid the sounds and lights swirling all around them for far too long already, and he was finding it difficult to be patient. He was only too aware of each second as it ticked by— precious seconds which raced inexorably toward the countdown of Daliah's fate.

Chaim Golan was still thinking, and Schmarya waited, knowing better than to rush the head of the Mossad.

Finally Golan shifted in his chair. His eyes sparkled merrily, but his voice was pained. "There is no time to call a special meeting and argue this case."

Schmarya shook his head. "It has to be tomorrow night. He has set it up to occur then, and the timetable cannot be altered."

Golan pursed his lips. "What impression did you get from him?" he asked. "Is he like the newspapers make out? Could this be some kind of adventure to alleviate a rich man's boredom?"

"Not at all. He is quite serious about this. He wants Abdullah stopped."

Golan swore under his breath. "Mecca! The Wailing Wall!

St. Peter's!" He shook his head angrily. "It proves what we have known all along. Abdullah is mad. He should have been terminated a long time ago. We would have all been much better off."

Schmarya shook his head. "All those euphemisms. Why can't anybody in the intelligence service use real words, like 'murder' or 'assassinate'? *Terminate!*" He snorted.

Golan chose to ignore that. "It's too bad we have so little time," he said. "From what you tell me, it sounds like we should mount a full-scale operation. Attacking a hundred trained terrorists on their own ground with only a handful of men is . . . well, suicidal."

"We have the element of surprise," Schmarya pointed out.

"That is about all we have," Golan countered dryly.

Schmarya put his glass down and leaned toward him. "How many men, Chaim?" he demanded in a whisper. "How many can you come up with?"

"Fifteen. Twenty." Golan shrugged. "Thereabouts. Some will not be available, others might be out of the country." He sighed and shook his head. "They are bad odds for good boys, Schmarya. Very bad odds."

"But they are well-trained. They are the best of their kind in the world."

"All the more reason not to waste them senselessly!"

Schmarya stared at him. "You yourself just admitted that anything is worth it if we can stop Abdullah. You're not going to throw this chance away, are you? It's the opportunity of a lifetime!"

"Then you trust Najib al-Ameer."

Schmarya nodded. "I believe he is sincere. It is as important for him to get rid of Abdullah as it is for us. In fact, we have much in common; many of his reasons are the same as ours."

Golan grunted. "Then why was he so involved with that hotbed of terrorists for so long, I ask you? For years, it was his money and his shipping routes that kept Abdullah in business."

Schmarya looked surprised. "Then you know all about him."

Golan's face was expressionless. "We've been keeping an eye on him," he said evasively.

Schmarya gave a bark of a laugh. "How thick is that dossier?"

"You'll keep your wondering to yourself," Golan advised grimly.

"What I can't understand is, if you found out so much, then why didn't you put a stop to him?"

"You know why." Golan gestured irritably. "He's untouchable. Nothing could be proven. Just because arms are shipped on his freighters and planes and large sums of money are channeled through a maze of Swiss accounts doesn't necessarily prove anything against *him*. Of course, we know it's him, but we'd have to prove it. He's no dum-dum, I can tell you that. He's been wise enough to distance himself so that if the shit ever hits the fan, it stops short of splattering him."

"He told me he wants out of the PFA."

"I can't imagine why." Golan's voice was heavily sarcastic. "Funny, how people who make a deal with the devil always find out too late that when you deal with the devil, you end up in hell. You'd think they'd get wiser earlier on, wouldn't you?"

"Chaim . . ." Schmarya said, a troubled look on his face.

Golan sighed heavily. "All right, all right," he said. "Against my better judgment, the answer is yes. I'll round up the men and weapons immediately. Just remember"—he wagged a cautioning finger—"for all practical purposes, this is a *private* endeavor. We have no knowledge about the attempt. Should one or more of our boys die, we will not acknowledge they are ours. And if we do get Daliah out, remember: not a word to the press about what really happened. We say it was a moderate splinter group of Abdullah's which attempted a coup, and that *they* released her. Is that understood?"

Schmarya nodded and held his gaze. "I'm grateful for your decision, Chaim," he said. "There is just one more thing. Also, Najib al-Ameer requests immunity."

"Immunity! A woman's been kidnapped and a man has been killed!"

"Daliah won't press charges—"

"And Elie Levin's death? Are we supposed to just forget that?"

"Under the circumstances, it might be wise. True, Najib al-Ameer's been involved with Abdullah. But it was Abdullah's men who did the killing."

"Schmarya, sometimes you try my soul."

"And you, you old putz? You don't try mine?"

The head of the Mossad shrugged.

In the Almoayyed palace:

In her second-floor suite, Daliah paced restlessly. She wore a pair of floppy silk lounging pajamas she had found in the closet, and she had fashioned her long hair into a single thick long braid that hung down her back. That way, she figured, her mane wouldn't get in the way of things. Earlier in the day, Khalid had dropped by, ostensibly to check upon her, and had whispered that if a rescue attempt was made, she should be prepared for it to be that very night. After that bit of news, there was no way she could hope to get any sleep. She didn't even try. Her nerves were too wound up. . . .

Monika yelled and kicked. Slashed her flattened hands through the air so that they blurred and whistled. Kicked with the other foot. Advanced. Yelled. Withdrew. She was sweating up a storm. Whenever possible, she practiced her judo and karate twice a day—in the morning right after she got up, and at night, just before bedtime. It pleased her that her reactions were better than ever. . . .

Khalid swallowed cupfuls of cold strong black coffee. He could have used sleep, but he had long ago found that his reactions were always better if he didn't sleep right before a mission. It took him too long to wake up fully, and tonight, of all nights, he didn't dare be groggy. . . .

At the far end of the palace compound, Hamid tiptoed around the utility room in one of the outbuildings and shone a powerful flashlight around. The thousands of thin, color-coded wires baffled him. He didn't know which ones to disconnect, so he decided to be on the safe side and disconnect them all. His hand shook and he broke out in a cold sweat as he began tearing all the wires loose, praying that a contingency alarm wasn't hooked up to any of the wires he was pulling. He was sure that bells would be sounding any minute. . . .

Ghazi stirred from his sleep, lumbered groggily into one of the bathrooms, urinated sloppily, and wandered back to his bed, where he fell back into a soundless, dreamless sleep. . . .

Surour was in the other bathroom, sitting on one of the two travertine toilet seats. His semiautomatic rifle was at his side, and his bandaged right hand was swelling up worse, but it was a pain he could bear. His chest swelled with pride. He was guarding his master while he showered. . . .

Under the twelve steaming shower jets which crashed on him from all four walls, Abdullah was feeling satisfied with himself. As he soaped himself vigorously, visions of glory filled his mind. It had already occurred to him that the Jewish actress was a chain around his neck and that the holy war was far more important. Tomorrow Daliah Boralevi would be shot and buried in the sand. . . .

* * *

Somewhere over Jordan:

Najib entered the dark cockpit of the 727-100 and took over copilot duties for a while. Long ago, he had discovered that helping to fly the big jet relaxed him and soothed his nerves. On this night, however, sitting in front of the multi-colored lights and glowing dials, he was discovering that for once it was only making him more tense. . . .

Dani was in one of the compact toilets, smearing camouflage gel over his face. He cursed as the jet hit turbulence. He was not in the least bit surprised to find that his skin was clammy and his hands were shaking. Not only was this suicidal mission fraying his nerves, but ever since he had been shot down by the Germans during the war, with his plane exploding in midair, it was all he could do to board a plane. . . .

Schmarya felt his pulse tripping, and knew without checking that his blood pressure had risen dangerously. He glanced around the luxuriously furnished cabin and wondered for the hundredth time whether any of them stood a chance of surviving. The odds were almost five to one. Against. . . .

And in Jerusalem:

Chaim Golan was feeling the wrath of a head of state. The meeting was informal, unofficial, and took place in the book-lined library of the prime minister's house. Chaim was beginning to wish he had turned down Schmarya Boralevi's request. Or better yet, that he'd never even heard of him.

The prime minister sat silently on a comfortable over-stuffed chair. Telephone lines to key people in the government were open, and the military had been put on full alert. Otherwise, there was nothing to do but wait. . . .

"See anything yet?" Dani asked as the clock inched past two-twenty-five A.M.

"No." Schmarya shook his head. Shielding the glare from the bright cabin with his cupped hands, he was peering out the square Perspex window. All he saw was blackness, blackness, and yet more blackness. The jet was streaking above the Rub' al-Khali, the Empty Quarter, and it lived up to its name. For the last two hours, there had not been a single light to be seen anywhere below. He glanced at his watch: ETA was in twenty minutes.

Turning away from the window, he pushed the control button on the side of his seat, which slowly swiveled the chair around, and glanced about the cabin. If it hadn't been for the deadly seriousness of the mission, it would have made for an extraordinarily amusing sight. Seated around the flying Arab palace were seventeen crack Israeli commandos, volunteers all, and all with faces smeared mat black and bodies encased in tight black stretch jumpsuits. They looked, he thought, more like futuristic chimney sweeps than commandos on a live-or-die mission. Only there was nothing amusing about it—a fact which the presence of the one man not in black confirmed. He was the Israeli military surgeon accompanying the mission. He would remain on the plane during the assassination-and-rescue attempt and treat any of the wounded men on the return flight. Schamrya felt an inordinate pride. He was honored to be among them. They were a group who believed in taking care of their own.

At the moment, everything seemed to be on a forward slant, and the plane was shaking. The turbulence increased as they descended into warmer air. On the floor were Uzi submachine guns, American M16-Al's, portable shoulder rocket launchers, flamethrowers, and an array of other greasy, high-tech West German, Soviet, and Israeli weaponry. They were ready to be grabbed up the instant before touchdown, and in the turbulence, they clattered and rattled metallically against one another.

Schamrya swiveled his seat further around and looked over at Dani, seated on the other side of the low table they shared. "Nervous, Dani?" Schamrya asked in a low voice.

Dani raised his head. He was a strange sight—all black face, white eyes, and white teeth. "Nervous?" he asked. There was just the slightest hesitation. "I suppose so." He gave a tight little smile. "Yes."

"I am nervous too. If it gives you any comfort, think of the old days. It's like bicycle riding: I don't think you can ever lose your touch. You used to be one of the best, you know."

"I'm old now."

Schamrya laughed. "You're young. *I'm* the one who's old. Too old to be playing war games, and far too old to dress up like it's Halloween." Oh, yes, he thought with satisfaction, Dani would be all right.

Najib, also black-faced to melt into the night, was making his way aft from the cockpit. He stopped at Schamrya's seat. "Captain Childs has just contacted the helicopter. It is in position five miles south of the palace. He will radio them again exactly five minutes before we touch down. That way it will arrive simultaneously with us."

Schamrya looked up at him. He was amazed at the man's calm—for that matter, at everyone's calm, his own included.

He glanced around. Seventeen crack troops, he thought, plus Dani, Najib, and myself. Twenty men. Twenty-two, if I count the two at the palace.

His face hardened. He could only hope that twenty-two of them would be enough. Not that the commandos weren't first-rate. They were superb; watching them drill had proven that. No matter what they did, they worked together as finely as the precisely tuned gears inside a Swiss watch, each of them a different articulated part of one host body: totally in synch, consummately courageous, and with an all-for-one-and-one-for-all Musketeer loyalty. If this mission succeeded, it would be because of them.

But, he reminded himself, Abdullah's forces of a hundred or so had more than mere numbers on their side. They had the messianic madness of their leader to inspire them, and, depending on how one looked upon them, they were the hundred heads of a very lethal hydra. It would be folly to discount the strength and fighting abilities of a lean, mean fighting machine. Abdullah and his men lived to destroy, and if they were half as good as it was claimed, then element of surprise or no, the small force of twenty and the two in the palace were headed into the face of death, never to return.

It was a sobering thought.

"Do you mind if I join you?" Najib asked, indicating the empty seat behind Schmarya.

"It's your plane," Schmarya said with a laugh. "Be my guest." He activated the swivel mechanism and did a ninety-degree turn in his chair so he would face him.

Najib nodded at Dani, who now sat behind Schmarya, and then dry-swallowed several times as he took a seat. As always, the change in cabin pressure clogged his ears. By habit he glanced at the computer map at the front bulkhead. There were fourteen minutes to go.

Eight hundred and forty seconds to zero hour.

Najib nodded to himself. He could only pray that Allah was on their side. The mission had to go like clockwork; a single foul-up could have endless ramifications. The fallout from this rescue mission would have far-reaching consequences for the Israelis, but most of all for him. For even if the mission were successful, if word somehow leaked out that he had joined forces with the Jews and mounted a mission against his own people, he would be *persona non grata* in the entire Arab world and would not have long to live. Even more hated than Jews were Arab traitors.

He tightened his lips grimly. Right now, it was best not to think of such things.

Schmarya watched Najib closely. He could tell from the shadow that came into Najib's eyes exactly what he was thinking. The thoughts were not that much different from his own.

Thirteen minutes.

Near the front of the cabin, the young Israeli captain in charge of the commandos got to his feet. He stood cockily in the center of the aisle, legs spread, hands resting on lean hips. "If you gentlemen will please give me your undivided attention for a moment," he called out in a strong voice. "I know we have been through all this already, but I'll go through it one last time since we haven't had that much time to drill. So listen carefully. Have your weapons in hand the moment we touch ground. We're coming in totally blacked out, and you'll be forewarned by the captain before the lights go out. We'll use the emergency slide chutes to exit the plane, and since it's going to be dark out, take extra care. The one thing we can't afford is for any of you to have an accident before the shooting begins. I don't have to tell you that there are few enough of us as it is. The helicopter seats six, which includes the pilot, and will drop us off inside the compound in relays of five. That's four trips. The alarms on the palace grounds should have been disconnected by now, but in case they weren't, or something goes wrong, be prepared for them to go off. I don't need to warn you that we're dealing with a zealous group of terrorists. Shoot first and ask questions later. We can't afford to take prisoners, and we certainly cannot afford to let a single one of us be taken. The instant the woman is found, fire off a red flare. Once Abdullah's death is confirmed, fire off a yellow one. When both have been fired, that is the signal to regroup and withdraw. Being a civilian, the woman goes on the first helicopter relay back to the plane. Any questions?" He looked around the cabin.

One of the commandos raised his hand.

"What is it, Meyer?" the captain asked wearily.

"My wife wants an Oriental carpet. Can we take souvenirs?" The men laughed.

"Shove it, Meyer," the captain said with conversational good cheer. He paused and looked around. "Check your weapons and get in gear."

Suddenly there was a lot of clicking and clattering going on, and the rustling of movements everywhere around. Dani reached under the low table and flipped a helmet across it to

Schmarya, who caught it, and tossed another further back to Najib.

Najib caught it like a football. "Is this really necessary?" He held up the helmet. "It feels so heavy."

"Better to curse it now than wish belatedly you'd had it on," Schmarya advised.

Najib looked at him and then nodded. He put it on and strapped it under his chin. Amazingly enough, it was a perfect fit.

Turning to the Perspex window, he looked at his reflection. Black helmet, black face. He smiled to himself. Even his own mother would not have recognized him. Now, if only no one at the palace did either.

Again he looked past Schmarya, toward Dani, and this time he caught his eye and held it for a long moment.

Dani met his gaze challengingly.

"I haven't had the opportunity to thank you for coming," Najib said softly. "I want you to know how much I appreciate it."

Dani shook his head. A faint smile crossed his lips. "It should be I who thank you. Daliah is my daughter, and I've been behaving childishly. I'm sorry if I was a little tough on you back on Cyprus."

"You had every right."

Dani shook his head. "No, I did not. I went far beyond my rights." He hesitated, looked away, then back at Najib. "I want you to know that Daliah is very lucky. Few men would have done what you are doing."

Najib laughed. "That is because few men could afford it."

"That is not what I meant. I just want you to know . . . well . . ." Dani looked away, suddenly embarrassed.

Najib did not prod him.

Dani's eyes came back around. "What I want to say is: I will not stand between you and Daliah."

Najib looked at him with surprise. Then a smile broke across his lips. But before he could reply, Captain Childs' flat voice came over the cabin speaker. "Five minutes until landing, gentlemen," he drawled. "The helicopter is taking off at this moment and will meet us at the runway. The palace is straight ahead on our left. We'll be passing over it, and we'll leave the window shades up so that you can get a look at the compound. Please extinguish all smoking materials. In fifteen seconds I will douse the cabin lights and turn off all external safety lights. We will be coming in totally blacked out, without even navigational lights, and I'd appreciate it if none of you mentioned this little fact to the aviation authorities. We are breaking every regulation in the book, and I happen to like flying." He paused. "Five seconds until lights-out."

And then the plane blacked out completely, both inside and out. Even the computer map faded. Only the dim red lights above the emergency exits glowed softly.

"Good luck, gentlemen," Captain Childs added, and then the fuselage gave a shudder as the landing gear came down.

There was a lot of commotion as all the men moved over to the left side of the jet. Najib activated his seat to swivel it around, and pressed his black face to the Perspex and looked down. There it was! Coming up ahead, and almost close enough to touch, the Almoayyed palace glowed like a multi-faceted beacon.

He turned to Dani one last time. "Good luck, friend," he said softly.

"Good luck," Dani said, equally softly, and added gently: "friend."

All around them, the men were commenting on the palace fortress. There wasn't one among them who wasn't impressed.

Dani was the only one who did not look down. He was sitting erectly, a submachine gun lying across his knees. It felt strangely light for its size, and oddly greasy. He clamped one hand on the grip and the other around the barrel. There was something strangely reassuring about it. It was almost as though it was an extension of his body. The years fell away to the exciting days of his youth. He felt strong and invincible, his animal instincts heightened. He felt the long-forgotten tightening inside his stomach, the wire-drawn tension in all his muscles, and finally the adrenaline charge letting go, as if a massive floodgate had been thrown open. He could almost feel himself growing ten feet tall. Once a soldier, he thought, always a soldier. It never faded from your blood.

And then the jet came in low over the rooftop of the palace.

Of all the countless rooms in the palace, Saeed Almoayyed's suite, which Najib had occupied, afforded the single best view of the runway. At the moment, the sliding windows were open to the night, and the air was brisk and chill. Khalid was seated in the dark, alone, a thermos of coffee at his side. Years spent staking out targets for Abdullah's terrorist activities and month-long stretches of having had to go to ground after various missions had been completed had honed his patience to that of a hunter. So seasoned by a lifetime of violence, he felt no hurry and no nervousness, not even the rising rush of adrenaline which in most men usually occurs in the lull directly before a battle. Later, when the shooting began, power would surge through him.

He could hear the unmistakable rumble of an approaching jet. He checked his digital watch. The red LED letters flashed 02:44:02. Fifty-eight seconds, and he would activate the runway lights with the remote-control unit at his side. He had tested it at noon, when the sun was brightest and the lights clicking on would be the least noticeable, attributed to the reflection of the sunlight. It had confirmed to him that the remote and the lights were in working order.

He got up from his chair and checked the ammunition clip, yanking it out by feel and then snapping it back into his semiautomatic rifle. Then he unsnapped the flap of his holster so that his revolver could be drawn without hesitation, and unbuttoned his big boxy fatigue pockets so that he could get to the grenades. He picked up the remote unit and checked his watch—02:44:59.

One more second.

He pushed the button of the remote unit, and in the darkness outside, the two strands of straight pearl necklaces shimmered whitely.

The whine of the approaching jet was very close now. Very low. It almost drowned out the clatter of an approaching helicopter.

He grinned to himself. The waiting was nearly over.

Daliah stood stock-still as the eerie whine, like the whistling of a dropped bomb, screamed to an ear-splitting crescendo. Then an explosive boom, which sounded like the end of the world, shook the palace to its foundations and rattled the windows in their frames.

Her heart was beating wildly. So Khalid was right: Najib's troops had landed.

"Far fucking out!" she said aloud.

Abdullah was in the *majlis*. Three tables had been shoved together to form an asymmetrical U in the center of the huge room, directly under the three-story-high stained-glass rotunda. Spread out on each surface was a map—one each of Jerusalem, the Vatican, and Mecca.

Like a general in his high-backed armchair, Abdullah sat inside the open end of the U. Three shaded marble-based fluorescent lamps—one on each table—cast a pool of white light on each map and threw his face into sharply angled, prominently ridged shadows. Earlier in the day he had had squads of men remove every stick of furniture from the enormous room, with the exception of the three tables, three lamps, a single black telephone, and his stately, chosen chair. Now, at last, the *majlis* was to his satisfaction: a carefully lit, exceptionally dramatic stage set worthy of its occupant.

Ghazi, black glasses in place, stood on guard several feet behind him, a burly unmoving statue with a semiautomatic slung over his shoulder by its webbing strap.

Abdullah nodded to himself. The *majlis* had become his combination throne room and war room, and he thought it quite fitting. He felt a bridled, barely contained power race inside him. All he needed was to unleash it at the appointed hour, and the world would be his. This, he thought, was surely how Mohammed had felt. Almighty and omnipotent. Filled with Herculean power.

Despite the ungodliness of the hour, Abdullah was wide-awake. He hadn't even tried to go to sleep. In fact, he felt like he would never again need as much as another hour's sleep for as long as he lived. He had never felt better or more alert. Everything had taken on an otherworldly clarity. All last night, and then the entire day long, and now far into tonight also, his mind had been bombarding him with bits and pieces of logistical information. No matter what else he tried to concentrate on, his glorious vision was overpowering and filled his mind to bursting. The countless tactical problems of destroying Mecca, the Wailing Wall, and St. Peter's were beginning to work themselves out; at times, it was almost as though he didn't even *have* to think; his subconscious was solving everything for him. Greatness begot greatness. The aphrodisiac of power was speed in his veins. He was filled with a buzzing nervous energy.

Finally Abdullah turned and gestured for Ghazi to come around and stand in front of the desk. He waited until Ghazi faced him, and then asked, "How does your hand feel?"

Ghazi shrugged. "Not too bad."

"We'll have it seen to soon," Abdullah promised. "When my half-nephew returns, I will tell him to fly a doctor in from Riyadh." He paused and held his bodyguard's gaze. "You realize, I hope, how important it was that you follow my orders and hurt yourself? Only through an action of such magnitude could I prove to Khalid and Najib how selflessly devoted you are to me."

Ghazi shrugged his huge shoulders.

Abdullah placed his elbows on the arms of the chair, steepled his hands, and went on warmly, "I am very glad for you and Surour, and you should both be proud of yourselves. How many other men will be able to say they marched directly by my side as I rewrote history? Who knows? Perhaps we will even enter Paradise together." His vulpine lips smiled with satisfaction. "It is not everyone who is chosen to serve Allah in such an awesome—"

He cocked his head as he heard a jet scratching the silence, becoming louder and louder, until, with a deafening roar, it shot past directly overhead, rattling the stained-glass panels of the skylight in their soaring domed frame. As the roar receded, he could hear a second sound, that of the clattering rotors of a helicopter.

"What did I tell you?" Abdullah told Ghazi. "There is my half-nephew now. You will have your hand seen to even sooner than I anticipated. As soon as he is brought to me, I will have him send the jet to Riyadh to fetch a doctor for you and Surour."

Ghazi's expression was bland. "I am all right. There is really no rush."

"Ah, but there is." Abdullah's eyes were alight with a silver fire. "Do not forget, Ghazi, that I am counting on you and Surour to protect me. I need you both in excellent shape to do that!"

"Yes," Ghazi replied. "If that is your wish."

"It is." Abdullah leaned forward and bent back over the map of Mecca.

Suddenly, three stories above him, the skylight lit up with all the rainbow colors of daylight as a white flare exploded. Soft turquoises and pinks and blues and greens dappled him and the sea of flokati in a wide radiant circle, so that he looked like a tiny target in the exact center of a giant rose window. He looked up, an expression of amazement on his face. Then his eyes filled with fury, but his voice remained calm. "I see I shall have to have a talk with the men. Sometimes they behave like children. Flares are nothing to play with!"

A bleak joy came into Ghazi's eyes. "Let me go and put a stop to this!"

"No, no, you stay here by my side," Abdullah told him briskly with an elegant wave of his hand. "I am almost finished for the night, and we will drop by the barracks before we go upstairs." As he bent over the map again, the approaching whickering sounds of a helicopter sounded much closer. He felt oddly disturbed. Then he shrugged the feeling away. Najib has indeed returned, he thought, and for another two minutes he gave the helicopter no further thought.

It wasn't until a second white flare brightened the skylight even further, bringing the colors of the stained glass to even richer, more vivid hues, that Abdullah realized his folly. The thought flashed through his mind just as the clattering rotors filled the *majlis* with unbearable noises, lingered, and then receded again, droning swiftly away. Already the first crack of gunfire rent the air, and the stunning truth froze him momentarily. Then he leapt from his chair and, Ghazi at his side, made a dash across the white carpet of the enormous empty room. Even before they reached the door, a projectile came crashing through the green-tinted windows at the far end of the room, and a shower of glass merged with a rocketing explosion. A great orange-and-black fireball bloomed and rose in a column, and its fiery wind knocked Abdullah and Ghazi off their feet and slammed them flat to the floor. The explosion seemed to suck all the air out of the room. The U-shaped desk area, where they had been only moments earlier, was showered in a massive hailstorm of colored glass as the dome exploded. It was a savagely beautiful and fleeting sight, like a column of magnified, multicolored fairy dust.

Abdullah shook his head to clear it; his ears rang from the blast, and the smell was ghastly—acrid cordite and some sort of kerosene propellant. The walls all around were pockmarked with shrapnel. The flokati was on fire, smoking heavily, smelling like a herd of burned sheep. The air in the *majlis* would soon be unbreathable. Miraculously, he and Ghazi had survived. He felt something warm and sticky on his face. He touched it tentatively. Blood. He had been cut by fragments of flying glass.

He felt a black, dizzying killing rage come over him. His *majlis*—his throne room and war room—the symbol of his omnipotence, had been destroyed.

Talons of fear dug into Abdullah's heart while his screeching curses became a shrill scream of terror, and he knew then that precious minutes had already been lost. Realization had taken too long to dawn. Now he knew what had disturbed him earlier.

Najib's jet was one thing, but there shouldn't have been a helicopter within a hundred and eighty miles.

He jumped to his feet. "Mobilize!" he screamed at Ghazi. "We are under attack!"

It was like the epicenter of a massive earthquake.

A series of shockwaves from an explosion somewhere within the palace rocked the floor and caused a tremor which sounded like a rumbling freight train passing by directly below. The walls shook so violently that beside her, a hairline crack slashed across the pink suede wall covering and tore it apart at the seams with a loud ripping noise. From behind her, in the living room, she could hear the crashes as the windows imploded and the Venetian mirror burst on the wall and went flying. A mad staccato rattling gave evidence of the expensive *objets* on the sideboards and tables dancing spastically and falling. Daliah shouted and pounded on the Nevelson doors with renewed vigor, but it was futile. No one was coming to get her, and the big bronze portals only vibrated and groaned. It would take a lot more than a little shaking to loosen *them*.

Then the shockwave passed as suddenly as it had come. She put her ear to the cold bronze door. Muffled shouts and screams came from somewhere out in the hall, and she shouted and pounded on the doors some more. After a moment she slumped against the wall. Her fists were beginning to hurt and her knuckles were bleeding. From the way things sounded, she wouldn't be at all surprised if the whole palace was soon blown to kingdom come—herself included.

Lesser explosions were reverberating with less force from somewhere outside on the grounds. Turning her head, she glanced once again back into the living room. Earlier, she had opened the windows and drawn the curtains aside so that she would have no trouble hearing the jet when it approached, and now, through the horizontal hairline cracks between the shutter slats, lightning flashes of red and orange burst and boomed like fireworks. With each tremor, the shutters rattled and shook, but like the bronze doors, they held fast.

Strangely enough, despite her anger and frustration, she was not the least bit frightened. Rather, she felt a thrill of exhilaration. Her heart surged warmly. Najib had come for her, just as he'd promised. Wonderful!

Not so wonderful. There was a terrible whistling noise and, again, an explosion rocked the walls and sent another shockwave rippling and rattling all over again. Clouds of plaster rained down from the ceiling, and the big marble floor tiles actually lifted, shifted, and did a little dance. All but one, which had popped up and cracked, settled back in place. Whatever missiles were being aimed at the palace, they were certainly starting to hit closer to her suite. Not wonderful at all.

The shouts out in the hall seemed to be getting closer now, and from somewhere right outside the shutters came the unmistakable roar of a helicopter swooping down yet once again. A moment later there was the staccato rat-tat-tat of machine guns. *Oh, God, don't let Najib get hurt!*

She glanced around fiercely. She had to get out of here somehow. If only there were something she could do.

She let out a gasp. Of course! Why hadn't she thought of it before?

Brandy! During her rummaging, she had come across a bottle of brandy in the sideboard!

She stood there hesitantly, her heart thumping, and then literally flew into the living room. She lunged for the floor, ducked instinctively, and put her arms protectively over her head as another explosion rocked the palace. A hailstorm of shrapnel rained against the outside of the shutters. Mad fingers of blue and white electricity jumped from the slats to the now glassless window frames and sizzled.

Keeping down and crawling on her belly across the floor on broken glass, she made it to the sideboard and yanked the doors open. The bottle was just where she'd seen it. She grabbed it by the neck. Courvoisier. Beautiful. On impulse, she kissed it.

Now, matches. She would need matches and a wick. No, not matches. A lighter! There was a table lighter on the nightstand.

She crawled madly into the bedroom, cursing the size of the rooms and the length of the crawl. When she reached the bedside, she lunged up for the lighter, blessed Ronson, and grabbed a pillow off the bed. She tore the case off it and giggled to herself. Courvoisier and a Pratesi pillowcase! It would make one hell of an expensive Molotov cocktail!

The brandy was a new bottle. She tore the wrapping around the neck and cursed as she broke a fingernail in the process. She ripped the pillowcase in shreds, twisted a length of it into a respectable wick, and poured enough brandy on it to soak it thoroughly. She sniffed. It smelled fruity and potent. Then she looked at the bottle and shrugged. Why not? She lifted it to her lips and took a swig for good measure. It went down like liquid velvet and radiated through her like a warm cloud.

She stuffed the soaked rag into the neck of the bottle. Clutching her homemade bomb in her left hand and the lighter in her right, she raced back out to the foyer.

Now let them come get me.

She didn't have long to wait.

"*Schnell!* Unlock it!" a shrill, guttural German voice screamed from the other side of the door.

Just her luck. It *would* be the German bitch.

"Well, here's to you, Monika," Daliah said fiercely to herself. As she heard the rattle of keys, she flattened herself against the wall so that she would be hidden behind the door when it opened, lit the tip of the rag, and averted her face as it flared gloriously into a crackling flame. "Cheers," she whispered soundlessly.

Slowly the door slid open toward her. Then her heart sank. Why were they hesitating? Why didn't they come in?

Hurry! Dammit, hurry before this thing blows up in my face!

"Up!" Najib screamed in at the helicopter pilot. "To the roof!"

He was was standing on the left landing skid and hanging on to the outside of the cabin while Dani was hanging on to the other side. Their heads were ducked against the noisy *whack-whack-whack* of the overhead rotor, and the whirlwind it stirred up tore at their faces.

"Up!" Najib screamed again.

"If you say so." The imperturbable pilot calmly took off, nosing the bird upward at a sharp angle, and the ground fell away below them. Najib glanced down. Beneath his feet, all hell had broken loose, and Abdullah's men were racing around in confusion. He grinned to himself. Usually it was they who called the shots; now, suddenly caught in a defensive position, they were not prepared for being on the receiving end of things. They were getting a taste of their own medicine. *Good.*

Dani looked up. Overhead, the old flares in the sky were dying out and falling, and another white one shot up into the sky, bursting into radiance and bathing the compound in dazzling, starkly surreal light. Then, lowering his gaze, he could see the men atop the compound walls racing around; as he watched, a rocket from a shoulder-held launcher burst into the wall, exploding a giant hole. As though in slow motion, chunks of concrete and screaming men went cartwheeling through the air.

The helicopter rose above the palace roof, swooped down, and hovered, scattering a cluster of terrorists. Najib and Dani both let off a burst from their hip-held automatics. Two men pitched off the roof, two more were mowed down screaming, and the remaining three fled for the roof door and disappeared.

Crouching, Najib jumped off the skid, rolled over twice, and keeping his head ducked against the whirring rotors, leapt neatly to his feet. Still in a crouch, he raced toward the roof door. On the other side of the whirlybird, Dani did the same and dived into position alongside him, waving back to the pilot to take off.

Najib looked at Dani and pointed to the roof door; the clatter of rotors was too loud for speech. Dani nodded, and together they dashed to the door and flattened themselves to either side of it.

"Cover me!" Najib shouted. He reached sideways gingerly for the door handle and then flung the door open to a bright rectangle of light. Dani leapt forward and let fly a burst of bullets; then, as he jumped back, Najib dashed inside and took the stairs down three at a time, Dani right behind him.

They were inside the palace. So it was not impregnable after all.

When they reached the landing, a spray of zinging bullets shot up from below and chipped bits of marble off the walls around them.

Dani propelled himself forward in a dancing spiral, loosened another burst, and danced back again. He heard a scream, and the firing stopped.

He glanced at Najib. "Where to now?"

Najib gestured downward with his thumb. "This is the third level. Unless they've moved her, Daliah's still down on the second." He tensed and listened. Bursts of gunfire were coming from somewhere below. He exchanged glances with Dani.

On impulse, he unstrapped his helmet and tossed it aside. "I can't hear well enough with it," he said. "And it cuts down on my peripheral vision." Then, as Dani took his off also, Najib raced down to the second-floor landing. Behind him, Dani grinned to himself. He was glad Najib al Ameer was on his side. He'd hate to have him for an enemy.

Daliah shrank back against the wall as the German girl and Surour burst into the foyer and headed straight into the living room. She waited a few seconds before sliding quietly out from behind the door. She tiptoed soundlessly after them. The flames of the Molotov cocktail blazed like a giant leaping torch, and the heat was so intense that she had to lean away from it.

It was then that Monika heard the crackling of the fire behind her and whirled around, her face contorting in rage. *"Nein!"* she yelled, and flung up her arms to shield her face as Daliah flung the Molotov cocktail at her feet.

It exploded with a roar and Monika screamed as a sheet of flame engulfed her and shot up to the ceiling. Daliah caught a glimpse of the German's clothes starting to burn, but she didn't wait around to see what would happen. She lunged for the door, slipping on the small prayer rug in the marble-floored foyer and, arms windmilling, skated on it past the imposing open Nevelson doors and out into the hall. Pausing only fractionally to glance both ways, she could already hear Monika's screams turning into shrill curses, and then the clatter of weapons was close behind.

That could only mean one thing. Surour and Monika had been stopped only momentarily. They were coming after her.

Without thinking, Daliah turned right and, clenching her fists like a sprinter, raced down the sculpture-lined hall. Shots cracked like thunder close behind her, and bullets *boinged* as they ricocheted off a giant owlish Maillot.

Daliah ducked low and zigzagged wildly to avoid the spray of bullets, her heart pounding as though it would burst.

She lunged sideways, down another bisecting corridor.

Without direction, she ran for her life.

Najib burst through the open doors of the suite in which Daliah had been kept prisoner, Dani at his heels. They both began to cough violently. There was a smoldering fire in the suite, and the air was thick with pea-soup smoke.

"Daliah!" Najib called out. "Daliah!"

There was no answer. He exchanged glances with Dani. Was she gone? Or was she somewhere in that blinding fog, passed out? . . . Dead? There was only one way to find out. "Follow me," he rasped grimly to Dani. "I'll take the bath-rooms. You look in the bedroom. Then we'll both check the living room."

After four minutes of choking and coughing, they ran back out into the hall, their lungs raw, their eyes streaming.

They took little comfort in the fact that she was gone.

"What now?" Dani panted.

"You take that side," Najib gasped, pointing to the right. "I'll go left."

They were closing in for the kill.

Daliah took no heed of the detonations erupting in various parts of the palace. It was all she could do to stay one hallway turnoff ahead of Monika and Surour. She couldn't be sure, but she had the terrible suspicion that she was running in circles. It was too late now to wish she'd asked

Najib for a lesson in the palace layout. All the sculptures looked the same, and she could have sworn she'd run past them before.

And then she suddenly knew she wasn't running around in circles after all. The hallway she was skidding down came to a windowless dead end. Two sets of closed double doors, one on either side, loomed tall. She chose the one on the left and struggled with it. *Locked.* In desperation she tried the one on the right. *Locked.* The thud of heavy boots sounded very close. As she turned slowly around, the breath caught in her throat. Monika and Surour were rushing toward her.

She was neatly trapped.

Scorched bright red, eyebrows and crew cut completely singed off, Monika's face was a hideous feral mask. With slow deliberation she tossed her automatic rifle aside. Then, signaling Surour to stay put, she walked slowly toward Daliah, clapping her hands as though she thoroughly enjoyed what was coming.

Daliah stood still as a wary statue.

And then fancy footwork and blurring arms turned Monika into a killing virago.

Schmarya hurried around in a swift running limp, his automatic shooting arcing bursts of scintillating tracers.

His eyes were everywhere at once, scanning the battle-field. He wasn't sure if he was imagining it or not, but it sounded as if the return fire was already starting to lessen. He kept his eyes peeled for the Israeli captain in charge of the mission.

He finally caught up with him on the far side of the palace, behind a makeshift shelter of lawn furniture next to the big underwater-lit swimming pool. "Captain, I've found a pocket of resistance in what I think is being used as a barracks building!" Schmarya was breathing heavily from the exertion, but his eyes glowed with a resolute fever. "I need a man with a rocket launcher. As soon as the barracks is destroyed, that should halve the resistance we're encountering."

The captain signaled to one of the men who held a heavy portable rocket launcher on his shoulder. "Perlman, go with him. Then come back here immediately. In a few minutes we'll start storming the palace."

Schmarya led Perlman in that swift, stiff-legged limp of his to the other side of the compound. Now he knew he hadn't imagined it. The terrorists had definitely been cut off. The outbuilding being used as a barracks and the palace itself were still strongholds, but their defenders had definitely been driven from outside the compound in to shelter. Thus far, the Israeli commandos were doing themselves proud.

Monika smiled. Insanely.

Daliah smiled right back at her. Tauntingly. Taking careful steps backward, she beckoned with both her hands for the German to come closer.

Monika stared at her, the insane smile turned savage, and an unholy darkness came down over her eyes. She lunged forward, and as Daliah took evasive action, she drew unexpectedly back again and started to walk deliberate flat-footed circles around her. The feint had told Monika what she needed to know. Daliah was no combat expert, but her reflexes were good and she'd had training—probably a little bit of this, and a little bit of that. Standard military training and some judo, maybe even a little bastardized karate thrown in. That one evasive tactic showed it all.

Monika's flame-blistered lips grinned, and she wiped sweaty hands on her fatigue pants. Then she continued her stalking circles, waiting to catch Daliah when her guard was down. It might be an interesting fight after all.

"Never be defensive. Whenever possible, take the offensive." The words of the military training sergeant, so long ago in the Negev, came back to Daliah in a flash. Well, so be it. She'd been defensive up to now, and it was time to show some fancy steps. She crouched forward, gorillalike, her fingers brushing the floor.

In response, Monika prepared her hands rigidly for *Wing Chun* chops.

A mere millisecond ticked, and then Daliah sprang into action; one second she had been stationary, and the next her feet should have connected with Monika's abdomen. But Monika had whirled aside and parried the attack.

"Ha!" Not wanting to lose the initiative, Daliah continued the offensive—hands slashing and slicing, feet whirling and kicking. With her every movement Monika was losing ground and was slowly but steadily being beaten back toward the Libyan. The German's moves were all defensive, deflective.

Surour could sense Monika's being beaten. By reflex, his submachine gun followed Daliah and his finger tightened on the trigger.

Daliah was oblivious of him and kept up her winning streak. She was smiling grimly and sweat was flying off her, but her movements were controlled and precise and confident. She went for the kill, a flat chop to Monika's throat.

The blow was paralyzing—for Daliah. She hadn't even seen Monika's left knee blurring up, but her kidneys exploded in a flare of crippling pain, and then the right knee caught her just under the rib cage. She buckled from the explosions racking her body and sagged slowly to her knees. Wrapping her arms tightly around her, she rocked forward and backward.

Monika turned her back on her and unconcernedly walked a few steps away. Daliah knew what she was doing—adding a dollop of insult to deftly applied injury, showing she had nothing to fear. Daliah's rising anger subdued the stabs of pain to bearable aches and triggered off a blast of adrenaline. She climbed slowly to her feet just as the German turned around.

For a long moment they locked eyes. And then, without warning, Monika grabbed her by the left wrist and left ankle and began whipping her around and around, as if Daliah were a merry-go-round horse gone out of control. Daliah experienced a horror of dizziness as she flew in ever-quickening circles through the air.

Jerking and writhing and screaming and kicking, Daliah struggled to free herself, but Monika, skinny and wiry as she was, was solid muscle. Daliah's struggles only seemed to intensify Monika's fury and speed.

Vertigo and the centrifugal pull blinded Daliah; she was a crazy carousel, going around and around and around and then, up, around, down, and . . .

Monika let go.

Daliah had the horrifying helpless sensation of whistling through empty space. She arched her head back and whipped her arms together in an overhead diving stance as the blurry white wall loomed. But Monika had misjudged. Instead of smashing headlong into the wall, Daliah was flung headlong down the hall—straight into Surour's belly.

It was as if a torpedo had been shot at him. The big Libyan let out a grunt and toppled backward, a spurt of wild automatic fire spraying holes in the ceiling. He broke Daliah's fall, and she collapsed on top of him. Strangely enough, she could feel no pain. There was only a dizzy disorientation. Try as she might, she just couldn't get her bearings. Everything was still spinning wildly out of control.

Then, as the vertiginous spinning started to slow, Daliah tried to stagger to her feet, but she reeled in a vain attempt to keep her balance and fell to her knees. Her senses seemed sluggish, and her body refused to obey her commands. Everything seemed fuzzy and far away, as though she and reality were light-years apart. She swallowed and shook her head, but the cotton would not leave her ears.

And then Monika cartwheeled into the finale. She was still rasping from her recent exertions, and sweat poured off her like sheets of hot rain. She reached down, grabbed hold of Daliah's single braid of hair, wrapped it around her right hand twice like a rope, and then yanked Daliah to her feet.

Daliah jerked up and let out a scream. Every nerve ending in her scalp screeched and sang and protested. Tears of pain stood out in her eyes.

She was bound to Monika by her own hair, but at least it was a very long rope of hair, so she had some maneuverability, and she used it to advantage, twisting and twirling unexpectedly, her elbows repeatedly smashing into Monika's clavicle. Again and again she battered repeated punishing blows into that exact same spot, concentrating on weakening it and waiting for the bone to snap under the pressure. With every blow, the German gaped openmouthed and expelled vast grunt after grunt of hot air mixed with sprays of saliva. Forgetting herself for a moment, Monika doubled over and loosened her grip on Daliah's hair.

Daliah moved fast, yanking the coil of braid from around Monika's hand and kneeing her neatly in the belly for good measure.

The German's eyes saucered, and another spray of hot air and saliva flew out of her lungs.

One more clean hit! Just one more . . . and I've got her!

But one more elbow ram became two. And two became three. And three . . .

Monika seemed to gather power with every blow she received. With superhuman strength she pounded a fist in Daliah's chest and flung her aside. Then, like a stunned wrestler in a ring, she slowly rose up straight, shook her head like a raging bull, and began to stagger in a wide circle around Daliah, her chest heaving as she took deep lungfuls of air and—*was it possible*—psyched herself up for another round.

Daliah kept turning, watching her carefully. Even so, she was not prepared when Monika came at her in a flash. Oblivious of all of Daliah's pokes and punches, the wiry German pinned Daliah's arms to her sides and enfolded her in an iron-armed bear hug. And began to squeeze.

It was like nothing Daliah had ever experienced. Effortlessly Monika lifted her off her feet, and although she struggled like a fish, wiggling, twisting, and even kicking Monika's shins, nothing seemed to make any difference. The woman was too mad or too strong or possibly both. The steely embrace tightened and tightened, a grotesque death hug.

With a series of involuntary gasps, Daliah flung her head back as far as it would go, bared her teeth, and then, with the speed of a starved vampire, caught Monika's right ear between her teeth. Daliah clamped her incisors into the cartilage with full force. Sharp enamel sliced neatly through gristle and tugged. Spurts of thick warm metallic blood filled her mouth, and she wanted to gag. Instead, she bit even deeper, jerked her head back, and . . .

A fountain of liquid crimson velvet sprayed out from where Monika's ear had been.

Monika instinctively loosened her grip, threw back her head, and screamed. Involuntarily, one of her hands let go of Daliah and she touched where her ear had been. Feeling nothing, her fingers clawed desperately. Her face contorted with disbelief. "My ear! You Jew bitch! What did you do with my ear?"

Daliah felt Monika's hot blood trickling down her throat, and with a massive effort to clear her mouth, she spat out the ear and the mouthful of blood into Monika's face.

Stunned, Monika now let go of her completely. She staggered backward in horror and brought her blood-wet hand away from where her ear had been and stared at the dripping red fingers. Then her eyes scanned the floor, and she let out a bellow when she saw the raggedly chewed piece of cartilage lying in a pool of blood.

Daliah knew she didn't have long. As soon as Monika got over the initial shock, she would be fiercer than ever. Daliah's only hope was to finish her off swiftly. She dived forward, her shoulder a battering ram.

Monika's arms flashed around Daliah again, swift as an octopus' tentacles, and renewed the crushing bear hug.

Daliah convulsed, her mouth dropping open and her eyes going wide with shock. She shook her head as the grip tightened, tightened, tightened like bands of constricting steel. She felt herself reeling as sanity receded and a fuzz-filled grayness washed over her.

She was asphyxiating.

She could feel the relentless pressure on her ribs beginning to stave them in, and her lungs were ready to explode. The constrictor grip had forced all the air out, and there was no way she could breathe in a new mouthful. Before her eyes, brilliant sparklers spun like whirlpools, and huge blue and pink chrysanthemums burst from bud to flower and faded. As the life seeped out of her, so too the grayness darkened to blackness. She felt suddenly giddy, as though she was spinning off into the ether of a drug-induced high.

She was not prepared for the gunshots. They sounded distant and weak, more like muffled, faraway pops. But Monika jerked backward. A look of surprise came into her eyes and, still clutching Daliah, she began to slide slowly to her knees. For a moment she knelt there, her arms clasped around Daliah's hips. Her entire back, from the shoulders to the base of her spine, was one giant open wound, all shredded red meat. Then the pressure at Daliah's hips slackened as Monika let go and toppled over backward, thudding horribly on the marble.

Daliah felt her freedom, but she could not see; everything was still twinkling stars and spinning whorls. Coughing violently, she drew back her head and gasped desperately for air. Then, as the patterns faded and the black became gray, her vision slowly came back. The first thing she saw was Surour, sprawled limply on the floor, blood frothing from a massive chest wound. Then, raising her eyes, she saw two men in black standing over him, automatic rifles lowered, their faces masks of black grease. She didn't recognize either of them.

One of the black-faced men came toward her, and she tried to scream hysterically, but no sound would come. Then the man spoke gently, and it was a voice she knew.

"Thank God, Daliah!" he said fervently, holding her tightly. "We got to you just in the nick of time. Another minute and . . ."

She just stared up at him. Her face went from fear to blankness, and then relief came flooding in. "N-N-Najib?" she asked in a trembly voice. She looked into his eyes, and then flung her arms tightly around his neck and buried her face in his chest.

She began to sob as the nightmare receded, the horror drifting away. He smelled of battle—of grease and cordite and sweat and fire—but she thought it was a delicious aroma. "Oh, Najib," she sobbed, her chest heaving. Now that sanity had returned, she was starting to shake all over. "I knew you would come!"

The second man in black face came up beside them. "Well," he asked with a huge white grin, "Doesn't your father deserve a kiss too?"

She pulled away from Najib. "Father!" she exclaimed, laughing and crying at the same time. "I didn't recognize you!"

"I can't imagine why," Dani laughed. "Come on, give your daddy a kiss, and then let's get you the hell out of here."

The helicopter was on the ground just inside the compound walls, shuddering and jumping in place, as though straining to lift off. The engine roar was so deafening it numbed Daliah's entire body and set her teeth on edge, and the prop wash from its whipping rotors fanned up a sea of turbulent dust all around. She shivered. The starry night was cold, and despite the fact that someone had draped a blanket around her shoulders, the chill was creeping into her bones.

"Statistics!" the Israeli captain demanded in a crisp shout in order to make himself heard above the helicopter's racket.

"The two wounded men who were flown over to the jet are our only casualties," a sergeant shouted back at him. "Besides us here, we have five men holding off the terrorist forces trapped in the palace. All our men are accounted for."

The captain nodded with satisfaction. The casualties they'd sustained were negligible. The two wounded men would mend, and there hadn't been a single death on their side. Considering the odds against them, things had turned out phenomenally well. He turned to Schmarya and frowned. "How many terrorists are holding the palace, do you think?"

"Thirty?" Schmarya shrugged. "Forty? Something like that."

"And Abdullah," the captain pointed out dryly. He shook his head gravely. "That means we have no choice but to go in and storm the place. Our orders were specific as far as Abdullah was concerned. He is to be terminated."

"It won't be easy," Schmarya warned. "We've enjoyed the element of surprise out here, but once inside, it'll be different. We're liable to be picked off like birds on a power line."

"I say we just blow up the palace," the captain said.

Schmarya frowned. "Is that feasible?"

"Sure. We have plenty of plastique already hooked up to the detonators. All we have to do is switch the timers on and place them where the fuel pipeline enters the palace. When it goes off . . ." The captain gestured expressively with his hands.

"No!" Najib said forcefully. His face was grimly set and the muscles in his jaws quivered.

They looked at him in surprise.

"It's the safest way," the Israeli captain explained concisely. "If we go in, our losses are likely to be heavy. The terrorists have had a chance to regroup."

"*No!*" Najib shook his head again and stared at the captain, his eyes dark and cold. "We have two friends in there," he said. "If it hadn't been for them, Captain, we would never have achieved what we already have. We owe it to them to get them out."

Schmarya nodded. "Yes," he agreed, "we do." He turned to the captain. "Regroup our men. We'll go in in five minutes." He turned to stride off.

Najib caught him by the arm. "You don't need to go in," he said.

Schmarya squinted at him. "I take it you have a better suggestion?"

"Yes." Najib nodded. "Start moving your men out and fly them in relays over to the jet. I'll go in alone. If Abdullah can be found, I've got the best chance of finding him. And as for Khalid and Hamid, only I know what they look like. Your men are liable to shoot them." He smiled. "So you see, I am the best choice."

Schmarya met his gaze steadily. "And if you're not successful?"

Najib's expression did not change. "Have the explosives put in place anyway, with the timers set for fifteen minutes. If I'm not out by then, let them go off."

Daliah was horrified. She could stand this no longer. She grabbed Najib's arm and shook it violently. "That's madness! Can't we just forget about Abdullah? Please, let's just leave! If we don't lay the explosives, the two men will be safe."

"And Abdullah?" Najib asked her. "The captain has his orders."

She flushed under that cold stare, but her eyes flashed green fire. "Forget about Abdullah! He's not worth the life of any of you!" she said vehemently.

Najib placed a hand on each of her shoulders and looked at her sorrowfully. "Try to understand. Abdullah has hundreds, perhaps thousands of supporters elsewhere. You know we have to cut him down while we have the chance. It may never come again."

She looked beseechingly at Schmarya. "Can't you talk some sense into him, Grandfather?"

"Mr. al-Ameer is right," Schmarya said heavily. "We have to make sure Abdullah is dead. Or would you rather spend the rest of your very short life waiting for him to catch up with us and have us all killed?"

She had no answer for that.

Najib turned to the Israeli captain. "Fifteen minutes, Captain. That's all I ask. If I don't find them by then, then let it blow." He paused and urged, "Have your men set the explosives, Captain. Now."

"We may not even have to resort to the explosives," the captain said grimly. "Look." He pointed at the palace.

At the gaping holes where the big windows of the *majlis* had been, a rosy glow flickered and pulsated brightly. And at the other end of the palace, where Daliah had been held captive, the closed metal shutter slats on the second floor glowed orange-pink. There were at least two major fires raging out of control inside the palace, and from the looks of them, they were spreading quickly. From the twisted, glassless *majlis* dome a thick column of sparks was swirling skyward like a swarm of fireflies.

"You see?" the captain said. "From the looks of it, I'd say it's just a matter of time before those fires spread and set off the pipeline by themselves."

"Be that as it may," Najib said, "it won't guarantee Abdullah's death. If I know him, he'll find a way to escape before it blows."

Dani stepped forward. "I'll go with you," he volunteered.

Najib shook his head. "No, you would only be a liability, my friend. This I must do by myself. Besides, I know the men, and I know the palace. All I need is for the helicopter to land me on the roof and wait fourteen minutes to pick me up."

Daliah pulled the blanket off her shoulders and tossed it to the ground. "I want to go on the helicopter with you."

Najib looked at her without expression. "No. You have already gone through enough."

She tightened her lips. "I'm *not* going into the palace with you! I just want to be on the helicopter when it lets you off and picks you up again!"

His brows snapped together. "It is out of the question," he told her firmly. "It's far too risky. If anything should happen to you now, then the entire mission will have been futile."

She raised her chin resolutely. "I'm going," she said quietly. "Just try to stop me."

In the helicopter, hovering just feet above the palace roof, Najib shouted last-minute instructions at the pilot.

"Your watch is synchronized with mine. If I'm not back on the roof by thirteen till, then you are to forget about me and take off. Don't wait around a minute longer. The explosives are set for twelve till. That gives you only sixty seconds to get out of here."

"But if you're not—"

"Then forget about me!" Najib reiterated. The sharpness of his voice left no room for argument.

The pilot turned away. "Yes, sir."

Najib twisted in his seat and kissed Daliah.

"Come back to me in one piece," she said in a strained whisper.

He swung around to the open door and jumped out.

In the lush gardens on the southeastern side of the palace, the Israeli captain hunkered down in the shrubbery, watching as his explosives expert attached the packets of plastique to the pipeline. "Set them for fifteen minutes," he told the corporal.

The corporal nodded and set the miniaturized digital timers and activated them by flipping a switch. A tiny red light glowed on each. He looked at the captain. "Fifteen minutes it is, sir," he said unnecessarily.

The captain nodded grimly. "Then let's get the hell out of here, Corporal."

"Yes, sir!"

Together they jumped to their feet and took off. A fusillade of gunfire from somewhere within the palace sprayed around them as they lunged through the flowerbeds and past a spraying fountain. Bits of earth flew up and danced all around them.

Just before they reached the path, a bullet grazed the captain's right shoulder and spun him around.

"Damn!" he swore angrily, and dived to the ground. Keeping his head down, he looked up for the source of the shots and saw movement behind a series of tall first-floor windows some thirty feet away. With knit brows he emptied an entire clip from his MAC-10 machine pistol and watched the sheets of glass burst and rain down in shards. For an instant there was silence. Then heads popped out from behind the now glassless windows and streaks of return fire flashed and rattled.

He tightened his lips grimly. How many terrorists were in that room, anyway? With al-Ameer making his way around alone inside the palace . . .

Not very good odds, the captain thought. He reached for one of the firebombs hanging on his belt. After tearing off its shield, he rose in a crouch and hurled it at the gaping window with all his might and then threw himself flat on the ground.

The explosion came with a thunderous roar. The window frames burst out into the garden in almost lazy slow motion, and chunks of masonry rained down. Inside the room a cloud of yellow-orange fire billowed up the walls. A screaming, flailing human torch staggered to the window and fell out.

"There," the captain muttered to himself. "That should even things out a little."

Najib wished he could afford the luxury of searching the palace methodically. Normally, it would have made sense to start on the third floor and work his way down to the first, but the palace was too huge and there were too many rooms and halls and storage areas. A thorough search could take hours, and he did not have hours. He had less than fifteen minutes, and those were running out fast. As it was, unless a major miracle happened, this palace would be his tomb.

He moved swiftly, drawn by the sound of sporadic gunfire and a rocking explosion from somewhere below. He would check that out first. His instincts told him to disregard the upper two levels and concentrate on the ground floor. That was where all the activity seemed to be centered, and there he might find Khalid and Hamid, and, if he was very lucky, Abdullah as well. All three of them had to be *somewhere* in this sprawling palace. But where?

He literally flew down the two flights of marble stairs from the roof, raced down the endless marble corridors of the second floor, tore across the mezzanine above the foyer, and then jumped down the last set of stairs four at a time. The octagonal fountain gurgled and sprayed with mocking aloofness.

Everywhere, signs of destruction met his eyes: shattered glass, gaping walls, spent shell casings, smashed furnishings, and smoldering upholstery. The fires were spreading even more swiftly than any of them had anticipated, fed as they were by the sumptuous fabrics, acres of carpeting, and walls sheathed in exotic woods. Even the normally fireproof marble walls and floors could not contain them: too many flammable building materials had been used. The Almoayyeds were going to have quite a spectacular ruin on their hands.

Najib crossed from the foyer into the first of the three huge adjoining rooms—the fifty-foot-long oval library—shielding his face from the heat with his forearm. The windows were completely blown out, frames and all. The gently curving ceiling-high bookshelves tilted into the room at crazy

735

angles, and fires were everywhere. Piles of burning books, scorched tulipwood tables, and overturned chairs gave evidence of a recent explosion. Two blackened bodies were sprawled on the floor.

He nodded to himself: this was the explosion he'd heard when he was coming down the stairs—a firebomb.

Still shielding his face from the heat, he crossed into the next room, a green-velvet-lined screening room with a semicircle of green velvet armchairs facing a huge movie screen. He let his arm drop. It was cooler in here, and miraculously, the room was untouched: the destruction had stopped just outside the door. But it wouldn't remain that way for long.

He stopped for a moment, turned around, and stared back at the burning library beyond. He frowned thoughtfully. There was nothing in there except burning books, ruined furnishings, and fires raging everywhere, but he trusted his instinct and returned to the library. He crept across the velvet carpeting, flattening himself against the wall. His eyes flickered around the huge room. One second passed. Two. He jumped back as a section of bookshelf tumbled over with a crash, and a wild shower of roiling sparks exploded to the ceiling. No, there was nothing. He must have imagined whatever it was that had caught his attention.

He was about to curse the waste of precious seconds and head back into the screening room when a click froze him in his tracks. Little chills lifted the hair at his neck. He knew that sound only too well—a gun's hammer.

"Slowly put your weapon down," a voice hissed harshly, and something hard and menacing poked him brutally in the spine. "This is no time to try any tricks."

He bent over and laid his automatic on the floor, then slowly straightened back up.

"Kick it away from you."

He gave the weapon a nudge with the toe of his boot, and it spun across the marble.

"Raise your arms above your head and turn around slowly." The gun barrel left his back and he turned.

He and the two men behind him stared at one another.

"Khalid!" Najib said with a flood of relief. "Hamid! Am I ever glad to see you!"

Khalid lowered his automatic, exchanging grins with Hamid.

Najib let his hands drop. "You've both got to get out," he told them urgently. "The helicopter will pick us up from the roof. In only minutes, the whole palace is going to blow. Listen—does either of you know where Abdullah is?"

"Ah, the traitorous triumvirate!" It was Abdullah's voice. "I am right here, to your left."

The three of them froze.

A section of the tilting, burning bookcases had swung outward, and Abdullah and Ghazi stepped soundlessly out from a concealed reading room. Both were armed with semiautomatics, aimed right at them.

The timer digits were down to 7:56.

Najib heard the ear-splitting groan of a collapsing bookcase at the far end of the blazing library, and he stared in morbid fascination as a giant section of ceiling-high shelves tipped away from the wall in slow motion and toppled inward, dumping tons of burned volumes to the floor. All around, the other shelves were swaying precariously.

He pulled his gaze back to Abdullah. If his half-uncle had even heard the crash, he gave no evidence of it. The madman was in another world entirely, a world where he was omnipotent and the fears of ordinary mortals mattered not at all. His messianic eyes had been on Khalid, and now they slid back to Najib, the triumph in them merged with feral cunning. "As soon as the attack started, I suspected that the three of you were behind it," he was saying, "and now it is proven. How convenient that you are all together. It will make punishing you for your treachery so much easier. You swore an oath to me, all three of you!" His eyebrows arched into a dark V, and he laughed crazily. "For breaking it, you will now die!"

"This is the last flight!" Dani shouted at Daliah. He threw his helmet aside and his hair whipped in the prop wash. "Get in!"

Daliah's eyes darted around. No one was trying to hold off the terrorists in the palace any longer; of the five commandos who had been doing that, four had already been ferried to the jet. Now the single one who had remained had joined them at the helicopter. Besides him, she counted herself, Dani, Schmarya, the Israeli captain, and the helicopter pilot. Everyone else had already been flown out to the runway. She looked back at her father. "But what about Najib?" she yelled.

Dani's expression was fierce. "Young lady," he roared, "if you don't hurry, there won't be *time* to come back and get him!"

Without another word, she ducked into the vibrating little

cabin. In less than ten seconds the rest of them had piled in behind her and the helicopter rose heavily and made a tight, sweeping turn. Below, the palace shrank in size and seemed to tilt. Fires were sprouting from every wing and every floor now, and then, suddenly, she saw that a new wall of flames was beginning to race toward the spot where the explosives had been planted.

Daliah shut her eyes, willing Najib to be safe. *Please don't die. Please come back to me.*

Then they were over the compound walls and the palace was behind them. It was a mere half-minute up-and-down hop. The runway was already coming up and the chopper descended. She could feel the shudder as the skids hit the concrete, and she opened her eyes. The men piled out, and she climbed into the front seat beside the pilot.

Dani leaned into the cabin. "Take good care of her!" he yelled to the pilot.

Then the helicopter rose once more.

At the pipeline, the timer flashed down to four and a half minutes.

Najib could sense the standoff drawing to a close. His eyes flicked from Abdullah and Ghazi, twenty feet in front of him, to Khalid and Hamid at his sides. He was trying to determine the exact moment when he should dive for cover. If he moved too soon, he would force Abdullah or Ghazi to pump him full of bullets. And if he moved too late, he would be shot anyway. No matter what he did, it seemed he was doomed.

He wanted to scream at them to hurry.

What were they waiting for? Squeeze the triggers! Get it over with! Shoot. Shoot! What's keeping—

And then his sideways glance caught Khalid's split-second nod, and he threw himself to the floor. The four automatic rifles blazed blue fire, and prolonged bursts of bullets crisscrossed over his head. Roars exploded in his ears, the vibrations of smashing bullets thundering and ricocheting all around him.

He saw Ghazi being thrown backward in a grotesque dance of death, his chest bursting into a splatter of crimson fragments. He seemed to hang suspended in midair, and then slowly collapsed.

The weapon flew from Abdullah's hands as his body, bursting blood from his belly, jerked and spun in a 360-degree turn. He stood hunched over, his wild eyes wide with surprise, and then staggered in short, wobbly steps.

As suddenly as it had started, the gunfire ceased. The crackling of the flames seemed inordinately loud. Najib thrilled as he realized he was unharmed. Behind him, he heard two heavy thuds of falling bodies and the clattering of weapons hitting marble.

Slowly he turned.

Khalid and Hamid had fallen across one another to form a human cross, their features frozen with the contortions of their last agony. Their eyes were wide and blank. Najib didn't need to feel their pulses. There was nothing he could do for them.

Sickened, he stumbled to his feet.

"Najib! No!" Abdullah's voice was an incredulous screech. "You can't be alive! You have to be dead!"

"No, it's you who are going to be dead!" Najib shouted. "You're leaking blood all over."

Abdullah stared down at his belly and staggered backward in horror. His demonic eyes were wide as he gingerly touched a stomach wound that was steadily pumping out blood. Disbelievingly he raised his dripping red hand to his eyes. "I'm shot!" he moaned, jerking his face back from his hand as if it were a viper. *"I'm going to die!"*

"Not soon enough!" Najib said grimly.

"Najib!" Abdullah's voice became shrill. "You can fly me out! To Riyadh—"

"No!" roared Najib. "Never! It is time you were flung into the fires of hell, where you belong!"

"Help me, Najib!" Abdullah pleaded. "I'm your half-uncle! We're family! You must—"

"I must nothing. Now at least the world will be that much safer and saner!"

Madness flared in Abdullah's eyes. "You fool! Do you think I have not prepared for this day? I have trained others to follow in my footsteps, to continue where I have left off." He roared with insane laughter, his mortal wound momentarily forgotten. "My people are in every country of the Middle East! I have had legions to choose from, and I have chosen well!"

"Ah, but you won't be here to see how good they really are, will you?" Najib taunted.

At that moment another of the blazing bookcases creaked and came crashing down. It landed thunderously between the two of them, and a wall of fire shot up to the ceiling, driving Najib backward. Through the curtain of fire he could see Abdullah as a hellish staggering shadow. His mad shouting rose even above the roar of the furious flames.

"You will die, Najib! All of you will die! The girl! Her family! *All of you!* The orders have already gone out! My people will see to it!"

"You lie!" Najib bellowed. Oh, for the love of Allah, it *couldn't* be true! "Even at the point of death, you lie!"

Abdullah shrilled with laughter. "You will never know for certain, though, will you?" His laughter rose and swirled and howled. "You never even knew it was *I* who shot Iffat, and not the Jews, did you?"

"You?"

"I had plans for you, and I knew that by blaming the Jews I would have your loyalty!"

Najib staggered, overwhelmed by the revelation. All those years he had been fanning his hatred for Daliah's family and the Jews, and all the while it had been Abdullah who was the cold-blooded murderer.

Najib was filled with a killing rage. For an instant an overpowering urge seized him—to dive through the fire and finish Abdullah off with his bare hands.

Then: You're an idiot, he told himself. Abdullah is finished, and if you don't get out of this funeral pyre and back up to the roof, you'll be finished too.

He hesitated for a mere millisecond, then turned and raced out into the foyer. He sped up the stairs to the mezzanine and plunged down the endless halls, past blazing rooms, heading for the stairs, racing the clock to the roof.

He didn't need a watch—his heartbeats were countdown enough: 1:04 . . . 1:03 . . . 1:02 . . . 1:01 . . .

"One more minute!" the helicopter pilot shouted. "We might not even have that long. The place looks like its ready to go up at any moment!"

Daliah looked down. She was on her knees, grimly clutching the sides of the open door for dear life as she leaned out over the edge of the helicopter into space. They were hovering twenty feet above the palace roof, and the rotors whipped the oily black smoke around in a swirling tornado. It seemed that orange flames were shooting up everywhere, grabbing for them. The roar of the fire had even drowned out the ear-splitting clamor of the helicopter.

"Do you see anything?" the pilot shouted.

Daliah did not reply. Her burning eyes were frantically searching the rooftop for Najib. *Of course he's not there. No one is still alive down there.*

"Sorry, lady!" the pilot yelled. "We gotta go! The heat's too intense for the rotor to bite!"

740

"No!" Daliah shouted. "He's *alive*! I know he is! We can't just leave him here to burn! I'd rather die first!"

"Hey, you're forgetting something, aren't you?" he shouted. "It's my ass too! We gotta go! *Now*!"

"There he is!" she screamed excitedly. "I saw him!"

"Where?"

"There! Down . . ." She pointed and then scowled. "Dammit! The smoke's hidden him!"

"Lady—"

"*There!* See him?" She pointed to their right. The pilot craned his neck and squinted. Sure enough, between breaks in the smoke he could see a lone figure waving both arms above him.

"Well?" Daliah shouted. "What are you waiting for? Let's set down and get him!"

"We can't set down," the pilot insisted. "The roof won't support us!"

"So what do we do?"

"There's a rope behind your seat. Toss it down to him. It's already attached."

Daliah ducked back inside, scrambled over the seat, and found it. She heaved it out the open door.

"Hang on!" the pilot shouted, and nosed the chopper toward the spot where they had last seen Najib.

Daliah leaned out again. Where *was* he? Surely the smoke wasn't *that* thick. He had to be there. He . . .

And there he was! Dashing toward the rope just as the roof directly under his feet began to buckle, crack, and—

She stared down in openmouthed horror.

It was caving in!

"Najib!" she screamed as she saw him lunge for the rope.

For a horrible split second she saw him outlined against an enormous gaping hole of yellow, and then there was a tremendous roar, as if all the fires of hell had burst through the earth. The helicopter surged skyward and sped away from the palace.

Daliah squeezed her eyes shut. *Too late! Oh, Najib, Najib . . .*

When the helicopter landed at the edge of the runway, she was still weeping, refusing to open her eyes. As the rotor clatter slowed, she could hear the screaming engines of the waiting jet. Somehow it no longer seemed important that she had escaped. She wished she had died in the conflagration with him. At least then they would be forever together.

Gentle hands prised her grip loose from the doorframe, and a soft, familiar voice was saying, "Daliah! Daliah! Ev-

741

erything's all right now, my love. *Daliah!* Look at me, my darling."

Her heart stopped. She was hearing things. She—

Strong arms engulfed her, and she slowly opened her eyes. The camouflage grease on his face had been supplemented by head-to-toe soot, and his hair and eyebrows were seared and frizzed, giving him the appearance of an electrocuted mad scientist.

Her pulse raced and her heart kicked in. He *had* caught hold of the rope! She let out a shout of joy. He was *alive!* And to prove it to herself, she threw her arms around him.

"We'd better hurry," the helicopter pilot's voice intruded. "The jet's ready to take off." Daliah pulled her head away from Najib's and looked over at the sleek silver plane. The pilot was right. The jet was straining and shuddering, the brakes barely holding it in place.

He was in the lair of the dragons.

The torrent of flames roared like a million bellowing beasts, and the boiling light was brighter than a thousand exploding suns. Lithe figures of gold leapt and dervishes danced around Abdullah, their flowing veils fluttering and billowing and surging in parodies of lovers' embraces.

He heard the roar of the flames as a choir, and through the fiery garments of the twisting, writhing dancers he caught glimpses of a golden staircase, and beyond that, behind the clouds of camphor steam from the boiling fountain, he caught tantalizing glimpses of towering gold doors.

They were the golden gates to Paradise.

He was in ecstasy.

The Exordium sang in his mind with a heavenly chant. *In the Name of Allah, the Compassionate, the Merciful. Praise be to Allah, Lord of the Creation, the Compassionate, the Merciful, King of Judgment day!*

Oblivious of the heat, he stretched out his hands, welcoming the flickering tongues of gold fire to dance along his sleeves. Slowly, arms extended, he staggered toward the golden staircase to Paradise. He was filled with glory and exquisite pain, awash with the climax of multitudinous orgasms. He could feel the fires of holiness cleansing his boiling blood, shooting up his legs in ravenous greed.

And then the sky was rent asunder, the stars scattered, the oceans rolled together, and the dragons all around turned on him and roared.

Abdullah screamed in madness as his flesh melted from his bones like dripping wax. In that ghastly split second before death he knew that he'd been tricked. This was not the way to eternal Paradise!

On this, his Judgment Day, Allah had flung him into the caldron of eternal hell.

They had almost reached the boarding stairs when the plastique exploded and the palace blew asunder. For an instant the night flashed and became day. Najib flung Daliah to the ground and shielded her with his body. The shockwave came in a roll and rocked the jet above them. A brief sandstorm whipped and lashed.

The heat wave that immediately followed felt hotter than the noonday sun. Debris rained for half a mile all around, and the pipeline across the sands ignited, creating a crackling curtain of fire as far as the eye could see.

Slowly Daliah crawled to her knees and looked around. The palace was gone.

And then Najib was helping her to her feet and they were scrambling the last few steps to safety.

The engines changed pitch as the 727-100 nosed down through shreds of white cloud on its final approach to Newark International. The thirteen-hour flight from Tel Aviv was nearly over. It had been unlike any flight Daliah had ever taken—and she grinned at the thought that this was a lifestyle to which she could become very easily and very, very quickly accustomed. She and Najib had spent most of the flight in the big luxurious bed in the aft cabin. What better way was there to while away all those thousands of miles than by making love and sleeping?

Still, she would be glad to be back on the ground. She was anxious to be back in New York and have Najib carry her across the threshold into her new home—four entire floors of the Trump tower. The first thing she intended to do was banish all the help and lock herself up with him for one entire glorious week. Just the two of them. *Alone.*

They could use the rest.

The last five days had been hectic. There had been the media circus to contend with, then Ari and Sissi's delayed wedding, and finally her parents had hosted an impromptu engagement party for her and Najib. She was pleased that Tamara found Najib delightful, and gratified that most of her parents' Jewish friends seemed, if not exactly overjoyed at the prospect of her marrying an Arab, at least accepting of that fact.

And then, finally, when they'd boarded the jet, she'd

gotten her wish—to be alone with Najib and not have to share him with anyone.

His proximity gave her a cozy, serene security. Was this the way she would always feel, she wondered, or would the novelty of wanting to be at his side at every moment wear off in time? She laughed at herself. As long as he was hers, and she was his, that was all that mattered.

She turned to him and clasped one of his hands in both of hers. He looked so handsome and so gentle, and yet under his noble features he was as strong as steel; if he hadn't been, she wouldn't even be alive. Passionate, sensuous, powerful; he was a man who could hold his own beside her. She didn't have to worry that anyone would ever make the mistake of calling him Mr. Boralevi.

"Do you know what I was just thinking?" she asked him softly.

"Were you maybe thinking what *I* was thinking?" he retorted with a wicked little laugh.

"Hmmm." She grinned back at him and drew him close. "I believe so."

He gave a little sigh. "Unfortunately, our fuel tanks are nearly empty. A thirteen-hour flight is all this plane can handle. Otherwise, I'd be the first to suggest circling for a while."

She wagged a finger at him. "In that case, you owe me one!"

"The moment we get home!" he promised fervently. Then he smiled. "It won't be long. Customs is only a formality, and then it's into the limo, across the river, and up in the elevator. Thirty minutes. Maybe forty, depending on the traffic." He grinned again. "Do you think you can wait that long?"

She sniffed and turned her face away. "If I'm forced to . . ."

A small welcoming committee was clustered in the terminal after they were rushed through customs.

"Yoo-hoo! Daliah!" The shrill Brooklynese shout came from Patsy Lipschitz; even a nearby jet taking off couldn't muffle her stridency.

"Oh, no." Daliah looked panic-stricken. She recognized Jerome and Patsy easily enough, but . . .

She did a double-take. A long stare proved that it really was Cleo, and Daliah let out a squeal of pleasure and rushed to her. "Miss Cleopatra, honey!" she cried, hugging her and laughing. Then she pulled back. "I almost didn't recognize you!"

The change Cleo had undergone during the past three weeks was astounding. Cleo's casual urchin look had been shed, along with the corn-rolled hair and ubiquitous men's trousers and T-shirts that had seemed to constitute her entire wardrobe. In fact, Daliah had never before seen her friend wearing a dress. Now, seeing her dressed like a lady for the first time, she could only stare as though struck dumb.

Cleo was a gorgeous sight, from the slim black turban with its foot-long black feather sticking rakishly up in the air, to the beautifully tailored indigo-and-black Jean-Louis Scherrer dress and the black kid gloves encircled with three huge gold bracelets on each wrist. She was even wearing makeup, and it was masterfully applied, accentuating her extraordinarily high cheekbones and adding a regal exoticism to the slight slant of her eyes.

It took a moment for Daliah to find her voice. "What's happened to you? Why the fancy get-up? Is there a wedding or a funeral?"

"These threads," Cleo announced succinctly, "are part of the new me." She stretched her magnificent elongated swan's neck and fluttered her lashes. "You better git used to it. I'm gettin' married in September!"

"Whoa!" Daliah blinked suspiciously and made a little gesture with a finger. "Back up there for a moment. You? Married? Since when were you the hausfrau type? Why, I don't even recall your telling me you were dating anybody after you broke up with Serge. Is it him? Did you two kiss and make up?"

"Rich Woman, you know *he's* ancient history."

"Rich woman?" Daliah burst out laughing. "I thought I was *White* Woman."

"You was till you met Daddy Warbucks, here." Cleo smiled at Najib and said, "Hel-*lo* there, handsome."

Daliah affectionately placed an arm around Cleo's waist. "Cleo, I want you to meet Najib; Najib, this is Cleo, my best friend, confidante, and sometime pain in the ass!"

Najib held out his hand, but Cleo ignored it and gave him a hug and kissed his cheek.

"And this is Jerome St.-Tessier, whom I've told you so much about," Daliah continued dryly. "And this is Patsy Lipschitz, my agent. And this . . ." Daliah frowned and looked at Cleo for help.

"This," Cleo said as she pulled the reluctant black man forward, "is Coyote."

Daliah stared at the tall man, and then at Cleo. "That's not the same Coyote who—"

"The very same." Cleo nodded happily. "How's he lookin'? Good, huh?"

Daliah looked at Coyote more closely. She had to admit that there was *some* resemblance to the pimp, but it just couldn't be the same man. This one was a tall, lean man who was well-groomed and handsome. In fact, he looked like a high-fashion model.

Daliah was dazed. "Miss Cleopatra, honey, you must forgive me. I feel like I'm in some sort of time warp. Would one of you kindly explain?"

Cleo grinned. "Well, while you were gone, Patsy came to see me. Seems she wanted to pump me for information about your whereabouts, and then remembered they was looking to cast a black chick in a feature film, so before you know it, she had me sign with her agency."

"And?" Daliah demanded. "Did it work out?"

"Uh-uh." Cleo shook her head morosely. "They didn't want me, but the same producers are castin' a prime-time TV crime series, and when I went to the audition, Coyote was with me and they wanted him! They tested him and he got the part. How you like that? So it's good-bye pimpin' an' hel-lo, Hollywood, hel-lo."

"Daliah . . ." Jerome grabbed her by the arm and pulled her aside. As usual, he looked sullen and moody, and she wondered what she had ever seen in him. He was handsome enough, and no one knew better than she how talented he was, but next to Najib he looked like a spoiled brat.

"We have to talk," he said in a low voice. "Before you do anything rash, I want you to know how I feel about . . . uh . . . things." He looked around pointedly. "Isn't there anyplace we can go and talk in private?"

She shook her head. "Sorry, Jer," she said. "Anything you have to say, you can say in front of Najib."

"All right." Jerome looked unenthusiastic but plunged ahead. "I missed you, dammit!" When Daliah didn't respond, he looked down at his feet, sighed, and looked back up at her. "Look, I want you to come back to me. I've found alternative financing for the movie, and we can still live and work together. What do you say? It'll be just like old times."

"I'm sorry, Jerome. It wouldn't be like old times. Things have changed. *I've* changed. And besides, I'm in love with Najib."

There was a hint of cruel anger in his laughter. "That's a joke! First, you walked out on me because Arabs wanted to finance your film, and now you won't come back to me because you're in love with one? Really, Daliah, I'm not a fool, you know."

"I never said you were, but that's the way things are. I'm sorry, Jer. I really am."

"Bitch," he hissed, and turned his back. Hands in pockets, he stared sullenly across the terminal.

Patsy took the opportunity to push herself in front of Daliah. "You were brilliant, dollcake!" she crowed. "Brilliant!" She grabbed Daliah's arm and started to walk her away from Jerome. "You know, that kidnapping was the best publicity stunt anyone's ever cooked up!"

Daliah stared at the gargantuan woman. She couldn't believe she was hearing this. "For your information, Patsy, what I went through was bloody hell! It wasn't make-believe like some fucking movie!"

"Of course it wasn't," Patsy agreed. "But that's beside the point. You're the talk of the country. It's made you real hot stuff. My phone's been ringing off the hook, and the offers have been pouring in. Bolotsky at Paramount's offering you six mil to do *one* film! *Six mil!* That's right up there with Brando and Hackman. Of course, Jerome's agreed to match it." She looked over at him. "Haven't you, Jerome?" she called out. She didn't wait for a reply. "That makes twelve mil for not even a year's worth of work. *And* Karl Lorimar's topped CBS Video's offer for the exercise tape by two hundred thou— *Daliah!*" Patsy stared at her. "Aren't you listenin' to me?"

Daliah sighed. "I'll think about it, Patsy. If I do decide to make another movie, I promise you'll be the agent, okay?"

"Daliah!" Patsy looked ready to faint. "What are you tryin' to tell me? Of course you'll make another movie! Why, the money—"

"Patsy," she said wearily, "in a few days I'll become one of the richest women in the world. A few million is a drop in the bucket. Now, *please* . . ."

Jerome and Patsy both started yelling so loud that she didn't even try to make out what either of them was saying. She drew up alongside Najib. It was then that they saw a horde of photographers, who must have been tipped off, come running. Daliah glanced up at Najib.

He seemed to read her mind. Leaning down to kiss her, he murmured, "We can run back through customs to the plane, and it can be back up in the air within forty-five minutes. That means we would be at the yacht in another thirteen or fourteen hours—"

"—and no one can bother us at sea." She smiled dazzlingly. "Verrrry interesting."

Laughing like children, they dashed back toward customs and the 727.

Epilogue

On September 3, 1983, Inge celebrated her ninetieth birthday. The local newspaper printed a front-page article about her, using a photograph she complained bitterly about, claiming she couldn't possibly look *that* old, and when the mayor came to congratulate her, she feistily said, "Come back when I turn one hundred, sank you very much." She had lost none of her spunk and was as lucid and spry as ever.

No tourists occupied the motel that Labor Day week. Inge had kept the Sou'westerner Motel purposely vacant so that it would be at the disposal of her friends. To discourage off-the-road tourists, the No Vacancy shingle was prominently lit, and soon the cabins were full of the guests of her choosing. From Tel Aviv came Tamara, Dani, Schmarya, Ari and Sissi, and their two children; from Lebanon came Najib's parents; and Daliah and Najib and their not-quite-two-year-old daughter, Jasmine, came up from Manhattan.

They arrived quietly, almost furtively, flying in on Najib's jet so that the press would not be aroused.

It was to be a quiet family affair.

There were no caterers, no musicians, and no local guests save for Otha, who, as the only concession to Inge's age, was grudgingly allowed to run the motel. The party took place in the biggest room—Inge's kitchen—and everyone pitched in. Colorful construction-paper chains crisscrossed overhead, and Sissi draped the utilitarian dinette chairs, which Inge wouldn't have dreamed of allowing to be replaced, with festive lengths of fabric, while Tamara fashioned cloth bows to stick onto the backs. Daliah arranged the voluminous buckets of flowers.

The food selection crossed all borders. Sissi prepared her Jewish specialties—whitefish and mazoh-ball soup and pungent red cabbage—and Najib's mother roasted a shank of lamb in the Middle Eastern manner and cooked up bistella. Otha added her Southern-fried chicken, kernel-studded cornbread, and hot dogs for the kids. Najib added a hamper of Middle Eastern delicacies and two king-size tins of caviar—

nutty-flavored golden osetra, and large-grained grayish beluga—as well as a case of 1979 Dom Perignon. Tamara and Daliah baked and decorated the birthday cake themselves, and if it didn't look exactly professional—with a mountain of icing drooping at one end—everyone exclaimed over it.

Throughout the day and long into the evening, the family ate, caught up on news and gossip, and doted on the children, the familiar sounds of English punctuated with occasional bursts of exotic Hebrew and Arabic. The family was, after all, a United Nations in microcosm. This was the third year in a row that they had congregated on Cape Cod to celebrate Inge's birthday, and the third of September had become known as the unofficial but acknowledged date of their family reunions. Inge, not tied to them by blood, but by bonds of love that were equally as strong, looked forward to these occasions, even though they left her feeling tired afterward and glad for the stretch of quiet ahead. But the weariness of age would not make itself felt for another day or so. Meanwhile, she reveled in the noise and laughter, and spoiled the children shamelessly.

If only Senda could have been here, Inge couldn't help thinking wistfully. How proud she would have been! The Boralevis had turned out far more special than anyone would have imagined. She eyed the people crowded into the kitchen. Two generations of film stars—Senda would have liked that. And a billionaire, an archaeologist, and Dani and Schmarya. . . . Senda and Schmarya had been too young, Inge reflected, and history had conspired to tear them apart. Given time and other circumstances, their love would have cemented. Inge smiled at the three toddlers. Jasmine, Ruth, and Asa. They were the future, and only time and God would tell what they would become, and she thought: Oh, they'll become something, all right. That's one thing I don't have to worry about. It's in their genes.

Tears welled up in her eyes as she wished again that Senda could have been part of the festivities and felt the love. But perhaps she *was* here in spirit, invisible and undetectable. Inge hoped so.

"Inge!" Daliah was bending down to fuss over her. "You're not crying, are you?"

Inge's cornflower-blue eyes flashed as she drew her head up. "You know me better than that, Daliah!" she declared indignantly.

Daliah kissed her cheek affectionately. "It's nearly sunset, and we're all going for a walk along the beach. Well?" She waited. "Are you coming or not?"

"In a minute, in a minute," Inge muttered, turning her head and wishing for some privacy so that she could sniffle and wipe her eyes without it becoming a family fuss.

Otha stayed behind in the cabin, as had been prearranged, ready to light the cake's candles when they returned, and the rest of them walked barefoot along the beach, slowly for the sake of Inge, Schmarya, and the elderly al-Ameers, a straggling, chattering group led by Inge's dog, Happy, running ahead and barking as he splashed around in the water or tugged at pieces of driftwood. Offshore, a large sailboat tacked into the spectacular gold-and-vermilion sunset, and Sissi pointed it out to Ruth while Asa tugged on her wind-blown skirt for attention.

Inge regarded the sight warmly. It was like a gentle painting, the way mother and children were posed. Sissi had that bronzed earthy look of an early Picasso mother. Her rich brown skin attested to the hours she spent out-of-doors on archaeological digs; her career as a bones-and-trinkets sleuth was well on its way toward international recognition with her recent discovery of a heretofore unknown tell in Samaria.

Inge's gaze switched to Ari. Sissi's husband's looks had matured over the past three years; he no longer had that lean, rakish sabra sleekness, but he was still exceedingly handsome. He was no longer a boy, but a man comfortable in his skin, and it showed. He was steadily working his way up the ladder in the Israeli parliament.

Ahead, Daliah and Najib were walking side by side, his arm around her shoulder and hers around his waist, their feet kicking up bubbles of frothy salt water. Najib's other hand was raised, holding on to Jasmine, who sat atop his shoulders, gripping tufts of his hair. Inge nodded to herself. Daliah and Najib were well-matched. To make certain that their respective careers did not damage their marriage through long absences from each other, Najib and Daliah had wisely moved to London for the two-month duration of the location shooting of her last film. Theirs was a marriage of commitment, love, and mutual respect.

The sky reflected pools of molten gold on the heaving green waves. Lacy breakers curled and rushed and spent themselves upon the incline of beach with a massive sigh. Inge nodded. Life is like that, she was thinking. We're each of us waves, formed out there beyond the horizon somewhere, and then let loose to make our own run through life.

She smiled as she listened to the chatter rising and falling, and the cries of gulls swooping overhead. For an instant, time merged and the telescoped years contracted. The dunes could easily be snowdrifts, she mused, and behind them the huge palaces could be hiding. Sand . . . snow . . . oceans and borders . . . in the end everything was one and the same.

Strange, how it took so many years to discover that.

The individual incidents of the past were hazier now, less lethal and heartbreaking than when they'd occurred. *Memories*. There were so many of them. Schmarya, so young and brash; Senda, caught in Prince Vaslav's tightly meshed net, forced to choose either saving Schmarya and losing him, or killing him and losing him. Giving up her heritage and religion for a life on the stage. Captivating St. Petersburg in those frantic prerevolution years. Geneva . . . New York . . . Hollywood. Tamara's incredible success, her tragic loss of Louis, and finally her joyous embracing of the heritage and religion her mother had forsaken. And now Daliah, so fervent in her beliefs, yet willing to break all the rules and cross any boundary to marry the man she loved. Inge shook her head. So many years had passed, and the painful memories no longer stabbed; time and happier days had reduced them to a bearable throb.

Life went on.

New generations of waves were making their run for the beach.

"Happy birthday to you, happy birthday to you, happy birthday dear Inge. Happy birthday to youuuu . . ."

The lights in the kitchen were off, and the cake, proudly carried in by Otha, glowed and flickered with a sea of tiny candles. Again Inge had that peculiar sensation of time merging. Chandeliers used to look like that cake, she thought, weighed down with a prince's ransom in candles. Reverse-tiered crystal birthday cakes, whole hallways of them glowing richly . . .

Tamara's voice intruded on her thoughts. "Well? Aren't you going to blow out the candles?"

Inge slid her a severe look. "Tamara, let me watch them burn, will you? How many more times do you think I will get to see a birthday cake?" But she smiled with pleasure and finally, to loud applause and cheers, leaned toward the candles and blew them out, with the help of everyone else except Daliah.

As soon as the candles were snuffed, their flames popped

right back up again, brighter than ever. Daliah clapped a hand over her mouth to stifle her laughter.

Confused, everyone leaned toward the cake and blew even harder.

The candles went dark. And then continued blazing merrily.

Daliah howled so hard with laughter that tears streamed down her cheeks.

The others blew a third time, and by then they all roared and howled and screeched. It was a full five minutes before they recovered from the trick candles.

When the laughter had subsided, the ritual of Dom Perignon was begun. Crystal flutes were filled and handed round—though the elderly al-Ameers, being strict Muslims, had a mixture of apple juice and mineral water instead.

Najib scraped back his chair, stood up, and raised his glass. "I would like to propose a toast," he announced, and looked down at Inge, who, despite her pleasure, flashed him one of her stern looks. "To a very special lady, this family's adopted grandmother and matriarch, without whom we would not be gathered here today . . ." He raised his glass even higher. "I give you Inge Meier, a damn fine lady if ever there was one."

"Hear! Hear!" Tamara shouted.

Arms reached across the table, glasses chimed, and everyone sipped slowly and appreciatively. The champagne was a good year, dry, and icy cold.

"Thank you, Najib," Inge said, her face pink and her ears warm from the accolade. As he sat back down, she added sharply, her eyebrows arched in mock exasperation, "You didn't have to overdo it, you know. You make me sound so old." But she leaned over to pat his arm.

"To Inge." Now it was Schmarya's turn. He paused, the glass raised, his left hand tucked in the small of his back as he looked down at her. "You've kept the family together through war and revolution, through good times and a lot of bad. Without you, we would be scattered to the four winds, and when I say we have everything to thank you for, we all know that that is an understatement." He smiled at her, and knew by her faraway look that they were both seeing the past. *Both seeing Senda.* Memories ached softly and tugged at them like gentle breezes, the pictures in their minds crystal clear, as though only days had passed, not more than six decades. Senda seemed to waltz and drift just beyond eyesight, like an elusive ghost.

One by one, the others got up to make their toasts. Then the cake was sliced and heaped on gold-edged plates and handed around. After a few bites, Inge's guests trouped out and returned with beautifully wrapped gifts, which Inge, naturally, had to unwrap in front of them all. It was like Christmas. Inge looked overcome. "You shouldn't have, any of you!" she scolded severely. Tears of happiness rolled unchecked down her cheeks and she wept with happiness. "But I am so glad you did!"

As flashbulbs clicked and videotapes rolled to record the celebration, Jasmine suddenly took center stage, her little face mugging and running the gamut from laughter to pouts. She positively basked in the attention of the lenses, and was like a clown in constant motion.

As Tamara watched her plump granddaughter, something slowly began to stir in her.

That natural gift for performing in front of a camera, heedless of the people all around.

The image seared her mind like a strobe, and she shook her head to clear it.

Jasmine's performance was building, and she started to do imitations of the Smurfs, her favorite cartoon characters. Tamara could only watch her in wonder.

That effortless ease at imitation.

That natural affinity between lens and performer.

Those sly eyes, looking around to see if she had everyone's attention.

Ripples of whispery gooseflesh danced up and down Tamara's arms. In startled amazement she looked to Daliah to see if she had seen. Daliah caught her glance, indicating she had, and they raised their eyebrows and turned slowly to Inge, who had seen too. Once more, all three women looked back toward Jasmine, and then at each other. Could it be? they wondered silently.

When Jasmine finished her performance, Inge caught the child and hugged her to her scrawny bosom. "I would say you definitely have the Boralevi talent," she whispered with a smile. She gently stroked the girl's lustrous dark hair with both shriveled, age-spotted hands. "Mind you, it's still too early to tell, but I do believe I can detect a little of Senda, Tamara, and Daliah in you, young lady. What do you say? Do you want to grow up to become a star?"

The magic moment was like a munificent wave of warmth. As though drawn by a magnet, the four of them—Inge, Tamara, Daliah, and Jasmine—drew together and linked their arms around each other.

We are links of the same chain, Inge thought happily, her eyes misty. *You see, Senda? You are here after all. Part of you lives on in each of us, just like part of us will live on in the memories of Jasmine, and her children, and her children's children. So it was, and so it will forever be.*

"Now, come with Aunt Inge," Inge finally whispered to Jasmine. "It's late and time for beddy-bye. I'll tuck you in myself, and we'll both get a good night's sleep, eh?" She took the little girl by the hand. "That way, we'll be rested when we go shopping in town tomorrow. Aunt Inge's going to buy you a glassy new dress."

Tamara and Daliah smiled after them. Much had changed over the years, but when Inge became very, very emotional, she still tended to bungle her English.